Praise for *Mason & Dixon*

"Awash with light and charm, rich with suggestion and idea, stuffed with the minutiae of another time and world. *Mason & Dixon* is less a book to read through than to read in, to savor paragraph by paragraph."
—Paul Skenazy, *San Francisco Chronicle*

"As a fellow-novelist I could only envy it and the culture that permits the creation and success of such intricate masterpieces. This almost feels like the last great fiction of our dying era. Though I'm sure it won't be, I must admire its sense of the bright farewell, the clear passing overseas of the torch that Peacock, Dickens, Lawrence, and Conrad bore. You'll not find a better, this next time round." ·
—John Fowles, *The Spectator*

"A dazzling work of imaginative re-creation, a marvel-filled historical novel . . . Exceptionally funny."
—Michael Dirda, *The Washington Post Book World*

"*Mason & Dixon* will make you want to curse American history, then turn around and bless it, because nowhere else but America could you find a zany literary genius like Thomas Pynchon." —Malcolm Jones Jr., *Newsweek*

"Splendid . . . *Mason & Dixon*—like *Huckleberry Finn*, like *Ulysses*—is one of the great novels about male friendship in anybody's literature."
—John Leonard, *The Nation*

"Pynchon always has been wildly inventive, and gorgeously funny when he surpasses himself: the marvels of this book are extravagant and unexpected."
—Harold Bloom, *Bostonia*

"This is the old Pynchon, the true Pynchon, the best Pynchon of all. *Mason & Dixon* is a groundbreaking book, a book of heart and fire and genius, and there is nothing quite like it in our literature, except maybe *V.*, and *Gravity's Rainbow.*" —T. Coraghessan Boyle, *The New York Times Book Review*

"A unique and miraculous experience . . . A tale of scientific triumph and an epic of loss."
                                                          —Paul Gray, *Time*

"This is the book of a lifetime."   —Frank MacConnell, *Commonweal*

"It is a sad and beautiful and nutty and profound book. . . . All I can do is doff my cap."   —Luc Sante, *New York*

"An astonishing and wonderful book."
                          —Louis Menand, *The New York Review of Books*

"Very grand and mad and beautiful . . . I can't remember ever having reviewed a more original novel . . . If America produces a novel to come near this marvelous, proliferating thing this decade, I promise to eat it."
                                          —Philip Hensher, *Spectator*

"A masterpiece."   —Ted Mooney, *Los Angeles Times*

"A contemporary *Don Quixote* or *Canterbury Tales*—or more accurately the *Iliad* and *Odyssey*, with heavy splashes of Woody Allen and the Marx Brothers. Pynchon's not only back, but he's left us all in the dust again, with only the sound of his laughter echoing far in front of us."
                                          —Jim Knipfel, *New York Press*

"With *Mason & Dixon* we're again in the generous hands of one of American literature's true masters."   —Rick Moody, *The Atlantic Monthly*

Also by Thomas Pynchon

Mason & Dixon

Thomas Pynchon

Mason  Dixon

An Owl Book
Henry Holt and Company
New York

Henry Holt and Company, Inc.
Publishers since 1866
115 West 18th Street
New York, New York 10011

Henry Holt® is a registered
trademark of Henry Holt and Company, Inc.

Published in Canada by Fitzhenry & Whiteside Ltd.,
195 Allstate Parkway, Markham, Ontario L3R 4T8.

Library of Congress Cataloging-in-Publication Data
Pynchon, Thomas.
Mason & Dixon / Thomas Pynchon.
p.   cm.
ISBN 0-8050-5837-0
1. Mason, Charles, 1728–1786—Fiction.   2. United States—History—
Colonial period, ca. 1600–1775—Fiction.   3. Surveying—United
States—History—18th century—Fiction.   4. British—United States—
History—18th century—Fiction.   5. Frontier and pioneer life—
Pennsylvania—Fiction.   6. Frontier and pioneer life—Maryland—
Fiction.   7. Surveyors—United States—Fiction.   8. Dixon,
Jeremiah—Fiction.   I. Title.
PS3566.Y55M37   1997   97-6467
813'.54—dc21   CIP

Henry Holt books are available for special promotions and
premiums. For details contact: Director, Special Markets.

First published in hardcover in 1997 by
Henry Holt and Company, Inc.

First Owl Books Edition 1998

Designed by Betty Lew

Printed in the United States of America
All first editions are printed on acid-free paper.∞

1   3   5   7   9   10   8   6   4   2

The author wishes to thank the John D. and
Catharine T. MacArthur Foundation.

For Melanie,
and for Jackson

Mason & Dixon

One

Latitudes and Departures

I

Snow-Balls have flown their Arcs, starr'd the Sides of Outbuildings, as of Cousins, carried Hats away into the brisk Wind off Delaware,— the Sleds are brought in and their Runners carefully dried and greased, shoes deposited in the back Hall, a stocking'd-foot Descent made upon the great Kitchen, in a purposeful Dither since Morning, punctuated by the ringing Lids of various Boilers and Stewing-Pots, fragrant with Pie-Spices, peel'd Fruits, Suet, heated Sugar,— the Children, having all upon the Fly, among rhythmic slaps of Batter and Spoon, coax'd and stolen what they might, proceed, as upon each afternoon all this snowy Advent, to a comfortable Room at the rear of the House, years since given over to their carefree Assaults. Here have come to rest a long scarr'd sawbuck table, with two mismatch'd side-benches, from the Lancaster County branch of the family,— some Second-Street Chippendale, including an interpretation of the fam'd Chinese Sofa, with a high canopy of yards of purple Stuff that might be drawn all 'round to make a snug, dim tent,— a few odd Chairs sent from England before the War,— mostly Pine and Cherry about, nor much Mahogany, excepting a sinister and wonderful Card Table which exhibits the cheaper sinusoidal Grain known in the Trade as Wand'ring Heart, causing an illusion of Depth into which for years children have gaz'd as into the illustrated Pages of Books...along with so many hinges, sliding Mortises, hidden catches, and secret compartments that neither the Twins nor their Sister can say they have been to the end of it. Upon the Wall, banish'd to this Den of Parlor Apes for its Remembrance of a Time better forgotten, reflecting most of the Room,— the Carpet and Drapes a little fray'd, Whiskers the Cat stalking beneath the furniture, looking out with eyes finely reflexive to anything suggesting Food,— hangs a Mirror in an inscrib'd Frame, commemorating the "Mischianza," that memorable farewell Ball stag'd in '77 by the British who'd been Occupying the City, just before their Withdrawal from Philadelphia.

This Christmastide of 1786, with the War settl'd and the Nation bickering itself into Fragments, wounds bodily and ghostly, great and small, go aching on, not ev'ry one commemorated,— nor, too often, even recounted. Snow lies upon all Philadelphia, from River to River, whose further shores have so vanish'd behind curtains of ice-fog that the City today might be an Isle upon an Ocean. Ponds and Creeks are frozen over, and the Trees a-glare to the last slightest Twig,— Nerve-Lines of concentrated Light. Hammers and Saws have fallen still, bricks lie in snow-cover'd Heaps, City-Sparrows, in speckl'd Outbursts, hop in and out of what Shelter there may be,— the nightward Sky, Clouds blown to Chalk-smears, stretches above the Northern Liberties, Spring Garden and Germantown, its early moon pale as the Snow-Drifts,— smoke ascends from Chimney-Pots, Sledging-Parties adjourn indoors, Taverns bustle,— freshly infus'd Coffee flows ev'ryplace, borne about thro' Rooms front and back, whilst Madeira, which has ever fuel'd Association in these Parts, is deploy'd nowadays like an ancient Elixir upon the seething Pot of Politics,— for the Times are as impossible to calculate, this Advent, as the Distance to a Star.

It has become an afternoon habit for the Twins and their Sister, and what Friends old and young may find their way here, to gather for another Tale from their far-travel'd Uncle, the Revd Wicks Cherrycoke, who arriv'd here back in October for the funeral of a Friend of years ago,— too late for the Burial, as it prov'd,— and has linger'd as a Guest in the Home of his sister Elizabeth, the Wife, for many years, of Mr. J. Wade LeSpark, a respected Merchant, active in Town Affairs whilst in his home yet Sultan enough to convey to the Rev^d, tho' without ever so stipulating, that, for as long as he can keep the children amus'd, he may remain,— too much evidence of Juvenile Rampage at the wrong moment, however, and Boppo! 'twill be Out the Door with him, where waits the Winter's Block and Blade.

Thus, they have heard the Escape from Hottentot-Land, the Accursèd Ruby of Mogok, the Ship-wrecks in Indies East and West,— an Herodotic Web of Adventures and Curiosities selected, the Rev^d implies, for their moral usefulness, whilst avoiding others not as suitable in the Hearing of Youth. The Youth, as usual, not being consulted in this.

Tenebræ has seated herself and taken up her Needlework, a piece whose size and difficulty are already subjects of Discussion in the House, the Embroidress herself keeping silence,— upon this Topick, at least. Announc'd by Nasal Telegraph, in come the Twins, bearing the old Pewter Coffee-Machine venting its Puffs of Vapor, and a large Basket dedicated to Saccharomanic Appetites, piled to the Brim with fresh-fried Dough-Nuts roll'd in Sugar, glaz'd Chestnuts, Buns, Fritters, Crullers, Tarts. "What is this? Why, Lads, you read my mind."

"The Coffee's for you, Nunk,— " " "— last Time, you were talking in your sleep," the Pair explain, placing the Sweets nearer themselves, all in this Room being left to seize and pour as they may. As none could agree which had been born first, the Twins were nam'd Pitt and Pliny, so that each might be term'd "the Elder" or "the Younger," as might day-to-day please one, or annoy his Brother.

"Why haven't we heard a Tale about America?" Pitt licking Gobbets of Philadelphia Pudding from his best Jabot.

"With Indians in it, and Frenchmen," adds Pliny, whose least gesture sends Cookie-crumbs ev'rywhere.

"French Women, come to that," mutters Pitt.

"It's not easy being pious for both of us, you know," Pliny advises.

"It's twenty years," recalls the Rev^d, "since we all topped the Allegheny Ridge together, and stood looking out at the Ohio Country,— so fair, a Revelation, meadow'd to the Horizon— Mason and Dixon, and all the McCleans, Darby and Cope, no, Darby wouldn't've been there in 'sixty-six,— howbeit, old Mr. Barnes and young Tom Hynes, the rascal...don't know where they all went,— some fought in the war, some chose peace come what might, some profited, some lost everything. Some are gone to Kentucky, and some,— as now poor Mason,— to Dust.

7

" 'Twas not too many years before the War,— what we were doing out in that Country together was brave, scientifick beyond my understanding, and ultimately meaningless,— we were putting a line straight through the heart of the Wilderness, eight yards wide and due west, in order to separate two Proprietorships, granted when the World was yet feudal and but eight years later to be nullified by the War for Independence."

And now Mason's gone, and the Revd Cherrycoke, who came to town only to pay his Respects, has linger'd, thro' the first descent of cold, the first drawings-in to the Hearth-Side, the first Harvest-Season meals appearing upon the next-best Dishes. He had intended to be gone weeks ago, but finds he cannot detach. Each day among his Devoirs is a visit, however brief, to Mason's grave. The Verger has taken to nodding at him. In the middle of the night recently he awoke convinc'd that 'twas he who had been haunting Mason,— that like a shade with a grievance, he expected Mason, but newly arriv'd at Death, to help him with something.

"After years wasted," the Rev^d commences, "at perfecting a *parsonical Disguise,*— grown old in the service of an Impersonation that never took more than a Handful of actor's tricks,— past remembering those Yearnings for Danger, past all that ought to have been, but never had a Hope of becoming, have I beach'd upon these Republican Shores,— stoven, dismasted, imbécile with age,— an untrustworthy Remembrancer for whom the few events yet rattling within a broken memory must provide the only comfort now remaining to him,— "

"Uncle," Tenebræ pretends to gasp, "— and but this Morning, you look'd so much younger,— why I'd no idea."

"Kindly Brae. That is from my Secret Relation, of course. Don't know that I'd phrase it quite like that in the present Company."

"Then...?" Tenebræ replying to her Uncle's Twinkling with the usual play of Eye-lashes.

"It begins with a Hanging."

"Excellent!" cry the Twins.

The Rev^d, producing a scarr'd old Note-book, cover'd in cheap Leather, begins to read. "Had I been the first churchman of modern times to be swung from Tyburn Tree,— had I been then taken for dead, whilst in fact but spending an Intermission among the eventless corridors of Syncope, due to the final Bowl of Ale,— had a riotous throng of medical students taken what they deem'd to be my Cadaver back beneath the somber groins of their College,— had I then been 'resurrected' into an entirely new Knowledge of the terms of being, in which Our Savior,— strange to say in that era of Wesley and Whitefield,— though present, would not have figur'd as pre-eminently as with most Sectarians,— howbeit,— I should closely resemble the nomadic Parson you behold today...."

"Mother says you're the Family outcast," Pitt remarks.

"They pay you money to keep away," says Pliny.

"Your Grandsire Cherrycoke, Lads, has ever kept his promise to remit to me, by way of certain Charter'd Companies, a sum precise to the farthing and punctual as the Moon,— to any address in the World, save one in Britain. Britain is his World, and he will persist, even now, in standing sham'd before it for certain Crimes of my distant Youth."

"Crimes!" exclaim the Boys together.

"Why, so did wicked men declare 'em...before God, another Tale...."

"What'd they nail you on?" Uncle Ives wishes to know, "strictly professional interest, of course." Green Brief-bag over one shoulder, but lately return'd from a Coffee-House Meeting, he is bound later this evening for a slightly more formal version of the same thing,— feeling, here with the children, much as might a Coaching Passenger let off at Nightfall among an unknown Populace, to wait for a connecting Coach, alone, pedestrian, desiring to pass the time to some Revenue, if not Profit.

"Along with some lesser Counts," the Rev^d is replying, " 'twas one of the least tolerable of Offenses in that era, the worst of Dick Turpin seeming but the Carelessness of Youth beside it,— the Crime they styl'd 'Anonymity.' That is, I left messages posted publicly, but did not sign them. I knew some night-running lads in the district who let me use their Printing-Press,— somehow, what I got into printing up, were Accounts of certain Crimes I had observ'd, committed by the Stronger against the Weaker,— enclosures, evictions, Assize verdicts, Activities of the Military,— giving the Names of as many of the Perpetrators as I was sure of, yet keeping back what I foolishly imagin'd my own, till the Night I was tipp'd and brought in to London, in Chains, and clapp'd in the Tower."

"The Tower!"

"Oh, do not tease them so," Tenebræ prays him.

"Ludgate, then? whichever, 'twas Gaol. It took me till I was lying among the Rats and Vermin, upon the freezing edge of a Future invisible, to understand that my name had never been my own,— rather belonging, all this time, to the Authorities, who forbade me to change it, or withhold it, as 'twere a Ring upon the Collar of a Beast, ever waiting for the Lead to be fasten'd on.... One of those moments Hindoos and Chinamen are ever said to be having, entire loss of Self, perfect union with All, sort of thing. Strange Lights, Fires, Voices indecipherable,— indeed, Children, this is the part of the Tale where your old Uncle gets to go insane,— or so, then, each in his Interest, did it please ev'ryone to style me. Sea voyages in those days being the standard Treatment for Insanity, my Exile should commence for the best of Medical reasons."

Tho' my Inclination had been to go out aboard an East Indiaman (the Rev[d] continues), as that route East travers'd notoriously a lively and youthful World of shipboard Dalliance, Gale-force Assemblies, and Duels ashore, with the French Fleet a constant,— for some, Romantic,— danger, "Like Pirates, yet more polite," as the Ladies often assur'd me,— alas, those who controll'd my Fate, getting wind of my preference at the last moment, swiftly arrang'd to have me transferr'd into a small British Frigate sailing alone, upon a long voyage, in a time of War,— the *Seahorse*, twenty-four guns, Captain Smith. I hasten'd in to Leadenhall Street to inquire.

"Can this be Objection we hear?" I was greeted. "Are you saying that a sixth-rate is beneath you? Would you prefer to remain ashore, and take up quarters in Bedlam? It has made a man of many in your Situation. Some have come to enjoy fairly meaningful lives there. Or if it's some need for the Exotic, we might arrange for a stay in one of the French Hospitals...."

"Would one of my Condition even know how to object, my Lord? I owe you everything."

"Madness has not impair'd your memory. Good. Keep away from harmful Substances, in particular Coffee, Tobacco and Indian Hemp. If you must use the latter, do not inhale. Keep your memory working, young man! Have a safe Voyage."

So, with this no doubt well-meant advice finding its way into the mid-watch sounds of waves past my sleeping-place, I set sail upon an Engine of Destruction, in the hope that Eastward yet might dwell something of Peace and Godhead, which British Civilization, in venturing Westward, had left behind,— and thus was consternation the least of my feelings when, instead of supernatural Guidance from Lamas old as time, here came Jean Crapaud a-looming,— thirty-four guns' worth of Disaster, and only one Lesson.

2

To Mr. Mason, Assistant to the Astronomer Royal,
At Greenwich
Esteem'd Sir,—

As I have the honor of being nam'd your Second, upon the propos'd
Expedition to Sumatra, to observe the Transit of Venus, I hope I do
not err, in introducing myself thus. Despite what Re-assurances
you may have had from Mr. Bird and Mr. Emerson, and I hope
others, as to my suitability,— yet, yourself being Adjunct to the
Prime Astronomer of the Kingdom, 'twould be strange,— not odd of
course, but unexpected, rather,— if you did not entertain a professional Doubt, or even two, as to my Qualifications.

Tho' 'tis true, that in my own Work I have recourse much more
often to the Needle, than to the Stars,— yet, what I lack in Celestial experience, I pray I may counterpend with Diligence and a
swift Grasp,— as, clearly, I cannot pretend to your level of Art, Sir,
gladly would I adopt, as promptly as benefit from, any suggestions
you might direct toward improving the level of my own.

In this, as in all else,—
Y'r obd't s'v't.
Jeremiah Dixon.—

A few months later, when it is no longer necessary to pretend as much
as they expected they'd have to, Dixon reveals that, whilst composing
this, he had delib'rately refrain'd from Drink. "Went thro' twenty Revi-
sions, dreaming all the while of the Pint awaiting me down at The Jolly

Pitman. Then the Pint after that, of course, and so forth.... Growing more desirable with each stricken Phrase, if tha follow me,— "

Mason in turn confesses to having nearly thrown the Letter away, having noted its origin in County Durham, and assumed it to be but more of the free provincial advice that it was one of his Tasks to read thro' in the Astronomer Royal's behalf, and respond to. "Yet, 'twas so sincere,— I instantly felt sham'd,— unworthy,— that this honest Country soul believ'd me wise.— Ahhrr! bitter Deception...."

> To,— Mr. Jeremiah Dixon
> Bishop Auckland, Co. Durham.
> Sir,—
>
> I have yours of the 26th Ult. and am much oblig'd for your kind opinion.— Yet I fear, the Doubts may with justice fall more upon your side, for I have never taught anyone, upon any Subject, nor may I prove much skill'd at it. Howbeit,— pray you hesitate not, in asking what you like, as I shall ever try to answer honestly,— if probably not *in toto*.
> Each of us is to have his own twin Telescope, by Mr. Dollond, fitted with the latest of his marvellous Achromatics,— our Clock by Mr. Shelton,— and of course the Sector by your Mr. Bird,— none but the best for this Party, I should say!
> Wishing you a journey south as safe as His Ways how strange, may allow, I wait your arrival in a Spirit happily rescu'd by your universally good Name, from all Imps of the Apprehensive,— an Exception most welcome, in the generally uneasy Life of
> y'r obdt. Svt.,
> Charles Mason

3

I was not there when they met,— or, not in the usual Way. I later heard from them how they remember'd meeting. I tried to record, in what I then projected as a sort of *Spiritual Day-Book,* what I could remember of what they said,— tho' 'twas too often abridg'd by the Day's Fatigue.

("Writing in your sleep, too!" cry the Twins.)

O children, I even dream'd in those Days,— but only long after the waking Traverse was done.

Howsobeit,— scarcely have they met, in the Saloon of Mason's Inn at Portsmouth, than Mason finds himself coming the Old London Hand, before Dixon's clear Stupefaction with the Town.

"Eeh! Fellow was spitting at my Shoes…? Another pushing folk one by one into the Gutters, some of *them* quite dangerous to look ah'…? How can Yese dwell thah' closely together, Day upon Day, without all growing Murderous?"

"Oh, one may, if one wishes, find insult at ev'ry step,— from insolent Stares to mortal Assault, an Orgy of Insult uninterrupted,— yet how does one proceed to call out each offender in turn, or choose among 'em, and in obedience to what code? So, one soon understands it, as yet another Term in the Contract between the City and oneself,— a function of simple Density, ensuring that there never be time enough to acknowledge, let alone to resent, such a mad Variety of offer'd Offense."

"Just so,— why, back in Bishop, it might take half the night to find an excuse to clash someone i' the Face, whilst in London, Eeh! 'tis the Paradise of the Quarrelsome, for fair."

"You'd appreciate Wapping High Street, then,— and, and Tyburn, of course! put that on your list."

"Alluring out there, is it?"

Mason explains, though without his precise reason for it, that, for the past Year or more, it has been his practice to attend the Friday Hangings at that melancholy place, where he is soon chatting up Hangmen and their 'Prentices, whilst standing them pints at their Local, The Bridport Dagger, acquiring thus a certain grisly intimacy with the Art. Mason has been shov'd about and borne along in riots of sailors attempting to wrest from bands of Medical Students the bodies of Shipmates come to grief ashore, too far from the safety of the Sea,— and he's had his Purse, as his Person, assaulted by Agents public and private,— yet, "There's nothing like it, it's London at its purest," he cries. "You must come out there with me, soon as we may."

Taking it for the joke it must surely be, Dixon laughs, "Ha, ha, ha! Oh, thah's a bonny one, all right. Eeh."

Mason shrugging, palms up, "I'm serious. Worse than that, I'm sober. A man's first time in town, he simply can't miss a hanging. Come, Sir,— what's the first thing they'll ask when you get back to County Durham? Eh? 'Did ye see them rahde the Eeahr at Taahburn?' "

Is it too many nights alone on top of that fam'd Hill in Greenwich? can this man, living in one of the great Cities of Christendom, not know how to behave around people?— Dixon decides to register only annoyance. "Nooah, the first thing they'll ask is, 'Did thoo understand 'em the weeay theey talk, down theere...?' "

"Oh, damme, I say, I didn't mean,— "

So Dixon for the second time in two minutes finds himself laughing without the Motrix of honest Mirth,— this time, a Mr. Mason–how-you-do-go-on laugh, sidewise and forbearing, the laugh of a hired Foil. Feeling it his Duty to set them at Ease, Dixon begins, "Well. There's this Jesuit, this Corsican, and this Chinaman, and they're all riding in a greeat Cooach, going up to Bath...? and the fourth Passenger is a very proper Englishwoman, who keeps giving them these scandaliz'd Glances...? Finally, able to bear it no longer, the Corsican, being the most hot-headed of the three, bursts out, and here I hope You will excuse my Corsican Accent, he says, ''Ey! Lady! Whatta Ye lookin' ah'?' And she says,— "

Mason has been edging away. "Are you crazy?" he whispers, "— People are staring. *Sailors* are staring."

"Eeh!" Dixon's nose throbbing redly. "You have heard it, then. Apologies," reaching to clasp Mason's arm, a gesture Mason retreats from in a Flinch as free of deliberation as a Sneeze. Dixon withdrawing, broken into a Sweat, "Why aye, it took me weeks of study to fathom that one, but I see You've a brisk Brain in Your gourd there, and I'm pleas'd to be working with such as it be...?" Resolutely a-beam, pronouncing the forms of *You* consciously, as if borrowing them from another Tongue.

The two sit staring, one at the other, each with a greatly mistaken impression,— likewise in some Uncertainty as to how the power may come to be sorted out betwixt 'em. Dixon is a couple of inches taller, sloping more than towering, wearing a red coat of military cut, with brocade and silver buttons, and a matching red three-corner'd Hat with some gaudy North-Road Cockade stuck in it. He will be first to catch the average Eye, often causing future strangers to remember them as Dixon and Mason. But the Uniform accords with neither his Quaker Profession, nor his present Bearing,— a civilian Slouch grown lop-sided, too often observ'd, alas, in Devotees of the Taproom.

For Dixon's part, he seems disappointed in Mason,— or so the Astronomer, ever inclined to suspicion, fears. "What is it? What are you looking at? It's my Wig, isn't it."

"You're not wearing a Wig...?"

"Just so! you noted that,— you have been observing me in a strange yet, I must conclude, meaningful way."

"Don't know...? Happen I was expecting someone a bit more...odd...?"

Mason a-squint, "I'm not *odd* enough for you?"

"Well it is a peculiar station in Life, isn't it? How many Royal Astronomers are there? How many Royal Astronomers' Assistants are there likely to be? Takes an odd bird to stay up peering at Stars all night in the first place, doesn't it...? On the other hand, Surveyors are runnin' about numerous as Bed-bugs, and twice as cheap, with work enough for all certainly in Durham at present, Enclosures all over the County, and North Yorkshire,— eeh! Fences, Hedges, Ditches ordinary and Ha-Ha Style, all to be laid out...I could have stay'd home and had m'self a fine Living...?"

"They did mention a Background in Land-Surveying," Mason in some Surprize, "but, but that's it? Hedges? Ha-Has?"

"Well, actually the Durham Ha-Ha boom subsided a bit after Lord Lambton fell into his, curs'd it, had it fill'd in with coal-spoil. Why, did You think I was another Lens-fellow? O Lord no,— I mean I've been *taught* the lot, Celestial Mechanics, all the weighty lads, Laplace and Kepler, Aristarchus, the other fellow what's his name,— but that's all Trigonometry, isn't it...?"

"Yet you,— " how shall he put this tactfully? "you *have* look'd... ehm...through a...ehm..."

Dixon smiles at him encouragingly. "Why aye,— my old Teacher, Mr. Emerson, has a fine *Telescope* Ah believe the word is, encas'd in Barrel-Staves tho' it be, and many's the Evening I've admir'd the Phases of Venus, aye those and the Moons of Jupiter too, the Mountains and Craters of our own Moon,— and did You see thah' latest Eclipse...? canny,— eeh...Mr. Bird, as well, has shar'd his Instruments,— being kind enough, in fact, just in this last fortnight, to help me practice my observing and computing skills,— tho' so mercilessly that I was in some doubt for days, whether we'd parted friends...?"

Mason, having expected some shambling wild Country Fool, remains amiably puzzl'd before the tidied Dixon here presented,— who, for his own part, having despite talk of Oddity expected but another over-dress'd London climber, is amus'd at Mason's nearly invisible Turn-out, all in Snuffs and Buffs and Grays.

Mason is nodding glumly. "I must seem an Ass."

"If this is as bad as it gets, why I can abide thah'. As long as the Spir-its don't run out."

"Nor the Wine."

"Wine." Dixon is now the one squinting. Mason wonders what he's done this time. " 'Grape or Grain, but ne'er the Twain,' as me Great-

Uncle George observ'd to me more than once,— 'Vine with Corn, beware the Morn.' Of the two sorts of drinking Folk this implies, thah' is, Grape People and Grain People, You will now inform me of Your membership in the Brotherhood of the, eeh, Grape...? and that You seldom, if ever, touch Ale or Spirits, am I correct?"

"Happily so, I should imagine, as, given a finite Supply, there'd be more for each of us, it's like Jack Sprat, isn't it."

"Oh, I'll drink Wine if I must...?— and now we're enter'd upon the Topick,— "

"— and as we are in Portsmouth, after all,— there cannot lie too distant some Room where each of us may consult what former Vegetation pleases him?"

Dixon looks outside at the ebbing wintry sunlight. "Nor too early, I guess...?"

"We're sailing to the Indies,— Heaven knows what's available on Board, or out there. It may be our last chance for civiliz'd Drink."

"Sooner we start, the better, in thah' case...?"

As the day darkens, and the first Flames appear, sometimes reflected as well in Panes of Glass, the sounds of the Stables and the Alleys grow louder, and chimney-smoke perambulates into the Christmastide air. The Room puts on its Evening-Cloak of shifting amber Light, and sinuous Folds of Shadow. Mason and Dixon become aware of a jostling Murmur of Expectancy.

All at once, out of the Murk, a dozen mirror'd Lanthorns have leapt alight together, as into their Glare now strolls a somewhat dishevel'd Norfolk Terrier, with a raffish Gleam in its eye,— whilst from somewhere less illuminate comes a sprightly Overture upon Horn, Clarinet, and Cello, in time to which the Dog steps back and forth in his bright Ambit.

> Ask me anything you please,
> The Learnèd English Dog am I, well-
> Up on ev'rything from Fleas
> Unto the King's Mon-og-am-eye,
>
> Persian Princes, Polish Blintzes,
> Chinamen's Geo-mancy,—

Jump-ing Beans or Flying Machines,
Just as it suits your Fan-cy.

I quote enough of the Classickal Stuff
To set your Ears a-throb,
Work logarith-mick Versèd Sines
Withal, within me Nob,
— Only nothing *Ministerial,* please,
Or I'm apt to lose m' Job,
As, the Learnèd English Dog, to-ni-ight!

There are the usual Requests. Does the Dog know "Where the Bee
Sucks"? What is the Integral of One over (Book) d (Book)? Is he married? Dixon notes how his co-Adjutor-to-be seems fallen into a sort of
Magnetickal Stupor, as Mesmerites might term it. More than once,
Mason looks ready to leap to his feet and blurt something better kept till
later in the Evening. At last the Dog recognizes him, tho' now he is too
key'd up to speak with any Coherence. After allowing him to rattle for a
full minute, the Dog sighs deeply. "See me later, out in back."

"It shouldn't take but a moment," Mason tells Dixon. "I'll be all right
by myself, if there's something you'd rather be doing...."

With no appetite for the giant Mutton Chop cooling in front of him,
Mason mopishly now wraps it and stows it in his Coat. Looking up, he
notes Dixon, mouth cheerfully stuff'd, beaming too tolerantly for his
Comfort.

"No,— not for me,— did you think I was taking it for myself?— 'tis for
the Learnèd Dog, rather,— like, I don't know, perhaps a Bouquet sent to
an Actress one admires, a nice Chop can never go too far off the Mark."

Starting a beat late, "Why aye, 'tis a...a great World, for fair...? and
Practices vary, and one Man certainly may not comment upon— "

"What...are you saying?"

Dixon ingenuously waving his Joint, eyes round as Pistoles. "No
Offense, Sir." Rolling his Eyes the Moment Mason switches his Stare
away, then back a bit late to catch them so much as off-Center.

"Dixon. Why mayn't there be Oracles, for us, in our time? Gate-ways
to Futurity? That can't all have died with the ancient Peoples. Isn't it
worth looking ridiculous, at least to investigate this English Dog, for its
obvious bearing upon Metempsychosis if nought else,— "

There is something else in progress,— something Mason cannot quite confide. Happen he's lost someone close? and recently enough to matter, aye,— for he's a way of pitching ever into the Hour, heedless, as Dixon remembers himself, after his father passed on.... "I'll come along, if I may...?"

"Suture Self, as the Medical Students like to say."

They go out a back door, into the innyard. A leafless tree arches in the light of a single Lanthorn set above a taut gathering of card-players, their secret breathing visible for all to try to read, and Wigs, white as the snow on the Roofslates, nodding in and out of the Shadows.

Sailors, mouths ajar, lope by in the lanes. Sailors in Slouch-Hats, Sailors with Queues, puffing on Pipes, eating Potatoes, some who'll be going back to the Ship, and some who won't, from old sea-wretches with too many Explosions in their Lives, to Child-Midshipmen who have yet to hear their first,— passing in and out the Doors of Ale-Drapers, Naval Tailors, Sweet-shops, Gaming-Lairs, upstart Chapels, calling, singing Catches, whistling as if Wind had never paid a Visit, vomiting as the Sea has never caus'd them to.

"Happen his Dressing-Room's close by," Dixon suggests, "— in with the Horses, maybe...?"

"No one would keep a talking Dog in with Horses, it'd drive them mad inside of a Minute."

"Occurs often, does it, where you come from?"

"Gentlemen," in a whisper out of a dark corner. "If you'll keep your voices down, I'll be with you in a trice." Slowly into their shifting spill of lantern-light, tongue a-loll, comes the Dog, who pauses to yawn, nods, "Good evening to ye," and leads them at a trot out of the stables, out of the courtyard, and down the street, pausing now and then for nasal inquiries.

"Where are we going?" Mason asks.

"This seems to be all right." The Learnèd English Dog stops and pisses.

"This dog," Mason singing *sotto voce*, "is causing me ap-pre-hen-sion,— surely creatures of miracle ought not to, I mean,...Flying horses? None of them ever— "

"The Sphinx...?" adds Dixon.

"My Thought precisely."

"Now, Gents!" 'Tis a sudden, large Son of Neptune, backed by an uncertain number of comparably drunken Shipmates. "You've an interest in this Dog here?"

"Wish'd a word with him only," Mason's quick to assure them.

"Hey! I know you two,— ye're the ones with all the strange Machinery, sailing in the *Seahorse*. Well,— ye're in luck, for we're all Seahorses here, I'm Fender-Belly Bodine, Captain of the Foretop, and these are my Mates,— " Cheering. "— But you can call me Fender. Now,— our plan, is to snatch this Critter, and for you Gents to then keep it in with your own highly guarded Cargo, out of sight of the Master-at-Arms, until we reach a likely Island,— "

"Island..." "Snatch..." both Surveyors a bit in a daze.

"I've been out more than once to the Indies,— there's a million islands out there, each more likely than the last, and I tell you a handful of Sailors with their wits about them, and that talking Dog to keep the Savages amused, why, we could be kings."

"Long life to Kings!" cry several sailors.

"Aye and to Cooch Girls!"

"— and Coconut-Ale!"

"Hold," cautions Mason. "I've heard they *eat* dogs out there."

"Wrap 'em in palm leaves," Dixon solemnly, "and bake 'em on the beach...?"

"First time you turn your back," Mason warns, "that Dog's going to be some Savage's Luncheon."

"Rrrrrraahff! Excuse me?" says the Learnèd D., "as I seem to be the Topick here, I do feel impell'd, to make an Observation?"

"That's all right, then, Fido," Bodine making vague petting motions, "— trust us, there's a good bow-wow...."

A small, noisy party of Fops, Macaronis, or Lunarians,— it is difficult quite to distinguish which,— has been working its way up the street and into Ear-shot. Thro' several window-panes, moving candlelight appears. Hostlers roll about disgruntled upon feed-sack Pillows and beds. Unengaged Glim-jacks look in, to see if they can cast any light on matters.

The Dog pushes Mason's Leg with his Head. "We may not have another chance to chat, even upon the Fly."

"There is something I must know," Mason hoarsely whispers, in the tone of a lover tormented by Doubts, "— Have you a soul,— that is, are you a human Spirit, re-incarnate as a Dog?"

The L.E.D. blinks, shivers, nods in a resign'd way. "You are hardly the first to ask. Travelers return'd from the Japanese Islands tell of certain *religious Puzzles* known as *Koan,* perhaps the most fam'd of which concerns your very Question,— whether a Dog hath the nature of the divine Buddha. A reply given by a certain very wise Master is, 'Mu!' "

" 'Mu,' " repeats Mason, thoughtfully.

"It is necessary for the Seeker to meditate upon the *Koan* until driven to a state of holy Insanity,— and I would recommend this to you in particular. But please do not come to the Learnèd English Dog if it's religious Comfort you're after. I may be præternatural, but I am not supernatural. 'Tis the Age of Reason, rrrf? There is ever an Explanation at hand, and no such thing as a Talking Dog,— Talking Dogs belong with Dragons and Unicorns. What there are, however, are Provisions for Survival in a World less fantastick.

"*Viz.*— Once, the only reason Men kept Dogs was for food. Noting that among Men no crime was quite so abhorr'd as eating the flesh of another human, Dog quickly learn'd to act as human as possible,— and to pass this Ability on from Parents to Pups. So we know how to evoke from you, Man, one day at a time, at least enough Mercy for one day more of Life. Nonetheless, however accomplish'd, our Lives are never settled,— we go on as tail-wagging Scheherazades, ever a step away from the dread Palm Leaf, nightly delaying the Blades of our Masters by telling back to them tales of their humanity. I am but an extreme Expression of this Process,— "

"Oh I say, Dog in Palm Leaf, what nonsense," comments one of the Lunarians, "— really, far too sensitive, I mean really, Dog? In Palm Leaf? Civiliz'd Humans have better things to do than go about drooling after Dog in Palm Leaf or whatever, don't we Algernon?"

"Could you possibly," inquired the Terrier, head cocked in some Annoyance, "not keep saying that? *I* do not say things like, 'Macaroni Italian Style,' do I, nor 'Fop Fricasée,'— "

"Why, you beastly little— "

"Grrrr! and your deliberate use of 'drooling,' Sir, is vile."

The Lunarian reaches for his Hanger. "Perhaps we may settle this upon the spot, Sir."

"Derek? You're talking to a *D-O-G?*"

"Tho' your weapon put me under some Handicap," points out the Dog, "in fairness, I *should* mention·my late feelings of Aversion to water? Which may, as you know, signal the onset of the Hydrophobia. Yes! The Great H. And should I get in *past* your Blade for a few playful nips, and manage to, well, break the old *Skin,*— why, then you should soon have caught the same, eh?" Immediately 'round the Dog develops a circle of Absence, of about a fathom's radius, later recall'd by both Astronomers as remarkably regular in shape. "Nice doggie!" " 'Ere,— me last iced Cake, that me Mum sent me all 'e way from Bahf. You take i'." "What think yese? I'll give two to one the Fop's Blood'll be first to show."

"Sounds fair," says Fender Bodine. "I fancy the Dog,— anyone else?"

"Oughtn't we to summon the Owners...?" suggests Mr. Dixon.

The Dog has begun to pace back and forth. "I am a British Dog, Sir. No one owns me."

"Who're the Gentleman and Lady who were with you in the Assembly Room?" inquires Mason.

"You mean the Fabulous Jellows? Here they come now."

"Protect you from sailors?" wails Mrs. Jellow, approaching at a dead run over the treacherous Cobbles of the Lane, "Oh, no, thank you, that was not in our Agreement." Her husband, pulling on his Breeches, Wig a-lop, follows at a sleepy Amble. "Now you apologize for whatever it was you did, and get back in that Stable in your lovely straw Bed."

"We were wondering, Ma'am," Bodine with his hat off, quavering angelically, "would the li'oo Doggie be for sale?"

"Not at any price, Topman, and be off wi' you, and your rowdy-dowing Flock as well." At her Voice, a number of Sailors in whose Flexibility lies their Preservation from the Hazards of Drink, are seen to freeze.

"Do not oppose her," Jellow advises, "for she is a first-rate of an hundred Guns, and her Broadside is Annihilation."

"Thankee, Jellow,— slow again, I see."

"*Oh* dear," Bodine putting his hat back on and sighing. "Apologies, Sir and Madam, and much Happiness of your Dog."

"You are the owners of this Marvel?" inquires Mason.

"We prefer 'Exhibitors,' " says Mr. Jellow.

"Damme, they'd better," grumphs the Dog, as if to himself.

"Why, here is The Pearl of Sumatra!" calls Dixon, who for some while has been growing increasingly desperate for a Drink, "And a jolly place it seems."

"Fender-Belly is buying!" shouts some mischievous Sailor, forever unidentified amid the eager Rush for the Entry of this fifth- or sixth-most-notorious sailors' Haunt upon the Point, even in whose Climate of general Iniquity The Pearl distinguishes itself, much as might one of its Eponyms, shining 'midst the decadent Flesh of some Oyster taken from the Southern Sea.

"How about a slug into y'r Breadroom, there, Fido?"

"Pray you, call me Fang.... Well, and yes I do like a drop of Roll-me-in-the-Kennel now and then...."

Inside, seamen of all ranks and ratings mill slowly in a murk of pipe-smoke and soot from cheap candles, whilst counter-swirling go a choice assortment of Portsmouth Polls in strip'd and floral Gowns whose bold reds, oranges, and purples are taken down in this light, bruised, made oily and worn, with black mix'd in everywhere, colors turning ever toward Night. Both Surveyors note, after a while, that the net Motion of the Company is away from the Street-Doors and toward the back of the Establishment, where, upon a length of turf fertiliz'd with the blood and the droppings of generations of male Poultry, beneath a bright inverted Cone of Lanthorn Light striking blue a great ever-stirring Knot of Smoke, and a Defaulter merry beyond the limits of cock-fight etiquette suspended in a basket above the Pit, a Welsh Main is in progress. Beyond this, a Visto of gaming tables may be made out, and further back a rickety Labyrinth of Rooms for sleeping or debauchery, all receding like headlands into a mist.

The Learnèd D., drawn by the smell of Blood in the Cock-Pit, tries to act nonchalant, but what can they expect of him? How is he supposed to ignore this pure Edge of blood-love? Oh yawn yes of course, seen it all before, birds slashing one another to death, sixteen go in, one comes out alive, indeed mm-hmm, and a jolly time betwixt, whilst the Substance we are not supposed to acknowledge drips and flies ev'rywhere....

"There, Learnèd," calls Mrs. Jellow brusquely, "we must leave the birds to their Work." Beneath the swaying Gamester, the general pace of the Room keeps profitably hectic. From the Labyrinth in back come assorted sounds of greater and lesser Ecstasy, along with percussions upon Flesh, laughter more and less feign'd, furniture a-thump, some Duetto of Viol and Chinese Flute, the demented crowing of fighting-cocks waiting their moment, cries in Concert at some inaudible turn of a card or roll of the Fulhams high and low, calls for Bitter and Three-Threads rising ever hopeful, like ariettas in the shadow'd Wilderness of Rooms, out where the Lamps are fewer, and the movements deeper with at least one more Grade of Intent...At length the Dog halts, having led them to where, residing half out of doors, fram'd in cabl'd timbers wash'd in from a wreck of long ago, an old piece of awning held by a gnaw'd split, ancient Euphroe between her and the sky with its varied Menace, sits Dark Hepsie, the Pythoness of the Point.

"Here," the Dog butting at Mason, "here is the one you must see."

Instantly, Mason concludes (as he will confess months later to Dixon) that it all has to do with Rebekah, his wife, who died two years ago this February next. Unable to abandon her, Mason is nonetheless eager to be aboard a ship, bound somewhere impossible,— long Voyages by sea being thought to help his condition, describ'd to him as Hyperthrenia, or "Excess in Mourning." Somehow the Learnèd Dog has led him to presume there exist safe-conduct Procedures for the realm of Death,— that through this Dog-reveal'd Crone, he will be allow'd at last to pass over, and find, and visit her, and come back, his Faith resurrected. That is as much of a leap as can be expected of a melancholick heart. At the same time, he smokes that the Learnèd English D.,— or Fang, as now he apparently wishes to be known,— in introducing them thus, is pursuing an entirely personal End.

"Angelo said there'd be a Package for me?"

"Quotha! Am I the Evening Coach?" The two rummage about in the Shadows. "Look ye, I'll be seeing him later, and I'll be sure to ask,— "

"Just what you said last time," the Dog shaking his head reprovingly.

"Here, then,— a Sacrifice, direct from me own meager Mess, a bit of stew'd Hen,— 'tis the best I can do for ye today."

"Peace, Grandam,— reclaim thy Ort. The Learnèd One has yet to sink quite *that* low." The Dog, with an expressive swing of his Head, makes a dignified Exit, no more than one wag of the Tail per step.

"Your ship will put to Sea upon a Friday," Hepsie greets Mason and Dixon, "— would that be a Boatswain's Pipe into the Ear of either of you Gents?"

"Why, the Collier Sailors believe 'tis bad luck...?" Dixon replies, as if back at Woolwich before his Examiners, "it being the day of Christ's Execution."

"Nicely, Sir. Thus does your Captain Smith disrespect Christ, Fate, Saint Peter, and the god Neptune,— and withal there's not an insurancer in the Kingdom, from Lloyd's on down, who'll touch your case for less than a sum you can never, as Astronomers, possibly afford."

"Yet if we be dead," Dixon points out, "the Royal Navy absorbing the cost of a burial at sea, what further Expenses might there be?"

"You are independent of a Family, Sir."

"Incredible! Why, you must be a very Scryeress...?" Dixon having already spied, beneath her layers of careful Decrepitude (as he will later tell Mason), a shockingly young Woman hard at work,— with whom, country Lout that he is, he can't keep from flirting.

But Mason is now growing anxious. "Are we in danger, then? What have you heard?"

Silently she passes him a soil'd Broadside Sheet, upon which are printed descriptions of varied Services, and the Fees therefor. "What's this? You won't do Curses?"

"My Insurance? Prohibitive," she cackles, as the young fancy the old to cackle. "I believe what you seek is under 'Intelligence, Naval.'"

"Half a Crown?"

"If you insist."

"Ehm...Dixon?"

"What? You want me to put in half of thah'?"

"We can't very well charge...this...to the Society, can we?"

"Do I shame you, Sir?" Hepsie too 'pert by Decades.

"Oh, all right," Mason digging laboriously into his Purse, sorting out Coins and mumbling the Amounts.

Dixon looks on in approval. "You spend money like a very Geordie. He means no harm, lass...?" beaming, nudging Mason urgently with his Toe, as Bullies shift about in the Dark, and Boats wait with muffl'd Oars to ferry them against their will over to a Life they may not return from. The smell of the great Anchorage,— smoke, Pitch, salt and decay,— sweeps in fitfully.

"Sirs, attend me," the coins having silently vanish'd, "— Since last year, the Year of Marvels, when Hawke drove Conflans upon that lee shore at Quiberon Bay, the remnants of the Brest fleet have been understandably short of *Elan,* or *Esprit,* or whatever they style that stuff over there,— excepting, now and then, among the Captains of smaller Frigates, souls as restless to engage in personal Tactics as dispos'd to sniff at national Strategy. Mortmain, Le Chisel, St.-Foux,— mad dogs all,— any of them, and others, likely at any time to sail out from Brest, indifferent to Risk, *tête-à-tête* as ever with the end of the World, seeking new Objects of a Resentment inexhaustible."

"*Oh* dear," Mason clutching his head. "Suppose...we sail upon some other Day, then?"

"Mason, pray You,— 'tis the Age of Reason," Dixon reminds him, "we're Men of Science. To huz must all days run alike, the same number of identical Seconds, each proceeding in but one Direction, irreclaimable...? If we would have Omens, why, let us recall that the Astronomer's Symbol for Friday is also that of the planet Venus herself,— a good enough Omen, surely...?"

"I tell you," the young Impostress merrily raising a Finger, "French Frigates will be where they will be, day of the week be damn'd,— especially St.-Foux, with *La Changhaienne.* You know of the *Ecole de Piraterie* at Toulon? Famous. He has lately been appointed to the Kiddean Chair."

Mason and Dixon would like to stay, the one to fuss and the other to flirt, but as they now notice, a considerable Queue has form'd behind them. There are

Gamesters in Trouble, Sweet-Hearts untrue,
Sailors with no one to bid them adieu,

Roistering Fops and the Mast-Pond Brigade, all
Impatient to chat with the Sibylline Maid, singing,

Let us go down, to Hepsie's tonight,
Maybe tonight, she'll show us the Light,—
Maybe she'll cackle, and maybe she'll cry,
But for two and a kick she won't spit in your Eye.

She warn'd *Ramillies* sailors, Beware of the Bolt,
And the Corsica-bound of Pa-oli's Revolt,—
From lottery Tickets to History's End,
She's the mis'rable, bug-bitten sailor's best friend, singing,
Let us go down, &c.

"Nice doing Business with you, Boys, hope I see yese again," with an amiable Nod for Dixon.

Back at the Cock-fights, Fender-Belly Bodine comes lurching across their bow, curious. "So what'd she have to say?"

Something about crazy Frigate Captains sailing out of Brest, is all either of them can remember by now.

"Just what she told my Mauve, and for free. Good. We'll have a fight, Gents. And if it's Le Chisel, we'll have a Stern-chase, too. Back on old H.M.S. *Inconvenience,* we wasted many a Day and Night watching that fancy Counter get smaller by the minute. And when he'd open'd far enough from us, it pleas'd him to put out the Lanthorn in his Cabin, as if to say, '*Toot fini,* time to *frappay le Sack.*' Skipper saw that light go out, he always mutter'd the same thing,— 'The Dark take you, Le Chisel, and might you as readily vanish from my Life,'— and then we'd slacken Sail, and come about, and the real Work would begin,— beating away, unsatisfied once more, against the Wind." Foretopman Bodine pausing to squeeze the nearest Rondures of a young Poll who has shimmer'd in from some Opium Dream in the Vicinity. Like Hepsie, Mauve is far from what she pretends. Most men are fool'd into seeing a melancholy Waif, when in reality she's the most cheerful of little Butter-Biscuits, who has escap'd looking matronly only thanks to that constant Exertion demanded by the company of Sailors. She and Hepsie in fact share quarters in Portsea, as well as a Wardrobe noted, even here upon the Point, for its unconsider'd use of Printed Fabricks.

"She's a wonderful old woman, 's Hepsie," says Mauve. "Fortunes have been won heeding her advice, as lost ignoring it. She tells you beware, why, she has reckon'd your Odds and found them long.... She is Lloyd's of Portsmouth. Believe her."

Later, around Dawn, earnestly needing a further Word with Hepsie or the Dog, Mason can find no trace of either, search as he may. Nor will anyone admit to knowing of them at all, let alone their Whereabouts. He will continue to search, even unto scanning the shore as the *Seahorse* gets under way at last, on Friday, 9 January 1761.

4

Had it proved of any help that the Rev^d had tried to follow the advice of Epictetus, to keep before him every day death, exile, and loss, believing it a condition of his spiritual Contract with the world as given? When the French sail came a-twinkling,— with never-quite-invisible death upon the Whir fore and aft, with no place at all safe and only the unhelpful sea for escape, amid the soprano cries of the powder-monkeys, the smell of charr'd wood, the Muzzle's iron breath,— how had these daily devotions, he now wondered, ultimately ever been of use, how, in the snug Shambles of the *Seahorse?*

To the children, he remarks aloud, "Of course, Prayer was what got us through."

"I should have pray'd," murmurs Cousin Ethelmer, to Tenebræ's mild astonishment. Since appearing in the Doorway during a difficult bit of double-Back-stitch Filling two Days ago, return'd from College in the Jerseys, he has been otherwise all Boldness.

"Not seiz'd a Match? Not gone running up and down the Decks screaming and lighting Guns as you went? Cousin." The Twins consult each the other's Phiz, pretending to be stricken.

Ethelmer smiles and amiably pollicates the Rev^d, and less certainly Mr. LeSpark, his own Uncle, as if to say, "We are surrounded by the Pious, and their well-known wish never to hear of anything that sets the Blood a-racing."

Brae looks away, but keeps him in the corner of her eye, as if to reply, "Boy, Blood may 'race' as quietly as it must...."

Mr. LeSpark made his Fortune years before the War, selling weapons to French and British, Settlers and Indians alike,— Knives, Tomahawks, Rifles, Hand-Cannons in the old Dutch Style, Grenades, small Bombs. "Trouble yourself not," he lik'd to assure his Customers, "over Diameter." If there are Account-books in which Casualties are the Units of Exchange, then, so it seems to Ethelmer, his Uncle is deeply in Arrears. Ethelmer has heard tales of past crimes, but can hardly assault his Host with accusations. Ev'ryone "knows,"— that is, considering Uncle Wade as some collection of family stories, ev'ryone remembers. Some Adventures have converg'd into a *Saga* that is difficult to reconcile with the living Uncle, who sends him bank-drafts on Whims inscrutable that catch the Nephew ever by surprise, frequents the horse-races in Maryland, actually once fed apples to the great Selim, and these days doesn't mind if Ethelmer comes along to visit the Stables. At the late Autumn Meet, gaily dress'd young women, fancier than he thought possible, had wav'd and smil'd, indeed come over bold as city Cats to engage Ethelmer in conversation. Tho' young, he was shrewd enough to smoak that what they were after was his Plainness, including an idea of his Innocence, which they fail'd to note was long, even enjoyably, departed.

"He wants *whah'?*"

Mason nodding with a sour Smile.

"Out of our Expenses? shall it leave us enough for Candles and Soahp, do You guess?"

"No one's sure, Captain Smith having not himself appear'd before the Council,— rather, his Brother came, and read them the Captain's Letter."

"An hundred pounds,— apiece...?"

"An hundred Guineas."

"Eeh...that suggests they expect someone to come back with a counter-offer...? As it isn't huz, who would thah' be?"

"It comes down to the Royal Soc. or the Royal N." As Mason has heard it, the Council mill'd all about, like Domestick Fowl in Perplexity,

repeating, "Proportional Share!" in tones of Outrage, "— Pro-*portional?
Sha-a-are?*"

"Leaving this, this Post-Captain the right to Lay it Out, as he calls it,
at his Pleasure."

"Some Captain!— step away from a Privateer, by G-d." Aggriev'd voices
echoing in the great stairwell, Silver ringing upon Silver,— sugar-Loaves
and assorted Biscuits, French Brandy in Coffee,— Stick-Flourishes, motes
of wig-powder jigging by the thousands in the candle-light.

"Immediately raising a particular Suspicion,— unworthy of *this* Captain, goes without saying, and yet,— "

"— not to be easily distinguish'd from petty Extortion."

"Quite the sort of behavior Lord Anson's forever on about eradicat-
ing...."

"...and other remarks in the same Line," reports Mason. "They were
just able at last to appoint a Committee of Two to wait upon Lord Anson
himself, who took the time to inform them that in the Royal Navy, a Ship
of War's Captain is expected to pay for his own victualing."

"Really," said Mr. Mead, "I didn't know that, m'Lord,— are you
quite— I didn't mean that,— of course you're *sure*,— but rather,— "

"His Thought being," endeavored Mr. White, "that all this time, we'd
rather imagin'd that the Navy— "

"Alas, Gentlemen, one of Many Sacrifices necessary to that strange
Servitude we style 'Command,' " replied the First Lord. "Howbeit, 'twill
depend largely on how much your Captain plans to drink, and how many
livestock he may feel comfortable living among,— hardly do to be slipping in goat shit whilst trying to get ten or twelve Guns off in proper
Sequence, sort of thing. At the same time, we cannot have our Frigate
Captains adopting the ways of Street Bullies, and this Approach to one's
guests, mm, it does seem a bit singular. We'll have Stephens or someone
send Captain Smith a note, shall we,— invoking gently my own pois'd
Thunderbolt, of course."

"Oh Dear," Capt. Smith upon the Quarter-deck in the Winter's
grudg'd Sunlight, the Letter fluttering in the Breeze,— from the direction of London, somewhere among a peak'd Convoy of Clouds, a steady
Mutter as of Displeasure on High, "and yet I knew it. Didn't I. Ah,—
misunderstood!"

Far from any Extortion-scheme, it had rather been the Captain's own Expectation,— the fancy of a Heart unschool'd in Guile,— that they would of course all three be messing together, Day upon Day, the voyage long, in his Quarters, drinking Madeira, singing Catches, exchanging Sallies of Wit and theories about the Stars,— how else?— he being of such a philosophickal leaning, and so starv'd for Discourse, it never occurr'd to him that other Arrangements were even possible....

"I assum'd, foolishly, that we'd go in equal Thirds, and meant to ask but your Share of what I hop'd to be spending, out of my personal Funds, upon your behalf,— not to mention that buying for three, at certain Chandleries, would've got me a discount,— Ah! What matter? Best of intentions, Gentlemen, no wish to offend the First Lord,— our Great Circumnavigator, after all, my Hero as a Lad...."

"We regret it, Sir," Dixon offers, "— far too much Whim-Wham."

Mason brings his Head up with a surpris'd look. "Saintly of you, considering your Screams could be heard out past the Isle of Wight? Now, previously unconsulted, *I* am expected to join this Love-Feast?"

Dixon and the Captain, as if in Conspiracy, beam sweetly back till Mason can abide no more. "Very well,— tho' someone *ought* to have told you, Captain, of that *Rutabageous Anemia* which afflicts Lensmen as a Class,— the misunderstanding then should never have arisen."

"Gracious of You, Mr. Mason," cries Dixon, heartily.

"Most generous," adds the Captain.

'Tis arrang'd at last that they will be put in the Lieutenant's Mess, which is financ'd out of the Ship's Account,— that is, by the Navy,— and take their turns with the other principal Officers in dining with the Captain, whose dreams of a long, uneventful Voyage and plenty of Philosophick Conversation would thus have been abridg'd even had the *l'Grand* never emerg'd above the Horizon.

On the eighth of December the Captain has an Express from the Admiralty, ordering him not to sail. "Furthermore," he informs Mason and Dixon, "Bencoolen is in the hands of the French. I see no mention of any plans to re-take the place soon. I am sorry."

"I knew it...?" Dixon walking away shaking his head.

"We may still make the Cape of Good Hope in time," says Capt. Smith. "That'll likely be our destination, if and when they cut the Orders."

"No one else is going there to observe," Mason says. "Odd, isn't it? You'd think there'd be a Team from somewhere."

Capt. Smith looks away, as if embarrass'd. "Perhaps there is?" he suggests, as gently as possible.

As they proceed down the Channel, "Aye, and that's the Tail of the Bolt," a sailor informs them, "where the *Ramillies* went down but the year February, losing seven hundred Souls. They were in south-west Weather, the sailing-master could not see,— he gambl'd as to which Headland it was, mistaking the Bolt for Rome Head and lost all."

"This is League for League the most dangerous Body of Water in the world," complains another. "Sands and Streams, Banks and Races, I've no Peace till we're past the Start Point and headed for the Sea."

"Can this Lad get us out all right?"

"Oh, young Smith's been around forever. Collier Sailor. If he's alive, he must have learn'd somewhat."

Passing the Start-Point at last, the cock's-comb of hilltops to starboard, the Ship leaning in the up-Channel wind, the late sun upon the heights,— more brilliant gold and blue than either Landsman has ever seen,— the Cold of approaching Night carrying an edge, the possibility that by Morning the Weather will be quite brisk indeed..."Su-ma-tra," sing the sailors of the *Seahorse*,

> "Where girls all look like Cleo-
> Pat-tra,
> And when you're done you'll simply
> Barter 'er,
> For yet another twice as
> Hot, tra-
> La la-la la-la la-la la—
> La la la, la..."

From the day he assum'd command of the *Seahorse*, Capt. Smith has lived in a tidy corner of Hell previously unfamiliar to him. Leaving the rainswept landing, rowed out into the wet heaving Groves of masts and spars upon Spithead, 'mid sewage and tar and the Breath of the Wind, he had searched, with increasing desperation, for some encouraging first sight of his new command, till oblig'd at last to accept the remote scruffy Sixth Rate throwing itself like a tether'd beast against its anchor-cables. Yet, yet,…through the crystalline spray, how gilded comes she,— how corposantly edg'd in a persisting and, if Glories there be, glorious light…and he knows her, it must be from a Dream, how could it be other? A Light in which all Pain and failure, all fear, are bleach'd away….

He'd been greeted at the Quarter-deck by a Youth of loutish and ungather'd appearance, recruited but recently in a press-gang sweep of Wapping, who exclaim'd, "Damme! Look at this, Boys! An officer wha' knows enough to come in out of the rain!"

Trying not to bark, Capt. Smith replied, "What's your name, sailor?"

"By some I be styl'd, 'Blinky.' And who might you be?"

"Attend me, Blinky,— I am the Captain of this Vessel."

"Well," advised the young salt, "you've got a good job,— don't fuck up."

Steady advice. He haunts his little Raider like a nearly unsensed ghost, now silent upon his side of the Quarter-deck, now bending late and dutifully over the lunar-distance forms. "He wishes to be taken as a man of Science," opines the Rev^d upon first meeting the Astronomers, "— perhaps he even seeks your own good opinion. Mention'd in a report to the Royal Society? However you do that sort of thing." Choosing to stand with the ingenious and Philosophickal wing of the Naval profession rather than its Traditional and bloody-minded one, though he would fight honorably, Capt. Smith does not consider his best game to be war.

The Vessel herself, however, enjoys a Reputation for Nerve, having proved it at Quebec, fearless under the French batteries of Beauport, part of a Diversion whilst the real assault proceeded quite upon the other flank, out of the troop-carrying ships that had sailed past the city, further upstream. Thenceforward is her Glory assur'd. She has done her duty in the service of a miracle in that year of miracles, 1759, upon whose Ides of March Dr. Johnson happen'd to remark, "No man will be a sailor who has contrivance enough to get himself into a jail; for being in a ship is being in a jail, with the chance of being drowned."

Some would call her a Frigate, though officially she is a couple of guns shy, causing others to add the prefix "Jackass,"— a nautical term. Neither Names nor modest throw-weights have kept her from mixing it up with bigger ships. Capt. Smith has long understood that tho' a Sea Horse may be born in spirit an Arab stallion, sometimes must it also function as a Jackass,— a Creature known, that is, as much for its obstinacy in an argument as for its trick of turning and using its hind legs as a weapon. "Therefore I want the best gun crew for the Stern Cannon. Let this Jackass show them a deadly kick."

When the *l'Grand* comes a-looming, nevertheless, the Captain is more than a little surprised. Why should Monsieur be taking the trouble?— knowing the answer to be "Frigate Business," built into the definition of the command. In return for freedom to range upon the Sea, one was bound by a Code as strict as that of any ancient Knight. The *Seahorse's* Motto, lovingly embroider'd by a certain Needlewoman of Southsea, and nail'd above the Bed in his Cabin, reads *Eques Sit Æquus.*

"Now, *Eques*," according to the helpful young Revd Wicks Cherry-coke, "means 'an arm'd Horseman.' "

"Ranging the Land," Dixon suggests, "as a Frigate-Sailor the Sea."

"Later, in old Rome, it came to mean a sort of Knight,— a Gentleman, somewhere between the ordinary People and the Senate. *Sit* is 'may he be,' and *Æquus* means 'just,'— also, perhaps, 'even-temper'd.' So we might take your ship's Motto to mean, 'Let the Sea-Knight who would command this Sea-Horse be ever fair-minded,'— "

"— trying not to lose his Temper, even with boil-brain'd subordinates?" the Captain growling thus at Lieutenant Unchleigh, who stands timidly signaling for his attention.

"Um, what appears to be a Sail, South-Southwest,— although there is faction upon the question, others insisting 'tis a Cloud...."

"Damnation, Unchleigh," Capt. Smith in a low Voice, reaching for his Glass. "Hell-fire, too. If it's a Frenchman, he's seen us, and is making all sail."

"I knew that," says the Lieutenant.

"Here. Don't drop this. Get up the Mast and tell me exactly what and where it is. Take Bodine up with you, with a watch and compass,— and if it proves to be a sail, do try to obtain a few nicely spac'd magnetickal

Bearings, there's a good Lieutenant. You'll note how very Scientifick we are here, Gentlemen. Yet," turning to a group of Sailors holystoning the deck, "ancient Beliefs will persist. Here then, Bongo! Yes! Yes, Captain wishes Excellent Bongo *smell Wind!*"

The Lascar so address'd, crying, "Aye, aye, Cap'n!," springs to the windward side, up on a rail, and, grasping some Armful of the Fore-Shrouds, presses himself far into the Wind, head-rag a-fluttering,— almost immediately turning his Head, with a look of Savage Glee,— "Frenchies!"

"Hard a-port," calls the Captain, as down from the Maintop comes word that the object does rather appear to be a Sail, at least so far unaccompanied, and is withal running express, making to intercept the *Seahorse*. "Gentlemen, 'twould oblige me if you'd find ways to be useful below." The Drum begins its Beat. They have grown up, English Boys never far from the Sea, with Tales of its Battles and Pirates and Isles just off the Coasts of Paradise. They know what "below" promises.

At first it seems but a Toy ship, a Toy Destiny.... T'gallants and stay-sails go crowding on, but the wind is obstinate at SSW, the *Seahorse* may but ever beat against it, in waters treacherous of stream, whilst the *l'Grand* is fresh out from Brest, with the wind on her port quarter.

" 'Twas small work to come up with us, get to leeward,— from which the French prefer to engage,— and commence her broadsides, the *Seahorse* responding in kind, for an hour and a half of blasting! and smashing! and masts falling down!"

"Blood flowing in the scuppers!" cries Pitt.

"Did you swing on a rope with a knife in your teeth?" asks Pliny.

"Of course. And a pistol in me boot."

"Uncle." Brae disapproves.

The Rev^d only beams. One reason Humans remain young so long, compar'd to other Creatures, is that the young are useful in many ways, among them in providing daily, by way of the evil Creatures and Slaughter they love, a Denial of Mortality clamorous enough to allow their Elders release, if only for moments at a time, from Its Claims upon the Attention. "Sad to say, Boys, I was well below, and preoccupied with sea-

37

surgery, learning what I needed to know of it upon the Spot. By the end of the Engagement I was left with nothing but my Faith between me and absolute black Panic. Afterward, from whatever had happen'd upon that patch of secular Ocean, I went on to draw Lessons more abstract.

"Watching helplessly as we closed with the *l'Grand*, I felt that with each fraction of a second, Death was making itself sensible in new ways.... We were soon close enough to hear the creak and jingling of the gun tackle and the rumble of trucks upon the deck, then to see the ends of the rammers backing through the gun-ports, and vanishing as cartridges and wads were pushed into place, and the high-pitch'd foreign jabbering as we lean'd ever closer....

"Broadsides again and again, punctuated by tacking so as to present the Guns of the other Side,— ringing cessations in which came the Thumps of re-loading, the cries of the injur'd and dying, nausea, Speechlessness, Sweat pouring,— then broadsides once more. Each time the firing stopp'd, there seem'd hope, for a Minute, that we'd got away and it was over,...until we'd hear the Gun-Tackle being shifted, and feel in the dark the deck trying to tilt us over, charg'd with the moments, upon the downward Roll, just before the Guns, vibrating in a certain way we had come to expect,— and when it came no more, we stood afraid to breathe, because of what might be next.

"The Astronomers and I meanwhile endur'd intestinal agonies so as not to be the first to foul his breeches in front of the others, as the Spars came crashing from above, and the cannon sent sharp Thuds thro' the Ship like cruel fists boxing our ears, knocking cockroaches out of the overhead,— Blows whose personal Malevolence was more frightening even than their Scale,— the Ship's hoarse Shrieking, a great Sea-animal in pain, the textures of its Cries nearly those of the human Voice when under great Stress."

Altho' Dixon is heading off to Sumatra with a member of the Church of England,— that is, the *Ancestor of Troubles*,— a stranger with whom he moreover but hours before was carousing *exactly like Sailors*, shameful to say, yet, erring upon the side of Conviviality, will he decide to follow Fox's Advice, and answer "that of God" in Mason, finding it soon enough with the Battle on all 'round them, when both face their equal chances of imminent Death.

Dissolution, Noise, and Fear. Below-decks, reduced to nerves, given in to the emprise of Forces invisible yet possessing great Weight and Speed, which contend in some Phantom realm they have had the bad luck to blunder into, the Astronomers abide, willing themselves blank yet active. Casualties begin to appear in the Sick Bay, the wounds inconceivable, from Oak-Splinters and Chain and Shrapnel, and as Blood creeps like Evening to Dominion over all Surfaces, so grows the Ease of giving in to Panic Fear. It takes an effort to act philosophickal, or even to find ways to be useful,— but a moment's re-focusing proves enough to show them each how at least to keep out of the way, and presently to save steps for the loblolly boy, or run messages to and from other parts of the ship.

After the last of the Gun-Fire, Oak Beams shuddering with the Chase, the Lazarette is crowded and pil'd with bloody Men, including Capt. Smith with a great Splinter in his Leg, his resentment especially powerful,— "I'll have lost thirty of my Crew. Are you two really that important?" Above, on deck, corpses are steaming, wreckage is ev'ry-where, shreds of charr'd sail and line clatter in the Wind that is taking the Frenchman away.

What conversation may have passed between the Post-Captain and the Commandant? He wore the Order of the Holy Ghost, the white Dove plainly visible thro' the Glass,— St.-Foux, almost certainly, yet commanding a different Ship. What was afoot here? Had the Frenchman really signal'd, "France is not at war with the sciences"? Words so mag-nanimous, and yet..."Went *poohpooh*, he did. Sort of flicking his gloves about. 'I'm westing my time,' he says, 'You are leetluh meennow,— I throw you back. Perhaps someday we meet when you are biggair Feesh, like me. Meanwhile, I sail away. *Poohpooh! Adieu!*' "

"Nevertheless," Capt. Smith had replied, "I must give chase."

One of those French shrugs. "You must, and of course, may."

But she is too wounded. They watch the perfect ellipse of the *l'Grand*'s stern dwindle into the dark. At last, well before the midwatch, Captain Smith calls off the Chase, and they come about again, the wind remain-ing as it has been, and with what sail they have, they return to the Ply-mouth Dockyard.

Some at the time said there had been another sail, and that the Frenchman, assuming it to be a British Man o' War, had in fact broken off, and headed back in to Brest as speedily as her condition would allow. Some on the *Seahorse* thought they'd seen it,— most had not. ("Perhaps our guardian Angel," the Rev^d comments, "— instead of Wings, Topgallants.")

A Year before, Morale aboard the *l'Grand,* never that high to begin with, had seem'd to suffer an all but mortal blow with news of the disaster to the Brest fleet at Quiberon Bay. In calculating her odds *vis-à-vis* the *Seahorse,* the Invisible Gamesters who wager daily upon the doings of Commerce and Government must have discounted her advantage in guns and broadside weight, noting that a crew so melancholick is not the surest guarantee of prevailing in a Naval Dispute. Yet, considered as a sentient being, the French Ship continued to display the attitude of an undersiz'd but bellicose Sailor in a Wine-shop, always upon the *qui vive* for a scrap, never quite reaching the level of Glory it desir'd, always *téton dernier* of the Squadron, ever chosen for the least hopeful Missions, from embargo patrols off steaming red-dawn coasts below the Equator to rescue attempts beneath the Shadows of the mountainous Waves of winter storms in the Atlantic,— forever unthank'd, disrespected, laboring on, beating now alone at night back into Brest for new spars and rigging and lives.

> "Ooh,
>   La,
>   Fran...
>   -Ce-euh! [with a certain debonair little Mordant upon "euh"],
> Ne
> Fait-pas-la-Guerre,
> Con-truh les Sci-
>   -en-
>   ceuhs!"

— sung incessantly till the Ship made Port, and then by the Working-Parties at the Quai, with the sour cadences of Sailors in a Distress not altogether bodily,— humiliated, knowing better, yet unable to keep from humming the catchy fragment, its text instantly having join'd the Company of great Humorous Naval Quotations, which would one day also include, "I have not yet begun to fight," and, "There's something wrong with our damn'd ships today, Chatfield."

Long after Nightfall, Mason and Dixon, officially reliev'd of their Medical Duties, reluctant to part company, go lurching up on Deck, exhausted, laughing at nothing,— or at ev'rything, being alive when they could as easily be dead. Despite the salt rush of Wind, they can no more here, than Below, escape caught in the Drape of the damag'd Sails, the Reek of the Battle past,— the insides of Trees, and of Men…. They have to prop each other up till one of them finds something to lean against. "Well, what's this, then?" inquires Mason.

"More like a Transit of Mars…?"

"With us going 'cross *its* Face."

"Were I less of a cheery Lad, why, I'd almost think…"

"It has occurr'd to me."

"They knew the French had Bencoolen,— what else did they know? Thah's what I'd like to know."

"Are you appropriating that Bottle for reasons I may not wish to hear, or,— ah. Thankee." They pass the Bottle back and forth, and when it is empty, they throw it in the Sea, and open another.

5

If ever they meant to break up the Partnership, this would've been the time. " 'Twas all so out of the ordinary," Mason declares, "that it must have been intended,— an act of Him so strange, His purposes unknown."

"Eeh,— that is, I'm not sure which one tha mean."

Mason instantly narrows his eyes. "Who else could— oh. Oh, I see. Hum...a common Belief among your People?"

"All thah' Coal-Mining, I guess."

In the crucial moments, neither Mason nor Dixon had fail'd the other. Each had met the other's Gaze for a slight moment before Duty again claim'd them,— the Vapors rising from the Wounds of dying Sailors smoothing out what was not essential for each to understand.

For the moment, they know they must stand as one, tho' not always how. Arriv'd in Plymouth Dockyard, drafting the letter to the Royal Society, thro' the dark hours, each keeps rejecting the other's ideas. The Candles tremble with the Vehemence of their Speech. They are well the other side of Exhaustion, and neither has bother'd to keep his defensive works mann'd against the other. With what they've lately been through together, it seems quite beside the point for them to do so. At least they are past that. Each knows, that is, exactly how brave and how cowardly the other was when the crisis came.

"Say, 'If You might arrange for us each to have a Regiment,— a Frigate being impractical, given our Ignorance of how to sail, much less fight, one,— we should be happy to proceed to war upon any people, in any quarter of the Globe His Majesty should be pleas'd to send us to,— ' "

"Dixon, think,— what if they should say yes? Do you want to command a Regiment?"

"Why,...say, 'tis nothing I'd rule out, at this stage of my life,— "

"You're a Quaker, you're not suppos'd to believe in War."

"Technically no longer a Quaker, as they expell'd me back at the end of October from Raby Meeting, just before I came to London,— so I guess now I may kill anyone I like...?"

Mason pretends interest, having already heard about it in his briefing by the R.S. "And will any personal difficulties attend that, do you think?"

"We've all of us,— the same Quaker Families, Dixons, Hunters and Rayltons in particular, again and again,— a long history in Durham of being toss'd out for anything, be it drinking, getting married by a Priest, working for the Royal Society, whatever someone didn't like. To some Christians, Disfellowship is a hard Blow, for they have been allow'd to know only others of their Congregation. But Quakers are a bit matier, the idea being to look for something of God in ev'ryone...? The Denomination's less important. Ah mean, Ah've met Anglicans before...?"

"I wonder'd why you never stare at me much."

"Eeh, Ah've even seen the Bishop of Durham. One of the very biggest among thee, correct? A Prince in his own lands. No,— I've no problem with Anglicans."

"Thank ye. I welcome the return of at least an Hour's more Sleep each Night otherwise spent in Fretfulness upon the Question. Be assur'd, I have run across the odd Quaker as well,— Mr. Bird of course coming to mind,— and have ever found you Folk as peaceable in your private Discourse, as you are Assertive in your Publick Doings."

"That's what people say, for fair."

There they sit, drinking up their liquor allowance, feeling no easier for it, trying to understand what in Christ's Name happen'd out in the Channel. Neither is making much sense. They will talk seriously for half an hour about something completely stupid, then one will take offense and fall silent, or go off somewhere to try to sleep. Out in the hall they keep running into each other, Wraiths in night-clothes.

"What if we said," Mason appearing to have given it some Thought, " 'In view of an apparent Design, by well-known Gentlemen, to put me in harm's way— ' "

" 'Huz.' "

"If you like. — exposing an undermann'd Warship to a certain Drubbing, Questions must emerge. Why could not the French Admiralty have been advis'd, via Father Boscovich or another available messenger, of the *Seahorse*'s approximate Route, her destination and purpose?' "

"Eeh, Mason, come, come. They would have attack'd anyway. Why would they believe any story from the English, be the Messenger King Louie Himself?"

"A little Sixth-Rate! What possible mischief could it get into? What possible threat to France?"

" 'Tis call'd, in that jabber over there, *Une Affaire des Frégates,*— 'An Affair of the Frigates.' "

"Of Forces less visible, I fear."

"Here,— any more of that Golden Virginian about? 'Twill settle our wits." In what each is surpriz'd to note for the first time as a companionable Silence, they prepare Pipes, find a Dish in the Cupboard and a live Coal in the Fire, and light up.

Wrapt tightly, as within Vacuum-Hemispheres, lies the Unspoken,— the concentration of Terror and death of but two afternoons ago, transpir'd without one word, in brute Contempt for any language but that of winds and masses, cries and blood. Impenetrable, it calls up Questions whose Awkwardness has only increas'd as the Astronomers have come to understand there may be no way of ever finding the Answers.

"Did the Captain signal? Did they read it, and attack despite it?"

"Or *because of it*...?"

It seems not to belong in either of their lives. "Was there a mistake in the Plan of the Day? Did we get a piece of someone else's History, a fragment spall'd off of some Great Moment,— perhaps the late Engagement at Quiberon Bay,— such as now and then may fly into the ev'ryday paths of lives less dramatick? And there we are, with our Wigs askew."

"Happen," Dixon contributes in turn, "we were never meant at all to go to Bencoolen,— someone needed a couple of Martyrs, and we inconveniently surviv'd...?"

"What a terrible thing to say."

" 'Terrible,' well, as to 'Terrible'..." And what they cannot speak, some of it not yet, some of it never, resumes breathless Sovereignty in the wax-lit Rooms.

In swift reply comes a Letter of Reproach and Threat from the Royal Society. Someday Mason and Dixon may not dream as often of the Battle with the Frenchman,— but this Letter they will go back to again and again, unable to release it.

"Not even the courtesy,— Damme! of a personal Reply,— 'tis rather the final draft of some faceless committee. To my Heart's Cry, my appeal to Bradley for Guidance, Apprentice to master, confiding candidly my fears, trusting in his Discretion,— to a four years' Adjunct, his Protégé even longer,— instead of Comfort or Advice, he betrays my Confession to some Gang of initial'd Scoundrels, leaving them the task of bringing us to the level of Fear needed to get us back aboard that dreadful Ship."

"Yet others," carefully, "might hear in it a distinct Voice, indeed quite full of personal Heat."

Mason shrugs. "Who, then? 'Twas Morton his Signature,— " his Eyebrows rak'd a shade too high for it to be other than a request to let this go.

"Ordinarily, Ah'd allow it to depart upon the Tides of Fortune...?" says Dixon, "— but as I'm included in this charge of Cowardice, if it be a Matter between thee and Dr. Bradley, why, I hope tha'd tell me somewhat of it...?"

"You suppose this is Bradley's voice? I think not, for I know him,— Bradley cannot write like this, even simple social notes give him trouble. '...Whenever their circumstances, now uncertain and eventual, shall happen to be reduced to Certainty.' Not likely."

"Eeh, thah's deep...? 'Reduc'd.' "

"As if...there were no single Destiny," puzzles Mason, "but rather a choice among a great many possible ones, their number steadily diminishing each time a Choice be made, till at last 'reduc'd,' to the events that do happen to us, as we pass among 'em, thro' Time unredeemable,— much as a Lens, indeed, may receive all the Light from some vast celestial Field of View, and reduce it to a single Point. Suggests an optical person,— your Mr. Bird, perhaps."

"Then tha may rest easy, mayn't thee, if it's I who's being reprov'd by *my* Mentor, for a change...?"

Thus sleeplessly on both continue to rattle, whilst Plymouth reels merrily all 'round them, well illuminated, as a-scurry, thro' the night.

"Lightning doesn't strike twice," suggests Dixon.

"Correct. It strikes once, as it just lately did for me out there. Now 'tis your turn."

"Hold, hold...? Are tha sure of thah'...?"

6

"The Interdiction at Sea," it seems to the Rev[d], "was patently a warning to the Astronomers, from Beyond. Tho' men of Science, both now confess'd to older and more Earthly Certainties, being willing then and there to give up Bencoolen, offering rather to observe the Transit from any other Station yet in reach,— Skanderoon was mention'd,— but the Royal S. wrote back in the most overbearing way, on about loss of honor, strongly threatening legal action if Mason and Dixon were to break their contract, *force majeure* or no, even when it was pointed out yet again that Bencoolen lay in the hands of the French, anyway. No matter that the Astronomers were right and the R.S. wrong,— they had to comply."

"But why?" laughs Brae in exasperation, waving her Needle and Floss about. "Why weren't they simply more flexible in London? Just send the *Seahorse* someplace else?"

"So they did, when next our Astronomers put to sea."

"Having, I hope, *splic'd their Main-Brace* well,— g'd Evening, all." 'Tis Uncle Lomax, sliding in from the day at his Soap-Works, smelling of his Product, allowing the cheeriness of the Sot to overcome the diffidence of a man in an unpopular calling,— for "Philadelphia Soap" is a Byword, throughout the American Provinces, of low Quality. At the touch of water, nay, damp Air, it becomes a vile Mucus that refuses to be held in any sort of grip, gentle or firm, and often leaves things dirtier than they were before its application,— making it, more properly, an Anti-Soap. He steers a Loxodrome for the cabinet where ardent Spirits are kept for Guests of the Wet Persuasion, and pretends to weigh his Choice.

So off we sail again (the Rev^d continues), this time in convoy with another, larger Frigate,— the idea being, Children, always to get back up on the Horse that has nearly killed one. Especially if it's a Sea Horse. I am quarter'd with Lieutenant Unchleigh, a rattle-head. "Damme, Sir,— a Book? Close it up immediately."

" 'Tis the Holy Bible, Sir."

"No matter, 'tis Print,— Print causes Civil Unrest,— Civil Unrest in any Ship at Sea is intolerable. Coffee as well. Where are newpapers found? In those damnable Whig Coffee-Houses. Eh? A Potion stimulating rebellion and immoderate desires."

I feel a certain Gastrick Desolation. What will be his idea of Diversion ashore? Nothing to do with Coffee, I suppose,— tho' this Route to India be known as a Caffeinist's Dream. What else may he not abide? My Berth a Prison, unseamanlike Behavior abounding, the very Ship a Ship of Death. How is any of this going to help restore me to the "ordinary World"?— the answer, which I am yet too young to see, being that these are the very given Conditions of the "ordinary World." At the time, my inward lament goes something like this,—

> Where are the wicked young Widows tonight,
> That sail the East India Trade?
> Topside with the Captain, below with the Crew,
> Beauteously ever display'd.
> Oh I wish I was anyplace,
> But the Someplace I'm in,
> With too many Confusions and Pains,—
> Take me back to the Cross-Roads,
> Let me choose, once again,
> To cruise the East India Lanes.

Frigate Captains are uncomfortable with sailing in formation,— 'tis to be turn'd to fussing about forever with Jib and Staysail, by someone senior with an oppressively tidy Theory of Station-keeping. The Aversion of the *Seahorse*'s new Captain to group manœuvres indeed extends to sailing with even one other warship, as the captain of the *Brilliant*, 36, will discover before they are out of the Channel.

In the brisk weather, there seems little sense in dawdling. The impatient Capt. Grant keeps closing the gap between himself and the ship ahead, often drawing up to a distance that allows Sailors easily to converse in ordinary tones, till at last the *Brilliant* signals to the *Seahorse*, "Observe Standard Interval,— Comply." After a moment's Cogitation, Grant signals back, "Oh." Having given orders to make to windward, he repairs to his Cabin to fetch from a Chest a curiously embellish'd Jolly Roger, said to be of the Barbadoes, won at Swedish Rummy of a Sailing-Master off the old H.M.S. *Unreflective.* Now, having gather'd enough open sea, he cheerfully comes about, hoists his black Announcement, and runs full before the breeze, knifing through the swell as if intending to ram the *Brilliant.* The other Captain returns this Jollification by clearing for Battle. If not for the timely appearance of sail in the direction of Brest, who knows how far the Affair might have been taken?

"Insane," Mason shuddering in fear only partly exaggerated. "How can the Admiralty allow such Men freely to set to sea, in these murderous machines of war?"

"A Quaker might say, 'tis war thah's insane, and Frigate captains only more open about it...?"

"What,— All War,— no exceptions? You go about in this,— forgive me,— this Coat, Hat, and Breeches of unmistakably military color and cut,— "

"Upon the theory that a Representation of Authority, whose extent no one is quite sure of, may act as a deterrent to Personal Assault."

"— not to mention this Ocean of Ale flowing thro' you, day after day, Sundays not exempt,— a Potable well known for provoking Truculence,— "

"Hold,— tha're saying Wine-Drinkers are the meek who'll inherit the Earth?"

"Preferably that part of it with a sunward slope, and well-drain'd, aye,— and what of it, Mustard-Grinder?"

"Ale does not make me violent," Dixon explains, "— I am violent by nature. Ale-drinking, rather, slows me down, increasing the chances I'll fall asleep before I cause too much damage. I could summon witnesses, if tha'd like...?"

By this point they are well out to Sea, bound for Tenerife to take on water and wine (hence the priority of the Topick), and then as far East as a mysterious seal'd Dispatch, handed to the Captain at Plymouth just before they cast off, will command. "Oh, that's all right," Mason waving grandly, "I'll take your word for it." And together as the sun goes down o'er the starboard Bow, they sing.

> We swore up and down, that we'd sail nevermore,
> Thro' waters infested by French-men,
> Whilst in Safety and Smugness, all dry on the Shore,
> Kept Morton and all of his Hench-men,—
> Yet a Shark is a Shark, in the day or the dark,
> Be he Minister, fish or King's Be-ench-man,
> With a Munch and a Crunch and the Lunch shall be free!
> And Good-bye, Royal Soci...e-tee!
> [Refrain]
> For we're off to the Indies, off to the East,
> Ho for the Fables and Ho for the Feast,—
> Grov'ling like Slaves in the Land of the Turk,
> There's nought an Astronomer won't do for Work.

From the time they clear'd the Lizard, Capt. Grant has made no secret of where *he's* been these dreary months since Quiberon Bay,— camp'd like a Gypsy upon a waiting-list, is where, ever laboring to empty his mind, seeking to become but the sleek Purity of Ink upon Paper, trusting in the large-scale behavior of Destiny to bring him, even in this wretched Lull, a Ship, any Ship,— until he saw the *Seahorse,* and amended this to, well, *almost* any Ship....

It had done his Hopes little good to see her so wounded, tho' he understood the Immortality of Ships,— new masts stepp'd in and Yards set, Riggers all over her, new preventers and Swifters and Futtock-Staves, one miserable reeving at a time,— yet slow as Clock-hands, Wood, Hemp, and Canvas Resurrection would proceed. Three weeks and she was whole again, waiting in Sutton Pool. Grant's orders were to follow the *Brilliant* when the *Brilliant* should be order'd to depart, and then stand by for further Advice.

This came by way of an Admiralty Fopling, standing up in the Gig that brought him out, waving a seal'd Sheaf of Papers. "You're to head South, and open these at Tenerife," a Smirk possessing the young Phiz as whiskers had not so far been able to do. "Now this is an instrument of Receipt,— "

Muttering, Capt. Grant surreptitiously flicked the Quill, trying to spatter ink-drops upon the Visitor's snowy lac'd Stock, as he pretended to blurt, "Yet Sir, I must confide this to someone, the Truth being,— "

" 'Truth'...?" A look of unaccustom'd Astonishment. "Perhaps I am not your ideal Confidant," he mumbled, "— divided Loyalties sort of thing...."

Feverishly, Capt. Grant continued, "— I find my thoughts ever wand'ring, that is, you see, to the Topick of Bencoolen, and to the Rumor that my Predecessor was order'd there in full knowledge that 'twas already in the hands of the French,— rendering his whole trip rather pointless, and naturally the Thought then did occur to me, well, what if my orders are to some equally impossible Destination? Except that now it seems I may not know till Tenerife."

"Not my Desk, really, so terribly sorry," descending again to the Gig, calling back, "yet chin up, perhaps it is a British Destination, or will be so by the time you get there,— so much more swiftly than the Trade Winds, these Days, do the Winds of Diplomacy blow."

"Boy, ye're sending me 'pon a damn'd fool's errand."

"Ah,— your first, Sir?"

He couldn't very well call the Sprout out, could he?— especially as he recognized too easily the malapert youth he himself had once been, the Offense he'd offer'd merely by being present,— down to the matching Waistcoat and Queue-Tie, in the same choice of citrick-yellow. He settled for loading and priming a Pistol, aiming it across the water, and allowing the Youth to decide whether to cower in the Boat or jump into the Water.

At this turn of his Life, Capt. Grant has discover'd in his own feckless Youth, a Source of pre-civiliz'd Sentiment useful to his Praxis of now and then *pretending to be insane,* thus deriving an Advantage over any unsure as to which side of Reason he may actually stand upon. Not till they're well at Sea, with a Fortnight more till they sight the Peaks of

Tenerife, does he find Mason busy at the same Arts, morose and silent, beetle-back'd against the Wind, keeping Vigil all day and night of 13 February, the second Anniversary of his Wife Rebekah's passing, touching neither Food nor Drink,— with no one upon the Ship, including Capt. Grant, willing to approach too near,— till the final eight Bells, when Mason reaches for a Loaf and a Bottle and becomes upon the instant convivial as anyone has ever seen him.

The Sailors, having mark'd in both Men these rapid changes of Aspect, are determin'd to keep a wary eye,— tho' Madness at Sea is not quite as worrying as fire or theft, being indeed so of the essence of a Frigate's crew that one might as well speak of "Hemp at Sea" or "Wood at Sea." It's a Village, after all, 's a Frigate,— and what is a Village, without Village Idiots? Ev'ryone on board knows who the Madmen are, and that they are here as security against the Forces of Night,— "Don't want the French hurting my Mate here, do I. Jus' 'coz half the time he thinks he's Admiral Hawke,— "

"Noted, noted. Now unhand me, I say!"

"There, there, your Lordship."

"— Common Swab."

This ship's history has, however, prov'd too hectick for its Military Band. The Frigate life is not for ev'ryone,— it seems wherever this one put in, whenever any sailor went over and fail'd to return, he was a *Seahorse* musician. One by one, thro' the years of the Rivalry with France, the little Combination dwindl'd,— upon the North American Station, they lost their Inner Voices, halfway thro' the West Indies their Continuo,— until, home again, the Hautboy-player having been one night absorb'd into that Other World of which Wapping is the anteroom, the *Seahorse* found herself down to a single Fifer, to whom it fell, the noontide the Frenchman appear'd, to inspire the Lads into battle with his one silver Pipe.

None, later, could say,— tho' sure the Moment was enough,— the deepening bowel-fear as the ships drew slowly together, the *l'Grand* growing ever larger, smaller details ever more visible, the *Seahorse*'s Crew, understanding that nothing would go away now, and that Shot was inevitable, 'morphosing to extensions of a single Engine homicidal,— in that general and ungovernable Tip of Soul, what allow'd us to hear the

Musick so keenly?— the Fife being of standard Military issue, tun'd in that most martial of Scales, B-flat major, stirring in all who heard it, even Philosophers, the desire to prevail over a detestable Enemy,— its Performance recall'd as "virtually Orchestral." Amid the Blasts, the heavy tun'd Whirrs of enemy Shot, the mortal Cries, could the Instrument ever be heard,— "Hearts of Oak," "Rule, Britannia,"— aching for the phantom polyphony no longer on board, trying to make up for the other Voices by Efforts of Lip as difficult as any of Limb, proceeding among the Gun-Tackle.

Slowcombe had been press'd from a tavern in Wapping where he clearly ought not to've been, mischievous Lad,— having learn'd the Art of his Instrument from the fam'd Hanoverian Fifer Johann Ulrich, whom the Duke of Bedford had brought in after the previous War to instruct his Regimental Winds. "You'll ask, what's a Royal Artilleryman doing in a Sailor's Haunt? Aye, nowt but a low, mud-bound Gunner, surrounded by them who must be both Gunners and Seamen,— hoping, I confess, to pass as one of them. Is ours not the Age of Metamorphosis, with any turn of Fortune a possibility? So, upon that Night, did I pass abruptly from Soldier to Sailor, in less than the swallowing of a cheaply opiated Pint, and found, but for the inconvenience of it, a Dream come true,— there being Soldiers' sorts of Lasses, I mean, and Sailors' sorts, and a quiet Brotherhood who appreciate the Sailors' Lasses who be left, for all the reasons we know, unattended. And now tell me, for I'll ne'er tell you, of the short and devious Fifer out trolling for trouble, creeping 'round, sniggering, peeping up Skirts,— yet ah, my Lads, most times all it took was to bring out the Fife, and finger upon it some brief Air,— eight Bars of any little Quantz Etude, and usually she was mine."

"Rather stick the Pig and hear it squeal," comments Jack "Fingers" Soames, a viperish Lad whose eponymous Gesture, made in answer to all Overtures, however ritual or ev'ryday, strangely lacks any hostile Intent, being expressive rather of a deep-held wish, so far as may be possible within the Perimeter of a Sixth-Rate, to be left alone. All but the most resolutely matey of Ship's Company are content to oblige him. He enjoys the solitude that results,— never idle, obeying commands Outer and Inner, perfecting maritime Skills,— amid, but not of, a floating Village of others just as busy living lives he's no desire to enter. "So you got married, does that mean you forgot how to fuck yourself?" " 'Nice day'? do you know Bollocks?— go get hit by Lightning."

The only crew member he has ever been Civil to is Veevle, legendary thro'out the Royal N. for being impossible to wake to stand Watch. Countless hundreds of Ship-mates have tried without issue to rouse the somniac Tar. The Admiralty is understood secretly to have plac'd in Escrow a £1,000 reward for the first who should succeed.

Audible methods, such as screaming, having been early discourag'd by others requiring sleep, his would-be Awakeners have tried hitting the Soles of Veevle's Feet with Rope-ends, introducing Cockroaches up his Nose, and rolling him over and administering Enemas of Lucas the Cook's notorious Coffee, which in several sworn instances has restor'd life to certified Cadavers. Nothing works. They whisper elaborate Promises. They light Slow-Matches and place them between his Toes. They wrap him in his Hammock and lower him over the Side, and at the touch of the Waves, he but makes a snuggling motion, and begins to snore. It is soon widely appreciated that one must catch Veevle whilst awake, and trick him into standing someone else's Watch, whereupon he becomes the smartest and most estimable of Seamen.

"Cheerly. Cheerly, then, Lads...."

"Excuse me, Captain, problem with the Euphroes again."

"Get O'Brian up here, then, if it's about Euphroes, he's the one to see."

"Hey t'en, Pat. Scribblin' again, are ye? More Sea stories?" Not only does O'Brian know all there is to know and more 'pon the Topick of Euphroes, and Rigging even more obscure,— he's also acknowledg'd as the best Yarn-Spinner in all the Fleets. "Euphroe Detail again."

They are in the southern Latitudes at last, hence the need for Awnings,— the shipboard routine settl'd into, the Boatswain, Mr. Higgs, turning ev'ryone to upon the Project of tidying up the work of the Riggers at Plymouth, who've left far too many Ends untuck'd for this Deck-Tyrant, born under the sign of Virgo, so obsessive about neatness in Knot-work, as to provide a source of Amusement for the Captain, who finds him an ideal Subject to practice being insane upon. "A Phiz of Doom! we can't have this! Worse than idle Whistling!" Mr. Higgs obliges the section not on Watch to attend Instruction in Lashings, Seizings, the art of making a Turk's Head that might fool a Harem Girl. "You may think no one'll get close enough to see it, but a Thousand details, each nearly invisible, all working together, can mean the difference between a ship that goes warping and kedging in to a Foreign Port, and one that Makes an Entrance. And which will the Scoundrels think of meddling with first, eh? Now I want to see each of ye hauling me taut a Matthew Walker, that England shall be proud of,"— implying that somewhere there is a Royal Museum of Splices, Hitches, and Bends, where their Work may one day lie upon Display. Some in the Narcosis of the Cruise are more than eager to adopt Mr. Higgs's Obsessedness as to Loose Ends, becoming many of them quite picky indeed, scrutinizing the Rigging, often whilst fifty feet up in its Midst, for unsightly Dribblings of Stockholm Tar, Hooks too carelessly mous'd, fray'd Throat-Seizing among the Dead-eyes.

Other Sailors look for alternatives to Ennui even more extreme.

"Where's Bodine?"

"Last I saw of him was out the end of the fore t'gallant Yard, with his Penis in the Jewel Block,— quite enjoying the Friction, to Appearance."

"You men are that desperate for Entertainment?"

"Do we seem to you a care-free Lot, Sir? 'Tis quite otherwise. Bodine, among his shipmates, is indeed reckon'd fastidious,— the steps from Boredom to Discontent to Unwise Practices are never shorter than aboard a Sixth-Rate upon a long Voyage, Sir." One or two chess players hold out for perhaps an extra week,— then 'tis *Sal Si Puedes,* and they, too, are biting off their toenails, growing Whiskers, piercing Ears, putting upon View, for a fee, fictitious Sea-Creatures that others must bend down to see, becoming thereupon subject to Posterior Assault.

In such a recreational Vacuum, the Prospect of crossing the Equatorial Line soon grows unnaturally magnified, as objects in certain Mirages and Apparitions at Sea,— a Grand Event, prepared for weeks in advance. Fearless Acrobats of the upper Courses and hardened Gunners with prick'd-in black-powder Tattoos are all at once fussing about, nitter-nattering like a Village-ful of housewives over trivial details of the Ceremony of Initiation plann'd for those new to this Crossing, and dropping into Whispers whenever these "Pollywogs,"— namely, Mason,

Dixon, and the Revd Cherrycoke,— happen near. Members of the Crew are to take the parts of King Neptune and his Mermaid Queen, and their Court, and the Royal Baby,— a rôle especially sought after, but assign'd by Tradition to him (Fender Bodine is an early favorite in the Wagering) whose Paunch, oozing with Equatorial Sweat, 'twill be most nauseating for a Pollywog to crawl to and kiss,— this being among the more amiable Items upon the Schedule of Humiliation.

"Why?" the Twins wish to know. "It sounds more like Punishment. Did somebody make it a crime to cross the Equator?"

"Sailors' Pranks, Lads,— ignoring 'em's best," huffs Uncle Ives. "And a foolish rowdy-dow over some Geometers' Abstraction that cannot even be seen."

"But that for one Instant," the Rev^d points out, "our Shadows lay perfectly beneath us. To change Hemispheres is no abstract turn,— our Attentions to the Royal Baby, and the rest of it, were Tolls exacted for passage thro' the Gate of the single shadowless Moment, and into the South, with a newly constellated Sky, and all-unforeseen ways of living and dying. So must there be a Ritual of Crossing Over, serving to focus each Pollywog's Mind upon the Step he was taking."

"We'd suppos'd it fun," frowns Pliny.

"Your getting thump'd about and all, Uncle," explains Pitt.

"Has either of you," inquires the Rev^d, "ever had a Basin-ful of Spotted Dick slung into your Face?" The Twins, deciding that this is not an actual Threat, voice approval of the Practice. "Yes, boys, it does sound sportive enough,— except for the part that no one ever tells you about,— "

"Tell us!" cries Pitt.

"Not sure I ought...the same indeed being true of Puddings and the more Cream-like Pies,— "

"Tell us, or you're Salt Pork," stipulates Pliny.

"Well, then, Lads,— *it goes up your Nose.* Yes. You know what Pond-water feels like up there, I'm sure, but imagine...thick, cold, day-before-yesterday's Spotted Dick,...curdling, spots of Mold, with all those horrible Raisin-bits, hard as Gravel,— "

"And if it goes far *enough* up your Nose," adds Uncle Lomax with a monitory tremolo, "Well. Then it's in your *Brain,* isn't it?"

In the Lull whilst the Boys consider this, the Rev[d] slips back into his tale.

On southward the *Seahorse* gallops, as if secure forever in a warm'd, melodious Barcarole of indolent days, when in fact 'twill be only a few degrees of Latitude more till we pick up the Trade Wind, and hear in its Desert Whistle the message Ghosts often bring,— that 'tis time, once again, to turn to. And, in denial of all we thought we knew, to smell the Land we are making for, the green fecund Continent, upon the Wind that comes from behind us.

The Astronomers have a game call'd "Sumatra" that the Rev[d] often sees them at together,— as children, sometimes, are seen to console themselves when something is denied them,— their Board a sort of *spoken Map* of the Island they have been kept from and will never see. "Taking a run in to Bencoolen, anything we need?" "Thought I'd nip up the coast to Mokko-Mokko or Padang, see what's a-stir." "Nutmeg Harvest is upon us, I can smell it!" Ev'ry woman in "Sumatra" is comely and willing, though not without attendant Inconvenience, Dixon's almost instantly developing Wills and Preferences of their own despite his best efforts to keep them uncomplicated,— whereas the only women Mason can imagine at all are but different fair copies of the same serene Beauty,— Rebekah, forbidden as Sumatra to him, held in Detention, as is he upon Earth, until his Release, and their Reunion. So they pass, Mason's women and Dixon's, with more in common than either Surveyor will ever find out about, for even phantasms may enjoy private lives,— shadowy, whispering, veil'd to be unveil'd, ever safe from the Insults of Time.

7

Trying to remember how they ever came to this place, both speak of Passage as by a kind of flight, all since Tenerife, and the Mountain slowly recessional, having pass'd like a sailor's hasty dream between Watches, as if, out of a sea holding scant color, blue more in name than in fact, the unreadable Map-scape of Africa had unaccountably emerg'd, as viewed from a certain height above the pale Waves,— tilted into the Light, as a geometer's Globe might be pick'd up and tilted for a look at this new Hemisphere, this haunted and *other* half of ev'rything known, where spirit-powers run free among the green abysses and the sudden mountain crests,— Cape Town's fortifications, sent crystalline by the Swiftness, rushing by from a low yet dangerous altitude as the Astronomers go swooping above the shipping in the Bays, topmen pointing in amazement, every detail, including the Invisible, set precisely, present in all its violent chastity. A town with a precarious Hold upon the Continent, planted as upon another World by the sepia-shadow'd Herren XVII back in Holland (and rul'd by the Eighteenth Lord, whose existence must never be acknowledg'd in any way).

The moment Mason and Dixon arrive, up in the guest Suite sorting out the Stockings, which have come ashore all a-jumble, admiring the black Stinkwood Armoire with the silver fittings, they are greeted, or rather, accosted, by a certain Bonk, a Functionary of the V.O.C., whose task it is to convey to them an assortment of Visitors' Rules, or warnings. One *might* say jolly,— one would have to say blunt. "From Guests of our community, our Hope is for no disruptions of any kind. As upon a ship at sea, we do things here in our own way,— we, the officers, and you, the passengers. What seems a solid Continent, stretching away Northward for thousands of miles, is in fact an Element with as little mercy as the Sea to our Backs, in which, to be immers'd is just as surely, and swiftly, to be lost, without hope of Salvation. As there is nowhere to escape to, easier to do as the Captain and Officers request, eh?"

"Of course," Mason quickly.

"We've but come to observe the Sky...?" Dixon seeks to assure him.

"Yes? Yes? Observe the Sky,— instead of what, pray?" Smiling truculently, the Dutchman glowers and aims his abdomen in different directions. " 'Of course,' this isn't a pretext? To 'observe' anything more Worldly,— Our Fortifications, Our Slaves,— nothing like that, eh?"

"Sir," Mason remonstrates, "we are Astronomers under the commission of our King, no less honorably than ten years ago, under that of his King, was Monsieur Lacaille, who has since provided the world a *greatly* esteem'd Catalogue of Southern Stars. Surely, at the end of the day, we serve no master but Him that regulates the movements of the Heav'ns, which taken together form a cryptick Message,"— Dixon now giving him Looks that fail, only in a Mechanickal way, to be Kicks,— "we are intended one day to solve, and read," Mason smoking belatedly that he may be taking his Trope too far.

For the Dutchman is well a-scowl. "*Ja, Ja,* precisely the sort of English Whiggery, acceptable among yourselves, that here is much better left unexpress'd." Police Official Bonk peers at them more closely. It is nearly time for his midday break, and he wants to hurry this up and get to a Tavern. Yet if Mason is acting so unrestrain'd with a Deputy direct from the Castle itself, how much more dangerous may his rattling be in the hearing of others,— even of Slaves? He must therefore be enter'd in the Records as a Person of Interest, thereby taking up residence, in a pen-and-paper way, in the Castle of the Compagnie. Into the same Folder, of course, goes a file for the Assistant,— harmless, indeed, in some Articles, simple, though he appears,— pending the Day when one may have to be set against the other.

Although rooming at the Zeemanns', the Astronomers are soon eating at the house behind, owing to the sudden defection of half the Zeemann kitchen Slaves, gone quick as that to the Mountains and the Droster life. This being just one more Domestick Calamity,— along with Company Prices, collaps'd Roofs, sand in the Soup,— that the Cape Dutch have come to expect and live thro', Arrangements are easily made, the Vrooms' having been Neighbors for years. At mealtimes Mason and Dixon go out by the Zeemanns' kitchen, on past the outbuildings, then in by way of the back Pantry and Kitchen to the Residence of Cornelius Vroom and his wife, Johanna, and what seems like seven, and is probably closer to three, blond, nubile Daughters. Mealtimes are a strange combination of unredeemably wretched food and exuberantly charming Company. Under the Table-cloth, in a separate spatial domain such as Elves are said to inhabit, feet stray, organs receive sudden inrushes of Blood,— or in Mason's case, usually, Phlegm. Blood, clearly rushing throughout Dixon, is detectable as well in faces and at bosoms and throats in this Jethro's Tent they've had the luck to stumble into.

Cornelius Vroom, the Patriarch of this restless House-hold, is an Admirer of the legendary Botha brothers, a pair of gin-drinking, pipe-smoking Nimrods of the generation previous whose great Joy and accomplishment lay in the hunting and slaughter of animals much larger than they. Vroom is a bottomless archive of epic adventures out in the unmapped wilds of Hottentot Land, some of which may even hold a gleam of truth, in among the narrative rubbish-tip of this Arm-chair Commando, wherein the mad Rhino forever rolls his eye, the killer Trunk stands erect and a-bellow, and the cowardly Kaffirs turn and flee, whilst the Dutchman lights his Pipe, and stands his Ground.

One Morning, the Clock having misinform'd him of the Hour, as he hurries to Breakfast thro' the back reaches of the two Yards,— edging past a bright-feather'd Skirmish-line of glaring poultry, a bit more forward than the usual British Hen, who stalk and peck as if examining him for nutritional Purposes,— Mason only just avoids a collision with Johanna Vroom, that would have scrambl'd her apron-load of fresh-gather'd eggs, and produc'd, at best, Resentment, instead of what now, even through Mason's Melancholickally smok'd Lenses, appears to be Fascination.

How can this be? Assigning to ev'ry Looking-Glass a Coefficient of Mercy,— term it μ,— none, among those into which he has ever gaz'd, seeking anything but what he knows will be there, has come within screaming distance of even, say, 0.5, given the Lensman's Squint, the Stoop, and most of all, in its Fluctuation day by day, the Size of a certain Frontal Hemisphere, ever a source of Preoccupation, over whose Horizon he can sometimes not observe his Penis.

Between Greenwich and the Cape, however, he was pleas'd to note a temporary reduction of Circumference, owing to sea-sickness and the resulting aversion to even Mention of food, though he did achieve a tolerance at last for ship's Biscuit,— Dixon, for his part, having by then develop'd a particular Taste for Mr. Cookworthy's Portable Soup, any least whiff of which, of course, sent his partner queasily to the lee rail.

As if Dixon had come ashore with Slabs of the convenient yet nauseating Food-Stuff stowed about his Person, the women of the Colony unanimously avoid him. Not only was he swiftly deem'd eccentric,— he knows well enough the looks Emerson took whenever he came in to Darlington Market,— how fiercely did his Students then all leap to his defense!— but more curiously, from their first sight of him, the Dutch have sifted Dixon as unreliable in any white affairs here. They have noted his unconceal'd attraction to the Malays and the Black slaves,— their Food, their Appearance, their Music, and so, it must be obvious, their desires to be deliver'd out of oppression. "The English Quaker," opines Mrs. De Bosch, the Doyenne of Town Arbitresses, "is rude, disobedient, halfway to a Hindoo, either sitting in trances or leaping up to begin jabbering about whatever may be passing through on its uncomplicated journey from one ear to the other. S.N.S., my Children,"— Simply Not Suitable. But Mason is another story. Mason the widower with that Melancholick look, an impassion'd, young-enough Fool willing to sail oceans and fight sea-battles just to have a chance to watch Venus, Love Herself, pass across the Sun,— in these parts exotic even in his workaday earth tones, coming in starv'd from the Sea with all those strange Engines, and obviously desperate for a shore-cook'd meal. None of this has appear'd to him in any mirror he's consulted.

Until June, most of their obs will be of Jupiter's Moons playing at Duck and Ducklings, and of fix'd Stars such as Regulus and Procyon, as well as the zenith-Star at the Cape, Shaula, the Sting in the Tail of the Scorpion,— all so as to establish the Station's Longitude as nearly as possible. Many nights in that Season proving to be stormy or clouded over, there will be plenty of time for Mischief to shake her Curls, pinch some color into her Cheeks, and, assuming ev'ryone 'round here is not yet dead, feel free to make a few Suggestions.

"Meet my Daughters," Cornelius is ever pleas'd to introduce them to Strangers, "— Jemima, Kezia, and Kerenhappuch." They are, in fact, Jet, Greet, and Els, as he fails, in fact, to be quite Job.

Jet, sixteen, is obsess'd by her Hair,— as if 'twere a conscious Being, separate from her, most of her activities thro' the long Cape Quotidian are directed by its needs,— from choosing Costumes to arranging Social schedules, to assessing, from the way they behave when in its Vicinity, the suitability of Beaux.

The middle Daughter Greet having chosen good Sense as a refuge when she was seven, Attention to her Hair,— as her older sister has more than once chided,— is limited to different ways of covering it up. Withal, "I am the Tavern-Door 'round here," she cries of her *Rôle* as Eternal Mediatrix, for should Els grow too frolicksome, Greet must team up with Jet to restrain her,— yet, should Jet pretend to wield Authority she hasn't earned, Greet must join with Els in Insurrection.

Els, tho' a mere twelve by the Calendar back home, down here in the Southern World began long ago the active Pursuit of Lads twice her age, not all of them unwilling. Of the three Sisters, she seems devoted most unreflectively to the Possibilities of Love, her judgment as to where these may best be sought being the nightly Despair of her Sisters. She never needs to touch her Hair, and it is always perfect.

Cornelius Vroom, anxious as others in the House upon the Topick of Nubility and its unforeseen Woes, has forbidden his daughters to eat any of the native Cookery, particularly that of the Malay, in his Belief that the Spices encourage Adolescents into "Sin," by which he means Lust that crosses racial barriers. For it is real,— he has known it to appear, more than once, here and up in the country, where his Brothers and their families live. He keeps loaded Elephant-Guns in both the front hallway and the *Dispens* in back. Deep in the curfew hours, in bed with his pipe, he imagines laughter outside the windows, even when the wind drowns out every sound,— slave laughter. He knows they watch him, and he tries to pay close Attention to the nuances of their speech. Somewhat as his Neighbors each strenuous Sunday profess belief in the Great Struggle at the End of the World, so does Cornelius, inside his perimeter of Mauritian smoke at the hour when nothing is lawfully a-stir but the Rattle-Watch and the wind, find in his anxious meditations no Release from the coming Armageddon of the races,— this European settlement so precarious, facing an unknown Interior with the sea at their backs, forced, step after step, by the steadfast Gravity of all Africa, down into it at last.... It is another way of living where the Sea is ever higher than one's Head, and kept out only provisionally.

The first moment they find themselves in a Room together, Jet hands Mason a Hair-Brush. "There's a bit in back I can't reach,— please give it a dozen Strokes for me, Charles?"

"Nor does she allow just anyone do this," Greet entering, crossing, and exiting, "I hope you feel honor'd, Sir," with a look back over her shoulder that is anything but reproachful. A moment later she's back, with Els, who comes skipping over to Mason, and without a word, lifting her skirts, sits upon his lap in a sinuous Motion, allowing the Lace Hems to drop again, before squirming about to glance at his Face. "Now then, my English Tea-Pot," reaching to pinch his Cheek, by now well a-flame, "shall I tell you what she really wants you to do with that Hair-Brush?"

"Els, you Imp from Hell, I shall shave your Head. Mr. Mason is a Gentleman, who would never have such designs upon my bodily Comfort," putting out her hand for the return of the Hair-Brush, "— would you, Charles?"

Mason sits, torpedo'd again. To refuse to return the Brush would be to issue an Invitation she might accept. Yet if he hands it back, she'll shrug and go flitting on, tossing her Hair about, to someone marginally more interesting, and he'll face Hour upon insomniack Hour with the Fevers of erotick speculation ever dispell'd by the Cold Bath of Annoyance at himself. Els continues meanwhile to reposition her nether Orbs upon Mason's Lap, to his involuntary, tho' growing Interest. Greet comes over to place her hand on his Brow. "Are you well, Sir? Is there anything I may bring you?" Fingertips lightly descending to his already assaulted Cheek, her eyes Crescent and heated. Her Lips, at least as he will recall this later, beginning to part, and come closer.

"Girls." Johanna bustling in. "You are disturbing Mr. Mason, 'tis obvious, and," switching to Cape Dutch, "in here it begins to smell like the Slaves' Chambers." The three maidens immediately snap to Attention, lining up in order of Height, trying without success to avoid all Gaze-Catching.

When they've been sent away cackling, their mother places an unpremeditated hand upon Mason's arm. "As a man of Science, you understand the role of Humors in adolescent behavior, and will not respond, I hope, too passionately. Is that the word, 'Passionately'?"

"Good Vrou, rest easy,— these days Passion knows me not,...alas."

She gazes long enough at his Member, still erect from the posterior Attentions of her youngest Daughter, before looking him in the eye. "I cannot imagine, then, how 'twill be, once you and It are re-acquainted."

"Should that occur," says Mason, fatally but not yet mortally, "pray feel welcome to attend and observe at first hand." She looks away at last, and in the Release Mason feels an Impulse to smite the Wall repeatedly with his Head. "Then again, your Duties may oblige you to be elsewhere."

She brushes against him on her way out the other Door, raking him with a glistening stare. "O, too late for that, good Sir, far too late."

What is wrong with this family? He feels stranded out at the end of some unnaturally prolong'd Peninsula of Obligation, whilst about to be overwhelm'd by great Combers of Alien Lusts. He now recognizes the Hair-Brush Dilemma in a different form. This time, whatever he may say in reply, will be taken and 'morphos'd, however Johanna wishes. He feels a sudden rush of Exemption. It does not matter what he says.

That night, the Sky too cloudy for Work, Mason is awaken'd by the naked Limbs of a Slave-girl, who has enter'd his Bed. Dixon is not yet return'd, tho' 'tis well past the Gunfire. "What the Deuce!" is his gallant greeting. "And,— who are you, then?" He recalls having seen her in the company of various Vroom Girls.

"Austra, good Sir,— 'tis a common name here for Slaves."

" 'The South.'..." He is peering at her in the moonlit room. "I am Mason. Charles Mason."

She takes his Chin betwixt her Thumb and Finger. "A few basic points, Sir. First, no unnatural Activities. Second, no Opium, no *Dagga*, no Ardent Spirits, no Wine, and so on. Third, their Wish is that I become impregnated,— if not by you, then by one of you."

"Ehm..."

"All that the Mistress prizes of you is your Whiteness, understand? Don't feel disparag'd,— ev'ry white male who comes to this Town is approach'd by ev'ry Dutch Wife, upon the same Topick. The baby, being fairer than its mother, will fetch more upon the Market,— there it begins, there it ends."

"What, no Sentiment, no Love, no— Excuse me? 'Approach'd'? Ahrr! Of course,— was I imagining m'self the first? And you, how many of these expensive little slaves have you borne her?"

"Why be angry with me, Sir? She is the Mistress, I do as she bids."

"Why, in England, no one has the right to bid another to bear a *child?*"

"Poh. White Wives are much alike, and all their Secrets are common knowledge at the Market. Many have there been, oblig'd to go on bearing children,— for no reason but the man's pride."

"Our Women are free."

" 'Our'? Oh, hark yourself,— how is English Marriage any different from the Service I'm already in?"

"You must marry an Englishman, and see."

"Not today, Sailor. Yet take warning,— the Mother will set her three Cubs upon ye without Mercy, and make her own assaults as well, all of it intended to keep *this* rigid with your Desire,— and the only one in the House you'll be allow'd to touch is me."

" 'This'? I say, what's that you're doing there? You really ought not to— "

"Having but an innocent Squeeze, Sir. Keep me in Mind. I'll tell them I couldn't wake you up." She proceeds carefully as she may to the door, expecting at ev'ry step to be assaulted,— he snorts, and paws the Counterpane, but doesn't charge. Exiting, looking back over a dorsal 'Scape immediately occupying all of Mason's Attention, "See you tomorrow at Breakfast,— remember to save one of those 'cute Frowns for me." And Damme, she's off.

Next morning, none of the five Sprites is able to engage the Eyes of any other. Dixon wolfs down griddle cakes and Orange-Juice, whilst Mason glumly concentrates upon the Coffee and its Rituals. Cornelius comes in briefly to light his Pipe and nod before proceeding to his Work, which involves a good deal of screaming at the Slaves. Mason's Day, long and fatiguing, is spent popping in and out of doors, being caught alone in different rooms with different females of the household, by others, who then contrive to return the favor. Only slowly does it dawn on him that this goes on here all the time,— being likely the common Life of the House,— and that he but happens to have stumbl'd into it as some colorful Figure from the Fringes of the World, here for a while and then gone, just enough time for ev'ryone, barring some unannounc'd bolt of Passion finding a Target, to make use of him, perhaps not quite time enough for them to come to despise him.

So Mason prays for clear nights and perfect seeing,— nonetheless, his throat closes and dries, his heart's rhythm picks up whenever the Clouds cover the Sunset, and the Fog rolls swiftly all the way up to the Observatory, and over it, and on up, and he knows he'll be facing anywhere up to five distinctly motivated Adventuresses, each of whom, as in some fiendish Asian parlor-game, is scheming against the other four, the field having shifted from Motives of Pleasure to Motives of Reproduction and Commerce. Its being for them a given that nothing of a Romantick nature will occur,— nothing does. Mason is usually left with an inflexible Object, which, depending upon the Breeches he's wearing that day, not to mention the Coat, is more or less visible to the Publick, who at any rate, as it proves, are quite us'd to even less inhibited Displays.

Dixon does his best not to mention it, waiting rather for Mason either to brag, or to complain.

Eventually, "I know what you're looking at. I know what you're thinking."

"Who? I? Mason."

"Well, what am I suppos'd to do about it?"

"First, get out of thah' House."

Mason makes quick Head-Turns, to Left and Right, and lowers his Voice. "Whilst you've been out rollicking with your Malays and Pygmies,...what have you heard of the various sorts of Magick, that they are said to possess?"

Dixon has in fact heard, from an assortment of Companions native to the Dutch Indies, Tales of Sorcery, invisible Beings, daily efforts to secure Shelter against Demonic Infestation. "They are not as happy, nor as childlike, as they seem," he tells Mason. "It may content us, as unhappy grown Englishmen, to think that somewhere in the World, Innocence may yet abide,— yet 'tis not among these people. All is struggle,— and all but occasionally in vain."

Mason cocks his head, trying to suppress a certain Quiver that also gives him away when at Cards,— a bodily Desire to risk all upon a single Trick. "Would you happen to enjoy *Entrée* to this world of Sorcery? I am anxious as to Protection...."

"A Spell...?" Dixon suggests.

"Emphatickally not a Love-Potion, you understand, no, no, quite the contrary indeed."

Dixon, to spare himself what might else prove to be Evenings-ful of Complaint, says, "I've met people who are said to possess a special Power,— the Balinese Word is *Sakti*. It has not, however, always been successful against Dutchmen. Would this be a *Hate* potion, then, that tha require?"

"Well, certainly not Hate. Inconvenient as Love, in its own way,— no, more of an Indifference-Draught, 's more what I had in mind. 'Twould have to be without odor or Taste, and require but a few Drops,— "

"I could have a look about, tho' 'tis more common here to accept what they happen to offer...?"

Difficult indeed are the next few Nights as Dixon, searching the Malay Quarter for an Elixir to meet Mason's specifications, beneath lampless staircases, in the bloody lulls of cock-fights, is merrily insulted from one illicit Grotto to another. Oh, they've heard of the Philtre, all right, 'tis quite in demand, in fact, as much by one Sex as the other. As the Company seeks to confine all the Dutch of the Cape Colony behind a Boundary it has drawn, and to rule them radially from a single Point, the least immoderate of Feelings, in such a clos'd Volume, may prove lethal. Over the Mountains, to keep all tranquil, entire Tribes work day and night shifts, trying to supply a lively Market. Imitations and Counterfeits abound.

Mason is not seeking the Potion for himself,— rather, his Scheme is to introduce it into the Soup-Bowl of his Hostess, who is kept tun'd to her own dangerous Pitch thro' the Attentions of a number of young Slave-girls chosen for their good looks,— they haunt her, whisking the flies from her skin, oiling it when the South-easter makes it dry as Pages of a Bible, draping it with silks from India and France. They feed her pome-granates, kneeling quickly to lick off the juice that runs down her hand before it reaches her sleeve. Cornelius has a Peep in from time to time. Though he usually departs with an Erection, it is possible that he is feel-ing the pain of an ineptly shot Beast. But his Expression doesn't change. He sucks upon his Pipe, removes it from his mouth to cough, and, con-tinuing to cough, ambles away.

In Johanna's intrigue to bring together Mason and her senior slave, however, 'tis the Slavery, not any form of Desire, that is of the essence. Dixon, out of these particular meshes, can see it,— Mason cannot. Indifferent to Visibility, wrapt in the melancholy Winds that choir all night long, persists an Obsession or Siege by something much older than anyone here, an injustice that will not cancel out. Men of Reason will define a Ghost as nothing more otherworldly than a wrong unrighted, which like an uneasy spirit cannot move on,— needing help we cannot usually give,— nor always find the people it needs to see,— or who need to see it. But here is a Collective Ghost of more than household Scale,— the Wrongs committed Daily against the Slaves, petty and grave ones alike, going unrecorded, charm'd invisible to his-tory, invisible yet possessing Mass, and Velocity, able not only to rattle Chains but to break them as well. The precariousness to Life here, the need to keep the Ghost propitiated, Day to Day, via the Company's merciless Priesthoods and many-Volum'd Codes, brings all but the hardiest souls sooner or later to consider the Primary Questions more or less undiluted. Slaves here commit suicide at a frightening Rate,— but so do the Whites, for no reason, or for a Reason ubiquitous and unaddress'd, which may bear Acquaintance but a Moment at a Time. Mason, as he comes to recognize the sorrowful Nakedness of the Arrangements here, grows morose, whilst Dixon makes a point of treating Slaves with the Courtesy he is never quite able to summon for their Masters.

Yet they entertain prolong'd Phantasies upon the Topick. They take their Joy of it. "Astronomy in a Realm where Slavery prevails...! Slaves holding candles to illuminate the ocular Threads, whilst others hold Mirrors, should we wish another Angle. One might lie, supine, Zenith-Star position, all Night,...being fann'd, fed, amus'd,— ev'ryone else oblig'd to remain upon their Feet, ever a-tip, to respond to a 'Gazer's least Velleity. Hahrrh!"

"Mason, why thah' is dis-gusting...?"

"Come, come, and you're ever telling me to lighten up *my* Phiz? I have found it of help, Dixon, to think of this place as another Planet whither we have journey'd, where these Dutch-speaking White natives are as alien to the civilization we know as the very strangest of Pygmies,— "

" 'Help'? It doesn't help, what are tha talking about...? Tha've a personal Interest here, thy Sentiments engag'd, for all I know."

"Ahrr! My Sentiments! Sentiments, in this Place! A Rix-Dollar a Dozen today, tomorrow wherever the Company shall peg them,— the Dutch Company which is ev'rywhere, and Ev'rything."

"Somewhat like the Deists' God, do tha mean?"

"Late Blow, late Blow,— "

"Mason, of Mathematickal Necessity there do remain, beyond the Reach of the V.O.C., routes of Escape, pockets of Safety,— Markets that never answer to the Company, gatherings that remain forever unknown, even down in Butter-Bag Castle. I'd be much oblig'd if we might roam 'round together, some Evening, and happen we'll see. Mind, I'm seldom all the way outside their Perimeter,— yet do I make an effort to keep to the Margins close as I may."

"And I'm making no Effort, is that it, you're accusing me of Servility? Sloth? You're never about, how would you know how hard I'm working? Do not imagine me taking any more Joy of this, than you do."

"Come, then. There's too much Sand in the Air tonight for any decent Obs,— Zeemanns and Vrooms all cataleptick from these Winds, none shall miss us,— mayn't we be carefree Mice for a few Hours, at least...?"

He receives a blurr'd and strangely prolong'd Gaze. "I wish I knew where my Affection for you runs,— one moment 'tis sure as the heart-yarn of a Mainstay, the next I am entertaining cheerfully Projects in which your Dissolution is ever a Feature."

"Calling off the Wedding, again. We must try not to weep...?" For an instant both feel, identically, too far from anyplace, defenseless behind this fragile Salient into an Unknown, too deep for one Life-Span, that begins directly behind Table Mountain.

They do, to be sure, go out that Evening, as into various others together, in search of Lustful Adventure, but each time Mason will wreck things, scuttling hopes however sure, frightening off the Doxies with Gothickal chat of Headstones and Diseases of the Mind, swilling down great and occasionally, Dixon is told, exceptional Constantia wines with the sole purpose of getting drunk, exploding into ill-advis'd Song, losing consciousness face-first into a Variety of food and Drink, including more than one of the most exquisite *karis* this side of Suma-tra,— that is, proving a difficult carousing partner, block'd from simple enjoyment in too many directions for Dixon to be at all anger'd,— rather marveling at him, as a Fair-goer might at some Curi-osity of Nature.

Mason, no less problematick indoors than out, being an uneasy sleeper, begins at about this time to dream of some Presence with a *Krees* or Malay Dagger, of indistinct speech, yet clear intention to Dowse for the Well-Spring of Mason's Blood. He wakes up screaming, repeatedly. At length Austra, expressing the will of both Houses, sends him to talk with a certain Toko, a Negritoe, or Asian Pygmy, of a Malay tribe call'd the Senoi. It is their belief that the world they inhabit in their Dreams is as real as their waking one. At breakfast each morning, families sit and report their Dreams to one another, offering advice and opinions *passim,* as if all the fantastical beings and events be but other villagers, and village Gossip.

"They live their Dreams," Mason reports to Dixon, "whilst we deny ev'rything we may witness during that third of our Precious Span allotted, as if Sleep be too much like Death to advert to for long...." It is at some point that night, after securing the second Altitude of Shaula, that the Astronomers agree to share the *Data* of their Dreams whenever possible. After those initiatory Hours together upon the *Seahorse*, having found no need to pretend a whole list of Pretenses, given thereby a windfall of precious time, neither is surpriz'd at how many attunements, including a few from dream-life, they may find between them.

"Heaven help me," Mason muttering sourly, "my Dreams reveal this Town to be one of the colonies of Hell, with the Dutch Company acting as but a sort of Caretaker for another...Embodying of Power, 's ye'd say, altogether,— Ev'ryday life as they live it here, being what Hell's colonials have for Routs and Ridottoes,— "

"Why," Eye-Lids clench'd apart, "my own dreams are very like, tho' without the Dutch Company,— more like a Gala that never stops.... Think thee 'tis all this Malay food we're eating ev'ry day...?"

Mason has a brief excursion outside himself. "You're enjoying this miserable Viper-Plantation! Why, Damme if you're not going to miss it when we're shut of it at long last. Arh, arh! What shall you do for *Ketjap?*"

"They must sell it somewhere in London...?"

"At ten times the price."

"Then I shall have to learn a Receipt for it."

The next time the tall Figure with the wavy Blade approaches him, Mason, willing to try anything, stands his ground, and with the help of certain Gloucestershire shin-kicking Arts, actually defeats his Assailant. "Keep your Face down," Mason tells the Adversary. "I do not wish to see your Face."

"You must then demand something from him," Toko has advis'd. "Some solid Gift you may bring back with you."

"The *Krees*," says Mason. Silently, the bow'd Figure throws it on the Ground to one side. Mason stoops and picks it up. "Thank you." When he wakes, there it is, the Point lying nearly within the Portal of one Nostril,— a wrong turn in his Sleep might have been the End. Despite its look of Forge-fresh Perfection, 'tis not a Virgin Blade,— tiny Scratches, uncleansable Stains, overlie one the other in a Palimpsest running deep into the Dimension of Time.

"Happen 'twill be those Girls, teasing with thee…?"

"Why thankee, Blight, what would a Day be without a Common-sense Remark from you?"

"One of us must provide a Datum-Line of Sanity, and as it seems unlikely to be thee,— "

"Aahhrr! The most intimate of acts, the trustful sharing of a Dream, taken and us'd against the Master, by his own sly 'Prentice!"

"Begging thy Mercy, Sir, let us not venture into the *terre mauvais* of professional Resentment, or we shall certainly miss the culmination of Shaula, that Sting e'er pois'd above the Pates of this unhappy People, to strike which, and which not, who can say…?"

"The very voice of Responsibility Astronomick,— was ever Star-gazer more fortunate than I, to be seconded to this Angelickal Correctness. And yet despite you, Dixon, do you know what, the Imp calls,— it advises me, 'Whom better to bore with the unabridg'd tale of your woeful treatment by the World you so desperately wish to be lov'd by, aye, unto Ravishment, than this unreflective Geordie here? At least he understands some Astronomy,' is usually how it goes."

" 'And being your Second,' " Dixon bats back, " 'he has no choice *but* to listen.' "

"Just so, and take Notes if you wish, for someday, Lad, you'll be running your own Expedition, bearing all the weight of Leadership, which crusheth a man even as it bloateth his Pride…. Aye, miraculous,— perhaps with some luck you'll come to know the Relief indescribable of shedding that Load, dumping months, even years, of accumulated Resentment in one great— "

"Eeh, if tha don't mind?"

"Oh. Oh, of course, I hadn't realiz'd. 'Tis but our uninhibited Earthiness, we of lower degree, we're forever speaking of shit, you see, without much— Damme, I say, I said 'shit,' didn't I?— Oh, shit, I've said it again,— No! Twice!" Smacking himself repeatedly upon the Dome.

"Be easy, Mason, it's all right."

"You'll report me now."

"Be happy to, if I thought anyone would believe it...?"

"Wouldn't want you getting into any trouble," Mason unable to refrain from adding, "— Spanish Inquisitors or whatever...."

"Indulge me, Sir, that word again was...?"

"Oh, for Heav'n's sake, 'Authorities,' if you like, if that's not too sectarian for you."

"I am not a fucking Jesuit, Mason. If Jesuits are manipulating me, then are we two Punches in a Droll-booth, Friend,— for as certainly would it be the East India Company who keep *thee* ever in Motion."

"Ah,— and how is that, exactly?"

"Someday, someone will ask, How did a baker's son get to be Assistant to the Astronomer Royal? How'd a Geordie Land-Surveyor get to be his Second on the most coveted Star-gazing Assignment of the Century? Happen 'twas my looks...? thy charm...? Or are we being us'd, by Forces invisible even to thy Invisible College?"

"Whatever *my* Station," bristling, "I have earn'd it. Tho' frankly, I have wonder'd about you. A collier's son,— a land-sale collier at that,— surely there's more wealth and respect in sea-coal?"

"Aye, and we're Quakers as well, is there a *Nervus Probandi* about someplace?"

"Merely have I gone on puzzling,— as, without influence, nothing may come of a Life, and however briskly you may belabor me with Mr. Peach,— yet who, I ask myself thro' the Watch when Sleep comes not, may it have been, between mouthfuls of 'Sandwich,' as the spotted Cubes went a-dancing, who dropp'd the decisive word about you? Don't tell me Emerson, or Christopher Le Maire."

"Why, 'twas John Bird...? Thought ev'ryone knew thah'. As Mr. Bird's Representative in the Field,— my duty's to tend the Sector,— pray nothing goes too much amiss, requiring me to fix it...? Eeh! I'm the Sector Wallah!"

Mason's response is a *Reverse Squint*,— each Eye, that is, doing the opposite of what it usually does when he peers thro' a Telescope. Dixon finds it, briefly, disorienting. Mason even seems to be trying to smile in apology. "The Arts of leadership in me how wanting, as all alas must know,

I bear this command only thanks to a snarl'd and soil'd web of favors, sales, and purchases I pray you may ever remain innocent of. You are right not to accept my Command,— well, not all the time, as I may hope,— "

"Am I giving that impression, I'm sure I didn't mean to...?"

"You're the mystery, Dixon, not I. I'm but a Pepper-corn in the Stuffata, stirr'd and push'd about by any Fool who walks by with a Spoon, entirely theirs,— no mystery about any of them, dubious set of Cooks tho' they be, nough' but the same old Criminals, some dating back to Walpole. But your lot, now,— well, they're a different sort, aren't they?"

"Recall last year, Ingenuous,— Clive's in London by the first of August. By the eleventh of September,— that is, the next thing anyone knows,— the Assignments are chang'd, with thee no longer his brother-in-law's second, rather leading a Team of thy own, replaced by an unknown Quantity. What am I to make of this? We scarcely know Maskelyne. Who is Robert Waddington, anyway?"

"One of the Lunarian Stalwarts, teaching the Mathematicks out near the Monument someplace, Intimate, indeed Housemate, of one of the Piggotts, those eminent advocates of taking the Longitude by Lunar Culminations."

"Maskelyne's sort of Lad...?"

(As Maskelyne will later tell Mason, Waddington from the outset was afflicted with a Melancholy lighter and faster, tho' no less lethal, than the traditional Black sort. "So how be ye, Robert?"

"Two weeks in Twickenham, how am I suppos'd to be? Strawberry Hill, Eel-Pie Island, haven't I seen it all?"

"Yet the Fishing, 'tis said— "

"Oh, Bleak easily the length of a man's hand. Ye take 'em with a Maggot that dwells only upon that Reach,— quite unknown to the rest of Britain. And if Beetles be your Passion, why, the Beetle Variety there! Fair stupefies one."

"Piggotts all well, I trust?"

A long stare. "Where's the Local 'round these parts, then?"

"A moment's Walk, tho' not as easy to get back from."

"Hum. Bit like Life, isn't it?"

And that was in early January, with the Transit of Venus yet six Months off. They were going to be left together upon St. Helena, an island that, according to rumor, often drove its inhabitants insane.)

"Tom Birch did happen to mention that 'twas Maskelyne who'd given him Mr. Waddington's address. He show'd me his Note-Book. Maskelyne had written it in himself. It appears he preferr'd as his co-adjutor the friend of the Piggotts to the Friend of the Peaches,— thus allowing me to proceed in a single unprotected little Jackass Frigate, instead of his own giant India-man, in a Convoy, with half the Royal N. there as well to keep them safe...."

"Allowing Dr. Bradley to step in, obtaining for thee the leadership of an additional Observing Team."

"And choosing you upon advice from Mr. Bird, Author of the most advanc'd Astronomickal Device in Creation. Yes, yes, upon the face of it, quite straightforward, isn't it?...And yet, d'ye not feel sometimes that ev'rything since the Fight at sea has been,— not a Dream, yet..."

"Aye. As if we're Lodgers inside someone else's Fate, whilst belonging quite someplace else...?"

"Nothing's as immediate as it was.... We might have died then, after all, and gone on as Ghosts. Haunting this place, waiting to materialize,— perhaps just at the moment of the Transit, the moment the Planet herself becomes Solid...."

"Even by then," the Rev^d declares, "upon some Topicks, the Astronomers remain'd innocent. That few usually believ'd this, might have prov'd more than once an Advantage, in their Strivings with the Day,— had they known how disingenuous they appear'd, they could have settl'd for much more than they ended up getting."

"Oh, Uncle, how can you reckon so?"

"By others who did far less, and receiv'd more."

"And they're all Dead," says Ethelmer, "so what's it matter?"

"Cousin." Tenebræ holding a Bodkin in at least an advisory way.

Ethelmer scowls in reply, what was a lambent Spark in his Eyes now but silver'd, cold Reflection.

"Brae, your Cousin proceeds unerringly to the Despair at the Core of History,— and the Hope. As Savages commemorate their great Hunts with Dancing, so History is the Dance of our Hunt for Christ, and how we have far'd. If it is undeniably so that he rose from the Dead, then the Event is taken into History, and History is redeem'd from the service of

Darkness,— with all the secular Consquences, flowing from that one Event, design'd and will'd to occur."

"Including ev'ry Crusade, Inquisition, Sectarian War, the millions of lives, the seas of blood," comments Ethelmer. "What happen'd? He liked it so much being dead that He couldn't wait to come back and share it with ev'rybody else?"

"Sir." Mr. LeSpark upon his feet. "Save that for your next Discussion with others of comparable wisdom. In this house we are simple folk, and must labor to find much amusement in Joaks about the Savior."

Ethelmer bows. "Temporarily out of touch with my Brain," he mumbles, "Sorry, ev'rybody. Sir, Reverend, Sir."

8

As the Days here slip by, whilst the Transit yet lies too distant for him quite to believe in, Dixon, assailed without mercy by his Sensorium, almost in a swoon, finds himself, on Nights of Cloud, less and less able to forgo emerging at dusk, cloaked against the Etesian wind, and making directly for the prohibited parts of town. Somewhere a Tune in the musical Mode styl'd, by the East Indians, *Pelog,* which they term appropriate to evening, bells quietly with him as he goes, keeping the rhythm of his stride, and he begins to whistle briskly along. After months of being told by Masters-at-Arms that he might not whistle aboard ship, any resumption of the vice comes as a freedom almost Torpedick, particularly here, as he follows these increasingly unlighted lanes of hammered dust, with Lawless Bustle at ev'ry Hand, black slaves carrying gamecocks, looking for a Spot Contest, *Bandieten* exil'd from Batavia with their Retinues of Pygmies, Women in Veils, Drosters down on business, Sailors to whom ev'ry Port of Call's but another Imitation of Wapping, and along the way, at each dimmed crossing, Cape Malays waiting with Goods to sell, all of whom have soon come to know Dixon.

"Here, *Tuan!* Best *Dagga,* cleaned, graded, ready for your flame…"
"Real Dutch gin, bottles with th' original seals, yes! Intact as virgins…"
"Latest *ketjap,* arriv'd Express from Indo-China, see? Pineapple, Pumplenose, Tamarind,— an hundred flavors, a thousand blends!" Invisible through the long Dutch workday, life in the Cape Night now begins to unwrap everywhere. Dixon smells the broiling food, the spices,

the livestock, the night-blooming vines, the ocean voracious and immense. He is acquiring a nasal map of the Town, learning, in monitory whiffs, to smell the Watch,— pipes, sheep-fat suppers, pre-Watch gin,— and to take evasive action…learning to lurk, become part of the night, close enough to slave-borne lanthorns passing by to feel their heat as easily as he may scent the burghers' wives through the curtains of their sedan chairs,— the St. Helena coffee, English soap, French dampness. In the distance the nightly curfew cannon barks, announcing Dixon's transition to the state of Outlaw.

He feels like a predatory Animal,— as if this Town were ancient to him, his Hunting-Ground, his Fell so mis-remember'd in nearly all Details, save where lie the Bound'ries he does not plan to cross. Tho' how can there be any room for excess in this gossip-ridden Town, crowded up against the Mountains that wall it from the virid vast leagues of Bushmen's Land beyond? as behind these carv'd doors and Gothickal Gates, in the far Penumbræ of sperm tapers, in Loft and *Voorhuis,* in entryways scour'd by Dusk and blown Sand, these Dutch carry on as if Judgment be near as the towering Seas and nothing matter anymore, especially not good behavior, because there's no more time,— the bets are in, ev'ry individual Fate decided, all cries taken by the great Winds, and 'tis done. Temporally, as geographically, the End of the World. The unrelenting Vapor of debauchery here would not merely tempt a Saint,— Heavens, 'twould tempt an Astronomer. Yet 'tis difficult, if not impossible, for these Astronomers to get down to a Chat upon the Topick of Desire, given Dixon's inability to deny or divert the Gusts that sweep him, and Mason's frequent failure, in his Melancholy, even to recognize Desire, let alone to act upon it, tho' it run up calling Ahoy Charlie. "How could you begin to understand?" Mason sighs. "You've no concept of Temptation. You came ashore here *looking* for occasions to transgress. Some of us have more Backbone, I suppose…."

"A bodily Part too often undistinguish'd," Dixon replies, "from a Ram-Rod up the Arse."

Jet slides by in the narrow Hallway. "Don't forget to-night, Charles," she sings.

"I'll remember," mutters Mason, adjusting his Wig.

Dixon beams after her, then back at Mason. "Engaging Youngster…?"

"She is a fine young Woman, Dixon, and I shan't hear a Word more."

"Tell me," blinks Dixon, "what'd I say?" But Mason has already clamber'd away up the Stairs. Passing thro' the Hallway a bit later, Dixon observes Mason now in deep conversation with Greet, the two of them nervous as cats. "Mutton Stew this evening, I'm told," Dixon cries in cheery Salute. The Girl shrieks, and runs off into the Kitchen.

Mason snarls. "Time hanging heavy, 's that it? What can I do to help? Just name it."

"Why aye,— perhaps when the Ladies have retir'd,— " Thus bickering they pass into the Dining-Room. After the Cape custom, the Dutchman has lock'd his front door for the evening meal, which he now regards, smoldering, less predictable than an Italian Volcano.

"I see you have discovered another Cape delicacy, Mr. Dixon," Johanna in an effort not to get into any verbal exchange with Mason, whilst her husband is in the room, "— our Malays call it *ketjap.*"

"Girls, don't even want you looking at it. Filthy Asian stuff," Cornelius commands thro' clouds of aromatic pipe-smoke. "Even" (puff) "if something has to be done" (puff) "to cover up the taste of this food." Another volcanickal Emission, whilst he grimly attacks his slice of the evening's mutton in Tail-fat. Over the course of its late owner's life, the Tail has grown not merely larger and more fatty, but also, having absorbed years of ovine Flatulence ever blowing by, to exhibit a distinct Taste, perhaps priz'd by *cognoscenti* somewhere, though where cannot readily be imagin'd.

Dixon meanwhile is struggling with the very Chinese Concoction, or rather with its slender Bottle, out of whose long neck he finds he has trouble getting the stuff to flow. "Strike her upon the bottom," whispers Els, "and perhaps she will behave." Dixon does a quick triple-take among the faces of the women, a Jocularity poised upon his Tongue but peering out warily, not quite trusting the open. He notes, at the far corner of his visual field, Mason attempting to hide behind, perhaps even beneath, the food on his plate. Cornelius, president inside his blue tobacco Fumulus, seems unaware of the tangle of purposes in the room. Greet is playing vigorously with locks of her Hair, trying to remember what her sisters above and below think she does and doesn't know at this point in the *Saga*, as against what her Mother believes. What Mason may be thinking is of course unimportant to any of them.

At last, the relentless Supper done, the Vrooms, as is their Custom, retire out front to the *Stoep*, Johanna and the Girls swiftly choosing Seats to Windward of Cornelius and his Watch-fire, leaving the Astronomers to light what Pipes they may in self-defense.

"There is something irresistibly perverse," as the Rev^d then noted, "about a young white woman sitting upon a Stoep in the evening, among a steady coming and going of black servants meant, as in the Theater of the Japanese, to be read as invisible, whilst she poses all a-shine, she and her friends. According to which steps they sit upon, and which are then claim'd by the Feet of young Sparks who might wish to linger, the possible viewing-angles, for both Parties, are more or less multiplied, each combination of Steps having its own elaborate Codes for what is allow'd, and what transgresses, from Eye-play to the readjustment of skirts and underskirts, and the length of time 'tis consider'd proper to gaze. Some Belles like to 'boss' their male Slaves about in front of the young men, whilst others wish to be caught gazing after Girl-slaves with unconceal'd envy. Over the Range of their Desires, they are shameless, these Dutch girls of all ages, for they are the Girls of the end of the world, and the only reason for anyone to endure church all day Sunday is to be reminded of the Boundaries there to be o'erstepp'd. The more aware of their Sins as they commit them, the more pleas'd be these Cape folk,— more so than Englishmen, who tend to perish from the levels of Remorse attending any offense graver than a Leer."

Slowly, gravely, the Younkers dance up and down the Steps in the Evening. Their talk is of Roof-tops, Arch-ways, Sheds, and Warehouses— any place secure from Traffick long enough for a Skirt to be lifted or Breeches unbuckl'd. Johanna keeps looking over at Mason, as if offering to translate. A young Gallant arrives bearing a diminutive three-string'd Lute, and dropping to one Knee before Jet,— tho' she has delegated the sighing to her sisters,— sings his own original Pæan to Cape Womanhood,—

> Oh,
> Cape Girrl,
> In the Ocean Wind,
> Fairer than the full Moon,
> Secret as a Sin,—

You're a,
Light Lass,
So the Lads all say,
Sitting on your Stoep, hop-
-Ing Love will pass today...
You keep your Slaves about,
As don't we all,
Yet no one in love is brave,
And even a Slave may fall...
In love with,—
Cape Girl,
When South-Easters blow,
Thro' my Dreams, I know,
To your Arms I'll go,
Cape Girl, don't say no.

"And self-Accompanied, Wim!— what *is* that tiny Object in your Lap that you've been whanging your Triads upon, there, and so rhythmic-ally, too?"

"Found this down at that Market near the Gallows,— 'tis a Fiji Islander's Guitar, first introduc'd there two hundred years ago by Por-tuguese Jesuits, according to the Malay that sold me it."

"I see the Jesuit part clearly enough," Greet remarks.

"So long as you don't grasp it," murmurs Els.

'Tis an open enough Game, with a level of Calculation, among these Daughters of the Low Country, no less forgiving than the sort of thing that may be heard, any slack-time, among the Girls in the Company Brothel at the Slave Lodge,— two distinct Worlds, the Company maintaining their separation, setting Prices, seeking as ever total control, over the sex industry in Cape Town. Yet do there remain a few independents, brave girls and boys who are young enough to enjoy the danger of going up against the Compagnie. Sylphs of mixed race, mixed gender, who know how to vanish into the foothills, and the Droster Net-work, even finding safety beyond, in the land of the Hottentots. Yet 'tis difficult to leave the life in town, to give up that sudden elation, when the ships appear 'round the Headlands, Spanish Dollars everywhere in golden Infestation, every woman in town, from the stoniest white Church-Pillar to the giddiest black Belle in from the Hinterland, at once coming alert, and even sometimes a-jangle. The taverns are jumping, sailors bring their pipes and fiddles ashore, *Dagga* smoke begins to scent the air, voices lift, music pulses, the nights bloom like Jasmine.

'Tis then Mason and Dixon are most likely to be out rambling among all the Spices armies us'd to kill for, up in the Malay quarter, a protruded tongue of little streets askew to the Dutch grid, reaching to the base of Table Mountain. The abrupt evening descends, the charcoal fires come glowing one by one to life, dotting the hill-side, night slowly fills with cooking aromas,— shrimp paste, tamarinds, coriander and cumin, hot chilies, fish sauces, and fennel and fœnugreek, ginger and *lengkua.* Windows and doorways open to Lives finite but overwhelming, households gathering against the certain night....

Greet Vroom slips away with Austra to follow the Astronomers. "They visit different Kitchens, and eat," she reports back to her sisters, nodding her head, a little out of breath. "They wander about, eating and talking. Every now and then they'll step into one of those seamen's taverns."

"What do they eat?"

"*Everything.* Half of it is food you wouldn't *dream* of!

> Out in the Dark where the Malays all feast,
> Spices and Veg'table Treats from the East,
> Peppers as hot as the Hearth-sides of Hell,
> Things that Papa has neglected to tell,—
> Curried wild Peacock and Springbok Ragout,
> Bilimbi Pickles, and Tamarinds, too,
> *Bobotie, Frikkadel,* Fried Porcupine,
> Glasses a-brim with Constantia Wine, singing,
> Pass me that Plate,
> Hand me that Bowl,
> Let's have that Bottle,
> Toss me a Roll,'
> Scoffing and swilling, out under the Sky,
> Leaving the Stars to go silently by.

"Greet,— uncomb'd, sentimental Greet," Jet gushes. It occurs to no one that what has driven the Astronomers up the slopes of Table Mountain may be, at last, the Table Vroom. The pipe smoke, the Sheep-fat, the strange Dinner-ware, everything, dishes, spoons, *Yes* even twinkling through the mutton broth at the bottom of one's spoon, are these,— well, stories,— Battles, religious Events, Personages with rapt Phizzes standing about in Rays from above, pointing aloft at who knows what, violent scenes of martyrdom from the religious wars of the previous century, obscure moral instructions written in all-but-unreadable lettering, and in Dutch withal,— framing the potatoes on one's plate, or encircling some caudal Stuffata being passed from eater to eater, and rotated as it goes, so that each gets to view a separate episode of some forever obscure doctrinal dispute.... Soon enough Mason and Dixon are desperate. Pretending astronomical Chores up at the Observatory, Bowls and Cutlery conceal'd in their Cloaks, they steal away, thinking of Oceanick Fish, African Game, hot Peppers, spices of the East.

"I believe in Vibrations," declares Mason, "— I believe, that Vibrations from that horrid family get *into their food,* which is difficult enough to enjoy to begin with,— "

"And?"

"I'd rather be out here."

"Why aye,"— as far projected into the Sea, each will confide, as Land may go, out blessedly alone upon the furthest Point, nothing beyond but the uninterrupted planetary Seas of the 40's, the West Wind Express, and the Regions of Ice, and the Mystery at the exact Other Pole,— the night Fog creeping like quicksilver, all but surrounded by a Waste where the Seas might grow higher than either Astronomer can imagine without Fear, set up and waiting for a Southern Star, Lumina of a shapely Constellation unnam'd, forever below any British Horizon, to culminate.

They have come upon a Queue forming up a dark street, and decide to join it, Dixon in his red coat, boots with three-inch heels, and mysteriously cockaded hat, Mason, after an hour before his traveler's Mirror, having assum'd rather a darken'd, volish neutrality. As they move slowly toward the makeshift kitchen-tent, more and more of its candle-lit interior may be seen. A man in a Sarong cooks as though possessed, running about with a *Krees* to gaze too long at whose bright wavy edge might put a Man's Thumbs a-prickle, as his Mind in a Bind,— poking embers precisely into huge gusts of flame, stirring the contents of various pots, peeling Garlick, deveining and Butterflying shrimps, slicing vegetables, boning and filleting fish, performing perhaps a dozen such Tasks more or less simultaneously with this single Implement, whilst beds of embers glow, and from iron pans rise huge clouds of smoke and steam, so fragrant that breathing them is like eating the first Plate-ful of a large Meal,— and his wife hands the food out the window and collects the money, and older children carry and prepare whilst younger ones tend the babies in the dark, watching the Progress of the *Krees,* which they have seen fly, heard sing, and, in the presence of a pure well, felt a-tremble, there being an odd number of waves to its Blade, signifying Alliance with the correct Forces.

"Amazing," Mason somehow having fallen into conversation with one of the Children. "In my country, near my Home, since the Mills came, our pure Wells have been well hidden, and we must now ask Dowsers, who use long Hazel Wands in much the same way, to find them."

"Have the Dutch conquer'd your land, too?"

"Oh, dear me, no,— " Mason prim'd to chuckle in condescension till Dixon, infernally a-beam, says, "William of Orange, what about him? Tha wouldn't style thah' a Conquest?"

"Captain Jere, Good Evening, the Satay Deluxe as usual?"

"Looks bonnie, Rakhman,— what are those yellow bits there?"

"Mangoes. Still on the green side tonight, but tomorrow,— tomorrow's the Day."

Accordingly, next morning at the first risen Gull's cry, "Eeh, Mason,— the Mangoes are in!"

"Bring me back a likely one," Mason mutters, "and perhaps I shan't kill you." Yet out of something like Duty ow'd his Senses, he finds himelf shambling down to the Market, yawning in the sun, there to behold Mountains of the Fruit apparently all come to Ripeness at the same Moment,— causing a Panic, for all must then be pick'd in a short time from the Groves up-country and rush'd directly to Town, to lie in these towering Heaps, waiting to be lifted and apprais'd, as they find the Reverend Wicks Cherrycoke doing when they arrive.

"Well met, Gentlemen! What a Morning! One feels as Adam felt,— even better, as Eve."

"I shall kill him now," Mason declares.

"Eeh, get the old Nozzle down upon this one, Mason,— a Beauty, 's it not?" The Aroma captures Mason's Attention. "Aye, tha'd better eat thah' one now thy Nose has been all over it."

"Why don't I throw it at you instead?" They are soon retir'd to a nearby Stoep, where they sit eating Mangoes. Neighboring Stoeps are similarly occupied.

"Thought you'd sail'd," Dixon says.

"The *Seahorse* proceeds without me. East of the Cape, Captain Grant was pleas'd to inform me, men of Christ are not desir'd,— tho' why, he refus'd to say, even when I suggested that if clergy be bann'd, then what is contemplated out there must be too terrible to speak of, in any way but secretly."

"I, personally, am looking for that B-st-rd St.-Foux," Captain Grant declar'd. "My *Seahorse* is a damn'd snappy little Package, and I suppose I've grown to love her, for her Honor is become important to me."

"Shall I be safer in Cape Town?" inquir'd the Rev.^d

"Safe enough. You shouldn't have long to wait. Indiamen come thro' all the time, tho' they are most inflexibly anti-clerickal Folk,— their Cargo spaces are purposely built a Tun short to avoid the law that requires a Chaplain on board,— so you'd do better to represent yourself in some other line of work."

"Tha could pretend to be an Astronomer," Dixon says, "— all tha need to know, I can teach thee in five minutes."

"Surveying won't even take that long," snaps Mason. "Piss runneth downhill, and Pay-Day is Saturday,— now you're a qualified Fence-runner."

The Rev.^d holds aloft a Mango, as if 'twere a Host. "Had I gone, I should have miss'd this. Regard how the fruit takes its shape and feel from this great seed-case within, which the Spanish call *el Hueso*, 'the Bone.' This Mango handles like flesh,— to peel it is to flay it,— to bite into it is to eat uncook'd Flesh,— though I can imagine as well uncomfortable religious questions arising."

Mason, who has been shock'd by impieties far more venial, might have shar'd his Moral Displeasure were the Topick not Food, allowing him promptly to advert to his own Iliad of dietary Misfortune here among the Dutch. "Their emphasis upon roots,— the eternal boiling,— the absence of even salt, we have already review'd. 'Tis the Sheep,— Heaven forfend we should ever find a Moment without Sheep in it. Sheep, where I come from, are more important than all but a few humans. A boy is as likely to learn to skate upon a Shearing-floor as upon the Ice. The smell, at some times of year sensible for Miles, of Sheep, and wool-fat, and that queasy Nidor of Lambs baking in ovens meant for bread...the very nasal Patina that met me here, upon entering my first Dutch house, of Mutton-fat vaporiz'd and recondens'd, again and again, working its way insidiously, over the years of cooking, into all walls, furniture, draperies, within a certain radius of that kitchen,— ahrrhh! How foolishly did I believe I'd escap'd these perfumes of Gloucestershire,— nay,— at the Dutchman's Table, I am return'd to them, as to a kind of Hell."

The young clergyman nods in apparent sympathy. "Then eating Malay food seems a cheap enough Deliverance,— bearing in mind that the cuisine of a people whose recreations include running *Amok* is necessarily magickal in purpose and effect, and no one is altogether exempt." Later that night, writing in his Journal, adding,— "Lamb of God, Eucharist of bread,— what Mr. Mason could not bear, were the very odors of Blood-Sacrifice and Transsubstantiation, the constant element in all being the Oven, the Altar wherebefore his Father presided."

A few pages later, he admits, "Of course, 'twas none of my affair,— yet such was the unease of those Days, as I waited for a Ship to convey me further East, that I sought distraction in the study of other Lives,— usually without their Principals knowing of it. So found we ourselves, for the moment, as some might say beached, just here, upon the Brink of all the Indies, before the Unfolding, fearful and inexhaustible, of the East."

9

Despite all wish to avoid it, here they are, Vrou Vroom and Mason, in an upper Bedroom, in unshutter'd afternoon light swiftly fading, harkening to each sound in the House, waiting for the "Bull's Eye," a strange dark cloud with a red center, to appear over Table Mountain, and grow swiftly, till but minutes later the North-Wester shall sweep upon them. "I am not one of these Cape women," she is whispering, "— tho' I have ever envied their reputations. Next to Cornelius, so dreamt I, must other men figure as Adonises, and I should certainly have my pick. Alas. Whenever in earnest I have tried to flirt, each time my choice proves to be *worse* than Cornelius. I ought to've given up, and settled for being a Churchly ideal."

"And instead?" Mason finds to his surprize that he cannot refrain from inquiring, his Jealousy nonetheless more peevish than substantial.

Misunderstanding, she hangs her head, in lewd innocence erring upon the side of Eros, and whispers, "— I have chosen to be a very wicked woman."

"Who it seems will commit any sin."

Giggling awkward as a Girl, her face a-glow,— the first time he's observ'd her thus. She has been trying to unbutton her Bodice...the trembling in her hands and the failing light resist her...at last with a small growl she grabs both sides of the Garment and rips it in two, or, actually, twain. The light in the room is darkening with unnatural speed, turning her nipples and mouth black as ashes, her fair hair nearly invisible. There is a sudden hammering upon the Door. Mason jumps up and runs 'round the Room twice before locating the Window, which, without looking back, he raises, climbs thro', and vanishes from with a receding wail and a Thump somewhere below.

In runs Jet. "Charles, we've only five minutes,— Oh hello, Mamma."

"What would Mr. Mason be doing here, my Imp?" inquires merry Johanna.

"What's happen'd to your Bodice?"

In a corner, the Darkling Beetle rustles in its Cage, its Elytra the same unforgiving white as the great sand-waste call'd 'Kalahari' lying north of here, where the creature was taken up, brought Leagues overland to the Cape with hundreds of its kind, arriving hungry and disoriented, to be set out with others, like a great sugar-iced Confection, at some Harbor-side Market frequented by Sailors and the Strange. So far in its Life, it has never seen Rain, tho' now it can feel something undeniably on the way, something it cannot conceive of, perhaps as Humans apprehend God,— as a Force they are ever just about to become acquainted with....

The storm arrives, and goes on for the next three days. Cornelius, up-country, is prevented by floods from returning. The logistics are both simple and hellishly next to impossible, for tho' the Guest rooms at Zeemanns' lie empty,— Dixon being across town at a certain Malay establishment, rain'd in like ev'ryone else,— and Mason is known for not responding to knocks upon the door, yet is Johanna oblig'd to arrange plausible absences from her daily schedule, with dozens of sets of eyes, within the house and outside it, scrutinizing her every step.

No sooner, for example, is her Mother out the door than in comes bouncing Els, all a-soak. "It's fantastic!" she cries. "The Season I live for! Come, Charles. Do the English kiss in the Rain?"

Down the street somebody's roof collapses in a sodden rumble. All structural Surfaces here, even Vertical ones, touch'd by Rain, begin at once to take up Water like great rigid Sponges, and after enough of it, dissolving, crumble away. A Bell upon a Roof-top begins to ring. Fruit Peels lie squash'd and slippery in the Gutters that run down to the Canals, where the Slaves are out in the Storm, doing their Owners' Laundry, observing and reading each occurrence of Blood, Semen, Excrement, Saliva, Urine, Sweat, Road-Mud, dead Skin, and other such

Data of Biography, whose pure form they practice Daily, before all is lixiviated 'neath Heaven. In the rainy-day Shadows beneath the Arcades, Pipesful of Tobacco pulse brightly, and bob about in front of watchful Faces. Ev'rything smells of wet Lime and Sewage. A stray'd Sheep cowers against a Wall too high for it, bleating fretfully. Mason is not having fun. "Chase me," at last demands the mischievous Snip, and away she shoots up the Lane and gone. No matter how he rotates his hat, Mason cannot prevent a Stream of Water from funneling somewhere onto his Person. He arrives back at the Vrooms' skidding in the Mud, Wig-powder running down his Shoulders and Lapels in a White-Lead Wash. The Door is lock'd. Inside he hears Els and her sisters laughing. Furious, he stalks thro' the down-pour around to the back, locates a Ladder, and props it against a Balcony whose Window seems open, but when he gets to it, is not. With no more than a precarious hold upon the Balcony, Mason now feels activity beneath his Soles, and looks down in time to see the Ladder being deftly abstracted and taken 'round the Corner in malicious fun by Jet, who is for some reason feeling under-appreciated today. As he hangs there in Misery, tasting Ocean Salt in the Wind, watching in a spirit of Distance, "Soon," he mutters aloud, "to be Detachment," the Bolts connecting the House to the Balcony, which was never meant to bear much more weight than that of an adolescent Female's Foot, begin to slide, protesting with horrid sucking Shrieks, out of the Lime and Sand that have held them there so ornamentally till now. "What," he is heard to exclaim, "— not again?" before jumping clear of the falling Iron-work, landing, mercifully without more than Contusions and Pain, upon the soak'd Earth. This time he decides to lie for a while, as he imagines in Surrender to the Forces of Nature, allowing Heaven's Rains to visit as they will. After a bit he notices a peculiar weight to the Drops striking his Face, and withal a distinctly *lateral* motion, as of something actually crawling—

"Ahrrh!" He plucks from his Face a Beetle, about half an inch long and emitting green light as if bearing a Candle within. He rolls his Gaze wildly about,— all 'round him, all over Cape Town, as 'twill prove, these Insects, swept here over Mountains and Deserts, are falling. It is not a message from any Beyond Mason knows of. It is an introduction to the Rainy Season.

"What'd we respectfully request? Skanderoon, wasn't it? only to be anointed with the suppos'd contents of our cowardly Breeches, and sent here, where they know how bad the seeing is. What madness are they about? We'll be lucky to see the Sun here,— and how many Years will give us clear Nights enough to fix our Latitude and Longitude?"

"It wouldn't be like this in Skanderoon," Dixon agrees. "They say, 'tis nearly Europe there."

"Fabulous Skanderoon," sighs Mason. They are presently part-singing, to a sort of medium-tempo Cuban Rhythm,

> Skan-deroon,
> I'd rather be in, Skanderoon,
> Tho' 'twould have to be quite soon,—
> This June,—
> In Skan-
> Deroon!
> Not far away,—
> Lesser Asia, so they say,—
> Minarets and Palms a-sway,
> We might lounge about all day,—
>
> Stuf-fing our Gobs,—
> With Turkish Delight,—
> Securing our Obs,—
> Then beginning, the Night...
>
> Crescent Moon,
> Caravan, and Muezzin's Tune,
> I'll not be forgetting soon
> Souvenirs of, Skanderoon!

What a Hope. Rain rules now, and shall, until October. The Girls follow Mason one afternoon up to the Observatory, up onto the first slopes of the Mountain where they are forbidden ever to go,— "Father says because of the African Boys," they proclaim solemnly to Austra, who laughs merrily.

"Boys! Babies, rather. Stay close to me,— I'll protect you." She wishes to add, " 'Tis not with them your debit grows, but with the African Women from whom you take, take without pause or apology," but aloud says, "Just try to wear something over your Hair,— the only blond they see up where we're going is when the Kommando ride through, and the sight of it sometimes causes them to act in haste."

"I shall let mine blow wild," Els cries.

"Cover my Hair?" Jet astonish'd. "As, I haven't better things to do?"

"You'll want to keep it out of the Wind," says Greet.

"And end up with Shawl Hair? I think not, Greet." But they are by now too far ascended for her to return home unaccompanied. They are ascended into Africa. At some point all note that they can no longer hear the Town. That is all it takes, to deliver them into Africa. They can see the Bay, and the Sea beyond, and the Ships and Boats, but the girls have lost the Voices and Percussion and rough Breath of the Town,— they are of the Continent now, and the Town is a Spectacle in a Museum of Marvels, and the Rain-Beetles are in Song. And who gazes back upon it, too long or even too sentimentally, may never see it again. Or may turn to Salt, and be white for Eternity.

Mason, far ahead of them, an earthen Trudging among the Lanes, appears to be making for a curious, squat Cylindrick Structure with a Cone-shap'd roof, perch'd high enough to keep above the morning Fog,— or so the Astronomers hope.

" 'Tis a Gnome's House!" whispers Els.

Jet is gazing at the ends of large fistfuls of her Hair. "Look at these,— these should have been soaking in Egg-Whites half an Hour ago,— do you know what happens if I miss one day? They're already split beyond belief,— "

"Has anyone notic'd the Light?" inquires Greet. For the Sun is darkening rapidly, whilst striking to a remarkable Hellish Red all surfaces that not so long ago were reflecting the simple Day-light.

"What?— Never been this close to the Bull's Eye?" Austra smiles grimly. "Welcome to the Droster Republick, Misses. Up here, some believe the Bull's Eye lives, and goes about…selecting those it shall *take*."

"We must ask Mr. Mason for Shelter," cries Jet. They flee, all shivers and screar..s, a-splash up the hill-side to the Observatory just as the Storm breaks, arriving at the Door-Way soak'd through. Mason is not cowering, he will later explain,— tho' he is sorry if that's what it look'd like,— rather standing guard over the Instruments,— whilst Dixon, no less warily, opens the Door, and in tumble the Bunch of them, rowdy and wet.

The Carpenter of the *Seahorse* and his men have put up a structure solid as a Man o' War, tarr'd the Roof and all the joints, rigg'd a couple of Blocks in a Gun-Purchase Arrangement allowing the Gentlemen to slide the Shutter open and clos'd from inside. "Get her down to the Water, step a Mast, put up some Canvas, and ye may sail her home," the Carpenter assur'd them. It holds six snugly,— less awkwardly if, as Jet and Els now discover, two lie together upon one Astronomer's Couch,— as, promptly, do Austra and Greet, upon the other.

The storm drums at the Cone above, which sheds the Rain in Sheets. There is nothing to drink but Cape Madeira, a thick violet Liquid one must get thro' six or seven Bottles of even to begin to feel at ease. There is no Question of Working, all Drudgery Logarithmick having been brought up to Date, the Clock seen to, the Shutter-Tackle made secure.

"Now then," Mason rapping upon the Table's Edge with a sinister-looking Fescue of Ebony, whose List of Uses simple Indication does not quite exhaust, whilst the Girls squirm pleasingly, "as you young Ladies *have* been kind enough to visit during School-Hours, we must be sure that your Education advance upon *some* Topick,— wherefore our Lesson for today shall be, the forthcoming Transit of Venus."

Cries of, "Oh, please, Sir!" and "Not the Transit of Venus!"

"Then what in the World are thee up here for," Dixon's Eye-Balls ingenuously gibbous, "if not out of Curiosity as to what we do?"

They all take looks at one another, Austra at length detaching to smirk at Mason and cast her Eyes heavenward, where the Roar of the Storm goes on unabating. Her blond Procuresses all begin to expostulate at once, and Mason understands that the vocal assaults of the Vroom Poultry are not inborn, but rather learn'd in this World from their Owners.

"Ladies, Ladies," Mason calls. "— You've seen her in the Evening Sky, you've wish'd upon her, and now for a short time will she be seen in the Day-light, crossing the Disk of the Sun,— and do make a Wish then, if you think it will help.— For Astronomers, who usually work at night, 'twill give us a chance to be up in the Day-time. Thro' our whole gazing-lives, Venus has been a tiny Dot of Light, going through phases like the Moon, ever against the black face of Eternity. But on the day of this Transit, all shall suddenly reverse,— as she is caught, dark, embodied, solid, against the face of the Sun,— a Goddess descended from light to Matter."

"And our Job," Dixon adds, "is to observe her as she transits the face of the Sun, and write down the Times as she comes and goes…?"

"That's all? You could stay in England and do that," jaunty little Chins and slender Necks, posing, and re-posing, blond girls laughing together, growing sticky and malapert.

The Girls are taken on a short but dizzying journey, straight up, into the Æther, until there beside them in the grayish Starlight is the ancient, gravid Earth, the Fescue become a widthless Wand of Light, striking upon it brilliantly white-hot Arcs.

"Parallax. To an Observer up at the North Cape, the Track of the Planet, across the Sun, will appear much to the south of the same Track as observ'd from down here, at the Cape of Good Hope. The further apart the Obs North and South, that is, the better. It is the Angular Distance between, that we wish to know. One day, someone sitting in a room will succeed in reducing all the Observations, from all 'round the World, to a simple number of Seconds, and tenths of a Second, of Arc,— and that will be the Parallax.

"Let us hope some of you are awake early enough, to see the Transit. Remember to keep both eyes open, and there will be the three Bodies, lined up perfectly,— the Heliocentric system in its true Mechanism, His artisanship how pure." The Girls keep their Glances each looping 'round the others, like elaborately curl'd Tresses, trying to see if they should be understanding this, or,— being cruel young beauties ev'ry one,— even caring.

10

As Planets do the Sun, we orbit 'round God according to Laws as elegant as Kepler's. God is as sensible to us, as a Sun to a Planet. Tho' we do not see Him, yet we know where in our Orbits we run,— when we are closer, when more distant,— when in His light and when in shadow of our own making.... We feel as components of Gravity His Love, His Need, whatever it be that keeps us circling. Surely if a Planet be a living Creature, then it knows, by something even more wondrous than Human Sight, where its Sun shines, however far it lie.

— Revd Wicks Cherrycoke, *Unpublished Sermons*

"Show us upon the Orrery," suggests Pliny.

"I get to light the Sun," cries Pitt, dashing for the card-table, where the Tapers are kept in a drawer.

Tenebræ finds herself, in the general convergence upon the Machine in the corner, quite close to her Cousin Ethelmer, who is trying to remember how old she is. He cannot recall her looking quite this,— he supposes, nubile. And how old does it make him, then? Briefly he beholds the gray edge of a cloud of despair, promises himself to think about it later, smiles, and sallies, "Remember the time you snipp'd off a lock of your hair, and we fashion'd it into a Comet, and placed it in the Orrery?"

"That grew back a long time ago, Cousin."

"When you were quite a bit shorter, as well. I almost had to sit down to kiss you hello. Yet now,— um, that is,— "

"Dangerous territory, Sir."

"How so? an innocent peck upon the cheek of a child?"

"Had you thought to inquire of the Child," Tenebræ's chin rising slowly, "you might have found your education further'd in ways unexpected, 'Thelmer." Ethelmer for a split second is gazing straight up into her nostrils, one of which now flares into pink illumination as Pitt's Taper sets alight the central Lanthorn of the Orrery, representing the Sun. The other Planets wait, all but humming, taut within their spidery Linkages back to the Crank-Shaft and the Crank, held in the didactic Grasp of the Revd Cherrycoke. The Twins, push'd to the back, content themselves with the movements of the outermost Planets, Saturn and the new "Georgian," but three years old. Dr. Nessel, the renown'd German Engineer, last spring show'd up unexpectedly in Philadelphia, having travers'd the Sea under wartime conditions, to add free of charge the new Planet to the numerous Orreries he had built in America. In each Apparatus, he fashion'd the Planet a little differently. By the time he got to Philadelphia, he was applying to the miniature greenish-blue globes *Mappemondes* of some intricacy, as if there were being reveal'd to him, one Orrery at a time, a World with a History even longer than our own, a recognizable Creator, Oceans that had to be cross'd, lands that had to be fought over, other Species to be conquer'd. The children have since pass'd many an hour, Lenses in hand, gazing upon this new World, and becoming easy with it. They have imagin'd and partly compos'd a Book, *History of the New Planet,* the Twins providing the Wars, and Brae the scientifick Inventions and Useful Crafts.

"Here then," the Rev^d having smoothly crank'd Venus, Earth, and the Sun into proper alignment, "— as seen from the Earth, Venus,— here,— was to pass across the Disk of the Sun. Seen from Cape Town, five and a half hours, more or less, Limb to Limb. What Observers must determine are the exact Times this Passage begins and ends. From a great many such Observations 'round the world, and especially those widely separated north and south, might be reckon'd the value of the Solar Parallax."

"What's that?" Pitt and Pliny want to know.

"The size of the Earth, in seconds of Arc, as seen by an observer upon the surface of the Sun."

"Don't his feet get blister'd?" hollers Pitt, with his brother goading him on, "— isn't he too busy hopping about? and what of his Telescope, won't it melt?"

"All of these and more," replies the Rev[d], "making it super-remarkable, that thro' the magick of Celestial Trigonometry,— to which you could certainly be applying yourselves,— such measurements may yet be taken,— as if the Telescope, in mysterious Wise, were transporting us safely thro' all the dangers of the awesome Gulf of Sky, out to the Object we wish to examine."

"A Vector of Desire."

"Thankee, DePugh, the phrase exact." DePugh is the son of Ives LeSpark, like Ethelmer home on a Visit from School, in this case from Cambridge,— traveling the Atlantick to and fro by Falmouth Packet as easily as taking the Machine to New Castle. He has shown an early aptitude with Figures. God be merciful to him, silently requests the Rev[d].

Somebody somewhere in the World, watching the Planet go dark against the Sun,— dark, mad, mortal, the Goddess in quite another Aspect indeed,— cannot help blurting, exactly at The Moment, from Sappho's Fragment 95, seeming to wreck thereby the Ob,—

"O Hesperus,— you bring back all that the bright day scatter'd,— you bring in the sheep, and the goat,— you bring the Child back to her mother."

"Thank you for sharing that with us...recalling that this is Sun-Rise, Dear, -*Rise*, not sun-*Set*."

"Come! She's not yet detach'd!"

"Let us see. Well, will you look at that." A sort of long black Filament yet connects her to the Limb of the Sun, tho' she be moved well onto its Face, much like an Ink-Drop about to fall from the Quill of a forgetful Scribbler,— sidewise, of course,— "Quick! someone, secure the Time,— "

This, or odd behavior like it, is going on all over the World all day long that fifth and sixth of June, in Latin, in Chinese, in Polish, in Silence,— upon Roof-Tops and Mountain Peaks, out of Bed-chamber windows, close together in the naked sunlight whilst the Wife minds the Beats of the Clock,— thro' Gregorians and Newtonians, achromatick and rainbow-smear'd, brand-new Reflectors made for the occasion, and ancient Refractors of preposterous French focal lengths,— Observers lie, they sit, they kneel,— and witness something in the Sky. Among those attending Snouts Earth-wide, the moment of first contact produces a collective brain-pang, as if for something lost and already unclaimable,— after the Years of preparation, the long and at best queasy voyaging, the Station arriv'd at, the Latitude and Longitude well secur'd,— the Week of the Transit,— the Day,— the Hour,— the Minute,— and at last 'tis, "Eh? where am I?"

Astronomers will seek to record four Instants of perfect Tangency between Venus's Disk, and the Sun's. Two are at Ingress,— External Contact, at the first touch from outside the Sun's Limb, and then Internal Contact, at the instant the small black Disk finally detaches from the inner Circumference of the great yellow one, Venus now standing alone against the Face of the Sun. The other two come at Egress,— this time, first Internal, then external Contact. And then Eight more years till the next, and for this Generation last, Opportunity,— as if the Creation's Dark Engineer had purposedly arrang'd the Intervals thus, to provoke a certain Instruction, upon the limits to human grandeur impos'd by Mortality.

The Sky remains clouded up till the day of the Transit, Friday the fifth of June. Both the Zeemanns and the Vrooms speed about in unaccustom'd Bustle, compar'd to the Astronomers, who seem unnaturally calm.

"Dutch Ado about nothing," Mason remarks.

Dixon agrees. "And they're usually so stolid, too...?"

Els comes skidding across the floor in her Stocking Feet, heading for the Kitchen with an Apron's load of Potatoes. "Nothing to worry about!" she cries, " 'twill clear up in plenty of time!" Even Cornelius is up on the Roof, scanning the Mists with a nautical Spy-Glass, reporting upon hopeful winds and bright patches. " 'Tis ever like this before a Cloudless Day," he assures them. The Slaves speak inaudibly, and are seen to gaze toward the Mountains. They have never observ'd their owners behaving like this. They begin to smile, tentatively but directly, at Mason and Dixon.

Of whom one is insomniac, and one is not. Afterward, none in the Household will be able to agree which was which. Drops of what proves to be *ketjap* in the pantry suggest Dixon as the sleepless one, whilst a Wine-Glass abandon'd upon a chicken-Battery indicates Mason. The Rattle-Watch make a point of coming by ev'ry hour and in front of Zeemanns' singing out the Time of Night, adding, "And all's clouded over yet!"

Somehow, ev'ryone is awake at first Light. "The Sun ascended in a thick haze, and immediately entered a dark cloud," as Mason and Dixon will report later in the *Philosophical Transactions*. Clock-time is 0 Hours, 12 Minutes, 0 Seconds. Twenty-three minutes later, they have their first sight of Venus. Each lies with his Eye clapp'd to the Snout of an identical two-and-a-half-foot Gregorian Reflector made by Mr. Short, with Darkening-Nozzles by Mr. Bird.

"Quite a Tremor," Mason grumbles. "They'll have to ascend a bit more in the Sky. And here comes this damn'd Haze again."

Upon first making out the Planet, Dixon becomes as a Sinner converted. "Eeh! God in his Glory!"

"Steady," advises Mason, in a vex'd tone.

Dixon remembers the Tale Emerson lov'd to tell, of Galileo before the Cardinals, creaking to his feet after being forc'd to recant, muttering, "Nonetheless, it moves." Watch, patiently as before the Minute-Hand of a Clock, become still enough, and 'twould all begin to move.... *This,* Dixon understands, is what Galileo was risking so much for,— this majestick Dawn Heresy. " 'Twas seeing not only our Creator about his Work," he tells Mason later, "but Newton and Kepler, too, confirm'd in theirs. The Arrival, perfectly as calculated, the three bodies sliding into a single Line...Eeh, it put me in a Daze for fair." Whatever the cause, the times he records are two to four seconds ahead of Mason's.

"With all the other Corrections to make, now must we also introduce another, for observational impatience," supposes Mason,— "styling it 'Leonation,' perhaps,— "

"As well might we correct for 'Tauricity,' " replies Dixon, "or Delays owing to Caution inflexible."

The girls have also been observers of the Transit, having cajol'd a Sailor of their Acquaintance into lending them a nautickal Spy-Glass, and smoak'd with Sheep-tallow Candles their own Darkening-Lenses,— taking turns at the Glass, even allowing their Parents a Peep now and then,— Jet breathing, "She's really there," Greet adding, "Right on time, too!" and Els,— hum,— we may imagine what Els was up to, and what transpir'd just as the last of the Black Filament, holding the Planet to the Inner Limb of the Sun, gave way, and she dropp'd, at last, full onto that mottl'd bright Disk, dimm'd by the Lenses to a fierce Moon, that Eyes might bear.

As before the Transit the month of May crept unnaturally, so, after it, will June, July, August, and September hasten by miraculously,— till early in October, when Capt. Harrold, of the *Mercury*, finds a lapse in the Weather workable enough to embark the Astronomers, and take them to St. Helena in. By which time, ev'ryone is more than ready for a change of Company. The North-West Rains have well possess'd the Town,— all Intrigue lies under Moratorium, as if the Goddess of Love in her Visitation had admonish'd all who would invoke her, to search their Hearts, and try not to betray her quite so much.

After the Transit, Astronomers and Hosts walk about for Days in deep Stupor, like Rakes and Doxies after some great Catastrophe of the Passions. The Zeemanns' servant difficulties being resolv'd, the Astronomers return to that Table, and for the next four months pursue Lives of colorless Rectitude, with the Food no better nor worse, waiting upon the Winds. In the Mountains, the Bull's Eye is sovereign. All over Town, Impulse, chasten'd, increasingly defers to Stolidity. Visiting Indian Mystics go into Trances they once believ'd mindless enough, which here prove Ridottoes of Excess, beside the purpos'd Rainy-day Inanition of the Dutch. The Slaves, as if to preserve a secret Invariance, grow more visible and distinct, their Voices stronger, and their Musick more pervasive, as if the Rain were carrying these from distant parts of Town. Johanna and the Girls, after a brief few weeks in a nun-like withdrawal from the Frivolous,— Jet going so far as to cover her hair with a diaphanous Wimple she has fashion'd of Curtain-stuff,— are all back to their old Theatrics, this time to the Delight of a trio of young Company Writers lately arriv'd at False Bay, Mr. Delver Warp and the Brothers Vowtay, coming home from Bengal non-Nabobickal as when they went out, with only enough in their pockets to draw the interest of Cape Belles, who are far less particular than the Vrooms, and fearful that if they don't get it, 'twill be as soon gambl'd away into the Purses of Sea-Sharpers. Corrupted by India, yet poor,— ungovernably lewd, yet unwrinkl'd,— and withal, what a Heaven-sent Source of White Blood are these Lads! Johanna can almost see those Babies now, up on the Block, adorable enough to sell themselves, kicking their feet in the air and squealing,— and she grows monomaniackal in her Pursuit, whilst Austra finds herself calculating which of the Sprigs shall be easiest to seduce, and which, if any, more of a Challenge....

Presently, from across the back-Yards jealously patroll'd by their predatory Hens, come once again sounds of feminine Merriment. Mason looks over at Dixon. "At least they're back to normal over there," he remarks. "For a while, I puzzl'd,— had the Town undergone some abrupt Conversion? Had I, without knowing it?"

Dixon recalls when Wesley came to preach at Newcastle,— "His first sermon in the North-East,— the congregations immense,— all the Side, and beyond, transform'd,— belonging to the Spirit. It lasted for Weeks after,— tho' it may have been months, for all I knew of Time in those Days,— I was a Lad, but I could make it out. Little by then surpriz'd me, yet this was the canniest thing upon the coaly Tyne since Harry Clasper out-keel'd the Lad from Hetton-le-Hole...? Nothing like it again, that I've noatic'd...? Until this Transit of Venus...this turning of Soul, have tha felt it,— they're beginning to talk to their Slaves? Few, if any, beatings,— tho' best to whisper, not to jeopardize it too much...?"

"The Dutch are afraid," Mason is able to contribute, "unto Death."

"Why, Aye. So do I recollect myself, the first time it happen'd to me...?"

Mason suspicious, sniffing Enthusiasm,— "To you? Do they allow you to talk about that?"

"I've been booted out of Raby Meeting, haven't I...? I can reveal all the mystick secrets I wish...?"

"One first must keep one's Hat on one's Head, correct?"

"Aye, the Spirit ever fancies a bonny Hat,— but the fairly principal thing, is to sit quietly...? It took me till well out of my Youth to learn, tho' now I'm not sure I remember how, any more...?"

"That's it? Sit quietly? And Christ...will come?"

"We spoke of it as the Working of the Spirit, within. 'Tis a distinct Change from the ev'ryday...tha wouldn't be able to miss it, should it happen...?"

"Yet then, you say, it passes...."

"It abides,— 'tis we who are ever recall'd from it, to tend to our various mortal Requirements...? and so another such Visit soon becomes necessary,— another great Turning, and so forth...? Howbeit, 'tis all Desire,— and Desire, but Embodiment, in the World, of what Quakers have understood as Grace...?"

Starting about then, rain-bound, whenever he may, Mason contrives to sit in some shutter'd room, as quietly as he knows how, waiting for a direct experience of Christ. But he keeps jumping up, to run and interrupt Dixon, who is trying to do the same, with news of his Progress,—

"Jere! I think it almost happen'd! D'ye get a kind of rum sensation here,"— touching the center of his Forehead,— "is that it?"

"Mason, first tha must sit,— not jump up and down like thah'...? And then, sit quietly. Quietly...." Back they go, till Mason in his Chair, falling asleep, topples with a great Crash, or Dixon decides he'll step out after all, nip down to The World's End, and see what the Cape Outlawry may be up to.

Little by little, as weeks pass, the turn of Spirit Mason and Dixon imagine they have witness'd is reclaim'd by the Colony, and by whatever haunts it. Any fear that things might ever change is abated. Masters and Mistresses resume the abuse of their Slaves, who reply in Bush tongues, to which, soon enough hoarse with Despair, with no hope of being understood, they return, as to childhood homes.... Riding in and out of Town now may often be observ'd White Horsemen, carrying long Rifles styl'd "Sterloops," each with an inverted Silver Star upon the Cheek-Piece.

When Mason and Dixon encounter Vrooms in the Street they bow, and pass, with each exchange lapsing closer to Silence. By the time the

Southeaster has advanc'd to the Circumference of the Day, there remains nothing to say to them, nor to any who have been their Hosts. "I warn'd you all," Mrs. De Bosch lilts, triumphant, "did I not, ev'ryone. Nor should I be much surpriz'd, if those frightful Instruments they brought, have serv'd quite another Purpose here."

When they leave the Cape, no one is there at the Quay to say good-bye but Bonk, the police official who earlier greeted them. "Good luck, Fellows. Tell them at the Desk, I was not such a bad Egg, no?"

"What Desk is that," ask Mason and Dixon.

"What Desk? In London, off some well-kept Street, in a tidy House, there will be someone at a Desk, to whom you'll tell all you have seen."

"Not in England, Sir," Mason protests.

For the first and final time they see him laugh, and glimpse an entire Life apart from the Castle, in which he must figure as a jolly Drinking Companion. "You'll see!" he calls as they depart for the Ship in the Bay. "Good Luck, Good Luck! Ha! Ha! Ha!" Resounding upon the Water ever-widening between them.

"What made them leave home and set sail upon dangerous seas, determining where upon the Globe they must go, was not,— *Pace* any Astrologists in the Room,— the Heavenly Event by itself, but rather that unshining Assembly of Human Needs, of which Venus, at the instant of going dark, is the Prime Object,— including certainly the Royal Society's need for the Solar Parallax,— but what of the Astronomers' own Desires, which may have been less philosophical?"

"Love,— I knew it," Tenebræ all but sighs. " 'Twas Love for the Planet Herself."

"Nothing like your own, of course," beams her Uncle. "I recollect that when you were no more than Three, you saw Venus through your Papa's fine Newtonian for the first time. 'Twas in the crescent Phase, and you said, 'Look! the Little Moon.' You told us that you already knew the Moon had a little Moon, which it play'd with."

"We would go outdoors, long after bed-time, up to the pasture," she is pleas'd to recall, "— the Observatory wasn't built yet. The Ponies would all stand together, quite cross, and watch us as we came up, their eyes flashing in the light from our Lanthorns, and I always thought I could hear them muttering, for it was clear we were disturbing them."

"Did they bite you?" inquires Pitt.

"Hard?" adds Pliny.

"Rrr!" she raises her Hoop as if to hurl it at them.

"Do find a way," advises Aunt Euphrenia, careering into the room, with her Oboe and an armload of sheet-music, "to wrangle with less Noise, or your old Uncle will have to sell you, as a Brace, to the *Italians* rumor'd to live South of this City, where you shall have to learn to sing their vulgar Airs, and eat Garlick ev'ry day, as shall ev'ryone else,— "

"Hooray!" shout Pitt and Pliny. "For Breakfast, too!"

"Tra-la, say, Food Perversion? nothing to do with the Cherrycoke side of the family," sniffs Aunt Euphrenia, producing the most wicked-looking of Knives, and beginning very carefully to carve a Reed for her Instrument from a length of Schuylkill-side Cane. "Yes lovely isn't it?" she nods after a while, as if responding to a Pleasantry. " 'Twas given me by the Sultan. Dear Mustapha, 'Stuffy' we call'd him in the Harem chambers, amongst ourselves..."

When Brae, once, and only once, made the mistake of both gasping and blurting, "Oh, Aunt,— were you in a Turkish Harem, really?" 'twas to turn a giant Tap. "Barbary Pirates brought us actually 's far as Aleppo, you recall the difficult years of 'eighty and 'eighty-one,— no, of course you couldn't,— Levant Company in an uproar, no place to get a Drink, Ramadan all year 'round it seem'd,— howbeit,— 'twas at the worst of those Depredations, that I took Passage from Philadelphia, upon that fateful Tide...the Moon reflected in Dock Creek, the songs of the Negroes upon the Shore, disconsolate,— " Most of her Tale, disguis'd artfully as traveler's Narrative, prov'd quite outside the boundaries of the Girl's Innocence, as of the Twins' Attention,— among the Domes and Minarets, the Mountain-peaks rising from the Sea, the venomous Snakes, miracle-mongering Fakeers, intrigues over Harem Precedence and Diamonds as big as a girl's playfully clench'd fist, 'twas Inconvenience which provided the recurring Motrix of Euphrenia's adventures among the Turks, usually resolv'd by her charming the By-standers with a few appropriate Notes from her Oboe,— upon which now, in fact, her Reed shap'd and fitted, she has begun to punctuate her brother Wicks's Tale, with scraps of Ditters von Dittersdorf, transcriptions from Quantz, and the *Scamozzetta* from *I Gluttoni*.

II

"The St. Helena of old had been as a Paradise," avers Euphrenia. "The Orange and Lemon-Groves, the Coffee-Fields,— "

"Gone before your Time, Euphie."

"Does that mean I am forbidden to mourn them? They are mine as much as anyone's, to mourn."

"I'd be last to lay any sort of claim," says the Rev^d, "— whilst the Astronomers were sailing there from the Cape, I was journeying on, quite the other way, to India, and then past India.... St. Helena was a part of the Tale that I miss'd, and along with it the Reverend Dr. Maskelyne, who has continued, even unto our Day, as Astronomer Royal, publishing his Almanack and doing his bit for global Trade."

"Something wrong with that, Wicks?" inquires Mr. LeSpark.

"Only insofar as it is global, and not Celestial," replies the Rev^d, with a holy Smirk master'd in his first week of Curacy.

The Merchant of Purposeful Explosion throws an arm across his Brow. "Your Halo blinds me, Sir. Aye, most Italian,— Joy of it, I'm sure."

"More of this Brandy ought to dim it some." Genial Uncle Lomax, grinning mischievously at his older Brother, pours the Rev^d another Beaker-ful. From outside, frozen Rain sweeps briefly yet pointedly at the glossy black Window-Panes.

"Then how are we ever to know what happen'd among the three of 'm upon that little-known Island?" Uncle Ives a bit smug, ev'ryone thinks.

"Well, let us see. Maskelyne was there the better part of a Year,— aware, from early on, that he could not obtain the Observations he wanted, owing to a defective Plumb-line suspension on the Sector, yet there, enisl'd, remaining,— twenty-nine years old, first time he's been away from home, and he's facing months in what proves to be,— those whose bed-time is nigh, stop your Ears,— an infamous Port of Call, quite alone in the mid-Atlantic, a Town left to shift as it may, dedicated to nought but the pleasures of Sailors,— which is to say, ev'ry species of Misbehavior, speakable and not."

"Tides and Lunars cannot have provided the Reverend Maskleyne full occupation,— one is understandably curious as to what else may've befallen him."

"Something must have," the Revd Cherrycoke agrees, "— else he should have emerg'd mad as all sooner or later go, upon that Island."

"An attack of Reason," suggests Mr. LeSpark.

"What's the Mystery?" Ethelmer shrugs. "Didn't Days take twenty-four Hours to pass, as they do now?"

Brae peers thro' the candle-light. "Why Coz, how interesting."

The idea, in making Port at St. Helena, is to keep to windward, get South-east of the Island, and let the Trade Winds carry you to the coast,— which you then follow, generally northward, till you come 'round to the lee side, and on into the harbor of James's Town,— where despite appearances of Shelter, the oceanic Waves continue to beat without ceasing, the Clamor wind-borne, up across the Lines and the Parade, all being reduced to Geometry and optical Illusion, even what is waiting there all around, what is never to be nam'd directly.

Once ashore, the Astronomers hear the Ocean everywhere, no Wall thick, nor Mind compos'd, nor Valley remote enough to lose it. It shakes the Ground and traverses the Boot-soles of the Watch, high in the ravines. The floorboards of Taverns register its rhythmick Blows, as they have the Years of Thumps from the swinging boots of Seamen whose destinies were sometimes to include Homicide, as if keeping Faith with that same Brutal Pulse, waiting upon a Moment, needing but the single sighting,— sworn to, vanish'd,— the terrible Authorization.

Tho' the sun nightly does set below the Island's stark horizon, what Mason sees, from his first Nightfall there, is Darkness, *rising up* out of the sea, where all the carelessly bright day it has lain, as in a state of slumber...whilst at dawn, that same Darkness, almost palpably aware of his Regard, appears to withdraw, consciously, to a certain depth below the Atlantick Surface. In the Astrology of this island, the Sun must be reckoned of less importance than Darkness incorporated as some integral, anti-luminary object, with its own motions, positions, and aspects,— Black Sheep of the family of Planets, neither to be sacrificed to Hades nor spoken of by Name....

Sirius, which Maskelyne remains here to observe, is the Island's Zenith-Star, as is Gamma Draconis for Greenwich. (Englishmen are born under the Dragon, St. Helenians under the Dog. At Bencoolen Mason and Dixon would have been under inconstant Mira, in the Whale. These signs are the Apocrypha of Astrology.) Ev'ry Midnight the baleful thing is there, crossing directly overhead,— the Yellow Dog. There inverted among the Wires, all but flowing. Treacly, as you'd say,— would even a Portsmouth Poll wear such a vivid, unhealthy shade of Yellow?

A very small town clings to the edge of an interior that must be reckoned part of the Other World. No change here is gradual,— events arrive suddenly. All distances are vast. The Wind, brutal and pure, is there for its own reasons, and human life, any life, counts for close to nought. The Town has begun to climb into the Ravine behind it, and thus, averaged overall, to tilt toward the sea. After Rain-Storms, the water rushes downhill, in Eagres and Riffles and Cataracts, thro' the town, rooftop to rooftop, in and out of Windows, leaving behind a shiv'ring Dog from uphill, taking away the Coffee Pot, till leaving it in its turn somewhere else, for a Foot-Stool,— thus bartering its way out to sea. The Horizon has little use for lengthy sunsets. Creatures of the Ocean depths approach the shore-line, as near as the little Coves where the water abruptly becomes Lavender and Aquamarine, remaining to observe, deliberate in their movements, without fear.

For years, travelers have reported that the further up into the country one climbs, the more the sea appears to lie *above the Island,*— as if suspended, and kept from falling fatally upon it, thro' the operations of Mysterion impenetrable on the part of a Guardian.... As if in Payments credited against the Deluge, upon no sure Basis of Prediction, the great Sea-Rollers will rise, and come against the Island,— reaching higher than the Town with the Jacobite Name, tho' perhaps not quite to the ridgeline above it. For anyone deluded enough to remain down at sea-level, there must come a moment when he finds himself looking upward at the Crests approaching. The Public Trees quite small in Outline below them. The Cannon, the Bastions, of no Avail. Did he choose, more prudently, to escape to the Heights, he might, from above, squinting into spray whose odor and taste are the life of the sea, behold a Company of Giant rob'd Beings, risen incalculably far away over the Horizon, bound this way upon matters forever unexplain'd, moving blind and remorseless across the Sea, as if the Island did not exist.

Not as spectacular, older residents declare, as the Rollers of '50. Then, it seem'd, 'twas the Triumph of a Sea gone mad, and the Island must be lost.... Being part of a general Exodus to high ground, one may not pause for too long to gaze and reflect upon the fastnesses of empty water-plain, the Sun-glare through the salt Mists after the sleepless climb thro' the Dark,— the only Choices within one's Control, those between Persistence and Surrender. Within their first week upon the Island, all visitors have this Dream.

Out upon Munden's Point stand a pair of Gallows, simplified to Pen-strokes in the glare of this Ocean sky. A Visitor may lounge in the Evening upon the Platform behind the Lines, and, as a Visitor to London might gaze at St. Paul's, regard these more sinister forms in the failing North Light,— perhaps being led to meditate upon Punishment,— or upon Commerce...for Commerce without Slavery is unthinkable, whilst Slavery must ever include, as an essential Term, the Gallows,— Slavery without the Gallows being as hollow and Waste a Proceeding, as a Crusade without the Cross. Down at the end of the great Ravine that runs up-country from the sea, beneath the cliffs, along the Batteries, in the evenings, Islanders looking to catch the breeze will nightly promenade. If one ignores the guns darkly shining and the arm'd Sentries, the Island might be fancied an East Indiaman of uncertain size, and these crepuscular parades to and fro, a Passengers' turn upon her Weather-decks,— though at closer inspection each Phiz might suggest less a Traveler's Curiosity, than some long-standing acquaintance with the glum, even among the women who appear, each Sunset.

Besides those resident here for purposes of Nautickal Amusement, the Birds of passage thro' St. Helena make up a mix'd flock,— Convicts being transported to the South Seas for unladylike crimes in England, with St. Helena one of the steps in their Purgatory,— young Wives on their way out to India to join husbands in the Army and Navy, a-tremble with tales, haunting the Day like a shadow from just beneath the Horizon ahead, of the Black Hole of Calcutta,— and Company Perpetuals, headed out, headed home, such shuttles upon the loom of Trade as Mrs. Rollright, late of Portland, who keeps opium in her patch-box and commutes frequently enough upon the India run to've had four duels fought over her already, though she has yet to see her twenties out. Almost to a woman, they confess to strange and inexpressible Feelings when the ship makes landfall,— the desolate line of peaks, the oceanic sunlight,— coming about to fetch the road, losing the Trade-Wind at Sugar-Loaf Point, hugging the shore and playing the eddies, the identickal Routine, 'twas O G-d are we here again,— whilst to First-Timers another Planet, somehow accessible from this.

"There's one a-sop with the Dew," Dixon remarks, "— in the Claret-color'd Velvet there, with the Chinese Shawl, and the Kid Boots...? She seems to recollect thee, for fair."

"Tyburn Charlie! well prick me with a Busk-Pin and tell me 'twas all a Dream. 'Tis I,— little Florinda! Yes, you do remember,— but last Year,— " and she sings, in a pleasant Alto,

> 'Twas the Fifth Day of May, in
> The Year of our Lord, Seven-
> -Teen hundred sixty and Zero,
> That the Brave Lord Ferrers
> Ascended the Steps, of
> The Scaffold, as bold as a Hero...

Mason amiably joining in, they continue,

> 'I am ready,' said he, 'If you'll
> Quote me your Fee,'— to the
> Cruel Hangman's Eye sprang a Tear-oh,—

'Of your silver-trimm'd Coat,
I'll admit I made note,
But must no longer claim it, oh dear, oh!'
[Refrain]
'O, my, O Dear O!
You must think I've the morals of Nero!
Be it dangle 'em high, or strangle 'em low,
Hangmen have Feelings, or didn't ye know?'

The year after Rebekah's death was treacherous ground for Mason, who was as apt to cross impulsively by Ferry into the Bosom of Wapping, and another night of joyless low debauchery, as to attend Routs in Chelsea, where nothing was available betwixt Eye-Flirtation, and the Pox. In lower-situated imitations of the Hellfire Club, he hurtl'd carelessly along some of Lust's less-frequented footpaths, ever further, he did not escape noting, from Pleasure,— the moonlight falling upon the lawns, the trees, the walks, claiming the color of desire, as to represent all that Passion, seething within that small corner of Town, the music through the leaves, each washed in moon-white,— to the Fabulators of Grub-Street, a licentious night-world of Rakes and Whores, surviving only in memories of pleasure, small darting winged beings, untrustworthy as remembrancers...yet its infected, fragrant, soiled encounters 'neath the Moon were as worthy as any,— an evil-in-innocence....

("Uncle, Uncle!"
"Hum, hum, howbeit,— "
"Another Cup, Sir?")

'Twas then that Mason began his Practice, each Friday, of going out to the hangings at Tyburn, expressly to chat up women, upon a number of assumptions, many of which would not widely be regarded as sane.

Rol-ling out the Edge-ware Ro-o-oad,—
To where they climb a Ladder-to-go, to sleep,—
The crowd is all a-tiptoe and the skies are bright, 'tis
A lovely day to come and have a Peep.—
He'll drop right thro' the Floor [tick-tock]

He'll dance upon the Air [knock-knock]
Whilst 'neath the Deadly Never-Green
'Tis merry as a Fair,— and
If you're luc-ky to be short enough,
With no-place much to stare,
Why, you might not even know, you're, there...

Turn'd thirty-two but days before, Mason, as a gift of Festivity to himself, attends the much-heralded Hanging of Lord Ferrers for the murder of Johnson, his Steward. What seems the entire world of Fashion has assembl'd, with each trying to outdress ev'ry other. Nonce-Hats, never before seen, many never to be seen again. Wigs as elaborately detail'd as Gowns. Coats especially commission'd for the occasion, with a classic Thirteen-Turn Noose Motif to the Braiding, and the Smoking Pistol depicted in Gold Brocade. As Mason, feeling shabby, curses himself for not having worn a more stylish outfit, he notes a young Woman observing him,— when he meets her Gaze, she immediately switches it away with a look of annoyance, not with Mason, it pleases him to fancy, so much as with herself, for happening to be the one caught staring,— there being scores of good reasons why no further degree of Fascination will develop from this. Judging by her escort, she's some rising Beauty of the Town, whose Looks more than excuse an absolute lack of taste in any matter of Costume, whilst at the same time she finds herself mysteriously drawn to snuff-color'd and, frankly, murkier Statements, such as Mason's, here.

"Hallo, d'you think he'll get much of a hard-on, then?" is her Greeting. "They say that agents of Lady F. are about, betting heavily against it."

Mason gapes in despair. He'll be days late thinking up any reply to speech as sophisticated as this. "In my experience," he might say, " 'tis usually the Innocent who get them, and the Guilty who fail to."

"How very curious." She will not blink, tho' her nostrils may flare. Her escorts will titter,— and her little Dog Biscuit, alone scenting her onset of interest, will begin to act up. "Could Remorse ever really unman any of you?"

"Why no.— 'Tis rather that Surprize invigorates us."

Flirtatiously, she scowls, as Mason goes rattling on morosely,— "Take the noted Highwayman Fepp, but last week, most likely not insane, being mov'd by the Mathematicks of his wealth, or rather lack of it, more than by any criminal Passion,— the *Membrum Virile* was remarkably flaccid, at least according to the Jobbers who cut him down,— "

"And subsequently up," chirps the Maiden.

"— for consider that the Murderer cannot, in the Moment, know the ecstatic surprise of the Innocent, having borne within him, from Life's beginning, an acquaintance with the sudden Drop and Snap of its End. He dreams about it, sometimes when awake. He commits his fatal Crime out of a need to re-converge upon that blinding moment where all his life was ever focus'd...."

Her eyes have grown enormous and moist,— the Bodice of her Gown squeaks gently at its Seams, her Modesty-Piece flutters as if itself perplex'd. The Fops accompanying her having been freed to resume their chief interest, the Exchange of Gossip, even Custodial Eyes are elsewhere. "Sir," she murmurs, "I have ever sought a man such as yourself— " There is a sudden roar from the crowd, half for and half against, as His Lordship's carriage arrives, and the fourth Earl steps out. Seamen throw unchewable Sausages and half-eaten scones, brightly dress'd Women throw Roses. "Hideous suit," remarks one of the Fops, "— what's that Shade, some kind of Fawn? altogether too light for the occasion." "I do like the Silver bits, though," comments his Friend, Seymour. All manner of retainers in black livery bustle about, the one attracting the most Notice being the Rope-bearer,— for 'tis rumor'd that Lord Ferrers is to be hang'd, at his request, with a Rope of Silk. The bearer is a slight figure in black velvet, whose skin in the high sunlight appears paper-white. All the way from the Tower, atop the bright jinglings of the Carriage,— expensively encrusted and plated by highly-paid Italians,— like a Miniature propell'd, in its strange slow Progress, by some invisible Child,— is the fatal Rope held aloft, perfectly white upon a black Silk Cushion, for the inspection of all the straining Eyes. "Well it's still 'emp for me," someone remarks, "— all things being equal, if not all Men."

"Aye, Silk's what they fancy out in India, with their Thuggee,— over the wall, in your Window, *kkkk!* Job's done, another tasty Bite for old Kalee,— that's their Goddess, as you'd say. Silk,— it's scarcely there, and yet..."

"*Kkkk!*"

"Precisely my point."

Orange-girls and beggars, ale-pots, gaming in the Dirt, purses wafted away, glances intercepted, dogs bravely a-prowl for Scraps, as hungry Blademen for Dogs, Buskers wandering and standing still, with a Wind from the Gallows bringing ev'ry sigh, groan, and Ejaculation over the heads of the crowd to settle upon their hearing like Ash upon the Hats of spectators at a Fire, the Day wraps and fondles them as Mason and the temporarily heedless beauty move together thro' the crowd, till they reach a Barrow with Awnings rigg'd against the Sun. "Wine!" cries she, "oh let's do!"

"This Château Gorce looks interesting," says Mason, "although, as the day is mild, perhaps a chill'd Hock would be more...*apropos.*"

"If not *de Rigueur,*" she replies.

"But of course, *Chérie.*" They laugh at the *Piquance* of these *Mots,* and sip Wine as the imbécile Peer goes along toward his Doom,— till some kind of problem arises with the new Trap-door Arrangement, today's being its first Use at any publick Proceeding.

"These frightful Machines!" she pretends to lament, "— shall our Deaths now, as well as our Lives, be rul'd by the Philosophers, and their Army of Mechanicks?"

"That Trap's probably over-constructed," Mason has already blurted, "hence too heavy, and bearing sidewise upon the Lever and Catch,— " He notes a sudden drop in the local Temperature.

"You are...a man of Science, then?" looking about, tho' not yet with Panick.

"I am an Astronomer," Mason replies.

"Ah...existing upon some sort of Stipend, I imagine. How...wonderful...I'd taken you for one of the better sort of Kiddy, the way you were turn'd out, quiet self-possession, I mean, one usually is able to tell,— alas, 'tis just as Mr. Bubb Dodington warn'd me,— 'Florinda,' said he, 'you are too young to appreciate men either in their wide diversity, or for the pitiable simplicity of what they really want. Can you guess what that is, my Wren?' His Wren. Well,— it might've been one thing, mightn't it,— and then again— "

"Excuse me, did I hear you, I'm sure inadvertently, mention that you receive…Assessments of Character, from Bubb Dodington? the ancient Fitch of legend? That relick from a signally squalid Era in our Nation's Politickal History,— *that* Bubb Dodington?"

"Georgie is a particular Friend," she flares, in a way that suggests Experience upon the Stage. "If he may advise the Princess of Wales as to matters constitutional, he may advise me, whatever he wishes. He grows older, and a life of super-human excess is at last presenting its Bills,— whose demands turn ever harsher with the days,— even at the Interest, yet a Bargain. Will you have as much to say, Star-Gazer, when it is your time?"

Mason lets his Head drop, abjectly. "There's one, says Pearse, as he fell in the Well…. The truth is, Madam, that I have envied your Friend the honesty of his Life. Tho' being an Earl help'd, of course,— "

"If you mean that you envy his openness as to his Desires,— I collect there are things you yourself may wish to do, that you haven't quite the Words for?" And gazing at him quite steadily, too.

"I?" Mason's Soles beginning to ache, his Brain unable to muster a thought. What he does not, consequently, understand, is that, having reckon'd him harmless, she has decided to get in a bit of exercise, in that endless Refining which the Crafts of Coquetry demand, using Mason as a sort of *Practice-Dummy.*

"You did have me going, Florinda."

"Well I hope so, I'm sure. Tell me, then,— are you still gazing at the Stars for Simpleton-Silver?"

"You remember that?"

"Why, you're not saying, Charlie, that there are too many Men in my Life for me to remember? Surely 'tis not the aggregate Total of all Men, but how many *kinds* of Men, that matters?— and that Figure is manageable, thankee."

James's Town, snug in its ravine, the watchfires high above keeping the nights from invasion, settles into the darkness. Smells of Eastern cooking pour out the kitchen vents of the boarding-houses, and mix with that of the Ocean. The town is for a Moment an unlit riot of spices, pastry, fish and shellfish, Penguin Stuffatas and Sea-Bird Fricasées. Upon the swiftly darkening sea-prospect, in outline now appears a Figure that lacks but a Scythe in its Grasp, to turn all thoughts upon the Brevity of Life. "Dad-dums!" she cries. "Over here! Charlie, my fiancé, Mr. Mournival."

"I meet so many of Florrie's old Troupe," the tall cadaverous Person-age, whose Eyes cannot be clearly seen, hisses in the Twilight. "Charlie, Charlie...You must have been one of the Zanies?"

"Your Theatrical sense,— uncanny Sir," murmurs Mason. "Allow me to present my co-adjutor, whose repertoire of Jest is second only to what resides in the Vatican Library,— Mr. Dixon."

"A Chinaman, a Jesuit, and a Corsican are riding up to Bath..."

12

Mason, Dixon, and Maskelyne are in a punch house on Cock Hill called "The Moon," sitting like an allegorickal Sculpture titl'd, *Awkwardness*. It is not easy to say which of them is contributing more to sustaining the Tableau. Mason is suspicious of Maskelyne, Maskelyne struggles not to offend Mason, and Dixon and Maskelyne have been estrang'd from the instant Dixon, learning of Maskelyne's Residence at Pembroke College, Cambridge, brought up the name of Christopher Smart.

"Durham Lad...? He became a Fellow at Pembroke...?"

A Gust of Panic crosses Maskelyne's face briefly, then his Curatickal Blank returns. "Mr. Smart was our perennial Seaton Prize-winner.— He left two years after I arriv'd,— our Intimacy being limited to Meal-times, when I brought his Food to the Fellows' Table, and fetch'd away his soil'd Napery and his gnaw'd Bones. Sometimes, after they'd all gone, we of the Scullery would eat their Leavings,— his may have been among 'em, I did not distinguish closely,— I was a Lad, and not all aware of how uncomfortable a Life it must have been. To live at Cambridge, to step where Newton stepp'd? I would have become a servant's servant."

"Newton is my Deity," Dixon rather blurts, ignoring Maskelyne's efforts to show polite astonishment by raising one eyebrow without also raising the other, "and Mr. Smart, why I knew him when I was small, a rather older Lad, who came to Raby on his School Vacations, his Father being Steward of the Vane Estates down in Kent, You see, as was mah Great-Uncle George of Raby." Maskelyne now has his Eye-balls roll'd to

Heaven, as if praying for Wing'd Escape. "So both of us quickly learn'd our way 'round the Larders, the trysting places, the passageways inside the Walls, where our Errands often took us, Mr. Kit's being usually to or from the Chapel. I can recall no-one marking in him any unkind moment,— tho' he did seem, each time he return'd to Raby, a bit more preoccupied."

"In 'fifty-six, I believe, he was confin'd in a Hospital for the Insane," says Maskelyne, his Field-Creature's Eyes a-sparkle. "And releas'd, I have heard, the Year before last, mad as when he went in."

"Why aye," Dixon grimly beams, "it must have been thah' Raby Castle, that did it to him...?"

"Well it certainly wasn't Pembroke," Maskelyne sniffs. "Indeed, 'twas only when poor Smart gave up Cambridge, that his mind began to leave him."

"Away from those healthy Surroundings...?" Dixon replies, with clench'd Amiability.

There is Commotion as the Landlord, Mr. Blackner, and several Regulars, leaning to hear, lose all idea of their centers of Gravity, and staggering in the puddles of Ale that commonly decorate the Floor of The Moon, go crashing among the furniture.

Mason, as if newly arriv'd, speaks at last. "Forget not London itself, as a pre-eminent author of Madness,— Greenwich to Grub-Street, the Place is not for ev'ryone,— drawn tho' we be to the grandeur, the hundred Villages strewn all up and down the great Inlet from the Sea, and the wide World beyond,— yet for many, the Cost, how great."

Maskelyne, choosing to hear in this a rebuke, snaps, "Perhaps too many damn'd *Gothickal Scribblers* about, far too many's what did for Mr. Smart," seeming in his turn to allude to Mason's earlier-announc'd preferences in Entertainment.

As Mason considers some reply, Dixon gallantly fills in. "Why, Grub-Street Pub-Street, Sir. *The Ghastly Fop? Vampyrs of Covent Garden?* Come, come. Worth a dozen of any *Tom Jones,* Sir."

This receives Maskelyne's careful Smirk. He fancies it a Smile, but 'tis an Attitude of the Mouth only,— the eyes do not engage in it, being off upon business of their own. The impression is of unrelenting wariness. "I'd expected such to lie up Mr. Mason's Lane,— hadn't suppos'd your own tastes to run there as well. Excellent way to pass those Obless Nights, I'd imagine, reading each to the other?"

Mr. Blackner has appear'd. "I always fancied the one about the Italian with no Head, that'd be, now, *Count Senzacapo,* do any of you know that one?"

"Excellent choice, Sir," Dixon as it seems cheerily, "— that Episode with the three peasant girls,— "

"— and those Illustrations!" The Lads lewdly chuckling.

"Yet surely," Maskelyne all but whining, "there's far too much of it about? Encouraging," his Voice dropping, "all these melancholick people." He gestures 'round the Room with his head. "This Island, especially,...is full of them. Six months I've been here,— too many idle Minutes to be fill'd, soon pile up, topple, and overwhelm the healthiest Mind,— "

"Sirius Business," cackles the Proprietor, sliding away to other Mischief.

"*Damn* the fellow," Maskelyne clutching his Head.

"Something else coming, here," Dixon advises.

Mason looks up. "Aahhrr! the Natives from the Kitchen,— Maskelyne! what is it, a Cannibal Sacrifice?— "

"No!" Maskelyne screams, "Worse!"

"Worse?" Dixon murmurs, by which time all can see the Candles upon the great iced Cake, being borne out to them as its Escort burst into "For He's a Jolly Good Fellow."

Mr. Blackner brandishes an invisible Spoon. "Assembl'd it myself, Sir, tho' my Apprentice here did the Icing."

"They found out!" whispers Maskelyne, "— but how? Do I talk in my sleep, whilst they listen at the Door? Why would I mention my birthday in my sleep? 'Twas last week, anyway."

"Congratulations, much Joy," wish Mason and Dixon.

"Twenty-nine's Fell Shadow! O, inhospitably final year of any Pretense to Youth, its Dreams now, how wither'd away...tho' styl'd a Prime, yet bid'st thou Adieu to the Prime of Life!...There,— there, in the Stygian Mists of Futurity, loometh the dread Thirty,— Transition unspeakable! Prime so soon fallen, thy Virtue so easily broken, into a Number divisible,— penetrable!— by six others!" At each of Maskelyne's dismal Apostrophes, the Merriment in the Room takes another step up in Loudness, tho' muffl'd in Cake. The Ale at The Moon, brew'd with the runoff from up-country, into whose further ingredients no one has ever inquir'd closely, keeps arriving, thanks to Maskelyne, now fully a-bawl,— "Fourth Decade of Life! thy Gates but a brief Year ahead,— tho' in this place, a Year can seem a Century,— what hold'st thou for the superannuated?"

"Marriage!" shouts a Sailor.

"Death!"

"The Morn!" All the Pewter rings with dour Amusement.

"Ye're a cheery lot for being so melancholick," Maskelyne raising his Tankard. "When are you leaving? I'll miss you."

Mason and Dixon have been looking over at each other in some Agitation. When Maskelyne at last takes himself outdoors, Dixon sits up briskly,— "Just reviewing this,— I am to leave you for at least three months in the company of this Gentleman? Is thah' more or less,— "

"Dixon.— The Sector...doesn't...work."

"Whah'...!"

"The Sisson instrument,— someone's put the Plumb-line on wrong. The change he's looking for in the position of Sirius, would span but a few seconds of Arc,— yet the Error owing to the Plumb-line is much greater,— enough to submerge utterly the Result he seeks. Yet he continues here under Royal Society orders,— as now, apparently, do we."

"Tha talk like a sober man."

"Who can get drunk in this terrible place?"

"Cock Ale Tomorrow! Cock Ale Tomorrow!" screams a Malay running into the Room, holding by the Feet a dead Fighting-Cock trailing its last Blood in splashes like Characters Death would know how to read.

"Why, then 'tis damn'd Bencoolen all over again."

"With as little freedom to demur. Yet I might find a way to fix his Plumb-line for him."

"Would thee at least let me have a look at it? Before I leave, thah' is...?"

"Pray you, do not even bring up the Topick of Instruments with him. The one he's oblig'd to go on with, will he nill he, has far more than money invested in it."

"Nonetheless, 'tis the Friendly thing to do,— I'm John Bird's Field Rep, aren't I,— certainly know my way 'round a Sector,— tricks with Beeswax and Breath that few have even heard of,— "

Back comes Maskelyne, fussing with his Queue. "Think about it!" Mason whispers in some panick, as the other Astronomer locates his Seat, sits, and peers at them suspiciously.

Dixon with a beefy grimace meant to convey righteousness, "Nah,— I'm going to ask him."

"Fine! fine, go ahead,— I withdraw from this in advance, it's between you two."

Dixon's eyebrows shoot Hatward, signaling Mischief. "Eeh, well *thah's* too *bahd*, Meeaahson,— my Question to Mr. Maskelyne was to've been, Pray thee Sir, might I buy the next Round out of my own Pocket, blessèd be thy own Generosity for fair, of course,— "

"Ahhrrhh!" Mason brings his Head to the Table-top in a controll'd thump, as Mr. Blackner immediately appears with three gigantic Pots of today's Cock Ale. "Rum Suck, Gents, and if Mr. Mas-son, can resist it, why then you Gents may divide this third Pot betwixt ye, Compliments of the House." Mr. Blackner's Receipt for Cock Ale is esteem'd up and down the India Route, and when these Malays stop in Town with their traveling Cock-Fights, the *Main* Ingredient being suddenly plentiful, Cock Ale, as some might say, is in Season. Mr. Blackner prefers to soak the necessary dried Fruit Bits in Mountain, or Málaga Wine, instead of Canary, and to squeeze the Carcass dry with a cunning Chinese Duck-Press, won at Euchre from a fugitive aristocrat of that Land, in which Force may be multiplied to unprecedented Values, extracting mystick Humors not obtain'd in other Receipts.

Maskelyne looks from one Astronomer to the other. "Excuse me for asking,— and as a Curate only,— lies there between you, some lack of complete Trust?"

"More like a Lapse of Attention," mutters Mason, reaching for one of the Ale-Cans.

"It seem'd a perfectly friendly Request," Maskelyne keeps at it. "Is he often on at you like this, Mr. Dixon? Shall I have to guard my own Tongue?"

"Doesn't work. Whatever you say, from 'Good Morning' on, he'll find somethin' in it...?"

"Yet if you *could* refrain from 'Good Morning,'" Mason advises Maskelyne, "the rest of the Day would fall into place effortlessly."

"I shall miss your good advice, Mr. Dixon."

When inform'd that he must return to the Cape directly, Dixon remains strangely calm. " 'Tis said of the French Astronomers, that they never turn their Instruments, be it out of Pride or Insouciance or some French Sentiment we don't possess, whilst what seems to distinguish us out here, is that we do. We reverse our Sectors, we measure ev'rything in both Directions. It follows, if we've two clocks, that we must find out all we may of their separate Goings, and then, exchanging their positions in the World, be it thousands of Leagues' removal, note the results. 'Tis the British Way, to take the extra step that may one day give us an Edge when we need one, probably against the French. Small Investment, large Reward. I regard myself as a practitioner of British Science now."

"I'll be sure to pass the Word along to London," Maskelyne gentle as Lye.

When Mason and Dixon arriv'd in St. Helena, the observers' Teams exchang'd Clocks,— Dixon, barely ashore, turning about and taking the Shelton Clock back to the Cape by the next ship out, and Mason setting up the Ellicott Clock in Maskelyne's Rooms in James's Town. For a short while, the two Clocks stood side by side, set upon a level Shelf, as just outside, unceasingly, the Ocean beat.... However well sprung the Bracket arrangements, these Walls were fix'd ultimately to the Sea, whose Rhythm must have affected the Pendula of both clocks in ways we do not fully appreciate,— the Pendulum as is well known, being a Clock's most sensitive Organ of communication,— here allowing the two to chat, in the Interval between the one's being taken from its Shipping-Case and the other's being nail'd up in its own, to go with Dixon to the Cape. Both are veterans of the Transit of Venus, as well as having been employ'd, Hour upon dark Hour, in Astronomers' work, from Equal-Altitude Duty to the Timing of Jupiter's Moons, which back and forth like restless Ducklings keep vanishing behind their Maternal Planet, only quickly to reappear. "You'll be on Duty twenty-four hours, is what it comes to," the Ellicott Clock advises. "Along with the usual fixation upon one's rate of Going...."

"So, what's it like in Cape Town?" the other wishes to know.

"The air is ever moist, as you'd say," replies the Ellicott Clock,— whose only knowledge of the Cape has been gather'd in the Rainy Season,— before going on then to recite a list of Horologick Ailments it currently suffers from, from Sluggish Main-spring to Breguet's Palsy, the other's Bob swinging along in Sympathy.

"Then I collect, all there's not Water-proof'd."

"They do take advantage of ev'ry Break in the Weather to make it more so."

"Alas, and what else, then? The Dutch Clocks, what are they like?"

"Hmm...of course much will depend upon you. Some get along with Dutch Clocks quite well.... Haven't Dutchmen, for Generations, been living with Dutch Clocks in the House, after all,— even whilst they sleep? Indeed, 'tis exactly that Dutch Stolidity of Character that's requir'd, for their Clocks strike each Quarter-hour, and without warning,— BONGGbing! sort of effect. Takes a certain Personality, 's what I'm saying."

The Ellicott Clock is referring to the absence of a striking-train, which in British Clocks can usually be heard in Motion a bit before the Hammer begins hitting the bell. But in those Cape Clocks that happen, like the Vrooms' and Zeemanns' to've been made in Holland, 'tis rather Cams upon a separate Wheel, gear'd to the Minute Hand, that cause the striking,— so there is never warning.

"Um," says the other. "And how'd your British Observers react to that?"

"Mason, being the more phlegmatick of the two, kept silent longer, his rage however rising bit by bit at each unannounc'd Striking, till at last it must brim over. Dixon,— in whose Care you'll be,— preferr'd to express himself otherwise, choosing, each time he was caught unawares, to...well, scream,— and most vexedly too, aye sets a Time-piece's Rods to humming, damme 'f it don't."

"I must hope that my own remain less resonant with his Cries, then. Mustn't I."

"Ah, he soon relents, and vows never again to be assaulted so rudely,— yet sure as time, fifteen minutes later, 'twill happen again. He could never, not even upon his last day there, remember that that Dutch Clock was going to strike." They share a Tremolo of amusement.

"Wonderful chatting with you like this. Well! let's just tick these off once more,— there're the Rains, the Rudeness of the native Clocks, the Mental Instability of the Astronomer 'pon whom I shall be depending utterly…anything we've left out?"

"The Gunfire at the Curfew, which has never once been on time,— and might easily lead, in the uncaution'd, to a loss of Sanity."

"In that case, allow me to thank you for your part in preserving mine,— tho' I do so in advance, for who knows when next we'll meet?"

"Next Transit of Venus, I suppose."

"Eight years hence! Do hope it's not that long."

"Time will tell.…"

"Anything you'd like to know about St. Helena? or Maskelyne?"

"I hear Steps coming."

"Quickly then,— Maskelyne is insane, but not as insane as some, among whom you must particularly watch out for— "

Too late. 'Tis Dixon and a Ship's Carpenter, and before either Clock can bid the other Adieu, the Shelton Clock is taken, crated up, and stow'd aboard the taut and lacquer'd Indiaman straining at her Anchor-Cables to be out in the Trades again. And indeed, what they wanted to talk about all along, was the Ocean. Somehow they could not get to the Topick. Neither Clock really knows what it is,— beyond an undeniably rhythmick Being of some sort,— tho' they've spent most of their lives in Range of it, sometimes no more than a Barrel-Stave and a Hull-Plank away. Its Wave-beats have ever been with them, yet can neither quite say, where upon it they may lie. What they feel is an Attraction, more and less resistible, to beat in Synchrony with it, regardless of their Pendulum-lengths, or even the divisions of the Day. The closest they come to talking of it is when the Shelton Clock confides, "I really don't like Ships much."

"Ha! Try being below the water-line in one that's under attack sometime."

"Not sure I want to hear about that."

"Thank you. There's never much to tell, so I have to embellish. 'Tis a task I am happy to avoid."

When Dixon and the Shelton Clock are alone at last, "Well! Here we are, sailing back to Cape Town, and all for thee! Eeh! So! Thoo're a Clock! Interesting Work, I'll bet…?" The Clock cannot compensate for a fine quivering in its Pendulum, which Dixon notices. Tha've probably been hearing Tales about me. Setting a-jangle all the sensitive Clockwork about with m' Screaming. Yet, think of these episodes as regular Tonicks, without which tha might succumb to the Weather, which can get unusual, or the ways of the Dutch...?"

"Watch out for the Pox," Dixon in turn advises his Co-adjutor, just before stepping into the Boat. "You thought the Cape was something,— this place...it's..." shaking his head, "risky. A Fair of damn'd Souls, if tha like." Clouds loom, Ocean rains approach.

"As if there'd ever be any time.— Now, what of Maskelyne?"

"Oh...he should watch out for it, too...?"

"Ahr..."

"I am resolv'd upon no further criticism of any Brother Lens," Dixon with eyes rais'd sanctimoniously. "Even one to whom Right *Ascension* may require a Wrong or two.— Howbeit, thoo know him better than I...?"

"You seem to be saying, that I should look out for myself."

"Did Ah say thah'? Ah didn't say thah'...?" as he sees Mason's head begin its slow lateral Reciprocation, "*thoo* said thah'."

"Thankee, Dixon. Always useful, talking these things over. Well. Convey my warm sentiments to any there who may yet feel such for me."

"Thah' won't take long."

"Mind y'self, Jere. Mind the Clock."

"See thee at Christmastide, Charlie."

13

Intent upon picking his way back over the wet Rocks to the Sea-Steps, ascending with the same care, Mason doesn't notice Maskelyne till he's ashore and nearly upon him. It seems an odd place to find him, unless he's here for the departure of a ship,— and upon this Tide, only Dixon's is bound away. Withal, Mason doubts that he wishes to be seen,— his Eyes, on detecting Mason, performing a swift Passado.

"My Early Stroll," he greets Mason. "Up most of the Night, anyway, Stargazer's Curse. Mr. Dixon and the Clock successfully embark'd, I trust."

Mason nods, gazing past the little Harbor, out to Sea. None of his business where Maskelyne goes, or comes,— God let it remain so. The Stars wheel into the blackness of the broken steep Hills guarding the Mouth of the Valley. Fog begins to stir against the Day swelling near. Among the whiten'd Rock Walls of the Houses seethes a great Whisper of living Voice.

"Shall we enter again the Atlantick Whore-House, find Breakfast, and get to work?"

At this hour, Lanthorns through Window-Glass beckon ev'rywhere. "It certainly isn't Cape Town," Mason marvels. Sailors a-stagger, Nymphs going on and off Shift, novice Company Writers too perplex'd to sleep, Fish-Mongers in Tandem with giant Tunas slung betwixt 'em consid'rately as Chair riders, Slaves singing in the local patois, Torches a-twinkle ev'rywhere,— and no Curfew. John Company, unlike its Dutch counterpart, recognizes here the primacy of Tide Tables, and, beyond them, of the Moon,— ceding to her de facto rule over all arrivals and departures, including Life and Death, upon this broken Island, so long ill us'd.

They cross the Bridge, go along the Main Parade, the Waves ever beating, and past the Company Castle, pausing at the bottom of the principal Street. "Tho' small in secular Dimensions," Maskelyne gesturing in at the Town, "yet entering, ye discover its true Extent,— which proves Mazy as an European City...no end of corners yet to be turn'd. 'Tis Loaves and Fishes, here in James's Town, and Philosophy has no answer." He appears lucid and sincere.

"Then" (Mason, as he reviews it later, should likely not have blurted) "if someone wish'd to disappear for a while, yet remain upon the Island,— "

The bright eyes begin to blink, as if in some Code. "Of course, forever would be easier,— because of the Sea, that is."

Mason isn't sure he wants to know what this means. "Of course, but, say for a Se'nnight?"

" 'Twould depend who's in Pursuit."

"Say, Honorable John."

"Hum. The first two or three days'd be easy,— assuming one had a perfect knowledge of the Town and the Island,— for the initial Search-Parties would be of younger Writers and 'Prentices, too new here to know even the Castle in its true Extension, disruptive lads, intimidating, alerting ev'ry Soul to the Imminence of a Search Island-wide,— that is, thro' this entire World,— "

"You've, ehm, certainly thought this out...."

"You were inquiring upon your own Behalf, I'd assum'd.... No need for *me* to disappear. Oh, Dear, the Royal Soc's quite forgotten all about old N.M., Esq. Lounging his life away waiting at the King's Expense for the Home Planet to move along. But now at the very Instant there is work to be done at last, the Heav'ns have provided me— "

"Yes?" inquires Mason, pleasantly enough.

"— a veteran Astronomer, with a brilliant Success to his Credit, to share in my simpler, meaner Duties."

"Mr. Waddington, I collect, being...somehow unavailable for the Honor."

Maskelyne shrugs. "No sooner did the Planet detach from the Sun's further limb than 'twas D.I.O. for Mr. Waddington."

Waddington left, in fact, three weeks after the Transit. "I don't do Parallaxes of Sirius, I don't do Tides," he mutter'd as they made their Farewells, "I don't do Satellites of Jupiter, all it says in my Contract is one Transit of Venus,— and that's what I did. If you wish me to observe the next, there'll have to be a new Contract."

"Easy Passage to ye, Robert," replied Maskelyne equably, "moonlit Nights and successful Lunars all the way," as he turn'd, toward the Town, and the Whores' Quarter again by the little Bridge, and the somber Cleft of the Valley ascending in back of it all, to go and re-engage with his Tasks.

"This Island," Maskelyne sighs, "— not ev'ryone's Brochette of Curried Albacore, is it?" Waddington express'd his displeasure upon their Indiaman's first sight of Lot and Lot's Wife, and the grim Company Fort at Sandy Bay,— not a Day of his Engagement was to pass, without the Island providing new ways to disappoint him. Too few Streets, too many Stares, the Coffee seeming to him adulterated with inferior Javas, obviously broken from Company Cargoes by enterprizing Pursers....

"Surely not," Mason alarm'd.

"Be easy. 'Twas his Phantasy. Afterward, appearing before the Royal Society, he prais'd St. Helena, and its Governor, very extravagantly and generously, having withal, on the way Home, got his Lunars beautifully,— the Captain forgave him the cost of his Passage, they came that near,— tho' the Weather grew so thick at the end that they were all the way in to Portland Bill before anyone saw Land, Waddington being heard to let out a heart-felt cry of Joy, that at least he'd liv'd to see England again."

"I must try to honor his precedent," Mason supposes, "mustn't I."

"You mean you won't help me with the Tidal data either? A couple of Sticks to be set in the Water, where's the Hardship?"

"I meant, rather, that I must obtain Lunars in quantity and of a Quality to match. If I weren't intending to help, I should have sail'd with Dixon, away from this,— that is,— "

"Pray you. There is no Comment upon the Island so unfavorable, that I've not heard already from Waddington, or utter'd myself. For a while I firmly believ'd this Place a conscious Creature, animated by power drawn from beneath the Earth, assembl'd in secret, by the Company,— entirely theirs,— no Action, no Thought nor Dream, that had not the Co. for its Author. Ha-ha, yes imagine, fanciful me. I tried to walk lightly. I did not want It feeling my Foot-Steps. If I trod too hard, I would feel It flinch. So I try not to do that. So might you. All, even the large population here of Insane, go about most softly. What Authority enforces the Practice? Governor Hutchinson? The Company Troops? I suggest that more than either, 'tis the awareness of living upon a *Slumbering Creature,* compar'd to whose Size, we figure not quite as Lice,— that keeps us uniquely attentive to Life so precarious, and what Civility is truly necessary, to carry it on. Hence, no Curfew. To live, we must be up at all hours. Every moment of our Waking, pass'd in fear, with the possibility ceaseless of sliding into licentiousness and squalor,— "

"Ah! Well now ye've brought the Topick up,— "

"Sir. Ye may speak lightly in London of these things, but here we may, only at our Peril. You have not yet seen Squalor, Sir,— be advis'd that you now live in the Metropolis of that Condition."

Mason is sweating heavily, thinking, Dixon has left me alone here with a *dangerously insane person.* And, and why did Waddington *really* have to leave so quickly? Hey? Fool?— why, 'tis plain as Day, his Departure had Panick written all over it! Obviously, one must live in perpetual caution, here, *never* to Alarm Maskelyne. Ahhrr....

Mason begins by trying to slow down his usually convulsive shrugging. "I'm...but newly come."

"What are you saying? Hey? That I should have left with Waddington? How? Why are you caressing your Hat so forcefully? Obs of Sirius must be taken as far apart as possible, mustn't they,— at least six months of what the World no doubt sees as Idleness, whilst the Planet, in its good time, cranketh about, from one side of its Orbit to the other, the Base Line creeping ever longer, the longer being the better...how is any of that my fault?" Is he expecting an answer? They have pass'd thro' the level part of the Town, and begun to climb.

"You think me neglectful?" Maskelyne with an unsettl'd frown. "You can tell me freely, how I seem to you. Alone in this place, how am I to know anything, even of how I look? Wore my Wig for a while, but ev'ryone gave it such queer Stares? There's not a Looking-Glass of any useful size 'pon the Island. Too luxurious to merit the Lading. No one here knows how he appears to anyone else, save for some Maidens down by the Bridge, who are said to possess Rouge-Boxes with miniature mirrors set inside the Covers, that allow them to View their Features, tho' one at a Time. All that is not thus in Fragments, is Invisible. And if my Character as well be experiencing some like 'Morphosis, some Veering into Error, how am I to know? Perhaps you are sent, upon this Anti-Etesian Wind unbearable, as Correction,— to act as my moral Regulator.— How we've all long'd for one of those, hey?"

With any number of ways to respond to this, Mason chooses a Silence, which he hopes will not be taken as unsociable, and they climb on.

As the Island's only Harbor out of the Wind, James's Town knows slumber but fleetingly. Sailors speak of it, before and after coming ashore, as of a place visited in an Opium Dream. Musick ev'ry time a Door or shutter comes open, Torches trailing scarves of flame ever rising. Chuck-farthing players in the Alley-way. Ornamental Lanthorns scarcely bigger than the Flames they hold, dangling from the Wrists of young Ladies with business at this Hour,— "All the Rage in Town just now," Maskelyne assures Mason. "These Girls flock to the Indiamen as much for the Shopping, as for the Sailors,— taking up one novelty upon the next, discarding each as lightly as they choose another...a mix'd lot, as you see, African...Malay...the odd Irish Rose...."

"Oo Reverend, who's your attractive friend?"

"Now now, Bridget.... Yes, a lovely Day to you,— " waving amiably. "Not that one ever lacks for wholesome Activities, here, one can picknick up the Valley. Visit Sandy Bay. Improve one's mind, study Vortices, learn Chinese. Drink." He pretends now to reel in astonishment before an Entry, in a Wall more Brick than Lime, above which swings a Sign depicting a White Luminary with the face of a Woman of the Town, multiply-patch'd to indicate Behavior she might, upon Acquaintance, prove to be a Good Sport about.

"Ah, ha. Amazing! Why, here again's The Moon. Care to pop in?"

Inside, a chorus of pleasant-looking young Women begin to sing,—

> Well Sailor ahoy,
> Put down that Harpoon,
> You're a fortunate Boy,
> For ye've beach'd on The Moon,
> And we Moon Maidens hope,
> We shall know ye quite soon,
> 'Tis the end of our Rope,—
> We need Men, in The Moon.
> [refrain]
> Ah, Men in The Moon,
> A miraculous Boon,
> Midnight and Noon, we need
> Men in The Moon!

What but Maskelyne's local? "Usual Sir Cloudsley, Gov? and the Madeira for your friend? Mr. Mas-*son,* excellent. Mr. Dixon successfully embark'd, I trust?"

"Once again, a Pleasure," Mason squints.

The landlord, Mr. Blackner, is that extremity of Quidnunc which, given enough time, necessarily emerges upon a small Island surrounded by Ocean for thousands of Soul-less leagues in ev'ry direction, where the village-siz'd population have only one another to talk about, and anyone newly arriv'd is feasted upon with an eagerness match'd only in certain rivers of South America. Everyone comes to know what everyone else knows,— and the strange mind-to-mind Throb may be felt distinctly, not to mention apprehensively, by the New-comer.

As soon as Mr. Blackner, by way of this remarkable intelligence-gathering Mirror, discover'd Maskelyne's connections to Clive and the East India Company, he began announcing the news to Visitors, some of them no more than common Seamen, with a jerk of the Thumb in Maskelyne's direction,— "That's Clive of India's brother-in-law, over there. Right by the Crock of Gin?"

"Out in the Wind a bit too long again, Mr. B."

"My Oath,— the Celebrated Super-Nabob his brother-in-law, right before your eyes,— and he has two Brothers, and Clive of India's *their* brother-in-law, too." Sometimes actually bringing over to Maskelyne the wary pint-clutching Visitor, "Here, Nevil my Lad,— who's your brother-in-law? Go ahead, tell him."

Annoying himself each time, Maskelyne, reluctant to fuss, wishing only to have it over with, replies, "Aye, 'tis Lord Clive."

"But,— Clive of *India?*" the shrewd Visitor will wish to make sure.

"That very Hero, sir, has the great good fortune to be married to my sister."

"Ah yes, yes," their Host far too avid, "that of course'd be Miss Peggy."

For this sort of thing he has receiv'd nearly audible glares,— 'tis a finely pois'd arrangement here at The Moon. In return for suffering the familiarities of a celebrity-mad Knit-wit, Maskelyne is allow'd to run up a Tab, already legendary even in a hard-drinking port like this, that might finance a small War,— chargeable to the Royal Society of course, and beyond them, should they demur above a sum Mr. Blackner is not certain of (which will disagreeably prove to be but five shillings per Day), to the wealthy-without-limit Clive of India. Maskelyne may also feel the weight of Family Tradition, his brother Edmund, known as Mun, ten years before, on his way out to the Carnatic as a young Company Writer, having also visited The Moon, and not cared for it much,— suggesting it might, however, be just young Nevil's sort of place. Maskelyne is still trying to work out what that might be.

Later, up at the Upper Observatory upon Alarum Ridge, Mason tries to have a look at the Plumb-line Suspension without appearing too blatant about it, Maskelyne having grown ever more fretful,— not to mention resentful. On the Day of the Transit, Mason and Dixon had obtain'd Times for all four contacts internal and external of Venus and the Sun, whilst here at St. Helena, just at the crucial moment of first contact, a Cloud had appear'd, and made directly for the Sun. How Maskelyne's heart must have sunk. He'd been warn'd not to place his observatory too low, had known of Dr. Halley's difficulties with the early Fog that often fill'd the great Ravine. Upon hearing of Maskelyne's ill-fortune, Mason understands that his Task will be never to appear pleas'd in front of him,— nor for that matter to respond to any of his Stiletto-Flourishes, which will prove to be frequent.

"Of course not all are chosen for the Cape,— you Lads had the Pearl of the Lot, damme 'f you didn't." Maskelyne's voice, in such times of stress, edges toward a throat-bas'd Soprano.

" 'Twas the only port we could make in time." If Mason repeats it once, in this St. Helenian Sojourn, he does so a thousand times,— suggesting an average of ten times per Day.

"Damme if you're not simply bless'd, aye, and blessèd as well, I've a Curacy, you may trust me in that Article. As for the rest of us, why, what matter that all *Curricula* are brought in the ill-starr'd Instant each to the same ignominious Halt, poor Boobies as *we* be.

"Yet there go I, repining at what really was too much, too quickly,— not only the Weather, you do appreciate, for even had the seeing been perfect that day, there'd yet have been the d———'d Sector, do forgive me, 'tis the matter of the Plumb-line, *falsum in unum* Principle, how can I trust anything I may see thro' it, now?

"Especially here. Somewhere else it might not have matter'd as much, but it's disturbing here, Mason,— don't you think? Aren't you feeling, I don't know,— disturb'd?"

"Disturb'd? Why, no, Maskelyne, after the Cape I find it quite calming here, in a Tropical way, pure Air, Coffee beyond compare,— from Bush to Oast unmediated!— the Sky remarkably productive of Obs,— what more could a man ask?"

"*What more—* " slapping himself smartly once upon each cheek, as if to restrain an outburst. "Of course,— I am being far too nice, aye and no doubt namby-pambical as well,— *ha* ha, ha,— after all, what's being confin'd upon the Summit of a living Volcanoe whose History includes violent Explosion, hey? which might indeed re-awaken at any *moment*, with nought to escape to in that lively Event, but thousands of Leagues of Ocean, empty in ev'ry direction,— Aahckk! Mason, can y' not feel it? This place! this great Ruin,— haunted…an Obstinate Spectre,— an ancient Crime,— none here will ever escape it, 'tis in the Gases they breathe, Generation unto Generation,— Ah! 'Tis *it!* There! Look ye!"— pointing beyond the circle of Lanthorn-light, his features clench'd uncomfortably.

The first time Maskelyne carried on thus, Mason became very alarm'd. He already suspects that the Island enjoys a Dispensation not perhaps as relentlessly Newtonian as Southern England's,— and as to whose Author's Identity, one may grow confus'd, so ubiquitous here are signs of the Infernal. Howbeit, after some number of these Seizures, Mason no longer feels quite so oblig'd to react. It is thus with some surprize and a keen rectal Pang that his leisurely Gaze now *does* detect something out there, and quite large, too, that should not be,— a patch of Nothing, where but the other moment shone a safe Wedge of Stars Encyclopedically nam'd. "Um, this Observatory, Maskelyne? The Company's provided you some sort of, that is,... Armory?"

"Ha! a set of French Duelling-pieces, with the Flints unreliable. Take your pick,— does it matter? against What approaches, Shot is without effect." The Visitant,— by now more than Shadow,— has crept toward the Zenith, engrossing more and more of the field of Stars, till at length rolling overhead and down toward the Horizon.

"Weatherr," Mason almost disappointed. With that, rain begins to fall, dense and steaming, sending him cursing outside to make secure the sliding Roof, whilst Maskelyne occupies himself inside with a fresh Pipe, snug as Punch in his Booth. Mason feels less resentful than resign'd, preferring anyway the certain uproar of Elements he knows, to the spookish fug of Maskelyne's Sermons upon the Unknown. Soon the Rain-Fall is spouting from all three corners of his Hat at once, regardless of what Angle he places his Head at.

Later, Obless, reluctant to sleep, they open another bottle of Mountain. Outside this ephemeral Hut, anything may wait. Mountains sharp and steep as the Heights of Hell. The next Planet, yet without a name,— so, in The Moon, have they been solemnly assur'd.— A little traveling Stage-Troupe, is St. Helena really, all Performance,— a Plantation, sent out years since by its metropolitan Planet, which will remain invisible for years indeterminate before revealing itself and acquiring a Name, till then this place must serve as an *Aide-Mémoire*, a Representation of Home. Many here, Descendants of the first Settlers, would never visit the Home Planet, altho' some claim to've been there and back, and more than once. "What if 'twere so?" declares Maskelyne. "Ev'ry People have a story of how they were created. If one were heretickal enough, which I certainly am not, one might begin to entertain some notion of the Garden in Genesis, as an instance of extra-terrestrial Plantation."

Maskelyne is the pure type of one who would transcend the Earth,— making him, for Mason, a walking cautionary Tale. For years now, after midnight Culminations, has he himself lain and listen'd to the Sky-Temptress, whispering, Forget the Boys, forget your loyalties to your Dead, first of all to Rebekah, for she, they, are but distractions, temporal, flesh, ever attempting to drag the Uranian Devotee back down out of his realm of pure Mathesis, of that which abides.

"For if each Star is little more a mathematickal Point, located upon the Hemisphere of Heaven by Right Ascension and Declination, then all the Stars, taken together, tho' innumerable, must like any other set of points, in turn represent some single gigantick Equation, to the mind of God as straightforward as, say, the Equation of a Sphere,— to us unreadable, incalculable. A lonely, uncompensated, perhaps even impossible Task,— yet some of us must ever be seeking, I suppose."

"Those of us with the Time for it," suggests Mason.

One cloudless afternoon they stand in the scent of an orange-grove,— as tourists elsewhere might stand and gape at some mighty cataract or chasm,— nose-gaping, rather, at a manifold of odor neither Englishman has ever encountered before. They have been searching for it all the long declining Day,— it is the last Orange-Grove upon the Island,— a souvenir of a Paradise decrepit.... Shadows of Clouds dapple the green hillsides, Houses with red Tile roofs preside over small Valleys, the Pasture lying soft as Sheep,— all, with the volcanic Meadow where the two stand, circl'd by the hellish Cusps of Peaks unnatural,— frozen in midthrust, jagged at every scale. "Saint Brendan set out in the fifth century to discover an Island he believ'd was the Paradise of the Scriptures,— and found it. Some believ'd it Madeira, Columbus was told by some at Madeira that they had seen it in the West, Philosophers of our own Day say they have prov'd it but a Mirage. So will the Reign of Reason cheerily dispose of any allegations of Paradise.

"Yet suppose this was the Island. He came back, did he not? He died the very old Bishop of the Monastery he founded at Clonfert, as far from the Western Sea as he might, this side of Shannon. Perhaps that was Paradise. Else, why leave?"

"A Riddle! Wondrous! Just the Ticket! Why, ere 'tis solv'd, we may be back in England and done with this!"

"The Serpent, being the obvious Answer."

"What Serpent?"

"The one dwelling within the Volcanoe, Mason, surely you are not ignorant upon the Topick?"

"Regretfully, Sir,— "

"Serpent, Worm, or Dragon, 'tis all the same to It, for It speaketh no Tongue but its own. It Rules this Island, whose ancient Curse and secret Name, is Disobedience. In thoughtless Greed, within a few pitiably brief Generations, have these People devastated a Garden in which, once, anything might grow. Their Muck-heaps ev'rywhere, Disease, Madness. One day, not far distant, with the last leaf of the last Old-Father-Never-Die bush destroy'd, whilst the unremitting Wind carries off the last soil from the last barren Meadow, with nought but other Humans the only Life remaining then to the Island,— how will they take their own last step,— how disobey themselves into Oblivion? Simply die one by one, alone and suspicious, as is the style of the place, till all are done? Or will they rather choose to murder one another, for the joy to be had in that?"

"How soon is this, that we're talking about?"

"Pray we may be gone by then. We have our own ways of Disobedience,— unless I presume,— express'd in the Motto of Jakob Bernouilli the second,— *Invito Patre Sidera Verso,*— 'Against my father's wishes I study the stars.' "

Mason pauses to squint and shake his head free of annoyance. "How do you know anything of my Father's wishes? Do you mean, that because he is only a Miller and a Baker, he would naturally oppose Star-Gazing, out of Perverse and willful Ignorance?"

"I mean only that in our Times, 'tis not a rare Dispute," Maskelyne assures him. "Reason, or any Vocation to it,— the Pursuit of the Sciences,— these are the hope of the Young, the new Music their Families cannot follow, occasionally not even listen to. I know well the struggle, mine being with Mun especially, tho' Peggy as well would rag me...they cozen'd me once into casting her Horoscope, with particular reference to the likelihood of her being married any time soon. 'Twas but a moment's work to contrive the Wheel of a Maiden's dreams,— Jupiter smiling upon Venus in the house of partnerships, Mars exactly at the mid-heaven, Mercury with smooth sailing ahead, not a retrograde body in sight. Was I thank'd? Rather, one simple Horo, and 'twas 'Nevil the Astrologer,' thenceforward."

"Not as insulting as 'Star-Gazer,' anyway."

"And what if I did cast a Natal Chart or two whilst at Westminster,— and of course later, at Cambridge, when I found I could get sixpence,— well. I suppose you've lost respect for me now," this being their second week up on the Ridge, with confession apt to flow like the "water that cometh down out of the country" noted in ancient Maps of this place.

"You got *sixpence?* I never did better than three, and that was with all the Arabian Parts thrown in as Inducement."

"Oh, don't I remember those, Lens-brother,— 'tis our Burden. Kepler said that Astrology is Astronomy's wanton little sister, who goes out and sells herself that Astronomy may keep her Virtue,— surely we have all done the Covent Garden turn. As to the older Sister, how many Steps may she herself indeed already have taken into Compromise? for,

> Be the Instrument brazen, or be it Fleshen,
> [Maskelyne sings, in a competent Tenor]
> Star-Gazing's ever a Whore's profession,—
> (Isn't it?)
> Some in a Palace, all Marble and Brick,
> Some behind Hedges for less than a kick, tell me
> What's it matter,
> The Stars will say,
> We've been ga-zing, back at ye,
> Many a Day,
> And there's nothing we haven't seen
> More than one way,
> Sing Derry o derry o day...

[Recitative]

Now some go to Bath, where, like candle and Moth, even men of the Cloth seek them out. Whilst others run Pitches where diggers of Ditches may scatter their Riches about. Tho' the tools of their Trade may be differently made, for their Arts they are paid, all the same,— 'Pon Astronomer's Couch or Coquette's, all avouch, 'tis a reckless Debowch of a Game....

> There are Stars yet to see,
> There are Planets hiding,
> Peepers are we, with a Lust abiding,
> Some style it 'Providence,'
> Others say, 'God,— '
> Some call it even, and some call it Odd,
> Yes but what's it matter,
> The Stars will say,
>   &c.

"We've a while before Sirius,— " Maskelyne flush'd with Song, "what say I do yours now, and you do mine later?"

"What?" Mason begins to edge toward the Tent opening.

"Your natal Chart, Mason. Have you ever had it done?"

"Well..."

"It's all right, neither have I,— perhaps most Lens-folk would rather not know. But as we're old Charlatans together, maroon'd here in this other-worldly Place, and withal sharing the same Ruling Planet,— rather, Goddess,— to whose least sigh we must attend, or risk more than we ought,— eh?"

Mason blinks. Is it the Altitude? Hardly do to get into a Kick-up with Clive of India's brother-in-law, he supposes. Hey? What if this isn't Insanity? and no worse than the frantic chumminess of Exile.... Ahrrh, yet suppose, more harshly, that 'tis Bradley whom Maskelyne wishes to snuggle up to,— Mason having run into any number of amateur Star-gazers with the same ideas about access to the A.R.,— back Home, 'twas possible to wave them Adieu till they be absorb'd back into the human Nebulosity of the Town,— but here in a Tent in the middle of the 360-degree Ocean,— what choice does he have?

"Date of Birth?"

"Don't know. They had me baptiz'd May Day, and that's the day I mark."

"So you were born some weeks earlier, perhaps in Aries, even Pisces.... Less probably, in Taurus, yet,— " he is giving Mason the heavy O.O.

"If it's helpful, I am told that of the Qualities observ'd in my comportment, those of the classick Taurean prevail,— Persistent, Phlegmatick, Provok'd only with great difficulty,— our Passion of Titanick Scope, our Fate, ever to be prick'd at by small men in spangl'd Costumes."

"First of May, then, shall we?" So Maskelyne goes to work. By Dark-Lanthorn-Light, his face a-glimmer and smooth as wax, whilst the Sea crashes up to them past the baffling of vertiginous Peaks and Ravines, he pencils out a Wheel, and begins to fill it with Glyphs and Numerals. At one point, as if without thinking, he reaches back and releases his Queue, and hair swings forward to either side, curtaining him and his bright eyes with the calculations. Soon he is passing wordless remarks such as "Hmm!" and "Yaacch!,"— Mason beginning to huff somewhat, feeling like a Model to whom an Artist is making cryptic Suggestions. "There," says Maskelyne at last. "Will ye look at all those Venus aspects...La, la, la.... Where's that Mountain, again?"

"You're right, after all, I'd rather not know. Sorry to've put ye to all this trouble,— "

"First of all, doesn't it seem odd, that you and Mr. Dixon, with your natal signs rul'd by Venus and the Sun respectively, should have lately, as partners, observ'd the conjunction of those very two bodies,— the Event occurring, as well, in the Sign of the Twins?"

Shrugging, "Chance of a Sun ruler, one in twelve. Chance of a Venus ruler, two in twelve,— Chance of the Pair, two in one hundred forty-four,— a Coincidence appealing, yet not overwhelming."

"Yet as Odds,— say, upon a Race,— "

Tho' it takes Mason a while to recognize it, Maskelyne has been trying to convey the Dimensions of his Curiosity. As a man of Religion, he has often enough sought among the smaller Probabilities for proofs of God's recent Attendance, has practis'd Epsilonics for the sake of stronger Faith, as what deep-dyed Newtonian would not? One in seventy-two, or point zero one four, is not a figure he can be quite comfortable with. 'Tis not quite Miraculous enough, there's the very Deuce of it. And if not quite a clear Intervention by the Creator, not quite from Heaven, then what Power is this an Act *of?*

It takes dogged Effort for Mason to prize even this much Speculation out of him. Yet what else after all is there to do in this miserable Place, but smoke Pipes and discuss God,— as newly met guests at some Assembly might discuss a common Acquaintance but lately withdrawn?

"Your natal Jupiter lies in Gemini,— the very Sign in which the late Transit occurr'd, of which you Lads made that very fine Ob. Traditionally, Wealth from Collaboration,— yet both Mercury and Venus are in Aries,— possibly your Natal Sign,— favoring Independence, Leadership,— and both lie blessedly Sextile to your Moon in Aquarius…humane, inclin'd to Science, a devotee of Reason…'tho squar'd by your Sun of course.…" He has fallen into a kind of mystickal Bustling, like a Gypsy at the Fair. "But dear oh dear, not much sign of Mr. Dixon at all…nothing closer than your Mars in Virgo, standing two and a half Degrees in from the Cusp with Leo, suggesting you make him a truculent and wary neighbor." His shiny-eyed, vixenish Phiz peering out of all that loose Hair.

"You take a deep Interest in Mr. Dixon?"

A Parsonickal spread of Hands. "Shallow curiosity, Sir,— the amateur Observer's Curse. Yet, now ye've rais'd it,— have there been others, who…have taken an Interest in him? Who can they be,— and what may they expect?"

"Well. It can't be the Honorable E.I.C., can it? Or you'd know. Wouldn't you."

"As much as you. There being the fitful Rumor that your Mr. Peach will be nam'd a Director."

"As well as a Long-Establish'd Truth," Mason, later, will fear he snapp'd back, "that your Lord Clive may have anything he damn'd wishes. What of it? Any repayment I may owe Sam Peach, is many orders of Magnitude beneath the Arrangements proper to,— " pausing to deepen his Voice, "Clive,— of In-dia,"— Mason having found that inflecting the Name thus, whilst reliably nettling Maskelyne, also seems strangely to amuse him.

"We are quite the Pair, then,— that is, I presume," peering at Mason, "both Subjects of the same Invisible Power? No? What is it, think ye? Something richer than many a Nation, yet with no Boundaries,— which, tho' never part of any Coalition, yet maintains its own great Army and Navy,— able to pay for the last War, as the next, with no more bother than finding the Key to a certain iron Box,— yet which allows the Britannick Governance that gave it Charter, to sink beneath oceanick Waves of Ink incarnadine."

"Bless us!" Mason cries. "Another Riddle! Hold, permit me to guess...."

"Or perhaps, like our Tapster, you entertain *Fancies,* as to my relations with Lord Clive. Splendid! Out of Dark Policy do I encourage it in all, as little as object to it,— yet the Truth is so drab, Mason, indeed, since Peggy and he return'd, I've been to Berkeley Square but once, not seen them above thrice more,— ever in Company, certainly not in Private. Clive and I do not play Whist together, nor in Disguise haunt the Snares of Ranelagh,— he did not bring me back a jewel'd Telescope, nor am I his Connection in London for the purchase of Opium. Seldom if ever does he, upon the least movement of my Eyebrow, rush forward insisting I take Waggon-Loads of Oriental Treasure."

"Being the very least I should've expected,— what are Brothers-in-law for? Perhaps, wishing any Gifts to you to be appropriate, he yet remains unclear as to the Range of your Interests."

"He's not yet ready to make use of me, that's all. Someday he must...I've been paid for...it shan't cost him anything." Maskelyne's Phiz, with its one-sided smile and wary eyes and need for Complicity, would not have grown this cautious, had some blows not already landed. Whatever his Bargain, he is not happy with it. Mason, who as yet hasn't seen the terms of his own, is but apprehensive.

"Here we are," Maskelyne plaintively, "Englishmen in the bloom of Sanity, being snatch'd away, one by one, high and low, ev'ryday, like some population of distraught Malays waiting for the call of *Amok,*— going along, at what we style Peace with the Day,— all at once, Bang-o! another 'un out in the Street waving the old *Krees,*— being British of course, more likely a butter-knife or something,— yet with no Place, no

Link upon the Great Chain, at all safe,— none however exalted,— no and that is why I fear so, dear Colleague, for my sister, and for the great Soldier whose Fate is hers…," peering out now from a burrow of Anxiety, dug one long sour midwatch upon the next.

Mason has no way to tell how deliberate this is. Maskelyne, as all London, has known about Clive's use of Opium,— yet what Comfort can Mason give him? Such things have ended badly before,— whilst Maskelyne has ever presented an Enigma. Long before they met, Mason felt his sidling Advent, cloak'd as by Thames-side Leagues of Smoke and Mists. At last,— at first,— he saw the introductory Letter, as Dr. Bradley in the Octagon Room brought it fretfully to and fro, muttering, "Damn difficult to make out, seems to be instructing me in the matter of Lunar Distances,— yet somehow I can't quite…here, see if you can make any sense,— " letting go of it, allowing the document to flutter Earthward faster than Mason could dive to catch it, and disappearing toward the Observers' Kitchen.

At first, and then upon re-reading, he could make no more sense of the Letter than Bradley had done. One of Mason's chores as Assistant was to review just such Correspondence. Since the Longitude Act of 1714, which offer'd Prizes up to twenty thousand Pounds for a reliable way to find the true Longitude at Sea, the Observatory had become a Target for Suggestions, Schemes, Rants, Sermons, full-length Books, all directed to Bradley's Attention, upon the Problem of the Longitude. Though some were cagy, hinting at Amazing Simplicity and Ingenious Devising, whilst giving no details, most of the letters were all-out philosophick confessions, showing either an unhealthy naïveté, or an inner certainty that the Scheme would never work anyway. For many, it was at least a chance to Rattle at length to a World that was ignoring them. Others were more passionate as to the worth of their Inventions, though employing Arts more of the Actor-Projector than of the Geometer. Occasionally Insanity roll'd a sly Eye-ball into the picture. Treatises on "Parageography" arriv'd, with alternative Maps of the World superimpos'd upon the more familiar ones. Many,— as had the elder Cabot upon his deathbed,— claim'd to've been told the Secrets of the Longitude by God (or, as some preferr'd, Thatwhichever Created Earth and her Rate of

Spin). Others told of Rapture by creatures not precisely Angels, nor yet Demons,— styl'd "Agents of Altitude." That they were taken aloft and shewn the Earth as it appear'd from the Distance of the Sun, and that the Navigator of the Vessel us'd a kind of Micrometer, whose Lines were clapp'd to the Diameter of the Earth, and that the measuring device read 8.75 seconds of Arc, "not in our numbers of course, not until accurately transnumerated, from theirs.— More than happy to share details of this toilsome Conversion, upon duly authorized request.— Yet, as there now exists no further need for a foreign expedition to obtain the Earth's Solar Parallax from the Transit of Venus, You would oblige me by recalling your own Parties and using what influence you can with Astronomers of other Principalities, as well as among the Jesuits &c." A retir'd Naval officer wrote from Hampshire of the great Asymmetrick Principle he had discover'd, "an invisible Grain built into Creation, whereby, 'tis less work to rip than to cross-cut, to multiply than to divide, to take the Derivative than the Integral,— and, coming to my Point,— to obtain the Latitude than the Longitude. For the one, we need only know the Sun's elevation at Noon,— yet from the difficulty of finding the other, enter-prizes have founder'd, fleets have perish'd, treasure unreckonable lies beneath th' indifferent Sea. The solution is simple enough, though lengthier. I have practis'd its Elements from various Quarter-decks, in all conditions from close-reef'd to becalm'd,— my Zero Meridian not upon Greenwich, nor Paris, but a certain Himalayan Observatory, in Thi-bet, the Book of Tables I consult being reduced from Observations made there by the celebrated Dr. Zhang, then, as now, in exile. These are not Lunars, nor yet Galileans, but based upon the very slow Progress of what is undoubtedly a Planet, though no one else claims to've seen it, near η Geminorum."

Bradley ask'd Mason to read that part aloud, twice. "Aye, the Star I do recall,— lying upon the Zodiacal Path, a Pebble, a Clod, just in front of Castor's left foot, perhaps eternally about to be kick'd," if Bradley, who was never mistaken, was not mistaken, "— hence 'Propus,' though Flamsteed, paronomastickally disposed, call'd it 'Tropus' because it mark'd the turning point of the Summer Solstice."

"Although," Mason attentively foot-noting, "that Point presently lies somewhat to the east."

"Well,— you know just about where we mean, then, Charles. I do seem to recollect, now...well within the Field...aye, some kind of blur...a greenish blue. Perhaps I noted it down. Welcome to have a look, on your own Time of course, make sure you fix it with your Lady, they don't like it when you're up at night you know...prowling about...believe in their Hearts that men are Were-wolves, have you noticed? Never mind— you never heard a thing...."

And before the Echo had quite gone, in came Susannah, the lightest of dove-gray fans beneath her Eyes,— as if knowing her destiny, Mason thought, ashamed as he did at how it sounded, helpless before the great Cruel Unspoken,— the Astronomer's desire for a son,— and her fear that she might find, in their next Attempt, her own dissolution.... Yes, he had entertain'd such vile Conjectures, as who would not? He'd also imagin'd her lounging about all day, scoffing Sweets, shooing admirers out different doorways whilst admitting others, answering spousal importunities thro' Doors that remain'd shut, issuing Bradley ultimata and extravagant requisitions. Chocolates. A Coach and Six to go to her Mantua-Maker's. A full season's Residence at Bath. A Commission abroad for an Admirer grown inconvenient....

Not all Predators are narrow-set of Eye. In Town, some of the more ruthless Beauties have gone far disguis'd as wide-eyed Prey. Such a feral Doe was Susannah. If Bradley knew of this, 'twas an Article of his sentimental Service long agreed to.

The absence of further children after Miss Bradley was a secret Text denied to Mason. He seeth'd with it, a Beast in lean times, prowling for signs, turn'd by any Scent however contradictory,— or, to a Beast, unbeastly. She was back in Chalford. Had she ever slept with Bradley again? Did she have Bradley on her Name, but Mason on her Mind? Did she dream of Mason now as he'd once dreamt of her? Was that Oinking upon the Rooftop?— Their Trajectories never, Mason thought with dismay, even to *cross*,— tho' he'd've settl'd for that,— one passionate Hour, one only, then estrangement eternal, so craz'd had he been after Susannah Peach.

> I was only sixteen, upon your wedding day,
> I stood outside the churchyard, and cried.

And now I'm working for the man, who carried you away,
And ev'ry day I see you by his side.

Sometimes you're smiling,— sometimes you ain't,
Most times you never look my way,—
I'm still as a Mill-Pond, I'm as patient as a Saint,
Wond'ring if there's things you'd like to say.

Oh, are you day-dreaming of me,
Do you tuck me in at Night,
When he's fast asleep beside you,
Are those Fingers doing right?
How can Love conquer all,
When Love can be so blind? and you've got
Bradley on your Name,
And Mason on your Mind....

When it falls Mason's turn at Maskelyne's natal Chart, he grows unaccustomedly cheery, breezing through the computation and filling in the last Aspect with a Flourish. "There's the old Horo. Now, let us have a look, shall we. Hum."

"Pray you, Moon aspects only,— spare me the rest."

"Poh, Superstition. Your Moon is in Taurus, and making a grand trine with Mars and Venus. Wish ye Joy of that, I'm sure. No Squares...*no Squares?* Mercy." A Snort. "You're Fortune's little Pet. Abnormal number of trines and sextiles, as well,— in ev'ry Combination,— yet another promise of Good Luck. Jupiter and Mercury in your birth Sign,— Mercury's retrograde, but then Mercury's always retrograde,— hey?"

"The fell *Datum!*" cries Maskelyne. "I slip down streets unnam'd to the salons of unregister'd Rhetorick-Masters, where all struggle to teach me, yet continues it my curse, that the World cannot understand me when I express myself. My letters are ignor'd, my monographs rejected. Mercury retrograde! Tiny, fleet Trickster, yet counterponderating all these Blessings Astrologickal!"

"Excuse me? I'm not actually sure that I— "

"Ah! Now 'tis you, even you, Mason! What use are Trines and Sextiles, if Human Discourse be denied me? Fly on, fly on, Midge of Mischief,— thou hast triumph'd!"

Mason understands that he may if he wishes see himself thro' Duty at St. Helena by baiting Maskelyne thus, any time he has a Velleity to. He also understands how quickly the amusement value of this will fade. "Usually," he feels nonetheless impell'd to suggest, "a Messenger going the other way is returning, after having deliver'd his Message someplace else."

Maskelyne frowns and begins to consider this. The next day, after smoking a while in silence, "Perhaps that's it. Explains a good deal, doesn't it? A Message that never came to me. How shall I proceed?— waste what scrap of Life-Span remains to me, attempting to find out what it was?"

"According to this Chart," advises Mason, "you'll find out sooner or later. Refrain from struggle, allow your Life to convey it to you when it will, and as in all else, Bob's your Uncle. Or in this case, Brother-in-Law."

14

Mason, up on the Ridge, finds himself wondering about Dixon,— whether he has arriv'd safely at the Cape,— what, if he be there, he may be doing at a particular moment,— given the time of day or night, and Weather unknown. "Our daily lives to distant Stars attuned," he writes in a Letter to Dixon he then decides not to send,—

("Just a moment," Pitt says.

"You saw this Document?" inquires Pliny.

"Good Lads!" cries Uncle Ives, blessing each with a Pistole. "No, no, don't thank me, the only condition is that you spend it wisely. Prudently invested, it could provide you a tidy Fund by the time you're establish'd enough as Attorneys to need a friendly Judge now and then. Be better of course if you were partners. Confuse people."

"Our idea, actually," says Pitt, "is for one of us to run away and pretend to lead a Wastrel's Life, whilst the other applies himself diligently to the Law,— "

"— making it even less possible to tell you apart," declares their Aunt Euphie.)

Mason can calculate roughly when Dixon may be at the Snout, watching Jupiter and its Harem of moons, and when up in the Malay quarter, inspecting some Harem of his own. He imagines Dixon learning to cook a *Khari* with orange leaves, re-inventing the *Frikkadel*, putting that G-dawful *Ketjap* in ev'rything.

Believing he has walked away from the Cape and successfully not looked back, to see what Plutonian wife, in what thin garment, may after all have follow'd,— tho' none of them is anyone's Eurydice, he knows well enough who that is,— or would be, were he Orpheus enough to carry a Tune in a Bucket,— Mason continues to wonder, how Dixon has brought himself to turn, and then, to appearance imperturbable as a Clam, go back in,— back to Jet, Greet, Els, Austra, Johanna, the unsunn'd Skins, the Ovine Aromas, the Traffick to and from the Medicine-Cabinet at all hours, the Whispering in the Corners, the never-ending Intrigues,— whilst coiled behind all gazes the great Worm of Slavery. No hour of the Chapter-Ring is exempt from the echoes of Heated Voices off unadorn'd Walls. The Girls, having raided their Father's Snuff Supply, dashing about, colliding and dreamy, and talking to no effect....

By the time Dixon arrives, a number of stories have just begun to circulate...the Town pretends to be shock'd. Church services, far from the Ordeals Johanna has expected, turn lively at last, with smirks and stares and eye-avoidance, in full knowledge that ev'ryone knows ev'ryone else's secrets,— she feels she's being admitted at last to the adult life of the Cape...tho' nothing, understand, for all the racing up and down stairs and hanging out windows, has really "happen'd," as these matters are reckon'd,— so that she feels like an imposter, too, which is not without its own thrill of shame, before the Faces of the Congregation, where within the Brass-bound mercilessness of Sunday, these multiple acts of sisterhood will continue, till after a while the focus shifts to some new Bathsheba.

Cornelius, for his part, is not having quite so easy a time of it. Suddenly, wherever he goes, Dixon finds this unstable Butter-box up the wrong end of some Elephant Gun swiveling ever in Dixon's direction, as if the Dutchman had decided to accept him as a fair substitute for Mason. Through the streets, in the great South-East wind, the wig-snatching, flame-fanning, judgment-warping Wind, they chase, Cornelius presently setting the Fork'd Support in the blowing dirt, with some smoldering naval slow-match he carries in his teeth igniting a giant full Dutch-ounce blast whose Ball ricochets off the roof-tiles, sending small

Slides of red fragments into the street a good ten feet wide and short, windage calculations out here being matters more of Sentiment than of Science. He pauses to reload, his hair-tie loos'd and then blown away downwind whilst Dixon lopes on, unwilling to believe that the Dutchman can still feel unrequited enough to want to go through this exercise again,— until the next great crack, echoing from the hillside, as the hor-netting sphere this time explodes a watermelon at a nearby market stand, and the greengrocers head for cover. As the Dutchman, unhurried, stolid, probably insane, is reloading for yet *another* onslaught, this time Musketoon-style with a great pink Fist-ful of bullets, Dixon, having had enough, turns and makes a run at him. There seems to be time. As he gets near, he sees white all 'round Vroom's irises, and though it may not matter in a short while, knows that the Dutchman has never faced a charging animal in his life,— until now, it seems, for he stands para-lyzed, powder horn slipping from his grasp, screaming, "No! I am *sup-posed* to do this!"

Dixon takes the weapon gently away. "My life, for that ass Mason's? Excuse me, the Mails, I've not been getting my *Gazette*,— was there some amendment to the Code of Honor that no one told me of?"

"This is not about Honor, it is about Blood!"

"Aye, and were you a Malay Lad I shouldn't be that surprised...? but as you're a Dutch Lad, well, well, this 'running amok' business,— not that much in your people's line, is it, there's a good fellow...," coaxing him along before the wind, "same as we don't see that many Malays, do we really, standing about in wooden shoes, eh? fingers stopping up holes in the Dike sort of thing, no we don't, now just around this corner, good,— a little *Soupkie* ought to be just the Ar-ticle...?— "

"*Soupkie*," the Dutchman in a stricken monotone, nodding.

"Through this door, Mynheer,— there he is,— Abdul, you son of a sea-camel. We need a crock of your Special reserve gin, with the unusual herbs in it,— have the Nautch Girls come in yet? Eeh, well,— we'll just be over here, in the Corner...?"

"Ice. Ice."

"Quite so, Cornelius,— I may call you that mayn't I,— Ice Abdul by all means and perhaps two pipes as well?" He waves Cornelius into the Tavern. "My Local,— The World's End."

They retreat to a dark corner and for the next several hours, in a fragrant Nebulosity that provides comfort when Dixon cannot, go a-sorting in some detail thro' the Vrooms' domestic Sadness. Dixon is astonished at its depth, though it all becomes difficult to follow after a while. The fire roars, above it the Haunch of some Animal unfamiliar to Englishmen is slowly turn'd, and basted. A Phillippino guitar player strums a careless Suite of Nautical Melodies, at the end of each of which he grins, "Not done yet! More to come, *Sí?*" Tallow candles gutter and go out, as others are relit elsewhere in the Room. The wind hoots up and down the alley-ways, Table Bay slowly but measurably is blown seaward, the Town being borne away from the Shore-line at the same rate, and as the evening falls, in from all this peculiar Weather, hair and costumes blown and tangl'd, wearing Cast-offs from the days of the Sumptuary Laws, which the Slaves who got them either sold again promptly, or could not bring themselves to wear, in Ticklingburgs and Paduasoy, Swanskin and Shalloon, Brabant Lace and Ostrich-Feather Hats, here enter a Parade of curiously turned-out young creatures, most of whom appear to know Dixon,— each to go sit at a table-ful of Sailors, take a pipe or a drink, and eventually leave with a nautical Prize in tow. The Phillippino strums passionate minor-key Declarations of Longing. The Smoke in the room, though chiefly from tobacco, includes as well that of Opium, Hemp, and Cloves, so that anyone who walks in must become intoxicated, merely by standing and breathing.

Dixon came ashore intending to clear Mason's Name of all Suspicion before Cornelius, if not before the Town, but somehow no opening for this has occurred. "Here's what we'll do," proposes Cornelius now, gravely giddy, "— we will go to the Company Lodge, where the women are of all races, sizes, and specialties. We'll use my membership to get in, and you, that is the Royal Society, will then pay for everything."

"I am happy to see you thus return'd to what the Dutch must reckon Sanity," replies Dixon, for whom the Scene before them has begun to break up into small swarming Bits of Color, "and of course I'd be nothing but delighted...?"

The Company Seraglio smells of sandalwood and burning Musk. There is difficulty at the Door, regarding some unpaid Dues.... The

Barometer in the ebony case upon the Wall cannot be read, the Lettering too intricate, the Numerals possibly in some System other than the Arabic. There is no column of Mercury, no moving Pointer. Yet Pressure may be read by the Adept, remaining invisible until sought for.... The Instrument hangs above a velvet *Meridien* from France, near a painting of a mounted settler at dusk, somewhere out in Hottentot Land with his old smooth-bore athwart the Saddle, the Mountains between here and Home all grays, except for the sunset catching their Peaks a strange thinn'd luminous Red. And there. In the Shadows, all but painted over,—

Once again Dixon's unsuspicious Heart is surpriz'd. The first person to enter the Room is Austra, in a black velvet Gown and a leather collar, being leash-led by a tiny, expressionless Malay Sylph. It is evident from the Leer on Cornelius's Phiz, that the Tableau has been arrang'd for Dixon. There is enough time for her to recognize him, and know that he will not help her, either, before she passes into another Room, not looking back, to continue this slavery within Slavery.... At the moment of her Vanishing, he pays her full Notice for the first time,— tho' who could have avoided some Overspill from Mason's obsession? even with Mason seldom able to bore Dixon upon the Topick, Dixon most usually being out satisfying his more general Desire for anything, and on lucky Days everything, the World might be presenting to him, moment by moment. Had he not been under Siege rather by imps of Appetite indiscriminate, might he and Mason have become Rivals for her Attention? Thus stands he gawping after her.

"Let no one say that we cannot have Fun, when we must," Cornelius declares, thumping Dixon upon the Shoulder. "It is our Garden of Amusement, here."

Something a bit too Churchlike for Dixon, however,— a devotion to ritual and timing, the Space under-lit, what light there is as White as Wig-Powder, flowing from pure white candles, burning smoothly in the still air, and from bowls of incense close by, white Smoke in the same unwavering Ascent. Now in high Humor, Cornelius shows him secret Pornoscopes, conceal'd by fanciful room decorations, where Burghers may recline, grunting expressively, and spy upon one another in Activities that may be elephantine, birdlike, over in a flash, long as Church, enclos'd in hopeless desire for, revenge on, escape from some Woman, somewhere along these befabl'd and dolorous Company Lanes, someone said, some Woman....

The Opium-Girls are kept in a room of their own. That the substance is smoked in a Pipe has put it immediately in favor among the Dutch Gentlemen. Taken with tobacco, producing a vertiginous Swoon, such as might require most of an evening of drinking spirits to obtain, it seems to promise a great savings in time and cash, a thought these thrifty trades-men find enchanting. Before this Surrender to Sloth, however, Lust is schedul'd, splashing outside the Church-drawn boundaries of marriage, as across racial lines. Slave Women are brought here from ev'rywhere in this Hemisphere, to serve as dreamy, pliant shadows, Baths of Flesh darker than Dutch, the dangerously beautiful Extrusion of everything these white brothers, seeking Communion, cannot afford to contain,— whilst their wives, if adverted to at all, are imagin'd at home, sighing over needlework, or the Bible.

The Gunfire is at nine, in practice this curfew is stretched for as much as an hour, but by ten the sailors, so cheery, young, and careless with money, have to be out. After they are gone passes a silent period, an enshadowment which, prolonged past a certain point upon the Clock-Face, begins to rouse apprehension among the *filles*, for they know their Night has begun, and who is coming for them now, and some of what will be done to them. Many who have been to Rooms forbidden the others, report seeing, inside these, a Door to at least one Room further, which may not be opened. The Penetralia of the Lodge are thus, even to those employed there, a region without a map. Anything may be there. Perhaps miracles are still possible,— both evil miracles, such as occur when excesses of Ill Treatment are transform'd to Joy,— quite common in this Era,— and the reverse, when excesses of Well-being at length bring an Anguish no less painful for being metaphysickal,— Good Miracles. Even in a Polity sunny, bustling, and order'd as Cape Town, for reasons that mystify all (some blame the South-East winds, pointing to now-legendary examples of insane behavior in the dry season, whilst others whisper of magickal Practices of the Natives or Malays), howbeit, now and then, Madness will visit by Surprize, taking away to its Realm of Voices and Pain even a mind in the rosiest fullness of Sanity. When they are too dangerous to roam free, the town Madmen are kept as a responsibility of the Company, confin'd in padded rooms in the Slave Lodge. Sometimes for their amusement the Herren will escort a particularly disobedient employee to a Madman's cell, push her inside, and lock the door. Next to each cell is a Viewing Room where the gentlemen may then observe, through a wall of Glass disguis'd as a great Mirror, the often quite unviewable *Rencontre*. The Madmen are of every race, condition, and degree of Affliction, from the amiably delusionary to the remorselessly homicidal. Some of them hate women, some desire them, some know hate and desire as but minor aspects of a greater, Oceanick Impulse, in which, report those who survive, it is unquestionably better not to be included. Again, some do not survive. When the Herren cannot return their Remains to their villages, they dispose of them by sea, that the Jackals may not have them.

What so far there have been only rumors of, is a room nine by seven feet and five inches, being with Dutch parsimony reduc'd to a quarter-size replica of the cell at Fort William, Calcutta, in which 146 Europeans were oblig'd to spend the night of 20–21 June 1756. There persists along the Company nerve-lines a terrible simple nearness to the Night of the "Black Hole," some Zero-Point of history, reckoning whence, all the Marvels to follow,— Quebec, Dr. Halley's Comet, the Battle of Quiberon Bay, aye and the Transit of Venus, too,— would elapse as fugitive as Opium dreams, and mattering less.... To find the Black Hole in a menu of Erotic Scenarios surprizes no one at this particular end of the World,— Residents, visitors, even a few Seamen of elevated sensibility have return'd, whenever possible, to be urg'd along by graceful Lodge-Nymphs in indigo Dhotis and Turbans, dainty scimitars a-flash, commanding their naked "Captives" to squeeze together more and more tightly into the scale-model cell with as many Slaves,— impersonating Europeans,— as will make up the complement, calculated at thirty-six, best able to afford visitors an authentick Sense of the Black Hole of Calcutta Experience.

"If one did not wish to suffer Horror directly," comments the Rev[d] in his Day-Book, "one might either transcend it spiritually, or eroticize it carnally,— the sex Entrepreneurs reasoning that the combination of Equatorial heat, sweat, and the flesh of strangers in enforc'd intimacy might be Pleasurable,— that therefore might some dramatiz'd approach to death under such circumstances be pleasurable as well, with all squirming together in a serpent's Nest of Limbs and Apertures and penises, immobiliz'd in a bondage of similarly bound bodies, lubricated with a gleaming mixture of their own shar'd sweat, piss, and feces, nothing to breathe but one another's exhausted breaths, moving toward some single slow warm Explosion...."

(Tho' he does not of course read any of this aloud,— choosing rather to skim ahead to the Moral.)

"Behind our public reaction to the Event, the outrage and Piety, what else may abide,— what untouchable Residue? Small numbers of people go on telling much larger numbers what to do with their precious Lives,— among these Multitudes, all but a few go on allowing them to do so. The British in India encourage the teeming populations they rule to teem as much as they like, whilst taking their land for themselves, and then restricting the parts of it the People will be permitted to teem upon.

"Yet hear the Cry, O Lord, when even a small Metaphor of this continental Coercion is practis'd in Reverse, as 'twas in the old B.H. of C.

" 'Metaphor!' you cry,— 'Sir, an hundred twenty lives were lost!'

"I reply, 'British lives. What think you the overnight Harvest of Death is, in Calcutta alone, in Indian lives?— not only upon that one Night, but ev'ry Night, in Streets that few could even tell you how to get to,— Street upon desperate Street, till the smoke of the Pyres takes it all into the Invisible, yet, invisible, doth it go on. All of which greatly suiteth the Company, and to whatever Share it has negotiated, His Majesty's Government as well.' "

Cornelius has vanish'd into the Room of the Beasts, "A peculiarly Afrikaner Taste," he pauses to advise Dixon, "— you might not enjoy it!" A slender dark Arm, full of Bangles, emerges from the Door-way, and a practis'd Hand removes his Hat. "Let's go, Simba."

Dixon has some idea of roaming the Lodge, finding a secret Tunnel to the Castle, searching for Austra,— tho' what he will do then is less clear to him. He gets no further than a small on-Premises Tap-room, where, paus'd for what they are pleas'd down in these Parts to term "Ale," he encounters whom but Police Agent Bonk, wearing a Dressing-Gown of red Velvet galloon'd with Gold, sweating copiously and trying to get Drunk on Cape Madeira.

"You are back? When did you arrive?"

"Your Shop didn't know about it?"

"I am done with that. I am a Farmer now. This is my last night in Cape Town, tho' I might have remain'd here, as a Free Burgher. Tomorrow I put my Family in an Ox-waggon, and start North. Perhaps over the Mountains. Out of the reach of the Company, who desire total Control over ev'ry moment of ev'ry Life here. I could not for them longer work. The Mountains beckon'd, the vast Hottentot Land beyond.... And at last, do you know, a curious thing happen'd. The more the Company exerted itself,— Searches in the middle of the Night, property impounded,— the more Farmers up-country felt press'd to move North, away from the Castle. They styl'd it 'Trekking,' and themselves 'Trekkers.' The demands of my job,— the amount of Surveillance alone they wish'd,— were overwhelming. The Supervisors each week coming up with newer and less realistick Quotas. No time for anything. Out there are green rolling Leagues of farmland and Range, Bushmen for the most part docile, I am assur'd, wild Game ev'rywhere, and best of all no more Company orders to obey."

" 'Tis a brave Venture...?— much Success."

"I'm confident about most of it,— the one thing causing me some Apprehension,— do you mind if we,— that is, you're not in the middle of anything,— "

"Ev'ryone else's Fun, it seems."

"I can fire a Rifle when I'm standing still, you see,— it is the Shooting and Loading whilst on Horseback, that worries me. I don't know how to do it,— and 'tis said there's no use going out there if you don't. Now, I was leaning toward an Oortman, then I heard, no, they're too heavy, too much Powder to carry, you're better off with a *Bobbejaanboud,* you put the butt on the ground and muzzle-load from the Saddle, and if you're press'd for time, why simply hit the Ground with the Butt, and the powder comes out this over-siz'd Priming Hole and into the Pan,— but then I thought, Well, suppose I got the Oortman anyway, then enlarg'd the Hole myself...."

Dixon returns to the Vroom residence at Dawn, all but carrying an equally, tho' perhaps not likewise, exhausted Cornelius. Ev'ryone is up. The Daughters run about, regarding Dixon out of the corners of their Eyes. What enchanted Mason about these Girls, Dixon comes to realize, with some consternation, is their readiness to seek the Shadow, avoid the light, believe in what haunts these shores exactly to the Atom,— ghosts ev'rywhere,— Slaves, Hottentots driven into exile, animals remorselessly Savage,— a Reservoir of Sin, whose Weight, like that of the atmosphere, is borne day after day unnotic'd, adverted to only when some Vacuum is encounter'd,— a Stranger in Town, a Malay publickly distraught, an hour at the Lodge,— into which its Contents might rush with a Turbulence felt and wonder'd at by all. The Vroom Girls and their counterparts all over town are Daughters of the End of the World, smiling more than they ought, chirping when needful, alert to each instant of the long Day as likely as the next to hold a chance of Ruin. In their Dreams they ever return to Prisons of Stone, to Gates with Seals 'tis Death to break, the odor of soap and Slops, the Stillness of certain Corridors, the unchallengeable Love of a Tyrant, Yellow Light from unseen Watch-Fires flickering upon the Wall, and unexpectedly, rounding a particular Corner, to the tall Clock from Home, ringing the Quarter-Hour.

One by one the girls have grown up believing the Vroom Clock, a long-case heirloom brought from Holland, to be a living Creature, conscious of itself, and of them, too, with its hooded Face, its heartbeat, the bearing of a solemn Messenger. It stands deep in the House, in a passageway between the Front and the Back,— the two Worlds,— witness to everything that transpires within hearing-range with but its one Hour-Hand, and two Bells, a Great and a Small, for striking the Hours and Quarter-hours. They call it 'Boet,'— the traditional name, here, for an elder Brother.

When Mason and Dixon arriv'd with the Ellicott Clock, the Girls assum'd it was a Traveling Companion of the Englishmen. Later, when Dixon return'd with a different Clock, Mr. Shelton's, no-one notic'd but Greet. "Please go carefully," she takes him aside to whisper. "They think Charles and you've something to do with the Longitude. After you were gone, they came to believe, that the Royal Society's Clock, which you had with you, was able to keep Errorless Time at Sea,— a British State Secret,— we are apt to believe anything here. The East India Company is about to present two fabulous Clocks, of Gold encrusted with Diamonds, with tiny Clock-Work Birds and such, to the Emperor of China. 'Twould be far wiser of you, to hide this new Clock, and pretend that you are back for…some other reason."

"The Transit's run, Lass, all that remains is to find the Going of the Clock, and,— eeh,— why Greet, the very idea."

"They all know I'm in here with you." She seizes the two sides of her Bodice and tears it apart. A young Bosom appears, pale and pink. "Did you just do that? Shall I call out that you did? Or was it a Spontaneous Seam Separation, apt to happen to any Bodice, really?"

"Thou did it, Lass."

"They won't believe that."

"So they may say. But they know thee."

"Brutal Albion, you are making it difficult for me to love you." She presses together a few hidden Snaps, and the Bodice is once again complete. "Mr. Mason was never so cold."

"Mason is naturally affectionate. Tho' he appears not to know one end of a Woman from another, yet 'tis all he thinks about, when he has a moment to think. Would tha denounce me to the Company Castle, then?"

"Go carefully."

Down in the Castle, however, they are facing a Dilemma. There is an unpremeditated wave of Enthusiasm for two-handed Clocks currently sweeping over the Dutch, both here and back in Holland. Soon, during an interrogation, someone will wish to note the precise time that each question is ask'd, or action taken, by a clock with two hands,— not because anyone will ever review it,— perhaps to intimidate the subject with the most advanc'd mechanical Device of its time, certainly because Minute-Scal'd Accuracy is possible by now, and there is room for Minutes to be enter'd in the Records. Any new Clock in their Neighborhood is thus eligible for the Honor.

Word has finally reach'd them, however, of Dixon's connection with Christopher Le Maire. They assume, without Reflection, that the Jesuit must belong to some branch of the Dutch Le Maires, fam'd among whom were Jacob, navigator and explorer of the southern seas, and Isaac, the East India Company Director and speculator, notorious for having introduced to the Dutch Stock Exchange the practice of trading in Shares one did not actually own. And the Priest is currently teaching in Flanders, is he not? Accordingly, Dixon's Dossier is flagg'd in Yellow, which means, "Caution,— may be connected dangerously," allowing him to go on as ever at the Cape, running before any wind of Sensory delight, as the Church-Faithful carouse, Slaves conspire their Freedom, and Functionaries flee the Castle, and head for open Country.

15

Mason, convinc'd that he has been set upon a Pilgrimage by Forces beyond his ability at present to reach,— a Station of the Cross being his preferr'd Trope,— finds much to Puzzle in Maskelyne's insistence that they move to the other side of the Island, from enclosure to exposure, from Shelter to an unremitting and much-warn'd-against Wind. "The Attraction of Mountains," Maskelyne Jobates, whilst slowly 'round him The Moon becomes a Dormitory, "— according to Newton, these Peaks may hold enough Mass to deflect our Plumb-lines, thereby throwing off our Zenith Obs. We must therefore repeat these Obs at the other side of the Island, and take the Mean Values betwixt 'em."

"The Other Side,"— it does give Mason a Chill. If the Cape of Good Hope be a Parable about Slavery and Free Will he fancies he has almost tho' not quite grasp'd, then what of this Translocation? That Maskelyne's Obsessedness in the Article of Plumb-lines, may be a factor in the change, will not become apparent till too late. Days in a row now pass in which Maskelyne speaks of little but the faulty Suspension of the Sisson Instrument. "My career, my Life,— hanging from a damn'd Pin!" He takes to accosting strangers in The Moon and then in other taverns, subjecting them to long wearying recitations describing the malfunction in numbing detail, and what he has instructed be done to correct it, and how others have complied, or not,— a history without sentiment or suspense (save that in which the Plumb-line, as it proves faultily, hangs upon its Loop, and that upon its Pin).

"How did Waddington like it over there?" Mason inquires.

"He wouldn't go. Not even a Day-Excursion to Sandy Bay. 'I know the Score,' he said, again and again, 'I've seen them come in to Town from the Windward Side, I see what the Wind does to 'em, it is no condition I care to enter,' was how he put it."

"It doesn't sound all that appealing to me, either," allows Mason. "Yet, to cancel Error when possible,— it's like turning the Instrument, isn't it? An Obligation, not easily neglected."

"Ah, Neglect. Ah, Conscience."

Flank'd by the D——l's Garden and the Gates of Chaos, the Company Fort at Sandy Bay commands that inhospitable, luminously Turquoise Recess in the Shore, representing the level of Daring that John Company is expecting one day in its ideal Enemy,— the silent Windward-Side companion to the great Fort at James's Town, which ever bustles with Sentries, and martial Musick, whilst this one appears deserted,— Flagless, Walls unpierc'd, as if drawn in against the Wind. The Discipline here, tho' Military in name, is founded in fact upon a Rip-Rap of Play-Acting, Superstitions, mortal Hatreds, and unnatural Loves, of a solemnity appropriate to the unabating Wind, that first Voice, not yet inflected,— the pure Whirl,— of the very Planet. The Gunfire here is at Sunset, and aim'd full into the Wind, as if to repel an Onslaught. Years ago the Soldiers set up, and now continue as a Tradition, various Suicide-Banks and Madness-Pools, into which one may put as little as a sixpence,— more substantial Sums going into side-Wagers, and the Percentages of Widows' Shares being ever negotiable,— and thus convert this Wind into Cash, as others might convert it to a Rotary Impulse upon a Mill-Stone. Fortunes certainly the equal of many a Nabob's are amass'd, risk'd, and lost within a Night. "We are the Doings of Global Trade in miniature!" cries the Post Surgeon, who tries never to stir too far from the deepest rooms of the Fort, where the Wind may oppress him least, and is careful to include it in each daily Prayer, as if 'twere a Deity in itself, infinitely in Need, ever demanding....

Pois'd at length upon the last Cliff, with the eternal South-easter full upon them, Mason, knowing he cannot be heard, says, "Well,— Waddington may have had a point." Maskelyne nevertheless plucks from the Wind his Meaning, and later, indoors at Sandy Bay, replies, "It is not to all tastes, here. 'Tis said those who learn to endure it, are wond'rously Transform'd."

"Oh, aye, that Farmer last night who ran about barking, and bit the Landlorrrd's Wife,— verry diverting, Sir,— yet perhaps upon this Coast they be merely mad, finding as little welcome at James's Town, where Sobriety is necessary to Commerce, as those Folk might upon the Windward, where, against such helpless Exposure as this, a vigilant Folly must be the only Defense,— two distinct nations, in a state of mutual mistrust, within ten Miles' Compass, and the Wind never relenting, as if causing to accumulate in the Island yet another Influence that must be corrected for. Perhaps, if discover'd, 'twould be as celebrated as the Aberration of Light."

Maskelyne flushes darkly and seems to change the Topick.

"I was out upon the Cliffs today and fell in with one of the Company Soldiers here. German fellow. Dieter. Came out that he's in something of a spot. Enlisted in ignorance that anyplace like this could exist."

"Now he wants out," suggests Mason.

"A strangely affecting Case, nonetheless. I cannot explain it. He seem'd to know me. Or I him. Had you been there,— "

"He might have seem'd to know me as well?"

"Am I so unwary? Your Innuendo is not new to me,— yet, he has ask'd for no money. And what matter, that he knows of my connection with Clive?"

"*Oh* Dear. How'd that happen?"

"I told him."

"Ah."

"He was quite distraught, and but a Pace or two from the Edge of the Precipice. 'No one can help me,' he was crying, 'not Frederick of Prussia, nor George of England, nor the great Lord Clive himself,' and so forth,— and I being the only one within earshot able to say, 'Well, actually, as to Clive, you know,— ' What would you have done?"

"Were I in a position to offer Clive's Services to the Publick? Why, I don't know, Maskelyne. Determine first of all what percentage to take, I suppose...."

The German had stood there, in the late Sunlight, his Eyes enormous and magnetick, fixing the Astronomer where he stood, the Sea roaring below them, and in the Wind, Stock-ends, Kerchiefs, Queue-Ribands, all coming undone and fluttering like so many Tell-tales. "You...could really help?"

"I've been living over in James's Town," Maskelyne deferent, attempting to speak calmly. "This is the first time I've pass'd more than a Day over here,— yet I find already, that the Wind is having an Effect, upon my Nerves. Causing me to imagine things, that may not be so? Have you notic'd that?"

"The Wind owns this Island," Dieter inform'd him,— "What awful Pride, to keep a Station here. Who would ever invade, by way of this mortal Coast? If they surviv'd landing upon a Lee Shore, they must get inland in a day,— once into those Mountains, oblig'd to cross all that width of Purgatory, before descending upon James's Town.... Are the Dutch that crazy? ravening, lost to the world? The French? Three of their Men o' War, only the year before last, station'd themselves out there, lounging to windward, just in the middle of the Company's sea-lane, like village ne'er-do-wells hoping for a fight. They manag'd to intercept and chase four of the Company's China ships, who at last made a run for South America, finding refuge in the Bay of All Saints. We watch'd it all, as we had ev'ry day, day and night. The Sails, the Signals thro' the Glass...we swore to shapes in the Darkness, creeping ashore in the terrible Moon-Light...and what do your Hosts over there at James's Fort expect to see, coming down out of their Ravine? What last unfaceable enemy? When one night, out of habit, someone will look up at the Watch-fire upon the Ridge, and find there all black as Doom.— Overrun? all gone mad and simply walk'd away? How much time elaps'd, and how much remaining to the Town?

"The Company promis'd travel, adventure, dusky Maidens, and one Day, *Nawabheit*.... A silken Curtain opening upon Life itself! Who would not have been persuaded? So I enlisted, and without time to catch a breath was I posted here, to the Windward Side of St. Helena, God who hath abandon'd us.... We are spiritually ill here, deprav'd. You are Clive of India's Brother-in-Law. A word from you would set me free."

"Well, I'm, I haven't *that* much influence with the Company...and Clive has but recently return'd to England, whilst I," he shrugg'd, "am here. I suppose."

"And Shuja-ud-Daula, the Nabob Wazir of Oudh, is out there,— with an Army. Bengal, Sir, is a Magazine waiting to explode,— no time for your *Schwager* to be in England, when perhaps already too late it grows."

"His enemies among his own," Maskelyne supposed, "being inveterate as any Hindu Intriguer, and Leadenhall Street no simpler than the Bagh Bazaar, England is a Battle-Field to him, 'pon which he must engage. Since the Court of Directors' election, he has been lock'd in a struggle with Mr. Sullivan for the Soul of the Company. I am not sure how many favors he may command right now, even of the dimension you suggest."

"*Sobald das Geld in Kasten klingt,*" Dieter recited, sighing, "*Die Seele aus dem Fegefeuer springt.*"

Later, talking it over with Mason, "Tho' there be no escape from this place for me, the Logic of the Orbit, the Laws of Newton and Kepler constraining,— yet could I ransom at least one Soul, from this awful Wind, the Levy Money would not be miss'd."

"You said he asked for none."

"Not he. The Company. So they are paid the twenty pounds they paid him to enlist, it matters little who replaces him."

Does Maskelyne mean more, when he speaks of "the Wind"? May he be thinking of his own obligations to the East India Company, and the unlikelihood that anyone would ever ransom him? "We may sail with the Wind," he said once, "at the same speed, working all its nuances,— or we may stand still, and feel its full true Course and Speed upon us, with all finer Motions lost in that Simplicity."

The incident of the German Soldier, in Maskelyne's life, seems like St. Helena itself, the visible and torn Remnant of a Sub-History unwitness'd. None of what Maskelyne says about it quite explains the Power over his Sentiments, that Dieter exerts.

"You'll pay the money yourself?" Mason only trying to be helpful.

"I can't go to Clive, can I. Not for this."

Mason is almost unsettl'd enough by the Wind to ask, "For what, then, *will* you go to him?"

Some last Flinching of Sanity prevents him,— for where might the Discussion go? "What do you desire in the world? Is it in Clive's Power to bestow? How appropriate is it in Scale, for a Brother-in-law? What balance shall you owe him then?"

None of the words need ever be spoken,— tho' given the Wind, and its properties of transformation, there are no guarantees they will not be. Yet if Mason but remains silent, keeping his Wits about him and his Arse out of the Wind, who's to say that one day when this too has pass'd, back in England, among Colonnades, Mirrors, Uniforms and Ball-Gowns, Medals and Orders, Necklaces and Brooches incandescent,— and the Applause of Philosophickal Europe,— Lord Clive may not approach discreetly bearing an emboss'd Envelope,—

"You've been Commended most warmly, Sir, by my dear brother-in-law, as largely having restor'd him to Reason, after his prolong'd Residence at St. Helena had somewhat diminish'd it. Horrid Station,— one good Volcanick Eruption, why 'twould solve ev'rything.... But,— as I was saying, I needn't tell you, Nevil's Sanity is important to me, as I'm sure it must be to Lady Clive as well. I wish I knew some better way to express..." But being Clive of India, alas, does not. The stiff cream Object approaching Mason's Hand... "For preserving the Futurity of Astronomy in Britain..." Thus at the instant of first Exterior Contact, before Immersion of the Gift into a Coat-Pocket, all Honor Mason might take in the Moment is drain'd away, as even his Daydreams turn upon him, allowing among them Clive Anointing Maskelyne, as if in some particularly tasteless Painting destin'd to hang at the Greenwich Observatory,— "It has its Elements of Excess," Maskelyne will admit, "Clive's Tunick in partickular, and one or two of the attending Dignitaries' Hats...yet, see how he's drap'd me,— " Mason returns from these Excursions dejectedly mindful, like any moral Tumbler, that when Murder is too inconvenient, Self-sacrifice must do,— tho' 'tis not possible for him, to imagine Maskelyne as quite ever blazing enough for any grand, or even swift, Immolation,— 'twould be a Slow Roast, Years in length, that awaited any who might come spiraling in his way. Gleefully, prefacing each with a whisper'd, "Of course, this is but Romance," Mason then wallows in Reveries, more and more elaborate, of Mishaps for Maskelyne, many of them Vertical in Nature.

And here it is, upon the Windward Side, where no ship ever comes willingly, that her visits begin. At some point, Mason realizes he has been hearing her voice, clearly, clean of all intervention.... 'Tis two years and more. Rebekah, who in her living silences drove him to moments of fury, now wrapt in what should be the silence of her grave, has begun to speak to him, as if free to do so at last, all she couldn't even have whispered at Greenwich, not with the heavens so close, with the light-handed trickery of God so on display.

He tries to joke with himself. Isn't this suppos'd to be the Age of Reason? To believe in the cold light of this all-business world that Rebekah haunts him is to slip, to stagger in a crowd, into the embrace of the Painted Italian Whore herself, and the Air to fill with suffocating incense, and the radiant Deity to go dim forever. But if Reason be also Permission at last to believe in the evidence of our Earthly Senses, then how can he not concede to her some Resurrection?— to deny her, how cruel!

Yet she can come to him anywhere. He understands early that she must come, that something is important enough to risk frightening him too much, driving him further from the World than he has already gone. She may choose a path, and to all others Mask'd, a Shadow, wait for him. She can wait, now. Is this her redress for the many times he failed to attend her whilst she lived,— now must he go through it and not miss a word? That these furloughs from death are short does not console him.

Once, long before dawn, bidden he can scarce say how, Mason rises from his cot,— Maskelyne across the shelter snoring in a miasma of wine-fumes and an Obs Suit patch'd together from local sources, whose colors in the Gloom are mercifully obscur'd,— enters the Wind, picks his way 'cross Boot-slashing Rock up over the ridgeline and down onto the floor of a ruin'd ebony forest, where among fog-wisps and ancient black logging debris polish'd by the Wind, she accosts him shiv'ring in his Cloak. The Ocean beats past the tiny accidental Island. "I can't have Maskelyne finding me out here."

"I imagin'd you miss'd me," she replies in her own unmodified voice. Christ. The Moonlight insists she is there. Her eyes have broken into white, and grown pointed at the outer ends, her ears are back like a cat's. "What are you up to here, Charlie? What is this place?"

He tells her. For the first time since the *Seahorse,* he is afraid again.

"For the Distance to one Star? Your Lie-by was alone here for Months. He manag'd. Why do you remain?"

"Earth being now nearly an orbit's diameter distant from where she was, the Work requires two,— and I must do as others direct."

"But wait till you're over here, Mopery."

"You refer to...," he twirls his hand at her, head to toe, uncertain how, or whether, to bring up the topick of Death, and having died. She nods, her smile not, so far, terrible.

Telling Maskelyne is out of the question,— Mason believes he would sooner or later use it to someone's detriment. But when at last Dixon does come up the Sea-Steps at James's Town, Mason will seize his Arm and whisk him off to his local, The Ruin'd Officer, to tell him as soon as he can.

"Then She has come to me since...she came last night." They are sitting in front of, but not drinking, two glasses of Cape Constantia.

"Oh, aye...?"

Stubborn, heat in his face, "Damme, she was here.... Was it *not* her Soul? What, then? Memory is not so all-enwrapping, Dream sooner or later betrays itself. If an Actor or a painted Portrait may represent a Personage no longer alive, might there not be other Modalities of Appearance, as well?...No, nothing of Reason in it.— In truth, I have ever waited meeting her again." Nodding as if to confirm it.

He continues, tho' not aloud,— There is a Countryside in my Thoughts, populated with agreeable Company, mapped with Romantick scenery, Standing-Stones and broken Archways, cedar and Yew, shaded Streams, and meadows a-riot with wild-flowers,— holding therein assemblies and frolicks...and each time, somewhere by surprize goes Rebekah, ever at a distance, but damme 'tis she, and a moment passes in which we have each recognized the other,— my breath goes away, I turn to Marble,—

"Oh, Dixon. I am afraid."

Dixon, carefully, keeping back as far as he can get, stretches an arm and places his hand on Mason's shoulder.

Mason's feet remain tranquil. "Then," he is smiling to himself at the foolishness of this, of ev'rything, "what shall I do?"

"Why, get on with it," replies Dixon.

"Easy advice to give,— how often I've done it...."

"Even easier to take, Friend,— for there's no alternative."

"Do you believe what you're saying? How has Getting On With It been working out for you, then? You expect me to live in the eternal Present, like some Hindoo? Wonderful,— my own *Gooroo,* ever here with a sage answer. Tell me, then,— what if I can't just lightly let her drop? What if I won't just leave her to the Weather, and Forgetfulness? What if I want to spend, even squander, my precious time trying to make it up to her? Somehow? Do you think anyone can simply let that all go?"

"Thou must," Dixon does not say. Instead, tilting his wine-glass at Mason as if 'twere a leaden Ale-Can, he beams sympathetickally. "Then tha must break thy Silence, and tell me somewhat of her."

16

Here is what Mason tells Dixon of how Rebekah and he first met. Not yet understanding the narrative lengths Mason will go to, to avoid betraying her, Dixon believes ev'ry word....

'Twas at the annual cheese-rolling at the parish church in Randwick, a few miles the other side of Stroud. And May-Day as well, in its full English Glory, Mason's Baptismal day,— its own Breath being drawn again and again across the Brooksides, Copses, and Fields, heated, fragrant. Every young woman for miles around would be there, although Mason adopted a more Scientifick motive, that of wishing to see at first hand, a much-rumored Prodigy, styled "The Octuple Gloucester,"— a giant Cheese, the largest known in the Region, perhaps in the Kingdom.

Some considered it an example of Reason run amok,— an unreflective Vicar, worshiping at the wrong Altar, having convinced local Cheesemen to pool their efforts in accomplishing the feat. Scaled up from the dimensions of the classic Single Gloucester, not only in Thickness, but actually octupled in all dimensions, making it more like a 512-fold or Quincentenariduodecuple Gloucester,— running to nearly four tons in weight when green, and even after shrinkage towering ten feet high by the time it emerged from the giant Shed built at the outskirts of town especially for this unprecedented Caseifaction,— the extraordinary Cheese, as it slowly aged, had already provided material for months of public Rumor. In recent days, trying to contain their impatience, crowds had begun to gather outside the shed entrance, as if a royal birth were imminent. As gatherings of the People, in this part of England, often produc'd gastro-spiritual Distress among the Clothiers, there were also on hand a small body of Light Cavalry. When the Cheese was at last carefully rolled into publick View, those who were there remember a collective gasp, a beat of silence, then, "Well,— I knew it was going to be *big*, but— "..."How ever are they going to get it up to the Church?"... "Wonder what it tastes like?"

Traditionally, the cheeses to be blessed and ritually rolled thrice 'round the churchyard, and thence down a Hill, ordinary-sized Double Gloucesters, were carried to the site in wheeled litters of some antiquity, though such clearly, for this Behemoth, would not do. Someone finally located a gigantic Cotswold Waggon, painted brick red and sky blue, as were the spokes and rims, respectively, of its wheels. The Cheese, an equally vivid orange-yellow, had then to be carefully rolled off a kind of dock and on into the bed of the Waggon, where, like some dangerous large animal, it was secured with stout Cables in an erect position. As the sides of the Waggon were of spindles and not planks, the Cheese was visible to onlookers in its full Circumference.

The progress to Randwick Church was a Spectacle long to be remembered. Neighbor Folk of all conditions lined the route, at first, as the great Cheese swayed and loomed into view, silently in awe,— then, presently, as if strangely calmed by the Beams of a Luminary rising anew above each dip in the road,— calling out to the Cheese and its conveyors, calls which after not too long became huzzahs and even Hosannas. Drinkers tumbled out of the alehouses and toasted the majestic food product as it passed— "Let's have three cheers for the Great Octuple, lads!" Girls blew Kisses. Local youths from time to time would spring aboard, to help steady the cargo when the road-surface became difficult, able to tell one day of how they had escorted the great Cheese upon its journey, that famous first of May. Singing,

> Here's to the great, Octuple boys! the
> Mon-ster Cheese of fame,
> Let's cheer it with, a thund'rous noise,
> Then twice more of the same,—
> Oh the bells shall ring, and
> The guns shall roar,

For the won-derful Octuple Glo'r...
Aye, all the Lads, who push and who-pull,
Ev'ry Master, ev'ry Pupil
Single-ton and married Coople,
Eye at Win-dow, Door and Looph'le,
Ev'ry minim, dram and scruple
Of their Praise is Thine, Octuple!"

Of course Mason was there hoping to see Susannah Peach, even if it had to be from a distance, surrounded by cousins and friends. She would appear, as always, in silk. Her father, Samuel Peach, was a silk merchant of some repute, and a growing Power within the East India Company. Mason imagin'd her brought bolts of it, by Indians queu'd up in bright Livery, Silks without limit from the furthest of the far Eastern lands, the house in Minchinhampton soon drap'd ev'rywhere in bright spilled, intriguingly wrinkl'd yards of silkstuffs,— an hundred mirror'd candles casting upon it the fatty yellow light of a tropical sun. Savage flowers of the Indies, demurer Blooms of the British garden, stripes and tartans, foreign colors undream'd of in Newton's prismatics, damasks with epic-length Oriental tales woven into them, requiring hours of attentive gazing whilst the light at the window went changing so as to reveal newer and deeper labyrinths of event, Velvets whose grasp of incident light was so predatory and absolute that one moved closer to compensate for what was not being reflected, till it felt like being drawn, oneself, inside the unthinkable contours of an invisible surface. She could distinguish Shantung from Tussah and Pongee, being often quite passionate in her Preferences. "Would you like to learn Silk, Charles? It might mean Aleppo instead of India. Would that disappoint you?"

"No, Miss." He had visited her House when she wasn't there. He had enter'd her room. He had knelt by her Bed and press'd his face to the Counterpane of Silk to inhale what he could of her Scent. In the Sewing-Room, from down at Surface-level, he imagin'd from the Silk strewn so carelessly, a Terrain steeply wrinkl'd into mountainsides and ravines, through which pass'd dangerous Silk-route shortcuts, down upon which with the patience of Reptiles bands of arm'd men in colorful costume gaz'd, and waited. Waited to kidnap and unspeakably mistreat beautiful young Silk Heiresses....

Today he felt more than usually glum. His father's birthday gift to him had been a day off from duties at the Mill. All 'round him, ev'rybody else his age was flirting, chasing, and larking, whilst he trudged about, waiting at last only for the giant Cheese, which had been due to arrive, actually, some while ago. Susannah, as the daughter of a local dignitary, might be accompanying it upon its journey,— or might have stayed home altogether. He could see no one, withal, who was not by this point pair'd off. Not much use in staying, he suppos'd.... He started down the hillside by the church, planning at the bottom to pick up the road back in to Stroud, incompletely attentive to the slow Crescendo of cheering from the crowd above, and the wave of Children spilling down the Hill, and the first cries of Warning.

As he'd learn later, the Vicar had decided for reasons of safety to roll nothing greater than a Double Gloucester down the Hill,— yet as if ordain'd by some invariance in the Day's Angular Momentum, the Drag-Shoe on one side of the Octuple's Waggon broke away, causing the conveyance to slew, and slip down the side of a Hummock, and at last tip over, launching the Cheese into the Air, just before the Waggon (its Catapult) fell over with a great creak and jangle, Wheels a-spin, as meanwhile the enormous Cheese was hitting the Slope perfectly vertical,— bouncing once, startlingly orange against the green hillside, and beginning to roll, gathering speed. The first peripheral impression Mason had of it was of course a star-gazer's,— thinking, Why, the Moon isn't suppos'd to be out, nor full, nor quite this bright shade of yellow, nor for that matter to be growing in size this way,— about then smoaking belatedly where he was, and what was about to happen.

"Ahr! Mercy!" He threw his arms in front of his Face and succumb'd before the cylindrickal Onslaught, with a peculiar Horror at having been singl'd out for Misadventure... *The Victim of a Cheese malevolent,* being his last thought before abrupt Rescue by way of a stout shove, preceded by an energetick Rustling of Taffeta,— as he went toppling onto his face, grass up his Nose, hearing thro' his Belly the homicidal Ponderosity roll by without the interruption of a flatten'd Mason to divert it from its Destiny.

As he arose, slowly, holding his head, blowing out alternate Nostrils, her Voice first reach'd him. "Were it Night-time, Sir, I'd say you were out

Star-Gazing." She put upon her *r* the same vigorous Edge as his Father on a difficult day,— withal, "Star-Gazing" in those parts was a young man's term for masturbating. He might have said something then to regret forever, but her looks had him stupefied. If she was not, like Susannah, a Classick English Rose, neither was she any rugged Blossom of the Heath. He found himself staring at the shape of her mouth, her Lips slightly apart, in an Inquiry that just fail'd to be a Smile,— like a Gate-Keeper about to have a Word with him. What shadow'd Gates lay at her Back? What mystick Residence?

"My wish too intently these days," he declares to Dixon when it is possible to do so, "is to re-paint the Scene, so that she might bear somehow her fate in her Face, eyes guarded, searching for small injustices to respond to because she cannot bear what she knows will befall her,— yet Rebekah's innocence of Mortality kept ever intact...oh, shall this divide my Heart? she saw nothing, that May-Day, but Life ahead of her."

("There are no records of her in Gloucestershire," interrupts Uncle Ives.

"What, none? Shall none ever appear?"

"With respect to your Faith in the as-yet-Unmaterializ'd, Mason was baptiz'd at Sapperton Church, as were his Children,— yet he and Rebekah were not married there. So mayn't they have met elsewhere as well,— even at Greenwich?"

"Unless ghosts are double,— " " "— one walking, the other still," the Twins propose.)

Country Wife open and fair, City Wife a Creature of Smoke, Soot, Intrigue, Purposes unutter'd...her plainly visible Phantom attends Mason as if he were a Commissioner of Unfinish'd Business, representing Rebekah at her most vital and belov'd. Is this, like the Bread and Wine, a kindness of the Almighty, sparing him a sight he could not have abided? What might that be, too merciless to bear? At times he believes he has almost seen black Fumes welling from the Surface of her Apparition, heard her Voice thickening to the timbres of the Beasts...the serpents of Hell, real and swift, lying just the other side of her Shadow...the smell of them in their long, cold Waiting.... He gazes, at such moments, feeling pleasurably helpless. She occupies now an entirely new angular relation to Mercy, to those refusals, among the Living, to act on behalf of

Death or its ev'ryday Coercions,— Wages too low to live upon, Laws written by Owners, Infantry, Bailiffs, Prison, Death's thousand Metaphors in the World,— as if, the instant of her passing over having acted as a Lens, the rays of her Soul have undergone moral Refraction.

He tries teasing her with his earth-bound Despair. "Measuring Angles among illuminated Points, there must be more to it, 'Bekah, you see them as they are, you must."

"Oh, Charlie. 'Must.' " Laughter does not traverse easily the baffling of Death,— yet he cannot harden his heart enough to miss the old Note within,— 'tis sure, 'tis his own Rebekah. Her voice affects him like music in F-sharp minor, drawing him to the dire promise. "You believ'd, when you were a Boy, that the Stars were Souls departed."

"And you, that they were Ships at Anchor." She had, once,— as our Sky, a Harbor to Travelers from Ev'rywhere.

"Look to the Earth," she instructs him. "Belonging to her as I do, I know she lives, and that here upon this Volcanoe in the Sea, close to the Forces within, even you, Mopery, may learn of her, Tellurick Secrets you could never guess."

"I've betray'd you," he cries. "Ah,— I should have— "

"Lit Candles? I am past Light. Pray'd for me ev'ry Day? I am outside of Time. Good, living Charles,...good Flesh and Blood...." Between them now something like a Wind is picking up speed and beginning to obscure his View of her. She bares her Teeth, and pales, and turns, drifting away, evaporating before she is halfway across the slain Forest.

Erect after her dear Flesh impossible to him till Resurrection Day, he returns to his bed-clothes. In the Crepuscule, Maskelyne's Observing Suit is edging into Visibility. Great Waves of Melancholy, syncopating the Atlantick Counterparts not far away, surge against him. They might drown him, or bear him up,— he lies not caring, and fails to find Sleep again. Maskelyne, on the other side of the Tent, slumbers till Midday. "Hullo, Mason. Was that you, coming in about Dawn?"

"Not I." Unpremeditatedly.

"Hum,— Might it've been Dieter, d'ye think?"

"Dieter? Why would he be in the Tent?"

"The Wind."

"Ahrr,— that is, of course."

"He's not Dieter…at least not any more, he isn't."

Mason recalls that he has never met the German face to face. "How is the project for his Release getting on?"

" 'Tis someone else. You may be confus'd. Pray, erase Dieter from your Mind, and I shall be much oblig'd."

Mason, understanding little enough already, still resounding up and down his Center-Line with Rebekah's Visit, is abruptly certain that Dieter is a Ghost as well. How wise would it be, however, to share this Revelation with Maskelyne? "He is well, I trust," keeping at it for reasons he sees only after he has spoken.

" 'Well'! What are you saying, Mason? To be *not* well over here, is to be dead. How *you* have avoided that Fate, indeed puzzles me."

"Which leaves you,— are you 'well,' Maskelyne?"

" 'Tis Dieter who's in Peril here. Medically, I cannot speak,— yet as one of the Lord's Menials, I see his Soul insulted in ways Souls do not bear readily. Why did you not, rather, ask after him? His Fate has Consequences within my own."

Mason has begun in recent days hearing in the Wind entire orchestral Performances, of musick distinctly not British,— Viennese, perhaps, Hungarian, even Moorish. He finds he cannot concentrate. The Wind seems to be blowing cross-wise to the light incoming from Sirius, producing false images, as if, in Bradley's Metaphor for the Aberration, the Vehicle, Wind, has broken thro' some Barrier, and enter'd the nononsense regime of the Tenor, Light, whilst remaining attach'd to it. As supernatural as a Visitant from the Regime of Death to the sunny Colony of Life,— to be metaphorickal about it.…

"I think the two of ye need some time together," Mason, with what remains of his good Sense, suggests. "And to be honest, I haven't your resistance to this Wind. It is driving me insane." His Stomach warning him not to add, "*You* are driving me insane."

He runs without delay down to the Shingle and begins assembling a Signal-Fire, using his Coat to fan it, advising any Coasters that might come by, of his need of passage to the Leeward Side. The Price will be more or less Criminal.

Maskelyne waves good-bye from the Ridge. He wears a Canary Coat and Breeches Mason has never observ'd him in before, a Wig that even at this Distance causes a contraction of the Pupils, and a Hat, more obscurely, suggesting Optickal Machinery of uncertain Purpose. He seems to be on his Way to the Fort, perhaps into it. Perhaps that is where Dieter does his principal Haunting. Presently a Dhow ventures in, to Wading-Distance. "Good Ride to Jamestown! Twenty Rix-Dollars! Good Price!"

"Ten!" having no idea if he can afford it.

"Only as far as Friar's Valley."

"Break-neck," whispers a Voice clearly, tho' no one is there.

"To Break-neck," calls Mason.

"I've no wish to offend your Companion. Done."

17

Once 'round Castle Rock and the Needles, they can run before the Wind, down past Manatee Bay, and the great Ridge-line above wheeling as they rush on,— doubling at last the South-West Point, standing off from Man and Horse, Lines and Hooks drop over the side, and presently the Day's Meal is flopping about the Deck,— they have lost the Wind. The Absence stuns him. Breezes, Tides, and Eddies must now get them past this Coast. The Crew, who've been out in it for a few Days, find Mason's Discombob-ulancy amusing. That their Remarks are not in English sends him further a-reel. When they debark him at the mouth of Break-Neck Valley, two or three Miles from the Town, he is more than eager to be off.

He can smell the Town upon the Wind, the Smoke and Muck-Piles, long before he sees it. Awakening from a sort of Road-Trance, he finds himself before the Jenkin's Ear Museum, dedicated to the eponymous Organ whose timely Display brought England in against Spain in the War of '39. Not long after, Robert Jenkin went to work for the East India Company,— many styl'd it a quid pro quo,— being assign'd to St. Helena in '41 as Governor, and bringing with him the influential Ear, already by then encasqu'd in a little Show-case of Crystal and Silver, and pickl'd in Atlantick Brine. James's Town wove its Spell. Eventually, at Cards, Mr. Jenkin extended his Credit too far even for Honorable John. There remain'd the last unavoidable Object of Value, which he bet against what prov'd to be a Cross-Ruff, whence it pass'd into the Hands of Nick Mournival, an Enterpriser of the Town.

Mason is chagrin'd to find set in a low Wall a tiny Portico and Gate, no more than three feet high, with a Sign one must stoop to read,— "Ear of Rob[t] Jenkin, Esq., Within." Clearly there must be some other entry, tho' Mason can find none, not even by repeated Jumps to see what lies over the Wall,— to appearance, a Garden gone to weeds. Reluctantly at last he takes to his elbows and knees, to investigate the diminutive Doorway at close hand,— the Door, after a light Push, swinging open without a Squeak. Mason peers in. What Illumination there is reveals a sort of Ramp-way leading downward, with just enough height to crawl.

Owing to a certain *Corporate Surplus* accumulated at Cape Town, Mason's smooth descent is here and there in doubt,— each time, indeed, tho' but temporarily stuck, he comes near Panick. At last, having gain'd a slightly roomier sort of Foyer, hewn, it seems, from the Volcanick Rock of the Island, he is startl'd by a Voice, quite near.

"Good Day to you, Pilgrim, and thanks for your interest in a great modern secular Relic. Helen of Troy's face may've launch'd a thousand ships,— this is but one Ear, yet in its Time, it sent navies into combat 'round the Globe. Think of it as the closest thing you're apt to see to Helen's Face, and for one Pistole 'tis a Bargain."

"Bit steep, isn't it? Where, ehm, are you, by the way...the Echo in here,— "

"Look in front of you."

"Yaahhgghh,— "

"Ta-ra-ra! Yes, here all the time. Nick Mournival, formerly Esquire, now your Servant. Once a Company Director, now...as you see. Fortune's wheel is on the Rise or Fall where'er we go, but nowhere does it turn quite as furiously as here, upon this unhappy Mountain-Top in the Sea."

"You are Florinda's friend. We met before the Battery one evening,— she is well, I trust."

"She is flown. Some Chicken-Nabob traveling home with his Mother. Watch'd her work him. Masterful. She knew I was observing, and put on a Show. Her Stage Training,— humiliating, of course.— "

"Well," brightly, "where's the Ear then,— just have a look if I may, and be off?"

"Dear no, that's not how 'tis done, I must come along, to operate the Show."

"Excuse me,— Show...?"

Naïve Mason. First he must endure The Spaniard's Crime, The Ear Display'd to Parliament, the Declaration of War,— with Mournival speaking all the parts and putting in the sounds of Cannonades, and Storms at Sea, Traffick in Whitehall, Spanish Jabbering and the like, and providing incidental music upon the Mandoline from Mr. Squivelli's *L'Orecchio Fatale,* that is, "The Fateful Ear." A Disquisition upon Jenkin's Ear-*Ring,* "Aye, 'twas never Mr. J.'s Ear the Spaniard was after, but the great Ruby *in* it. For one silver shilling, you may view this remarkable Jewel, red as a wound, pluck'd from the Navel of an importantly connected Nautch-Dancer, by a Mate off a Coaster, who should've known better,— passing then from Scoundrel to Scoundrel, tho' Death to possess yet coveted passionately, from the Northern Sea to the farther swamps of the Indies, absorbing in its Passage, and bearing onward, one Episode after another, the brutal and dishonorable Tale of Bengal and the Carnatic, in the Days of the Company,— till it settl'd in to dangle beneath the fateful Lobe of Mr. Jenkin, and wait, a-throb with unluckiness, the Spaniard's Blade."

In the strait and increasingly malodorous space where they crouch, awash in monologue and vocal Tricks, Mason's only diversion is what Mr. Mournival, by now seeming more openly derang'd, styles "The Chronoscope," which, for a fee, may be squinted into,— here in all colors of the Prism sails the brig *Rebecca,* forever just about to be intercepted by the infamous *Guarda-Costa.* Mason's Squint is not merely wistful,— the ship's name is a Message from across some darker Sea,— as he has come to believe in a metaphysickal escape for the *Seahorse,* back there off Brest, much like this very depiction,— the Event not yet "reduc'd to certainty," the Day still'd, oceanick, an ascent, a reclaiming of light, wind express'd as its integral, each Sail a great held Breath.... Into just such a Dispensation, that far-off morning, had he risen... like a Child...India, all Islands possible, the open, inextinguishable Light...his last morning of Immortality.

"And finally, a salute to the career of Mr. Jenkin with the E.I.C., featuring his brief and not dishonorable tenure as Governor here." Nick Mournival's Tortoise Pick begins to vibrate upon the Notes of "Rule Britannia," as a life-siz'd portrait of Jenkin now shimmers into view, the missing Ear tastefully disguis'd by the excursions of a Wig of twenty years ago, and the Curriculum Vitæ is grandly recited.

All this while, the Ear reposes in its Pickling-Jar of Swedish lead Crystal, as if being withheld from Time's Appetite for some Destiny obscure to all. Presently 'tis noted by Mason,— he hopes, an effect of the light,— that somehow, the Ear has been a-glow,— for a while, too,— withal, it seems, as he watches, to come to Attention, to gain muscular Tone, to grow indeed quite firm, and, in its saline Bath, erect. *It is listening.* Quickly Mason grips himself by the head, attempting to forestall Panick.

"Aha." Mr. Mournival breaks off his narration. "Good for you, Sir. Some of them never do smoak it, you know. Yes of course Ear's been listening,— what're Ears for?— and to be honest, there's not much to do down here.... Ear may look small and brine-soak'd to some, but I can tell you she's one voracious Vessel,— can't get enough of human speech, she'll take anything, in any language,— sometimes I must sit and read to her, the Bible, the Lunar Tables, *The Ghastly Fop*, whatever comes to hand...'tis Ear's great Hunger, that never abates."

" 'Ear'?"

"Oh? What would you call her? 'Nose'?"

"I...but wish'd not to speak inappropriately,— " Mason's Eyes swiveling about more and more wildly, failing to locate the Egress.

"You're a Sporting Gentleman, I recognize your style, been to any number of London Clubs in me time, how'd you like to"— his Nudge, in this under-ground Intimacy, comes like an Assault,— "get a little closer, maybe...tell her something in private?" As much as the Space allows, he now flourishes a Key.

"Ehm, perhaps I'll just,— could you, actually, kindly, point me to the...Way out?"

Mr. Mournival has unlock'd the Vitrine, and reach'd into the Sea-Glow within. "You ought not leave, Sir, till you've spoken into Ear. She'll be a much better Judge of when you may go. And 'twill cost but a Rix-Dollar more,— "

"What!"

"Be advis'd, I am empower'd to use Violence, I've a Warrant from the Company,— "

"Here then,— take, take *two* Rix-Dollars,— why not? only Dutch money, isn't it, no more real than the Cape be, and that terrible Dream that has seiz'd and will not release them,— "

"Don't tell me," shrugs Mr. Mournival. "Tell Ear. It's just the sort of Chat-up she fancies. Treat for you today, Ear!" he cries, startling Mason into a back-twinge he would rather not have. "Go ahead, Sir. Put your Lips as close as as you care to."

"You're not altogether well," Mason points out.

"And more of us on the Leeward Side than you'd ever suspect.... There...so.— Better? Now whisper Ear your Wish, your fondest Wish,— join all those Sailors and Whores and Company Writers without number who've found their way down here, who've cried their own desires into the Great Insatiable. Upon my Solicitor's Advice, I must also remind you at this Point, that Ear only *listens* to Wishes,— she doesn't grant 'em."

Mason can scarce look into the blue-green Radiance surrounding the Ear,— in this crowded darkness, even the pale luminescence stuns...and just as well, too, for the Organ has now definitely *risen up* out of its Pickle, and without question is offering itself, half-cur'd and sub-terranean cold, to Mason's approaching Mouth. I have surviv'd the Royal Baby, Mason tells himself,— this can be done. The flirtatious Ear stands like a shell-fish,— vibrating, waiting.

His fondest Wish? that Rebekah live, and that,— but he will not betray her, not for this. What he whispers, rather, into the pervading scent of Brine and...something else, is, "A speedy and safe passage for Mr. Dixon, back to this place. For his personal sake, of course, but for my Sanity as well."

Helen of Troy, *mutatis mutandis,* might have smirk'd, yet even if the Ear were *able* to smirk, Mason wouldn't have notic'd, would he,— being preoccupied so with the Metaphysicks of the Moment. Till now, he has never properly understood the phrase *Calling into a Void,*— having imagin'd it said by Wives of Husbands, or Teachers of Students. Here, however, in the form of this priapick Ear, is the Void, and the very anti-Oracle— revealing nothing, as it absorbs ev'rything. One kneels and begs, one is humiliated, one crawls on.

"The Egress you seek lies directly before you, Sir,— " the Mandoline jingling a recessional Medley of Indian Airs as Mason climbs on. At the moment, all he wants to see is the Atlantic Sky. "Godspeed!" calls Nick Mournival, "— may you fare better in the life you resume, than ever did I in the one I abandon'd."

Having squirm'd past the last obstacle, Mason finds himself presently at Ground Level in the neglected Garden he glimps'd earlier. The Walls are markedly higher in here than he remembers them from the Street,— whose ev'ry audible Nuance now comes clear to him, near and far, all of equal Loudness, from ev'ry part of the Town,— but invisible.... In its suggestion of Transition between Two Worlds, the space offers an invitation to look into his Soul for a moment, before passing back to the Port-Town he has stepp'd from...a Sailors' waterfront Chapel, as some would say. He begins, like a Dog, to explore the Walls, proceeding about the stone Perimeter. Bright green Vines with red trumpet-shap'd Flowers, brighter indeed than the Day really allows...no door-ways of any kind...then Rain, salt from the Leagues of Vacant Ocean....

"I was in a State. I must have found the way out. Unless the real Mason is yet there captive in that exitless Patch, and I but his Representative."

When Dixon hears this, at last, a few days out in their Passage back to England, he sits staring at Mason. "Well,— this is going to seem uncoah', but as near as I can calculate, at exactly the instant you spoke into this Object, I heard, as out of a speaking-trumpet, your message. I was sitting in The World's End,— in some Wise that no Philosophy can explain, the Wind outside dropp'd for just long enough for me to hear. Of course I didn't recognize it as you, Mason,— so darken'd with echo and so forth was that Voice...?"

"Dixon, I am 'maz'd...my Wish, as well, you say.... Ahrr! You almost persuaded me,— why can you never just let it be?— you had the hook right in my Mouth, Sir."

"In Durham, we tend to let the Coarse Fish go...?"

"Oh, aye,— in favor of what, pray?"

"We look more for Carp, or Salmon-Trout, tho' naturally 'twould be a bit different down where tha do thy fishing,— a more predatory style no Doubt,— desperate, as tha'd say.... Only come up to Wearside some time, we'll teach thee how to wait."

"I am a Taurus, Friend. I know how to wait."

"Ever use a Ledger on thy Line?"

"A Lead Sinker, in the Frome? What a Hope,— something would eat it...? aye, so fast you'd never feel a thing...? I'm serious, Dixon. Lead? They esteem it a Delicacy."

" 'Tis just how I talk about places I don't fancy anyone else fishing in...?"

"For the Sake of the publick Health, nor should I,— not in those Clothiers' Sewer-Lines that were once my home Streams. We grew up feeling oblig'd to fish, yet certainly not to eat anything we caught. Too many cautionary Tales known to all."

"Much fishing at St. Helena?"

"I didn't leave Maskelyne in the best of mental health,— perhaps he's been here too long."

"With orbitally diametrick Obs as one's Plan, why there's never thah' much choice...? But life is so short." Dixon's Phiz now all piously of-course-I-never-gossip-but, "— Are you suggesting there's some other reason for his long Sojourn there, where five minutes is more than enough for some?"

"Mister, Dixon!" leaving Dixon just time to shrug unapologetickally, "what could that possibly be?"

"Six months...? a man can pass thro' an entire phase of his life in that time. Have an Adventure,— who knows?"

"You don't mean to raise the possibility of..."

"Friend Mason, who am I to say? 'Tis thoo's been with him since October. Have there been publick displays, Beauties unintroduc'd, mysterious absences? Sirius neglected? Happen he's only been going off to drink, as drinking does seem to take up an unco' Fraction of people's time here...?"

"I have come to believe, that Maskelyne lingers only because Bradley discover'd the Aberration, and achiev'd Glory, whilst trying to find the Parallax of London's Zenith-Star. Might not that great moment of Clarity beneath Draco, reasons Maskelyne, be repeated there, beneath the Great Dog?"

"He thinks he'll find something else, like the Aberration...?"

"He's careful, that's all. If there's anything to it, he'll know soon enough."

"Did I say anything? Ah don't even knaah the Lad...?"

"Nor I,— I'm speculating. *Suppose* that were it, 's all I'm saying.... And yet he stays on. He could've come back with us, couldn't he? Has he in the Strangeness of his Solitude, reach'd a Compact with the Island, as if 'twere sentient, has he in some way come to belong to it in Perpetuity? The Whores' Bridge, his Desert,— his Trial of Passage, Abstinence?"

"Or, in that place, Indulgence," Dixon reminds him.

They would rather discuss Maskelyne's Affairs, than what waits in England, in their own Futurity. Through his Correspondence, Maskelyne has heard of one Possibility, tho' 'tis far from a Reduction to Certainty. Following the Chancery decision the year before, as to the Boundaries between the American Provinces of Pennsylvania and Maryland, both Proprietors have petition'd the Astronomer Royal for assistance, using the most modern means available, in marking these out,— one of them being a Parallel of Latitude, five degrees, an Hundred Leagues, of Wilderness East to West.

"Why would Maskelyne tell us of this?"

"He'd not want it for himself. He'd rather see us permanently abroad,— then 'tis alone at last with Dr. Bradley."

"Would thou go to America?"

"I don't know that Bradley would recommend me again," Mason says. "For reasons we appreciate. Nor shall Maskelyne be too eager,— if it cannot advance the cause of Lunars, what use is it? Who? Waddington? Yourself? If you are interested, Dixon, after the Work you did at the Cape, you may likely write your own Contract."

"That good, was it?"

"Yes. Mine was lucky,— the Sector practickally did the Work,— but yours was good."

"Then they'll want to send us both again...? Won't they. Eeh,— a bonny gone-on,— the two of huz, in America."

"I don't think so."

18

Void of Course, back with Senses Boggl'd from War, Slavery, Successful Obs, the wind at St. Helena, unaccustom'd Respect from their Peers, Mason and Dixon wander about London like Tops a-spin, usually together, colliding from time to time and bouncing away smartly. They get to dine at The Mitre, tho' it is mid-afternoon and a Ploughman's Lunch of unintegrated Remnants of earlier meals. They address the Council of the Royal Society, and find they have nothing but good to say of all they have met at St. Helena and the Cape.

Dixon is soon departed Northward, his only Thought of The Jolly Pitman in Staindrop, an Idler's Haunt recall'd the more extravagantly as the Distance from Home increas'd. In London, Mason is less certain how to proceed. He must see his Boys, whom he cannot help missing, yet at the same time he dreads the Re-Union. In Town, he pays his Devoirs, and as Bonk predicted, is casually question'd, across what prove to be a Variety of Desks, by Agents of the Navy, the East India Company, the Royal Society, and the Parliamentary Curious, from King's Men to Rockingham Whigs, as to Vegetable Supply, Road-Widths, Shore-Batteries, Civilian Morale, Slave Discontent, and the like. He is releas'd at the sour gray end of afternoon into a City preparing for Night,— descending into Faith, from one Opportunity to the next, as once, early in his Grief for Rebekah, he descended into Sin.

The Cock Lane Ghost is all the Rage. Mason makes a point of going out to see what he can see. He finds at the fam'd Parsons Dwelling no

Ghost, but is amaz'd at the Living who arrive whilst he's there. "Imagine who's here when I'm not?" he is not fully conscious of having utter'd aloud. "That's Mrs. Woffington over there. Little Chap by her Side? Garrick. Aye."

Giddily exited into the Lane again, he resolves, upon Rebekah's next Visit, to ask if she mightn't just pop 'round here, for a look within the Walls. But the Days in London stretch on, until he understands that she will not come to him here,— that she wants him in Sapperton,— Home.

However content Rebekah may be, Mason's Sisters are unusually harsh in their treatment of him. The Boys regard him politely. He brings them a pair of Toy Ships, bought as a last-minute afterthought off a bum-boat in Santa Cruz Bay. They take them down to the Stream, leaving the Women to discuss his character, and Mason puzzles thro' with them what he may of the Rigging, re-express'd by Carvers living in Tenerife, after their memories of visiting ships from ev'rywhere. William is five. Doctor Isaac is three.

"It's from very far away," asserts Willy, more to Doc than to this incompletely recogniz'd man, whom it may be unwise to address. "It's not British."

"*Your* Boat?" Doc has no such caution in piping at Mason.

Mason has a look. "We carried more Guns, I think. There were not quite so many oddly-shap'd Sails. And of course as you note, these are blue. Exact shade of the Sea,— making them invisible Ships, as they sail along. Sneak right up on the French. Before they know it,— *Touché!*" Pretending to reach toward them with Intent to Tickle. They shrug out of range more than retreat, meantime eyeing him more curiously than before. Doc is closer to agreeable Laughter than his Brother, who believes it his Duty to be the Watchful One. Their boats ride the lenient Current together, in and out of the Shadows, ever in easy reach of rescue, the Boys shepherding them with Willow Wands, no more obtrusive in this Naval History than Gods in a Myth.

In the first weeks of July, Bradley falls ill, and gets steadily worse. On the thirteenth, in Chalford, he dies, and is put to rest with Susannah at Minchinhampton.

Mason rides over as he's done unnumber'd Times, trying not to think ahead. It does not much seem to matter. Too much lies unresolv'd for any Social Visit to clear away. He talks it over with himself.

"And Bradley knew..."

"Ev'rybody knew ev'rything. Except me. I only thought I did, so of course 'twas I who did the most screaming. Thro' the sleepless noontides Astronomers cherish, the emotion that rag'd within those admir'd walls could have shifted the Zero Meridian by seconds of Arc, into either Hemisphere, why who knows, even bounced it back and forth a few times.

"The indoor environment quickly became impossible to live in. That strange Parlor-Game commencing, Rebekah and I moving out of the Observatory, down to Feather Row, trudging up and down that hill at all Hours, with William going ev'rywhere in a sort of Sling,— then, before anyone quite realizes it, Susannah has mov'd in next door, Bradley begins visiting, at first penitent, then abject, soon he's there ev'ry night, takes to dropping in on *us,* hinting about, presently we're together as a foursome, boating upon the River, playing at Cards upon Nights of Cloud or Storm, Pope Joan, Piquet, Rebekah's sweet Voice, Susannah's hands never touch'd by Sunlight, impossible not to gaze at,— then we move up the hill again, whilst Bradley in some small flaring Snit takes our old Feather Row quarters...the Heavens wheel on, meantime."

Was he fated for these terrible unending four-door Farces? They do not always end luckily, as at the Cape, with ev'ryone's Blood unspill'd.

Young Sam Peach, Susannah's Brother, is there, and Miss Bradley, seventeen and despite her sleeplessness and Pallor, a-bloom,— and even with Bradley looking out of her face, more like her mother than Mason would ever have thought possible in the turn of a Socket, the Scroll of a Nose. He expects to disintegrate, but thro' the mercy of some curious Numbness, does not. They advise him, as gently as they've ever known how, that Bradley wish'd only the Family near. Any further word will be in the newspapers. Thus do Gloucestershire Nabobs deal with former Employees.

All the way back in to Stroud, episodes of the past flick at him like great sticky Webs. Some of us are Outlaws, and some Trespassers upon the very World. Everywhere stand Monitors advising Mason, that he may not proceed. He is a Warrior who has just lost his Lord.

Day into night, rain into starry heavens, when Rebekah crept from their bed to join Mason upon the Astronomer's Couch, Bradley's wraith stood over them, a lonely, weakly-illuminated picture of himself, compelled to watch them, to observe, yet wishing he did not have to hover so,— crying,— no louder than a Whisper,— "I am a Quadrant mounted upon a Wall, I must be ever fiduciary, sent into Error neither by Heat nor by Cold, that with which the Stars themselves are correlated,— finely-set enough for the Aberration of Light, but too coarse to read, with any penetration, the Winds of Desire." He was insanely in love with his young Wife, and had no way to estimate where the end of it might lie.

When young Miss Bradley and Rebekah went thro' their time of infatuation, talking long into the nights, Mason would come in from Observing to find them among the bed-clothes, and generally no room for him without waking one of them.

"How did you meet and marry him?" the girl wishes to know.

"My marriageable years had ebb'd away," Rebekah relates, "so slowly that I never knew the moment I was beach'd upon the Fearful Isle where no Flower grows. Days pass, one upon the next.... And then, against Hope,— lo, a Sail. There at the Horizon,— no idea how far,— a faint Promise of Rescue...a sort of Indiaman, as it prov'd."

"With an hundred handsome Sailors aboard, to choose from?" giggles Miss Bradley.

"But the one, alas, Impertinence.... A Pair of Gentlemen came to me one day and said, 'Here is the one you must marry,'— and put before me a small cheap sketch, in Sepia already fading, of Charles. Handsome and fine as any Nabob you'd wish for,— since you were about to ask, Princess Sukie,— and of course I knew he wouldn't look that fair in person, yet had I assum'd *some* Honesty from them,— so to find Picture and Man *quite* as different as they prov'd to be, well, did surprise me. ' 'Twas but a Representation,' they explain'd, repeatedly, till I quite lost count, having also ceas'd to know what the word meant, anyway."

"Who were these Gentlemen? Had they come from Grandfather Peach's Company?"

"A mystery, lass. They were turn'd out in that flash way of Naboblets, all Morning Tussah and braided Hats, tha may have seen such visiting at the Peaches' in the Country,— yet they might have been Buzz-men as easily, having some difficulties with the English Tongue, which, given my own, I may not judge."

"Where were ye wed?"

"Down near the East India Docks. 'Clive Chapel,' as they styl'd it then, a Nabob's Day-Dream, made to seem a Treasure-Cave of the East, with Walls of Crystal, Chandeliers of Lenses Prismatick, that could make the light of but a single Candle brighter than a Beacon, Prie-Dieux of Gold, Windows all of precious Gems instead of color'd Glass, depicting Scenes from the Wedding of Lord Clive and Miss Maskelyne,— her Gown entirely of Pearl, his Uniform Jacket of Burmese Ruby, their Eyes painstakingly a-sparkle with tiny Sapphires and Zircons."

"Heavenly...and their Hair?"

"Amber,— in its many shades.... And the Dignitaries attending, and their Ladies, each in a different Costume, each out-dazzling each,— the Clergy officiating,— the Views of Bombay in the Background,— well, it seem'd to go on forever. You could gaze and get lost. Perhaps I did."

"Or *he* might have."

"He got lost among the Stars. Years before he met me."

"Papa is like that. I know. They just...drift off, don't they?"

Bradley had reported upon the Comets of '23 and '37, but not, apparently, that of '44, one day to be term'd the finest of the Century. What came sweeping instead into his life that year, was his Bride, Susannah Peach. Did he make any connection at the time between the Comet, and the girl? Or again, in '57, another Comet-year, when she departed from his life?— though Mason would seem to be the one up there most ready to connect the fast-moving image of a female head in the Sky, its hair streaming in a Wind inconceivable, with posthumous Visitation,— hectic high-speed star-gazing, not the usual small-Arc quotinoctian affair by any means. It would have been Mason, desperate with longing, who, had he kept a Journal, would have written,—

"Through the seven-foot Telescope, at that resolution, 'tis a Face, though yet veil'd, 'twill be hers, I swear it, I stare till my eyes ache. I must ask Bradley's advice, and with equal urgency, of course, I must not."

First Susannah, then Rebekah. The nearly two years separating their deaths were rul'd by the Approaching Comet of Dr. Halley, which reach'd perihelion a month after Rebekah died,— dimming in the glare of the Sun, swinging about behind it, then appearing once more.... Whereupon, 'twas Mason's midnight Duty to go in, and open the shutters of the roof, and fearfully recline, to search for her, find her, note her exact location, measure her. On his back. And when she was so close that there could remain no further doubt, how did he hold himself from crying out after the stricken bright Prow of her Face and Hair, out there so alone in the Midnight, unshelter'd, on display to ev'ry 'Gazer with a Lens at his disposal? He could not look too directly...as if he fear'd a direct stare from the eyes he fancied he saw, he could but take fugitive Squints, long enough to measure the great Flow of Hair gone white, his thumb and fingers busy with the Micrometer, no time to linger upon Sentiments, not beneath this long Hovering, this undesired Recognition.

Up late between Stars, Mason listen'd downhill to the Owls as they hunted, and kill'd, himself falling into a kind of stunn'd Attendance but a step and a half this side of Dream.... In the Turning-Evil of this time, awaiting her sure Return, he seem'd one night to push through to the other side of something, some Membrane, and understood that the death-faced Hunters below were not moaning that way from any cause,— rather, 'twas the Sound itself that possess'd them, an independent Force, using them as a way into the Secular Air, its purposes in the world far from the Rodents of the Hill-side, mysterious to all.

The pitch of Lust and Death in the Observatory was palpable to, if seldom nameable by, those who came up there. "Phoh! beginning to doubt we'd ever get away again."

"In the Tales I was brought up on, they eat people in places like that. What is going on between those two?

Mason more than once had caught the old Astronomer watching Susannah with a focus'd Patience he recogniz'd from the Sector Room...as if waiting for a sudden shift in the sky of Passion, like that headlong change in Star Position that had led him to the discovery of the Aberration of Light,— waiting for his Heart to leap again the way it had then, after Night upon Night of watching a little Ellipse, a copy in miniature of how the Earth was traveling in its own Orbit, enacted by London's own Zenith-star, Caput Draconis, the Dragon's Head, looking for the Star's Parallax, as had been Dr. Hooke before him. When the Star inexplicably appear'd to be moving, it took him some time to understand and explain the apparent Disorder of the Heavens he was observing. "I thought 'twas meself,— all the Coffee and Tobacco, driving me unreliable." He also saw at the Time a Great Finger reaching in from the Distance, pausing at Draco and,— gently for a Finger of its size,— stirring up into a small Vortex the Stars there.

By the time Mason went to work for him, he was known and rever'd thro'out Europe, and in the midst of compiling a great Volume of Observations Lunar, planetary, and astral,— to interested Parties priceless, yet to their Lawyers pricey enough to merit Disputing over. By Warrant of Queen Anne, "Visitors" from the Royal Society were entitl'd annually to a Copy of all Obs,— now,— so Mason had heard being shouted in another room during his late moments with the Peaches,— as Queen Anne was dead these many years, so must be her Warrant, and as the Obs had ever belong'd to Bradley personally, so now did they to his Heirs and Assigns.

Had Susannah been but a means of getting those Obs into the Peach family, and the eager Mittens of Sam Peach, Sr.? Were they the Price of a Directorship in the East India Company? Once there was a child, having done her Job, would the little Operative have been free to return to Chalford, back into the Peach Bosom, whilst her Doting Charge fidgeted about with his Lenses and screw-Settings, at distant Greenwich?

Even Mason's Horse looks back at him, reproachful at this. An ungentlemanly Speculation. Who has not been an indulgent Husband? "Who ever set out to be an old fool with a young Wife?" Mason argues aloud. "Of course he ador'd her, his Governess in all things. How shall I speak?"

Sam could've told Tales'd chill any Father's Blood. His affections, as ever, with the Doctor, nonetheless, when they wed, did he welcome the Relief. Now may he welcome the Obs, too. Yet Mason, as Bradley's Assistant, perform'd many of them. Shall he put in a Claim for these? He thinks not, as he was really giving them to Bradley, all, for nothing more than, "Thank you, Mr. Mason, and well done."

19

In the bar of The George, what should he find, as the Topick of vehement Conversation, but Bradley again.

"I don't care how much glory he's brought England, he'll still have to pay for his Pints in here."

"Not likely now, is it? Poor Bugger."

"Howbeit,— he was in, don't forget, with Macclesfield and that gang, that stole the Eleven Days right off the Calendar. God may wait, for the living God's a Beast of Prey, Who waits, and may wait for years…yet at last, when least expected, He springs."

"Thank you, Rev,— now when do I get to sell Ale in your Chapel? Sunday be all right?"

"Nay, attend him,— the Battle-fields we know, situated in Earth's three Dimensions, have also their counterparts in Time,— and if the Popish gain advantage in Time's Reckoning, they may easily carry the Day."

"Why, that they've had, the Day and the Night as well, since 'fifty-two, when we were all taken over onto Roman Whore's Time, and lost eleven days' worth of our own."

Mason pretends to examine his shoe-buckle, trying not to sigh too heavily. Of the many Classics of Idiocy, this Idiocy of the Eleven Days has join'd the select handful that may never be escap'd. Some have held this Grudge for ten years,— not so long, as Grudges go. Now that misfortune has overtaken Bradley's life, do they feel aveng'd at last? He listens to the weary Hymn once more, as he has from his father, at this moment but walking-miles distant, still asleep, soon to wake....

"So what the D——l is yerr dear Friend Dr. Bradley up t', he and his Protectors? Stealing eleven Days? Can that be done?" It seem'd his Father had really been asking.

"No, Pa,— by Act of Parliament, September second next shall be call'd, as ever, September second,— but the day *after* will be known as 'September fourteenth,' and then all will go on consecutive, as before."

"But,— 'twill really be September third."

"The third by the Old Style, aye. But ev'ryone will be using the New."

"Then what of the days between? Macclesfield takes them away, and declares they never were?" With a baffled Truculence in his Phiz that made Mason equally as anxious to comfort the distress it too clearly signal'd, as to avoid the shouting it too often promis'd.

"We can call Days whatever we like. Give them names,— Georgeday, Charlesday,— or Numbers, so long as ev'ryone's clear what they're to be call'd."

"Aye Son, but,— what's become of the Eleven Days? and do you even know? you're telling me they're just...gone?" Would he not give this up? The shins of both men began to prickle with unmediated memories of violent collisions between Leather and Bone.

"Cheer ye, Pa, for there's a bright side,— we'll arrive instantly at the fourteenth, gaining eleven days that we didn't have to live through, nor be mark'd by, nor age at all in the course of,— we'll be eleven days younger than we would've been."

"Are you daft? Won't it make my next Birthday be here that much sooner? That's eleven Days older, idiot,— *older.*"

"No," said Mason. "Or...wait a moment,— "

"I've people asking me, what Macclesfield will do with the days he is stealing, and why is Dr. Bradley helping him, and I tell them, my son will know. And I did hope you'd know."

"I'm thinking, I'm thinking." He now began to quiz himself insomniac with this, wond'ring if his father had struggl'd thus with Mason's own earlier questions about the World. He invested Precious Sleep in the Question, and saw not a Farthing's Dividend.

Mr. Swivett, approaching a facial lividity that would alarm a Physician, were one present, now proclaims, "Not only did they insult the God-given structure of the Year, they also put us on Catholic Time. *French* Time. We've been fighting France all our Lives, all our Fathers' Lives, France is the Enemy eternal,— why be rul'd by their Calendar?"

"Because their Philosophers and ours," explains Mr. Hailstone, "are all in League, with those in other States of Europe, and the Jesuits too, among them possessing Machines, Powders, Rays, Elixirs and such, none less than remarkable,— one, now and then, so daunting that even the Agents of Kings must stay their Hands."

"Time, ye see," says the Landlord, "is the money of Science, isn't it. The Philosophers need a Time, common to all, as Traders do a common Coinage."

"Suggesting as well an Interest, in those Events which would occur in several Parts of the Globe at the same Instant."

"Like in the Book of Revelations?"

"Like the Transit of Venus, *eh Mr. Mason?*"

"Yahh!" Mason jumping in surprise. "Thankee, Sir, I never heard that one before."

"Mr. Mason," appeals Mr. Swivett, "you work'd beside Dr. Bradley, at Greenwich,— did the Doctor never bring the matter up? Weren't you personally curious?"

The George is clearly the wrong place to be tonight,— no easier than at Bradley's Bed-Side,— so remains he stunn'd at having been sent away, and with such unspeakable Coldness. Yet the spirited expedition into the Deserts of Idiocy Mr. Swivett now proposes, may be just the way for Mason to evade for a bit the whole subject of Bradley's dying without ever resolving what yet lies between them. A Gleam more malicious than merry creeps into his eyes. "Years before my time, tho' of course one was bound to hear things...," producing his Pipe, pouring Claret into his Cup, and reclining in his Chair. "Aye, the infamous conspiracy 'gainst th' Eleven Days,— hum,— kept sequester'd, as they say, by the younger Macclesfield,— intern'd not as to space, but rather...Time."

'Twas in that Schizochronick year of '52, that Macclesfield became President of the Royal Society, continuing so for twelve more Years, till his unfortunate passing. Among the Mobility, the Post was seen as a shameless political reward from the *Walpole-Gang,* for his Theft of the People's Time, and certain proof of his guilt.

"My Father required but four years as Earl of Macclesfield to bring the Name down," he complain'd to Bradley, around the time the Bill was in Committee, "descending thro' Impeachment, thro' Confinement in the Tower, into a kind of popular Attainder,— for the People are now all too ready to believe me a Thief as well. Would that I might restore to them their Days, and be done! Throw them open the Gates of Shirburn Castle, lay on the Barrels of Ale, and Sides of Beef, appear upon a Battlement with mystickal Machines, solemnly set back two hundred sixty-four Hours the hands of the Castle Clock, and declare again the Day its ancient Numbering, to general Huzzahs,— alas, with all that, who in G-d's Name among them could *want* eleven more Days? of what? the further chance that something *else* dreadful will happen, in a Life of already unbearable misfortune?"

"Yet we are mortal," whisper'd Bradley. "Would you spit, my Lord, truly, upon eleven more Days?" He laugh'd carefully. His eyes, ordinarily protuberant, were lately shadow'd and cowl'd. Macclesfield regarded his Employee,— for they were master and servant in this as in all else,— briefly, before resuming.

"My people are from Leek, in Staffordshire. For a while, during the summer, the sun sets behind one edge of Cloud Hill, reappears upon the other side, and sets again. I grew up knowing the Sun might set twice,— what are eleven missing days to me?"

Bradley, distracted, forgot to laugh at this pretty Excursion. "What happen'd when you discover'd the rest of the World accustom'd to seeing it set but once, Milord?"

Macclesfield star'd vacantly, his face gone in the Instant to its own Commission'd Portrait,— a response to unwelcome speech perfected by the Class to which he yet aspir'd. Bradley might never have spoken.

Below them the lamps were coming on in the Taverns, the wind was shaking the Plantations of bare Trees, the River ceasing to reflect, as it began to absorb, the last light of the Day. They were out in Greenwich Park, walking near Lord Chesterfield's House,— the Autumn was well advanced, the trees gone to Pen-Strokes and Shadows in crippl'd Plexity, bath'd in the declining light. A keen Wind flow'd about them. Down the

Hill-side, light in colors of the Hearth was transmitted by window-panes more and less optickally true. Hounds bark'd in the Forest.

Bradley was fifty-nine that year, Macclesfield four years younger, calling him James this, James that. The older man was in perpetual bad health, did not hunt, ride, nor even fish, had married foolishly, had been entirely purchas'd long ago, Aberration, Nutation, Star Catalogue, and all, tho' he'd denied it successfully to himself.... "Ev'ryone lies, James, each appropriate to his place in the Chain.... We who rule must tell great Lies, whilst ye lower down need only lie a little bit. This is yet another thankless sacrifice we make for you, so that you may not have to feel as much Remorse as we do,— as we must. Part of *noblesse oblige*, as you might say...is it so strange that the son of a lawyer who bought and then destroy'd in shame a once-honorable Title, should seek refuge in star-gazing? They betray us not, nor ever do they lie,— they are pure Mathesis. Unless they be Moons or Planets, possessing Diameter, each exists as but a dimensionless Point,— a simple pair of Numbers, Right Ascension and Declination.... Numbers that you Men of Science are actually paid, out of the Purses of Kings, to find."

"Fret not, Milord," replied Bradley, as if he were being paid to soothe the Patron, "— among Brother Lenses, all are welcome."

"Can you warrant me, that you did just now not insult me, James?"

Bradley imagin'd he caught a certain playfulness of Tone, but was unsure how much to wager upon that. "I have listen'd to my Lord insult himself for this last Hour,— why should I wish to join in, especially considering the respect I hold him in?"

"As a Lensman only, of course."

"You make it difficult."

They trudg'd thro' fallen Oak Leaves that sail'd and stirr'd about their Calves. They smell'd Chimney-Smoke. Blasted Autumn, invader of old Bones.

"Here," Mason explains to a small Audience at The George, "purely, as who might say, dangerously, was Time that must be *denied its freedom to elapse.* As if, for as long as The Days lay frozen, Mortality itself might present no claims. The Folk for miles around could sense a Presence,— something altogether too frightening for any of the regular servants at

Shirburn Castle to go near. Macclesfield had to hire Strangers from far, far to the east."

"The Indies?"

"China?"

"Stepney!"

His Lordship, as Mason relates, requir'd a People who liv'd in quite another relation to Time,— one that did not, like our own, hold at its heart the terror of Time's passage,— far more preferably, Indifference to it, pure and transparent as possible. The Verbs of their language no more possessing tenses, than their Nouns Case-Endings,— for these People remain'd as careless of Sequences in Time as disengaged from Subjects, Objects, Possession, or indeed anything which might among Englishmen require a Preposition.

"As to Gender,— well, Dear me but that's something else again entirely, isn't it, aye and damme if it isn't.... Howbeit,— thro' the good Offices of an Hungarian Intermediary,— "

Protest from all in the Company.

"Hey? Genders? Very well,— of Genders they have three,— Male, Female, and the Third Sex no one talks about,— Dead. What, then, you may be curious to know, are the emotional relations between Male and Dead, Female and Dead, Dead and Dead? Eh? Just so. What of love triangles? Do they automatically become Quadrilaterals? With Death no longer in as simple a way parting us, no longer the Barrier nor Sanction that it was, what becomes of Marriage Vows,— how must we redefine Being Faithful...?" By which he means (so the Rev[d], who was there in but a representational sense, ghostly as an imperfect narrative to be told in futurity, would have guess'd) that Rebekah's visits at St. Helena, if sexual, were profoundly like nothing he knew,— whilst she assum'd that he well understood her obligations among the Dead, and would respond ever as she wish'd. Yet how would he? being allow'd no access to any of those million'd dramas among the Dead. They were like the Stars to him,— unable to project himself among their enigmatic Gatherings, he could but observe thro' a mediating Instrument. The many-Lens'd Rebekah.

"Thro' the Efforts of Count Paradicsom, in any Case, a Band of these Aliens the Size of a Regiment, were presently arriv'd in Gloucestershire.

Bless us. Nothing like it since the Druids. They march'd in through the Castle gates playing upon enormous Chimes of Crystal Antimony, and trumpets fashion'd from the Bones of ancient Species found lying upon the great unbroken Plain where they dwell, their Music proceeding, not straight-ahead like an English marching-tune, but rather wandering unpredictably, with no clear beginning, nor end."

"Uniforms?"

"A sturdy sort of Armor head to toe, woven of the low Desert Shrubs of their Land."

"Ah, military chaps,— imposing, as you'd say?"

"Asiatick Pygmies," Mason says, "actually. Yet despite their stature, any Mob would have thought twice about challenging their right to colonize th' Eleven Days.

"Their Commission, that is, their Charter if you like, directed them to inhabit the Days, yet *not to allow the Time to elapse.* They were expected to set up Households, Farms, Villages, Mills,— an entire Plantation in Time."

"And say, do they live there yet? or, rather, 'then'? and have any of the days elaps'd, despite these enigmatick Gaolers?"

"Now and then, a traveler's report.... Geographickally, they're by now diffus'd ev'rywhere obedient to the New-Style Act,— some to America, some out to India,— vacant India! return'd unto wild Dogs and Serpents...the breeze off the Hoogli, blowing past the empty door-way of a certain...Black Hole?— and wherever they are, temporally, eleven days to the Tick behind us. 'Tis all an Eden there, Lads, and only they inhabit it, they and their Generations. 'Tis their great *Saga,*— the Pygmies' Discovery of Great Britain. Arriv'd they cannot say how, nor care, they sleep in our beds, live in our Rooms, eat from our Dishes what we have left in the Larders, finish our Bottles, play with our Cards and upon our Instruments, squat upon our Necessaries,— the more curious of them ever pursuing us, as might Historians of Times not yet come, by way of the clues to our lives that they find in Objects we have surrender'd to the Day, or been willing to leave behind at its End,— to them a mystery Nation, relentlessly being 'British,' a vast Hive of Ghosts not quite vanish'd into Futurity...."

"Then..."

"Aye and recall," Mason's Phiz but precariously earnest, "where you were, eleven days ago,— saw you anyone *really foreign* about? Very short, perhaps? Even...Oriental in Aspect?"

"Well,— well yes, now that you,— " recalls Mr. Hailstone, "right out in Parliament-Street, it was, a strange little fellow, head shaved ev'ry-where, red damask robes with gold embellishments, what could in the right circs be call'd a fashionable Hat, a sort of squat Obelisk,— and as cryptickally inscrib'd. Not that I paid all that much Attention, of course, tho' a good number of Citizens, themselves by way of Brims and Cock-ades displaying Headgear Messages a-plenty, were loitering about, try-ing to decipher this Stranger's Hat...the odd thing was, he didn't pay any of *us* the least heed. Imagine. Stroud Macaronis pok'd at him with their Sticks, Irish servants pass'd Leprechaun remarks, respectable Matrons of the town ventur'd to chuck him under the Chin. All reported a sur-prizing transparency, some a many-color'd Twinkling about the Fringes of his Figure."

"Of course,— for you saw him as he was, in the relative Vacuum of his Plantation,— whilst he, for his Part, believ'd you all to be prankish Ghosts he must not acknowledge, fearing who knows what mental harm. You haunted each other."

"Thus, from the Cargo of Days, having broken Eleven, precious, untranspir'd, for his Masters to use as they will, having withal conspir'd to deliver our Land unto these strange alien Pygmies, stands Bradley tonight, before the Lord's Assizes, his Soul in the gravest Peril, let us pray," and Revd Cromorne proceeds to what we in the Trade call Drop the Transom, voice falling to a whisper, Eyelids fluttering over Eyeballs of increas'd Albedo, Do excuse me, I'm talking to God here, be with ye as soon as we're done,—

Is Mason going to get angry and into a fight? Will he stand and announce, "This is none of God's judgment,— to be offended as gravely by Calendar Reform as by Mortal Sin, requires a meanness of spirit quite out of the reach of any known Deity,— tho' well within the resources of Stroud, it seems." And walk out thro' their stunn'd ranks to the Embrace of the Night, and never enter the place again? No.— He buys ev'ryone another Pint, instead, and resigns himself to seeking out his Family tomorrow,— tho' sure Agents of Melancholy, they sooner or later feel regretful for it, whilst Regret is just the sort of Sentiment that regular life at The George depends on having no part of. The Landlord is kind and forthright, the Ale as good as any in Britain, the Defenestration of the Clothiers in '56 has inscrib'd the place forever in Legend, and Good Eggs far outnumber Bad Hats,— yet so dismal have these late Hours in it been for Mason, as to make him actually look forward to meeting his Relations again.

2 0

The Boys circle about, not sure of him, tho' Doc has come running, as he has done each time, at the sound of the Horse, his own Motion far ahead of his earthly feet, the moment he spies Mason, stopping short and gazing intently. "Hello! All well, Papa?"

"Why, yes." Alighting, "Hello, Doctor Isaac. How's ev'ryone faring here?"

"Oh...we're all good?" He reaches up without hesitation to take Mason's hand, and they go in.

Today Mason is patient, and by and by the two have settl'd inside his slacken'd Perimeter. They live with their Aunt Hester, Mason's sister, and her husband, Elroy. Mason, having ridden up to the house prepar'd spiritually for Disrespect, Recrimination, bad Coffee, also finds Delicia Quall, the Clothier's daughter, in a colorful pongee gown at least an order of Magnitude too riotous for any casual Visit in these Parts. Before long it is distressingly clear, that she suffers from that uncontroll'd Need to be a Bride, known to Physicians as *Nymphomania,* in whose cheerful Frenzy nuances vanish, and ev'ry unattach'd man is a potential Husband.

"You're young enough," she ticks off item by item, "Your Sons need a Mother and I've been tending kids all my life. I can bake a Sally Lunn, whose Aroma alone is guaranteed to add Inches to any Waistline, even one as trim as your own, Charlie Mason. My Puddings are Legend even in Painswick. I was brought up in the Anglican Faith, and with enough

Spirits to drink, am said to be a merry companion. What were you look-ing for, exactly, in a second wife?"

" 'Licia, a Joy seeing you again, till this instant I wasn't aware I *was* looking. Yet I must have been, mustn't I?" At this moment, were he attending, he might have heard, from the direction of St. Kenelm's church-yard, a certain *subterranean Rotation.*

"What a faraway soul you can be, Mr. Mason," she smiles effort-fully,— "must I instruct you, that 'tis universal, upon this Planet, for a young widower to seek a new wife as soon as decency permits? Even wait an extra day, if he's shy."

"Thankee. So have I heard, and keep hearing, from so many well-wishers. Were I not under unbreakable Obligation,— "

"To whom? The Royal Society? A Room-ful of men in Wigs, droning away in the candle-light, that's where you'd rather be, than home at the Hearth with your next Wife, and little ones? And the Custard,— ruin'd! How could you!" to appearance self-persuaded, she draws back from him. "What sort of night-crawling creature are you, then?"

"Oh, be a friendly Girl," prays Mason.

"I am not dramatizing at the moment, Charles."

"Kiss me right now, Sweet-Heart."

"Twittering London Fop," she snarls, making to go off. The Boys come running in. "Auntie 'Licia!" "Don't go!" She gathers them in, flashing Mason a There-you-see Smirk, over their small nuzzling heads. "The time you took for your long Sea-Journey might be excus'd, as a remedy for excessive Grief. But you're back now, aren't you?"

"Not entirely, for now there's something else up. So I may be off again, and fairly soon,— "

"What?" shrieks Hester. "Where to, now? There's no work in England? You had a secure job at Greenwich once, what happen'd to that?"

"Times change, Hetty. I enjoy'd that Post by way of the Newcastle Gang, who languish now at politickal Death's Door. New sorts of Whig control the Appointments." Bradley is gone, that's it,— yet he will not whine,— not in front of the Boys. Nor may anyone 'round here even rec-ognize the Name. "The Pay's said to be good,— "

"Were I you," advises Delicia Quall, "I should stick to the matter of the Longitude, for that is where the Money's at."

"You have studied the Question.— True that in the short term, there'll be plenty of Almanack work, Lunars being the only practickal method at sea right now, and much cheaper than any Time-piece. But soon enough, sturdier offspring of Mr. Harrison's Watch will be showing their noontide Faces all about the Fleets, and Lunars will have had their day. The best we wretched Lunarians can ever hope for, is to share the Prize, which will prove at last a Tart cut too many ways to satisfy any. The real Fees nowadays, 'Licia, are to be earn'd abroad. For the first time real money is finding its way even into Astronomy,— Public Funds paying for entire Expeditions. It ages me to recall that Bradley, in discovering the Aberration, was obliged to rely upon the Generosity of those Nobility who shar'd his Passion for the Stars,"— an opening for someone at least to offer Condolences. None does.

"Where is it this time, Charlie?" asks his Sister Anne, but turn'd seventeen and eager to be out of the House, where she is an unpaid 'round-the-clock Menial.

"There're only Rumors, nothing's decided,— "

"Papa!" cries the demonick Doctor Isaac.

"Tell us, Sir?" pipes William. Their Eyes so round and unwavering.

Mason drops his head. "America."

This is greeted with an Uproar, as ev'ryone seeks to comment at once,— "For G-d's Sake, Charles," Hester in piercing disbelief, "you were lucky to come back alive once,— the Odds are well against you now,— you might be thinking of these Two, for a change," whilst the Boys thump and shout, "Snakes! Bears! Indians!" and the like, and the Tea-Kettle whistles furiously upon the Stove, and no one attends.

Whilst the Feminine Gales rage all about, Elroy draws Mason aside, offering a pipeful of Virginia. "This job in America,— you'll be Star-Gazing again?"

"They want Boundary-Lines, hundreds of Miles long, as perfect as they can get 'em. For that, someone must take Latitudes and Longitudes, by the Stars."

"And you'll be some time away, I imagine."

"I never meant the Lads to be a burden on you, or Hester, I can see poor Annie's running Night and Day,— Christ they're enormous, I don't even know them."

"And the next time you see them? Years, again? Charles, I esteem them as mine, for in this House all get the same Porridge, out of the same Pot,— you are off traveling more than you're here, whilst we'd be happy to take 'em. In which case, you'd have to sign over— "

"Ahhrrhh! Never!"

"Then there would be another Price, that you might not wish to pay."

He knows, roughly, what it is, and waits dumb as a Stone.

"When they're of Age, they'll both be apprentic'd to your Father at the Mill. Standard seven-year Contracts. He'll reimburse us till then, and we could well use that help, Charles."

"Why isn't *he* telling me this?"

"I represent your Father in this matter."

"You? you're a lawyer?"

"No, yet ev'ryone needs Representation, from time to time. If you go to America, you'll be hearing all about that, I expect."

A wonderful Dilemma. Meanwhile more and less distant Relations proceed thro' the Day to come at him from all directions, unerring as Swifts, pointing Fingers, shaking Fists, brandishing Sticks, all with Reasons he ought to stay in Sapperton, vividly recalling to Mason Reason upon Reason why, two years ago, he was happy to leave all this. Back then, of course, he had his Grief. But time has gone on, and absent the *Force majeure* that drove them, stunn'd, together for an Instant to agree, for the same service now, there will be a Price.

The Boys, up since before Dawn, mombly upon the Floor with Fatigue, lurch over to kiss him good-Night, as if he has never been away, and ev'ry night they have been kissing him so. As ever, he is surpriz'd by the fierceness of their bodies, their inability to hold back, the purity of the not-yet-dishonest,— 'twould take a harder Case than Mason not to struggle with Tears of Sentiment. His relations look on, variously grimacing, sneering, or pretending not to see, all recalling his difficulties, in particular with Dr. Isaac, in even touching his Sons. "I am ever afraid they'll draw away," he confesses to his little sister Anne, sitting in the Kitchen drinking Coffee, after the Boys have gone off to bed. "Who would not be? Willy doesn't remember me, Doc is too little,...and what has Hester been telling them about their Father?"

"That you'd be home soon," says Anne. "That you were away, upon a Mission for the King, but that soon, you would be with them again."

"Whilst she's selling them to their Grand-Dad."

"What else are we to do?"

He must talk with his Father about this. I am thirty-four, he tells himself, riding over at a morose trot. Whence come these rectal Flashes? What's the worst he'll do, assault me with a day-old Cob-Loaf? It is further possible that Elroy is making the whole thing up, as part of some elaborate Extortion Scheme, wagering that Mason will never be able to verify it.

"No, that's not quite it," his Father pretends to explain. "I said, that as I'd been paying some of their upkeep all along, all the time their father's been off touring the Tropic Isles, why the least I ought to have's a lien on their services, when they're old enough to work. Young Elroy never knows when I'm joking."

"Well, were you?"

"Was I what? Paying? of course I was paying. When am I ever not? No one else in this Family has any money, but by me. I'm the one soon or late you all come to."

"I meant, were you joking."

His smile suggests, *Soon I shall be unable to hear anything you say, and then I'll have escap'd you at last. Among ye, but not of ye.*

"How did you know about the job in America?"

"The Baker knows ev'rything."

"They don't know in London."

"When I heard that your Protector had died, I knew."

Shouting back and forth, as if above the sound of the Wind of Time. "I don't see the connection."

"I know. D'ye recall, that I warn'd you of Sam Peach?"

"You said he was not my friend."

"And was he, when you went to visit? How'd your *parrtickularr* Friend treat you?"

Of course his father would have heard about how he was turn'd away. That must have been his only reason for granting this Audience. "Gloat?" Mason inquires in a quieter ev'ryday Voice, "having a nice Gloat over it are we, how admirable, no wonder I've turn'd out this way."

The elder Mason smiles at him without warmth. "You're a Fool," he shouts. "Stay or go,— 'twill be me who ends up getting them both, I'm the neck of the great Family Funnel 'round here, ain't I? Were you planning to come in to Work today?"

Tho' 'tis not the first time Mason has been so berated, yet, he reflects, the Cob-Loaf would have been kinder.

In fact, far from the Ogre or Troll his son makes him out to be, Charles Sr. is a wistful and spiritual person. He believes that bread is alive,— that the yeast Animalcula may unite in a single purposeful individual,— that each Loaf is so organized, with the crust, for example, serving as skin or Carapace,— the small cavities within exhibiting a strange complexity, their pale Walls, to appearance smooth, proving, upon magnification, to be made up of even smaller bubbles, and, one may presume, so forth, down to the Limits of the Invisible. The Loaf, the indispensible point of convergence upon every British table, the solid British Quartern Loaf, is mostly, like the Soul, Emptiness.

"Wait till you've had the dough in your hands, Charlie," when they could yet talk without restraint, "and feel how warm, like flesh, how it gives off heat.— And if you set a Loaf aside, in a dark, quiet place, it will grow."

"Is it alive?" Young Mason had not wish'd to ask.

"Yes." A silence. "Would you like to have a go at some kneading, then." Weary more than patient, he expected the boy to say no. But as if the images of Flesh so intrigued him, that he must plunge his hands into the carnescent mass, young Mason presently did go to work at his father's Ovens. Mornings of Cock-crows in the dark, far up in the little valleys and echoing from the stones of town, horses a-stir, stable lads and serving-girls curling and turning on the earth floors, travelers dreaming, wives awakening,— young Mason kept thinking he could see dawn up the street, but dawn had not quite touch'd the Vale. His father work'd beside him, in light from two lanthorns, liquid, softened by years of flour-dust baked onto the reflectors,— watching his son in quick pulses of attention, but aware even so that the lad would rather be someplace else. In the next months, he would speak about duties to Charlie, who'd go along with it, tho' pulled at, the miller could tell, by something else, pull'd away from the silent loaves and the rumbling stones, out to London, the stars, the sea, India.

"Go ahead then, Charles," his mother, Anne Damsel, would call from someplace unseen.

"Talking to me?" the Baker kneading, without breaking his Rhythm, "or the little Starrrgazer?" putting in what Scorn he could afford. Mason, hands in the dough, watch'd his father openly, feeling the pain in his arms, the pale mass seething with live resistance,— hungry peoples' invention to fill in for times of no Meat, and presently a Succedaneum for Our Lord's own Flesh.... The baker's trade terrified the young man. He learn'd as much of it as would keep him going,— but when he began to see into it,— the smells, the unaccountable swelling of the dough, the oven door like a door before a Sacrament,— the daily repetitions of smell and ferment and some hidden Drama, as in the Mass,— was he fleeing to the repetitions of the Sky, believing them safer, not as saturated in life and death? If Christ's Body could enter Bread, then what else might?— might it not be as easily haunted by ghosts less welcome? Alone in the early empty mornings even for a few seconds with the mute white rows, he was overwhelmed by the ghostliness of Bread.

"What is it you think I do, then, when I'm up staring at the Sky in the middle of the night?" He stands there, as if hanging, under a sack of flour, hanging waiting, as if his father might stop work, and begin to chat with him.

The baker cocks an eyebrow. Whatever it is, he doesn't understand it, yet hesitates to start the Lad a-jabbering again. Is it his Wits? Slow-wittedness runs among the Damsel side, of course,— has for centuries. But how can his son so imperfectly grasp the nature of Work? Doesn't he even understand that he has to sleep sometime?

In fact, young Mason nods all the time, more than once with a risen raw Loaf for a pillow, his ear flow'd into intimately by the living network of cells, which seems, just before he wakes,— he insists he wasn't dreaming,— to contrive in some wise, directly in his ear canal, to speak to him. It says, "Remember us to your Father."

"What happens to men sometimes," his Father wants to tell Charlie, "is that one day all at once they'll understand how much they love their children, as absolutely as a child gives away its own love, and the terrible terms that come with that,— and it proves too much to bear, and they'll not want it, any of it, and back away in fear. And that's how these miserable situations arise,— in particular between fathers and sons. The Father too afraid, the Child too innocent. Yet if he could but survive the first onrush of fear, and be bless'd with enough Time to think, he might find a way through...." Hoping Charlie might have look'd at him and ask'd, "Are you and I finding a way through?"

He keeps trying. " 'Tis all one thing. From field, to Mill-stone, to oven. All part of Bread. A Proceeding. There'd be naught to knead or bake without this." He gestures toward where the great Stones move in their Dumbness and Power,— "The Grinding, the Rising, the Baking, at each stage it grows lighter, it rises not only in the Pans but from the Earth itself, being ground to Flour, as Stones are ground to Dust, from that condition taking in water, then being fill'd with Air by Yeasts, finding its way at last to Heat, rising each time, d'ye see, until it be a perfect thing." Picking up a Loaf and holding it to his face. Young Mason thinks he is about to eat it.

21

The towns around the Golden Valley didn't think much of one another,—as if combin'd in a League, not for Trade, but for purposes of Envy, Spite, and Vendetta. Living in a Paradise, they chose to enact a Purgatory, where the new Mill-Money flowing in seem'd not to preserve the Equilibrium of Meanness and Stultification they all thought they'd reach'd, so much as to knock all lop-sided again. The precise Geography of the Water-shed was now primary,— where Races might go, for Wheels to be driven and Workshops to be run from them...'twas like coming before the Final Judge and discovering that good and useful Lives, innocence of Wrong-doing, purity of Character, count for far less, than what He really wishes of us, something we have no more suspected than anyone in the Valley had ever imagin'd that the Flow of Water through Nature, along a Gradient provided free by the same Deity, might be re-shap'd to drive a Row of Looms, each working thousands of Yarns in strictest right-angularity,— as far from Earthly forms as possible,— nor that ev'ry stage of the 'Morphosis, would have its equivalent in Pounds, Shillings, and Pence.

"Yet some will wish but to flee,— to Gloucester, to London, to America,— anywhere but this Sink of village bickering." So, at least, did Charles represent his Needs for a future outside the Valley. Rebekah gazed back, an enigma to him, Eve in paradise,— or Eurydice in hell, yet to learn, after it was too late, where she'd been...his mind rac'd with ancient stories. How could he allow that she might have her own story?

How could he not choose the easier road, and refer her to some male character, the love-crazy Poet, the tempted Innocent? Was he supposed to light a pipe, pick her up, settle back, and read her all at one sitting? Was this what women wanted? Whom could he ask?

Had he gone to his father, already retreating into the unstirr'd Labyrinths of deafness (though they'd been shouting at each other all their lives), had the elder Charles for once showed some sympathy, who knows where they might have taken it? Instead, accepting that he must not love this young man as he had once, secretly, with all the mindless surrender of a mother, loved Charlie the baby, taking Charles Jr.'s arm, he would have steered him down a gradient of noise till they could shout comfortably. They'd be standing by the little pond, ducks drifting, gnats aswarm.... "Is she yawny then, too? Nobody's going to marry you, you young fool, unless there's something really wrong with her. What do women want? A good provider, not some stargazer who won't grow up."

"If the Position at Greenwich— "

"Sam Peach is not your friend. For every effort he makes on yerr behalf, there will be a price, and you may not enjoy paying it when it falls due."

All subjunctive, of course,— *had* young Mason gone to his father, this *might have been* the conversation likely to result.

They found a Hill-Top and pick-nick'd. Mason, she had already notic'd, search'd ever in the smoky distance, beyond the Observatory, and the winding of the River, for the East India Docks. "Do you dream of the far Indies?" she ask'd finally. "I do. I wish we might go."

He'd been in fact just about to tell her. It delighted him, this wordless Transgression of Cause and Effect. Aloud, "So we might." And her face turn'd to him. "What are you doing on the sixth of June 1761?"

Innocently expectant, "Oh, I'd have to look in my Calendar of Engagements.... Are you inviting me off to the Indies, then?"

"Sumatra, if we're lucky."

"If we're not?"

"Dunno. Hounslow Heath?"

"I meant,— would you go alone? Leave me here?"

"'Twould have to be together."

She was looking at him closely. He meant something else, but she couldn't quite see what. "Would we sail in an Indiaman?"

"Halfway 'round the world."

"Aye, and back,— and would we be Nabobs?"

"Alas, my 'Bekah, nor even chicken Nabobs,— though we might put aside enough to bespeak an Orrery, perhaps find employment as Operators, appearing in Public Rooms up and down the Coaching Routes."

"You won't have this job any more? Stargazer's Apprentice, or whatever it be."

"The Work has to go on," he told her. "Down here, the Rivalry with France, keen as ever,— out There, the Timeless, ev'rything upon the Move, no pattern ever to repeat itself.... Someone at Greenwich, ev'ry Night the Sky allows, must open the Shutters to its Majesty, and go in again to the unforgiving Snout and secure the Obs. If not me, someone."

"I can't believe Dr. Bradley wouldn't want you back."

"You see how he is,— his Age how merciless. By the time we return'd, we might no longer be able to look to his support."

"This sounds like Politics, 'Heart. I thought you gaz'd at Stars, and thought higher thoughts, you people."

"Arh, Arh! Alas,— not exactly. Astronomy is as soil'd at the hands of the Pelhamites as ev'ry other Business in this Kingdom,— and we ever at the mercy of Place-jobbery, as much as any Nincompoop at Court."

"Why, Disgruntlement. I had no idea."

Neither had he. "Kiss me anyway."

"Never kiss'd a...Placeman before."

"Play your Cards handsomely, ye shall have what we call the Newcastle Special."

"Humm.... And I shall learn Malay, Hindoo, Chinese, too. I'll be like one of those talking parrots. Oh, Mopery, you think I talk too much *now*, but Eastward bound, I shall never give those patient Ears a moment of rest, and you, unfortunate Lord, must suffer it, tho' count it a blessing my Wish was not to take lessons upon the Bag-pipes...."

As if this middle-aged Gothicism of Mason's were but some of the Residue, darken'd and sour'd, of an earlier and more hopeful Bottling of Self, he tells Dixon of how, one night near the Solstice, courting, they decided to ride South, to view Stonehenge by moonlight,— she close and snug upon the Pillion, wind rushing by, those expressive arms, all his back a-shiver and fingers aching,— presently falling in with the ancient Welsh cattle route call'd the Calfway, that ran from Bisley down to Chalford and up the other side of the Valley, toward the Salisbury Plain,— a day, a night, love beneath Hedges, sleep, another day,— arriving a few hours before sunset upon Midsummer Eve.

She was restless. She mov'd closer to him. "Charlie. It's very old, isn't it. What is it?"

"The old stargazers us'd it."

"It's too familiar. I've this feeling…I know the place, and *it knows me.* Could it be our ancestors? even so long ago, in your family, or mine?"

"Oh, we've been millers and bakers forever,— yet it might be some o' yours."

"We did have relations hereabouts."

"Then depend upon it,— if you mark the mass of these Stones, there must've once been full employment 'round here, and for many Years,— some of yours were bound to've been in on it…but dear oh dear, now won't Tongues be a-wag from Bisley to Stroud,— 'Lord in thy Mercy, he's married a Druid!'"

Their rhythm suddenly laps'd, hearing him speak the Verb lately so much upon her mind,— and more so than upon her lips,— having left her, for a moment, abash'd.

He snapp'd his Fingers. "But of course, you *are* Druid, aren't you,— frightfully awkward, tho' how would I've known, you don't *look* Druid particularly,— not as if I'd examin'd you as to religious beliefs or anything, is it…. So! Druid! Well, well,— do you still, ehm, put people in those wicker things, and set them on fire? hmm? or have you had a Reformation of your Faith as well?" He was smiling companionably, as if expecting some reply to this.

By surprize, she allow'd herself a merry laugh, made a fist, and slowly but meaningfully brought it to his Mouth. "And in Sapperton they'll say, 'Lord in thy Mercy, she's married an Idiot.'"

And as they ascended for the first time to the Observatory, she gave Charlie another of her open-handed smacks upon the Wig-top. "Druids! You have the Presumption to quiz with me about Druids!"

"Don't fancy it much, hey?" He stood with Bags and Boxes, already aching from the climb, yet aware that this was exactly how he'd prefer to come breezing into his new Position, helplessly burden'd and under affectionate assault by this handsome Lass, this particular one.

"Well look at it? It's peculiar isn't it? Are ye taking me to one of these sinister Castles, oh I've read about them,— secret Rituals, Folk in Capes and Hoods? Sex? Torture? Nuns and Monks? Why Charlie, the Idea."

"Hold, I never said,— excuse me, you've read about *what?*"

"And Night falling as well." They had heard an early Owl. "And what might go on in that part, there?"

"An ancient Well,— old as Stonehenge, anyway. Flamsteed us'd it for Obs in the Day-time. I'll show you it tomorrow, if I may."

And what sorts of Looks will she and Susannah be exchanging there in the courtyard of the Observatory, across the wind that bears away ev'rything spoken?— steps from the Zero Meridian of the World, the young Mistress in her Door-way, the Sorcerer's Apprentice's lower-born Wife, with her head inclin'd out of politeness, yet her eyes gazing out of Curiosity.... When does Rebekah begin to suspect that she is there to guarantee her husband's behavior?

He wants to dream for her a Resurrection, nothing Gothic, nor even Scriptural,— rather, a pleasant, pretty Ascent, some breezy forenoon, out of the tended Patch before the Stone, St. Kenelm's in the sunlight, Painted Ladies buffeted among swaying wild-flowers, all then rushing downward in a spectral blur as she rises above the valley, into the Wind, the shape of Sapperton in finish'd purity below, the Ridgeline behind her, cold, etch'd, that should have kept them from Oxford and Bradleys and all that came after.

He must keep reminding himself not to search the Boys' Faces too intently for Rebekah's. It makes them squirm, which gives him little Joy. Upon Days when he knows he will see them, he stares into his Mirror, memorizing his own face well enough to filter it out of Willy's and Doc's, leaving, if the Trick succeed, Rebekah's alone, her dear living Face,— tho' at about half the optickal Resolution, he guesses. When the time comes, he finds he cannot remember what he looks like. Withal, their Faces are their own, unsortably,— and claim the Moment.

"Will there be savages?" William asks. "Will you be afraid?"

"Yes,— and maybe."

"Will you have a Rifle?"

"I'll have a Telescope."

"Maybe they'll think it's a Rifle."

"Going where Mama go?" asks Doctor Isaac.

Someday, Mason almost replies. "Don't know." He picks the boy up, turns him upside down, and holds him by his feet. "Now then, what's this?"

"Me too!" cries Will.

One in each Arm, "I'll need to be at least this strong, in America." Each time he bids them farewell and rides away, he pretends there'll be at least one more Visit. They watch him depart, smaller in the Doorway than in his embrace, and at the Turn of the Road, hand in hand, go dashing off.

London is chang'd. There's less welcome than he discovers he's been wishing for. Ev'rywhere he looks are Squalid Mementoes of his History in the Town,— one Station after another upon a Progress Melancholick.

Mason has pimp'd for Maskelyne, that is his sin, what they whisper of even before his trailing Boot-sole has left the Carpet of the Foyer,— he has acquiesc'd in an elaborate Seduction of not only the Soprano within, but the comickal Basso at the Door as well. He knows what is happening. Yet at the same time, how can he know,— isn't he but a simple lad from the Country? Here comes this sly Cambridge Mathematician. By the time Mason smoaks his Game, 'tis too late, and he is all but pack'd off to America and well out of the way, whilst the interloper stops at home, making briskly what Interest he may.

That would be the Text of it, anyhow,— with Sermons upon it a-plenty, no doubt, to follow. The Pilgrim, however long or crooked his Road, may keep ever before him the Holy Place he must by his Faith seek, as the American Ranger, however indeterminate or unposted his Wilderness, may enjoy, ever at his Back, the Impulse of Duty he must, by his Honor, attend. Mason, not quite grown undeceiv'd as to Places that may no longer exist, nor yet quite reluctant enough, to be push'd into someone else's Notion of Futurity, is thus restricted to the outer

Suburbs that ring the Earthly City,— the Capital at the Heart of his Time,— not altogether banish'd from, tho' as little welcom'd into, that distant Splendor. By this Formula, any visit he makes with Maskelyne is fated to add a public component to what, in private, is already proving unendurable.

"Penance," Mason declares. They meet in London, Summer '63, at Mun Maskelyne's Rooms near New Bond Street, with Mason waiting to hear about the Engagement in America, and Nevil Maskelyne on the Eve of sailing off upon the Barbados Trials of Mr. Harrison's bothersome Watch. The eminent young Lalande, who has recently (in '62) succeeded J. N. Delisle in the chair of astronomy in the Collège de France, is likewise in town to view trials of the Chronometer, and to dine at The Mitre Club as well.

"He's but my age," remarks Maskelyne, "— adjunct Astronomer at the Paris Observatory before he was twenty-one. You, by contrast, were,— was it twenty-eight?— when you went to work for Bradley?"

"Withal, I am six years older than him to begin with," grunts Mason. "That gives him a jump of…what,— thirteen? fourteen years,— better get cracking, hadn't we.— Regard this, we're talking about Lalande again."

"For a Frenchman, he doesn't seem *that* difficult. Rather idolizes me, 's a matter of fact, tho' I can't imagine why.…"

Mason ought to reply, "Because he's too young to judge Character," but instead grimaces diplomatically.

"Aha! Here he comes now!"

"Nevil,— *Cher Maître!*" They are at one another's cheeks. Mason immediately suspects that Maskelyne has hir'd an Actor, a quasi-amateur Stroller at that, to impersonate the fam'd *Philosophe.*

"Dr. Bradley was the Lumina of our little Constellation of Astronomers, Sir," the Frenchman, to appearance sincere, greets Mason. "Lemonnier, my Mentor, worship'd him."

There is a Crash and a great voic'd Roar. A Woman shrieks, and several sets of footsteps hasten away. "Ah, and you'll get to meet Mun," his Brother in a Curatickal murmur.

Who now comes thumping in. "Just down from Bath, Nevil, need a good sleep to wake me up. Met this Herschel fella at the Octagon

Chapel, rather your sort of indiv., I'd imagine, Astrologer like your-self, frightfully damn'd talented Organist as well, goes without saying. Doo-doo doodley, doodley doodley doodley,— well you get the Idea.— Hul-lo, J.J., still in Town?— Who's this? Looks like he forgot where the Punch Bowl went. All in fun, Sir, and let us see what Nevil did give you to drink? Ah!" He pretends to back away in Terror from Mason's Cup. "The Lad means well, of course,— but he has no idea of Hospitality. Come along."

"I'll go along with you," says J. J. Lalande, "I'm off to Drury Lane to see *Florizel and Perdita.*"

"Both of them, eh?" Mun shaking his head in admiration. "You French,— say."

The next thing Mason knows, Night has fallen and he is in a Quarter of the City previously unknown to him. Fans of violet light, from Lan-thorns of tinted glass, reveal silent Crowds of hastening men and women. Odd Screams now and then break the determin'd Rush of Footfalls. Mun seems unconcern'd at the firmness of the Mobility's Grip upon them, once they have enter'd the Current. Soon he has vanish'd, leaving Mason to find his way back, tho' by now 'tis unclear if, thro' an Agency yet to be discover'd, he has not already, Wig and Waistcoat, been not so much transported as translated, to a congruent Street somewhere in America.

22

Fr. Christopher Maire, far from pallid, wearing no black beyond his Queue-Tie, neither wiry nor unnaturally fit, in Manner as free of the suave as of the pinguid, seems scarcely any Englishman's idea of a Jesuit. Yet he will confess, that earlier in life, during his Adventures in Italy with Fr. Boscovich in fact, he took time better us'd in spiritual Work to cultivate a more Loyolan Image,— proving quite unsuccessful at it, however,— remaining fair and spindle-shap'd as when he stepp'd off the boat, failing to rid his speech of Geordie coloration, nor ever achieving that opaque Effect of a Stiletto-Waver stuff'd into a Churchly Frock, which distinguishes *El Auténtico.*

Maire awaits Dixon in Emerson's front parlor,— outside, the traffic in and out of Hurworth creaks, and whistles, and clops. Those bound from Teeside across the Fells take a last opportunity to hark human Speech, before the long miles and unspoken-of but too well known Visits toward the end of the Day, when the cool'd light above the spoil-heaps favors them. And if any hint of the sinister were to accompany this Priest, 'twould be well in that Northern, bones-and-blood tradition, of beings like Hob Headless, said to haunt the road between Hurworth and Neasham, all of whose former Neighbors were agreed upon what a wholesome individual he once seem'd.

Emerson, bustling into the room bearing the remains of the Bloat Herring from Breakfast, directly adjoining upon the Plate an Ox-Tail from several Meals ago, and something that may once have been a Haggis, cries, "Now clap yersel's down," in an unnaturally vivacious tone.

'Tis no great leap for most to imagine William Emerson a Wizard. Interest in the Dark Arts is ever miasmatick in Durham, as if rising from the coal-beds,— old as Draconick Incursion, the scaly Visitors drawn by the familiar odors of Sulfur and Burning,— not to mention Ghosts in ev'ry Tavern, and Cannibals, impossible to Defeat, ranging the Fells.... Seekers come in from all 'round to Hurworth, where Emerson is ever available to cast a Horoscope, mix up a Philtre, find a stolen Purse. Not all his feats are benevolent,— once, out of Annoyance, he kept a neighbor Lad in a Tree for most of the Day, unable to stir, let alone descend...using a form of the very Technique which has found its late Exponent in Dr. Mesmer.

"In Paris," comments Cousin DePugh, his father happening for a Moment to be out of the Room, " 'tis all the Rage— indeed, *I* have been Mesmeriz'd."

"What,— " Ethelmer needling in among a general murmur of Dubiety, "by Mesmer himself, I suppose."

"Yes and Dr. M. was also kind enough to instruct some of us in what he knew,— "

"Mesmer charges an hundred Louis, 'tis well known," cries Euphie, "That's eighty-five pounds Brit, where's your poor Father getting money like that?"

"Oh, Franz gave us a Price, as there were so many of us, who wish'd to learn. By forgoing one Pint per Evening, for a Stretch somewhat longer than Lent, I soon had replenish'd my Funds. In fact, I don't ever recall telling Pa about it, and would be oblig'd, dear Cousin, um, that is..."

"Peach Not is ever my Policy, DePugh."

"I've become quite good at the Mesmerick Arts,— indeed I'm thinking of setting up a practice in America."

"New-York's the Place," advises Brae, "they've ev'rything there. But stay out of this Town, Coz, if you're looking to turn any Profit."

"Brae!" cries her father in a mock-offended Tone. "Anyone with the necessary Drive can make a go of it here. As Mr. Tox says in his *Pennsylvaniad,*— twenty-first or -second Book,

> 'A young man seeking to advance himself,
> Will get him to the nearest Source of Pelf.—
> And few of these are more distinctly Pelfier,
> Than,— Long Life, Queen of Schuylkill!— Philadelphia.' "

"I was thinking more of the West," says DePugh. "Little or no Medical equipment to weigh down one's Progress...the necessary Herbs, in those Wilds,— so 'tis said,— ev'rywhere to be found...and the Powers being already long known to Indian medicine-men, Business opportunities await the alert Practitioner, among Red, even as White, customers."

"More likely," his Uncle suggests, "any Doctors who're already there will run you out of town, if they don't kill you first, because they don't want the Competition."

"But it's America, Sir! Competition is of her Essence!"

"Nobody here wants Competition," Ives LeSpark re-entering, shaking his head gravely. "All wish but to name their Price, and maintain it, without the extra work and worry all these damn'd Up-starts require."

"More work for you, Nunk," supposes Ethelmer.

"We are like Physicians, there is always enough Work for us, as we treat the Moral Diseases," replies the Attorney, "nor are we any more dispos'd than our Brother Doctors to meeting other folks' Prices,— hence our zeal in defending Monopoly."

"A form of Sloth," notes the Rev^d, "that only Brutality can maintain for long, soon destroy'd if 'tis not abandon'd first."

"Rubbish," several Voices pronounce at once.

"Looks as if I'll need Fire-Arms," reckons DePugh.

"You know the Uncle to see, then," advises Aunt Euph.

"Already your Load increases," Brae puts in. "A Man oughtn't to be too weigh'd down."

"Franz told us we need bring but the proper Gaze."

"Hmm. Let us see."

"Be warn'd, Cousin...."

"He's Magnetick," says 'Thelmer.

Most of Hurworth (the Rev^d has meanwhile continu'd) believe William Emerson a practicing Magician. Sheep-tenders have reported flights, usually at dusk, Passages of shadows aloft that can only have been one of Emerson's classes out upon a Field-Trip, for he is teaching them to fly. Toward Sunset, when ev'ry least Ruffle in the Nap of the Terrain is magnified as Shadow, they'll be out looking for traces of Roman and earlier ruins. In the Twilight they ascend, one by one, dutiful Pupils, Caps tied firmly down, Rust Light upon the Wrinkles in their Clothing, to flock above the Village, before moving out across the Fells, following southwesterly the Ley-Lines he shows them, sighting upon the Palatine Residence at Bishop Auckland, whilst Chapel-Spires, roadside Crosses, pre-historic standing Stones, holy Spring-heads, one by one in perfect Line, go passing directly beneath,— until just at the river, over ancient Vinovium, the Flock will pause to re-group. He is teaching them to sense rather than see this Line, to learn exactly what it feels like to yaw too much to its port or starboard. The Ley seems to generate, along its length, an Influence,— palpable as that of Earth's Magnetism upon a Needle,— "That is," Dixon will avow years later to Mason, with every appearance of sincerity, "I knew I could feel those Lines."

"Bisley Church," recalls Mason, "with a history of unending village Meannesses,— false Surveys, 'cursèd Wells, vicious Hoaxes, ruin'd ceremonies, switch'd Corpses...and on into Stultification unending, traditional accounts of its construction suggesting, if not the intervention, then at least the cooperative presence of the D——l,— was meant for a field near Chalford,— but each night the stones were removed and transported in a right line, through the air, at brisk speed, to the church's present site. You can take a Map, draw a straight line from the Barrow near Great Badminton we call the Giant's Caves, to the Long Barrow near The Camp, and you'll observe it passes directly over Bisley, and might have been the church stones' route of transport, the ancient Barrows being known sources of, and foci for, the Tellurick Energies."

"Oh,— well our Leys were nowhere near as evil as thah'...? Flying them was indeed quite pleasant, yes quite pleasant indeed,— "

Over Wearside, here at Nightfall, exactly upon this Edge between sunlight too bright to see much by and moonlight providing another reading in coal-blue or luminous bone,— when spirits also are said in these parts to come out,— so beneath them now do the Dark-Age Maps, the long, dogged Roman Palimpsest, the earlier contours of Brigantum itself, emerge at a certain combination of low Sun-angle and Scholarly Altitude above the Fell,— coming up through the Spoil-heaps and the grazing, in colors of evening, in Map-makers' ink-washes, green Walnut, Weld, Brazil-wood, Lake, Terra-Sienna, Cullens-Earth, and Burnt Umber,— as Emerson meanwhile points out to his Flock the lines of the Roman baths and barracks and the temples to Mithras, the crypts in which the mysteries were pass'd on to novices, once long ago invisibly nested at the Camp's secret core, now open to anyone's curiosity. "The moral lesson in this," declares Emerson, "being,— Don't Die."

"The Romans," he continues, in class the next day, "were preoccupied with conveying Force, be it hydraulic, or military, or architectural,— along straight Lines. The Leys are at least that old,— perhaps Druidic, tho' others say Mithraic, in origin. Whichever Cult shall gain the honor, Right Lines beyond a certain Magnitude become of less use or instruction to those who must dwell among them, than intelligible, by their immense regularity, to more distant Onlookers, as giving a clear sign of Human Presence upon the Planet.

"The Argument for a Mithraic Origin is encourag'd by the Cult's known preference for underground Temples, either natural or man-made. They would have found a home in Durham, here among Pit-men and young Plutonians like yourselves,— indeed, let us suppose the earliest Coal-Pits were discover'd by Mithraist Sappers...? from the Camp up at Vinovia, poking about for a suitable Grotto,— who, seeking Ormazd, God of Light, found rather a condens'd Blackness which hides Light within, till set aflame...mystickal Stuff, Coal. Don't imagine any of you notice that, too busy getting it all over yerselves, or resenting it for being so heavy, or counting Chaldrons. Pretending it solid, when like light and Heat, it indeed flows. *Eppur' si muove,* if yese like."

Flow is his passion. He stands waist-deep in the Tees, fishing, contemplating its currents, believing, as Dixon will one day come to believe of the Wear, that 'twill draw out the Gout from his leg. Emerson has no patience with analysis. He loves Vortices, may stare at 'em for hours, if he's the Time, so far as they remain in the River,— yet, once upon Paper, he hates them, hates the misuse,— and therefore hates Euler, for example, at least as much as he reveres Newton. The first book he publish'd was upon Fluxions. He is much shorter than Dixon. He has devis'd a sailing-Scheme, whereby Winds are imagin'd to be forms of Gravity acting not vertically but laterally, along the Globe's Surface,— a Ship to him is the Paradigm of the Universe. "All the possible forces in play are represented each by its representative sheets, stays, braces, and shrouds and such,— a set of lines in space, each at its particular angle. Easy to see why sea-captains go crazy,— godlike power over realities so simplified...."

The Telescope, the Fluxions, the invention of Logarithms and the frenzy of multiplication, often for its own sake, that follow'd have for Emerson all been steps of an unarguable approach to God, a growing clarity,— Gravity, the Pulse of Time, the finite speed of Light present themselves to him as aspects of God's character. It's like becoming friendly with an erratic, powerful, potentially dangerous member of the Aristocracy. He holds no quarrel with the Creator's sovereignty, but is repeatedly appall'd at the lapses in Attention, the flaws in Design, the squand'rings of life and energy, the failures to be reasonable, or to exercise common sense,— first appall'd, then angry. We are taught,— we believe,— that it is love of the Creation which drives the Philosopher in his Studies. Emerson is driven, rather, by a passionate Resentment.

Upon concluding their Course of Study, Dixon's Class are brought in for a Valedictory Chat with Emerson.

"Your turn, Jeremiah. What's your aim in life?"

"Surveyor."

"What, Fool!— Staring yourself Blind...? Chaining through the Glaur...? Another damn'd Lamentation's added to the List,— 'Oink, oink.' "

A head-Shake, a Deferential Grin, yet, "These are busy times in Durham, Sir, the Demand for Enclosure having made Nabobs already of more than one plain Dodman. It may happen overnight, upon the Proceeds of but one Commission,— for, prudently invested,— ”

“Assuming you know what 'prudently' is, even so,— there are only so many of these big spenders. What happens when you run out of 'Squireocracy?”

“Business can but increase,— between enclosure and subdivision…? why there's work enough in Durham, the very day, for an hundred Surveyors.”

Emerson gazes at nothing anyone can make out, for a long time. “You and your Class-mates all know,” he murmurs at last, “of my confidence in Astrology,— yet here, facing thee, Plutonian Counter-example, must my Faith halt, and tremble. Regard th'self,— born under the Sign of the Lion, destin'd thereby for optimism, ambition, power in the larger World,— yet what do I behold instead, but a tepid, slothful Mope, with the Passions of a Pit-prop, whose dreams extend no further than siting Gazebos for jump'd-up Mustard-Farmers from Tow Law? whose naked Aim is but to accumulate Money, ever more Money, with as little work as possible? Tell me,— what natal Sign does that, I would have to say, exclusively, suggest to you?”

“The Bull,” mumbles Dixon, aware this is also Emerson's natal Sign, but not wishing to seem too pleas'd with it. “Don't think I haven't had the same thought, Sir, but I looked for it in the Parish records, and there I am, end of July.”

“Happen you've somewhat in the region of Pisces I don't know about? For *there's* the Sign of Enclosure…Leonian Fire kept ever within…? artfully hidden…? Aye, of course,— that must be it.”

“Why then advise me, as tha did from the outset, that my Destiny was to inscribe the Earth…? Why show any of us the Leys as tha did, and the great Roman streets,— direct as Shafts of Light's what tha call'd them.…”

“To weed out you who are too content with Spectacle,” Emerson replies.

“Of the Pupils thou've declined to teach further, there are enough of us to form a Club,” complains Dixon.

“You wanted only the flying, Jeremiah. 'Twas never about Flying.”

“What else could it've been…?”

"Fret not, you will execute Maps of breath-taking beauty, which is a form of Flight not at all dishonorable."

"Not what Ah have in mind, tho' Ah do thank thee, may I say Friend Emerson, now we're no longer master and— "

"Tha may not...? I am still Sir to you. Chain-carrier, go,— some fool's stately Ditches await thee."

Not that many years later, here is Dixon in his Teacher's Parlor, trying not to look at, much less eat, the Refreshments, observing instead the wordless messages between Emerson and Maire, and speculating as to who might have ow'd whom what, in arranging this Conference, in which Dixon seems to be some sort of desirable Package, if not Prize.

"I am off to St. Omer," the Priest says, "the merciless Environment of children, the company of most of whom I would not willingly have sought."

"Is it your Oath of Obedience?" The Geordie *O*, as if a Comment upon Maire's failure to seem Jesuit enough, prolonged only just short of giving offense.

Maire sighs. "You have never met one of us before?"

"Aye, mind yourself, Dixon, you've studied *De Litteraria Expeditione et Soforthia*,— show some respect."

Dixon, whose hat until now has been upon his head Quaker style, sweeps it off smartly enough, blurting, "Pray thee Sir, my admiration for thah' great Traverse, is match'd only by some of my feelings about Newton...?"

It gets him a wan smile. "I can imagine how you taught them that, William,— the march from Rome to Rimini, across plains and over mountains, with galloping Horses, Telescopes,— perhaps, knowing your ways, a few Brigands as well. How could it fail to appeal to boys' imaginations? I should be taking down Memoranda."

"I've tried to scribble an Angle or two whilst upon horseback," says Dixon, "— I stand 'maz'd to hear of Father Boscovich's long poem of the Tale at first Hand, that he wrote, as you went...?"

"Indeed, and in Scribe as fair as that produc'd upon an oak desk in a solid house far from the sea. 'Twill soon, I'm told, be printed in London. He did also alight now and then to attend to less literary Tasks, such as measuring two degrees of Latitude, for the first time in History, but,— let me draw back from the brink of Conjugate Capital Sin, and only add, that I commend and celebrate *mio caro Ruggiero,* as much as will satisfy you,— and may God be with him, in his present sojourn in London." His (as many suppos'd) secret Arrival the year before last, having been intended to reassure the British as to the continu'd Neutrality, in the present War, of the strategic Dalmatian Port of Ragusa,— Fr. Boscovich's birth-place, as it happen'd.

"What need of Deity," growls Emerson, "in London, among the Nabobs and philosophers? Stirring speeches to Diplomats...Glass of Madeira and a pipe at the jolly old Goose and Gridiron. Election to the hallow'd Society itself... Wonderful stuff, why aye,— yet what's his game, now, Kit?"

Nodding submissively, as if it had been coerc'd from him,— a silent "Very Well,"— "Brother Ruggiero wishes to measure a Degree, in America."

"How forthright, look at this."

"Latitude or Longitude?" inquires Dixon.

"Latitude. No further inland than necessary."

Emerson snorts. "No Rome to Rimini this time...?"

"He'd settle for a fraction of a Degree."

"He'll get none, Sir. This King will never allow Jesuit philosophers into British North America...? along either co-ordinate, be their motives unblemish'd as candle-wax,— and as to that,— what *are* your motives, why does the Society of Jesus after thirteen years suddenly want to start measuring Degrees again? How does it help you thump any more Protestants than you already do, basically?"

"Mayn't we be allow'd some curiosity as to the shape and size of the planet we're living on?" replies Maire, unblinking, just short of questioning the civility of his host.

"Why aye, so may we all...? But what your line-running Mate Boscovich also wants, indeed openly enough for word of it to've reach'd even the tilth-stopp'd Ears of this country Philosopher, is a great number of Jesuit Observatories, flung as a Web, all over the World it seems,— modeled somewhat, I'm told, upon the provisions made for observing the Transits of Venus. An obvious Question arises,— how often will Emplacements like that ever be needed? Any Celestial Event close enough for it to matter *which part* of the Earth 'tis observ'd from, being surely too rare to merit that sizable an investment...? Therefore,— " Emerson's notorious "therefore,"— intended, Dixon has at length discover'd, to bully his students into believing there must have been some train of logic they fail'd to see,— "the inner purpose, rather, can only be,— *to penetrate China*. The rest being but Diversion."

Maire, face forbearing, shrugs, "This is the Epoch of our Exile, William. Day upon Day, Jesuits are being expell'd from the kingdoms of Europe. Maria Theresa, God save her, is all but our last Protector. Our time here in the West may be more limited than any of us wishes to think about. Even within our Faith we are as itinerant Strangers. We must consider possible places of refuge...." He crosses his hands upon his Breast. "China...?"

Emerson sputters into his tea. "Eehh!— what makes you think the Chinese'll like you Jezzies any better than the Bourbons do?"

"They might. They're not Catholic."

"Nor would yese have to worry about Expulsion or Suppression, Chinese much preferring to,— " Emerson makes a playful Head-chopping gesture. "What charms as it frightens us plain folk," he goes on, "is how Jesuits observe Devotions so transcendent, whilst practicing Crimes so terrestrial,— their Inventions as wondrously advanced as their use of them is remorselessly ancient. They seem to us at once, benevolent Visitors, from a Place quite beyond our reach, and corrupted Assassins, best kept beyond the reach of."

"Fair enough," says the priest, "yet, Jeremiah, here you've a Choice at last, between staying at home, and venturing abroad...? For tho' your Faith teaches equality and peace, I've yet to meet one of you Quaker Lads who hasn't the inward desire to be led into some fight. (Lo, William, he blushes.) Why, if Authority and Battle be your Meat, lad, our Out-Fit can supply as much as you like. The Wine ration's home-made but all for free,— the Uniform's not to everyone's taste, yet it does attract the Attention of the ladies, and you'll learn to work all the Machines,—

So,—
Have,—
A,—

'Nother look,— at the Army that
Wrote the Book,— take the Path that you
Should've took— and you'll be
On your way!
Get, up, and, wipe-off-that-chin,
You can begin, to have a
Whole new oth-er life,—
Soldj'ring for Christ,
Reas'nably priced,—
And nobody's missing
The Kids or th' Wife! So,
Here's the Drill,
Take the Quill,
Sign upon the Line or any-
Where you will,
There's Heretics a-plenty and a
License to kill, if you're a
Brother in the S. of J.!"

At the close of which the Priest unhelpfully blurts, "(Celibacy of course being ever strictly enjoin'd.—) / If you're a Brother in the— "

"What, no fucking?" Dixon acting far too astonish'd, as some other-worldly Accompaniment jingles to a halt.

"Why, happen our vow of Chastity's the very thing that allows us to approach the Transcendent...?"

"Happen," growls Emerson, "it's what makes you so mean, methodical, and without pity."

"Rubbish. You like glamor jobs? travel, excitement? chance to look into any number of things you may have been wond'ring about both inside and outside. Your success with the Transit of Venus was a mark of God, that he remains in Sympathy with our Designs, which now are entwin'd with the Projected Boundary-Line Survey in America. You are a perfect candidate for the Position,— a working Land-Surveyor with astronomical experience. I can assure you of Calvert approval,— that you come of a Quaker Family must appeal to at least one major faction in Pennsylvania,— and further, to the morbid delight of certain *devotées* of monarchies past, your Family is closely associated with Raby Castle, and thereby the melancholy yet darkly inspirational Tale of Sir Henry Vane the younger."

"What, Jacobites in America? thought all thah' was over with...?" Dixon puzzles.

"Rather does the Tale go on, accumulating Power, told sweetly to Jacobite babes between the prayers and the Lullaby,— for Jacobites, like the Forces invisible that must ever create them, will persist. The Dispute did not end with Cromwell, nor Restoration,— nor William of Orange, nor Hanovers,— if English Soil has seen its last arm'd encounters, then the fighting-ground is now remov'd to America,— yet another use for the damn'd Place,— with Weapons likewise new, including fanciful Stuart Charters to American Adventurers, launch'd upon Futurity's Sea like floating Mines, their purposes not to be met for years, perhaps for more than one Life-span, their Mischief incalculable."

"Young Vane was never a Regicide," Dixon insists.

"O, thou Fool," needles Emerson, "he was treacherous as a Serpent."

"Yet 'round Raby, most believe 'twas the baseness of the father, in pursuing the destruction of Strafford, that caus'd the same fate to descend upon the son."

" 'Twas your Vane Junior gave Pym the notes, for Heaven's sake," Emerson grumbles.

"A copy of a copy,— " says Dixon, "useless as evidence, wouldn't you call thah' at least a venial sin, Friend Maire?"

"Wrong!" Emerson feigning horror, "now we'll be here all week...?"

The Jesuit, who has never master'd the European Art of expressive shrugging, spreads his hands. "What man may ever know, how much the son may have shared his father's resentment, when the Barony of Raby went to Strafford? It seems a shabby enough motive for one man, let alone two, to feel it worth another's life. Young Vane was twenty-seven,— about your age, Jeremiah. Had he no idea, of how easily those who pursue the Business of the World may resort to Murder? Perhaps he thought Pym and his people would use it only in private, as a negotiating point."

"Murder...?" Dixon perplex'd.

"Judicial Murder, Whelp," Emerson glares, "— words cost them nothing, Scriveners only a little more,— and lo! another Bill of Attainder or Sentence of Death, both in this our Day common as washing-bills, for the human life figures as nothing,— that being all the secret to Governance upon Earth."

"Whilst Heaven," Maire reminds him, "sets the worth of a Soul at Everything."

"Why aye, unless it be Indians of Paraguay, or Jews of Spain, or Jansenists across the way, and y' knaah I'd love to sit about and talk of Religion till Hell freezeth oahver,— especially Newton's Views upon Gravity and the Holy Ghost, tho' yese'll have to wait for my Volume upon the Subject, alas. Meantime, there being no Ale in the House,— "

"As if there ever would be," mutters the Jesuit.

"— and as in any case I find this standing Bitch quite soon a source of fatigue,— better," proposes Emerson, "we repair to my Local, The Cudgel and Throck." A moment Dixon has been dreading, for those who drink at this Ale-Grotto of terrible Reputation, do so out of a Melancholy advanc'd beyond his understanding. He has not quite made a connection between himself, in his own Publick-House Habitude, and these other but provisionally vertical Blurs of Sentiment, beyond a common fatality, for as many as might present themselves, of the doubtful comforts of Sadness.

Fr. Maire now removes his Cloak, revealing the snuff-color'd coat and breeches of a middling Town-Dweller. From an inner pocket he produces a costly Ramillies Wig, shakes it out in a brisk Cloud of scented Litharge, and claps it on, with a minimum of fuss, over his ascetic's Crop. "There. I am now Mr. Emerson's distant Cousin Ambrose, of Godless London."

" 'Godless' being just the note for the old Cudge," nods Emerson, as they go, "— 'tis the Poahpish, that's not overly welcome."

23

Indeed, one look at the place is enough to reconcile Fr. Maire to the possibility of having to leave it. As a member of the Society of Jesus, he has been in and out of some all but intolerable taverns, among which he believes he has seen the worst Great Britain has to offer,— withal, as a native of County Durham, he has been hearing Tales of this iniquitous Sink all his Life, tho' having till now successfully avoided it.

"Awhrr, God's blood, it's old Back-to-Front," they are greeted upon entering, "wi' two bumbailiffs he'll lose before sundown,— yet an honest Tapster has to put up wi' all sorts,— I imagine 'twill be Porter won't it, yes it would be…? Goblin! bloody bastard, do not even be thinking of biting my valued guests, or you shall be smit wi' the Gin Bottle again, yes y'shall…? Eeh, mind your Boots, lads, bit of unpleasantness there from last night, servants haven't quite gotten to it yet.…"

"Lovely day, Mr. Brain."

"Aye happen that'll change, too. Lud Oafery's been in and out,— and as nearly as we could understand him, he'd be looking for you, Doctor."

"He'll want another Spell," Emerson guesses. "That's if the last 'un work'd, of course.…"

"William, William," his "Cousin" admonishes.

"He buys me a Pint. Where's the Harm? This is Hurworth, not London, Namby. I do Horoscopes as well."

"Did mine," the Landlord avers, " 'twas all there in the Stars, the whole miserable story, but did I pay attention? Nooaahh...I was regretting the Sixpence, a fool with his eyes in the glaur."

Fr. Maire's eyebrows do take a Bounce when he hears the Price.

"Whah' then?" Emerson mischievously, "only the Church of Rome could quoahte yese any better."

"This place is even more depressing than I remember it," Dixon mutters, just audibly, in case anyone cares to discuss it.

"Oh, aye, 'tis no Jolly Pitman," Emerson snorts, naming Dixon's preferr'd Haunt at the edge of Cockfield Fell, close by the Road, where Miners and Waggoners seek refuge from a Nightfall pass'd alone, and where Travelers, no matter how many Miles they'll have to make up next day, choose to put in, rather than enter at Night that Looming Heath.

"There's Musick at the Pitman, anyway."

"Hold, hold, stand easy, we've Musick here," Mr. Brain producing from behind the Bar a batter'd Hurdy-Gurdy or Hum-Strum of antique design, left years ago by a Gypsy to settle a tab, "aye, Musick a-plenty, you need but ask,— wonderful to have Quality in,— Spot of Handel, perhaps?" whereupon he begins vigorously, though with no clear idea of how the Instrument works, to crank and finger, all in a G-dawful Uproar. The Dog Goblin, cowering eagerly, howls along. Emerson bears the Recital with an unexpected Calm, gazing at a Wall, as if imagining the Notes as they might appear upon some Staff as yet undevis'd, thumping time upon his knee. Dixon, whose mother, Mary Hunter, play'd each Day to her Children upon the Clavier, is less entertain'd.

"Ye'd find nothing like this in China, Jeremiah, Lad," cries Emerson.

"Mr. Dixon," declares the Jesuit, "at present, owing to the pernicious Cult of *Feng Shui,* you would find it a Surveyor's Bad Dream,— nowhere may a Geometer encounter an honest 360-Degree Circle,— rather, incomprehensibly and perversely, in willful denial of God's Disposition of Time and Space, preferring 365 and a Quarter."

"That being the number of Days in a year, what Human Surveyor, down here upon the Earth, would reject thah',— each Day a single, perfect Chinese Degree,— were 360 not vastly more convenient, of course, to figure with? Surely God, being Omniscient, has little trouble with

either...? all the Log Tables right there in His Nob, doesn't he,— "
Dixon, having been out tramping over the Fields and Fells for the past
few weeks, with Table and Circumferentor, still enjoying a certain
orthogonal Momentum, "and 365 and a quarter seems the sort of Division Jesuits might embrace,— the discomfort of all that extra calculation...? sort of mental Cilice, perhaps...?"

"Oh dear," Emerson's voice echoing within his Ale-can.

"Then again," says Maire, "there *is* a nice lad in Wigan who'd like the
Job."

"Bonnie then, and please convey my best.— Most Geordie Surveyors
make terrible Jesuit spies, I'm told."

"Look ye, Jeremiah," the Jesuit placing upon his sleeve a hand Dixon
briefly considers biting, "we would expect no reports, no *Espionage*, no
action of any kind,— for the marking of this Line will be undertaken,
with or without our Engagement,— we only wish Assurance that someone we know is there, materially, upon the Parallel. No more."

"Why, teach thy Grandam to grope Ducks...? If we're to have no communication, what matter where I may be?"

The meek Nod again. "In the all but inconceivably remote event we
did wish to reach you,— why aye, one does hear of Devices already in
position, which could find you faster than any known Packet or
Express."

"And...t'would be merely to say 'Whatcheer,' inquire after the
Weather, perhaps pass a few Spiritual Remarks, I presume,— not to
issue commands tha must already know I'd never o-bey."

"I'll send your Thoughts along. You don't seem eager for this."

"Ask Mr. Emerson. I'm but a county Surveyor,— not really at m' best
upon the grand and global type of expedition, content here at home,
old Geordie a-slog thro' the clarts, now and then, as if by magic, able to
calculate lines that may not be chain'd,— the Surveyor's form of walking upon Water.— May your Lancashire Lalande prove more boldly
dispos'd...?"

Emerson lifts his head, the ends of his Hair a-sop with Ale, and leers
at the Priest. "We had a wager upon this very Topick, I believe."

"No,— " gesturing with his own head at Dixon, "this is the one,
William, God's Instrument if ever I saw one. I'm not ready to concede."

"Hold,— am I a horse, in a horse-race, here? Friend Emerson's bet upon a sure thing then, for I don't fancy working for Jesuits,— no more than having others believe it's what I'm doing."

"You see?" Emerson beams, " 'Tis the Coldness, if you ask me,— aye, more than anything,— that absence of Pity."

"Pity? Oh, as to Pity,— " The Phiz of the Jesuit, who hasn't been missing too many Rounds, may be observ'd now in a certain state of Beefiness.

"You are twiddling about with that Wig," mutters Emerson, "so as to draw attention. Pray moderate it, *Coz.*"

"You wonder why I'm stuck over in Flanders, with a herd of Boys, all of them with Erections more or less twenty-four hours a day? a sinners' Paradise to some,— to others a form of Penance. Yea, 'tis Penance I do, for having once or twice, when it matter'd, unreflectively shewn an instant of this Pity whose value you cry up so...? well, I have learn'd, 'tis not for any of us to presume to act as Christ alone may,— for Christ's true Pity lies so beyond us, that we may at best jump and whimper like Dogs who cannot quite catch the Trick of it."

"What a Relief!" cries Dixon, "Whoo! no more Pity? Eehh, where's me Pistols, then...."

"The simpler explanation," Emerson with a distinct uvular component in his Sigh, "may be that none of you people has ever known a moment of Transcendence in his life, nor would re-cognize one did it walk up and bite yese in the Arse,— and in the long sorry Silence, grows the suspicion that Jesuits are but the latest instance of a true Christian passion evaporated away, leaving no more than the usual hollow desires for Authority and mindless O-bedience. Poh, Cousin,— Poh, Sir."

In now strolls Lud Oafery's friend and occasional Translator Mr. Whike, crying, "Eeh! were we having a little discussion as to the,— surely I heard the word,— Jesuits? not them again? that, that same secret cabal of traitorous Serpents, who seek ever to subvert our blessèd England before the Interests of Rome, and the Whore-House they call a Church,— *those* Jesuits? Why, here we'd thought there was no deep Conversation at The Cudgel and Throck."

"Hullo, Whike, I'm told Lud's been asking for me."

"His Mum, actually. Lud had to go down to Thornton-le-Beans, but he'll be back. Who's your not quite credibly turn'd-out Friend here? ('Tis the Wig, Sir,— needs the immediate Attentions of a Professional....) Just when I imagin'd I'd had all you lot sorted out at last!"

"Did I forget to introduce yese? And ordinarily I've the manners of a Lord."

"Which Lord was that?"

"Hadn't plann'd on this so early in the Day," Dixon in a low voice to Maire. To Whike, "Shall we get the Festivities going now, do tha guess, or would tha rather wait for thy Friend Lud,— 'tis all the same to me."

"Was yere Stu-dent ever like this, Sir? One of these big Lads that needs to be thumping away so at us smaller, wee-er folk? Sad, it is."

"Some might find it amusing, Whike," Emerson replies.

"Jeremiah. I am astonish'd. Were you actually planning to strike this perfectly pleasant, tho' strangely idle, young man? And I thought London taverns were quarrelsome!"

"Years ago, once and once only,— all in a spirit of Scientifick Inquiry,— I did, well, take hold of him,— "

Jumping back apprehensively, "Didn't ask me, did you?"

"Nor have tha let me forget it,— I only wish'd to pick him up, and throw him at that very Dart-Board over there, to see if his Head, which seem'd pointed enough, might stick...? And he's been on about it ever since,— all right then, Whike? Whike, I admit 'twas the improper way to test thee for Cranial Acuity,— I ought to have ta'en the Board from the Wall, brought it *to* thee, and then clash'd it upon thy Nob,— tha Bugger."

"I knew one day he'd feel remorse," carols Whike. "I accept yeer Apology most Graceful, Sir."

"Apology!" Dixon's face, as all would swear to later, having commenc'd to glow in the Murk. "Why, You little— "

All light from the outside vanishes, as something fills the Doorway. "Gaahhrrhh!" it says.

" 'Here then, don't be laying a finger on my Mate,' " Whike translates,— for 'tis Lud, back from Thornton-le-Beans, and his Mother, Ma Oafery, with him.

In the days of the '45,— guessing that the Young Pretender would travel ev'rywhere he could by way of those secret Tunnels known to

Papists from ancient times, which ran from most parish Churches away to other points of interest,— thro' that wond'rous Summer, Lads after Adventure haunted these dank passages, all over England, day and night, Dixon among them, walking his own Patrol up and down the Tunnel that ran from Raby Castle to Staindrop Church, down amid whose elegant Stone Facing and Root-Aromas he and Lud Oafery first met. Dixon was carrying a Torch,— Lud was not.

"Why bother," Lud explain'd, "when there's enough like you, who've brought their own light...? How much light can anyone need, just to get thro' a Tunnel, unless of course one stops to admire the Mason-work. Which is what you're doing, ain't it." He had a look. "This dates back to the time when Staindrop was the Metropolis of Stayndropshire with a *y*, and the very Pearl of Wearside. Right clash amid the best pool of Boring talent in England,— outside the House of Lords, of course,— where would this ancient Drift have gone, if not between Castle and Church?— either of which could afford it easily, for far less than a single Week's revenue...."

Lud in his ramblings claim'd to've been up and down ev'ry Tunnel in the County Palatinate of Durham,— some of them connected one to another, he said, so that any who truly needed to keep out of a Day-light so often perilous, might travel for great Distances, all under Ground.

"Ahrahr AHR, ahr-ahrahr," adds Lud, years later, in The Cudgel and Throck.

"Very old, these Diggings,— " reports Whike, "yet never wandering about under Ground, all bearing true as an Italian Miner's Compass between their Termini."

A Knowledge of Tunneling became more and more negotiable, as more of the Surface succumb'd to Enclosure, Sub-Division, and the simple Exhaustion of Space,— Down Below, where no property Lines existed, lay a World as yet untravers'd, that would clearly belong to those Pioneers who possess'd the Will, and had master'd the Arts of Pluto,— with the Availability of good Equipment besides, ever a Blessing. So, beneath the surfaces of English Parish-Towns, Bands of Pickmen once came a-stir like giant Worms, addressing themselves to Faces that would take them where they must...Fire-lit Earth Walls that betray'd nothing of what might lie a Shovel-ful away. Sometimes, 'twas told, a lucky Spademan might find buried Treasure,— "Huzzah, no more of this Earth-worming for me, tell the Master I'm off to London and the High Life, and oh yes here's a shilling for your Trouble,— " And sometimes, 'twas told, the Devil sent his own Dodmen, to lead the Diggers in grisly play 'round the Corner again and into the Church-yard, where Death in its full unpleasantness waited them, a Skull, in the instant of any Spade's burden, emerging from the Mud just at Eye-Level, smiling widely as in recognition, the Torches all at that instant guttering in some Vile breath out of the suburbs of Hell.

"The Diggers never knew what was likely to be ahead. They had to trust the Surveyors who kept above. Remember when I told you, Jere, that they were the Conscience of the Community, you pip'd up, that that was what ye'd be. And damme, so ye were!" Thus Whike's Version. Lud's merriment, even at half-voice, acts less to invite, than to intimidate.

"Is thah' what he said?" Emerson blinking his way into the Discussion.

"Thanking Whike for his good Faith, 'tis it, to the Comma. Lud, tha predicted then, solemnly, that our Ways would part,— that I would find my Destiny above, upon the Surface of the Earth,— whilst your own must lie quite the other way."

"Bit further down," nods Lud.

"How's Business been, down there?"

"Brisk as ever it gets upon thy Surface," replies Ma Oafery. "And thoo, Jere Dixon,— 'tis said tha'll be going to America, to build them a Visto of an Hundred Leagues or more...?"

"Sort of long Property-Line, Ma. Both sides want the Trees out of the way. Easier for getting Sights, tho' Ah wouldn't call it a Visto, exactly."

Lud beams. "When tha're down there in the Tunneling and can't see a thing...?" as Whike puts it, "tha feel ever one Foot-fall, ever one Turning, from collecting the Scheme Altogether." They whisper together, casting quick Glances at Father Maire. "Lud wishes to know," Whike relays at last, "Mr. Emerson's Cousin's Views, upon the Structure of the World."

"A Spheroid, the last I heard of it, Sir."

"Ahr *Ahr* ahr, 'ahr ahhrr!"

" 'And I say, 'tis Flat,' " the Jesuit smoothly translates. "Why of course, Sir, flat as you like, flat as a Funnel-Cake, flat as a *Pizza,* for all that,— "

"Apologies, Sir,— " Whike all Unctuosity, "the foreign Word again, was...?"

"The apology is mine,— Pizza being a Delicacy of Cheese, Bread, and Fish ubiquitous in the region 'round Mount Vesuvius.... In my Distraction, I have reach'd for the Word as the over-wrought Child for its Doll."

"You are from Italy, then, sir?" inquires Ma.

"In my Youth I pass'd some profitable months there, Madam."

"Do you recall by chance how it is they cook this 'Pizza'? My Lads and Lasses grow weary of the same Daily Gruel and Haggis, so a Mother is ever upon the Lurk for any new Receipt."

"Why, of course. If there be a risen Loaf about...?"

Mrs. Brain reaches 'neath the Bar and comes up with a Brown Batch-Loaf, rising since Morning, which she presents to "Cousin Ambrose," who begins to punch it out flat upon the Counter-Top. Lud, fascinated, offers to assault the Dough himself, quickly slapping it into a very thin Disk of remarkable Circularity.

"Excellent, Sir," Maire beams, "I don't suppose anyone has a Tomato?"

"A what?"

"Saw one at Darlington Fair, once," nods Mr. Brain.

"No good, in that case,— eaten by now."

"The one I saw, they might not have wanted to eat...?"

Dixon, rummaging in his Surveyor's Kit, has come up with the Bottle of *Ketjap*, that he now takes with him ev'rywhere. "This do?"

"That was a *Torpedo*, Husband."

"That Elecktrickal Fish? Oh...then this thing he's making isn't elecktrical?"

"Tho' there ought to be Fish, such as those styl'd by the Neopolitans, *Cicinielli*...."

"Will Anchovy do?" Mrs. Brain indicates a Cask of West Channel 'Chovies from Devon, pickl'd in Brine.

"Capital. And Cheese?"

"That would be what's left of the Stilton, from the Ploughman's Lunch."

"Very promising indeed," Maire wringing his Hands to conceal their trembling. "Well then, let us just..."

By the Time what is arguably the first British Pizza is ready to come out of the Baking-Oven beside the Hearth, the Road outside has gone quiet and the Moorland dark, several Rounds have come and pass'd, and Lud is beginning to show signs of Apprehension. "At least 'tis cloudy tonight, no Moonlight'll be getting thro'," his Mother whispers to Mr. Emerson.

"Canny Luck, it may have bought us Time." As both Teacher and resolute Rationalist, *Pace* Bourquelet and Nynauld, Emerson is convinc'd that the ancient popular belief in Were-Wolves, if it does not stem from, is at least reinforced by, the alarm'd reactions of mothers to the onset of Puberty in their sons. Once, at his first sight of it, he was alarm'd, too. Hair sprouting ev'rywhere, voices deepening, often to Growls, Boys who once went to bed early, now grown nocturnal. Mysterious absences occur. The family dog begins acting peculiar. Unusual Attention is paid to the Roast, just before it's popp'd in the Oven.... "Lord's sake, Betsy, what're you saying, that our Ludowick's a werewolf? Get a grip on y'self, woman!"

"Well there's none of it upon my side, is there."

"Oh, I see,— poor Uncle Lonsdale again,— who *was* releas'd, as you'll recall, with all apologies, the Blood proving to be, but from a hapless Chicken in the Road...."

"Yet the Vicar did testify, Dear, at the Assizes, that for five generations past,— "

"RRRR!"

"— oh good evening, Lud, my one would scarcely recognize you...."

"And that was when I said, 'We must go to Dr. Emerson,— he'll knaah whah' to do...?'

"Lud says, that he cannot tell, if you did know what to do. He adds, do not worry, for it amuses him."

"Lud, you're alive, are you not?"

"That wasn't quite his Question," Ma declares. "Would you pass me one of those pointed things?"

"Where's that bright Light coming from?" someone asks.

"The Clouds!" Ma Oafery running out to look. "Where'd they go? Oh, no! Look at that, will yese!" "That" being the Full Moon, just rising into a cloudless Night.

"Quick, the Shutters," squeals Whike, running to and fro.

"Lud, look ye what's over here, more 'Pizza,'— "

"Too late!" For Lud has seen the Full Moon, and now pursues it out into the Street, Whike at his Heels.

"I can't bear it when the Change comes," Ma laments. "It's getting harder for me even to look, tho' his own Mum must, mustn't she?— "

"He's changing," Whike calls back indoors to the rest of them, "— first, the Teeth, aye, and the Snout, and Claws,— now there goes the Hair, good, and he's, yes he's up on two legs now,— he's tying his Stock, fixing a Buckle, and here he is,— Master Ludowick,— "

In trips this shaven, somewhat narrow Youth, a Durham Dandy in Silver Brocade, Chinese Fastenings ev'rywhere in bright Gold, for Contrast,— and as a Finial, a curiously cock'd Hat with a long green Parrot Plume extending from it further than anyone present has even known a Feather to go. "Mother!" pipes the 'morphos'd Lud. "When *will* you do something about your Hair? Whike, stop touching me. Mr. Emerson, well met, turn about, so we may admire thy Buttons,— who's that, Jere Dixon? going over to America! knew they'd pop you one day, what was it, another Raid upon another Larder, I expect,— yet better than being hang'd, what-what, old Turnip?"

"Two, call it three nights," groans Ma Oafery, "ev'ry Month, no worse than the Flux, really,— he has memoriz'd several current Theatrickal Music-Pieces, and sings them to me thro' the Day. He tells Joaks I do not understand. He quizzes with me in Foreign Tongues. Yet am I a Mum,— I can tolerate it."

24

The most metaphysickal thing Mason will ever remember Dixon saying is, "I owe my Existence to a pair of Shoes." His Father, George Dixon, Sr., having ridden in late to Quarterly Meeting,— a wet night, ev'ryone gone to bed, a pile of Shoes left out to be clean'd,— in all the great quaquaversal Array, he sees only the pair belonging to Mary Hunter. Without planning it he has stoop'd, pick'd them up, pretending to move them back from the Fire lest they dry and crack. Who would own a pair of shoes like that, who'd have decided to wear them here to Meeting? Fancies herself a bit? A bit too much? He'll have to find out, won't he…?

George can tell a good deal by a pair of Shoes. As 'twas ever the custom Easter Mondays in County Durham, he'd run about Staindrop with other boys of the Fell to pull off the shoes of any Girls they met, and keep them till redeem'd with a gift. Older boys ask'd for a Kiss, younger boys were content with a Sweet, which Girls learn'd to carry a Bag of with them, upon that Day.

The minute he steps into Breakfast next morning,— so, one day, their daughter Elizabeth will come to believe,— they 'spy each other. More likely he's been up before the first bird, to ask the fellow cleaning all the Shoes,— finding out that she's Mary Hunter, from Newcastle. 'Tis a relative who introduces them at last. "Something about thy Shoes, Mary…?"

"My Shoes…?" A direct gaze.

George Dixon, out upon the Road so much that he has left back at the Stables any need in his Conversation to dismount, canters ahead. "Last night I took the Liberty of moving them back from the fire. I trust they're no worse for it."

"Thou must ask them." He is on one knee in a flash, a hand in each Shoe pois'd either side of his Face. Glancing up at her, "Well. How are thee," he addresses one Shoe, "not too wet, not too dry?" Causing it to reply, "Quite well, thanks," in a high-pitch'd voice that draws the attention of a number of small children nearby, "unless I am to be wet with tears of boredom, or dry from too little time walking out.— Why aye," in his ev'ry-day Voice, "and how's thy Sister?" "Eeh!" screeching back at himself in an ill-humor'd Ogress voice, "and have I started talking to gowks, then?" Shaking his own head, "I can't believe you're sisters, the one so sweet, the other— " "Watch yourself, Geordie," warns the screechy one.

Some Children have come tottering over to look at the source of these Voices. George Dixon, maybe too young to know trouble when he sees it, can't stop talking to himself. Some crazy Enterprizer, helpful Relations murmur, with a wild-cat coal operation out upon the Fell, whilst others wag their heads in dazed tho' not altogether comfortless unison,— and before any of them know it, the couple are, as they say around Staindrop, "gannin straights."

They are already connected in the Durham Quaker Web,— Mary's mother having died, her father, Thomas Hunter, took a second wife, who also died, and then a third. Eight years after his own death (Mary passing under the protection of her Uncle Jeremiah), the third wife and now widow, Elizabeth, got married again,— this time to Ralph Dixon, George's father.

"So...," taking off his hat and shaking out his hair, "we've each had her for a step-mother. What's that make us, then,— step-brother and step-sister-in-law...?"

"Yet that is not the Tale the Neighbors have preferr'd to tell. They have it, that Mamma, no sooner than my Father died, married *his* Father,— "

"So...she married thy grandfather...making thy mother also thy grandmother."

"Not too much of that over in Weardale, I imagine. Step-Grandmother, in fact...?"

"What would they do without Hunter women?"

He is tying his Hair back again with a brown grosgrain Ribbon,— she surprizes herself by staring at his hands and their patient way with what has prov'd to be a notable cascade of Hair,— as it comes less and less to frame his face, she understands that he's doing this on purpose, for her, offering, risking, his unprotected Face.

Mary Hunter was nearly eighteen when her father died and she became the ward of her Uncle, Jeremiah Hunter. He was fifty-four at the time. "Think of it as a Picturesque Affliction, my Dear." "Oh, Uncle…" Did she remain his Ward until she married George, twelve years later? It must have been with Uncle Jeremiah in mind that she nam'd her second son. George Sr., not altogether happy with the name,— too Scriptural,— would clutch his head whenever the baby let out a Peep, however good-naturedly, and exclaim, "Alas! The Lamentations of Jeremiah!" Whenever he heard these words, the baby would begin to give Beef in earnest, and his mother grimly to smile. As George Jr. learn'd to talk, he added the phrase to a Repertoire of Teasing Arts he was happy to share with his sisters. The difficulty was that little Jeremiah assum'd nearly all of this was being done to amuse him,— for he lov'd the older children with an unqualified and undaunted certainty, despite the energy bordering upon vehemence with which they lifted, swung, or pass'd him whilst inverted one to the other, and their tales of ghosts and creatures of the Fell, and the nick-naming, exclusions, and words kept secret from him,— 'twas all, to the unreflective Jelly-Belly, as he was known, huge Fun.

Neighbors came to think of his Mother as the cleverest woman ever to marry a Dixon. She pretended, however, that George was the clever one. "He usually reads my Mind," she told Elizabeth, "and if tha find an Husband who's fool'd as seldom, the happier thou'll be…? It saves thee all the day-in-and-day-out effort of trying to fool him,— fetch me that would you, beloved,— and upon the few occasions when thou *may* fool him,— why, it does wonders for thy Confidence."

"Tha've fooled him? Really, Mamma?"

"Once or twice. Beware a man who admires thy shoes. Thou may love him to distraction, but at the same time thou'll wish strongly to play tricks upon him, which though of an innocent nature, carry with them chances for misunderstanding. 'Tis not a pastime for the young,— I would urge thee for example to ease off upon the Raylton lad for the time being, and to concentrate upon thy Sums. Remember, she who keepeth the Books runneth the Business."

"He's so— "

"Yes."

"Oh, tha don't know."

"I know thee." A quick sweep of her palm down the Girl's Hair. "I see that gaupy Look."

His father died when Jeremiah was twenty-two, a fairly miserable stretch beginning for him then, tho' he never drank enough to interfere with field-work,— something he needed as much as ready access to Ale,— still young enough to arise little inconvenienced after a night's strenuous drinking, having led till now the merry Life of a Journeyman Surveyor, errant all through the North country, one Great Land-Holding to another, three-legged Staff cock'd over his shoulder, Circumferentor slung in a Pitman's bag along with dry Stockings and a small wheaten Loaf, spare Needles and Pins, Plummets, Pencils, scrap-paper, and jeweler's Putty for the Compass,— tho' Spaces *not yet enclos'd* would ever make him uneasy, not a promising mental condition for an outdoor job,— oblig'd to cross the Fell now and again, a dangerous and frightening place,— not only murderers abroad, but Spirits as well,— and Spirits not necessarily in human form, no,— the worst being, *almost in human form, but not quite*...now he long'd only, late at night, whispering to the familiar Floorboards, either to be kill'd and devour'd out there, or to become one of them, predatory and forever unshelter'd,— either way, transform'd.

He broke faith with ev'ry one he knew,— loans unhonor'd, errands unrun, silences unkept. His older sister Hannah married a Yorkshireman but three months after their Father's passing, and Jere show'd up at the Wedding and made a Spectacle of himself. "I'm best getting on with it, Jeremiah,— and so ought thee, and who are thee, to call me such things?" He was turning into a Country Lout, soon to be beyond reclamation.

Elizabeth, tearful and broken, had headed directly for the comfort of her Mother, both assum'd into a silent unapproachable cloud of mourn-

ing,— the boys being left each to his own way of soldiering on, the
Enemy who'd so unanswerably insulted them at their Backs now somewhere, and in and out of their sleep.... George got busier than he had to
be with one Scheme and another,— pulling Greenstone out of the Dyke
under Cockfield Fell, carving and fitting together stalks of Humlock for
another of his Gas-pipe Schemes, re-designing the Spur-gearing or the
Pump-seals out at the Workings. Jeremiah found himself indoors, perfecting his Draftsmanship, bending all day over the work-table, grinding
and mixing his own Inks,— siftings and splashes ev'rywhere of King's
Yellow, Azure, red Orpiment, Indian lake, Verdigris, Indigo, and Umber.
Levigating, elutriating, mixing the gum-water, pouncing and rosining the
Paper to prevent soak-through,— preparation he would once rashly have
hurried 'round or in great part omitted, was now necessary, absolutely
necessary, to do right. He must, if one day call'd upon, produce an overhead view of a World that never was, in truth-like detail, one he'd begun
in silence to contrive,— a Map entirely within his mind, of a World he
could escape to, if he had to. If he had to, he would enter it entirely but
never get lost, for he would have this Map, and in it, spread below, would
lie ev'rything,— Mountain of Glass, Sea of Sand, miraculous Springs,
Volcanoes, Sacred Cities, mile-deep Chasm, Serpent's Cave, endless
Prairie....another Chapbook-Fancy with each Deviation and Dip of the
Needle,

When night fell he would put his drafting things away, back into their
Velvet Nests in Pear-Wood cases, and go out to The Tiger or The Grey
Hound, seeking men who'd been friends of his father's, seeking somehow
to nod and smile them into remembering. Much of the Ale-borne Matiness others were to see in him was learn'd during this time, at great
effort, a word, a Gesture at a Time.

They told him often of things he didn't know, or thought he didn't, of
the Coal Business. Iliads of never-quite-straightforward dealings among
Owners, Staithemen, Collier-Masters, and Fitters,— who might have
own'd a particular Keel and who hadn't but said he did...'twas ever
something, for whilst business Tyneside might be done by one-year Contracts and fix'd Fees, here upon the Wear, all was negotiable.

Just before leaving for America, he spends as much Time as he may
at The Jolly Pitman, tho' now he is more likely to be the Story-teller.

Some are gone, yet are there some who say, "George would be proud of thee now."

"Will ye come with wee Dodd and me on my Keel, as ye did last time, Jere?"

"Why aye, Mr. Snow, and I thank thee...?"

So it is he now approaches the Harbor, down the River widening out of darkness, into a dawn singing of Staithemen and Keel-Bullies.... "How theer!" "Eeh, watcheer!"— the Fleets of Keels carried down and sailing up-stream, the Beam-Work of the first Staithes, penn'd upon the sunrise, both sides of the river a-rumble with, the coal in the shoots and the coal-filled waggons upon the wood rails, the Dyer's Bath of Morning, no redder than Twopenny Beer, spilling 'cross the World east of Chester-le-Street, punctuated by the Geometry of Tunnels, Bridges and earthwork Embankments sizable as Pyramids, the great inclin'd Waggon-Ways, whose Tracks run from the Mine-Heads inland for miles down to the Spouts upon Wear....

America, waiting, someplace. Going out to the collier *Mary and Meg,* bound again for London River, riding atop the Huddock, Dixon sees Fog, pale and shifting, approach like a great predatory Worm. He has snicker'd at Gin-shop tales of Keelmen lost in the fog, never expecting any such mishap in his own life, having ever plann'd to spend as much of it as he may upon dry land. But here it comes, the flanks of the aqueous Creature seething ever closer, as young Dodd the Peedee gives a shout of alarm, and Mr. Snow, in his Post of Keel-Bully, begins to swear vigorously. Already half the Shoreline is obscur'd. Far away upon the Shields a bell-buoy rings in the dank morning, and somewhere closer, upon now-invisible Rounds, yet goes the Bell of the Tagareen Man, ship to ship, Iron seeking Iron,— and then, like that, wrapped in the sulfurous Signatures of fresh Coal, have a Score of Savages appear'd out of the Sea-Fret, paddling Pirogues, shouting strange jibber-jabber, the words incomprehensible, yet the vowels unmistakably North British. How to explain this?

"That wild Indian sounds a bit like poor old Cookie, don't it?"

"They've painted themselves— "

"Aye, black as Coal-dust."

"How-ye,— " calls Mr. Snow, "What place is this?"

"Why, ye've floated to America, ye buggers!"

"Heer, we'll foy yese in…?"

"America…Eehh…?"

"Eeeh, y' Gowks!" A grappling hook, blackened and lethal, comes flying out of the Fret, just missing young Dodd and catching the Huddock. "They're attacking!" screams the Peedee, scrabbling in the coal. And just then, out there, like Hounds let loose, the church bells of America all begin to toll, peculiarly lucid in the fog, a dense Carillon, tun'd so exotically, they might be playing anything,— Methodist hymns, Opera-hall Airs, jigs and *gigues,* work songs of sailors, Italian serenades, British Ballads, American Marches.

"Now listen heer ye's," the Keel-Bully to Forces invisible, "there's nought to fear from huz, being but poor peaceable Folk lost in this uncommon Fret, who'll be only too pleased to gan wi' ye's, wheerever ye say." In a lower voice, to his own, "They want the Coal. Let them find us." Carefully, sensing the Tides thro' his Soles, he steers them further into the Obscurity. The others, keeping silent, may be anywhere. Snow reacts to ev'ry Splash, ev'ry shift of whatever is flowing past. Soon the Fog begins to clear.

They seem to rock beneath the Belfries of a great Estuarial Town. It smells like Coal. Ordinary Water-Birds coast above, quite at home. "Why I believe they're Geordies, as much as huz!" the Keel-Bully exclaims. Nor do they appear the faces of strangers. Yet where are Keelmen ever as silent as these have now fallen,— and why are the Faces beneath these Basin-crops so unmovingly resentful? Snow and even little Dodd know them. Some stood before the Assizes after the strikes of '43 and '50, and were sentenced to the Gallows, though 'twas later said they were transported to America. Why aye, if this be America, then here they are, in company with Alehouse champions of Legend carrying their Black-jacks big as Washing-tubs, celebrated Free-for-all Heroes, Keel racers from the coaly Tyne, worshiped even Wearside,— "Dobby, is it you, whatcheer!"— as if for Dixon ev'ry Phiz a-reel, ev'ry Can bought and taken, and nocturnal Voice lifted in harmony, down his Time, sooner or later would come to be reprised in this late-Day Invisibility,— and the Fret, for a moment, has made possible some America no traveler's account has yet describ'd, because as yet none has return'd, tho' many be the mates and dear ones who bide.

And when he sees the little Collier-Brig at last, her Sails not merely be-grim'd, but silken black, with Coal-Dust,— the *Mary and Meg*,— Dixon suffers a moment and a half of Dread, for her stillness in the Water, her evenness of Trim in a Light never seen upon the Shields.... Was it so, the first time,— did he simply miss it, with his Mind then pitch'd so immoderately further East? Or is this a particular and strong Message concerning America, meant not for him but for someone else, that he may only have got in the way of?

It is dangerous Passage, along the Coast down to the Thames and into the Pool, turning ever to Windward, often into the Teeth of Gales, among treacherous Sands, and the Channels ever re-curving, like great Serpents a-stir. Catching a windward Tide at the King's Channel, beating up toward the Swin, keeping out of the Swatchways and attending ever her Soundings, the *Mary and Meg*, threading nicely among Rocks, Shallows, a thousand other Vessels each bound its own way, desiring despite her ghostly look to live briskly whilst she may, brings Dixon at last to Long Reach, above Gravesend, guided to her Moorage in the Tier by the slowly rising Dome of St. Paul's, to Westward.

Tomorrow, he and Mason are to sign the Contract.

25

Miss Tenebræ, perplex'd, puts down her Embroidery. "This case, Uncle, languish'd in court for eighty years, yet just when Mason and Dixon happen to find themselves nicely between Transits of Venus, suddenly ev'ryone agrees there shall be the Survey in America. Aren't you at least suspicious?"

"You dark Girl. Must all be Enigmata? The Celestial Events were eight years apart,— the Term beyond Human Arrangement. Had the Survey taken longer, they'd have likely observ'd the second Transit from somewhere in America. As it was, running the Line would take them four of those years, with an extra year for measuring a Degree of Latitude in Delaware...."

The days before their Departure are Humid, splash'd into repeatedly by Rain. Upon their meeting again in London after a year and a Half, to sign their Contract with the Proprietors, who arrive back'd by Agents, Lawyers, and Bullies, Dixon, as soon as it is possible to do so,— the Sketch-Artists having dash'd in a few last Details and crept away,— takes off his Hat. "I was sadden'd to hear of Dr. Bradley's Death, Sir."

"Thank you for the Letter you wrote, Jeremiah."

Without agreeing to it, they find themselves, if but for Form's sake, out roistering in what proves to be a sort of sustain'd flow of Strong Drink, in which Mason will obscurely recall being included Gin, and Gin's

Hogarthian Society, winding up a Fortnight later in the unpromising Streets of Falmouth, a Town dedicated to Swift Communication, all Hurry, huge Sums at Stake, Veterinarians in Coaches-and-six, Brokers of News to and fro at the Gallop, last-Minute Couriers' Pouches, dilatory Visitors swimming back to Shore from another precise Departure, even as the next Packet after her makes ready to put to sea.

Mason's Nose approaches the Surface of his Ale, withdraws, approaches again. Presently, "If I only might have spoken with Bradley,— you recall our departure from Plymouth? Aye? He had put himself then to the labor of coming down,— between appointments with Pain, for the final Illness, as they said, was from Gravel. Upon the Landing, he kept apart from the others, even from cheery Mr. Birch, who was ev'rywhere at once...Mr. Mead and Mr. White pointing to various Lines and Tackle and correcting one another's Terminology... whilst betwixt Dr. Bradley and me, silent Conversation pass'd." Mason's Brow clearly unhappy. "I believe he had come to apologize," giving away this solemn confidence snappily as another might the Punch-Line of a Joak (for as I often noted, no matter what Sentiments might lie 'pon his Phiz, Mr. Mason was in the Habit of delivering even his gravest Speeches, with the Rhythms and Inflections of the Taproom Comedian). "I was loading an unreasonable weight of Hope upon that Mission, upon the Purity of the Event. Look ye at what I intended to escape. Rebekah lost, my Anchor to all I knew of Birth and Death,— I was adrift in Waters unknown, Intrigues and Faction within the Royal Society, as among Nations and Charter'd Companies. Foolishly seeking in the Alignment of Sun, Venus, and Earth, a moment redeem'd from the Impurity in which I must ever practice my Life,— instead, even this pitiable Hope is interdicted by the deadly *l'Grand,*— '...not at war with the sciences,'— Poh. In Plain Text, that Brass Voice announc'd,— 'The Business of the World is Trade and Death, and you must engage with that unpleasantness, as the price of your not-at-all-assur'd Moment of Purity.— Fool.' "

"Eeh! Tha were trans-lating all thah' French Jabber? hardly a bonny Sentiment, Mr. Mason."

"Mr. Dixon, I am cerrtain that you, as the unwaverring Larrk of the Sanguine, will find us a way past that."

Dixon's Smile acknowledging the Pronoun, "I imagine," he says carefully, "such Moments to lie beyond any Price that might be nam'd...?"

"Oh, I've had 'em for half a Crown sometimes," Mason mutters, "tho' of course your own Experience,— "

"Here's The Dodman. Might we go in this one, do tha guess...?"

"Why not? What's it matter? Savages, Wilderness. No one even knows what's out there. And we have just, do you appreciate, contracted, to place a Line directly thro' it? Doesn't it strike you as a little unreasonable?"

"Not to mention the Americans...?"

"Excuse me? They are at least all British there,— aren't they? The Place *is* but a Patch of England, at a three-thousand-Mile Off-set. Isn't it?"

"Eeh! Eeh! Thoo can be so thoughtful, helping cheer me up wi' thy Joaks, Mason,— I'm fine, really,— "

"Dixon, hold,— are you telling me, now, that Americans are *not* British?— You've heard this somewhere?"

"No more than the Cape Dutch are Dutch...? 'Tis said these people keep Slaves, as did our late Hosts,— that they are likewise inclin'd to kill the People already living where they wish to settle,— "

"Another Slave-Colony...so have I heard, as well. Christ."

"This from Quakers of Durham, whose Relations have gone there, and written back. There may be redeeming Qualities to the place. Who knows? The Food? The Lasses? Whatever else there is?"

"The Pay,— I suppose."

"Being from Staindrop," Dixon declares, " 'tis seldom at much personal Ease, that I discuss the Unpriceable,— yet, our last time out,— all for an Event that would occupy a few Hours, in some Places, but Minutes,— even with the late War as Precedent,— Hundreds of Lives for some log Palisado, Thousands in Sterling for some handful of Savages' Scalps,— even so, that Transit made no Market sense, whatso-fairly-ever...?"

"You think they paid us *too much?*" Fear of Enthusiasm immediately entering Mason's Gaze.

"There were moments when they must have thought so...?"

"Such as?"

"Oh, eeh, never mind."

"A certain Exchange of Letters? Correct?"

"*I* didn't say thah...?"

"The Letter to Bradley? You think that's what put us in the Stuffata? That when we sign'd the letter, we sign'd our careers away? Yet look ye here, we're hir'd again,— aren't we?"

"Out of nowhere...?"

"Surely we are rehabilitated,— all Suspicions wash'd away in the Stream of Time, all Resentments by Star-light heal'd.— What did we even do, that has to be absolv'd? We represented our unwillingness to proceed upon a fool's errand."

"Aye, and they replied, that we were cowards, and must proceed...?"

"Just so."

"Whereupon we touch'd our Hats, o-bey'd, and sail'd off in the same ship that had nearly been blown out from under us...? We did our Duty."

"And more,— not only getting for them their damn'd Transit Observations, but withal their damn'd Longitude,— "

"Their 'cursèd local Gravity,— "

"Damme, Dixon,— 'twas first-rate work,— surely that has preponderated against one Letter to Bradley,— rest his Soul,— yet, I cannot speak easily, even now, of my dismay at how he us'd me,— "

"You mean 'huz'...?"

"Very well,— tho' as to who may have felt more piercingly the harshness of the Reply, having presum'd, alas so foolishly, some Connection deeper than this hateful unending Royal Society Intrigue,— "

"Their infamy's no fresh News to me," Dixon quietly, "— what we must face is the probability that from now on, tho' we fight like Alexander and labor like Hercules, we shall always be remember'd as the Stargazers who turn'd Tail under fire."

"So might I have done," cries Mason, "had there been but room to turn it,— the irony how keen!"

"Eeh...? Well...I wasn't as scared as *thah'*, tho 'f course I did feel— "

"Hold,— who said I was scared?"

"Who?— Did I...?"

"Were you scared? I wasn't scared. You thought I was scared? I thought *you* were scared.— "

"I do recall a Disinclination, as who would not, to perish beneath the water-line of some, forgive me, miserable Sixth-Rate...?"

"Sounds like headlong panic to me," says Mason. "Thank goodness I was calmer about it."

"Calmer than what? An hour and a half of great Hellish Explosions and mortal screaming? Aye, Serenity,— we'll make a Quaker of thee yet."

"They'd decertify me out of Astronomy,— strictly C. of E. in this Trade,— I'd never micro in on another Star in that Town again. All the Pubs in Greenwich, shewn my Likeness,— aahhrr!"

"I cannot sound why they've hir'd us again...?"

"Nor I. They believe, however, that *we do* know why. In London, they credit us with a Depth of Motive at least equal to their own. They have to, otherwise they but spin, to no purpose. One may be altogether innocent of Depth,— well take yourself for example, forthright son of the Fells or if you like blunt Geordie,— "

"Eeh, aye,— yet I'm no stranger to intriguing, why tha need go no further than Bishop for thah', though there's plenty in Staindrop for fair,— yet are Londoners ever a-scan, ev'ry word tha speak, ev'ry twitch o' thy Phiz, for further meanings, present or not,— "

"They've but lately discover'd simple Metaphors.... Then ye find too late ye've insulted them,— or been quietly classified, or slander'd,— never knowing quite which word or gesture has done the job...."

" 'Tis call'd, I believe, Being from the Country...?"

Mason lets his head abruptly drop. "Yet, I thought I had quite got the Thames-side way of talking, the Philosophical Parlance, the fashions of the Day,— that the Bumpkin within had been entirely subdued."

"In Bishop we say, 'Ye may take the Boy out of the Country,— ' "

"Yes yes, 'but never the Country out of the Boy.' "

"Naa, that's not it,— 'But tha'll never take the Girl out of the City,' 's how we say it...?"

Mason is staring, shaking his head, "What...does that *mean?*"

"Something about Women?"

"You don't believe that they've forgiven us at the Royal Society."

"Nor ever shall...? Tho' eventually, 'tis they who'll look hasty and childish, whilst we'll be deem'd to've shewn a higher order of Courage than the World at present recognizes."

" 'Eventually'? *Oh* dear."

"Why aye, *we* shan't live to see it...?"

"So I shall die a documented Coward. Splendid. Attainted before the Ages, my Sons as well, oh thank you, Dixon, that's wonderful, that cheers me prodigious."

"Or," Dixon trying to speak clearly, "Co-adjutor in an honorable act of Defiance, taken in the full knowledge, that those Bastards upon high would slap us down...?"

"Oh, not I, as Chauncey said when the Bums came in,— I didn't assume any such thing.— Did you? That we were bound to fail?" He shakes his head vigorously, as if there is something upon it, that he wishes to dislodge. "Why on Earth did you sign the Letter?"

Dixon shrugs. "Emerson was right about them, they're evil folk, the lot, your Royal Society...? We had to resist them, somehow...?"

"Or, expressing it more hopefully, we tried to make a positive Suggestion, as to an alternative Station, reachable in time, taken from a list well known to all."

"Your suggestion of Scanderoon was particularly unfortunate," Maskelyne had rush'd to advise Mason, having led him into a Critique of his Cape Mission which seem'd to consist of ev'ry, to Maskelyne, flaw'd decision Mason had made.

"How?" Mason protested. "It wasn't my idea. Scanderoon was ever listed as one of the Alternates."

The little Muskrat. His eyes were unable to come to rest. He paced about far too energetickally. "I don't suppose Mr. Peach has ever spoken to you of the Levant Company...of that lively traffick in Muslins and Bombazines, passing thro' Aleppo, to the Sea, and the Warehouses of the Factors, at Scanderoon?"

"Mr. Peach does business with Aleppo,— no one who has learn'd Silk, can afford not to," Mason replied. "Yet, alas, unaccountably, it has remain'd absent from our Discourse."

"Jews," declar'd Maskelyne, regretting it in the Instant.

"Ah. Let me see if I'm following this. The Royal Society send Dixon and me to the Cape, thus incurring a Debt ow'd to Dutchmen, rather than to Jews, which any Stationing of Astronomers at Scanderoon would imply."

"Hastily he goes on to explain," now says Mason to Dixon, "that Overtures must be made by way of the East India Company, whose Westernmost Station is at Bagdad. Thence, up the Valley of the Euphrates, by way of Mosul, to Aleppo, which is the Turkey Company's eastern-most Factory, runs a private Communication,— Feluccas, Flights of miraculous Doves, Couriers with astonishing Memories, Rolling Eagres of messages, few upon Paper, up-stream and down,— having long connected, to a great reach of Intimacy, the two Companies. For Astronomers at St. Helena, or even at Bencoolen, all would be Arrang'd straightforwardly,— a clear Debt of Gratitude. But for Services of any 'Complexity,'— well, the Fees start going up,— the Company's Duty is not so clear. Particularly as the Turkey Company's route to India goes on losing custom to the Fleets that Honorable John keeps a-slinging each Day 'round the Cape into those prodigious Winds,— and whilst Janissaries, Sherifs, and Ottomans struggle to determine who shall rule over the Decline."

"What would Jews have requir'd of them, that Dutchmen would not?"

"Is...is this another Riddle?"

"Not wishing this to be taken as any but a Twinge of Curiosity," says Dixon, "— why has ev'ry Observation site propos'd by the Royal Society prov'd to be a Factory, or Consulate, or other Agency of some royally Charter'd Company?"

"Excuse me? you'd rather be dropp'd blindly, into a Forest on some little-known Continent, perhaps?— no Perimeters,— nor indeed chances of surviving,— in-Tree-guing, as the Monkey said. I think not. Philosophick Work, to proceed at all smartly, wouldn't you agree, requires a controll'd working-space. Charter'd Companies are the ideal Agents to provide that, be the Shore Sumatran or Levantine, or wherever globally, what matter?— Control of the Company Perimeter is ever implicit.

"In any case," says Mason to Dixon, "both Pennsylvania and Maryland are Charter'd Companies as well, if it comes to that. Charter'd Companies may indeed be the form the World has now increasingly begun to take."

"And I thought 'twas a Spheroid...?"

"Play, play,— trouble yourself not with these matters." Mason shivers. "Yet, I never told you how much I admir'd you, for going back to the

Cape,— for me, a Journey impossible. Should some Mischievous Power, in this World or Another, sentence me to repeat the Experience,— and knowing what I know now,— "

"There's the Catch, of course," Dixon pretending to be calm.

"What.— "

"Knowing what tha know now. Tha won't. That's part of the Price,— to drink from Lethe, and lose all thy Memories. Tha'll be considering the next World brand new,— nawh...? never seen thah' before!— and tha'll go ahead and make the same mistakes, unless tha've brought along a Remembrancer, as some would say a Conscience...? something stash'd in thy Boot-Strap to get thee going upon a cold Day,— and cold shall it be,— a part of thy Soul that doesn't depend on Memories, that lies further than Memories...?"

Mason regards him carefully. Something has happen'd, back in Durham. He puts on a stuffy Manner, that Dixon might rise to. "We don't have that in the Church."

"Why aye, you do...? If there were as much Silence in thy Masses, as in our Meetings, 'twould be evident even to thee."

"You're saying we jabber too much for you? no time to meditate, not Hindoo enough?— Bad Musick, too, I collect. Well. Any silences in *my* Church, thank you, are the sort most of us can't wait for to be over. All our worries, usually kept at bay by that protective Murmur of Sound, ye see, come rushing in,— Women, Work, Health, the Authorities,— anything but what you're talking about,— whatever that be."

"Mason,— shall we argue Religious Matters?"

"Good Christ. Dixon. What are we about?"

Two

America

26

For fourscore years, the Boundary Dispute
Had lain in Chancery, irresolute,
As Penns and Baltimores were born, and pass'd,
And nothing ever seem'd to move too fast.
Tho' Maryland's case be stronger on the Merits,
Yet Penn's the Friend at Court of certain Ferrets,
Who'll worry ev'ry dimly doubtful Acre
(The betting in the Clubs is with the Quaker).
Let Judges judge, and Lawyers have their Day,
Yet soon or late, the Line will find its Way,
For Skies grow thick with aviating Swine,
Ere men pass up the chance to draw a Line.
So, one day, into Delaware's great Basin,
With strange Machinery sail Mr. Mason,
And Mr. Dixon, by the Falmouth Packet,
Connected, as with some invis'ble Bracket,—
Sharing a Fate, directed by the Stars,
To mark the Earth with geometrick Scars.

— Timothy Tox, *The Line*

From the shore they will hear Milkmaids quarreling and cowbells a-clank, and dogs, and Babies old and new,— Hammers upon Nails, Wives upon Husbands, the ring of Pot-lids, the jingling of Draft-chains, a rifle-shot from a stretch of woods, lengthily crackling tree to tree and across the water.... An animal will come to a Headland, and stand, regarding them with narrowly set Eyes that glow a Moment. Its Face slowly turning as they pass. America.

At sunset they raise the Capes of Delaware, and lie to for the Night in Whorekill Road, just inside Cape Henlopen. The Astronomers hear Rails whistling, and a feral screaming in the Brakes, that the one imagines as Heat, and the other as Slaughter, tho' they do not discuss this. Somewhere a Channel-Buoy rings, reports arrive all night of Lights upon the Shore...Sailors prowl the Decks, losing Sleep. The sunrise comes chaste beyond all easy Wit. The Coffee is brew'd once, and then pour'd thro' its own Grounds again, by Shorty, the Cook. Among the morning Breezes, Capt. Falconer works his Vessel back out between the Hen-and-Chickens and the Shears, to the main Channel, and with a Pilot willing to take Packet-Wages aboard, begins threading among the bars and Flats of Delaware Bay, toward New Castle, where the Bay, narrow'd by then to a River, takes its great ninety-degree turn Eastward,— the Town wheeling away to larboard brick, white, grayish blue of a precise shade neither Astronomer has ever seen, Citizens and their Children waving, horses a-clop upon the paving-stones, white publick Trim-work shifting like Furniture upon the Sky.

Children, at that time Philadelphia was second only to London, as the greatest of English-speaking cities. The Ships' Landing ran well up into the Town, by way of Dock Creek, so that the final Approach was like being reach'd out to, the Wind baffl'd, a slow embrace of Brickwork, as the Town came to swallow one by one their Oceanick Degrees of freedom,— once as many as a Compass box'd, and now, as they single up all lines, as they secure from Sea-Detail, as they come to rest, none. Here is Danger's own Home-Port, where mates swallow the Anchor and have fatal failures of judgment. Where a Sailor who goes up an Alley may not return the same Swab at all.

'Tis the middle of November, though seeming not much different from a late English summer. It is an overcast Evening, rain in the Offing. In a street nearby, oysters from the Delaware shore are being cried by the Waggon-load. The Surveyors stand together at the Quarter-deck, Mason in gray stockings, brown breeches, and snuff-color'd Coat with pinchbeck buttons,— Dixon in red coat, Breeches, and boots, and a Hat with a severely Military rake to it,— waiting the Instruments, both, now, more keenly than at any time during this late sea-passage, feeling like Super-cargo, pos'd not before wild seas or exotick landscapes, but among Objects of Oceanick Commerce,— as all 'round them Sailors and Dock-men labor, nets lift and sway as if by themselves, bulging with casks of nails and jellied eels, British biscuit and buttons for your waistcoat, Ton-icks, Colognes, golden Provolones. Upon the docks a mighty Bustling proceeds, as Waggon-drivers mingle with higher-born couples in Italian chaises, Negroes with hand-barrows, Irish servants with cargo of all sorts upon their backs, running Dogs, rooting Hogs, and underfoot lies all the debris of global Traffick, shreds of spices and teas and coffee-berries, splashes of Geneva gin and Queen-of-Hungary water, oranges and shad-docks fallen and squash'd, seeds that have sprouted between the cob-blestones, Pills Balsamic and Universal, ground and scatter'd, down where the Flies convene, and the Spadger hops.

Stevedores are carrying trunks down the planks, or rolling Barrels down into waggons, where Horses, not much different from British farm horses, stand awaiting loads and journeys. Thoroughbred Cousins clitter-clatter in, hauling an open Carriage-Load of artfully dressed Maidens, who do not seem to be related to anyone on board, coming prancingly alongside, smiling and waving at everyone they can see. These are Philadelphia girls,— who, in the article of reckless Flirtation, the Sur-veyors will discover, put all the stoep-sitters of Cape Town quite in Eclipse. Dixon, playing the rural booby, grins and waves his hat. "Whatcheer, Poll, is it Thoo?"

> Philadelphia Girls,
> Philadelphia Ways,
> Heavenly Sights,
> Schuylkill-side Nights, and
> Phila-delphia Days…

Debarking passengers are scrutiniz'd by dock-side visitors with vary-ing Motives. Some are actually there to meet Passengers. Some have come to gather information. Others with an interest in the category of traveler term'd "unwary" have pass'd the Morning perfecting before pocket mirrors images of guilelessness. Appropriate Elements hover about the cargoes of small but interesting items such as Gemstones and Medicines, with Pilferage in mind. Vendors of all sorts have set up to address the Sailors, three weeks at sea. Those who do not stroll these Pitches one by one, ignore them, streaking past, eager to be in to Town before Evening's first illuminate Windows....

"Pass it by, Lads, 'tis not for you,— why should you ever need this marvelous Potion, prais'd by the most successful lovers of all time,— you there, ye've heard of Don Juan? Casanova? and how about Old Q, the Star of Piccadilly? What d'ye think keeps *him* so Brisk, eh?"

"Milkmaid in Your Pocket, right here Jack me Boy,— Milkmaid in Your Pocket,"— proving to be a curious portable Cup, equipp'd with a simple Siphon, for carrying about the Liquid of one's Choice, upon which one may then suck, "— whatever the Circs, during a card-game, out in the Street, back in the Ship."

"Her name is Graziana, Lads, a Daughter of Naples,— you that's been to Naples, heh, heh, and you that haven't, why this is your chance! she may not speak a word of English, but there's something she *can* do, and she's doing it right now! See her handle it,— see her flatten it,— see her toss it twirling in the Air, with all the female exuberance of her Race, and we haven't even gotten to the *Scamozz'* yet!"

"The Sign upon the Waggon says it all, Boys, 'Heaven or Bust,' those're the choices, you've been out around the World and you know it's true,— now what are you going to do about it? Go in another Tavern, follow like a train'd Dog another flashing of Satinette, wait one Card too many to gather up even a few small Coins,— stumble back to the Ship, single up all lines, out once again into certain Danger. What do you think Jesus feels like, when he sees you missing another Chance like that? Oh, He's watchin'. He knows."

The Revd MacClenaghan, a rousing Evangelist said to be much in the Whitefield Mold, has just been through Town, and the effects of his Passage appear everywhere. Snooty urban Anglicans for whom Christ has figured as a distant, minor Saint are suddenly upon the streets with their Wigs askew, singing original Hymns about rebirth in his Blood. Presbyterians in great Conestoga Waggons haunt the Approaches to taverns and inns, gathering up sinners of all degrees and persuasions, taking them far out into the Country, and subjecting them to intense sermonizing until they either escape, go to sleep, or find the true turning of Heart that needs no Authentication. Even Quakers are out in the Street, bargaining with unexpected pugnacity, for a share of this Population suddenly rous'd into Christliness.

"The New Religion had crested better than twenty years before," the Rev[d] Cherrycoke explains, "— by the 'sixties we were well into a Descent, that grew more vertiginous with the days, ever toward some great Trough whose terrible Depth no one knew."

"Or, 'yet knows.'" The intermittently gloomy Ethelmer. As so often, the Rev[d] finds himself looking for Tenebræ's reactions to the thoughts of her Cousin the University man. "All respect, Sir, wouldn't the scientifick thing have been to keep note, through the years after, of those claiming rebirth in Christ? To see how they did,— how long the certainty lasted? To see who was telling the truth, and how much of it?"

"Oh, there were scoundrels about, to be sure," says the Rev[d], "claiming falsely for purposes of Commerce, an Awakening they would not have recogniz'd had it shouted to them by Name. But enough people had shar'd the experience, that Charlatans were easily expos'd. That was the curious thing. So many, having been thro' it together.

"You should have seen this place the time Whitefield came. All Philadelphia, delirious with Psalms. People standing up on Ladders at the Church Windows, Torch-light bright as Midday. Direct experience of Christ, hitherto the painfully earn'd privilege of Hermits in the desert, was in the Instant, amid the best farmland on Earth, being freely given to a great Town of Burghers and Churchfolk.— They need only accept. How could the world have remain'd right-side-up after days like those? 'Twas the Holy Ghost, conducting its own Settlement of America. George the Third might claim it, but 'twas the Ghost that rul'd, and rules yet, even in Deistic times."

"Say." DePugh considering. "No wonder there was a Revolution."

"Hmph. Some Revolution," remarks Euphrenia.

"Why, Euph!" cries her sister.

"How not?" protests Ethelmer. "Excuse me, Ma'am,— but as you must appreciate how even *your* sort of Musick is changing, recall what

Plato said in his 'Republick',— 'When the Forms of Musick change, 'tis a Promise of civil Disorder.' "

"I believe his Quarrel was with the Dithyrambists," the Rev^d smoothly puts in, "— who were not *changing* the Forms of Song, he felt, so much as mixing up one with another, or abandoning them altogether, as their madness might dictate."

"Just what I keep listening for, 'Thelmer," Euphrenia nods, "in the songs and hymns of your own American day, yet do I seek in vain after madness, and Rapture,— hearing but a careful attending to the same Forms, the same Interests, as of old,— and have you noticed the way ev'rything, suddenly, has begun to gravitate toward B-flat major? *That's* a sign of trouble ahead. Marches and Anthems, for Triumphs that have not yet been made real. Already 'tis possible to walk the streets of New-York, passing among Buskers and Mongers, from one street-air to the next, and whistle along, and never have to change Key from B flat major."

"Ah. And yet…If I may?" The young man seats himself at the Clavier, and arpeggiates a few major chords. "In C, if ye like,— here is something the fellows sing at University, when we are off being merry,— 'To Anacreon in Heaven' 's its Name,— I'll spare ye the words, lest the Innocence of any Ear in the Room, be assaulted." Tenebræ has invented and refin'd a way of rolling her eyes, undetectable to any save her Target, upon whom the effect is said to be devastating. Ethelmer's reaction is not easy to detect, save that he is blinking rapidly, and forgets, for a moment, where Middle C is.

The Air he plays to them would be martial but for its Tempo, being more that of a Minuet,— thirty-two Measures in all,— which by its end has feet tapping and necks a-sway. "Here, I say, is the New Form in its Essence,— Four Stanzas,— sentimentally speaking, a 'Sandwich,' with the third eight 'Bars' as the Filling,— that Phrase," playing it, "ascending like a Sky-Rocket, its appeal to the Emotions primitive as any experienced in the Act of— "

"Cousin?— "

"— of, of Eating, that's all I was going to say…," hands spread in gawky appeal.

She shakes her Finger at him, tho' as the Rev^d can easily see, in nought but Play.

"And this is the sort of thing you lads are up to," he avuncularly rumbles, "out there over Delaware? Anatomizing your own drinking songs!— is nothing sacred, and is there not but a small skipping Dance-step, till ye be questioning earthly, nay, Heavenly, Powers?"

"Something's a-stir in Musick, anyway," quickly inserts Aunt Euphy, "— most of the new pieces us'd to be one Dance-Tune after another, or, for the Morning Next, a similar Enchainment of Hymns,— no connection, Gigue, Sarabande, Bourrée, la la la well a-trip thro' the Zinnias of Life, and how merry, of course,— but 'my' stuff, 'Thelmer,"— waving a Sheaf of Musick-Sheets,— "all is become Departure, and sentimental Crisis,— the Sandwich-Filling it seems,— and at last, Return to the Tonick, safe at Home, no need even to play loud at the end.— Mason and Dixon's West Line," Aunt Euphrenia setting her Oboe carefully upon the arm of her Chair, "in fact, shares this modern Quality of Departure and Return, wherein, year upon Year, the *Ritornelli* are not merely the same notes again and again, but variant each time, as Clocks have tick'd onward, Chance has dealt fair and foul, Life, willy-nilly, has been liv'd through...."

"As to journey west," adds the Rev^d helpfully, "in the same sense as the Sun, is to live, raise Children, grow older, and die, carried along by the Stream of the Day,— whilst to turn Eastward, is somehow to resist time and age, to work against the Wind, seek ever the dawn, even, as who can say, defy Death."

"A drama guaranteed ev'ry time a Reedwoman picks up her Instrument, Wick-Wax,— a Novel in Musick, whose Hero instead of proceeding down the road having one adventure after another, with no end in view, comes rather through some Catastrophe and back to where she set out from."

"No place like home, eh?" guffaws Lomax LeSpark.

"Doesn't sound too revolutionary to me," declares Uncle Ives. "Sounds like a good sermon aim'd at keeping the Country-People in their place."

"That's because you ain't hearing it aright, Nunk. 'Tis the Elder World, Turn'd Upside Down," Ethelmer banging out a fragment of the tune of that Title, play'd at the surrender of Cornwallis, " 'Tis a lengthy step in human wisdom, Sir."

"*Oh* dear oh dear, beware then," the Rev^d groans in a manner he has learn'd, if challenged, to pass off as Stomach distress. Ethelmer seems dangerous to him somehow, and not only because of Tenebræ,— toward whom these days he is undergoing Deep Avuncularity, with its own Jangle of Sentiments pure and impure. Yet, leaving all that out, there remains to the Boy a residue of Worldliness notable even in this Babylon of post-war Philadelphia,— a step past Deism, a purpos'd Disconnection from Christ....

"...South Philadelphia Ballad-singers," Ethelmer has meanwhile been instructing the Room, "generally Tenors, who are said, in their Succession, to constitute a Chapter in the secret History of a Musick yet to be, if not the Modal change Plato fear'd, then one he did not foresee."

"Not even he." His mathematickal cousin DePugh is disquieted.

"My point exactly!" cries Ethelmer, who has been edging toward the Spirits, mindful that at some point he shall have to edge past his Cousin Tenebræ. " 'Tis ever the sign of Revolutionary times, that Street-Airs become Hymns, and Roist'ring-Songs Anthems,— just as Plato fear'd,— hast heard the Negroe Musick, the flatted Fifths, the vocal *portamenti,—* 'tis there sings your Revolution. These late ten American Years were but Slaughter of this sort and that. Now begins the true Inversion of the World."

"Don't know, Coz. Much of your Faith seems invested in this novel Musick,— "

"Where better?" asks young Ethelmer confidently. "Is it not the very Rhythm of the Engines, the Clamor of the Mills, the Rock of the Oceans, the Roll of the Drums in the Night, why if one wish'd to give it a Name,— "

"Surf Music!" DePugh cries.

"Percussion," Brae, sweet as a Pie.

"Very well to both of ye,— nonetheless,— as you, DePugh, shall, one full Moon not too distant, be found haggling in the Alleys with Caribbean Negroes, over the price of some modest Guitar upon which to strum this very Musick, so shall you, Miss, be dancing to it, at your Wedding."

"Then you should be wearing this 'round your Head," suggests Brae quite upon her "Beat," "if you wish to work as a Gypsy." Handing him from her Sewing-Basket a length of scarlet Muslin, which the game Ethelmer has 'round his head in a Trice.

"More a Pirate than a Gypsy," Brae opines.

"Yet, just as Romantick, in its way...?"

27

" 'Demagogue'!" mutters Dr. Franklin. "Our excellent Sprout Penn, the latest of his crypto-Jesuit ruling family, and *his* Satanick arrangement with Mr. Allen, *his* shameless Attentions to the Presbyterian Mobility,— has the effrontery to speak of 'crushing this Demagogue'— well, well, aye, Demagogue...Milton thought it a 'Goblin word,' that might yet describe good Patriots,— "

"Good Patriots all!" cries the impulsive Mr. Dixon, raising his Cup.

Dr. Franklin observes them, one at a time, through the tinted lenses of Spectacles of his own Invention, for moderating the Glare of the Sun, whose Elevation upon his Nose varies, according to the message it happens to be inflecting, giving over all the impression of a Visitor from very far away indeed. The Geometers have encounter'd the eminent Philadelphian quite by chance, in the pungent and dim back reaches of an Apothecary in Locust-Street, each Gentleman upon a distinct mission of chemical Necessity, as among these shelves and bins, the Godfrey's Cordial and Bateman's Drops, Hooper's Female Pills and Smith's Medicinal Snuff, hasty bargains are struck, Strings of numbers and letters and alchemists' Signs whisper'd (and some never written down), whilst a quiet warm'd Narcosis, as of a drawing to evening far out in a Country of fields where drying herbal crops lie, just perceptibly breathing, possesses the Shop Interior, rendering it indistinct as to size, legality, or destiny.

Dixon is accosting at length a clerk who has taken him for one more English tourist hectically out in search of Chinamen's Drugs,— "Anything, ideally, with Ooahpium in it will do...? Al-cohol to keep it in solution of course...perhaps some For-mulation that would go well with the Daffy's Elixir of which we plan to purchase,— eeh, how many *Cases* was that again, Mr. Mason...?"

Mason glares back, too keenly aware of the celebrated American Philosopher's Eye upon them,— having hoped to project before it, somehow, at least the forms of Precedence,— but of course Dixon's rustic Familiarities have abolish'd, yet again, any such hope,— one more Station of the Cross to be put up with. "Any matter of Supply falls into your area, Dixon. Have a word with Mr. McClean if you're not sure," hearing how it sounds, even as he goes on with it.

Dixon remains cheery. "In thah' welcome Event," making a carefree motion in the Air with his Handkerchief, "an hundred Cases should do the trick, for this time out, anyway,— Now as to that Oahpiated article we were discussing,— "

"Aye, we call it a Laudanum, Sir,— compounded according to the original *Formulae* of the noted Dr. Paracelsus, of Germany."

"An hundred Cases?" screams Mason, "have you gone insane? This is a Church-going Province,— 'twill never be authoriz'd."

"Preventive against a variety of Ailments, Sir...?— excellent anti-costive properties,— given the Uncertainty of Diet,— "

"The Commissioners know all too well about Daffy's Elixir, and the uses 'tis put to," Mr. Franklin, who has been attending the exchange, here feels he must point out. "And being imported, 'tis only to be had, at prices charg'd in the English-shops. Now, for a tenth of that outrageous sum, our good Apothecary Mr. Mispick will compound you a 'Salutis' impossible to distinguish from the original. Or you may design your own, consulting with him as to your preferr'd Ratio of Jalap to Senna, which variety of Treacle pleases you,— all the fine points of Daffyolatry are known to him, he has seen it all, and nothing will shock or offend him." He raises a Finger. " 'Strangers, heed my wise advice,— Never pay the Retail Price.' "

"This is kind of you Sir, for fair...? Mr. Mason's choices, illustrative of a more *Bacchic* Leaning, enjoying Priority of mine, so must I rest content with more modest outlays, from my own meager Purse, alas, for any Philtres peculiarly useful to m'self...?"

Dr. Franklin shifts his Lenses as if for a clearer look at Dixon. A Smile struggles to find its way through lips purs'd in Speculation,— but before it quite may, being the sort of man who, tho' never seen to consult a Time-piece, always knows the exact Time, "Come," he bids the Astronomers abruptly, "— you've not yet been to a Philadelphia Coffeehouse? Poh,— we must amend that,— something no Visitor should miss,— I must transact an Item or two of Business,— would you honor me by having a brief Sip at my Local, The Blue Jamaica?"

"London," Mr. Mason is soon reporting, "is quite thoroughly charm'd by your Glass Armonica, thanks to the Artistry of the excellent Miss Davies."

"I have done my utmost to convince Miss Davies that, given the general Frangibility, use of any strong Vibrato could prove,— putting it as gallantly as possible,— unwise. Yet she plays so beautifully. My idle Toy has found itself fortunately arriv'd, among a small Host of *Virtuosi*. Heavens. The Mozart child,— and these Tales I keep hearing, of the young Parisian Doctor, Mesmer, who plays it, 'tis said, unusually well."

"Not the Magnetickal Gent?" says Mason.

"The very same. Known to the R.S. for some time, I collect."

"At The Mitre, he is ever reliable as a topick of lively Discourse."

"Where Franklin is a Member, and tha've scarcely been a Guest," Dixon may be muttering to himself. Aloud,— " 'Scuse me, Friend," briskly upon his feet, "where does one go over the Heap around here?"

Mr. Franklin points out to him a Door to the Yard, and when he is out of earshot, begins, it seems abruptly, to inquire about the Surveyor's "Calvert connections."

Mason is perplex'd. "I didn't know there were any. I imagin'd, that being of a Quaker family, he was deem'd acceptable to the Pennsylvanians, but have ever been at a loss to explain his appeal, if any, to the Marylanders."

"The Calverts are content to live in England,— as they are Catholics, their children are educated across the Channel, in St. Omer. One of the Jesuits teaching there is a certain Le Maire, who is native to Durham and a particular friend of Dixon's teacher, William Emerson,— "

"Yes. But you'd have to ask Dixon about the Jesuit. I know of him only as the partner of Roger Boscovich,— the two degrees of Latitude in Italy,— "

"— from Rome to Rimini, aye." Franklin, behind his Orchid-hued Lenses, waits for Mason to work out the Comparisons.

"What's going on, then?" Mason trying to peer, he hopes not as truculently as he feels, into the shadowy Lunettes.

"You might sometime find yourself discussing these matters with your Second,— "

"After which," Mason replies, as Franklin suddenly, with naked narrow'd eyes, looks over the tops of his Spectacles and nods encouragingly, "— I am to relate the Minutes of it all to you?"

Mr. Franklin replacing his "Glasses," "Not if it causes you Discomfort, Sir. Although some Discomforts may ever be eas'd by timely application of Ben's Universal Balm,— "

"— yet do others continue intractable. Why, Dr. Franklin, are you urging me to this, may I say, dismal choice?"

"Oh,— wagering against your loyalty," Franklin shrugs. "An elementary exercise,— and pray, do not feel you have in any way offended me,— as an adult, I am no stranger to Rejection, I have long learn'd to deal with it in Dignity, as a sane man would,— and without Resentment, motive for it though I may enjoy in Abundance."

"Sir, I cannot spy upon him for you. I am sorry the Politics here have become so, as one would say, Italian, in their intricacies. But my contractual Tasks alone will be difficult enough without— ah and here is Mr. Dixon."

"D'you know a lad nam'd Lewis? Said he knew you, Dr. Franklin."

"Where was this?" Franklin has begun twirling the hair upon either side of his Head, into long Curls.

"Just out in the Alley. He tried to sell me a Watch...? said it was a Masonick Astrologer's Model...? Signs of the Zoahdiahck...? Pheases of the Moon,— "

"You didn't— "

"Couldn't. Not unless one of you wants to lend me— "

"I'll go have a look," Mason rising. "Come along Dixon, and point him out?"

"Eeh, Ah think he's gone...?" Dixon now preoccupied with pouring the contents of a small Vial into his Coffee.

Mason, unable to insist without appearing to wish to consult out of Franklin's hearing, and needing to piss anyhow, shrugs and withdraws. The moment he vanishes, Franklin begins to press Dixon upon the Topick of Mason's "East India Company Connections."

"Is thah' the Dutch or the English one?" Dixon's Phiz altogether innocent. "Ah'm ever confounding 'em...?"

Franklin at last allowing himself to chuckle. "Friend Dixon,— Loyalty is a Gem, of Worth innate, Whose price is never notic'd,— till too late."

"We've had an Adventure or two, you see."

"Ah, me. Don't suppose the name Sam Peach of Chalford would ring a Bell...?"

With quizzical sincerity, "One of thoase lads in *The Beggar's Opera*...?— "

"Well, well, Mr. Dixon, be easy, I release you,— and look ye, here again is your Companion."

"The man's an entire Instrument-shop," says Mason, "— droll sort of friend for you to have, Dr. Franklin,— interesting Wig.... Told me a Riddle, in fact,— Why is the King like a near-sighted Gunner?— 'Well d——'d if I know,' I said back, 'but Dr. Franklin is sure to.' "

"Mr. Mason! Dear, dear. How would I know any such Joak? Or person?"

"Why, to help you find out how much,— " "— and how foolishly,— " "— we have to spend, perhaps!" sing Mason and Dixon.

"Phlogiston and Electric Fir-r-re,— " cries the eminent Philadelphian, "if I'm not the Biter bi-i-t. As you'd say, trans-parent, was I?... Awkward...should've just ask'd them at the Royal Society, being a member after all.... Indeed, I was among 'em at the time you fought the French Vessel,— in London, when you wrote to them...quite a Hub-Bub, Gentlemen! Tho' absent from the meeting which approv'd their reply to you,— innocent, you understand,— I did attend the next, a classick Display of those people at their worst. Taken one at a time,— dear Tom Birch, august Hadley the Quadrant's Eponym, Mr. Short, Dr. Morton,— excellent minds, invigorating Company,— but when they got all in a Herd,— bless us, the Stubbornness! They knew the French had Bencoolen and would be as content to sink the *Seahorse* there, as off Brest. They all knew. But they could never allow upstarts to advise them in matters of Global strategy. Alas, the British,— bloody-minded to the end, so long as it be somebody else's Blood. Thus the Board of Trade, thus the House of Commons.... Up there, day after day, instructing them, gently,— a Schoolmaster for Idiots.— Sooner or later, no offense, Gentlemen, Americans must fight them....

"Hurrah, howbeit?— for I am res-cued." He refers in his courtly way, to the arrival of a pair of young Women, both quite pleasant-looking, tho' deck'd out with what, even to the unschool'd Eye, seems willful Eccentricity, and who may or may not have been among those in the Carriage which had been earlier at the Landing.

"There he is!"

"Oh, Doctor!" more than vigorously nudging one another, and laughing at differing rates of Speed.

"These are Molly and Dolly," Franklin introduces them, "Students of the Electrickal Arts, whom I am pleas'd from time to time to examine, in the Sub-ject, ye-e-s.... If you've the Inclination tonight, Gentlemen, I am giving a recital, upon the Glass Instrument, at the sign of The Fair Anchor, upon Carpenters Wharf, just down from The London Coffee House. 'Tis a sort of,— what is the Word I grope for,— "

"Gin-shop," sings Molly.

"Opium den," cries Dolly.

"Ladies, Ladies...."

"Doctor, Doctor!" As the Philosopher, attempting to maintain his Hair in some order, is slowly absorb'd into a mirthful Cloud of tartan-edg'd Emerald Green and luminous Coral taffeta, Prints with a Lap-Dog Motif, ribbons with "Sailor Beware," "No free Kisses," "Be Quick about it," and other humorous slogans woven into them, Flounces and loose Hats and wand'ring Tresses, the Astronomers reckon it as good a moment as any to be off. Passing into the Street, they can hear Molly piping, "And she swore to me, she saw it glowing in the Dark...?"

Outside they stand, blinking. "I don't knaahw...?...Hadn't thoo imagin'd him as somehow more..."

"Organized. Aye. By Reputation, he is a man entirely at ease with the inner structures of Time itself. Yet, here he seems strangely..."

"Unfoahcused, as we Lensmen say…?"

Mason rolling his eyes, "Perhaps we should pop into that Fair Anchor this Evening, what think you?"

"Aye, happen those two canny Electricians'll be there…? Rather fancied old Dolly myself. Woman knows how to turn herself out, 'd tha noatice?"

Hearing what he imagines to be an Emphasis upon "two," Mason directs at Dixon an effortful smile, meaning, "Go ahead, but don't expect me to ascend wearily out of my Melancholia just so ev'rybody else can have their own idea of a good time,"— which happens to be the most Dixon would ever think of asking of him, anyhow. And withal, when they show up at The Fair Anchor that Night, it turns out to be Mason's sort of place nicely,— basic and bleak, discouraging ev'ry attempt, even grunting, that might suggest Conviviality, the wood Furniture carv'd upon, splinter'd and scarr'd, the Stale-Ale as under-hopp'd, as 'tis over-water'd. They secure a place along the Bar, and presently Mr. Franklin appears, having exchang'd his Orchid Spectacles for Half-Lenses of Nocturnal Blue. The occupants of the Room, hitherto strewn without more purpose than the human Jetsam of any large Seaport, all sit up at once, draw together, and with the precision of a long-rehears'd Claque, begin to chatter of Miss Davies, and Gluck, and ineluctably, Mesmer.

The Instrument awaits him, its nested Crystal Hemispheres, each tun'd to a Note of the Scale, carefully brought hither through reef'd-Topsail seas and likewise whelming Anxieties back at Lloyd's regarding the inherent Vice of Glass added to the yet imperfectly known contingencies of voyage by Ship,— brought to shine in this commodious Corner, beneath a portrait of some Swedish Statesman too darken'd with Room-smoke for anyone to be sure who it is any more,— Oxenstjerna, Gyllenstjerna, Gyllenborg, who knows?— discussions often becoming quite spirited, though, of course, conducted in Swedish. It has hung there, growing into its Anonymity, since the early times of the Swedish settlers,— gazing into the room, at the nightly dramas of lost consciousness and squander'd Coin, at gaming and roaring and varieties inexhaustible of Argument. Behind it rises a Flight of stairs, up and down which creeps a ceaseless Traffick. Many pause to stare over the false Mahogany Railing at Dr. Franklin seated at his Glass Armonica, or down upon the Figures and into the Décolletages of Molly and Dolly, who not only have show'd up, but have brought along two more young women with similar ideas about Fashion. "These Doxies," Mason mutters, "look ye,— they're staring at me. I can feel myself becoming Unreasonably Suspicious."

"Rest easy,— 'tis me they want," Dixon waving.

"Jerry! Charlie! Over here!" The Ladies seem delighted. Dr. Franklin waits for the parties to rearrange their seating, then strikes a C major chord. The room quiets instantly. He begins to play, rotating, by way of a Treadle Arrangement, the horizontal Stack of Glasses thro' a Trough of Water, to keep the Rims ever wet, and then simply touching each wet rim moving by, as he would have touch'd the Key of an Organ, to produce a queerly hoarse, ringing Tone. If Chimes could whisper, if Melodies could pass away, and their Souls wander the Earth…if Ghosts danced at Ghost Ridottoes, 'twould require such Musick, Sentiment ever held back, ever at the Edge of breaking forth, in Fragments, as Glass breaks.

Upon one of his intermissions, the Doctor, having secur'd a Pot of Ale, approaches the Geometers. "Come and meet Mr. Tallihoe, of Virginia," who proves to be anxious that they visit with Col° Washington, of that Province.

"You'll want to have a chat,— he's been out there, knows the country, the Inhabitants,— Surveyor, like yourselves."

Dixon here must suppress a Chuckle, knowing how it annoys Mason to be styl'd so. "Bad enough at the Cape, calling us both Astronomers,— " Mason has complained, and more than once. "I'm being insulted coming and going, it's not fair."

"He's said to be of a Wear Valley Family…? They told me to look him up…?"

At Dawn they are led to a remote cross-roads north of the City. Out of the cold Humidity rolls smoothly a Coach of peculiar Design. "But step aboard, Gents, and this Machine'll have yese in Mount Vernon ere Phœbus lift 'is Nob again."

"Is it safe?" inquires Mason.

"Perfectly,— 'tis the Road that's perilous!" Mr. Tallihoe shaking both their hands in fare-well.

"You're not coming along…?" Dixon collects.

"Not I. He'll not wish to see *me*. Lord's Mercy, no."

They ride all night, and neither sleeps. The Coach stops for nothing. Meals, each a distinct kind of "Sandwich," are pass'd to them down thro' a Hatch. The Remains, including Plates, are thrown out the Window, taken by the Wind. There are Newspapers and a Rack-ful of Books, and under the Driver's seat is a Cask of Philadelphia Porter, whose Tap extends within, for the use of the Passengers. When they must piss, they do so into glaz'd Jars, with Chinese Scenes upon them. By the time they consider pissing out the Coach Doors, so swiftly have they Travel'd, that they miss the Chance. The Driver is calling, "Potowmack just ahead, Gents!" He drops them off by the River, into the Slap and Scent of Winter upon the Wing, and points them uphill. Bearing nothing but what they may have stuff'd hastily into their Pockets, they begin the Ascent to Mount Vernon.

28

"In their Decadency these Virginians practice an elaborate Folly of Courtly Love, unmodified since the Dark Ages, so relentlessly that at length they cannot distinguish Fancy from the substantial World, and their Folly absorbs them into itself. They gaily dance the steps their African Slaves teach them, whilst pretending to an aristocracy they seem only to've heard rumors of. Their preferr'd sport is the Duel,— part of the definition of 'Gentleman' in these parts seems to be ownership of a match'd set of Pistols.

"To anyone who has observ'd slave-keepers in Africa, it will seem all quite ancient,— Lords and Serfs,— a Gothick Pursuit,— what, in our corrupted Days, has become of Knights and Castles, when neither is any longer reasonable, or possible. No good can come of such dangerous Boobyism. What sort of Politics may proceed herefrom, only He that sows the Seeds of Folly in His World may say."

— The Revd Wicks Cherrycoke, *Spiritual Day-Book*

Col^o Washington turns out to be taller than Dixon, by about as much as Dixon rises over Mason. "Enable us quite nicely to stand in a Shed if we keep a straight line," he greets them, "though Ah wonder why?" In this Province of the Unreflective, if the Colonel serves not as a Focus of Sobriety, neither is he quite the incompetent Fool depicted in the London press, rattling on, ever so jolly, about the whiz of enemy shot through the air, tho' how mean-spirited must we be to refuse Slack in the Sheets of Manhood to a gangling Sprig, sighting one day through the Eye-piece of a Surveyor's Instrument upon a Plummet-String, the next down the barrel of a Rifle at a Frenchman? In his mature person, tho' he will seem from time to time to allow his Gaze to refocus upon something more remote,— yet 'tis as little Fidgeting as Reverie, something purposeful, rather, allowing him to remain attentive to the Topick at hand. When he hears Dixon speak, he smiles, though owing to the state of his teeth he is reluctant to do so when in company,— a smile from Col° Washington, however tentative, is said to be a mark of favor,— "My people come from around your neck of the woods, I think, for I've relatives who talk the way you do."

Dixon cups an ear. "Happen I hear a fading echo of the old Pitman's Lilt...?"

The Col° shrugs. "Up in Pennsylvania they tell me I talk like an African. They imagine us here surrounded with our Tithables, insensibly sliding into their speech, and so, it is implied, into their Ways as well. Come. Observe this Pitcher upon the Table, an excellent Punch, the invention of my Man Gershom."

Out on the white-column'd porch, tumbler in fist, the large Virginian wants to talk real estate. "Sometimes a man must act quickly upon an opportunity, for in volatile times the chance may never come again. Just for example,— there is a parcel out past the South Mountain I'd like you to take a look at when you go by,— your Line, as I project it, passing quite close. Spotted it early in the War, kept it in mind ever since.... No reason you fellows shouldn't turn a Shilling or two whilst you're over here...and have ye consider'd how much free surveying ye'll be giving away,— as the West Line must contribute North and South Boundaries to Pieces innumerable? Don't suppose you have a copy of that Contract ye sign'd...well, no matter.... Yet I wonder at how you Boys have stirr'd up the land-jobbers. No one here regards the crest of the Alleghenies as the Barrier it was. You've only to look at the roads, some days the Waggons in a Stream unbroken,— new faces in ships arriving every day, nothing east of Susquehanna left to settle,— the French are out of the Ohio, the Scoundrel Pontiac is vanquish'd, the money is ready, Coffee-Houses in a frenzy of map-sketching and bargaining,— what deters us?"

"General Bouquet's Proclamation,— " Mason suggests, "no new Settlement west of the Allegheny Ridge-Line."

"Poh. The Proprietors won't enforce that."

"Whence then," replies Mason, "the Rumor that Mr. Cresap tried to bribe the General with twenty-five thousand acres, *not* to proclaim his Line?"

"Hum. Perhaps," chuckles Washington, " 'twas all the old Renegado dared promise,— and Bouquet may have wanted more,— as no Land may be had there now but by his Warrant, his Line might make of him an American Nabob,— as he was not offering his Services out of love for those inexpensive Tokens with which he is synonymous,— rather, the Lord ever Merciful, as in Bengal, sent us a Deliverer whose Appetite for Profit matches his self-confidence. 'Twas Business, more or less Plainly dealt. The next step will be to contract our Indian Wars out to Mercenaries,— preferably school'd in Prussian techniques, as it never hurts to get the best,— tho' many of these Hired professionals miss one pay-day and they're gone like Smoke. Could even be just before a decisive Battle,— forget it, damn 'em, they're off. Did you imagine Bouquet, or the Penns, to be acting out of tender motives, toward the Indians?"

"Why else refrain from expanding West," mildly inquires Dixon, "but out of a regard for the Humanity of those whose Homes they invade?"

"A motive even stronger and purer," frowns Colonel Washington, "— the desire to confound their enemies,— who chiefly are the Presbyterians settling the West, Proclamation-Shmocklamation,— Ulster Scots, who hate England enough to fight against her, now the French are departed,— tho' the cheerfully idiotic, who are numerous, believe such Sectarian passions to lie behind us. The Ulster Scots were dispossess'd once,— shamefully,— herded, transported,— Hostages to the demands of Religious Geography. Then, a second time, were they forc'd to flee the rack-rents of Ulster, for this American unknown. Think ye, there will be any third Coercion? At what cost, pray? Americans will fight Indians whenever they please, which is whenever they can,— and Brits wherever they must, for we will be no more contain'd, than tax'd. The Grenville Ministry ignore these *Data*, at their Peril."

"Mr. Grenville, alas, neglects to consult me in these Matters," says Mason.

"Wrote to him," adds Dixon,— " 'Tax the East India Company, why don't tha?' Did he even reply?"

"As a rule here," advises the Col°, "ye may speak your Minds upon any Topick Politickal. But on no account, ever discuss Religion. If any insist, represent yourselves as Deists. The Back Inhabitants are terrified of all Atheists, especially the Indians,— tho' Englishmen bearing unfamiliar Equipment across their land might easily qualify. Their first Impulse, upon meeting an Atheist, is to shoot at him, often at close range, tho' some of the Lancaster County Rifles are deadly from a mile off,— so running for cover is largely out of the Question. Besides, you cannot know what may be waiting among the Trees...."

"What's that Aroma?" Dixon blurts, knowing quite well, from the Cape, what it is.

"Ah, the new Harvest, how inhospitable of me. 'Tis but a small patch out back, planted as an Experiment,— if it prospers, next season perhaps we'll plant ten Acres, as a Market-Crop. With luck, between the Navy and the New-York Fops, we could get rid of it all, Male and Fimble, and see us some Profit. Always a few Shillings in Canary-Seed as well, worse comes to worst.— Here then,— Gershom! Where be you at, my man!"

An African servant with an ambiguous expression appears. "Yes Massuh Washington Suh."

"Gershom fetch us if you will some Pipes, and a Bowl of the new-cur'd Hemp. And another gallon of your magnificent Punch. There's a good fellow. Truly, Gentlemen, 'an Israelite in whom there is no guile.' "

Mason, recognizing the source as John 1:47, actually chuckles, whilst Dixon rather glowers. "At Raby Castle," he informs them, Phiz aflame, "Darlington liked to joak of his Steward, my Great-Uncle George, using thah' same quo-tation from the Bible. Yet only from Our Savior, surely, might such words be allow'd to pass, without raising suspicions as to amplitude of Spirit...? From the Earl of Darlington, the remark was no more than the unconsider'd Jollity one expects of a Castle-Dweller,— but to hear it in America, is an Enigma I confess I am at a loss to explain...?"

"Good Sir," the Colonel smiting himself repeatedly upon the head, unto knocking his Wig askew, "I regret providing the Text for an unwelcome association." He snatches the Wig completely off and bows his head, cocking one eye at Dixon. "The two Conditions are entirely separate, of course."

"I'm a Quaker," shrugs Dixon, "what am I suppos'd to do, call thee out?"

"Don't bother about that Israelite talk, anyhow," Gershom coming back in with a Tray, "it's his way of joaking, he does it all the time."

"Thou aren't offended?"

"As I do happen to be of the Hebrew faith," tilting his head so that all may see the traditional Jewish *Yarmulke*, attach'd to the crown of his Peruke in a curious display of black on white, "it would seem a waste of precious time."

"Say,— and cook?" beams George Washington. "Gersh, any them *Kasha Varnishkies* left?"

"Believe you ate 'em all up for Breakfast, Colonel."

"Well whyn't you just whup up another batch,— maybe fry us some hog jowls, he'p it slide on down?"

"One bi-i-i-g mess o' Hog Jowls, comin' raaight up, Suh!"

"Wait a minute," objects Mason. "Do the Jews not believe, that," glancing over at Dixon, "*the Article* you speak of, is unclean, and so avoid scrupulously its Flesh?"

"Please,— you don't think I feel guilty enough already? As it happens, the Sect I belong to, is concern'd scarce at all with Dietary Rules."

"— of any kind," adds the Col°, having inhal'd mightily upon his Pipe, whence now arises another aromatic Cloud. "Yet if a Jew cooking pork is a Marvel, what of a Negroe, working a Room? Yes, my Oath,— here is Joe Miller resurrected,— they applaud him 'round a circuit of Coaching-inns upon the roads to George's Town, Williamsburg, and Annapolis,— indeed he is known far and Wide, as a Theatrickal Artist of some Attainment, leaving him less and less time for his duties here,— not to mention an income *per annum* which creeps dangerously close to that of his nominal Master, me." He passes the Pipe to Dixon.

"He wants me to put it in Dismal Swamp Land Company shares," Gershom confides. "How would you Gentlemen advise me?"

Mason and Dixon make eye contact, Dixon blurting, "Didn't they tell us,— " Mason going, "Shh! *Sshhhh!*," Washington meanwhile trying to wave Gershom back into the house. Gershom, however, has just taken the Pipe from Mr. Dixon. "Thank you." Inhales. Presently, "Well! How are you, Gentlemen, you having a good time? That's quite some Coat you're wearing, Sir. It's, ah, certainly is red, ain't it? And those silver Buttons,— mighty shiny,— tell me, seriously now, you were planning to wear this, out into the Forest?"

"Why, why aye,— "

"Actually, bright red, it's quite *à la mode* out there, seen rather often,— down the barrels of cheap Rifles.— You'll be very popular with all kinds of Folk,— Delawares, Shawanese, Seneca,— Seneca fancy a nice red Coat.— So !" passing the Pipe to Mason, "I can see which one's the snappy Dresser,— whilst the Indians are shooting at him, the Presbyterians'll be after you, thinking you're something to eat,— 'It's a Buffalo, I'm tellin' ye, mon!' 'Hush, Patrick, it seem'd but a Squirrel to me.' 'So it's a Squirrel!' ffsss— *Pow!*"

"Oblig'd of course," squawks Mason, "ever so kind to imagine for me my Death in America...need no longer preoccupy myself upon the Matter, kind yes and withal a great relief,— "

Gershom turning to Dixon, "Is he always like this, or does he get indignant sometimes?"

"You see what I have to put up with," groans Col° Washington. "It's makin' me just mee-shugginah. Here, a bit of Tob'o with that?..."

"George."

"Oh-oh, stay calm, it's the Wife, just let me do the— ah my Treasure! excellent Gown, handsome Stuff,— allow me to present," and so forth. Mrs. Washington ("Oh, la, call me Martha, Boys") is a diminutive woman with a cheerful rather than happy air, who seems to bustle even when standing still. At the moment she is carrying an enormous Tray pil'd nearly beyond their Angles of Repose with Tarts, Pop-overs, Gingerbread Figures, fried Pies, stuff'd Doughnuts, and other Units of Refreshment the Surveyors fail to recognize.

"Smell'd that Smoak, figur'd you'd be needing something to nibble on," the doughty Mrs. W. greets them. "The Task as usual falling to that Agent of Domesticity unrelenting, the wife,— as none of *you* could run a House for more than ten minutes, in the World wherein most of us must dwell, without Anarchy setting in."

"I was suppos'd to be watching a Pot upon the fire," sighs Washington, "— matters more immediate claim'd my attention, one giving rise to yet another, till a certain Odor recall'd me to the Pot, alas too late,— another ruinous flaw in my Character, perhaps one day to be amended by me, though never to be forgiven by my Lady."

She shakes her head, eyes yawing more than rolling. "George, have a Cookie." He takes a Molasses ginger-bread man, closely examines its Reverse, as if to assure himself that his Wife hasn't somehow burn'd it, and is about to bite the head off, when something else occurs to him.

"Now you may have heard of the Ohio Company,— a joint adventure in which my late brothers had a few small shares. There we were, as deep in the savage state as men have been known to venture, often no clear line of Retreat, a sort of,— Marth, my Nosegay of Virtues, what's a piece of tricky weaving?"

"How," she replies, "pray, would I know? Am I a Weaver?"

"— a piece of tricky weaving," the Col⁰ has tried to continue, "— order, I mean to say, in Chaos. Markets appearing, with their unwritten Laws, upon ev'ry patch of open ground, power beginning to sort itself out, Line and Staff,— "

Mason and Dixon, in arranging for a fair division of labor, have adopted the practice, whenever two conversations are proceeding at once, of each attending one, with Location usually deciding who gets which. So it falls to Mason to defend his Profession against what he suspects is Mrs. W.'s accusation of unworldliness, whilst Dixon must become emmesh'd in Ohio Company history.

"— with our own forts at Wills and Redstone Creeks, and a Communication between.... As the East India Company hath its own Navy, why, so did we our own Army. Out in the wild Anarchy of the Forest, we alone had the coherence and discipline to see this land develop'd as it should be. Rest easy, that the old O.C. still exists," the Col⁰ is protesting, "tho' in different Form."

"Sounds like the After-life," Gershom remarks.

"If only we could've gotten the language we wanted in the Charter, the Tale might have been different. But our friends at Court are few, and now and then invisible, even to us."

"They fail'd to get the Bishop-of-Durham Clause," puts in Gershom.

"Look ye,— wasn't it like Iron Plate upon a Steam-Boiler for ev'ryone else? Virginia? The Calverts, the Penns? Ohio by precedent surely is entitl'd to one?"

"All respect, Colonel, those Grants," Gershom points out, "were more like fantastickal Tales, drafted in the days of some Kings who were not altogether real themselves. 'Twas a world of Masquing then, Fictions of faraway lands, what did they care? 'Bishop-of-Durham Clause? no problem with that,— how can we set you up, a Palatine Residence? 'tis yours,— you like cedar shakes, brick, traditional Stone approach, whatever, it's fine,— what's that, you want to put in a what, a Harem? why to be sure,— and how many Ladies would that be, Sir? of *course* you've a choice,— Lord Smedley, the Catalogue, please.' "

"Any Bishop-of-Durham Clause in America," says Dixon, "suggests a likeness, in the British Mind, between your Indians West of the Allegheny Ridge, and their Scots beyond Hadrian's Wall,— as the Bishop Prince's half of the bargain, is to defend the King against whatever wild cannibal Host lies North of us,— whose nightly Bagpipe-Musick, in the time of the 'Forty-five, could easily bring all within earshot to insomniack Terror by Dawn."

"Why, Sir," exclaims the Col°, "you might be describing a camp upon Monongahela, and the Death-hollows all night from across the River. The long watchfulness, listening to the Brush. Ev'ry mis'rable last Leaf. The Darkness implacable. When you gentlemen come to stand at the Boundary between the Settl'd and the Unpossess'd, just about to enter the Deep Woods, you will recognize the Sensation...."

"Yet, we sought no more than to become that encampment in the Night, that small refuge of Civilization in the far Wilderness."

"Trouble was, so'd the French," Gershom remarks.

"Thankee, Gersh."

Mason meanwhile is embark'd upon an Apologia for Astronomy and his own career therein. "The dispute is at least as old as Plato. Indeed, I feel like Glaucon in the Seventh Book of the 'Republic,' nervously listing for Socrates all the practical reasons he can think of for teaching Astronomy in the schools."

"Let's see, then, do I feel like Socrates...? Alas, Sir, I think not today,— nor Mrs. Socrates, neither,— that no doubt otherwise excellent Lady being, as I am told, far too busy with shrewish pursuits to bother with her Kitchen, and thus scarcely able to suggest to you, for example, this excellent Apricot Tart."

Mason is not sure, but thinks he has just detected a certain Cilial Excursion. "Obliged, Ma'am. All Lens-fellows, I mean, recognize that our first Duty is to be of publick Use. Hmm, oh, the Raspberry, too, then.... Thankee. Even with the Pelhams currently in Eclipse, we all must proceed by way of th' establish'd Routes, with ev'ry farthing we spend charg'd finickingly against the Royal Purse. We are too visible, up on our Hilltop, to spend much time among unworldly Speculations, or indeed aught but the details of our Work,— focus'd in particular these days upon the Problem of the Longitude."

"Oh. And what happen'd to those Transits of Venus?"

"There we have acted more as philosophical Frigates, Ma'am, each detach'd upon his Commission,— whilst the ev'ryday work of the Observatories goes on as always, for the task at Greenwich, as at Paris, is to know every celestial motion so perfectly, that Sailors at last may trust their lives to this Knowledge."

"Here," the Col° beams, "more fame attaches to the Transits,— Observers station'd all 'round the world, even in Massachusetts,— Treasuries of all lands pouring forth gold,— ev'ry Astronomer suddenly employ'd,— and all to find a true value for the 'Earth's Parallax.' Why, most of us here in Virginia wouldn't know a Parallax from a Pinwheel if it came on up and said how-d'ye do."

"Yet, what a Rage it was! the Transit-of-Venus Wig, that several women were seen wearing upon Broad Street, Husband, do ye remember it? a dark little round Knot against a great white powder'd sphere,— "

"And that Transit-of-Venus Pudding? Same thing, a single black Currant upon a Circular Field of White,— "

"— and the Sailors, with that miserable song,— "

> " 'Tis time to set sail, [sings the Col°]
> Farewell, Portsmouth Ale,

Ta-ta to the gay can-tinas,
For we're off, my Girl, to the end of the world
To be there, ere the Tran-sit of Venus.—
She's the something something,— "

"Goddess of Love," Martha in a pleasant tho' impatient soprano,

"— Shining above,
Without a bit of Meanness,
Tho' we'll have no more fun till she's cross'd o'er the Sun,
'Tis ho, for the Transit of Venus!
[Col° Washington joining her for the Bridge]
Out where the trade winds blow,
Further than Sailors go,
If it's not Ice and Snow,
'Twill be hotter than Hell, we know,
So!
Wave to your Dear, stow all your gear, and
Show a bit of Keenness,
Bid Molly adieu,
She isn't for you,—
For you're for the Transit of Venus!

By the last four Bars, they are facing and gazing at one another with an Affection having to do not so much with the Lyric, as with keeping the Harmony, and finishing together.

Gershom is presently telling King-Joaks,— "Actually they're Slave-and-Master Joaks, re-tailor'd for these Audiences. King says to his Fool, 'So,— tell me, honestly,— what makes you willing to go about like such a Fool all the time?' 'Hey, George,' says the Fool,— 'that's easy,— I do it for the same reason as you,— out of Want.'— 'What-what,' goes the King, 'how's that?'— 'Why, you for want of Wit, and I for want of Money.' "

The King is jesting with one of his Ambassadors. "Damme," he cries, "if you don't look like some great dishevel'd Sheep!" Ambassador replies, "I know that I've had the honor, several times, to represent your Majesty's Person."

The King, merry but distraught, asks leave of those at his Table, to Toast the Devil. "Why," says the Fool, "where that Gentleman resides, he is already well toasted.... Yet, I could never object to one of your Majesty's particular Friends."

The King takes a long coach-ride out into the country, and decides to walk back to the Palace, in company with his Fool. Growing at length fatigued, they learn, of a farmer they meet, that they've ten miles yet to go. "Maybe we'd better send for the Carriage," says the King. "Come on, George," replies the Fool, "— we can do it easily,— 'tis but five miles apiece."

Gershom follows these by singing "Havah Nagilah," a merry Jewish Air, whilst clicking together a pair of Spoons in Syncopation.

" 'Twas Céléron de Bienville who began the Dispute in 'forty-nine," recalls the Col° later, "when he voyaged South from Canada, landing upon the shore of Lake Erie, following French Creek to the Allegheny, where, to assert France's claims, he buried a lead plate, bearing the Royal Seal...thence by Battoe to the Ohio, and down it, past Allegheny, Beaver, Fish Creek, Muskingum, Kanahwah, Scioto, planting as he went these leaden Flags at the Mouths of each Stream in turn...."

"Lead?" Dixon, curiously.

"A Memorandum," it seems to Mason, "of other uses for the Metal, such as Shot,— another expression of that famous French contempt, not only to be prodigal with a base metal, but to bury it, in the dirt and the dark, as if that were the only way an Englishman might notice it."

"Oh, Sir, likely 'twas Practicality," beams Washington, "— Lead being cheaper than silver or gold, and if kept out of the Air that way, quite durable as well."

"Any metal in the form of a Plate," Dixon muses, "or Disk, might plausibly have an Electrickal Purpose."

"Have a word with Dr. Franklin," offers the Col°, "he'll know."

"Electricity, again." Mason gestures at his partner with his Thumb, shaking his head morosely. "Aye, 'tis the topick that most provokes his Disorder,— quite harmless of course,— comes over him without warning, suddenly he's on about his favorite Fluid, and no stopping him. Even Dr. Franklin can shed no light...the best physicians of the Royal Society,"— a shrug,— "baffl'd. We but hope, one day, he may regain his senses."

"A childhood Misadventure with a Torpedo," Dixon, with a brief move of his head toward Mason, confides, "— thus his Sensitivity at all References to the,"— whispering,— "*electrickal!*"

"Shocking!" Gershom remarks, and Mrs. W. beats Ta-ta-ma-ma smartly upon the Tabletop, whilst the Col° holds his Head, as if it ach'd.

"Yet not daz'd enough," Mason assures the Company, "nor too young, to miss recognizing, in the Torpedo, five-sixths of whose Length is taken up with these Electrical Plates, the Principle of all these Structures,— which is, that you must stack a great many of them, one immediately upon the next, if you wish to produce any effect large enough to be useful in, let alone noticed by, the World.— Aye, Dixon, well might you wag your Head,— wag away, may it circulate some sense. For what possible use a single plate, Lead or Gold, buried in the Earth, is, is beyond me."

"Perhaps only beyond our Sensorium, how Feeble," replies Dixon. "As were the Heavens, you may recall, but a short while ago, before Telescopes were invented...? Why may not these Plates collectively form a Tellurick Leyden-Pile? If not for storing quantities of simple Electrick Force, then to hold smaller charges, easily shap'd into invisible Symbols, decipherable by Means surely available to those *Philosophes*...."

"I fear the only message upon those Disks was a challenge, Sir,— a Provocation," asserts Washington. "The Surveyor's equivalent of a slap from a Glove."

And yet... (speculates the Rev[d]), what else? There remains a residue of Belief, out to the Westward, that the mere presence of Glyphs and Signs can produce magickal Effects,— for of the essence of Magic is the power of small Magickal Words, to work enormous physical Wonders,— as of coded inscriptions in fables, once unlock'd, to yield up Treasure past telling. So, Seals become of primary Moment, and their precise descriptions, often, matters of Life and Death, for one letter misplaced can summon Destruction immediate and merciless.

"You saw such Plates?"

"I dug a few of 'em up." Eyes etch'd in Crimson, the Col° is grinning at Dixon meaningfully, whilst Mrs. Washington grimaces in Warning. But Gershom is already on the way to fetch the Mementoes, calling mischievously, "Coming raaaight up, Suh! Bunch of Dead Weights,— beg pardon, Lead Plates (what'd I say?),— practically new, original Soil yet in place.... (Does the Gentleman know how to divert Guests?)"

What immediately draws Dixon's Attention is not the Royal Seal of France, but the markings upon the Reverse side. "Bless us, 'tis Chinese!"

"Chinese? Remarkable, Sir. The only Europeans who recognize such Writing, seem usually to be the...Jesuits."

"Excuse me...?" Dixon immediately upon the defensive, "Problem here, Colonel?"

"Depends," the Col° replies, with a Pause whose Heft all can appreciate, "— are you...*a traveling Man?*"

"Why aye," Dixon having learn'd of the Masonick password from a Lodge-member in Philadelphia, "and I'm traveling *West!*"

"West? Oh. Haw, haw! Well and so you are. Look ye,— 'tis simply this,— that from time to time, a Jesuit up North in Quebec will put off his skirts for Breeches, and cross the border in disguise, to work some mischief down here,— so a fellow has to be extra vigilant, is all. Report ev'rything to the Lodge, so that way somebody there can piece together a great many small items into a longer Tale,— perhaps even trace the movements, day to day, of these sinister intruders."

"Speaking as Postmaster-General," Dr. Franklin will later amplify, back in Philadelphia, "— I see our greatest problem as Time,— never anything, but Time. For any message to reach its recipient, we must reckon in a fix'd delay,— months by ship, days over Land,— whilst via the Jesuit Telegraph, *they* enjoy their d———'d Marvel of instant Communication,"— far-reaching and free of error, thanks to giant balloons sent to great Altitudes, Mirrors of para- (not to mention dia-) bolickal perfection, beams of light focused to hitherto unimagined intensities,— so, at any rate, say the encrypted reports that find their ways to the desks of highly-plac'd men whose daily task it is, to make sure they know everything,— appropriate to their places,— that must be known.

As expected of a Jesuit invention, timing and discipline are ev'rything. It is rumor'd that the Fathers limit themselves to giving orders, whilst the actual labor is entrusted to the Telegraph Squads, elite teams of converted Chinese, drill'd, through Loyolan methods, to perform with split-second timing the balloon launchings, to learn the art of aiming the beam, and, its reflection once acquir'd, to keep most faithfully fix'd upon it,— for like the glance of a Woman at a Ball, it must be held for a certain time before conveying a Message. "So we ever lag behind them, by gaps of Time none of us knows how to make up. If we could but capture one Machine intact, we might take it apart to see how it works.... Yet, what use? They'll only invent another twice as fiendish,— for here are conjoin'd the two most powerful sources of Brain-Power on Earth, the one as closely harness'd to its Disciplin'd Rage for Jesus, as the other to that Escape into the Void, which is the very Asian Mystery. Together, they make up a small Army of Dark Engineers who could run the World. The Sino-Jesuit conjunction may prove a greater threat to Christendom than ever the Mongols or the Moors. Pray that more than the Quarrel over *Feng Shui* divides them."

29

Cities begin upon the day the Walls of the Shambles go up, to screen away Blood and Blood-letting, Animals' Cries, Smells and Soil, from Residents already grown fragile before Country Realities. The Better-Off live far as they may, from the concentration of Slaughter. Soon, Country Melancholicks are flocking to Town like Crows, dark'ning the Sun. Dress'd Meats appear in the Market,— Sausages hang against the Sky, forming Lines of Text, cryptick Intestinal Commentary.

The Veery Brothers, professional effigy makers, run an establishment south of the Shambles at Second and Market Streets, by the Court House. Mason, in unabating Search after the Grisly, must pay a Visit.

"Can't just have any old bundle of Rags up there, even if 'tis meant to be burnt to ashes, can we," says Cosmo, "— our Mobility like to feel they're burning *something*, don't you see? Oh, we do Jack-Boots and Petticoats, bread-and-butter items the year 'round, yet we strive for at least the next order of Magnytude...."

"Here, for example, our Publick Beheading Model,— " adds his brother Damian, "or, 'the Topper,' as we like to call it, Key to ev'rything being the Neck, o' course, for after you've led them up to the one great Moment, how can you disappoint 'em wiv any less than that nice sa'isfying *Chhhunk!* as the Blade strikes, i'n't it, and will pure Beeswax do the Job? No,— fine for the Head and whatever, but look what you've got to chop at,— spine? throat? muscles in the neck? well,— not exactly Wax, is it? So it's on with the old Smock, lovely visit next door, scavenging among th' appropriately siz'd Necks for bones and suet and such. Then it's up to the Kiddy here to cover it all over and give it a Head with a famous, or better Infamous, Face. He's a rare Wax Artist, our Cosmo is. Likenesses almost from another World, perhaps not a World many of us would find that comfortable. Products of the innocent Hive, Sir, and beneath, the refuse of the daily Slaughter, yes there you have it, a grisly Amalgam, perhaps even a sort of Teaching,— sure you'd enter any dark-en'd Room *our* lads and lasses happen'd to be in, only upon ill advice indeed."

Which of course is exactly what Mason runs out and contrives to do, as soon as he gets a chance. He and Dixon go Tavern-hopping and find secret-society meetings in the back rooms of every place they visit. There is gambling, Madeira, carryings-on. Some invite them to join. Some they do join. "What, no floggings? No bare-breasted Acolytes in Chains? No ritual defloration? Drinking-games with Madeira, that's it?"

Some of these *Collegia*, learning that Mason's Name is Mason, claim to be Free-Masons of one Lodge and another. "Anyone whose name is Mason is automatickally a Member, the first of your Name likely having work'd as a Stonemason back in the Era of the great Cathedrals,— as you are descended from him, so are Free-Masons today descended from his Guild-Fellows. You are a Mason *ex Nomine*, as some might describe it." Unless, of course, 'twas an elaborate scheme to avoid paying for Drink.

In one of these Ale Venues, somewhere between The Indian Queen and The Duke of Gloucester, there proves to be a Back Room's back room,— for purposes of uninvited inspection a pantry, but in fact an Arsenal for various Mob activities. Anyone else out in search of Goth-ickal experiences might have found it neither quite ancient nor omi-nous enough to bother with. But Mason can ever locate those spaces most fertile for the husbanding of Melancholy. So now, blundersome, in he steps, candle-less as well, relying upon the light of a Lanthorn hang-ing outside the small Window, waiting for his eyes to adjust, making out first two Figures, then three, and at length the Roomful, erect, crowding close, without breath or pulse,— his immediate need is to speak, not challenging but pleading,— slowly, as he is able to make out more of the Faces, what he fears grows less deniable,— they are directing, nowhere but into his own eyes, stares unbearable with meaning he cannot grasp, as if,— he does not wish to examine this too closely,— as if they know him, and withal, *expect him....*

Mason is certain he saw at least one of them at the first Meeting with the Commissioners, the week previous,— tho', that being largely ceremonial, all the Faces then had been fram'd in more or less identical Wigs. Yet if he recognizes me, Mason asks himself now, why doesn't he speak? groping within for the Gentleman's Name, as the enigmatic Phiz continues, in the weak light, to sharpen toward Revelation.

As it will prove, all the Effigies in the back room bear Faces of Commissioners for the Boundary Line, tho' Mason, anxiously upon the lookout wherever in town they have to go, won't fully appreciate it till the second Meeting, on 1 December. The calm oval room has been furnish'd hastily, but minutes before their arrival, with a perfect Row of black comb-back'd Chairs for the Commissioners, set upon one side of a long Table, facing a Window revealing a late autumnal Garden,— white statues of uncertain Gender leaning in sinuous Poses,— and across the Table, two Chairs of ordinary Second Street origin and faux-Chippendale carving, unmatch'd, intended for the Astronomers, who will have little to look at but the Commissioners.

Luckily for Mason, the Gentlemen enter, not all in a Troop, but in ones and pairs, so giving him a few extra moments in which to work upon his Composure, which needs it. Those waxen Faces that gaz'd at him with such midnight Intent,— here are their daytime counterparts to greet him, with the same, O God in Thy Mercy, *the same look...*as if deliberately to recall the other night. But how could they, could anyone, know? has he been under Surveillance ever since landing here? And,— the Figures in that far back room, were they *not* Effigies at all, but real people, only *pretending* to be Effigies, yes these very faces,— ahrrhh! (What did he interrupt them at, then, in the lampless chamber, what Gathering he wasn't supposed to know about? And why couldn't he remember more clearly what had happen'd to *him* after he went into the Room? Was his Brain, in Mercy, withholding the memory?)

...As the Progress of Wax automata, by ones and twos, approaches, provoking, daring Mason to bring any of it up, the Possibility never presents itself to him, that all the Line Commissioners, from both Provinces, being political allies of the Proprietors, are natural and obvious Effigy Fodder to a Mobility of Rent-payers,— as will be later pointed out by Dixon, who now has begun casting him curious, offended looks. Neither has slept well for a Fortnight, amid the house-rocking Ponderosities of commercial Drayage, the Barrels and Sledges rumbling at all Hours over the paving-Stones, the Town on a-hammering and brick-laying itself together about them, the street-sellers' cries, the unforeseen coalescences of Sailors and Citizens anywhere in the neighboring night to sing Liberty and wreak Mischief, hoofbeats in large numbers passing beneath the Window, the cries of Beasts from the city Shambles,— Philadelphia in the Dark, in an all-night Din Residents may have got accustom'd to, but which seems to the Astronomers, not yet detach'd from the liquid, dutiful lurches of the Packet thro' th' October seas, the very Mill of Hell.

"Worse than London by far," Mason brushing away Bugs, rolling over and over, four sides at five minutes per side, a Goose upon Insomnia's Spit, uncontrollably humming to himself an idiotic Galop from *The Rebel Weaver*, which he attended in London just before Departure, instead of Mr. Arne's *Love in a Cottage*, which would have been wiser. Smells of wood-smoke, horses, and human sewage blow in the windows, along with the noise. Somewhere down the Street a midnight Church congregation sings with a fervency unknown in Sapperton, or in Bisley, for that matter. He keeps waking with his heart racing, fear in his Bowels, something loud having just occurr'd...waiting for it to repeat. And as he relaxes, never knowing the precise moment it begins, the infernal deedle ee, deedle ee, deedle-eedle-eedle-dee again.

The Rebel Weaver was set in the Golden Valley, being a light-hearted account of the late battles there between Weavers and Clothiers, with interludes of music, juggling, and tricksome Animal Life. "Strangely," Mason has reported to Dixon, "I was not appall'd,— tho' I've every reason to be." The plot, about a Weaver's son who loves the Daughter of a Clothier, and the conflict of loyalties resulting, presents nothing more troubling sentimentally, than the comick misunderstandings of an Italian Opera. One or two of the slower tunes, lugubrious to some Ears, he even yet fancies, tho' this damn'd Galop is another matter.

Upon his own side of the Bed, Dixon snores in a versatility of Tone that Mason, were he less anxious about getting to sleep, might be taking

Notes upon, perhaps to be written up and submitted to the *Philosophical Transactions,* so unexpectedly polyphonic do some passages emerge, all at the same unhurried, yet presently infuriating, *Andante.* Both men lie in the Clothing they have worn all day, Dixon as faithful to field-Surveyor's custom, as Mason to that of the Star-Gazer,— his quotidian dress, at Greenwich, having ever doubl'd as his Observing Suit. To sleep, one simply took off the Coat,— tho' Dixon has advis'd against this here. He is of course right. The Bugs run free,— American bugs, who so much resent being brush'd off Human Surfaces, that they will bite anyone for even approaching.

That's it, then. Himself a giant Bug, he rolls quietly from under the Counterpane and crawls from the Room,— dresses in the Hallway and upon the Stairs, and is soon insensibly translated into The Orchid Tavern, by Dock Creek, Hat beside him, Queue a-snarl, buying too many Rounds, enjoying viciously as any recreational Traveler the quaint Stridencies of a Politics not his own, yet, before Intoxication sets in, continuing to seek, somewhere in the perilous Text of Faction, Insult, and Threat, a Line or two of worth, to take home with him.

"Pennsylvania Politics? Its name is Simplicity. Religious bodies here cannot be distinguish'd from Political Factions. These are Quaker, Anglican, Presbyterian, German Pietist. Each prevails in its own area of the Province. Till about five years ago, the Presbyterians fought among themselves so fiercely, that despite their great Numbers, they remain'd without much Political Effect,— lately, since the Old and New Lights reach'd their Accommodation, all the other Parties have hasten'd to strike bargains with them as they may,— not least of these the Penns, who tho' Quaker by ancestry are Anglican in *Praxis,*— some even say, Tools of Rome. Mr. Shippen, upon whom you must wait for each penny you'll spend, is a Presbyterian, the City Variety, quite at ease as a member of the Governor's Council. As for the Anglicans of Philadelphia, the periodick arrival in Town of traveling ministries such as the Reverend MacClenaghan's have now split those Folk between traditional Pennites, and Reborns a-dazzle with the New Light, who are more than ready to throw in with the Presbyterians, against the Quakers,— tho' so far Quakers have been able to act in the Assembly as a body, and prevail,— "

"…Not sure I'm following this," Mason says.

"May you never have the need, Sir. 'Tis useful nonetheless, now and then, to regard Politics here, as the greater American Question in Miniature,— in the way that Chess represents war,— with Governor Penn a game-piece in the form of the King."

"Who'd be the Rockingham Whigs, I wonder?…"

At a short Arpeggio from the Clavier, a Voice thro' the Vapors announces, "The Moment now ye've all been waiting for…the Saloon of The Orchid Tavern is pleas'd to Present, the fam'd Leyden-Jar *Danse Macabre!* with that Euclid of the Elecktrick, Philadelphia's own *Poor Richard,* in the part of Death."

Eager Applause, as into the Lanthorn-Light comes a hooded, Scythe-bearing Figure in Skeleton's Disguise,— tho' the Instant it begins to speak, all sinister Impression is compromis'd. "Ah…? ex-cellent…. Now, if I might have a few Volunteers…from what obviously, here tonight, is the Flower of Philadelphian Youth…. Behold, Pilgrims of Prodigy, my new Battery,— twenty-four Jars crackling and ready." Dr. Franklin now throwing back his hood, to reveal Lenses tonight of a curious shade of Aquamarine, allowing his eyes to be view'd, yet conveying a bleak Contentment that discourages lengthy Gazing. "Come, Gentlemen,— who'll be next,— that's it, go-o-od, Line of Fops, all hold hands, Line of Fops, how many have we now,— dear me, not enough, come, one more, ever room for one more…." Thus briskly collecting into Line a dozen or so heedless Continentals, placing into the hands of the hindmost a Copper Cable from one Terminal of the Battery, and grasping the hand of the frontmost, Franklin reaches with the Blade of his Scythe to touch the other Terminal,— the Landlord at the same Instant dousing the Glim,— so that the resulting Tableau is lit by terrifying stark Flashes of Blue-white Light, amid the harsh Sputter of the Fulminous Fluid, and the giggling, and indeed Screaming, of the Participants, Snuff flying ev'rywhere and now and then igniting in Billows of green Flame, amid infernal Columns of Smoak.

The Battery having discharg'd, Light is restor'd,— the Company presently regaining enough Composure to note the Arrival of a Thunder-Gust, as Windows begin to rattle and Trees to creak, and the Landlord rushes about trying to Draw the Curtains,— as, thereby, the hearty

Opposition of these Electrophiles, whose wish is ever to observe their admir'd Fluid in its least mediated form.

"So much for Harlequin," cries Dr. Franklin, "Let us get out into the Night's Main Drama!— There's Weather-Gear for all, this Scythe here is the perfect Shape to catch us a Bolt, perhaps a good many,— better than a Key upon a Kite, indeed,— think of it as Death's Picklock,— come, form your Line...all here?" pulling his Hood up again, "— felonious Entry, into the Anterooms of the Cre-a-torr....Not joining us tonight, Mr. Mason?" Lowering his Lenses and staring for an Instant. Before Mason, from whom all comfort has flown, can quite reply, the Figure has turn'd and taken a Hand at the end of the Line,— the Door opens and the Wind and Rain blow in, Thunder crashes, and with odd strangl'd cries of Amusement, the Party of Seekers are plung'd out into the Storm, and vanish'd.

30

Upon the day appointed, pursuant to the Chancery Decision, the Commissioners of both Provinces, with Remembrancers and Correspondents, attended by a Thronglet of Children out of School, Sailors, Irishmen, and other Citizens exempt from or disobedient to the humorless rule of Clock-Time here, all go trooping down to Cedar Street and the House in Question, to establish its north Wall officially as the southernmost Point of Philadelphia. Fifteen Miles South of this, to the width of a Red Pubick Hair or R.P.H., will the West Line run.

The neighbors gather and mutter. "Well ye would think they'd wait a bit." "Eighty years, that isn't enough?" "Way this Town's growing, that South Point'll be across the street and down the Block before the Week's out." "Aye, moving even as we speak, hard to detain as a greas'd Pig." The Sector is borne in a padded Waggon, like some mechanickal Odalisque. Children jump, flapping their Arms in unconscious memory of when they had wings, to see inside. "Why not use the south Wall?" inquire several of them, far too 'pert for their sizes and ages. "The south Wall lies within private property," replies the Mayor's Assistant, "— so, as the southernmost Publick Surface, the Parties have agreed upon this north Wall here, facing the Street."

Mr. Benjamin Loxley and his Crew have been busily erecting an Observatory in a vacant Piece, nearby, mid the mix'd rhythms of Hammers, each Framer at his own slightly different Tempo, and blurted phrases of songs. "Done many of these, Ben?"

"First one,— but don't tell anybody. Pretty straightforward, regular Joists and Scantlings, nothing too exotick, beyond this Cone Roof, trying to accommodate the tall one, spacing the Collar-beams so he won't thump his Head when he stands up,— tho' they'll be spending most of their time either sitting, or 'pon their Backs,— "

"Hmm."

"Oh now, Clovis, your Bride is safe,— 'tis the only way for them to look straight up at the Stars that pass high overhead, these being the Best for the Latitude, as they say."

"Aye? and that great Telescope Tube thing ever pointing straight up? Heh, heh. Why's it got to be that big?"

"Don't break your rhythm, Hobab, I was quite enjoying it. The Gents wish to measure this quite closely,— find and keep the Latitude of their Line, to fractions of a second of Arc,— the Tube being the Radius of the Limb, see, a longer Tube will swing you a bigger Arc, longer Limb, longer Divisions, more room between the Markings, easier reading, nicer reading."

Mr. Chew appears to be making a Speech. "Shall we stop hammering till he's done?" Hobab inquires.

"Other Questions arise," Mr. Loxley gazing into the Distance. "Your notion of Futurity. Shall we continue to need Contracts with these people? How soon do you expect our Savior's Return may render them void? Considerations like that."

"I say whenever you can, give 'm all a Twenty-one-Hammer Salute," growls Clovis.

"I say take their Money, we don't have to love 'm," says Hobab.

"Or even marry 'm," adds young Elijah, the Swamper.

"Here are the Astronomers," Mr. Loxley notes, "perhaps you'd like to share some of your Analysis with them,— God grant ye clear Skies, Gentlemen," shouting over the newly percussive Activity of his Crew.

Dixon, removing his hat, tries out the Door-way, goes in, and lies supine upon the fresh-sawn Planking. Looking up, he sees Clovis, spread still as a Spider among the radial Rafters, watching him.

"Ask you something, Sir?...What thought have you given to getting that great Tube in the Door?"

"Oh, Mr. Bird calculated the whole thing, years ago, over in England. All on Paper."

"Before there was ever a Scantling cut?"

"Before there was ever a Screw cut for the Instrument."

"I'll study on it. Thank ye, Sir." He tips a nonexistent Hat and descends.

Mason looks in. "*Will* we get it in the Door, Dixon?"

Dixon stands up, carefully. "This is the very same Whimwham we had at the Cape…?"

"No Trouble, Gents, we'll make ye a Door it shall go in," promises the cheery Hobab.

"And out, too!" adds Elijah, from beneath a Load of Weatherboarding.

Dixon, as a Needle man anxious to obtain the latest Magnetick Intelligence of the Region that awaits them, Rumors reaching him of a Coffee-House frequented by those with an interest in the Magnetick, however it be manifested, shows up one night at The Flower-de-Luce, in Locust-Street. There, over the Evening, he will find, among the Clientele, German Enthusiasts, Quack Physicians, Land-Surveyors, Iron-Prospectors, and Watch-Thieves who know how to draw a Half-Hunter from one Pocket into another with the swiftness of a Lodestone clapping a Needle to its Influence. Strangers greet him as they might a Friend of ancient standing, whilst others, obviously seeking to shun his Company, glare whenever the Fumes of Tobacco allow them mutual Visibility. He has no idea what any of it is about. Gently tacking among the crowd, he arrives at the Bar. "Evening, Sir, what'll it be?"

"Half and Half please, Mount Kenya Double-A, with Java Highland,— perhaps a slug o' boil'd Milk as well…?"

"Planning on some *elevated* Discourse tonight?" jests the Coffee-Draper, swiftly and with little misdirection assembling Dixon's order. His Wig shines with a Nimbus in the strange secondary light from the Mirror behind him.

"This may seem an odd question, Sir,— but…have I been in here before?"

"Goodness no, yet how many times a day do I get ask'd that very thing. Diff'rent Visitors with diff'rent Expectations. You strike me as the English Tavern sort, and so you'll be noticing there's less Reserve 'round here than you may be us'd to,— tho' any who seek a Quarrel may readily find it, yea unto Dirks and Pistols, if that truly be your Preference.... Howbeit,— make yourself at home, and good Luck in America."

Dixon beamingly adverts to the early Crowd, here, immediately noticing Dr. Franklin's friend Dolly, tho' she's certainly not as eye-catchingly rigg'd out tonight as he's seen her before,— nor can he immediately 'spy any of her Companions. Soberly consulting a large Map upon a Mahogany Desk-top, she holds a pair of Silver Dividers, multiply-jointed, tending to White Gold in the Candle-light,— and refers repeatedly to a Book of Numerickal Tables, now and then gracefully walking the Instrument up, down, and 'cross its paper Stage. When she looks up at last, he guesses from her eyes that she knows he's been there, all the time. "Why Mr. Dixon. Well met." Holding out her hand, and before Dixon can begin to incline to kiss it, shaking his, as men do. "These *Data* arriv'd but this Instant, by the German Packet,— the latest Declination Figures. Our easterly movement, in Pennsylvania, as it's been doing in latter Years, decelerates yet,— here, 'tis four point five minutes east," as Dixon attentively gazes over her shoulder, "when in the year 'sixty, 'twas four point six. If you head South, 'twill be three point nine at Baltimore."

"Were these measur'd Heights," he murmurs, "a very Precipice."

"What could be causing it, do you imagine?"

"Something underground, moving Westward...?"

"Hush." Her Eyes rapidly sweep the Vicinity. "No one ever speaks of that aloud here,— what sort of incautious Lad are you, exactly?"

"Why, the usual sort, I guess."

"Well." She pulls him into an alcove. "Rather took you for an All-Nations Lad, myself."

"Been there." The serving-girls at The All-Nations Coffee-House are costumed in whimsical versions of the native dress of each of the coffee-producing countries,— an Arabian girl, a Mexican girl, a Javanese girl, and according to Dolly, a Sumatran girl as well,— a constantly shifting Pageant of allegorical Coffees of the World, to some ways of thinking, in fact, quite educational, tho' attracting a core Clientele louder, beefier, and altogether less earnest than Dixon by now expects to find in Philadelphia.

"Mm-Hmm...? Sumatran, tha say...?"

"You seem about to swoon, Sir."

He takes a delighted breath. "Ah don't know how much of my story tha may already have heard," bringing his Chair closer, "— or, to be fair to Mason, our story."

She shifts her own Chair away. "You and Mr. Mason are...quite close, I collect."

"Huz? We get along. This is our second Job together...? The Trick is all in stayin' out of each other's way, really."

"There are Arrangements in the World," she explains, "too sadly familiar to Women, wherein, as we say among us, with the one, you get the other as well,— "

"Lass, Lass...? Eeh, what a Suggestion. We'd make thah' one only to our Commissioners, I vouch.... Unless, that is, tha're indicating some interest in Mason?"

"Or asking 'pon Molly's behalf," her Eye-Lashes indulging in an extra Bat. "This gets very complicated, doesn't it?"

"Mason does need to be out more, for fair. Ah'm but thinkin' o' meself, here...? Ever been coop'd up with a Melancholick, for days on end?"

Dolly shrugs. "Oh, aye, Molly Sour-Apple. She's lucky I don't get like that. Two of us? Forget it."

"I find it hard work to be cheery all the time," says Dixon, "— as cheery as it seems I must."

"Really,— tell me all. The Way your Face begins to ache."

" 'Here's the Optimist,' wagging their Thumbs. Mr. Franklin must get thah' all the time...?"

"Mr. Franklin does not confide in me, nor would I encourage him to. He is too charming, too mysterious, entirely the wrong sort for a great Philosopher."

Dixon touches the end of his Nose. "Ow!" shaking his finger back and forth. "Needs some filing down. Do excuse me."

"My Tale is simple. I held my first Mariner's Compass when I was nine, an age when Girls develop unforeseen yet passionate Interests. I believ'd there was a Ghost in the Room. I walk'd with it, then, ev'ry-where. The first thing I understood was that it did not always point North...and it was the Dips and Deflexions I grew most curious about."

"In my Circumferentor Box, I learn'd to read what Shapes lay beneath the Earth, all in the Needle's Dance...? Upon the Fell, as if there were not enough already out there to bring me anxiety, I discover'd my Instrument acting as a *Cryptoscope,* into Powers hidden and waiting the Needles of Intruders, set up as a picket to warn Something within of any unannounc'd wishes to enter. No Creatures of the Fell I'd ever heard of enjoy'd that much Protection,— being shabby, solitary, notable more for the irrational fierceness of their Desires, than for any elegance or Justice in the enactment of them."

"You have impress'd them in Maryland," she informs him. "Cecilius Calvert, or, as he is styl'd by some, for his unreflective effusions, 'The Silliest' Calvert,— tho' not by me, for I consider him subtle,— believes you a Wizard, a Dowser of Iron."

"Close attention to the Instrument, a lot of Back-sighting, repetition, and frustration,— why disenchant them? If it's Weird Geordie Powers they wish, why W.G.P.'s they shall have, and plenty of them too...? Mr. Calvert offer'd me Port, in a Silver Cup...? Seem'd quite merry...?"

"In most places it is term'd, 'Giggling.' They are Geese, down there. They imagine, that you and your Instrument will make of them Nabobs, like Lord Lepton, to whose ill-reputed Plantation you must be drawn, upon your way West, resistlessly as the Needle. Then, Sailor among the Iron Isles,— Circumferentor Swab,— Beware."

31

One morning in late December, they wake to a smell of Sea-Weed and Brine. The Wind is sensibly colder,— before it swiftly run gray small clouds, more and less dark. Light, when it arrives, comes ever cross-wise. "Something wrong with the Town this morning," Dixon mutters.

"And what's that G-dawful twittering sound?"

"Styl'd 'Birds,' I'm told...?"

"How's it possible we've never heard any here before,— Dixon! Hold,— the Hammers! the Rip-Saws! the Meat-Waggons! the Screaming uninterrupted! what's happen'd?"

"Eeh...it's been Christmas, hasn't it...?"

"One of us," Mason declares, "must put on his Shoes and Coat, and go down into that Street, there, and discover the reason for this unsettling Silence."

"Eeh, so let's have Junior's Arse in the Roasting-Pan once again, shall we,— thah's bonny!" protests Dixon.

"Be practical,— if they kill you, and I remain safe, the loss to British Astronomy, if any, will go largely unnotic'd."

"Well,— put thah' way, of course,— where's m' Hat, then...?, not that one, thankee, Sir...?, no, I'll need the Broad-Brim today,— "

"You're going out as a Quaker?"

"Eeh! He has Costume-Advice for me now as well! He, who all too plainly exhibits his Need, when in Publick, ever to deflect Attention,— "

"— Inexpensive Salvo," Mason notes.

"Geordie Intuition, then," Dixon tapping his Head with the side of his Thumb, before pulling on a classick Philadelphia Quaker's Hat, differing in little but Size from thousands of others here in Town. "Trust mine. In London they may sift you by your Shoes,— but in this Place, 'tis Hat and Wig by which a man, aye and Woman too, may infallibly be known."

"They've been looking at, at my Wig, all this time? My Hat? Dixon,— you're sure?"

"Aye, and forming Opinions bas'd upon what they saw, as well...?"

"...Oh. Ehm, what, f'r example?"

"Eeh, what matter,— 'tis much too late...? they've all made up their minds about thee by now."

"Then I'll wear something else."

"So then they'll be on about thah',— 'Aye there he is, old Look Before Ye Leap,— *he*, bold enough to clap on anything as stylish as the Adonis? *eeh* no, 'tis but the tried and true for old Heavens What'll They Think o' Me.' "

"What,— my Wig, it isn't...adventurous enough, you're saying."

"Attend me, man, Molly and Dolly, remember them? discuss little but thy Appearance, and ways to modify it, at least in my hearing,— ruining, alas, and more than once, the promise of a Sparkish Evening,— thy Wig in particular provoking one of the greatest,— forgive me,— of all my Failures of Attention."

"It's a Ramillies, of the middling sort...bought some years since of a fugitive Irish Wig-Maker at Bermondsey...styl'd himself 'Mister Larry, Whilst Ye Tarry'...nothing remarkable at all about it. You say you've been spending time with— "

"Time and Coin and little else, aye but thah's another Tale, 's it not...? withal, my Reconnaissance mission awaits, and Damme, I'm Off!" And he is, Mason following so closely as nearly to have his Nose caught in the Jamb.

"Wait,— I was going out wi' ye!" Hopping down the stairs into his Shoes, attempting to button his Jacket, "How are you fitting that in, among all the Obs and Social Visits?"

"Fitting whah' in...?" Dixon staring in comick Dismay down toward his Penis, as he has seen Market-place Drolls do. The Snow this morning is ankle-deep, crepitous, with more on the way. The Street before the Inn seems deserted. "Odd for Wednesday Market...?"

" 'Tis another damn'd Preacher," Mason opines, "who's magnetiz'd the whole Population away to a Tent someplace. You know how they are, here. Flock to anything won't they, worldly Philadelphians."

The nearest Coffee-House, The Restless Bee, lies but a block and a half distant. There, if anyplace, should be News, up-to-the-Minute. On the way over, they begin at last to hear Ships' Bells and Boatswains' Pipes from the Docks, Children out coasting, dogs barking, a Teamster with a laden Waggon in a Snow-Drift, and presently indeed the crescent Drone and Susurrus of Assembly. Directly in front of The Restless Bee, they come upon a Circle of Citizens, observing, and in some cases wagering upon, a furious Struggle between two Men, one to appearance a City Quaker, whose Hat has been knock'd off,— the other, an apparent Presbyterian from the Back-Country, dress'd in Animal Hides from Head to Foot,— each having already taken a number of solid Blows from the other, neither showing any lapse of Pugnacity.

"Excuse me, Sir," Mason inquires of a Gentleman in full Wig, Velvet Coat, and Breeches, and carrying a Lawyer's Bag, "— what is the Matter here?"

The Attorney, after staring at them for a bit, introduces himself as Mr. Chantry. "Ye're from well out of Town if ye've not heard the news."

"Eeh," Dixon's Eyes seeking the Zenith.

"At Lancaster,— day before yesterday,— the Indians that were taking refuge in the Gaol there, were massacr'd ev'ry one, by local Irregulars,— the same Band that slew the other Indians at Conestoga, but week before last."

"So finishing what they'd begun," contributes an Apron'd Mechanick nearby. "Now the entire Tribe is gone, the lot."

"Were there no Soldiers to prevent it?" Dixon asks.

"Colonel Robertson and his Regiment of Highlanders refus'd to stir, toasting their Noses whilst that brave Paxton Vermin murder'd old people, small children, and defenseless Drunkards."

"Not being men enough to face Warriors, in a real Fight."

"Mind yeer Speech, Friend, or 'tis your Hat'll be on the Ground as well, and your Head in it."

"And here's to Matt Smith, and Rev^d. Stewart!"

"Here's Death to 'em, the cowardly Dogs!" Further Insults, then Snow-Balls, Fists, and Brickbats, begin to fly.

"This way, Gentlemen," Mr. Chantry helpfully steering the Surveyors to the Alley and thro' a back Entry into the Coffee-House, where they find Tumult easily out-roaring what prevails outside. With its own fuliginous Weather, at once public and private, created of smoke billowing from Pipes, Hearths, and Stoves, the Room would provide an extraordinary sight, were any able to see, in this Combination, peculiar and precise, of unceasing Talk and low Visibility, that makes Riot's indoor Sister, Conspiracy, not only possible, but resultful as well. One may be inches from a neighbor, yet both blurr'd past recognizing,— thus may Advice grow reckless and Prophecy extreme, given the astonishing volume of words moving about in here, not only aloud but upon Paper as well, Paper being waved in the air, poked at repeatedly for emphasis, held up as Shielding against uncongenial remarks. Here and there in the Nebulosity, lone Lamps may be made out, at undefin'd Distances, snugly Halo'd,— Servant-Boys moving to and fro, House-Cats in warm currents of flesh running invisibly before them, each Boy vigorously working his small Bellows to clear a Path thro' the Smoke, meantime calling out Names true and taken.

"Boy, didn't they tell you that Name is never to be spoken aloud in this Room?"

"Ha!" from somewhere in the Murk, "so ye've sneak'd in again, where yer face can't be seen!"

"I have ev'ry right, Sir,— "

"Boy, clear me a pathway to that infamous Voice, and we shall see,— "

"Gentlemen, Gentlemen!"

"There'll be Pistol-Play soon enough, by the looks of this new Express here, just arriv'd from over Susquehanna, for there's no doubt about it now,— the Paxton Boys are on the Move."

"Hurrah!"

"Shame!"

"How many, Jephthah?"

" 'Tis Micah. An hundred, and picking up Numbers by the Hour. So says it here." Smokers pause in mid-puff. The communal Vapors presently beginning to thin, human forms emerge in outline, some standing upon Chairs and even Tables, others seeking, in literal Consternation, refuge beneath the Furniture.

"The Boys say they're coming for the Moravian Indians this time."

"Indians, in Philadelphia?" Dixon curiously.

Mr. Chantry explains. Converted by the Moravian Brethren years before the last French war, caught between the warring sides, distrusted by ev'ryone, wishing only to live a Christian Life, these Indians were peacefully settl'd up near the Lehigh when the Rangers there came after them, but a few Weeks before the Conestoga murders, suspecting them of being in League with Pontiac, whose depredations were then at their full Flood. Tho' some of these People were slain, yet most escaped, arriving at Philadelphia in November,— "About the time you boys did, in fact,— 'spite of the Mob at Germantown, who nearly did for 'em,— and now an hundred forty Souls, from Wyalusing and Wecquetank and Nazareth, they're down at Province Island, below the City, where the Moravians and Quakers tend them,— the Army, given its showing at Lancaster, being no longer trusted."

"The Paxtons'll kill us all!" someone blubbers.

"Fuck 'em, they shan't have anyone here. Enough is enough."

"Our Line had better be set no nearer than Schuylkill, and the Ferries there brought back, first thing."

"How many Cannon have we in Town?"

Mason and Dixon look at each other bleakly. "Well. If I'd known 'twould be like *this* in America..."

In fact, when word arriv'd of the first Conestoga Massacre, neither Astronomer quite register'd its full Solemnity. The Cedar-Street Observatory was up at last,— Mr. Loxley and his Lads were done shimming and cozening square Members to Circular Purposes,— and after two days of Rain and Snow, Mason and Dixon were taking their first Obs from it. Mason did note as peculiar, that the first mortal acts of Savagery in America after their Arrival should have been committed by Whites against Indians. Dixon mutter'd, "Why, 'tis the d——'d Butter-Bags all over again."

They saw white Brutality enough, at the Cape of Good Hope. They can no better understand it now, than then. Something is eluding them.

Whites in both places are become the very Savages of their own worst Dreams, far out of Measure to any Provocation. Mason and Dixon have consult'd with all it seems to them they safely may. "Recall that there are two kinds of electricity," Dr. Franklin remark'd, "positive and negative. Cape Town's curse is its Weather,— the Electrick Charge during the Stormy season being ev'rywhere Positive, whilst in the Dry Season, all is Negative."

"Are you certain," Dixon mischievously, " 'tis not the other way 'round? That the rainy weather— "

"Yes, yes," somewhat brusquely, "whichever Direction it goes, the relevant Quantity here, is the size of the Swing between the two,— that vertiginous re-polarizing of the Air, and perhaps the Æther too, which may be affecting the very Mentality of the People there."

"Then what's America's excuse?" Dixon inquir'd, mild as Country Tea.

"Unfortunately, young people," recalls the Rev^d, "the word *Liberty*, so unreflectively sacred to us today, was taken in those Times to encompass even the darkest of Men's rights,— to injure whomever we might wish,— unto extermination, were it possible,— Free of Royal advice or Proclamation Lines and such. This being, indeed and alas, one of the Liberties our late War was fought to secure."

Brae, on her way out of the Room for a moment, turns in the Door-way, shock'd. "What a horrid thing to say!" She does not remain to press the Point.

"At the Time of Bushy Run," confides Ives LeSpark, "— and I have seen the very Document,— General Bouquet and General Gage both sign'd off on expenditures to replace Hospital Blankets us'd 'to convey the Small-pox to the Indians,' as they perhaps too clearly stipulated. To my knowledge," marvels Ives, "this had never been attempted, on the part of any modern Army, till then."

"Yes, Wicks?" Mr. LeSpark beaming at the Rev^d, "You wish'd to add something? You may ever speak freely here,— killing Indians having long ago ceas'd to figure as a sensitive Topick in *this* House."

"Since you put it that way," the Rev^d, in will'd Cheeriness, "firstly,— ev'ryone knew about the British infection of the Indians, and no one spoke out. The Paxton Boys were but implementing this same Wicked Policy of extermination, using Rifles instead,— altho',— Secondly, unlike our own more virtuous Day, no one back then, was free from Sin. Quakers, as handsomely as Traders of less pacific Faiths, profited from the sale of Weapons to the Indians, including counterfeit Brown Besses that blew up in the faces of their Purchasers, as often as fell'd any White Settlers. Thirdly,— "

"How many more are there likely to be?" inquires his Brother-in-Law. "Apparently I must reconsider my offer."

"Ev'ryone got along," declares Uncle Wicks. "Ye can't go looking for Sinners, not in an Occupied City,— for ev'ryone at one time or another here was some kind of Rogue, the Preacher as the Printer's Devil, the Mantua-Maker as the Milk-Maid,— even little Peggy Shippen, God bless her, outrageous Flirt even at four or five, skipping in and out, handing each of us Flowers whilst her Father frown'd one by one over our Disbursements. 'Papa's Work is making him sad,' the Miniature Temptress explain'd to us. 'My work never makes *me* sad.' 'What is your work, little Girl?' asks your innocent Uncle. 'To marry a General,' she replies, sweeping back her Hair, 'and die rich.' During the Occupation, having reach'd an even more dangerous Age, she had her Sights actually train'd upon poor young André, till he had his Hurricane, and march'd away, whereupon she sulk'd, tho' not without Company, till Arnold march'd in,— the little Schuylkill-side Cleopatra."

"Am I about to be shock'd?" inquires Tenebræ, re-entering.

"Hope not," DePugh blurts quietly.

"Well, DePugh."

"You've made an impression," mutters Ethelmer.

"Didn't mean to, I'm sure."

Tenebræ surveys the Pair. Unpromising. She sits, and bends to a Patch of Chevron-Stitch'd Filling.

Meanwhile, Mason and Dixon, a-jangle thro' Veins and Reins with Caffeous Humors, impatient themselves to speak, are launch'd upon the choppy Day, attending, with what Civility they may summon, the often reckless Monologues of others.

"The true War here is between the City and the back Inhabitants,—the true dying, done by Irish, Scots, Indians, Catholics, far from Philadelphia, as from any Ear that might have understood their final words. Yet is the City selling rifles to anyone with the Price, most egregiously the Indians who desire our Dissolution,— "

"The rivalry is withal useful to the British, our common Enemy, who thus gain the pretext for keeping troops forever upon our Land."

"Whilst their damn'd Proclamation Line, forbids to venture there those same back Inhabitants who took Ohio, at great suffering, from the French. These damn'd British, with their list of Offenses growing daily, have much to answer for."

"Oh, I tremble that Britain should ever have to reckon with the base cowards who left Braddock to die,— who will turn and flee at the stir of a feather, be it but upon some dead Turkey-cock. Oh,— let us by no means offer Offense to the scum of Hibernia, nor to the Jacobite refuse of Scotland, nor to any one of this mongrel multiplicity of mud-dwellers, less civiliz'd, indeed less human, than the Savages 'pon whom they intrude."

"Is he in here again? Someone, pray, kill him."

"Reason, Reason,— the Irish, Sir are school'd long and arduously in Insurrection, knowing how to take a Magazine, or raid a Convoy. Britain, tho' evoke she the tenderest feelings, has made it so."

Thus does the Lunch-Hour speed by. Soon there's a distinct feeling in the Rooms, of Afternoon. Maps have been brought and spread, Pigeons bearing Messages dispatch'd from under Roof-peaks by expert Belgians, resident here, to as far away as Lancaster County. Boys old enough to handle a Rifle are drilling out in Back. Younger brothers are active at the next Order of Minitude, with long Sticks, whilst down at the next, the Dogs run obsessively to and fro, all 'round the Edges, faces a-twist with Efforts to understand. Down the Street 'round the Corner, into the City at large, the Sailors grumble in their candle-less Ale-Hovels, the devout Man of Business looks ahead to an hour dedicated again to the Daily Question, the Child trembles at the turn in the Day when the ghosts shift about behind the Doors, and out in the Gust-beaten wilderness come the Paxton Boys...

Steadily on they ride, relax'd, in Poise,
Rifles a-thwart,— the dreaded Paxton Boys.
With Hunters' Eyes, and ancient Wrongs a-ranklin'
They soon come vis-à-vis with Mr. Franklin,
Whose Gaze behind empurpl'd Lenses hidden,
Cannot be seen, and so may not be bidden.
     — Tox, "The Siege of Philadelphia, or, Attila Turn'd Anew"

'Tis too cloudy for Obs tonight. Mason frets at the delay. As soon as they shall have taken Measurements enough to yield trustworthy Mean Values of the Zenith Distances of Algol, Marfak, Capella, and their other Latitude-Stars,— allowing them at last to compute the exact Latitude of the southernmost point of Philadelphia,— they can pack up and go looking for the next Observatory Site, someplace in that same Latitude, to the west of here.

"Can't be too soon for me," Mason mutters. They are returning to their rooms, from the Observatory. Tavern music and hoofbeats racket upon the brick, often for blocks.

"I was hoping we'd yet be in Town when those 'Boys' ride in," Dixon all but sighs.

"Why? The worst sort of Celtick Degenerates? Their Ancestors ate human flesh,— as their Relatives continue to, no doubt. They've tasted Blood, they'll shoot at anything, especially, ehm, Targets of bright Color which fail to blend enough, with the Environment. No, the best thing for this Party to do, is not dawdle, but simply get on with our Work,— basically, get out of this place, and if possible, lose the red Coat."

"Mason, reflect,— as we must go West, into the Forks of Brandywine,— and as these Barbarians of thine are advancing to the East, we are likely to meet them well before anyone in Philadelphia does...?"

Mason frowns. "Yet,— suppose we kept ever fifteen miles to the south,— any roads we'd have to cross leading up from the South, not down from Harris's Ferry,— the main body then ought to pass by to the north of us."

"Unless they've Rangers out, maybe even looking for huz...?" wistfully.

"Then you'd have your Adventure, after all. Tho' why should they bother?"

"Dunno...? Happen we're par-ticularly the Intruders they can't abide...? What must we look like? A sizable Band of Arm'd Pioneers, working for the Proprietors...? mystical Machinery they've never seen...? Up far too late at night, gazin' at the Heavens...? Why, what would thee think, were it revers'd?"

"Mightn't someone explain to them,— "

"We'd have to to draw within earshot, first,— if Tales I hear of their Rifles be true, why those German Gun-Smiths out there know how to send a Ball thro' a Pretzel, any Loop tha fancy, from a Mile away."

"You seem curiously merry at the Prospect."

"Merrily curious, rather, as to who commands them? Shall they really come against their Mother-City? Is this what America's going to be like? How, as a Quaker born, can I feel toward them any Sentiments, but those of grievous Offense,— yet how, as a child of the 'Forty-five, can my Heart fail to break, for the Lives they've been oblig'd to live? And such Inquiries along that Line."

They are just passing the Door of The Restless Bee Coffee-House, one of those remaining active all night, and, as little able to resist the sounds of Company, as to pass Nose-numb before the Perfumes of Celebes, they enter the Mid-watch Disputancy.

"Now then," Mason's Phiz presently wreathed in Delphic Vapors, "that's if ye'll excuse me,— counter-marching a bit, 'the 'Forty-five'? What would you possibly know, let alone remember, pray, of that fateful Year? You were a Child,— out there in a Pit-Cabin, wi' nowt but Spoil-Heaps to look at,— missin' it all, was the Tale ye told me, Lad!— Arrh! Arrh! The blithe piping of Youth, ever claiming a parrt in History,— I love it!" Somehow another fervent Cup is in his Hand, from which he sips at length, before singing,

> "When Night was Day
> And Day was Night
> Who, then, was the Jacobite?

"Eh? Of course you were far, far too young to appreciate those Grand Days of 'forty-five and -six, all too electrickal with Passion,— "

"Thee, Mason,— a Jacobite?"

"Anyone who was seventeen that summer, young Dixon, was a Jacobite."

Dixon does recall a band of Riders, cloak'd and mask'd, who clamor'd into Raby in the middle of the night. "I was watching from a Pantry window, down at Fetlock-level.... Boots, the Hems of Cloaks,— Tartan Patterns flashing ev'rywhere, tho' the Colors in that light were uncertain. Even now I believe that it was he...I could feel...something of such Moment...such high Purpose...I knelt, transfix'd. I would have done whatever he bade me. 'Twas the only time in my life I have felt that Surrender to Power, upon which, as I have learn'd after, to my Sorrow, all Government is founded. Never again. No more a Maiden as to thah', and thankee all the same."

"How so? He and his Forces came, and went, upon quite the other side of England,— the Irish side, most convenient to French Transport."

"And yet, could our Wishes have brought him..."

"Well. Our Wishes. However little I have to expect from my own, yet am I not grown quite so melancholick, as to in any way question those of others."

"Thoughtful of thee, Mason...?"

" 'Twas ever Sun-rise, Dixon, in those times,— I recall less well the Nights,— each morning bringing us in fresh news,— sightings of him ev'rywhere. We chose to loiter near the Houses with Pine Trees by 'em, such being a Coded Welcome to any Jacobite on the Run, as a sign of food and Shelter within."

"In Durham, sometimes when the Wind was fair, we could hear the Bag-Pipes, far away...we had never heard Music like it before...some Lads, aye and Lasses, would travel Miles to hear it.... Ah didn't much fancy it, sad to say, much too predatory, less accountable for how it sounded,— less human, the ever-inflated Bag allowing the Player to decouple Song from Breath. It *never paus'd for Breath.* Can you imagine how unsettling that may've been? Not as a Wild Creature in the night, for ev'ry Beast must roar, yet draw Breath,— whilst this...comes swelling, invisible, resistless. Something that has pass'd beyond the need for Breath."

"I remember,— 'twas how Wolfe's Men came to Stroud. Without Bag-Pipes at the Van, playing that Musick forbidden to all other Scots to play since 1745, and thereby doubly damn'd,— a-chaunting and a-keening all their loss, failure, hatred, may I say, of England,— frightening village after Village into Submission,— the Brits would never have prevail'd in India...in their Spoliation of Scotland they had learn'd the Power of that Cry that never Breathes, the direct Appeal to Animal Terror, and converted it to their Uses, leaving Loin-cloths besmear'd all up and down the Tropickal World. And here were they, as those for whom they march'd, doing the same to the Vale of my Birth and Blood.

"The Clothiers had made of children my Age Red Indians, spying upon them from the Woodlands they thought were theirs. We call'd them 'the White People,' and the House they liv'd in, 'the Big House.' Splendid boyhood, you might say, but you'd be wrong,— what I had imagin'd a Paradise proving instead but the brightly illustrated front of the Arras, behind which all manner of fools lay bleeding, and real rats swarm'd, their tails undulating, waiting their moment. I discover'd the Rulers who do not live in Castles but in housing less distinct, often unable to remain past Earshot of the Engines they own and draw their Power from. Imagine you're out late on a Spring night, riding along, with your Sweetheart, an Evening trembling with Promise, all the night an Eden,— "

"Should we be discussing this?"

"Yes,— because all at once one has blunder'd sheep-eyed upon yet one more bloody Mill,— a river turn'd to a Race, the Works lit up in the dark like a great hostelry full of ill-humor'd Elves. Any chances for a few sentimental hours nipp'd, as ever in Glo'rshire, as soon as they may arise. You, simple Geordie, inhabit a part of England where ancient creatures may yet move in the Dusk, and the animals fly, and the dead pop in now and then for coffee and a chat. Upon my home soil, the Ground for growing any such Wonders has been cruelly poison'd, with the coming of the hydraulick Looms and the appearance of new sorts of wealthy individual, the late-come rulers upon whom as a younger person I spied, silent, whilst holding savage feelings within. I was expell'd from Paradise by Wolfe and his Regiment. One Penetration, and no Withdrawal could ever have Meaning. My home's no more."

Does Dixon catch an incompletely suppress'd Lilt of Insincerity? Something's askew. "Thoo are in Exile, then...?"

"With London but the first Station. Then came the Cape. Then St. Helena. Now,— these Provinces. You were there, and are here. You must have seen it,— each time, another step further...."

"Away...? Away from...?"

"Perhaps not away, Dixon. No. Perhaps *toward*. Hum. Hadn't considered that, hey, Optimism? Exercise yer boobyish Casuistry 'pon that, why don't ye? Toward what?"

"I the Booby...? I...? When indeed,— " but how much further up-field can he bring that, before a Brush from one of Rebekah's potent Wings? "Toward what, then...?" yet in the tone of a Fop to a Bedlamite, concealing the demand, "Amuse me."

32

"And they proceeded to trade Blows," cries Pitt.

"Hurrah!" adds Pliny, "— they roll'd over and over, knock'd down the Tent, Mason got a Black Eye,— "

"— and Dixon a bloody nose!"

"And the axmen came running, their Coins a-jingle, the pass-bank Bully hastily recording their wagers upon narrow scraps of Elephant,— "

"Lomax,— " chides Euphie.

"Boys!" their Parents call. "Bed-Time."

"Us. To bed?" queries Pitt.

"Who should be listening to a Tale of Geminity," explains Pliny, "if not Twins?"

"Your Surveyors *were* Twins,— " "— were they not, Uncle?"

"Up to a point, my barking Fire-Dogs,"— the Rev^d having thought it over,— "as it seem'd to me, that Mason and Dixon had been converging, to all but a Semblance,— till something...something occurr'd between them, in 'sixty-seven or 'sixty-eight, that divided their Destinies irremediably...."

"Separated them?" cry the Twins.

"Perhaps this would be a good moment for us to abandon the Narrative," says Pitt.

"Best to remember them just this way," agrees Pliny, "before an inch of that Line was ever drawn."

"Bed-time for Bookends," calls their Sister. The Express Packet *Goose-down* is whistling all non-Children ashore, back to their storm-wreck'd Jetty, back to their gray unpromising Port-Town. There to bide far into the Night, exiles from the land their Children journey to, and through, so effortlessly.

"What about Indians?" asks Pitt, adhering to the Door-Jamb.

"You *did* mention Indians," mutters Pliny, around his Brother's Shoulder.

"Do the Surveyors get to fight anyone, at least?"

"Anyone kill'd?"

"A Frigate-Battle isn't enough for you Parlor-Apes?" the Rev^d smiting himself upon the Cheeks in dismay.

"Pontiac's Conspiracy?" Pitt hopefully.

"Broken, alas, whilst the Surveyors were in Delaware, running the infamous Tangent Line, with its Consort of correctional Segments."

"The Paxton Boys?"

"No likelier. Whilst they rode whooping and shooting upon Philadelphia, the Surveyors were out in the Forks of Brandywine, well south of the Invasion Route, with a new observatory up, and the Stars nimbly hopping the Wires for them, as they gaz'd from someplace here upon Earth's Surface, yet in their Thoughts how unmappable...."

"May we have Indians tomorrow, Uncle?"

"Of course, Pitt."

"Pliny, Sir."

"The Younger." Off they go.

Tenebræ, now the youngest of the company, brings in fresh candles and fills the Tea-kettle and puts it upon the Hearth. DePugh and 'Thelmer observe her covertly as she moves seemingly unaware of the effect her flex'd Nape, her naked Ear swiftly re-conceal'd by a shaken Tress, her Hands in the Firelight, are having upon them.

If Mason's elaborate Tales are a way for him to be true to the sorrows of his own history (the Revd Cherrycoke presently resumes), a way of keeping them safe, and never betraying them, in particular those belonging to

Rebekah,— then Dixon's Tales, the Emersoniana, the ghosts of Raby, seem to arise from simple practical matiness. Who, if not Mason, at any given moment, needs cheering? A cheerful Party-Chief means a cheerful Party.

"Directly before the Falmouth Packet sail'd," he begins, one night as they wait for a Star, "William Emerson presented me with a small mysterious Package...."

" 'Twill not be an easy journey,— " quoth he, "there'll be days when the Compasses run quaquaversally wild, boxing themselves, and you, into Perplexity,— or happen the Stars be absented for fortnights at a time, with your own Pulse, as ever, a suite of changing *Tempi*. Then will a reliable Ticker come in handy. This one, as you see, is too tarnish'd and wounded, for any British or French thief to consider worth an effort,— yet, Americans being less sophisticated, I'm oblig'd, Jeremiah, to enjoin ye,— be vigilant, to the point of Folly, if Folly it takes, in your care of this Watch, for within it lies a secret mechanism, that will revolutionize the world of Horology."

"Eeh! Calculates when she's over-charging, and by how much, something like thah'?"

"What it does do, Plutonian," Emerson told him, patiently, "is never stop."

"Why aye. And upon the hour it sings 'Yankee Doodle'...?"

"You'll see. 'Tis all in the design of the Remontoire."

"The first thing an Emerson pupil learns, is that there is no Perpetual-Motion," said Dixon, "which I am in fact all these years later still upset about, Sir,— perhaps in some strange way holding thee responsible."

"What're we to do...? 'Tis a Law of the Universe,— *Prandium gratis non est.* Nonetheless, if we accept the Theorem 'Hand and Key are to Main-spring, as Clock-train is to Remontoire,' then the Solution ever depends upon removing time-rates from questions of storing Power. With the proper deployment of Spring Constants and Magnetickal Gating, Power may be borrow'd, as needed, against repayment dates deferrable indefinitely."

"Sir,— why would thee entrust to me anything so valuable, in so unruly a Country? If it got into the wrong Pocket,— "

"If anyone tries to dis-assemble it to see how it works, upon the loosening of a certain unavoidable Screw, the entire Contraption will fly apart into a million pieces, and the Secret is preserv'd."

"But the Watch,— "

"Oah, another's easily built,— the Trick's uncommonly simple, once ye've the hang of it."

"Then why aren't these ev'rywhere? If we are arriv'd in the Age of Newton transcended...? Perpetual-Motion commonplace...? why's it yet a Secret?"

"Interest," chuckl'd Emerson, cryptickally. "In fact, Compound Interest! Eeh, eeh, eeh!"

Now what seems odd to Dixon, is that ten years ago, in *Mechanics, or, The Doctrine of Motion,* Emerson express'd himself clearly and pessimistickally as to any Hopes for building a Watch that might ever keep time at Sea, whose "ten thousand irregular motions" would defeat the regularity of any Time-Piece, whether Spring- or Pendulum-Driven. Whyever then this dubious loan of a time-keeper even less hopeful? Their history in Durham together has been one of many such Messages, not necessarily clear or even verbal, which Dixon keeps failing to understand. He knows, to the Eye-Blink, how implausible Emerson is, as the source of the Watch. Meaning he is an intermediary. For whom? Who in the World possesses the advanc'd Arts, and enjoys the liberal Funding, requir'd for the building of such an Instrument? Eeh,— who indeed?

On the Falmouth Packet coming over, alone with the Enigma at last, he inspects it at length, but is unable to find any provision for winding it,— yet one must be hidden *someplace....* "Damme," he mutters into the Wind down from Black Head, " 'tis Popish Plots again, thick as Mushrooms 'round the Grave of Merriment." Here they are, these Jezzies, being expell'd from one Kingdom after another,— whence any spare Time to devote to expensive Toys like this? He is a Newtonian. He wants all Loans of Energy paid back, and ev'ry Equation in Balance. Perpetual Motion is a direct Affront. If this Watch be a message, why, it does not seem a kind one.

At last, red-eyed and by now as anxiously seeking, as seeking to avoid, any proof, he delivers the Watch to Captain Falconer, for safe-keeping inside the Ship's strong-box, till the end of the Voyage,— finding the Time-Piece, upon arrival in Philadelphia, ticking away briskly as ever,— and the counter-rhythms of the Remontoire falling precisely as the Steps of a Spanish dancer. He hopes it might be confiding to him, that its Effect of perfect Fidelity, like that of a clever Woman, is an elaborate and careful Illusion, and no more,— to be believ'd in at his Peril.

"Like to listen?" Dixon offers, one day when he and Mason are out upon the Tangent Line.

"It's all right, I believe you." Mason's eyebrows bouncing up and down politely.

"Mason, it's true! I never have to wind it! Do you ever see me winding it?"

Mason shrugs. "You might be winding it while I'm asleep, or when screen'd, as we so often are one from the other, by Trees,— you might be engaging one of these Rusticks, keeping well out of my sight, to wind it regularly.— Do I have to go on?"

"Friend. Would I quiz with you 'pon something this serious? All our assumptions about the Conservation of Energy, the *Principia*, eeh…? our very Faith, as modern Men, suddenly in question like thah'…?"

"Had I tuppence for ev'ry approach made to Bradley upon the Topick of Perpetual-Motion, I should be elsewhere than this,— recumbent I imagine upon some sand beach of the Friendly Isles, strumming my *Eukalely,* and attended by local Maidens, whom I may even sometimes allow to strum it for me."

"Eeh, you are fair suspicious…? Listen to it, at least…?"

Watch to his ear, frown growing playful, Mason after a bit begins to sing,

> "Ay, Señorit-ta, it
> Can't, be sweet-ter, what
> Shall-we, do?
>
> What a *Fies-ta,* not
> Much *Sies-ta,* do you
> Think-so, too?
>
> Look ye, the, Moon-is ascend-ding,
> You no comprehend *ing-*
> *Glés,* it's just as well,—

For, I'm-in-your-Spell, what's
That-can't-you-tell? Ay, Seen-
Yo-ree-tah!

"Yes amusing little rhythm device,— not loud enough for ensemble work of course,— "

"Forgive me, Friend, I've again presum'd our Minds running before the same Wind. My deep Error."

Mason in reply begins to wag his Head, as at some unfortunate event in the Street, whilst Dixon grows further annoy'd. "Do tha fancy I've an easy time of it? With the evidence before me, gathering each day I doahn't wind the blasted Watch,— even so, I can't believe in it...? I know thah' old man's idea of Merriment! I am thrown into a Vor-tex of Doubts."

The Watch ticks complexly on,— to Dixon, sworn not to let it out of his sight, a Burden whose weight increases with each nontorsionary day. At last, at some Station ankle-deep in a classically awful Lower Counties Bog, he is able to face the possibility he's been curs'd,— Emerson, long adept at curses, having found himself, he once confess'd to Dixon, using the gift, as he grows older, in the service less of blunt and hot-headed revenge, than of elaborate and mirthful Sport,— directed at any he imagines have wrong'd him. Has Dixon finally made this List? Did he one day cross some Line, perhaps during a conversation he's forgotten but Emerson has ever since been brooding upon, perhaps in detail? Eeh! ev'ryone's nightmare in these times,— an unremember'd Slight, aveng'd with no warning. "What did I do?" confronting his teacher at last in a Dream, "to merit such harsh reprisal? Had I been that wicked to thee, I'd surely remember...?"

"You violated your Contract," Emerson producing a sheaf of legal Paper, each Page emboss'd with some intricate Seal, which if not read properly will bring consequences Dixon cannot voice, but whose Terror he knows.... "Where would you like to begin, Plutonian?"

'Tis now Dixon recalls the advice given Mason at the Cape, by the Negrito Toko,— ever vigorously to engage an Enemy who appears in a dream. He knows that to be drawn into Emerson's propos'd Exercise, is to fight at a fatal disadvantage upon his Enemy's ground. His only course is to destroy the Document at once,— by Fire, preferably,— tho' the nearest Hearth is in the next room, too far to seize the papers and run with them.... Emerson is reading his Thoughts. "Lo, a Fire-Sign who cannot make Fire." The contempt is overwhelming. Dixon feels Defeat rise up around him. It seems the Watch wishes to speak, but it only struggles, with the paralyz'd voice of the troubl'd Dreamer. Nonetheless, Dixon's Salvation lies in understanding the Message. Whereupon, he awakes, feeling cross.

Tho' sworn to guarantee the Watch's safety, he soon finds his only Thoughts are of ways to rid himself of it. In its day-lit Ticking, the Voice so clogg'd and cryptick in his Dream has begun to grow clearer. Drinking will not send it away. "When you accept me into your life," whispering as it assumes a Shape that slowly grows indisputably Vegetable,— as it lies within its open'd traveling-case of counterfeit Shagreen, glimmering, yes a sinister Vegetable he cannot name, nor perhaps even great Linnæus,— its Surface meanwhile passing thro' a number of pleasing colors, as its implied Commands are deliver'd percussively, fatally, "— you will accept me...into your Stomach."

"Eeeeh...," a-tremble, and Phiz far from ruddy, he shows up at the Tent of the camp naturalist, Prof. Voam,— who advises that, "as the Fate of Vegetables is to be eaten,— as success and Reputation in the Vegetable Realm must hence be measured by *how many* are eaten,— it behooves each kind of Vegetable to look as appetizing as possible, doesn't it, or risk dying where it grew, not to mention having then to lie there, listening to the obloquy and complaint of its neighbors. But, dear me,— as to objects of Artifice,— Watches and so forth..."

"Tell me, with all Honesty, Sir, regarding this Watch,— does it not seek to project an Appearance, not only appetizing, but also,— eeh!...Ah can't say it...?"

"Vegetables don't tick," the Professor gently reminds Dixon.

"Why aye, those that be *only Vegetables* don't. We speak now of a *higher form of life,*— a Vegetable with a Pulse-beat!"

"Beyond me. Try asking R.C., he enjoys puzzles."

Beyond R.C.,— a local land-surveyor employ'd upon the Tangent Enigma,— as well,— tho' he's not about to say so. From the Instant he sees the Watch, the *Mens Rea* is upon him. He covets it.— He dreams of it,— never calling it "the Watch" but "the Chronometer,"— in his mind conflating it with the marvelous Timepiece of Mr. Harrison, thus flexibly has the Story reach'd America of the Rivalry between the Harrisons and Maskelyne, to secure the Longitude,— and as much prize money as may be had from Longitude's Board.

"If a man had a Chronometer such as this," R.C. asks Dixon, "mightn't it be worth something to those Gentlemen?"

"A tight-fisted Bunch, according to Mason,— tha must open their Grip upon it with a Prying-Bar...?"

"Must be why they call it 'Prize' money," says R.C., "— I'll bet you find it temptin', tho', don't ye?"

"I'm not sure whose this is," Dixon replies carefully. "I'm keeping it for someone."

"A Gratuitous Bailment,— of course." R.C. trying his best not to look mean. As a Transit-Fellow, Dixon recognizes R.C.'s Complaint but too well,— the many years pass'd among combatants unremitting, unable by one's Honor to take sides however much over the Brim Emotions might run, assaulted soon or late by all Parties, falling at last into a moral Stuporousness as to the claims of Law,— in fact, perilously close oneself to being *mistaken* for a Lawyer, a bonny gone-on.

"Mmm-mm! Did ye see that, boys? Good enough to eat." Axmanly Wit at the Watch's expense, causes R.C. to glower and approach, often to fractions of an inch away.

"What're you in my Phiz for now, R.C.?"

"You don't want to be offending the wrong Folks," R.C. advises. No one knows what this means, but his point,— that he is too insane for ev'ryone else's good,— is made.

One midnight there is an uproar. Dogs bark. Axmen request Silence. The Surveyors are out of their Tents, up the Track somewhere taking Zenith observations. There is a crowd in front of Dixon's Tent. R.C. is caught in the light of Nathe McClean's Tallow-Dip, just as the last bit of Gold Chain, suck'd between his Lips like a Chinese Noodle, disappears.

"R.C., may be you're gittin' too mean to think straight any more?"

"I thought I heard someone coming."

"That was us. Shouldn't you've set it down someplace, 'stead of swallerin' it?"

"There wasn't Time."

"Now ye've more than ye know what to do with," quips Moses Barnes, to the Glee of his Companions.

"Don't you know what it is you swallow'd, R.C.?" Arch McClean slowly reciprocating his Head in wonder. "That's sixty Years of Longitude down there, all the Work 'at's come and gone, upon that one Problem, since Sir Cloudsley Shovell lost his Fleet and his Life 'pon the cruel Rocks of Scilly."

"What were my Choices?" R.C. nearly breathless. The thing was either bewitch'd, by Country Women in the middle of the night,— Fire, monthly Blood, Names of Power,— or perfected, as might any Watch be, over years, small bit by bit, to its present mechanickal State, by Men, in work-Shops, and in the Daytime. That was the sexual Choice the Moment presented,— between those two sorts of Magic. "I had less than one of the Creature's Ticks to decide. So I took it, and I gobbl'd it right down." His pink fists swing truculently, and he has begun to pout. "Any of you have a Problem with this?"

"As the Arm of Discipline here, I certainly do," declares Mr. Barnes, the Overseer of the Axmen, "for in an expedition into the Country, as upon a ship at sea, nothing destroys morale like Theft. Which, legally speaking, is what this is."

"Yet anyone may put an ear to his Stomach. The Watch is sensibly there, nor's he making a Secret of it.... We might more accurately say, an Act of Sequestration, its owner being denied the use of— "

"Aye, yet absent a Conversion to personal Use,— "

"O Philadelphia!" thunders Mr. Barnes, "have thy Barristers poison'd Discourse e'en unto the Rude who dwell in this Desert? What ever shall we do?" The Utterance being Mr. Barnes's cryptic way of requesting it, stone Silence falls over the Company. "Has anyone consider'd where we are?" All know that he means, "where just at the Tangent Point, strange lights appear at Night, figures not quite human emerge from and disappear into it, and in the Daytime, Farm animals who stray too close, vanish and do not re-emerge,— and why should anyone find it strange, that one Man has swallow'd the Watch of another?" Some style this place "the Delaware Triangle," but Surveyors know it as "The Wedge."

To be born and rear'd in the Wedge is to occupy a singular location in an emerging moral Geometry. Indeed, the oddness of Demarcation here, the inscriptions made upon the body of the Earth, primitive as Designs prick'd by an Iroquois, with a Thorn and a supply of Soot, upon his human body,— a compulsion, withal, supported by the most advanc'd scientifick instruments of their Day,— present to Lawyers enough Litigation upon matters of Property within the Wedge, to becoach-and-six a small Pack of them, one generation upon another, yea unto the year 1900, and beyond.

By early Youth, R.C. had become the kind of mean, ornery cuss his neighbors associated with years of Maturity. "Here comes old R.C., and don't he look sour'd today." 'Twas his Profession did it to him. As a young Surveyor, from the rude shocks attending his first boundary-dispute, he understood that he must exercise his Art among the most litigious people on Earth,— Pennsylvanians of all faiths, but most intensely the Presbyterians, hauling each other before Justices of the Peace, Sheriffs, Church Courts, Village Quidnuncs, anyone who'd listen, even pretend to, at an unbelievable clip, seeking recompense for ill treatment grand and petty. If he wish'd to pursue this line of Work, he would have to recognize the country-wide jostle of Polygons as a form of madness, by which, if he kept to a Fiduciary Edge of Right Procedure, he might profit, whilst retaining his Sanity. He infuriated the more bookish surveyors with his Approach, which includ'd avoiding Paper-work, walking the Terrain, and making noninstrumental guesses. "Looks about eighty-eight-thirty to me. Here,— " Eyes shut, Arms straight out to his sides, then swept together till the fingertips touch'd, Eyes open,— "That's it."

"How so?"

"By Eye," he twinkl'd sourly. "Most of these out here 'round the Wedge, ye can do by Eye," pronouncing it "Bah-ahy." By the time he turn'd his hand to the Problem of the Tangent Line, it seem'd but an accustom'd Madness, in a different form,— the geometrick Whimsicality of Kings, this time, and Kings-to-be.

In the months, and then the years, after he swallows the Watch, as the days of ceaseless pulsation pass one by one, R.C. learns that a small volume within him is, and shall be, immortal. His wife moves to another Bed, and soon into another room altogether, after persuading him first to build it onto the House. "Snoring's one thing, R.C., I can always do something about that," brandishing her Elbow, "— but that Ticking…"

"Kept me awake, too, at first, Phœbe,— but now, it rocks me to sleep."

"Best Wishes, R.C."

"Oh, suit yourself." R.C. can act as sentimental as the next young Husband, but his public *Rôles* require him to be distant and disagreeable. Besides, since he swallow'd the Watch, she's been noticeably less merry with him, as if cautious in its presence.

"Do you imagine it cares what we're doing out here, in the world outside? Say, Phœb, do be a Peach and come— "

"But R.C., it might be— "

"What?" his voice beginning to pitch higher. "Listening?"

"Taking it all down, somehow."

"You're the girl I married, damme 'f you're not." He knows she never quite sees what this means, and being none too sure himself, he never offers to explain it.

" 'Tis a national Treasure," declares Mr. Shippen,— "and whoever may first remove it from its present location, shall enter most briskly upon the Stage of World Business, there, will-he nill-he, to play his part.— All at the price of your own Life, R.C., of course, Chirurgickal Extraction and all, but,— that's Business, as they say in Philadelphia."

"I'll chuck it up, why don't I do that?" putting his finger down his Throat.

"Oh, may we watch?" cry the Children.

"Never say 'Watch' to your Father," advises Mrs. R.C.

"Ahhrrhh!" the Finger comes out bleeding. "Something bit me!"

"Likely trying to protect its Territory," his eldest Son assures him.

"How could it bite me? 'tis in my Stomach. 'Tis a Watch."

"Alter its shape, maybe? Who knows what's happening to it in there?"

"Where all is a-drip, disgusting and mushy with chew'd-up food,— "

"And acid and bile and it smells ever of Vomit,— "

"Eeeooo!"

"Enjoy yourselves, children, even at the expense of your poor suff'ring old Father if you're that desperate for merriment, no matter, go, mock, too soon will equal Inconvenience befall ye, ev'ry one, 'tis Life."

"We'll not go swallowing Watches, thankee."

"Not if you want to sneak up on an Indian someday, you won't."

"Hadn't plann'd on it, Pa."

"Figures he'll cash in on Longitude, instead he eats the Chronometer, some zany Dreamer I married." Of course Dixon has to tell Emerson. For weeks after the Express has curvetted away, he mopes about, as gloomy as anyone's ever seen him. "I was suppos'd to look after it...?"

"You wish'd release from your Promise," Mason reminds him. "Think of R.C. as *Force Majeure.*"

The Letter, in reply, proves to be from Mrs. Emerson. "When he receiv'd your News, Mr. Emerson was quite transform'd, and whooping with high amusement, attempted whilst in his Workroom to dance a sort of Jig, by error stepping upon a wheel'd Apparatus that was there, the result being that he has taken to his Bed, where, inches from my Quill, he nevertheless wishes me to say, 'Felicitations, Fool, for it hath work'd to Perfection.'

"I trust that in a subsequent Letter, my Husband will explain what this means."

There is a Post-Script in Emerson's self-school'd hand, exclamatory, ending upon a long Quill-crunching Stop. "Time is the Space that may not be seen.— "

('Pon which the Rev^d cannot refrain from commenting, "He means, that out of Mercy, we are blind as to Time,— for we could not bear to contemplate what lies at its heart.")

33

"Hope to have your Company at the Bridge....," writes Benjamin Chew, to the Surveyors. He means Mary Janvier's, at Christiana Bridge,— where the Line Commissioners find merry Pretext to gather, gossip, swap quids and quos, play Whist, drink Madeira, sing Catches, sleep late, or else stay up till the north-bound Mail-coach wheels in at seven A.M., and the Passengers all come piling out for Breakfast at The Indian Queen. Never know whom you'll run into. An hour's pause in the journey, wherein early Risers may practise, each day, upon a diff'rent set of Travelers. Flirting? Cards? Coffee and Chatter? the Hope is for a productive, when not amusing, Hour.

At this pleasant waterside Resort, gulls sit as if permanently upon Posts, Ducks enjoy respite from the Attentions of Fowlers, the mild haze thins and thickens, Sandwiches and Ale arrive in a relax'd and contingent way, official business is taken care of quickly, to make available more time for Drink, Smoak, and Jollification. Yet whilst the Marylanders, attun'd to Leisure, take the time as it comes, the Gentlemen from Philadelphia, their Watches either striking together with eerie Precision ev'ry Quarter-hour or, when silent, forever being consulted and re-pocketed, must examine for Productivity each of their waking Moments, as closely as some do their Consciences, unable quite to leave behind them the Species of Time peculiar to that City, best express'd in the Almanackal Sayings of Dr. Franklin.

In the Summer, toward Evening, Thunder-Gusts come slashing down off the Allegheny Front, all the way riding close above the trees flaring either side in wet and bright Waves upon each arrival of the Lightning, over Juniata then Susquehanna, tapping at the Windows of Harris's Ferry, skidding across the shake roofs of Lancaster and soaking the Town,— and on to Chesapeake and a thousand Tributaries each in its humid, stippl'd Turmoil, and the Inn, and the Gentlemen indoors at their Merriment, whilst Ducks of all sorts, lounging in the Weather as if 'twere sun-shine, fly into a Frenzy at each blast of Lightning and Thunder, then, immediately forgetting, settle back into their pluvial Comforts.

Tho' all are welcome here, Janvier's, like certain counterparts in Philadelphia, has ever provided a venue for the exercise of Proprietarian politics, by a curious assortment of City Anglicans and Presbyterians, with renegade Germans or Quakers appearing from time to time. Especially upon nights before and after Voting, the Rooms contain a great Ridotto of hopeful Cupidity. Strangers are view'd suspiciously. Mr. Franklin's confusion is toasted more than once. Rumors circulate that the Anti-Proprietarians have a Jesuit Device for seeing and hearing thro' Walls.

The Bar seems to vanish in the Distance. Hewn from some gigantick Tropical Tree, of a vivid deep brown wood all thro', further carv'd and wax'd to an arm-pleasing Smoothness, comfortable as a Bed,— no one has yet counted how many it can accommodate, tho' some have sworn to over an hundred. Environ'd by immoderately colored Colonial wall-paper, tropickal Blooms with Vermilion Petals and long, writhing Stamens and Pistils of Indigo, against a Field of Duck-Green, not to mention reliable Magenta, the Pulse of the Province ever reciprocates, a quid for a quo, a round for a Round, and ever another chance to win back the bundle one has wager'd away. And somewhere sure, the raising of Voices in debate politickal.

"Observe no further than the walls of London,— 'A harsh winter,— a cold spring,— a dry summer,— and *no King*.' Not Boston, Sir, but London. Your precious Teutonical dispensation,— Damme!— means even less upon these shores, Sir! I would say, the D——l take it, were he not already quite in possession."

328

"Treason, Sir!"

Mr. Dixon, cordially, "Now then, Sir!"

"Peace, Astrologer,— "

"Astronomer, if it please you," corrects Mr. Mason, without quite considering.

"At least I am about my business in the honest light of God's day,— what is to be said, of men who so regularly find themselves abroad at midnight?" The pious gentleman has worked himself into a state of heedless anger. Is it the innocent roasted Berry, that has put them all in such surly humor? No one else in the room is paying much notice, being each preoccupied by his own no less compelling drama. Smoke from their bright pale pipes hangs like indoor fog, through which, a-glimmering, the heavy crockery and silverware claps and rings. Servant lads in constant motion carry up from the cellar coffee sacks upon their shoulders, or crank the handles of gigantic coffee grinders, as the Assembly clamors for cup after cup of the invigorating Liquid. By the end of each day, finely divided coffee-dust will have found its way by the poundful up the nostrils and into the brains of these by then alert youths, lending a feverish edge to all they speak and do.

Conversing about politics, under such a *stimulus,* would have prov'd animated enough, without reckoning in as well the effects of drink, tobacco,— whose smoke one inhales here willy-nilly with every breath,— and sugar, to be found at every hand in lucent brown cones great and little, Ic'd Cupcakes by the platter-ful, all manner of punches and flips, pies of the locality, crullers, muffins, and custards,— no table that does not hold some sweet memento, for those it matters to, of the cane thickets, the chains, the cruel Sugar-Islands.

"A sweetness of immorality and corruption," pronounces a Quaker gentleman of Philadelphia, "bought as it is with the lives of African slaves, untallied black lives broken upon the greedy engines of the Barbadoes."

"Sir, we wish no one ill,— we are middling folk, our toil is as great as anyone's, and some days it helps to have a lick of molasses to look forward to, at the end of it."

"If we may refuse to write upon stamped paper, and for the tea of the East India Company find a tolerable *Succedaneum* in New-Jersey red root, might Philosophy not as well discover some Patriotic alternative to these vile crystals that eat into our souls as horribly as our teeth?"

Every day the room, for hours together, sways at the verge of riot. May unchecked consumption of all these modern substances at the same time, a habit without historical precedent, upon these shores be creating a new sort of European? less respectful of the forms that have previously held Society together, more apt to speak his mind, or hers, upon any topic he chooses, and to defend his position as violently as need be? Two youths of the *Macaronic* profession are indeed greatly preoccupied upon the boards of the floor, in seeking to kick and pummel, each into the other, some Enlightenment regarding the Topick of Virtual Representation. An individual in expensive attire, impersonating a gentleman, stands upon a table freely urging sodomitical offenses against the body of the Sovereign, being cheered on by a circle of Mechanics, who are not reluctant with their own suggestions. Wenches emerge from scullery dimnesses to seat themselves at the tables of disputants, and in brogues thick as oatmeal recite their own lists of British sins.

The attempt to relieve Fort Pitt continues, as do reverberations from the massacres at Conestoga and Lancaster. All to the West is a-surge and aflame. Waggons from over Susquehanna appear at all hours of Day and Night, Pots and Kettles, sacks of Corn, the Babies and the Pig riding inside. 'Tis the year '55 all over, and the Panick'd Era just after Braddock's Defeat. The Smell of a burn'd Cabin grows familiar again, the smell of things that are not suppos'd to be burn'd. Women's things. House things. Detecting it, if one's approach happens to be from downwind, is ever the first order of business.

The Star-Gazers are well away from Events. On the eighth of January, thirty-one miles more or less due West of the southernmost point of Philadelphia, they begin setting up their observatory at John Harland's farm.

"Ye'll not wreck my Vegetable Patch," Mrs. Harland informs them.

"We are forbidden, good Woman, as a term of our Contract and Commission, to harm Gardens and Orchards. We'll set up in a safe place,— pay ye fair rent, of course."

"Welcome one and all," cries Mr. Harland. "Ye fancy the Vegetable Patch, why ye shall have it too! We'll buy our Vegetables!"

Playfully swinging at her Husband with the Spade she holds, "Why here, Sirs?"

"Because your farm lies exactly as far south from the Pole as the southernmost point in Philadelphia," Mason informs them.

" 'Tis the same Latitude, 's what you mean. Then so's a great Line of farms, east and west,— why choose mine? Why not my neighbor Tumbling's, who has more land than he knows what to do with anyway?"

"Exactly fifteen miles due south of here," Dixon gently, "we'll want to set up another Post. 'Twill mark the Zero Point, or Beginning, of the West Line. The Point here in your Field, will tell what its Longitude is, as well as the Latitude of the south Edge of Philadelphia. It ties those two Facts together, you see."

"That wasn't my question."

"Mr. Tumbling fir'd his Rifle at us," says Dixon.

"And what made you think I wouldn't?"

"We gambl'd," suppose Mason and Dixon.

"I'll just fetch down the Rifle," offers Mrs. Harland.

Harland is frowning. "Wait. Why didn't you Lads measure south from Philadelphia first, and *then* come West?"

"Going south first, we should have had to cross the Delaware, into New-Jersey," Mason explains, "and when 'twas time to turn West, fifteen miles down, the same River by then become much enlarg'd, to cross back over it, would have presented a Task too perilous for the Instruments, if not to the lives of this Party,— all avoided by keeping to dry land. Hence, first West, and then South."

"And at the end of your last Chain," says Mrs. Harland, "here *we* are." She goes off waving her hands in the air, and her Husband will be getting an Ear-load soon.

Overnight, in John Harland's Field, appears an organiz'd Company of men, performing unfamiliar Rituals with Machinery that may as well have been brought from some other inhabited World. ("Aye," Dixon agrees, "the Planet London. And its principal Moon," nodding at Mason, "Greenwich.") The farmer can hear them at midnight, when a whisper will carry a mile, as in the Day-time, conversing like ship-captains through Speaking-Trumpets. Numbers. Words that sound like English but make no sense. Of course he starts finding reasons to go back there and look about. He comes upon the Astronomers scribbling by beeswax light, before a tent pitch'd beneath a wavelike slope in the Earth, a good sledding hill, part field, part woods, this being a region of such mariform grades. They have been bringing the Instrument into the Meridian. "Because of the way Earth spins," Mason explains, "the Stars travel in Arcs upon the Sky. When each arrives at the highest point of its Arc, so are you, observing it in the Instant, looking perfectly Northward along your Meridian."

"So the Trick would be knowing when it gets to that highest Point."

"And for that we have the equal-Altitude Method.... We are waiting just at the Moment upon Capella. Have a look?"

Harland slouches down beneath the Eye-piece. "Thought this was meant to bring 'em nearer?"

"The Moon," says Dixon, "Planets...? Not the Stars...?"

"Of a Star," Mason adds, "we wish to know but where it is, and when it passes some Reference."

"That's it?"

"Well, of course, one must manipulate the various Screw-Settings precisely, read the Nonius, and an hundred details besides I'd but bore you with,— "

"Seems fairly straightforward. This moves it up and down..."

"Bring Capella to the Horizontal Wire," suggests Dixon.

"Hey!" Mason in a tone not as vex'd as it might be, "who's the certified Astronomer, here?"

"Child's Play," murmurs Mr. Harland, handling the Adjusting Screws and Levers with a Respect both Mason and Dixon immediately note.

"Tha take the Time it crosses the Wire rising, and then the Time it crosses, when setting. The Time exactly half-way between, is the Time it cross'd the Meridian."

"This one's not rising,— 'deed, 'tis gone below the Line,— "

" 'Tis the Lens. Ev'rything in the image we see is inverted."

"The Sky, turn'd upside down? Wondrous! You are allow'd to do this?"

"We're paid to do this," declares Dixon.

"Kings pay us to do this," adds Mason.

" 'Tis like a Job where you work standing upon your Head," marvels John Harland. He steps back, gazing upward, comparing the Creation as seen by the Naked Eye, with its Telescopick Counter-part. "I am unsteady with this."

"Knowing the time of Culmination, allowing for how fast or slow the Clock's going, we may compute the Time of the next such Culmination, be out There the next Night, and upon the Tick, turn the Instrument down to the Horizon, direct an Assistant bearing a Lanthorn till the Flame be bisected by the Vertical Wire, have him drop a Bob-Line there, and Mark the Place. And that's North."

"That's what you were roaring about, thro' those horns all night?"

"Why, what else...?"

"Are you looking into Futurity?"

"Is it what your Neighbors believe?"

"What they hope, aye."

"Would that we were."

Yet this is when he grows shy of regarding them directly,— as if it might be dangerous to risk more than sidelong Glances.

By February they have learn'd their Latitude closely enough to know that the Sector is set up 356.8 yards south of the Parallel that passes thro' the southernmost point of Philadelphia, putting them about ten and a half seconds of Arc off.

"Ye'll be moving the Observatory, I collect?" says Mr. Harland.

"No need to,— we'll merely remember to reckon in the Off-sett."

In March a Company of Axmen, using Polaris to keep their Meridian, clear a Visto from John Harland's farm fifteen Miles true south, to Alexander Bryant's farm. How can Harland not go along? The Wife is less enchanted,— "John, are you crazy? All this Moon-beaming about, and it's past time to be planting,— over at Tumbling's they've got it till'd already."

"You plant it, Bets," Harland replies, "and rent out what you don't. This means five shillings ev'ry day I work,— silver,— British, real as any Spade. You do it. You know how, you do fine, I've seen you, just don't put in too many 'them damn' flowers, is all." He will come north again to find she's taken a neat square Acre and planted it to Sun-flowers, soon spread without shame upon the hill-slope, a disreputable yellow that people will see for miles. In its re-reflected glow in the corner of the Field in back, a newly-set chunk of Rose Quartz is shining strangely. At certain times of the day, the sun will catch the pink grain just right and ah! you might be transported beneath the Sea, under the Northern Ice.... Here is Harland, among the Sunflowers, having Romantic thoughts for the first time. Bets notices it. He is chang'd,— he has been out running Lines, into the distance, when once Brandywine was far enough,— and now he wants the West. The meaning of Home is therefore chang'd for them as well. As if their own Fields had begun, with tremendous smooth indifference, to move, in a swell of Possibility.

In April Mason and Dixon, using fir Rods and Spirit Levels, measure exactly the fifteen miles southward, allowing for the ten and a half Seconds off at the north end. In May they find their new Latitude in Mr. Alexander Bryant's field, then remeasure the Line northward again,— "Think of it," Dixon suggests, "as a Chainman's version of turning the Sector." By June, having found at last the Latitude of their East-West Line,— 39°43'17.4",— they are instructed to proceed to the Middle Point of the Peninsula between Chesapeake and the Ocean, to begin work upon the Tangent Line. By the end of the Month, they have chain'd north from the Middle Point to the Banks of the Nanticoke.

One reason given for bringing Mason and Dixon into the Boundary Dispute was that nobody in America seem'd to've had any luck with this fiendish Problem of the Tangent Line, which had absorb'd the energies of the best Geometers in the Colonies, for more Years than would remain to some, their lives to the Great Cypress Swamp a Forfeit claim'd. Field parties had gone out in '50, '60, and '61, ending up east and west of previous Tangent Points by as much as four tenths of a mile. 'Twas infuriating. 'Twas like tickling a Fly under its wing-pit, with a long and wobbly Object such as a fishing-pole.

The idea was to start from the exact middle of the Delaware Peninsula,— defin'd, quite early in the Dispute, as the "Middle Point,"— and run a line north till it just touch'd the arc of a circle of twelve miles' radius, centered upon the Spire of the Court House in New Castle, swung from the shore of Delaware, around counter-clockwise, westward, till it met its Tangent Line. That's presuming there was a Tangent Line there to meet it, and so far there wasn't. The problem seem'd intractable. From the Middle Point, you wanted to somehow project a Line about eighty miles northward, through swamp and swamp inhabitants, that would at the far end *just kiss,* at a single Tangent Point, the Twelve-mile Arc,— making a ninety-degree Angle with the radius, drawn from the Court House Spire, out to that point. Somebody must have imagin'd the Tangent as some perfect north-south line, some piece of Meridian, that would pass through the Middle Point *and* be exactly twelve miles from New Castle at the same time. But it couldn't do that and run true North, too,— 'twas more Royal Geometry, fanciful as ever. Any Line from the Middle Point one wish'd to end up tangent to the Twelve-Mile Arc, would have to be aimed about three and a half degrees west of true North. Not only did this Arc pass too far West, but it also fail'd to reach far enough North to touch 40° latitude,— which was the northern boundary of the Baltimores' grant from Charles II,— thus making of the Lower Counties an exclave of Pennsylvania, *inside Maryland.* Yet how could either King have foretold that the younger William Penn might wish the Lower Counties one day contiguous with upper Pennsylvania?

So was it drawn. Then ev'ryone waited for the Astronomers from London to come and verify the rude Colonials' work.

For ev'ry surveyor who forsook his hearthside in the Weeks of Chill when the crops were in, and the leaves were flown and sights were longer, to go out into the Brush and actually set up, out of pure Speculation, where there might be a few square inches of dry land, and try to turn the angles and obtain the star shots, getting in addition snake-bit, trapp'd in sucking Mud, lost in Fog, frozen to the Marrow, harass'd by farmers, and visited by Sheriffs,— for ev'ry such Field-Man there were dozens of enthusiastic amateurs, many of them members of the clergy, who from the comfort of their Fires sent the Commissioners an unceasing autumn-wind full of solutions,— which came in upon foolscap and Elephant and privately water-mark'd stock, fluttering in the doors, drifting into corners,— you'd have thought it was Fermat's Last Theorem, instead of a County Line that look'd like a Finial upon something of Mr. Chippendale's.

"Yes well of course *that's* a Question of taste, but,— look at the way it *leans,* just enough to be obvious,— honestly Cedric, it's so predictably Colonial, as if,— 'Oh they don't even know how to find North over there, well we must send our Royal Astronomers to tidy things up mustn't we,— ' sort of thing when in fact it's once more the dead Hand of the second James, who went about granting all this Geometrickally impossible territory,— as unreal, in a Surveying way, as some of the other Fictions that govern'd that unhappy Monarch's Life."

Or, "Once upon a time," as the Rev^d re-tells it for Brae, "there was a magical land call'd 'Pennsylvania.' In settlement of a Debt, it was convey'd to William Penn by the Duke of York, who later became James the Second. And James had been granted the land by his brother Charles, who at the time was King.

"To understand their Thinking, however, would require access to whatever corner of the Vatican Library houses the Heretick Section, and therein the concept, spoken of in hush'd tones, when at all, of *Stupiditas Regia,* or the Stupidity of Kings. And Queens, of course, O alarmèd Tenebræ, not to mention Princesses,— yes Stupidity even afflicts those, you would think perfect, Creatures as well."

"How so?" Tenebræ coolly carrying on with her acufloral Meditations. "There have I'm sure been non-stupid Princesses, indeed a good many, Uncle. Whereas Kings and Princes are so stupid, they pretend maps that can't be drawn, and style them 'Pennsylvania.' " Picking up a Fescue, she leans toward the Map upon the Wall, recourse to which over the years has settl'd no one knows how many such Disputes, "King Charles begins at a Meridian Line Somewhere out in the untravel'd Forests,— here, five degrees of Longitude West of Delaware Bay. Then this not very learnèd Brother finds the point where his desolate Meridian crosses the Fortieth Parallel of North Latitude. 'Tis of course in a huge blank space on the Map. Here. At the south-western and least accessible corner of the Grant,— where, at *this* remote intersection of Parallel and Meridian, is to be anchor'd the entire Scheme. Running *eastward* from there, the royal Brothers expect the Forty-Degree Line somewhere to encounter James's Twelve-Mile Arc about New Castle,— "

"Oh, twelve miles ought to do it. We don't want to say thirteen, because that's so unlucky."

"Fourteen would engross for you Head of Elk," Charles observes, "but 'twould push too far West, this vertical Line, here,— "

"The Tangent Line, Sir."

"I knew that."

"Charles and James," the Rev^d sighing, "and their tangle of geometrick hopes,— that somehow the Arc, the Tangent, the Meridian, and the West Line should all come together at the same perfect Point,— where, in fact, all is Failure. The Arc fails to meet the Forty-Degree North Parallel. The Tangent fails to be part of any Meridian. The West Line fails to begin from the Tangent Point, being five miles north of it."

Indeed, a spirit of whimsy pervades the entire history of these Delaware Boundaries, as if in playful refusal to admit that America, in any way, may be serious. The Calvert agents keep coming up with one fanciful demand after another, either trying to delay and obstruct as long as possible the placing of the Markers, or else,— someone must suggest,— giddy with what they imagine Escape, into a Geometry more permissive than Euclid, here in this new World. During the negotiations, Marylanders suggest locating the exact center of New Castle by taking a sheet of paper showing a map of the Town, trimming 'round the edges till only the Town remains, and then shifting this about upon the point of a Pin, till it balances, and at that center of gravity pricking it through, as being the true center of the Town.

Yet, if the Twelve-Mile Arc be taken as the geometrical expression of the Duke of York's wish to preserve from encroachment his seat of Government, then must there project a literal Sphere of power from the Spire atop the State-House, whose intersection with the Earth is the Arc,— unalterably Circular, not to be adjusted by so much as a Link to agree with any Tangent Line.

Oblig'd, for meetings with the Commissioners, to sleep in New Castle a Night or two, the Surveyors discover the Will of the second James at close hand. South, tho' not far enough, lie the Bay, and the open

Sea. Before subsiding to perhaps but a single deep hour of stillness broken by no more than the Voices of frogs and the stirring of the salt fens, the sounds dominating the fallen night are the Cries of Sailors behind the doors of Taverns, and the jingling and Drone of the Musick that pleases them. The hypnagogic Citizenry lie wond'ring if these sailors, some of whose Ships carry guns, would defend the Town, should some Catholick war-ship, or more than one, advance upon them, torches flaming black and greasy, Ejaculations in Languages unfathomable....

"Spanish privateers, and Frenchmen, too," their Hosts are pleas'd to relate, "were us'd to come up the River, bold as Crows, to attack the little villages and Plantations. We never felt as secure at night as you in Philadelphia. Any seaborne assault upon that City would mean first the Reduction of New Castle, for 'tis the Key to the River. Now it is difficult to remember, but fifteen years ago in the era of Don Vicente López, there was an apprehensive Edge in this Town as soon as the Sun went down, that did not grow dull till dawn. Tho' by day the busy Capital of the *de facto* Province of Delaware, with night-fall we became a huddl'd cluster of lights trembling into the coming Hours, from lanthorns, candles, and hearths, each an easy target upon the humid Shore. Many of us adopted forms of nocturnal Behavior more typical of New-York, staying up the Night thro', less out of the Desire to transgress than the Fear of sleeping anytime other than in the Day-light hours."

The great Scepter atop the Court House continues in the dark to radiate its mysterious force. The stock are gone to sleep. The fish and the Wine were excellent. Rooms fill with tobacco Smoke,— insomnia and headaches abound. Cards emerge from Cherry-wood Recesses. Occupants of the Houses along the River stir among the lumps in their Mattresses, ready at any Alarm to wake. Their dreams are of Spanish Visitors who turn out to be unexpectedly jolly, with courtly ways, rolling eyes, passionate guitars, not a homicidal thought in the Boat-load of 'em. Ev'ryone ends up at an all-night Ridotto, with piles of mysterious delectable Mediterranean food, "Sandwiches" made of entire Loaves stuff'd with fried Sausages and green Peppers, eggplants, tomatoes, cheese melted ev'rywhere, fresh Melons mysteriously preserv'd thro' the Voyage, wines whose grapes are descended from those that supplied Bacchus himself. New Castle dreams, drooling into and soaking Pillows, helpless before the rapacious, festive fleet.

> How swiftly might the Popish scourge descend,—
> Another Don Vicente, Havoc's Friend,
> Another vile and ringletted Señor,
> Another Insult to our sov'reign Shore.
> — Timothy Tox, *Pennsylvaniad*

Through July they continue North, thro' swamps, snakes, godawful humidity, thunder-gusts at night, trees so thick that even with thirty axmen, each chain's length seems won with Labor incommensurate,— waking each glaucous Dawn into sweat and stillness, to struggle another Day, with no confidence that at the correct Distance, they will pass anywhere near the Tangent Point, much less touch it exactly.

On paper, the Tangent Line's inclination reminds Dixon of the road between Catterick and Binchester,— in fact, on up to Lanchester, though one had to look for it,— part of the Romans' Great North Road. To amuse himself in his less mindful moments, he would travel out to the old Roman ruins above the Wear and sight southward down the middle of the road, for it ran straight ahead as a shot. Nothing so clear or easy as that in Delaware, however. Dixon mutters to himself all shift long. "If we set up over there, then this great bloody Tree's in the way,— yet if we wish to be clear of the Tree for any sight longer than arm's length, we must stand in Glaur of uncertain Depth,— looking withal from Light into Shadow...."

"I appreciate it," says Mason, "when you share your innermost thought-processes with me in this way,— almost as if, strangely, you did trust me."

"After these Months? Who would?"

In August they finally go chaining past the eighty-one-mile mark, which they figure puts them a little beyond the Tangent Point, wherever it is, back there. They take September, October, and November to find it, as nicely as Art may achieve, computing Offsets and measuring them, improving the Tangent Line by small Tweaks and Smoothings, until they can report at last that the ninety-degree Angle requir'd, between the Tangent Line and the twelve-Mile Radius from the Court House to the Tangent Point, is as perfect as they can get it,— which means, as it will prove, off by two feet and two inches, more or less.

In December they discharge the Hands and pause for the Winter, at Harlands', at Brandywine. "To a good year's work." Dixon raising a pewter Can of new Ale. "And pray for another."

"To Repetition and Routine, from here to the End of it," Mason gesturing reluctantly with his Claret-Glass…even so, more festive than he's been for a while.

"Routine! Not likely! Not upon the West Line! Who knows what'll be out there? Each day impossible to predict,— Eeh! pure Adventure…?"

"Thankee, Dixon, a Comfort as ever, yes the total Blindness in which we must enter that Desert, might easily have slipp'd my mind, allowing me a few pitiable seconds' respite from Thoughts of it how welcome,— alas, 'twas not to be, was it, at least, nowhere in range of your Voice."

"*Ehw* deah…imagin'd I'd been taking rather the jolliest of Tones actually, my how awkward for you…?"

Another Holiday flare-up, of many preceding, which at first had sent Harlands of all ages cringing against the walls or scrambling up the Ladder, yet soon subsided to but one more sound of untam'd Nature to be grown us'd to out here, like Thunder, or certain *Animal Mimickries* at night, from across a Creek. Each time, the Surveyors apologize for their behavior,— then, presently, are screaming again. Apologize, scream, apologize, scream,— daily life in the Harland house grows jagged. After a Christmastide truce, with the rest of the winter waiting them, perhaps more of it than any can imagine themselves surviving without at least one serious lapse in behavior, the Surveyors decide to travel to Lancaster, perhaps in hopes that the imps of discord will fail to pursue them 'cross Susquehanna.

34

Lancaster Town lies thirty-five miles' Journey to the West. "What brought me here," Mason wrote in the Field-Record, "was my curiosity to see the place where was perpetrated last Winter the Horrid and inhuman murder of 26 Indians, Men, Women and Children, leaving none alive to tell."

" 'Me,' notes Uncle Ives, " 'my,'— sounds like Mason went by himself."

The Rev^d nods. "Dixon told me, that Mason had meant to go alone,— but that at the last moment, mindful of the dangers attending Solitude in a Town notorious for Atrocity, he offer'd to add Muscular Emphasis, tho' Mason seem'd unsure of whether he wanted him there or not."

They— presume "they,"— reach Lancaster 10 January 1765, putting up at The Cross Keys. The Public Rooms are crowded with Lawyers, Town Officials, Justices, Merchants, and Mill-owners,— the middling to better sort, not a murderously drooling backwoodsman in sight,— unless they include their Guide, pick'd up about a minute and a half inside the Town Limits, who may once or twice have undergone a loss of salivary control,— Mason soon enough on about how quaint, how American, Dixon rather suspecting him of being in the pay of the Paxton Boys, to keep an eye upon two Hirelings of their Landlord and Enemy, Mr. Penn.

"Here for a look at the Massacre Site, are you, Gentlemen? I can always tell. Some bring Sketching-Books, some Easels, others their Specimen-

Bags, but all converge thro' the same queer Magnetism. I quite understand, tho' others about may not,— 'twould do to mind one's belongings,— yet I must not bite the Backs that ignore me.... The first stop upon any Tour is acknowledg'd to be The Dutch Rifle, whither the Boys, hush'd be the Name ever spoken, having left their Horses at Mr. Slough's, repair'd just before the Doing of the Deed. Step this way, pray yese."

When they see what is upon the Tavern Sign, Mason and Dixon exchange a Look,— the Weapon depicted, Black upon White, is notable for the Device upon its Stock, a Silver Star of five Points, revers'd so that two point up and one down,— a sure sign of evil at work, universally recogniz'd as the Horns of the D———l. No-one would adorn a Firearm with it, who was not wittingly in the service of that Prince. This is not the first Time the Surveyors have seen it,— at the Cape, usually right-side-up, it is known as the Sterloop,— a sort of good-luck charm, out in the Bush. But ev'ry now and then, mostly on days of treacherous Wind or Ill-Spirits, one or both had spied upon a Rifle an inverted Star, much like what they observe now, against the Sky, plumb in the windless Forenoon.

"I told ye the last time, that last time was the last time, Jabez," comes a Voice from a high Angle,— Mason and Dixon, peering upward, observe the Landlord, whose Pate appears to brush the beams above him, in a vex'd Temper.

"Ever a merry Quip," cries Jabez, nimbly stepping behind the Surveyors and propelling them in ahead.

They are examin'd skeptickally. "Not from the Press, are you?"

" 'Pon my Word," cry both Surveyors at once.

"Drummers of some kind's my guess," puts in a Countryman, his Rifle at his Side, "am I right, Gents?"

"What'll we say?" mutters Mason urgently to Dixon.

"Oh, do allow me," says Dixon to Mason. Adverting to the Room, "Why aye, Right as a Right Angle, we're out here to ruffle up some business with any who may be in need of Surveying, London-Style,— Astronomickally precise, optickally up-to-the-Minute, surprisingly cheap. The Behavior of the Stars is the most perfect Motion there is, and we know how to read it all, just as you'd read a Clock-Face. We have Lenses that never lie, and Micrometers fine enough to subtend the Width of a Hair upon a Martian's Eye-ball. This looks like a bustling Town, plenty of activity in the Land-Trades, where think yese'd be a good place to start?" with an amiability that Mason recognizes as peculiarly Quaker,— Friendly Business.

"Then why are yese askin' Jabez 'bout th' Massacree?" inquires a toothless old Coot with an empty Can, which Dixon makes sure is promptly fill'd.

"Aye! How do we know ye're not just two more Philadelphia Fops, out skipping thro' the Brush-wood?"

"He approach'd us," Mason protests.

"We're men of Science," Dixon explains, "— this being a neoclassickal Instance of the Catastrophick Resolution of Inter-Populational Cross-Purposes, of course we're curious to see where it all happen'd.— "

"You can't just come minuetting in from London and expect to understand what's going on here," advises Mr. Slough.

"This is about Family, sure as the History of England. Inside any one Tribe of Indians, they're all related, see? Kill you one Delaware, you affront the Family at large. Out here, if it's Blood of mine, of course I must go out and seek redress,— tho' I'll have far less company."

"Each alone lacking the Numbers, our sole Recourse is to band together."

"These were said to be harmless, helpless people," Dixon points out in some miraculous way that does not draw challenge or insult in return. Apprehensive among these Folk, Mason, who would have perhaps us'd one Adjective fewer, regards his Geordie Partner with a strange Gaze, bordering upon Respect.

"They were blood relations of men who slew blood relations of ours," Jabez explains.

"Then if You know who did it, for the Lord's sake why did You not go after them?"

"This hurt them more," smiles a certain Oily Leon, fingering his Frizzen and Flint.

"Aye, they go on living, but without dear old Grandam,— puts a big Hole in the Blanket, don't it?"

"You must hate them exceedingly," Mason pretending to a philosophickal interest actually far more faint than his interest in getting out of here alive.

"No," looking about as if puzzl'd, "not any more. That Debt is paid. I'll live in peace with them,— happy to."

"Mayn't they now feel oblig'd to come after you?" asks Jere Disingenuous. He notices Mason just visibly creeping toward the Door.

"Not this side of the River, nor this side of York and Baltimore Road. 'Tis all ours now. They answer to us here."

"What's the complaint?" demands Oily Leon. "We're out here as a Picket for Philadelphia,— we've clear'd them a fine safe patch, from Delaware to Susquehanna. Now may they prance about foolish as they may."

"Aye, Penns, handing us and our children about like Chattel,— "

"Damme,— like Field Slaves!"

"— dared they ever leave England and come here, they should find harsher welcome than any King."

"Here's a Riddle,— if a cat may look at a King, may a Pennsylvanian take aim at a King's enforcer?"

"Sir!" The murmuring is about equally divided, as to whether this is going too far, or not far enough.

"Their Cities allow them Folly," a German of Mystickal Toilette advises the Astronomers, "that daily Living upon the Frontier will not forgive. They feed one another's Pretenses, live upon borrow'd Money as borrow'd Time, their lives as their deaths put, with all appearance of Willingness, under the control of others mortal as they, rather than subject, as must Country People's lives and deaths be, to the One Eternal Ruler. That is why we speak plainly, whilst Cits learn to be roundabout as Snakes. Our Time is much more precious to us."

"What. Our Time not precious!" guffaws a traveling sales Representative. "Why, you're welcome, Cousin, to try and get thro' twenty-four Hours of Philadelphia Time, which if it don't kill you, will cure you, at least, of your Illusions about us."

"Excuse me," says Dixon, "I meant to ask...? Whah's thah' smoahkin' Object in thy Mouth, thah' tha keep puffin' on?"

"Not much Tobacco where you Boys are from? Down Chesapeake, why they've nothing but.— Endless Acres, Glasgow shipping fender-to-fender in the Bays, why Tob'o, Hell, they use it for money! Smoke your Week's Pay! This form of it, Sir, 's what we call a 'Cigar.' They come in all

344

sorts, this particular one being from Conestoga, the Waggon-Bullies there style it a 'Stogie.' The Secret's in the Twist they put into the handful of Leaves whilst they're squeezin' it into Shape. Sort of like putting rifling inside a Barrel, only different? Gives the Smoke a Spin, as ye'd say? Watch this." He sets his Lips as for a conventional, or Toroidal, Smoke-Ring, but out instead comes a Ring like a Length of Ribbon clos'd in a Circle, with a single Twist in it, possessing thereby but one Side and one Edge....

("Uncle?"

"Hum? Pray ye,— 'tis true, I was not there. Yet, such was the pure original Stogie in its Day....")

Tho' nothing much has been said, the Surveyors are surpriz'd to discover that ev'ryone's been saying it for several Hours. The only thing that has grown clearer is Jabez's motive in offering to be their Guide. Soon Lamps are lit, and the Supper-Crowd has come in, and Mason and Dixon, no closer to having seen the site of the Massacre, Heads a-reel with smoke, return to their Rooms.

Does Britannia, when she sleeps, dream? Is America her dream?— in which all that cannot pass in the metropolitan Wakefulness is allow'd Expression away in the restless Slumber of these Provinces, and on West-ward, wherever 'tis not yet mapp'd, nor written down, nor ever, by the majority of Mankind, seen,— serving as a very Rubbish-Tip for subjunctive Hopes, for all that *may yet be true,*— Earthly Paradise, Fountain of Youth, Realms of Prester John, Christ's Kingdom, ever behind the sunset, safe till the next Territory to the West be seen and recorded, measur'd and tied in, back into the Net-Work of Points already known, that slowly triangulates its Way into the Continent, changing all from subjunctive to declarative, reducing Possibilities to Simplicities that serve the ends of Governments,— winning away from the realm of the Sacred, its Borderlands one by one, and assuming them unto the bare mortal World that is our home, and our Despair.

"Yet must the Sensorium be nourish'd," Mason, insomniack, addresses himself in a sort of Gastrick Speech he has devis'd for Hours like these, "...as the Body, with its own transcendent Desires, the foremost being Eternal Youth,— for which, alas, one seeks in vain thro' the Enthusiasts' Fair, that defines the Philadelphia Sabbath,— the best

Offer heard, being of Bodily Resurrection, which unhappily yet requires Death as a pre-condition...."

He finds himself pretending Rebekah is there, somewhere, and listening. She has not "visited" since St. Helena. Mason cycles back to the Island, a Memory-Pilgrim with a well-mark'd Itinerary Map, to recapitulate Exchanges in the Ebony Clearing, the empty Wall'd Patch, the Lines at Dawn before the Atlantick Horizon....

The next Day, he creeps out before Dixon is awake, and goes to the Site of last Year's Massacre by himself. He is not as a rule sensitive to the metaphysickal Remnants of Evil,— none but the grosser, that is, the Gothickal, are apt to claim his Attention,— yet here in the soil'd and strewn Courtyard where it happen'd, roofless to His Surveillance,— and to His Judgment, prays Mason,— he feels "like a Nun before a Shrine," as he later relates it to Dixon, who has in fact slept till well past noon, as Shifts and Back-shifts of Bugs pass to and fro, inspecting his Mortal Envelope. "Almost a smell," Mason quizzickally, his face, it seems to Dixon, unusually white, "— not the Drains, nor the Night's Residency,— I cannot explain,— it quite Torpedo'd me."

"Eeh! Sounds worth a Visit...?"

"Acts have consequences, Dixon, they must. These Louts believe all's right now,— that they are free to get on with Lives that to them are no doubt important,— with no Glimmer at all of the Debt they have taken on. That is what I smell'd,— Lethe-Water. One of the things the newly-born forget, is how terrible its Taste, and Smell. In Time, these People are able to forget ev'rything. Be willing but to wait a little, and ye may gull them again and again, however ye wish,— even unto their own Dissolution. In America, as I apprehend, Time is the true River that runs 'round Hell."

"They can't all be like thah'...?"

"Go and see,— and d——'d if I'll share any more Moments like that with you."

"Eeh! As it suits thee. 'Tis how to suit myself, that's the Puzzle. Quaker Garb will send them into a war-like Frenzy, whilst the Red Coat will strike them sullen and creeping, unable to be trusted at any Scale...?"

"You might go as Harlequin," Mason replies, unsooth'd, "or Punch."

Dixon has a fair idea of how little Mason cares for this Continent. He himself has been trying to keep an open Mind. Having been a Quaker all his Life, his Conscience early brought awake and not yet entirely fallen back to sleep, he now rides over to the Jail as to his Duty-Station, wearing a Hat and Coat borrow'd of Mason. He is going as Mason.

He sees where blows with Rifle-Butts miss'd their Marks, and chipp'd the Walls. He sees blood in Corners never cleans'd. Thankful he is no longer a Child, else might he curse and weep, scattering his Anger to no Effect, Dixon now must be his own stern Uncle, and smack himelf upon the Pate at any sign of unfocusing. What in the Holy Names are these people about? Not even the Dutchmen at the Cape behav'd this way. Is it something in this Wilderness, something ancient, that waited for them, and infected their Souls when they came?

Nothing he had brought to it of his nearest comparison, Raby with its thatch'd and benevolent romance of serfdom, had at all prepar'd him for the iron Criminality of the Cape,— the publick Executions and Whippings, the open'd flesh, the welling blood, the beefy contented faces of those whites.... Yet is Dixon certain, as certain as the lightness he feels now, lightness premonitory of Flying, that far worse happen'd here, to these poor People, as the blood flew and the Children cried,— that at the end no one understood what they said as they died. "I don't pray enough," Dixon subvocalizes, "and I can't get upon my Knees just now because too many are watching,— yet could I kneel, and would I pray, 'twould be to ask, respectfully, that this be made right, that the Murderers meet appropriate Fates, that I be spar'd the awkwardness of seeking them out myself and slaying as many as I may, before they overwhelm me. Much better if that be handl'd some other way, by someone a bit more credible...." He feels no better for this Out-pouring.

Returning to their Rooms, he finds Mason reclin'd and smoking, looking up guiltily from a ragged Installment of *The Ghastly Fop*.

"When were tha thinking of leaving this miserable Place?"

"My Saddle-Bags are pack'd, I merely take the time waiting you to satisfy myself that the shockingly underag'd Protasia Wofte has not yet succumb'd, before the wicked Chymickal Assaults of the Ghastly F."

"Whom are we working for, Mason?"

"I rather thought, one day, you would be the one to tell me."

"My Bags are never *un*pack'd. May we do this without Haste, avoiding all appearance of Anxiety?"

"I am cool," Mason replies.

In the Instant, both feel strongly drawn by the Forks of Brandywine, Mrs. Harland's Bean Pies and Rhubarb Tarts, the Goose-Down Bedding, the friendliness of the Milk-maids, the clement Routine of Observation. Gently they disengage from Lancaster. Each Milestone passes like another Rung of a Ladder ascended. Behind,— below,— diminishing, they hear, and presently lose, a Voicing disconsolate, of Regret at their Flight.

35

"Facts are but the Play-things of lawyers,— Tops and Hoops, forever a-spin.... Alas, the Historian may indulge no such idle
Rotating. History is not Chronology, for that is left to Lawyers,—
nor is it Remembrance, for Remembrance belongs to the People.
History can as little pretend to the Veracity of the one, as claim
the Power of the other,— her Practitioners, to survive, must soon
learn the arts of the quidnunc, spy, and Taproom Wit,— that
there may ever continue more than one life-line back into a Past
we risk, each day, losing our forebears in forever,— not a Chain
of single Links, for one broken Link could lose us All,— rather, a
great disorderly Tangle of Lines, long and short, weak and strong,
vanishing into the Mnemonick Deep, with only their Destination
in common."

— The Revd Wicks Cherrycoke, *Christ and History*

"Why," Uncle Ives insists, "you look at the evidence. The testimony. The
whole Truth."

"On the contrary! It may be the Historian's duty to seek the Truth, yet
must he do ev'rything he can, not to tell it."

"Oh, pish!"

"Tush as well."

" 'Twasn't Mr. Gibbon's sort of History, in ev'ry way excellent, that I
meant,— rather, Jack Mandeville, Captain John Smith, even to Baron

Munchausen of our own day,— Herodotus being the God-Father of all, in his refusal to utter the name of a certain Egyptian Deity,— "

"Don't say it!"

"What,— seek the Truth and not tell it! Shameful."

"Extraordinary. Things that may not be told? Hadn't we enough of that from the old George?"

"Just so. Who claims Truth, Truth abandons. History is hir'd, or coerc'd, only in Interests that must ever prove base. She is too innocent, to be left within the reach of anyone in Power,— who need but touch her, and all her Credit is in the instant vanish'd, as if it had never been. She needs rather to be tended lovingly and honorably by fabulists and counterfeiters, Ballad-Mongers and Cranks of ev'ry Radius, Masters of Disguise to provide her the Costume, Toilette, and Bearing, and Speech nimble enough to keep her beyond the Desires, or even the Curiosity, of Government. As Æsop was oblig'd to tell Fables,

> 'So Jacobites must speak in children's rhymes,
> As Preachers do in Parables, sometimes.'

Tox, *Pennsylvaniad,* Book Ten of course...."

"Hogwash, Sir," Uncle Ives about to become peevish with his Son, "Facts are Facts, and to believe otherwise is not only to behave perversely, but also to step in imminent peril of being grounded, young Pup."

"Sir, no offense meant. I was but pointing out that a single Version, in proceeding from a single Authority,— "

"Ethelmer." Ives raises a monitory Eye-brow. "Time on Earth is too precious. No one has time, for more than one Version of the Truth."

"Then, let us have only Jolly Theatricals about the Past, and be done with it,— 'twould certainly lighten my School-work." Mr. LeSpark's Phiz grows laden with Menace.

"Or read Novels," adds Aunt Euphrenia, her tone of dismissal owing more to her obligations as a Guest than her real Sentiments, engag'd more often than she might admit, with examples of the Fabulist's Art.

As if having just detected a threat to the moral safety of the company, Ives announces, "I cannot, damme I cannot I say, energetically enough insist upon the danger of reading these storybooks,— in particular those known as 'Novel.' Let she who hears, heed. Britain's Bedlam even as the French Salpêtrière being populated by an alarming number of young persons, most of them female, seduced across the sill of madness by these irresponsible narratives, that will not distinguish between fact and fancy. How are those frail Minds to judge? Alas, every reader of 'Novel' must be reckoned a soul in peril,— for she hath made a D——l's bargain, squandering her most precious time, for nothing in return but the meanest and shabbiest kinds of mental excitement. 'Romance,' pernicious enough in its day, seems in Comparison wholesome."

"Dr. Johnson says that all History unsupported by contemporary Evidence is Romance," notes Mr. LeSpark.

"Whilst Walpole, lying sick, refus'd to have any history at all read to him, believing it must be false," declares Lomax, gesturing with his Brandy-wine Glass.

"As if, at the end, he wish'd only Truth? Walpole?" Euphie plays an E-flat minor Scale, whilst rolling her eyes about.

"What of Shakespeare?" Tenebræ still learning to be disingenuous, "Those *Henry* plays, or the others, the *Richard* ones? are they only make-believe History? theatrickal rubbish?" as if finding much enjoyment in speaking men's names that are not "Ethelmer."

"Aye, and *Hamlet?*" suggests the Rev^d, staring carefully at the youngsters in turn.

Her eyes a lash's width too wide, perhaps, "Oh, but Hamlet wasn't real, was he?" not wishing to seem to await an answer from her Cousin, yet allowing him now an opening to show off.

Which Ethelmer obligingly saunters into. Of course he has the *Data.* "All in all, a figure with an interesting Life of his own,— alas, this hopping, quizzing, murderously irresolute Figment of Shakespeare's, has quite eclips'd for us the man who had to live through the contradictions of his earthly Life, without having it all re-figur'd for him."

"Then, did he 'really' have a distant cousin named Ophelia," Tenebræ inquires, a shade too softly to be heard by any but Ethelmer, "and did he, historically, break her Heart?"

"More likely she was out to break his,— being his foster-sister actually, working on behalf of his enemies, tho' with no success. A minor figure, who may have charm'd Shakespeare into giving her more lines than she merits, but who does not charm the disinterested Seeker."

"Did he love anyone, then? besides himself, I mean...."

"He ended up marrying the daughter of the English King, 's a matter of fact, and later, in addition, the quite intimidating Hermuthruda, Queen of Scotland."

"What about that Stage strewn with Corpses?" wonders Uncle Lomax. "Two wives!"

"Barbary Pirates take as many as they wish," twinkles Euphie.

"O Euphrenia, Aunt of Lies," Tenebræ shaking her Finger in pretended sternness.

"Mercy, Brae,— I was nearly one myself. Hadn't been for the old Delusse, here, you'd be calling me 'Ayeesha' now. Had to run the Invisible Snake Trick that time, none too reliable in the best o' Circs...." She plays a sinuous Air full of exotick sharps and flats. The Company redeploy themselves in the direction of Comfort, as the moistly-dispos'd Uncle Lomax steers again for the Cabinet in the corner, presently returning with a bottle of Peach Brandy.

Upon his first Sip, the Rev^d reels in his Chair. "Why bless us, 'tis from Octarara."

"Amazingly cognizant, Wicks."

"I once surviv'd a Fortnight, Snow-bound," replies the Rev^d, "upon little else. 'Twas at Mr. Knockwood's, by Octarara Creek, in the terrible winter of 'sixty-four–'sixty-five, when, after four years, the Surveyors and I once more cross'd Tracks...."

'Twas a more tranquil time, before the War, when people moved more slowly,— even, marvelous to say, here in Philadelphia, where the *bustling* might yet be distinguish'd from the *hectic*. There were no Sedan Chairs. Many went about on foot. Even Saint Nicholas was able to deliver all his Gifts, and yet find time for a brisk Pint at The Indian Queen.

I was back in America once more, finding, despite all, that I could not stay away from it, this object of hope that Miracles might yet occur, that God might yet return to Human affairs, that all the wistful Fictions necessary to the childhood of a species might yet come true,...a third Testament.... I had been tarrying over Susquehanna, upon a Ministry that had taken me out among the wilder sort of Presbyterians, a distinct change from the mesopotamian Mysticks of Kutztown or Bethlehem. A bug-ridden, wearying, acidic Journey. Among these folk,— good folk, despite litigious and whiskey-loving ways,— I was not welcome. In my presence dogs howled, milk turn'd, bread failed to rise. Moreover, a spirit of rebellion was then flickering across the countryside, undeniable as the Northern Lights, directed at Britain and all things British, including, ineluctably, your miserable Servant. What we now style "The Stamp Act Crisis" was in full flower. The African Slaves call'd it "the Tamp." Unusual numbers of Riders were out ev'ry Night. The Province seem'd preparing for open warfare. Whiteboys and Black Boys, Paxton Boys and Sailor Boys,— a threat of Mobility ever present.

Thro' this rambunctious Countryside, a Coach-ful of assorted Travelers make their way Philadelphiaward, each upon his Mission. The purposefully jovial Gamer Mr. Edgewise, in whose purse already lie more of my Chits than he really likes to have out at any given time, has won from me a sum we both must view, less as any real Amount, than as a Complication to be resolv'd at some unnam'd date. I lose yet again,— "Why, damme Rev just write me another note, what's it matter the color of the paper, who has any cash anyway?" Business then, in this Province, Wagering included, was conducted overwhelmingly by way of Credit,— the Flow of Cash was not as important as Character, Duty, a complex structure of Debt in which Favors, Forgiveness, Ignominy were much more likely than any repayment in Specie. Mr. Edgewise is traveling with his Wife, who, when she must, regards him with a Phiz that speaks of the great amounts of her time given over, in a philosophickal way, to classifying the numerous forms of human idiot, beyond the common or Blithering sort, with which all are familiar,— the Bloody-Minded I., for example, recognized by the dangerous sea of white all around the irises of the eye-balls, or the twittering

Variety, by the infallible utterance "Frightfully." Then one has Mr. Edgewise....

We have passed, tho' without comment, out of the zone of influence of the western mountains, and into that of Chesapeake,— as there exists no "Maryland" beyond an Abstraction, a Frame of right lines drawn to enclose and square off the great Bay in its unimagin'd Fecundity, its shoreline tending to Infinite Length, ultimately unmappable,— no more, to be fair, than there exists any "Pennsylvania" but a chronicle of Frauds committed serially against the Indians dwelling there, check'd only by the Ambitions of other Colonies to north and east.

Our Coach is a late invention of the Jesuits, being, to speak bluntly, a Conveyance, wherein the inside is quite noticeably larger than the outside, though the fact cannot be appreciated until one is inside. For your Benefit, DePugh, the Mathematickal and Philosophickal Principles upon which the Design depends are known to most Students of the appropriate Arts,— so that I hesitate to burden the Company with information easily obtain'd elsewhere. That my Authorial Authority be made more secure, however, it may be reveal'd without danger that at the basis of the Design lies a logarithmic idea of the three dimensions of Space, realiz'd in an intricate Connexion of precise Analytickal curves, some bearing loads, others merely decorative, still others serving as Cam-Surfaces guiding the motions of other Parts.—

("We believe you, Wicks. We do. Pray go on.")

Bound through the nocturnal fields, the land asleep, the sky pressing close, losing at an ever-unadjourned game of All-Fours, dyspeptic from the fare at the last inn, restlessly now and then scanning the dark outside for any Light, however distant, I was bounced out of a disgruntled reverie by the Machine's abrupt slowing and eventual halt, out in the middle of a Night already grown heavy with imminent snow. Waiting at the Roadside were two Women, who prov'd to be mother and daughter, dresses flowing as homespun was never suppos'd to, and Faces that were to drive me, later that night, unable to sleep, beneath the Beam of my writing-lanthorn, to diaristic excess.— Yet, how speak of "Luminosity" in that pre-snowlight, or say "flawless," or, in particular, "otherworldly," when in fact in Cisalleghenic America, apparitions continue,— Life not yet having grown so Christian and safe that a late traveler may not, even in this Deistically stained age, encounter a Woman of just such unearthly fairness, who will promise him ev'rything and end by doing him mischief. Indeed, already in the course of this journey we had encountered what may well have been a Victim, fix'd and raving in the batter'd road, of some such Night-Interception. As the pair of Creatures boarded the Machine, I mutely ask'd,— not "pray'd," for all my Prayers in those Days must be Questions,— Are these now come for me, to be my own guides across the borderlands and into Madness?

But to my surprise and perhaps disappointment, their eyes will meet no one else's. As the Machine again gathers speed, it becomes clear that the young women intend to sit in companionable but perfect silence, for the entire journey. One by one, around the traveling Interior, small private lanthorns begin to glow, whilst I, long accustomed to finding beauty only among the soiled and fallen,— having thereby supposed a moral invariance as to beauty and innocence in women,— grow distracted at the very Conjunction,— undeniable, overwhelming, each with her hair tucked away 'neath a simple cap of white Lawn, tied under the chin, so that her face is the only part of her body exposed,— Faces innocent of all paint, patches, or pincering, naked as Eve's own.

Mr. Edgewise leans forward to introduce himself in a mucilaginous voice he would have described rather as cordial. "And how far would you ladies be traveling this fine evening?"

Because of the net outflow of light from her face, the daughter is seen instantly to blush, whilst the mother, with a level gaze but without smiling, replies, "To Philadelphia, Sir."

"Why, 'tis Sodom-upon-Schuylkill, Ma'am!" the blunt but kindly Traveler rolling his eyes about expressively. "What possible business could be taking a Godly young woman down into that unheavenly place?"

"My story must be only for the ears of the Lawyer I go to hire, Sir," she answers quietly, in the same determin'd voice.

All of us stare, each in his own form of astonishment. "You intend,"— it happens that I am first to speak,— "to engage the services,— forgive me,— of…a Philadelphia Lawyer? Good lady, surely there is some recourse less…extreme? Your family, your congregation, the officials of your Church,— "

She is gazing at my clerical collar, within which I must appear shackl'd secure as any Turk's slave. "Are you one of these? The English Church, *net?*"

How might I speak of my true "Church," of the planet-wide Syncretism, among the Deistick, the Oriental, Kabbalist, and the Savage, that is to be,— the Promise of Man, the redemptive Point, ever at our God-horizon, toward which all Faiths, true and delusional, must alike converge! Instead, I can only mumble and blurt, before the radiance of these young Pietists, something about being between preferments at the moment, so askew in my thoughts that I've forgotten my new Commission, and indeed the Purpose of my Journey,— even using "interprebendary" again, after promising a Certain Deity that I would refrain. But her innocent attention has reach'd unto the dead Vacuum ever at the bottom of my soul,— humiliation absolute.

Mr. Edgewise, a devotee of machinery, the newer the better, produces a Flask of curious shape and surface, devised in Italy by a renowned Jesuit artificer, out of which, to the wonder of the company, the Gambler now begins to pour steaming-hot coffee into a traveler's cup he has by him, and hands it to the young woman, who introduces herself as Frau Luise Redzinger, of Coniwingo. As she continues to sip more and more eagerly at the refreshing liquid,— which Mr. Edgewise is content to keep providing ever more of, out of the strange and apparently inexhaustible Flask,— before long she finds herself talking quite readily.

"Philadelphia, Sirs, can hold little to surprise me. My sister lives in the most licentious Babylon of America, though they are pleased to call themselves 'Bethlehem,' so. Liesele happened to marry a Moravian, now a baker of that town,— the two having met upon the ship that carried us all here. Her destiny was to be fancy, as it was mine to be plain, I who do not know one grape wine from another,— whilst Liesele, already, between her first and second letters to me, had slid steeply into a gaudy Christianity aroar with Putzing and gay distraction, little to be distinguish'd from that of Rome,— having, indeed, its own Carnival, its gluttony and lustfulness, and the Trombone Choir, imagine, a wonder their minister is not addressed as *Pope,* so." At this the daughter gives a small gasp. But Frau Redzinger has grown flushed and cheerful, as if this address to a coach-ful of strangers were perhaps more speech than she has allow'd herself, save among her own sex, in who knows how long.

"Child, child, 'twould be far more sensible to forgive your sister," murmurs Mistress Edgewise, taking the young woman's hand. "You must both pass beyond it, dear." Her husband huffs forward, intending a similar Courtesy toward the young Woman's knee, but is deflected by a wifely stare, that contrives to look amused, tho' indisposed to bantering.

Frau Redzinger gestures expansively with her coffee cup, which is luckily, for the moment, empty. "Oh, yes, I am a bad sister, a bad wife and Christian, I am the one who must be forgiven, somehow, but,— " she regards us each for a moment, her chin atremble, "of whom here would I ask it? Of course I resent Liesele, I envy her life. She has her husband."

At which looseness of tongue the daughter, at last, protests. But too late, for her Mother has rush'd on, as we now go rushing along down the Communication, above us our Jehu son of Nimshi taking chances he would never have taken in the Daylight.

" 'Twas not the same as being struck by lightning,— we've lightning over Schuylkill that's every bit the equal of Mr. Franklin's famous city-lightning, folk who've been hit by ours, speak of being 'prison'd in a thunderous glory'...but Peter was only bringing hops in to the cooling-pit, the most ordinary of tasks,— slipped in the dust, fell in the Pit, with the dried hops nearly twenty feet deep, hot from the Kiln, you can squeeze them together almost forever, drowning in them is easy, last year it was a church person over at Kutztown, even the odor of the pollen is deadly, the man's wife said, *that it took him into a poison'd sleep,*— but neither of us was with her husband when it happened, it is not a place women go, I was in the fields, with the other women and the last of the harvest, the way it is, we work only with the living Plants, so we tend the

Bines all summer,— soon as the Cones are picked, and dead, it is then the Men take over, *net?*

"I don't know what I might have done…. The hops buoy'd him up, but not so much,— when help arrived, they said they could see only his hand above the cones, releasing their dust and terrible fumes as his struggling broke them,— by the time Jürgen could anchor himself, there was only my husband's one finger, reaching back into this world, his poor finger. The force it took to pull him out…no physician anywhere could have put it back to what it was. Peter would call it his sacramental finger, his outward and bodily sign of the Other thing that had happened to him down in that miserable suffocation. He bore it without shame, rather…with bewilderment."

Certain herbal essences in massive influxion, as I feel it my duty to assure her, have long been known and commented upon, as occasions of God-revealing. She nods emphatically.— As weeks passed, she tells us, Peter Redzinger's account chang'd, from a simple tale of witness, to one of rapture by beings from somewhere else, "long, long from Pennsylvania," as he expressed it,— and always at the center of the Relation, unwise to approach, an unbearable Luminosity.

As God has receded, as Deism has crept in to make the best of this progressive Absence, more and more do we witness extreme varieties of human character emergent,— Cagliostro, the Comte de St.-Germain, Adam Weishaupt,— Magicians with Munchausen tales and ever more extravagant effects,— Illuminati, Freemasons, Elect Cohens, many of whom, to my great curiosity, have found their way into Pennsylvania. They wander the town streets, they haunt the desert places, they are usually Germans. Woe betide the credulous countryman who falls under their influence,— or, as in the case of Peter Redzinger, is transform'd into one of them.

Another American Illumination, another sworn moment,— and where in England are any Epiphanies, bright as these? Bring anything like one,— any least Sail upon the Horizon of our Exile,— to the attention of an Established Clergyman, and 'twill elicit nought but gentle Reproofs and guarded Suggestions, which must sooner or later include the word "Physician."

These times are unfriendly toward Worlds alternative to this one. Royal Society members and French Encyclopædists are in the Chariot, availing themselves whilst they may of any occasion to preach the Gospels of Reason, denouncing all that once was Magic, though too often in smirking tropes upon the Church of Rome,— visitations, bleeding statues, medical impossibilities,— no, no, far too foreign. One may be allowed an occasional Cock Lane Ghost,— otherwise, for any more in that Article, one must turn to Gothick Fictions, folded acceptably between the covers of Books.

"They say Peter is seen now over Susquehanna, *aus dem Kipp,* wandering from one cabin to another, anywhere two or more Germans may be gathered together, with his Tales of the Pit. He calls it preaching,— so, to no one's surprize, do others. Some even follow him, Redzingerites, for whom his enlightenment by way of nearly drowning is the central event. Their view of Baptism does not, need I say, stop at Total Immersion. I imagine him by now a creature of the Forest. Perhaps I have mistaken my own destiny for his, and his Elevation," sighing, "has prov'd my Enearthment."

She speaks, it unfolds, of the Redzinger Farm, an hundred-acre Parcel close to, if not actually in, Maryland,— no one will know until the English Surveyors come through. The Proprietors of both Provinces have been offering lower Land prices, sometimes even exemption from the Quit-rent, to any who'll settle near Boundaries in dispute. Peter Redzinger has always known good land, he can look at it and tell you, if you ask, what it will bear in Abundance, what it will not tolerate. This place, as he recogniz'd from frequent visits to it in Dreams since he was young, would give him back anything he wished. "When he walk'd it, he discover'd he was dowsing it with his feet, and for more than Water, too, and had to keep his Shoes on, because upon his bare soles he could not withstand *Die Krafte,* the Forces? It whispers to him. He can almost make out the words."

Sometimes he tried to talk to Luise about this, but with such difficulty that she always ended up thinking about her sister in Bethlehem, and the Dancing she might be missing, after all. "...And it comes from the wind moving through the underbrush...it is inside of the Wind, and they are real words, and if you listen…" She must have known quite early, that the Hoppit, or something as decisive, was waiting for them. Meanwhile, maize and morning glories, tomatoes and cherry trees, every flower and Esculent known to Linnæus, thriv'd. The seasons swept through, Mitzi, and then the Boys, were born, Luise and Peter built a Bakery, Smokehouse, Stables, Milk-barn, Hen-coop, Hop-kiln, and Cooling-pit. His brothers, and their families, live nearby. Like many in Lancaster County, they all have Fields planted to Hops and Hemp. Each Crop, for its own reasons of Peace and War, is in rapidly growing demand, and fetching good prices.

Grodt, one of the farmers whose land adjoins the Redzingers', has long coveted their farm, and furthermore believes that both farms are located in Maryland. Under Maryland law, he knows he may get a warrant to resurvey his land, and in the process include any vacant land it happens to adjoin,— the property Line will be allow'd to stretch about and engross it,— by virtue of the Resurvey, it will become his. (Many were the elephantine tracts swallowed at one nibble, in those times, by the country Mice thereabouts.) Land defined as vacant includes land once settled but now "in escheat," meaning gone back to the Proprietor, usually for non-payment of taxes,— Luise has been paying the Quit-rents to Pennsylvania, but Grodt, contending that she dwells in Maryland and owes more back taxes there than she can ever pay, believes the land is escheatable.

"I am no attorney," I try to console her, "but his case sounds doubtful."

"If he goes ahead," warns Mr. Edgewise, "obtains a warrant, pays the caution money, has title, then it's his, if no one can prove the land *isn't* escheatable." All now fall to arguing about Land-Jobbery, the discussion growing at times spirited and personal. Everyone in the Coach, it seems, has suddenly become a Philadelphia Lawyer.

"Why," Mrs. Edgewise demands to know, "must this subject rouse quite so much Passion?"

The Purveyor of Delusion confers upon his wife a certain expression or twist of Phiz I daresay as old as Holy Scripture,— a lengthy range of Sentiment, all comprest into a single melancholick swing of the eyes. From some personal stowage he produces another Flask, containing, not the Spruce Beer ubiquitous in these parts, but that favor'd stupefacient of the jump'd-up tradesman, French claret,— and without offering it to anyone else, including his Wife, begins to drink. "It goes back," he might have begun, "to the second Day of Creation, when 'G-d made the Firmament, and divided the Waters which were under the Firmament, from the Waters which were above the Firmament,'— thus the first Boundary Line. All else after that, in all History, is but Sub-Division."

"What Machine is it," young Cherrycoke later bade himself good-night, "that bears us along so relentlessly? We go rattling thro' another Day,— another Year,— as thro' an empty Town without a Name, in the Midnight...we have but Memories of some Pause at the Pleasure-Spas of our younger Day, the Maidens, the Cards, the Claret,— we seek to extend our stay, but now a silent Functionary in dark Livery indicates it is time to re-board the Coach, and resume the Journey. Long before the Destination, moreover, shall this Machine come abruptly to a Stop...gather'd dense with Fear, shall we open the Door to confer with the Driver, to discover that there is no Driver,...no Horses,...only the Machine, fading as we stand, and a Prairie of desperate Immensity...."

36

The driver, having observed through the gusting low clouds, candle-lit Windows in the Distance, now notifies those of us below, that we are approaching an Inn. The Ladies begin to stir and pat, lean together and discuss. Men re-light their Pipes and consult their watches,— and, more discreetly, their Pocket-books. The rush of the Weather past the smooth outer Shell, a surface lacquered as secretly as the finest Cremona Violin, smoothly abates, silences, to be replaced by the crisp shouts of Hostlers and Stable-boys. We observe Link-men waiting in a double line, as if at some ceremony of German Mysticks, their torches sparking intensely yellow at the edges as they illuminate the falling Snow-Flakes.

In the partial light, the immense log Structure seems to tower toward the clouds until no more can be seen,— tho' the clouds at the moment are low,— whilst horizontally sprawling away, into an Arrangement of courtyards and passageways, till likewise lost to the eye, such complexity recalling Holy Land Bazaars and Zouks, even in the wintry setting,— save that in this Quarter nothing is ancient, the logs are still beaded with clear drops of resin, with none of the walls inside attached directly to them, the building having not yet had even a season to settle. The pots in the kitchen are all still bright, the Edges yet upon the Cutlery, bed-linens folded away that haven't yet been romp'd, or even slept, among.

This new Inn is an overnight stop for everybody with business upon the Communication, quite near a rope ferry across Bloomery Creek, one of the thousand rivers and branches flowing into Chesapeake. Waggoners are as welcome as Coach parties, and both sorts of Traveler, for the time being, find this acceptable. There's a long front porch, and two entrances, one into the Bar-room, the other into the family Parlor, with Passage between them only after a complicated search within, among Doors and Stair-cases more and less evident.

Meanwhile, the Astronomers, returning from Lancaster, are attending the Day's cloudy Sky as closely as they might a starry one at Night. "Can't say I'm too easy with this weather," Mason remarks.

"Do tha mean those white flake-like objects blowing out of the north-east...?"

"Actually, I lost sight of the Trees about fifteen minutes ago."

"Another bonny gahn-on tha've got us into...? Are we even upon the Road?"

"Hold,— is that a Light?"

"Don't try to get out of it thah' way."

"I am making it snow? Is this what you mean to assert, here?— how on earth could I do that, Dixon, pray regard yourself, Sir!"

"Tha pre-dicted a fair passage back to the Tents, indeed we have wager'd a Pistole,— "

"You would, of course, mention it."

Bickering energetickally, they make their way toward the lights and at length enter the very Inn where your Narrator, lately arriv'd, is already down a Pipe and a Pint,— only to be brought to dumbfounded silence at the Sight of one whom they've not seen since the Cape of Good Hope.

"Are we never to be rid of him, then...?" cries Dixon.

"An Hallucination," Mason assures him, "brought on by the Snow, the vanishing of detail, the Brain's Anxiety to fill the Vacuum at any Cost...."

"Well met, Sirs," I reply. "And it gets worse." I reach in my Pockets and find and unscroll my Commission, which, all but knocking Pates, they read hastily.

"Party Chaplain...?"

"Who ask'd for a Chaplain?"

"Certainly not I...?"

"You don't mean *I*,— "

" 'Twas part of a side-Letter to the Consent Decree in Chancery," I explain helpfully, "that there be a Chaplain."

"Most of 'm'll be Presbyterians, Rev...? When they're not German Sectarians, or Irish Catholics...?"

"The Royal Society, however, is solidly Anglican."

"Chaplain," says Mason.

"Eeh," says Dixon.

As torch- or taper-light takes over from the light of the sunset, what are those Faces, gather'd before some Window, raising Toasts, preparing for the Evening ahead, if not assur'd of life forever? as travelers come in by ones and twos, to smells of Tobacco and Chops, as Fiddle Players tune their strings and starv'd horses eat from the trough in the Courtyard, as young women flee to and fro dumb with fatigue, and small boys down in strata of their own go swarming upon ceaseless errands, skidding upon the Straw, as smoke begins to fill the smoking-room...how may Death come here?

Mr. Knockwood, the landlord, a sort of trans-Elemental Uncle Toby, spends hours every day not with Earth Fortifications, but studying rather the passage of Water across his land, and constructing elaborate works to divert its flow, not to mention his guests. "You don't smoak how it is," he argues, "— all that has to happen is some Beaver, miles upstream from here, moves a single Pebble,— suddenly, down here, everything's changed! The creek's a mile away, running through the Horse Barn! Acres of Forest no longer exist! And that Beaver don't even know what he's done!" and he stands glaring, as if this hypothetickal animal were the fault of the patient Listener.

The weather continues to worsen. Taproom Regulars come in to voice openly Comparisons to the Winter of '63 and '64, the freezing and Floods. New casks of peach Brandy are open'd daily. The Knockwoods begin to raise their voices. "But I was saving that one."

"For what? The Book of Revelations? These are cash customers."

The Assembly Room is not Bath. Here congregate all the Agentry of the Province, Land-Jobbers and Labor Crimps, Tool-Mongers and Gypsy Brick-Layers, as well as the curious Well-to-do from further East, including all the Way back across the Ocean. The Waggoners keep together, seeking or creating their own Snugs, and the Men of Affairs arrange for Separate Rooms. Those that remain, tend to run to the quarrelsome.

"Where may one breathe?" demands one Continental Macaroni, in a yellow waistcoat, "— in New-York, Taverns have rooms where Smoke is prohibited."

"Tho' clearly," replies the itinerant Stove-Salesman Mr. Whitpot, drawing vigorously at his Pipe, "what's needed is a No-Idiots Area."

The youth at this makes a motion, less threatening than vex'd, toward the Hanger he wears habitually at his side,— tho' upon which he happens, at the moment, to be sitting. "Well, and you're a Swine, who cares what a Swine thinks?"

"*Peevish* Mr. Dimdown," coos Mrs. Edgewise, reaching behind the youth's ear and underneath his Wig to produce a silver pistole she has no intention, however, of offering to him, "do re-sheathe your weapon, there's a good young gentleman." Mistress of a diverting repertoire of conjuring tricks with Playing-Cards, Dice, Coins, Herbs, Liquids in Flasks, Gentlemen's Watches, Handkerchiefs, Weapons, Beetles and Bugs and short Excursions up the Chain of Being therefrom,— to Pigeons upon occasion, and Squirrels,— she has brought, to the mud courtyards of trans-Susquehannian inns, Countryfolk from miles about to gather into a crepuscular Murmur, no fabl'd Telegraph so swift as this Diffusion among them of word that a Magician is in the Neighborhood. In this Autumn cold, out in the Rain, beneath the generally unseen rising of the Pleiades, has she been trouping on, cheerfully rendering subjunctive, or contrary to fact, familiar laws of nature and of common sense.

Despite her Skills in Legerdemain, her Husband seldom, if ever, will allow her to accompany him upon his gaming Ventures. Ever subject to Evaporations of Reserve, she will now and then inquire why not, receiving the dyspeptic equivalent of a Gallant Smile. "Madam, to visit yea even gaze upon such Doings would I fear my honey'd Apiary prove no easy burden to Sensibilities as finely rigged out as your own, therefore must I advise against it, with regret yet vehemence as well, my tuzzy-muzzy."

"I know your 'vehemence.' It is of little account with me."

"Among my acquaintance," remarks Mr. Dimdown, fondling his Hanger, "no woman would dare address her Husband in that way, without incurring a prolonged chastisement."

"As the phrase, scientifickally, describes Life with Mr. Edgewise, your Acquaintance need not, on this Occasion at least, suffer disappointment."

In a distant corner, Luise and Mitzi are engag'd in a Discussion as to Hair. "I want it all different lengths," fiercely, "I don't want to fasten it close to my head. I don't want to cover it. I want people to see it. I want *Boys* to see it."

" 'Tis a brumal Night, for behold, it sweepeth by," announces Squire Haligast from the shadows, resuming his silence as everyone falls silent to attend thereupon,— for the gnomic Squire, on the rare occasions he speaks, does so with an intensity suggesting, to more than one of the Guests, either useful Prophecy or Bedlamite Entertainment.

This is the Room Mason and Dixon descend into, where all is yet too new for the scent of hops and malt to've quite worked in,— rather, fugitive odors of gums and resins, of smoke from pipes and fires, of horses upon the garments of the company, come and go, unmix'd. The winter light creeps in and becomes confus'd among the glassware, a wrinkl'd bright stain.

"You're the Astronomers," Mr. Knockwood greets them. "The Rev^d has been speaking of you." When they come to explain about the two Transits of Venus, and the American Work filling the Years between, "By Heaven, a 'Sandwich,' " cries Mr. Edgewise. "Take good care, Sirs, that something don't come along and *eat* it!"

His pleasure at being able to utter a recently minted word, is at once much curtailed by the volatile *Chef de Cuisine* Armand Allègre, who rushes from the Kitchen screaming. "Sond-weech-uh! Sond-weech-uh!," gesticulating as well, "To the Sacrament of the Eating, it is ever the grand Insult!"

Cries of "Anti-Britannic!" and "Shame, Mounseer!"

Mitzi clutches herself. "No Mercy! Oh, he's so 'cute!"

Young Dimdown may be seen working himself up to a level of indignation that will allow him at least to pull out his naked Hanger again, and wave it about a bit. "Where I come from," he offers, "Lord Sandwich is as much respected for his nobility as admired for his Ingenuity, in creating the great modern Advance in Diet which bears his name, and I would suggest,— without of course wishing to offend,— that it ill behooves some bloody little toad-eating foreigner to speak his name in any but a respectful manner."

"Had I my *batterie des couteaux*," replies the Frenchman, with more gallantry than sense, "before that ridiculous little blade is out of his sheath, I can bone you,— like the Veal!"

"Stop it," admonishes the Rev^d, "both of you,— not all the Sensibilities here are grown as coarsen'd as your own. The Eponym in dispute," he continues to point out to the Macaroni, "better known these Days as Jemmy Twitcher, withal, is a vile-mouthed drunkard, a foolish gambler, and a Sodomitical rake, who betrayed his dear friend for the sake of,— let us say, a certain Caress, from the feeble hand of *Georgie*, Jack Bute's pathetic Creature."

"By Heaven, a Wilkesite!" cries Mr. Edgewise, "right here among us, imagine it, my Crown of Thorns!"

"The Lord's long Night of gaming draws to a close," pronounces Squire Haligast, "— the Object in its Journey, comes nigh, among the excursions of Chance, the sins of ministers, the inscriptions upon walls and Gate-posts,— the birth of the 'Sandwich,' at this exact moment in Christianity,— one of the Noble and Fallen for its Angel! Disks of secular Bread,— enclosing whilst concealing slices of real Flesh, yet a-sop with Blood, under the earthly guise of British Beef, all,— but for the Species of course,— Consubstantiate, thus…the Sandwich, Eucharist of this our Age." Thereupon retracting his head into the recklessly-toss'd folds of his neck-cloth, and saying no more.

"Precisely so," blares Mr. Edgewise, striking his wife smartly upon the Leg,— "oh, beg pardon, m' dear, thought it was meself I was thumping upon, well well a long night of gaming for us all isn't it? even if it is usually in the daytime, day after quo-not-to-mention-quid-tidian day now ain't that correct, my cheery Daw!"

At table next morning, instead of the gusts of grease-smoke she expected venting from the kitchen, Luise Redzinger is agreeably surpriz'd to find Fragrances already familiar from her own cooking, and withal strange deviations,— what she later will identify as Garlick, for one, and a shameless over-usage of Butter in place of Lard, for another. "Do you not consider it a sin, even in the English church?" she accosts Revd Cherry-coke. "You could not find this even in Bethlehem at Christmastide." The object is a *Croissant*,— "a sort of ev'ryday Roll among the French, who put Butter in all they cook, Madam," the worldly Mr. Edgewise instructs her,— half a dozen more of which her Daughter, less scandalized, has already accounted for,— though no fingers in the room go altogether ungreased by these palatable pastries, which keep arriving from some distant oven, one great steaming platter-ful after another. "More likely the Devil's work," sniffs the beauteous Sectarian, "than any Frenchman, so." But with a strange,— what indeed is later thought to be hopeful,— Lift, at the end of it.

"Well then," bustles their host, "how'd you like to meet him in person?"

She gasps. Whenever she tells the story after that, she will put in, "My heart stopped, almost,— for I thought he meant the Devil." But he means his newly-hired Chef, the diminutive and athletic Monsieur Armand Allègre, whose white Toque, "half again as tall as he," she has noticed once or twice flashing in the kitchen doorway, even thro' pipe-murk and this dark Daybreak,— more brightly, in fact, than there is light to account for. "Here, Frenchy! Venayzeesee! One of our Guests wishes to present her compliments!" He winks at the eaters at nearby tables, Lord Affability.

"Gentle Sir," Frau Redzinger fixing him with a gaze whose calmness is precarious at best, "he may cook whatever he pleases,— I will not preach him a sermon."

"Oh, he's a good sort, you needn't worry, he's not all *that* French! Here then,— "

Introduced by their jocund host, the Frenchman sweeps off his Toque, causing a trio of Candles nearby to gutter for a moment, and stands before her exposed in his true altitude, hardly taking breaths, as she, meantime, 'tis clear to one or two of the Company, sits likewise trans- fix'd, the croissant in her posed hand shedding flakes, as a late flower its petals. By the unabated noise in the room, it would seem the moment has passed unremark'd. She, as if becoming aware of the (as it now turns out) already half-eaten Article she holds, shakes it slowly at him in reluctant tribute. "How...did you do this?"

"Madame,— I am even now about to begin a new batch of the Crois- sant Dough...I would be honored, if you would care to observe our little Kitchen at work...." From somewhere producing a simple turned hick- ory cylinder, some twenty inches long and perhaps two across,— "My Rolling-pin,"— urging her to take it in her hesitant hands, appreciate the weight, the smoothness, and give it a sample roll or two upon the table.

Frowning, curious, she complies. Presently, her voice lower, "It pays well, this Job, *net?*" He shrugs, his thoughts elsewhere. "Were it Thou- sands," sighing as if they were the only two in the room, and forcefully grasping his own face by the cheeks, "yet would you behold...the face of Melancholy. Alas. Once the most celebrated chef in France,— now alone, among foreign Peasants and skin-wearing Primitives, with no chance of escaping. And even if I could, where would I go? when all civilized,— I mean, of course, French,— soil is forbidden to my foot, even in the Illinois, even in the far mountains of Louisiana, *It* would seek me out, and remain, with motives too alien for any human ever to know."

" *'It'!* How dreadful. Who dislikes you so much?"

" 'Who,' alas...a human pursuer, I perhaps could elude."

Fascinated herself, she has miss'd completely his effect upon Mitzi, who is sitting there flush'd and daz'd, with as clear an incipient case of the Green Pip as Mrs. Edgewise has met with since her own Girlhood. She leans from an adjoining Table. "Do you wish to faint, child?" Cour- teously the girl's eyelids and lashes swing downward, at least for as long as she can bear it, till presently in a weightless Languor sweeping up again for another quick glance at Armand. The older Woman straightens again, shaking her head with a smile in which ordinary Mirth, though present, is far from the only Element,— as meanwhile M. Allègre proceeds, before a room-ful of what, to his mind, must seem unfeeling barbarians, to recite his Iliad of Inconvenience.

37

"I was the youngest of four brothers. Each of us, one by one, was well placed in life, until my turn came,— when, our Father's Fortunes' having experienc'd an unforeseen reversal, there remain'd only money enough to send me to Paris and apprentice me to the greatest chef in France,— which is to say, in the World.— "

This is greeted with cries of, "Really, Mounseer!" "The world of Amphibia, perhaps," and "Here Frenchy,— try a nice British Sausage Roll!" "*Oh* dear," murmurs Mr. Knockwood, awaiting the ominous scrape of chair-legs along his new floor-planking.

For years (the Frenchman goes on), I grunted 'neath Loads of water and firewood, Sacks of Flour, Tubs of Butter. Everything the *Maître* considered below standard I got to eat, thus learning in the most direct way, the rights and wrongs of the Food. 'Twas another year before I was permitted to hold a Whisk. No one offer'd to teach me anything. Learning was to be all my responsibility. Year by year, sleepless and too often smileless, I acquir'd the arts of *la Cuisine*,— until, one day, at last, I had become a Chef. And presently, as these things unfold, Paris was at my feet.

I'll say it for you,— poor Paris! Here were great Houses getting into violent feuds over my *pâtés*, the Queen commenting upon my *Blanquette de Veau.* I quickly grew too self-important to understand that it was my Novelty they were after, not my cooking,— a realization I delay'd for longer than prov'd wise....

I was visited one day by a certain well-known Gentleman-*Detective* of the Time,— let us call him Hervé du T.,— whilst in the most critical Passage of a very demanding Sauce. The man had no idea of what he had put in jeopardy. In the Kitchen, one of the most useful Skills, is knowing when best, and when not, to deploy *un Accès de Cuisinier,* which properly executed has been known to freeze entire arm'd Units in their Tracks. The Obsession lighting the Eyes of my Visitor, however, far outshone anything I knew how to summon,— I was intrigued,— God help me, Madame, I listened.—

At this point Armand catches sight of Mason and Dixon, who are attempting to bring their Breakfast to an undisturb'd corner of the Saloon. "Ah! how curious that this Instant, Gentlemen, I was about to advert to your Brother in Science, whom perhaps you have even met, the immortal Jacques de Vaucanson."

Mason squints thoughtfully, Dixon shifts his Hat about till presently nodding, "Why aye, thah's it,— the Lad with the mechanickal Duck...?"

"Too true, alas. A Mechanician of blinding and world-rattling Genius, Gentlemen, yet posterity will know him because of the Duck alone,— they are already coupl'd as inextricably as...Mason and Dixon? Haw-hawhawnnh. The Man Voltaire call'd a Prometheus,— to be remember'd only for having trespass'd so ingeniously outside the borders of Taste, as to have provided his Automaton a Digestionary Process, whose end result could not be distinguish'd from that found in Nature."

"A mechanickal Duck that shits? To whom can it matter," Mr. Whitpot, having remov'd his Wig, is irritably kneading it like a small Loaf, "— who besides a farmer would even recognize Duck Waste, however compulsively accurate? And when might any country person get to see this Marvel to begin with, if its only engagements were in Parisian *Hôtels?*"

"Some," the Frenchman bristles, "might point rather to a Commitment of Ingenuity unprecedented, toward making All authentic,— perhaps, it could be argued by minds more scientifick, 'twas this very Attention to Detail, whose Fineness, passing some Critickal Value, enabl'd in the Duck that strange Metamorphosis, which has sent it out the Gates of the Inanimate, and off upon its present Journey into the given World."

What I was told then (Armand continues), remains even today high treason to reveal,— this was bigger than the Man in the Iron Mask,— Kingdoms, Empires indeed, had begun to sway, since the fateful moment when one of Vaucanson's Servants enter'd the Atelier, to find the Duck hovering a few feet above a Table-top, flapping its Wings. There was no need to scream, tho' both of them did, anyway. The Secret was out. Within an hour, the Duck was well flown.

" 'Twas not of M. Vaucanson's Device, then?"

"*Ha,* ha ha, what a droll remark, I must tell Madame la Marquise de Pompadour, next time we '*faisons le Déjeuner,*' she will be so amus'd.... No, ingenuous one,— the 'Design' was of quite a different order, an entirely new Bodily Function in fact, and no one, including the great Engineer himself, knows what happen'd...."

Vaucanson's vainglorious Intent had been to repeat for Sex and Reproduction, the Miracles he'd already achiev'd for Digestion and Excretion. "Who knows? that final superaddition of erotick Machinery may have somehow nudg'd the Duck across some Threshold of self-Intricacy, setting off this Explosion of Change, from Inertia toward *Independence, and Power.* Isn't it like an old Tale? Has an Automatick Duck, like the Sleeping Beauty, been brought to life by the kiss of...*l'Amour?*

"Oo-la-la," comes a voice from the corner, "and toot ma flute."

"Frenchies,— marvelous i'n't it," comments another, "ever at it, night and day."

"Savages," hisses the Gallic miniature.

"Pray, Monsieur, go on," Frau Redzinger with a glance of reproach at the room in general.

"For you, Madame." He gestures broadly with his giant Toque, and continues.—

My visitor had grown quite agitated by now. " 'Twas his own *Hubris,*— the old mad Philosopher story, we all know, meddl'd where he shouldn't have, till laws of the Unforeseen engag'd,— now the Duck is a Fugitive, flying where it wishes,— often indeed visiting the Academy of Sciences, where they have learn'd that the greater its speed, the less visible it grows, until at around a Thousand Toises per Minute, it vanishes entirely,— but one of many newly-acquir'd Powers, bringing added

Urgency to finding it as quickly as possible, before this 'Morphosis carries it beyond our Control. Which is precisely where you may do us a Service, Sir."

"But my gifts…scarcely lie in this direction."

"Recollect, *cher Maître,* as I do with senses even today a-tremble, your *Canard au Pamplemousse Flambé.* It is unique in Civilization. Not to mention the sublime *Canard avec Aubergines en Casserole*…mmhhnnhh! I embrace them! The immortal *Fantaisie des Canettes*…,"— and much more, including Dishes I'd all but forgotten. I should have stood unmov'd, but I'd gone a-blush. "Oh, those old Canards," I murmur'd.

"You see, when one looks in the files of the Ministries, and of other Detectives, for that matter, invariably, under the Heading, 'Duck,' the two Humans whose Names most often appear, are Vaucanson, and yourself. Again and again. Can there be a Connection?— the Automaton apparently believes so, having somehow, quite recently, become *aware of you.* Since then, its Resentment on behalf of all Ducks,— and not only those you personally may have cook'd,— has grown alarmingly. Without doubt, it is forming a Plan, whose details you may not wish to know."

"But this is dangerous! What if its Brain be affected by now? And if it be blaming me for Wrongs I never knew I was committing?"

"Ah! it might seek you out, mightn't it,— and, in the Monomania of its Assault, grow careless enough to allow my Agents at last to apprehend it. That would be the Plan, anyhow. Agreed, you must consider how best to defend yourself,— wear clothing it cannot bite through, leather, or what's even more secure, chain-mail,— its Beak being of the finest Swedish Steel, did I mention that, yes quite able, when the Duck, in its homicidal Frenzy, is flying at high speed, to penetrate all known Fortification, solid walls being as paper to this Juggernaut…. One may cower within, but one cannot avoid,— *le Bec de la Mort,* the…'Beak of Death.'"

"Wait, wait," trying not to upset him further, "reprising this,— you wish me to act as a sort of…Decoy? to attract the personal Vengeance of a powerful and murderous Automaton…*Bon.…* For this, I might require a small Fee, in advance?"

"Of course. Here is your small Fee,— you see this Pistol? I will *not* fire it into your head, eh?"

"Only a thought.— "

I was sav'd, if that is the word, by a loud terrifying Hum outside. The Detective, with a frighten'd cry, ran swiftly and irrevocably from the Room, leaving me in great Anxiety, as reluctant to follow, and continue in his arm'd company, as to stay, and face an Arrival perhaps even more perilous. I stepp'd out to the Terrace, to look. The Noise was circling overhead, as if its Source,— surely the Duck,— were contemplating a course of action,—

And there! there it was, my future Nemesis! Ah! As I watch'd, it began its long glissade, directly toward me,— the Stoop of an unreasonably small and slow Predator. With plenty of time to escape, quite unlike ordinary Prey myself, I remain'd staring, whilst in defiance of Newton the metallick Marvel floated gently down...till it alit near me, upon one of the Railings of the Terrace, with barely a sound. It faced me...its ominous Beak crank'd open...it quack'd, its eye holding a certain gleam, and began to speak, in a curious Accent, inflected heavily with linguo-beccal Fricatives, issuing in a fine Mist of some digestive Liquid, upon pure Faith in whose harmlessness I was obliged to proceed.

"So," spray'd the Duck,— "the terrible Bluebeard of the Kitchen, whose Celebrity is purchas'd with the lives of my Race. Not so brave now, eh?"

"Thousands in France slay, cook, and eat Ducks ev'ry day. Why single me out?"

"What more natural Enemy for the most celebrated Duck in France, than the most celebrated Chef?"

Hadn't M. du T. made nearly the same remark about the two Dossiers? Had the Duck gain'd access to these? How? "I am not your Enemy," I protested. "I may even be your Friend."

"At least until you contrive to make a dish of me, eh? Be advis'd, I am provided with extensive Alarms, that not a feather be molested, but 'twill trigger Consequences disagreeable. Would you like to try it? eh? go ahead, the Breeze from your moving hand will be enough."

"Be assur'd of the total Safety, when I am present, of ev'ry excellent Feather," surpriz'd to hear a strange Flirtatiousness in my voice, "yours, may I say, being most uncommonly— "

"*Attend, Flatteur*,— there may be one way for you to deflect my Wrath,— an inconsequential Task you may wish to do for me. I've a request to make of Vaucanson, and the Clock-work is ticking."

"Why not just fly over there and ask him?"

"Sir, he does not wish me well,— I cannot say why,— I hear, that he has hired an Attorney,— an infallible sign of Hatred, if you ask me...."

"Then, perhaps, you must hire one yourself."

"You wish me," the Duck spreading its wings as if to invite inspection, "to walk in, hand him my Card, 'How d'ye do, spot of bother with the Human who design'd me'?— I think not. Withal, my Case would be weak,— he would no doubt present me as some poor Wretch ever connected, by way of this celebrated inner Apparatus, to Earth, but to nothing as transcendent as,"— a wing-shrug,— "*l'Amour*.... Whilst presenting himself as doing me a great Favor,— failing to consider that I might not miss what I never possess'd."

("Hear, hear," Mason tapping the side of his Coffee-Mug with the Jam-Spoon.

Dixon looks over. "Eeh,— are you crazy yet, Mason?"

The French cook moves his Eyebrows about. "That was what it said, Messieurs. And by then, Curiosity overcoming my good sense...")

"So," I ask'd the Duck, "— is this why you're suddenly able to fly, and whatever else by now...?"

"That's certainly what it feels like...tho' as for this 'Love,'— I still don't even know what it's suppos'd to be."

"Indeed,— then, do you meet no other Ducks, in your,— um that is,— "

"Exactly," ruffling all its Feathers excitedly, "— aside from the clock-tower Cocks of Strasbourg and Lyon, how many other mechanickal Fowl have I, exactly, to choose from?— excepting, *bien entendu*, the Fatal Other...."

"Pardon,— who?"

"My Duplicate,— that other Duck, which Vaucanson has kept ever on hand, ready to waddle into the Lights to become the 'Vaucanson's Duck' the World would come to know, should this experiment upon me've fail'd. In the Atelier we have often cross'd Paths. In fact our Thoughts have not remain'd so *philosophique* as to avoid the growth of a certain...Fascination.

"So it is that I now commission you, to go to my Creator, and pray upon my behalf his Permission, to take this very Duck out for the evening,— I have tickets to the Opéra,— 'tis Galuppi's *Margherita e Don Aldo.* We could stop for a bite at L'Appeau, they have my table there, you must know of Jean-Luc's *Insectes d'Etang à l'Etouffée,—* "

"Wait, wait, this other Duck,— it's male? female? For that matter, which are you?"

"*Moi?* Female, as it happens. The other, being yet sexually unmodified, is neither,— or, if you like, both. Any Problem?"

"The arrangement you wish me to make for you...'twould fall, I regret, in a Realm of the Erotick, where, alas, I've no experience,— "

"For a Frenchman, this is refreshing. Unhappily, my 'Morphosis ever proceeding, I enjoy as little choice of a Broker, as of a Partner."

"Why should Vaucanson agree? If he is your enemy, he may also demand a price, such as your return to his Atelier."

"Details for you to work out. In Italian opera, the young Soprano's Guardian may always be deceiv'd." The Duck flapp'd its Wings, rose in the Air, and with a Hum, singing a few bars of "Cálmati, Mio Don Aldo irascibile," crank'd up to speed and vanish'd.

"But this is French Tragedy!" I call'd after. Had the shock of acquiring an erotick Self driven the Creature insane? Was that it? I was a Chef, not a Match-maker for Automatick Ducks. *Merde!*

Nonetheless, in nearly total ignorance of the path I was choosing, nor knowing even how to reach Vaucanson, I set out to see what favors I might convert,— so entering the little-known world of the Automatophile Community, learning swiftly that the Duck's curious 'Morphosis was a common topick of Gossip at Court, with Mme. la Marquise de Pompadour, as Hervé du T. had hinted, vitally interested. Spies were ev'rywhere, some working for this redoubtable Lady, with her Jansenists and *Philosophes,* others for Parties whose Fortunes would have intermesh'd more and less naturally with those of any Flying Automaton,— the Jesuits, of course, the British, the Prussian Military,— along with Detectives upon missions Bourbon and Orleanist, Corsican Adventurers, Martinist Illuminati, a

Grand Mélange of Motive.... As no one was what he,— and, for the most part delightfully, she,— claim'd, no one told or expected the truth. Long were the nights, as a-riot with Hepatomachy and Pursuit, as the days a-tangle with Rumor and Faithlessness,— not to mention wayward Barouches, opiated Chablis at Pick-nicks unforeseen, Ear-rings lost and found, invisible Street-Singers echoing 'round the Corners, the Melancholy of the City at sunset,— a descent, like passing into sleep, uneasy and full of terror till we be establish'd once more within the Evening, as within the Evening's first Dream....

My efforts to reach Vaucanson were not without Repercussion. Engagements disappear'd. People cross'd streets to avoid me. Unfamiliar men loung'd against the walls of my neighborhood, as if waiting for instructions. I spent much of my time at the Soupçon de Trop, a local *Repaire* for Kitchen-Workers of all Ranks, finding in their numbers Safety for a while, at least from human Enemies,...but soon enough, the Duck got wind of my Whereabouts,— having learn'd in the meantime that vibrating back and forth very quickly, whilst standing still, would produce the same effect of Invisibility as linear movement,— and, at first to the Amusement, and later to the Annoyance, of my Colleagues, began paying regular visits, emerging to deliver me one reproof upon another, announced only by that distressing Hum.

Only in that Phase of Night when Drunkenness prevail'd and less and less imported, did I even dare reply. "Why do you obsess me? go seek out Vaucanson yourself. I know he's dangerous, but, my God, you're invisible, faster than anything known, you penetrate walls,— you're more than a match for him." I knew as I cozen'd thus the Duck, how carelessly provoking it all must sound, yet such was the Desperation I liv'd in, redefining Shame with each sunrise, that what might once have matter'd to my Pride, now quite often fail'd even to claim my Attention. Whenever I began to list for her the Obstacles, the Daily Intrigues, the Assaults and Deceptions that ever delay'd my Mission upon her behalf, she would proclaim, thro' candle-lit iridescences of vocal Spray, "Duress? Duress is not an Issue,— for Life is Duress."

I once would have inquir'd coolly, what an Automaton might know of Life, but now I only sat silent, unconsciously having assum'd what I later learn'd was that Hindoo *asana*, or Posture, known as "the Lotus." At what moment the Duck may have taken her leave, who but the Time-Keeper knoweth? Time, however, had acquir'd additional Properties.

Mysteriously, from about that date, I found myself beneath a Protection unseen, yet potent. Thugs who approach'd me in the Street were suddenly struck in mid-Body vigorously enough to throw them for Toises along the Cobbles, where they lay a-cowering, trying to remember their Prayers. A Wine-cask, falling spontaneously out of an upper Window directly at my Head, was invisibly deflected, to smash open harmlessly, in spatter'd red radii, upon the Pavement. In the path of a runaway coach-and-six, I was suddenly lifted by the back of my collar, into the Air, above the Hats and Faces of the rapidly gathering Crowd, and convey'd to Safety. I could attribute such a degree of Protection (in which I fail'd, till too late, to see the component of Love) to nothing but the Duck,— which soon enough declar'd her Sentiments, leaving me a plain opening,— but to my shame, I could say nothing. How could anyone? I took refuge in wild theorizing,— if Angels be the next higher being from Man, perhaps the Duck had 'morphos'd into some Anatine Equivalent, acting as my Guardian,— purely, as an Angel might…. Or, perhaps, as Ducklings, when their Mother is not available, will follow any creature that happens along, so might not an Automaton, but newly aware of its Destiny as a Duck, easily fasten upon the first human, say, willing to remain and chat, rather than go running off in terror,— and come to define this attachment as Love?…Or, was it something she'd glean'd from some Italian Opera,— that an Intermediary in the Employ of a Soprano Character might soon find himself in her Embrace as well? These and other speculations swiftly carried me close to a dangerous Ecstacy, in which Vaucanson's "erotic Apparatus" never occurr'd to me as a possible Cause. My colleagues of course saw ev'rything. "Armand, Armand, you have ruined a notable career, made enemies in the highest places,— "

"— can no longer work in this town even as a sub-scullion,— "

"*Voilà*, and yet he sits, laps'd in this strange Supernaturalism. Paris is no longer for you, my Friend, you belong somewhere else,— in China! in Pennsylvania!"

Everyone at least knows of China,— but imagine, till then I had never heard of Pennsylvania. They meant, as it turn'd out, a place in America, where Religious Eccentricity of all kinds was not only tolerated, but publickly indulg'd,— where

> Schwenkfelders might past Unitarians brush,
> And Wesleyites scarce from Quakers raise a blush,

as great Tox has it. The Miraculous lay upon ev'ry hand,— in the days that follow'd, I was much entertain'd with tales of fertile lands, savage Women, giant Vegetables, forests without end, Marshlands seething with shell-fish, Buffalo-Herds the size of Paris. Increasingly I wondered if somewhere in that American Wilderness there might be a Path, not yet discover'd, to lead me out of my Perplexity, and into a place of Safety from what was by now a long list of Persecutors, unhappily including the Duck, whose Affection had grown multiplex with daily Difficulties. At a time when I needed any work I could get, she resented even the few Hours that might take me elsewhere to create some Vulgarian's Luncheon, in which the cost of any mistake would be fatally high,— she grew jealous, imagining that I was seeking the company of some other Duck.... "We mate for life. Alas, my poor Armand."

"As you yourself have pointed out, there's but one other in the World,— "

"Aha! My Virgin Double,— somewhere upon a Shelf, in one of Vaucanson's many clandestine workshops, oh yes and by the way, what progress have you made, upon that simple Errand, wait, let me guess,— another barrier arisen? another note gone astray? or is it something more sinister, such as your desire to have the other for yourself? Eh? Look, he sweats, he trembles. Admit it, Betrayer."

My social life had fallen to pieces. I could no longer show my face down at the Soupçon. The Duck was my Shadow night and day. She started waking me up to criticize some item of my attire from days before, my choice of Company, and at last, unacceptably, my Cooking. Three in the morning and we sat bickering about my Beet Quiche...beneath it her Iron Confidence in the power conferr'd by her Inedibility...being artificial and deathless, as I was meat, and of the Earth...my only hope was that her 'Morphosis would somehow carry her quite beyond me, and soon. Meanwhile, Paris having grown impossible, I resolv'd secretly to leave for America.

Feeling like a young man in a Fable, who has us'd up all but one Wish, I sent out my last note, held my breath, and was lucky,— upon the basis of a Chill'd Brain Mousse, invented to celebrate the Peace of Aix-la-Chapelle, I was able to secure passage to Martinique, and thence, through months of trans-shipment, in ev'rything from Pirogue to Pirate Ship, at last to New Castle upon Delaware, where I stepp'd ashore in the moonless Dark,— as it was said, that the people there did not interfere with these nocturnal Landings, being ever in dread of the French and Spanish Privateers....

"Here then, you *wretched* little Frog!" The Company groans. It is Mr. Dimdown, Hanger in hand. The Frenchman picks up his *Hachoir,* and raises one eyebrow.

38

'Tis determin'd afterward, that Mr. Dimdown, heretofore unacquainted with any confinement longer than hiding in the Root-Cellar till the Sheriff took his leave, had been drinking steadily whatever Spirits came to hand, for the three days previous, attempting, as he explains, "to get the Time to pass differently, that's all."

Mr. Knockwood comes from around the Bar whilst Mrs. Knockwood, sorting her Keys, heads for the Musketoon in the China-Cabinet.

"And furthermore," Mr. Dimdown in a fury, "how dare you you fabulating little swine pretend to any knowledge of America, having sneak'd onto our Shores 'pon your miserable Belly,"— and so on.

"There, there, now, Gentlemen," the Landlord slowing his Address as much as he can afford to, whilst keeping an eye upon his Wife's progress with the Powder Horns, Funnel, and Shot, "Mr. Dimdown, mind my Chef now, I can't afford to lose him. And you, Frenchie,— "

"Filthy frog! Deet adyoo!" Mr. Dimdown makes a murderous Lunge with his Blade, straight at the Chef's unprotected Heart. Immediately, Inches short of its target, the Weapon, from no cause visible to anyone, leaves Dimdown's Grasp and sails across the Room in a slow, some might say insolent Arc, directly in among the blazing Logs of the Hearth, where none may reach.

" 'Twas…Magnetism or something," protests Mr. Dimdown, "and withal I stumbl'd,— or was deliberately tripp'd up. Look ye,— how am I to retrieve my Bleeder now? The heat will ruin the Steel. Damn you, Mon-soor."

"Thus," intones the Frenchman, with a twirl of his Toque, "the very Duck, in action. You have seen for yourselves. You have borne Witness. Her capacity for Flight having increased to ever longer Distances, in the years between then and now, till one day, not even the vast Ocean might deter her,— *Voilà!*— I wake to find her perch'd at the end of the Bed, quacking merrily as a Milk-maid. Yes, she has follow'd me even to the New World, whether in affection or hatred, who can say,— that 'tis Passion, none may dispute,— and once again, I am besieged, as she continues upon her strange Orbit of Escape from the known World, whilst growing more powerful within it."

To Luise, this is beginning to sound like Peter Redzinger all over again. Upon an Impulse, nevertheless, she places a somewhat larger than Parisian Hand,— a callus'd working Hand, cut and healed in a thousand places, sun-brown, hair-tucking, needle-nimble,— upon his arm. A close observer, did one attend, might see him begin to flicker 'round the edges. "Oh, Monsieur. An Angel, so?"

"Perhaps, Madame, it is merely the price I must pay for having left France,— yet, to be honest, coming from a place where people starve to death every night, if I must suffer the Duck's inscrutable attendance, in Exchange for this Miracle of Plenty,— then, 'tis a Bargain. On market days in New Castle or Philadelphia, my Heart yet soars as ever it has done,...like a dream.... Have you ever wanted to cook *everything*,— the tomatoes, terrapins, peaches, rockfish, crabs, Indian Corn, Venison! Bear! Beaver! To create the Beaver *Bourguignon*,— who knows, perhaps even the...the Beaver *soufflé, non?*" He is gesturing excitedly.

"Sure, the Indians know how to cook Beaver," she tells him, "there's some Glands you have to take out, and much Fat to trim, but when 'tis done right? Ach,...as good as anything from a German kitchen, plain or fancy."

"You have actually,"— he gazes at her,— "that is...*eaten...*"

In the days they are to remain snow-bound, a triangle will develop among the incorruptible Pietist, the exil'd Chef, and the infatuated

Duck. Strangely, given her great powers for Mischief, the Duck does nothing to harm Luise, indeed extends to her the same invisible Protection,— as if sensing a chance to observe "Love" at first hand, invisibly. Thus do Armand and Luise, never knowing when she may be there watching, find one more Obstacle in the way of bodily Desires,— "She's being quite sympathetic about all this, don't you think?"

"I don't know, Armand. Are you sure you've told me ev'rything?"

"My Dearest! How could you even..."

"She seems to know you...so well."

It does not, however, in fact take long for the Duck to grow far less certain than before, that she even wishes an erotick Life. Meanwhile, in their Niveal Confinement, the behavior of the Company grows ever less predictable. "And over my head," relates Squire Haligast, "it form'd an *E*-clipse, an emptiness in the Sky, with a Cloud-shap'd Line drawn all about it, wherein words might appear, and it read,— 'No King...' "

"Thank you for sharing that with us, Sir," snarls the dependably viperous Mr. Whitpot, the first upon whom the Squire's oracular charm has begun to lose its grasp. As days of snow and snow-clouds in dark unpromising shades of Blue pass one into another, the readiness of immoderate Sentiment to burst forth upon any or no occasion is felt by all to be heightening dangerously. Even young Cherrycoke struggles with it, rosy Phiz a-glimmer, seated at a Table of local Dutch Manufacture, writing in his Memorandum-Book, as the snow lapses in wet silence 'cross the rhombic Panes before him, whilst from his Pen, in bright, increasingly bloody Tropes, speculation upon the Eucharistic Sacrament and the practice of Cannibalism comes a-spurting. It had begun in Scholarly Innocence, as a Commentary upon an earlier Essay by Brook Taylor (the Series and Theorem Eponym), "On the Lawfulness of Eating Blood."

Mr. Knockwood observes from an upstairs Window a depth of Snow nearly level with its Sill, and worrying about the supply of Air in the Rooms below, rushes to find, and ask, the Astronomers. And what has happen'd to the Light? are there Snow-Eclipses? Down in the Pantry, Armand and Luise are embracing, outdoing the Sparkishness of even Philadelphian Youth (yet again, perhaps that is only what people bring out upon days when gossip is scarce, honoring the rest of the time their manifest Innocence),— whilst Mitzi, out in this taupe daylight, is hanging about the stable-hands and Scullery Boys, swinging her Hair, flashing her eyes, getting into conversations that she then tries to prolong to some point she can't clearly enough define to herself. She's grown up with murderous Indians in the Woods all 'round, painted bare skins and sharpen'd Blades, she has a different sense of Danger than do these mild estuarial Souls, with their diet of fish, like a race of house-cats, so. Yet what she really wishes to prolong, may be the state of never knowing exactly how safe she may be among the English Fisher-Boys, as at first, at each new fall of Snow, she has thrill'd, knowing it means at least one more day of isolation with the Inn's resident Adonises,— or, as Armand, feeling increasingly Paterfamilial, prefers, Slack-jaw'd Louts. Lately, however, the Winter has begun to oppress more than encourage her hopes. She actually starts looking about for Chores to do, offering Armand her help in the Kitchen, still a-blush ev'ry time they speak,— Luise, as he is joyous to learn, having taught her at least the Fundamentals. Soon he is allowing her to prepare salads, and confiding minor Arcana of French *Haute Cuisine*,— its historical beginnings among the arts of the Poisoner,— its need to be carried on in an Attitude of unwavering Contempt for any who would actually chew, swallow, and attempt to digest it, and come back for more,— the first Thousand Pot-lid settings, from Le Gastreau's fam'd article in the *Encyclopédie*,— the Pot-Lid being indeed a particular Hobby-Horse of Armand's, upon its proper Arrangement often hanging the difference between success and failure. "Off, on, all the way on, partly off, crescents of varying shape, each with its appropriate use,— you must learn to think of the Pot, as you look down upon it, as a sort of Moon, with Phases...tho' keeping in mind Voltaire's remark about Gas- and As-tronomers."

The Rev[d] looks on with interest. The Frenchman fascinates him. With his recent animadversions upon the Lord's Supper, he is attending more to Food, and its preparation. "I thought I had put behind me," he writes, "the questions of whether the Body and Blood of Christ are consubstantiate with, or transubstantiated from, the Bread and Wine of the Eucharist,— preferring at last to believe, with Doctors such as Haimo of Halberstadt, that the outward Forms are given to bread and wine as an act of God's Mercy, for otherwise we should be repell'd by the sight of real human Flesh and Blood, not to mention the prospect of eating it. Thus to God's attributes must be added the skills of a master Chef, in so disguising a terrible reality. The question I cannot resolve is whether real Flesh and real Blood are themselves, in turn, further symbolick,— either of some mystickal Body of Christ, in which participants in the Lord's Supper all somehow,— mystickally, to be sure,— become One,— or of a terrible Opposite…some ultimate Carnality, some way of finally belonging to the doom'd World that cannot be undone,— a condition, I now confess, I once roam'd the Earth believing myself to be seeking, all but asphyxiated in a darkling innocence which later Generations may no longer fully imagine.

"But since those days of young hopes, illusory daybreaks, and the uncanny sureness of Nerve, I have been down into other quarters of the City of Earth, seen and smell'd at village Markets, hung amid the flies and street-dust with the other animal meat, Human Flesh, offer'd for sale…. In America some Indians believe that eating the flesh, and particularly drinking the blood, of those one has defeated in battle, will transfer the 'Virtues,' as theologians might call 'em, from one's late opponent, to oneself,— a mystickal Union between the Antagonists, which no one I have consulted is quite able to explain to me. It raises the possibility that Savages who appear to be Enemies are in fact connected somehow, profoundly, as in a Covenant of Blood, with War for them being thus a species of Sacrament. This being so, as a practical matter out here, the Warriors-Paths must be deem'd holy, and transgression of them serious, to a degree difficult to imagine in the common British Foot-path dispute. We must either change our notions of the Sacred, or come to terms with these Nations,— and sooner rather than later."

Late in the day after his assault upon Armand, Mr. Dimdown answers a Knock at the door of his Room, to find Mitzi Redzinger, holding out his Hanger cautiously by its Strap. "I clean'd it up as best I could," she murmurs, gazing at anything but him. "A bit of Soot, nothing worse. And I sharpen'd it for you."

"You *what?*"

"Armand has taught me how." She has stepp'd into the room and shut the door behind her, and now stands observing him, surpriz'd at how tatter'd seems his Foppery in the Day-time.

"No one sharpens this but me, this is genuine Damascus Steel, for Heaven's sake,— here, then, let us see the Damage." Taking what seems far too long, he peers up and down the newly glitt'ring Edge, and is soon making ornamental Lunges and Passes in the Air, presenting each Leg a number of times for her Consideration, adjusting his Cuffs and Stock unceasingly. "Hmm. Appears that you may understand something about Blades...." A complicated assault upon a Candle-stick. "Feels a little slow. Us'd to be faster. Is there a fruitful lawsuit here? yes perhaps I shall take Knockwood to court, if Spring ever comes,— say, Frowline, your Cap,...what d'you think you're doing?"

The Goose. She is untying her Cap, then taking it slowly off, unbinding and shaking out her Hair. She is making it ripple for him. She is getting it to catch the winter Light thro' the Window. She is so flabber-gasting this Macaroni with it that he seems to fall into a contemplative Daze before the deep Undulations, a Dreamer at the Edge of the Sea. Outdoors, the Snow is upon the Glide yet again, and soon 'twill be Night. She remembers all the Leagues of Snow-cover'd Terrain between here and the Redzinger Farm, all going dark, the City she cannot quite believe in that lies ahead, her Father's Resurrection and Departure, her Mother's visible Change, and lastly her own, which she can as little command as explain,— Breasts, Hips, Fluxes, odd Swoons, a sharpening Eye for lapses of Character in young Men. "The Lord provides," her Mother has told her. "Wisdom comes to us, even as it appears to leave Men. You won't need to go all the way to Philadelphia. Nor much further than the Town, upon Market Day, so."

He has begun apologizing for his Assault upon the Frenchman. " 'Twas vile of me. I know you are his Friend,— I wish there were some way...?"

"Simply tell him. Isn't it done among you?"

"Go into that Kitchen? You've seen his Battery,— the Knives, the Cleavers? Mrs. Dimdown rais'd no Idiots, Frowline."

"Oh, if you knew Armand." She laughs merrily.

"I am become a Target for his Instruments edg'd and pointed. There, our Relation appears at a Stand-still."

"But recall, that no one here has ever seen Armand cut anything. That's why he's teaching me how to,— so that I can do what he can no longer bear. Perhaps it is my Mother's doing,— he has forsworn Violence in the Kitchen,— not only toward Meat, but the Vegetables as well, for as little now can he bring himself to chop an Onion, as to slice a Turnip, or even scrub a Mushroom."

"Perhaps you oughtn't to be telling me. A man needs his Reputation."

"But as a veteran Bladesman, you would never take advantage of him, I'm sure?"

His face grows pink and swollen, a sign she knows,— she has been blurted at by young men. Feeling behind her for the Door-knob, she is surpriz'd to find herself several steps from it, well within the Room. "Mr. Dimdown, I trust you are well?"

"Philip," he mumbles, "actually," putting his Hanger back in its Scabbard. "As you have confided in me, so may I admit to you, that I have never, well that is not yet, been obliged to, uh in fact,…"

"Oh, I can see you've never been in a Duel." She pushes aside some hair that may be screening the full effect of the Sparkle in her eyes.

"Ruin!— Ah! You must despise me."

She shrugs, abruptly enough to allow him to read it, if he wishes, as a sympathetick Shiver. "We have had enough of fighting, out where we live,— it is not to me the Novel Thrill, that some Philadelphia Girl might think it." Taking up hair that has fallen forward over her right Shoulder, she shifts the Locks back, and slowly leftward, tossing her head from time to time.

Ignoring this opening, all a-fidget, "Are you the only one that can see it, or does ev'ryone know that I've never been out? as if, engrav'd upon my Head, or something?"

"Calm…Philip. I'll tell no one."

In lurches the Landlord. "Your mother's looking for you, Miss." Flourishing his Eyebrows at them both.

"Trouble," mutters young Dimdown.

"He wishes to apologize to Monsieur Allègre," Mitzi quickly sings out, "isn't that it, Sir?"

"Uhm, that is,— "

"Excellent, I can arrange that," and Mr. Knockwood dashes off again.

"I'm putting my life in your hands, here," says Philip Dimdown. "No one else is what they seem,— why should you be?"

'Tis only now that Mitzi, at last, finds herself a-blush, this being her very first Compliment, and a roguish one at that. He seems at once considerably wiser, if no older.

And presently, in the afternoon Lull between meals, the peace is made, the two men shaking hands at the kitchen door, and commencing to chatter away like two Daws upon a Roof-top. Luise comes by with a Tray-ful of Dutch Kisses, provoking witty requests, most of which, though not all, she avoids gracefully.

"Damme for a Bun-brain, Mounseer,— as if I'd actually impale the greatest Cook in the Colonies,— "

"But your movement with the Blade,— so elegant, so *professionel.*"

"Not exactly the great Figg, I regret to say,— indeed, never closer to the real thing, than private Lessons, at an establishment in New-York, from a Professor Tisonnier.— "

"But I knew him! in France!— *Oui,* he once commented upon my brais'd Pork Liver with Aubergines,— offer'd to teach me the St. George Parry if I'd give him the Receipt."

"He was esteem'd for that, indeed, and for his Hanging Guard,— I'd show you it, but I wouldn't want to nick up the old Spadroon."

"Damascus steel, 's it not? Fascinating. How is that Moiré effect done?"

"By twisting together two different sorts of Steel, or so I am told,— then welding the Whole."

"A time-honor'd Technique in Pastry as well. The Armorers of the Japanese Islands are said to have a way of working carbon-dust into the steel of their Swords, not much different from how one must work the Butter into the Croissant Dough. Spread, fold, beat flat, spread, again and again, eh? till one has created hundreds of these prodigiously thin layers."

"Gold-beating as well, now you come to it," puts in Mr. Knockwood, "— 'tis flatten and fold, isn't it, and flatten again, among the thicknesses of Hide, till presently you've these very thin Sheets of Gold-Leaf."

"Lamination," Mason observes.

"Lo, Lamination abounding," contributes Squire Haligast, momentarily visible, "its purposes how dark, yet have we ever sought to produce these thin Sheets innumerable, to spread a given Volume as close to pure Surface as possible, whilst on route discovering various new forms, the Leyden Pile, decks of Playing-Cards, Contrivances which, like the Lever or Pulley, quite multiply the apparent forces, often unto disproportionate results...."

"The printed Book," suggests the Rev^d, "— thin layers of pattern'd Ink, alternating with other thin layers of compress'd Paper, stack'd often by the Hundreds."

"Or an unbound Heap of Broadsides," adds Mr. Dimdown, "dispers'd one by one, and multiplying their effect as they go."

The Macaroni is of course not what he seems, as which of us is?— the truth comes out weeks later, when he is discover'd running a clandestine printing Press, in a Cellar in Elkton. He looks up from the fragrant Sheets, so new that one might yet smell the Apprentices' Urine in which the Ink-Swabs were left to soften, bearing, to sensitiz'd *Nasalia*, sub-Messages of youth and Longing,— all about him the word repeated in large Type, LIBERTY.

One Civilian leads in a small band of Soldiers. "Last time you'll be seeing that word."

"Don't bet your Wife's Reputation on it," the Quarrelsome Fop might have replied. Philip Dimdown, return'd to himself, keeps his Silence.

"If we choose to take the Romantic approach,— "

"We must," appeals Tenebræ. "Of course he was thinking about her. How did they part?"

"Honorably. He kept up the Fop Disguise till the end."

"Impossible, Uncle. He *must* have let her see...somehow...at the last moment, so that *then* she might cry, bid him farewell, and the rest."

"The rest?" Ives alarm'd.

"After she meets someone else."

"Aaahhgghh!" groans Ethelmer.

"Never ends!" adds Cousin DePugh.

39

"All right then, if tha really want to know what I think,— "

"Of course."

The Surveyors have been at this since Noon. Squire Haligast predicts an end to the general Incarceration by tomorrow. Ev'ryone not yet reel'd away into Madness prays that it be so, for no one here can bear much more Company.

"Without meaning offense, then...? 'tis against Nature."

"What! to mourn my Wife?"

"Not to be seeking another...?"

For a moment Mason inspects his Co-Adjutor's Shins,— then his eyes shift away, and grow unfocus'd. "Were we in Gloucester, I should expect, naturally, to hear such useful advice as this. 'Tis the expected thing. Simple country Procedure. Alas, I may have stopt in London for too long, breathing its mephitic airs, abiding too close to its Evil unsleeping. I know I have been corrupted,— but perhaps it has unmann'd me as well."

"You're just not getting out enough...?"

"Out! Out where?" Gesturing at the Window, "White Mineral Desolation, unvarying and chill,— "

"Out of your Melancholy."

Try as he may, Mason can detect in this nought but kind Intent. "I only hope you're not suggesting anyone in our immediate Company,— I mean, *you* haven't been,— that is, what am I saying, of course you've...," his eyes happening to fall upon Dixon's Stomach, whose size and curvature seem different to him, somehow (the Figure of it indeed changing, one day to the next, the rest of us watching in some alarm its Transition from a Spheroid vertically dispos'd, to one more wide than high). "Ah. 'Tis someone in the Kitchen. Am I right?"

"Either that or I'm pregnant," holding his Corporation and gazing down at it. "If so, 'twould be by Maureen, for I've been true to no other,— she being the one you'll recall who bakes— "

"— the Pies," Mason is joyous to enumerate, "the Tarts, the, the Jam-stuff'd Dough-nuts, the lengthy Menu of French Crèmes and Mousses, the Fruit-Cakes soak'd in Brandy be it Feast-day or no,— "

"Stop...?" cries Dixon, "tha're making me hungry."

"Ahrrh...," warns Mason.

"Sure you wouldn't like to just pop back to the Bake-house, take a chance that she's in, find one or two of those iced Waffles, aye she or her friend Pegeen, happen you've seen her, the Red-head with the Curls...? Wears green all the time...?"

"There it is. Damme! you persist.— Whenever I begin to imagine we're past this.— One or two malicious Jokes, that's fine, I'm a good Sport,— but pray you, grant me a Respite, no Pegeens."

"Perhaps I'm only trying to get thee to eat something. This self-denying has its limits,— tha're down to skin and bones with it, 'tis an Affliction Sentimental, in which Melancholy hath depress'd thy Appetite for *any Pleasure*."

"Hold,— you're sitting there like Henry the Eighth, advising *me* upon Dietary matters? Regard yourself, Sir,— how are we to do accurate work in the Field, with you subtending so many Degrees of it, even at the Horizon?— What is this Spheroid you bear," tapping Dixon's Belly, "or rather lug about, like some Atlas who doesn't plan to bring the Globe all that far?"

" 'Tis prolate, still," with a long dejected Geordie O. "Isn't it...?"

"I'm an Astronomer,— trust me, 'tis gone well to oblate. Thanks for your concern at the altitude of my spirits,— but what you're really seeking, is an Accomplice in the pursuit of your own various fitful Vices."

...

So, by the time the Snow abates enough to allow them to rejoin the Harlands, the Surveyors, having decided thereafter to Journey separately, one north and one south, to see the country, return to the Harlands the use of their Honeymoon Quilt, and kindly allow John Harland to toss one of his new silver Shilling Pieces, which lands Heads, sending Mason North and Dixon South. Next time, they agree to reverse the Directions.

"Happen I'll find someplace warm at last," Dixon a bit too cheerfully.

"See here, I hope we'll go ahead with it,— I mean, it's been like a Booth-load of Puppets swinging Clubs all about, hasn't it."

"Ah know, Ah'm as unquiet as thee,— why aye, we must spread out, the one thing we knoaah of this Place, is, that Dimension Abounds...?"

("Dixon was first to leave," the Rev^d relates, "and with no indication in the Field-Book of where he went or stopp'd, let us assume that he went first to Annapolis,— "

"How 'assume'?" objects Ives. "There are no *Documents,* Wicks? Perhaps he stay'd on at Harland's and drove all of *them* south, with his drunken intriguing after ev'ry eligible,— meaning ev'ry,— Milkmaid in the Forks of Brandy-wine."

"Or let us postulate two Dixons, then, one in an unmoving Stupor throughout,— the other, for Simplicity, assum'd to've ridden,— as Mason would the next year,— out to Nelson's Ferry over Susquehanna, and after crossing, perhaps,— tho' not necessarily,— on to York,— taking then the Baltimore Road south, instead of the one to Frederick, as Mason would,— south, to Baltimore, and thro' it, ever southing, toward Annapolis, and Virginia beyond. Tho' with suspicions as to his Calvert Connections already high, Dixon might have avoided Maryland altogether, instead of tempting Fate.")

He comes into Annapolis by way of the Rolling-roads, intended less for the Publick than for the Hogsheads of Tobacco being roll'd in to Market from distant Plantations, night and day, with two or three men to each Hogshead,— African Slaves, Irish Transportees, German Redemptioners and such, who understand well enough that others might also prefer to travel this way. In Town, Dixon roams unfocus'd from Waggoners' Taverns to harbor-front Sailors' Dens,— "Only looking for that Card-game," he replies if ask'd, and if they say, "What Card-game?" he beams ever-so-sorry and retreats from the Area, feigning confusion about ev'rything save the way out, for one Tavern is as likely as another to provide opportunities for Mischief.

He has certainly, and more than once, too, dreamt himself upon a dark Mission whose details he can never quite remember, feeling in the grip of Forces no one will tell him of, serving Interests invisible. He wakes more indignant than afraid. Hasn't he been doing what he contracted to do,— nothing more? Yet, happen this is exactly what they wanted,— and his Sin is not to've refus'd the Work from the outset.—

When they later re-convene at Harlands', Mason gets around to inquiring of Dixon, what was his Purpose, in entering Maryland.

"Bait. Make myself available. Like Friend Franklin, out in the Thunder-Gusts...?"

"You wish'd to be...stricken? assaulted?"

"I'm content with 'Approach'd'...? Yet no French Agents, nor Jesuits in Disguise, have announc'd themselves,...nor have Freemasons cryptickally sign'd to me.... Yet I suppose my own *Surveillor* might be secreted anywhere in our Party, among our Axmen, Cooks, or Followers, noting ev'rything."

In Williamsburg at last, Dixon feels he has come to the Heart of the Storm. There can be no more profit in going any further South,— this will have to do for whatever he may learn.

The Tobacco Plantations lie inert, all last season's crop being well transported to Glasgow by now, and the Seeds of the next not yet in Flats.... Whilst the Young, who seem to be at ev'ry hand, take their Joy of Assemblies and River-Parties, Balls and Weddings,— others, *longer in the Curing-Shed,* rather hasten to explore at last the seasonless Vales of Sleep, with trusted,— how else?— African Slaves to stand in Cordons all 'round, and keep each Dreamer safe. Dixon rides into Town, a Maze-like Disposition of split-rail Fences, a Dockyard's worth of Ship-lap Siding, a quiet Profligacy of Flemish Bond to be found upon vertical Surfaces from Pig-Ark to Palace. The last Seed-Pods hang, black and unbreach'd, from the Catalpa Trees. Swains by Garden Walls rehearse the Arts of Misunderstanding. Some nights, the Wind, at a good Canter, will as easily freeze tears to uncreas'd Faces, as Finger-tips to waistcoat Buttons. There is an Edge to Young Romance, this year, that none of those testing its Sharpness may recognize, quite yet.

The Stamp Act has re-assign'd the roles of the Comedy, and the Audience are in an Uproar. Suddenly Fathers of desirable Girls are no longer minor Inconveniences, some indeed proving to be active Foes, capable of great Mischief. Lads who imagin'd themselves inflexible Rivals for life, find themselves now all but Comrades in Arms. The languorous Pleasantries of Love, are more and more interrupted by the brisk Requisitions of Honor. Over the winter-solid Roads, goes a great seething,— of mounted younger Gentlemen riding together by the dozens upon rented horses, Express Messengers in love with pure Velocity, Disgruntl'd Suitors with Pistols stuff'd in their Spatterdashes, seal'd Waggons not even a western Black-Boy would think of detaining. The May Session of the Burgesses, the eloquent defiance of Mr. Patrick Henry, and the Virginia Resolutions,— that Dividing Ridge beyond which all the Streams of American Time must fall unmappable,— lie but weeks ahead. At the College, Dixon may hear wise Prophecy,— at the State House, interested Oratory,— but there proves no-place quite as congenial to the unmediated newness of History a-transpiring, as Raleigh's Tavern. Virginians young and old are standing to toast the King's Confoundment. When it's his own turn to, Dixon chooses rather to honor what has ever imported to him,— raising his ale-can, "To the pursuit of Happiness."

"Hey, Sir,— that is excellent!" exclaims a tall red-headed youth at the next table. "And ain't it oh so true…. You don't mind if I use the Phrase sometime?"

"Pray thee, Sir."

"Has someone a Pencil?" The youth finds a scrap of paper, and Dixon lends him his Lead "Vine," that he uses for sketching in the Field. "Surveyor? Say," it occurs to him, scribbling, "are you Mason, or Dixon?"

"Tom takes a *Relative* interest in West Lines," quips the Landlord, "his father having help'd run the one that forms our own southern border."

"Upon the Topick of West Lines," Dixon assures him, "any Advice would be more than welcome,— anything."

" 'Twas Colonel Byrd that began it,— Pa, with Professor Fry, continu'd it. My guess is, the Professor did most of the Mathematickal

Work,— for I know Pa was ever impatient with that. He would wear out books of Tables, so vehemently did he consult them.

"Colonel Byrd's segment is the oldest, run long before my time. He recorded each Day in a Field-book,— not only the Miles and Poles travers'd, but more usefully all the Human Stuff,— the petty Resentments, the insults offer'd and taken, the illnesses, the cures, the Food they ate, the Spirits they drank, the Ladies of all Hues, who captur'd their various eyes, now and again...."

"Is it printed, and sold?"

"Not yet. When it shall be, I hope that ev'ry Surveyor will read it as a term of his Apprenticeship,— my father styl'd it one of the great Cautionary Tales of the Vocation."

"As to...?"

"Joint Ventures. Particularly when half the Commissioners live north of the other half. In Colonel Byrd's history, the Carolinians in the Party were envious, gluttonous, slothful Degenerates all,— somehow owing to the difference in Latitude. 'Twould not surprise me if Pennsylvanians were to entertain similar opinions of their own Neighbors to the South, including Virginia. This land of Sensual Beasts."

Three young Ladies are peeping 'round the Door-Way, like shorebirds at the edge of the Water, stepping nicely in and out of that Aura of Tobacco-Smoke that Men for centuries have understood keeps women away as well as were they Bugs. "I'm going in," declares the boldest of the Girls, actually then proceeding two or three steps inside, before crying, "Eehyeww!" and skipping in Retreat. Then another would try,— and "Eeyooh!" and out again, and so forth, amid an unbroken stream of close Discussion,— their desire for Romantick Mischief thus struggling with their feminine abhorrence of Tobacco.

Dixon beams and waves at them. "Are all Virginian Ladies as merrily dispos'd?"

"Ev'rywhere but at Norfolk, where talk of Passion far outweighs its Enactment,— indeed, the Sailors' Paronomasia for that wretched Place, is 'No-Fuck.'"

"They'll be wishing to Dance, I think," judges young Tom. "We've been hearing that Musick for a while, now."

"But watch your Form, Sir, if Dueling be not your preferr'd Pastime, for one wrong Dance-step, Leg before Wicket, as you might say, and no shortage of Virginia Blades about to defend a Lady's Honor,— 'twill be out at Dawn wi' you."

Sure enough, no more than twenty steps into the Assembly Room, and eight Measures into a lively Jig with a certain "Urania," Dixon is aware of a perfum'd flickering upon one Cheek, which proves to be the Glove of her Fiancé, Fabian.

"Did they tell You I was a Quaker, Sir, and would not fight?— "

"They did,— which is why I suggest we settle this at Quoits, Sir,— Megs at forty Feet, Ringers only."

"Eeh, most agreeable," says Dixon, instead of, as he will insist he meant to say, "— if so, they are quizzing with you, Sir,— in fact I am a Transported Felon of the most Desperate Stripe, to whom, in the great Feast of Sin, Murder is but an Hors d'Oeuvre...?"

"We have found Quoiting," Fabian is explaining, "similar enough to Pistols to satisfy us, with the same long and narrow Field, the *Rencontre*, if one wishes, at Dawn, the two Megs driv'n in the ground at a Distance negotiable, the Metal hurtling thro' the Air, even, if you listen closely enough, a certain Hum,— "

"Thah' was negotiable? I might have said thirty feet? Eeh! too focus'd, I imagine, upon the part where ev'ryone gets to stay alive...?"

At Dawn they go trooping out, the lot of them, to a Quoiting-Ground near the Water. When there's just light enough to see the other Meg by, the Contest begins. After each Disputant wins a game, and they agree not to play the third, receiving each a Kiss of equal Vivacity from the fair Pretext herself, all repair to Breakfast amid smoky and sodden good Companionship.

Returning north,— mud Tracks, black wet Branching of Trees overhead, as Revelations of Earth out thro' the Snow,— Dixon, inhabiting Silence, waits, Clop after Clop, Mile after Mile, for some kind of sense to be made of what has otherwise been a pointless Trip. Somewhere between Joppa and Head of Elk, lightless within and without, he begins to Whistle, and presently to sing.

Polecat in the Parlor,
Hound-Dog up the Tree,
Continental Ladies
Are Riddle enough for me...

In all Virginia, tho' Slaves pass'd before his Sight, he saw none. *That* was what had not occurr'd. It was all about something else, not Calverts, Jesuits, Penns, nor Chinese.

40

Having mark'd the sixth Anniversary of Rebekah's Passing, Mason leaves the Forks of Brandywine and proceeds north, arriving in New-York by way of the Staten Island Ferry,— the approaching Sky-line negligible but for a great Steeple, far to port, belonging to the Trinity Church, at the head of Wall-Street, where he will attend services on Sunday. But then there is Monday Night.

"The Battery's the spot to be," he is inform'd by all he meets who know the Town. It proves to be a testimonial to Desire, for upon a Cold Night of Wind that tears the Flames from the Torches, and sends waves against the Sea-Wall, yet along that Lee Shore, amorous Gaits more cautious for the wet Footing, go well into the Midnight a Parade of needful Citizens, Faces ever bent from the assault of Wind smooth as Light, toward the empty Path, the unapproachable Shadow, Acts never specified. Mason, seeing no point, joins them for a while nonetheless. It all proceeds wordless as a Skating-Party. Presently he has fallen in with a certain Amelia, a Milk-Maid of Brooklyn, somehow alone in New-York without funds. "Here then. You've not eaten." He is correct. At a Tavern in Pearl-Street, she scoffs down several Chops, a Platter of Roasted Potatoes, her bowl of Fish Chowder and his, before Mason has butter'd his Bread. A Clock strikes the Hour. "Oh, no!" They must run to catch the last Ferry back to her farm upon Long-Island. A bittersweet passage, Ferries ev'rywhere upon that cold and cloud-torn Styx, Bells dolefully a-bang in the Murk, strange little gaff-rigg'd coasters and lighters veering all over the Water, stack'd high abovedecks with Cargo,— a prosperous Hell.

Amy is dress'd from Boots to Bonnet all in different Articles of black, a curious choice of color for a milkmaid, it seems to Mason, tho', as he has been instructed ever to remind himself, this is New-York, where other Customs prevail. "Oh, aye, at home they're on at me about it without Mercy," she tells him, "I'm, as, 'But I *like* Black,'— yet my Uncle, he's, as, 'Strangers will take you for I don't know what,' hey,— I don't know what, either. Do you?"

"How should I— "

"You're a stranger, aren't you? Well? What would you take me for?"

Days later, riding back to Brandywine through the Jerseys, he will rehearse endlessly whether she said "would you take me," or "do you take me," and ways he might have improv'd upon "Um...," his actual Reply. She does glance back with an Expression he's noted often in his life from Women, tho' never sure what it means.

The "Uncle" seems young for one of that Designation, his Hair a-shine with some scented Pomade, side-whiskers shav'd to quite acute Angles, his hand ever straying to consult the over-siz'd and far from ornamental Dirk he wears in a Scabbard upon his Belt. With Mason he is genial but guarded,— toward Amy, however, even Mason detects insinuations of reprisal to come. "All her Funds? even the Pennies little Ezekiel gave her, to buy him Sweets? Oh, Amelia. Dear oh dear. Was she careless, was that it? Did she look in the Window of some English Shop and see a Frock she fancied? Did one of those awful big-city Dips fly by and lift her whole Bundle, perhaps as an Exercise? Is that what happen'd, 'Amelia'?"— pronouncing the name with such Vexation, that Mason faces the inconvenient Dilemma of stepping in as a Gentleman must,— yet on behalf of someone he has cross'd a River with under, it now appears, an assum'd Name. Where is his Loyalty presum'd to lie? It isn't as if they've been at all, as you'd say, intimate, is it?...Fortunately, by this point in his Deliberations, Amelia, in a suggestive Tone, is murmuring, "I know I've been ever so wicked, Uncle,...but the Gentleman has been very kind...."

Causing a redirection of the avuncular Gaze upon Mason, for reasons he will grasp only later, when Dixon explains it to him back in Camp, with Gestures, some of them impatient. "We all appreciate a kind Gentleman 'round here," the young man offers, as into the Parlor behind him now slide an assortment of Rogues weirder than any Mason has yet seen, be it at Portsmouth, or the Cape, or even Lancaster Town.

"Look what Pussy's brought in," leers a Half-Breed with a braided Queue.

"Brit, by the look of him," cries a short, freckl'd seaman in whom Stature and Pugnacity enjoy an inverse relation. "— long way from home ain't you old Gloak?"

"Who does your Wigs, Coz?"

"There there, my Lads, think of the Impression we must be making, when we ought to be showing our Guest that here in Brooklyn, we can be just as warm and friendly as they are over in New-York. We're not Country-folk, after all. We've seen 'em all, all manner of Traveler, saints and sinners, green and season'd, some who could teach Eels to wriggle and some who were pure fiduciary Edge, and I'll tell you, this one...I don't know. What do you think, Patsy? He's not so easy to read. You've done the Ferry-boat Lurk, you know all the Kiddies, what say you?"

Someone who in different Costume might easily be taken for a Pirate of the Century past, gives Mason the up-and-down. "New one on me, Cap'n. The diff'rently-siz'd Eye-balls suggest a life spent peering into small Op'nings. Yet he's not a Bum-bailiff, nor a bum's assistant,— lacks that, what you would call, cool disinterest."

"Amen to that," cries the lewd Half-Breed.

"Where would his Interests lie, do you think?" inquires Uncle. Ev'ry-one looks at Amelia.

" 'Xcuse me? I'm suppos'd to know? I'm sure I was, as, 'Ahoy, Sailor,' and Stuff?" she exclaims at last.

"What's he been peeping into, then?" the truculent Sailor yells. General again is the Merriment.

"I observe the Heavens," Mason seeking thro' the force of his upward gaze some self-Elevation, "I am a Cadastral Surveyor, upon a Contractual Assignment," in a tone inviting a respectful hush.

Instead of which, Amelia, squealing in alarm,— "Cad! Ass?— Eeeoo!"— jumps backward, into the not entirely unwelcoming embrace of her "Uncle," whilst a number of Dogs begin to wail, as it seems, disappointedly, and a thick-set Irishman, announcing in a pleasant voice, "I'll kill him, if you lot would rather not," begins to load his Pistol.

"There there, Black-Powder, now put it away,— Sir, the lad's confus'd, hates the English King and all his subjects as well,— best to tell him you're French, use an Accent if you can manage it,— no, killing him is out of the question, Blackie, for you see, he's the renown'd Astronomer, M'syeer Maysong."

"Nor am I 'ere to gathair the *Intellizhonce*,"— as Blackie's Eyes narrow thoughtfully,— "on be'alf of anyone, for pity's sake. Were it not for your Niece,— "

"Ah.— "

"Pray ye Captain,— I am well into my thirty-seventh Year,— "

"My point exactly. You see how she is. A Dew-Drop, trembling upon the morn of Womanly awakening, not yet assaulted by that Day you and I well know,— let alone savag'd, us'd up, and thrown aside."

"Quotha. She strikes me rather as a resourceful young woman, independent in her ways."

"Others would say willful. One day soon, someone will have to ask her to stop wearing black Cloth, as it all comes here from England,— yet who among us is eager for the task? they'll hear her across the River."

"No black Cloth? Rum little gesture to insist upon."

"It goes to the Heart of this," snarls the Half-Breed, Drogo. "All the Brits want us for, is to buy their Goods. The only use we can be to them, is as a Herd of animals much like the Cow, from whose Udders, as from our Purses, the contents may be periodickally remov'd,— well,— if all we have to withhold from them, be a few pitiable Coins, then so let us do,— hoping others may add to the Sum."

Hum…"may add"…Mason, squinting into a neutral corner, considers this. Upon the one hand, he has heard Highwaymen address Travelers they wish to rob in tones less direct,— upon the other, if they are willing to call it a Bribe, Mason is certainly willing to discuss the size of it.…

"As it happens, Sir, yours may be just the helping hand we need. Be you familiar with any Aspect of Telescopick Repair?"

"Enough not to cause too much Damage."

In the Silence following, ev'ryone but Mason exchanges Looks. "Oh, he's all right," decides "Amy" 's "Uncle," whose Sobriquet (for few here use Christian Names) is "Captain Volcanoe." "If he reads the Papers, he knows what we are....Sir,— when there is light enough,— would you mind having a look?"

The Telescope stands in its own Window'd Observatory at the Top of the House, before it the Edge of the River, behind it a green Plain strewn with Groves and Homesteads, and stems of Smoke in wand'ring Ascent, their Yearnings how like our own.... The Instrument seems to be point-ing down toward the Ship-Yards across the River,— commanding a View, in fact, of all the Docking along Water-Street, and, more obliquely, of the River-front, down to the White-Hall Slip at the South end of the Island, unto Governor's Island beyond, and the Buttermilk Channel. A Field-Marshal's Dream.

"Here," mutters Mason.— " 'Tis design'd to be aim'd upward, y'see, not down, for one thing. All the relevant screw-adjustments on this Model end, effectively, at the Horizon. For, as with our Thoughts, to aim downward is to risk,— ahrrh," squinting into the Eye-piece. "Something has knock'd these Lenses quite out of Line. You need to re-collimate."

"How long will that take to fix?"

"You really need a Frenchman for a job like this,— that is,— "

"Hey! You're a Frenchman, you said."

"*Oui*, I meant, of course, I am your Man! What Tools are there?" Not many. The subtle and ingenious M. Maysong must unscrew the fastening-Rings with Blacksmith's Tongs, padded with the remains of a Hat which has met with some violent Misadventure almost certainly including Fire. Sheep and Poultry wander in and out of his Atelier. Black-Powder looks in frequently, brandishing a different Weapon each time. "Do I make ye twitchy, Sir? Capital!"

Feeling not quite a Prisoner, Mason works thro' the Day. From across the River come the sounds of Mauls upon Pegs, Ship-fitters' Ejacula-tions, the squeal of lines in Sheaves, Thuds and far-carrying Cries, Ships' Bells, Chandlers' Dogs hungry all day, Bumboats crying their Merchandise. Members of the Collectivity climb the Ladder, to appear-ance but curious in a friendly way, and soon the room is full of young

Men and Women in avid Disputation. Someone brings up "Sandwiches," and someone else a Bottle, and as night comes down over New-York like a farmer's Mulch, sprouting seeds of Light, some reflected in the River, the Company, Mason working on in its midst, becomes much exercis'd upon the Topick of Representation.

"No taxation— "

"— without it, yesyes but Drogo, lad, can you not see, even thro' the Republican fogs which ever hang about these parts, that 'tis all a moot issue, as America has long been perfectly and entirely represented in the House of Commons, thro' the principle of Virtual Representation?"

Cries of, "Aagghh!" and, "That again?"

"If this be part of Britain here, then so must be Bengal! For we have ta'en both from the French. We purchas'd India many times over with the Night of the Black Hole alone,— as we have purchas'd North America with the lives of our own."

"Are even village Idiots taken in any more by that empty cant?" mutters the tiny Topman McNoise, "no more virtual than virtuous, and no more virtuous than the vilest of that narrow room-ful of shoving, beef-faced Louts, to which you refer,— their honor bought and sold so many times o'er that no one bothers more to keep count.— Suggest you, Sir, even in Play, that this giggling Rout of poxy half-wits, *embody* us? Embody *us?* America but some fairy Emanation, without substance, that hath pass'd, by Miracle, into *them?*— Damme, I think not,— Hell were a better Destiny."

"Why," exclaims the Captain, " 'tis the Doctrine of Transsubstantiation, which bears to the Principle you speak of, a curious likeness,— that's of course considering members of Parliament, like the Bread and Wine of the Eucharist, to contain, in place of the Spirit of Christ, the will of the People."

"Then those who gather in Parliaments and Congresses are no better than Ghosts?— "

"Or no worse," Mason cannot resist putting in, "if we proceed, that is, to *Consubstantiation,—* or the Bread and Wine remaining Bread and Wine, whilst the spiritual Presence is reveal'd in Parallel Fashion, so to speak,— closer to the Parliament we are familiar with here on Earth, as whatever they may *represent,* yet do they remain, dismayingly, Humans as well."

Ev'ryone stops eating and drinking to stare at him. "Parley Voo?" inquires Blackie. "Hey?"

"All respect, Sir, 'tis not near as fussy as that. We'd rest content with someone in Parliament along the Lines of Mr. Franklin recently, in London, someone that side of the Herring, looking out for the interests of the Province,— walking in to that Board of Trade,— 'Right, then, here I am in person,'— turning on that damn'd Charm,— "

"Aye, an agent for Parliamentary business,— working for us, not some Symbol of the People who won't care a rat's whisker about his Borough, who will indeed sell out his Voters for a chance to grovel his way to even a penny's-worth more Advantage in the World of Global Meddling he imagines as reality."

"Yet Representation must extend beyond simple Agentry," protests Patsy, "— unto at least Mr. Garrick, who in 'representing' a rôle, becomes the character, as by some transfer of Soul,— "

"You want someone to go to London and pretend to be an American who hates stamp'd Paper, something like that? Send over Actor-Envoys? Stroller-Plenipotentiaries? Appalling."

"Not that bad a Thought,— and consider Preachers, as well. Mr. Garrick's said to envy Whitefield's knack for bringing a Congregation to Tears, simply by pronouncing 'Mesopotamia.' "

"If we'd but had *someone* there, why there might be no miserable Stamp Tax now,— and till we have someone, that can prevent the next such, why, the Stamp Act is simple Tyranny, and our duty's to resist it."

Mason expects shock'd murmurs at this,— that there are none shocks him even more gravely, allowing him a brief, careening glimpse at how far and fast all this may be moving,— something styling itself "America," coming into being, ripening, like a Tree-ful of Cherries in a good summer, almost as one stands and watches,— something no one in London, however plac'd in the Web of Privilege, however up-to-the-minute, seems to know much about. What is happening?

"...Even Playing-Cards,— they want to take a Shilling the Pack. If *your* Parliament go ahead with this, we'll have a Summer like the World has never seen."

"Not my Parliament," Mason alertly.

"Do I take it, then, that you own no Property, wherever 'tis you're from, Sir?"

"What Rooms in my Adult Life have not been rented to me," Mason reckons, "have been included among the terms of my employment."

"Then you're a Serf. As they call it here, a Slave."

"Sir, I work under Contract."

"Someone owns you, Sir. He pays for your Meals and Lodging. He lends you out to others. What is that call'd, where you come from?"

"Why, and if you are free of such Arrangements," Mason shrugs, "hurrah thrice over and perhaps one day you may instruct all the rest of us in how, exactly."

"So we shall." The tone balanc'd upon a Blade's Edge, between Pity and Contempt.

Mason, not wishing to look into his eyes, carefully scrapes the Blacking from around a Set-Screw, then with the worn Tip of a Hunting Knife removes it, a Quarter-turn at a time. "I have had this Promise in Philadelphia, as well,— from Coffee-House Cabals and such."

"We are in Correspondence," says the Captain, "as are all the Provinces one with another. You may wish to pass that on to London. This is Continental, what's happening."

Amelia, attach'd to an avuncular Sleeve, is gazing at Mason with new interest. "Didn't know you were famous," she murmurs, "working directly for the King, the Cap'n says,— well, I'm, as, 'maz'd."

"Alas, no longer. Out in the Woods these days, running lines for a couple of Lords in a squabble...."

"An exercise in futility! I can't believe you Cuffins! In a few seasons hence, all your Work must be left to grow over, never to be redrawn, for in the world that is to come, all boundaries shall be eras'd."

"You believe Christ's return to be imminent," Mason feigning Heartiness, "— that is surely wonderful news, brother! In my own Faith, we believe the same,— except possibly for the 'imminent' part."

"Is this worth explaining to him?" Drogo asks the Captain.

"Degrees of Slavery, Sir. Where in England are you from?"

A Mask-dropping Sigh.

"Stroud, G-d help me."

"Then you have known it."

"I have encounter'd Slavery both at the Cape of Good Hope, and in America, and 'tis shallow Sophistry, to compare it with the condition of a British Weaver."

"You've had the pleasure of Dragoons in your neighborhood? They prefer rifle-butts to whips,— the two hurt differently,— what otherwise is the difference in the two forms of Regulation? Masters presume themselves better than any who, at their bidding, must contend with the real forces and distances of the World,— no matter how good the pay. When Weavers try to remedy the inequality by forming Associations, the Clothiers bring in Infantry, to kill, disable, or deliver up to Transportation any who be troublesome,— these being then easily replaced, and even more cheaply, by others quite happy to labor in Silence."

"Yet Slaves are not paid,— whereas Weavers,— "

"Being from Stroud, Sir, I think you know how Weavers are paid,— tho' Wolfe preferr'd to settle the Pay-list with lead and steel, keeping his hand in between Glorious Victories, thinking he'd use weavers for target practice, nasty little man, hated Americans, by the way,— 'Contemptible cowardly dogs who fall down dead in their own Shit,' I believe was the way he phras'd it...."

Mason recalls well enough that autumn of '56, when the celebrated future Martyr of Quebec, with six companies of Infantry, occupied that unhappy Town after wages were all cut in half, and the master weavers began to fiddle the Chain on the Bar, and a weaver was lucky to earn tuppence for eight hours' work. Mason in those same Weeks was preparing to leave the Golden Valley, to begin his job as Bradley's assistant, even as Soldiers were beating citizens and slaughtering sheep for their pleasure, fouling and making sick Streams once holy,— his father meantimes cursing his Son for a Coward, as Loaves by the Dozens were taken, with no payment but a Sergeant's Smirk. Mason, seeing the Choices, had chosen Bradley, and Bradley's world, when he should instead have stood by his father, and their small doom'd Paradise.

"Who are they," inquires the Rev^d in his Day-Book, "that will send violent young troops against their own people? Their mouths ever keeping up the same weary Rattle about Freedom, Toleration, and the rest, whilst their own Land is as Occupied as ever it was by Rome. These forces look like Englishmen, they were born in England, they speak the language of the People flawlessly, they cheerfully eat jellied Eels, joints of Mutton, Treacle-Tarts, all that vile unwholesome Diet which maketh the involuntary American more than once bless his Exile,— yet their intercourse with the Mass of the People is as cold with suspicion and contempt, as that of any foreign invader."

"We shall all of us learn, who they are," Capt. V. with a melancholy Phiz, "and all too soon."

Wednesday Morning, Mason waves good-bye at the Dock, where they've all come down to the Ferry, and Patsy boards with him, to see him across, and past the Inconveniences of New-York. Arriv'd at last in the Jerseys, Patsy claps him on the Shoulder. "We could be at War, in another Year. What a Thought, hey?"

"I do not enjoy regular Luncheon Engagements with these people, but I am close enough to tell you this,— they will not admit to Error. They rely upon colorful Madmen and hir'd Bullies to get them thro' the perilous places, and they blunder on. Beware them."

"Thank you, Sir. It must have cost you at least a few Years of believing otherwise, and I appreciate it. We all do."

Coming back down thro' the Jerseys, Mason and his Horse abruptly disjoin. "Met some boys," says the Field-Book Entry for Sunday the twenty-fourth, "just come out of a Quaker Meeting House as if the De——l had been with them. I could by no means get my Horse by them. I gave the Horse a light blow on the head with my Whip which brought him to the ground as if shot dead. I over his head, my Hat one way wig another, fine sport for the Boys." In the Foul Copy, he writes, "for ye D——l and the Boys," but this does not appear in the Fair Copies the Proprietors will see. All thro' the Monday he lies in bed, his Hip a Torment, no Position any less painful than another. What had happen'd? What unforeseen Station, what Duty neglected? What had his Horse boggl'd at? it being well known that Horses may detect Spirits invisible to human Sensoria.

"Mason's Strike-over here is of the Essence," opines Uncle Ives. "He knows that the Boys, releas'd from the Silence of the Meeting into that

Exuberance which to soberer spirits is ever a sign of the Infernal, yet did not cause his Animal's behavior. What was there, too much for the Horse to remain in the Road, that his own Sensorium was too coarse or ill-coded, to detect?"

"The D— "

"Not in this House, 'Thelmer," warns his Uncle Wade.

"Pigs are known to smell the Wind," remarks Aunt Euphrenia, busy at the Valves and Cocks of the Coffee-Urn.

"Saul who is also Paul, upon his way to Damascus," adds the Rev^d, "smit by the Glory and Voice of the risen Christ, is Christ's in the instant. Many of us long to be taken in the same way,— many are."

Recovering from his Fall, Mason in fact spends his waking time reading I Corinthians, in particular Chapter 15, in which Paul's case for Resurrection proceeds from Human bodies to Animal Bodies, and thence to Bodies Celestial and Terrestrial, and the Glories proper to Each, to Verse 42,— "So also is the Resurrection of the Dead."

"Excuse me?" Mason aloud. " 'So also'? I don't see the Connection. I never did."

"Of course not, dear Mopery,— it comes of thinking too much, for there is a Point beyond which Thought is of little Service." It is not Rebekah, not exactly, tho' it may have been one of those clear little Dreams that lead us into the crooked Passage-ways of Sleep,— tho' he would insist, as ever to Dixon, that he was not sleeping at the time of the Visit.

If he does not yet treasure, neither does he cast away, these Lesser Revelations, saving them one by mean, insufficient one,— some unbidden, some sought and earn'd, all gathering in a small pile inside the Casket of his Hopes, against an unknown Sum, intended to purchase his Salvation.

41

"Ran into them once at a Ridotto, actually," acknowledges Mr. LeSpark. "Must've been that first year or two."

"John!"

"Ages before we met, my Treasure."

"But my Nonpareil, you know how I resent and begrudge even the least allusion to any Life of yours, before we met." At this the Rev^d blinks, and may be seen slightly to cringe, for he knows his Sister.

"Thus depriving me," LeSpark at least game, "of all but, what's it been now...ten years? twenty?"

"Fifteen, my stout Chestnut. As before me you had no Life, fifteen is your true Age, putting you yet in the Bloom of Youth...."

"Um, Zab," the Rev^d can't keep from inquiring, "you...regard your Husband, as some sort of...Sprout?"

She pretends to think about this for a while. "Zabby!" Mr. LeSpark in a hurt tone.

"Would this Ridotto, Sir, have been at Lepton Castle, by Chance?"

"The very Oasis, Wicks. We'd done some Business out that way, I and his Lordship,— I'd a standing Invitation from them to pop in whenever I wish'd."

"Didn't know I'd married Quality, did you?" Elizabeth chirps.

" 'Twas a part of the Expedition I miss'd, Zab, and, as the Surveyors were on about it for weeks after, was often to be reminded of,— the infamous Lepton Ridotto."

In those days, out past the reach of civic Lanthorns, as of Nail-hung Lamps in Sheds, and Tallow Dips, and the last feeble Rush-Light,— beyond, in the Forest, where the supernatural was less a matter of Publick-Room trickery or Amusement, Mr. LeSpark, as he tells it, was us'd to visit with potential customers, as well as tour his sources of supply,— Gunsmithies, Forges, Bloomeries, and Barrel Mills,— passing as in a glide, thro' the Country, safe inside a belief as unquestioning as in any form of Pietism you could find out there that he, yes little JWL, goeth likewise under the protection of a superior Power,— not, in this case, God, but rather, Business. What turn of earthly history, however perverse, would dare interfere with the workings of the Invisible Hand? Even the savages were its creatures,— a merchant's Pipe-Reverie, and, if consider'd as a class of Purchasers-at-retail,— well,— more admirable even than Dutch housewives, in the single-minded joy with which they brows'd and chose....

In his first Trips out, he engag'd local Guides, who kept to the shadows and did not speak, to show him the way to the well-guarded, and in the estimate of some, iniquitous, Iron-Plantation of Lord and Lady Lepton. Each time, 'twas like stepping across out of the difficult world and into that timeless *Encyclopedia-Light*, where Apprentices kept a monastic silence, entirely dedicated to the tasks at hand, did not fall asleep in mid-afternoon, nor moon about in states of Erection for hours at a time. All noxious smokes and gases were being vented someplace distant, invisible. The dogs loaf'd, well fed, in the alleyways. Iron in an hundred shapes was being produced, exactly to plan. The women chatted as they work'd in a small studio of their own, casting from small Crucibles specially formulated Batches of Steel. Sunlight flooded thro' open'd windows, the faces of the workers remaining attentive, uninflected, eyes only upon the Work. This, LeSpark must remind himself, each time he rounded one particular unfolding of the Trail,— Hazel branches parting, river noise suddenly in the air, Dogs on route and at the Gallop,— this was how the world might be. To see with nothing but this Simplicity, to take only these unpolluted Breaths, to leave the shop after the last of the light, with a face as willingly free of Affliction as that presented at Dawn,— 'twas a moment, hard come by out here, of viewing things whole, and he grew with each Visit more and more to depend upon it.

It is something he cannot explain to many people,— he knows that few distinguish between the Metal itself, and the Forms it happens to end up in, the uses it is widely known for being put to, against living Bodies,— cutting, chaining, penetrating sort of Activities,— a considerable Sector of the iron market, indeed, directed to offenses against Human, and of course Animal, flesh.... "All too true," he can imagine himself saying, "yet, once you have felt the invisible Grasp of the Magnetic, or gazed, unto transport, as the Gangue falls away before the veined and billowing molten light, oh the blinding purity...."

"Oh, Mr. LeSpark," being the likely reply.

"What is not visible in his rendering," journalizes the Rev^d to himself, later, "is the Negro Slavery, that goes on making such no doubt exquisite moments possible,— the inhuman ill-usage, the careless abundance of pain inflicted, the unpric'd Coercion necessary to yearly Profits beyond the projectings even of proud Satan. In the shadows where the Forge's glow does not reach, or out uncomforted beneath the vaporous daylight of Chesapeake, bent to the day's loads of Fuel from the vanishing Hardwood Groves nearby, or breathing in the mephitic Vapors of the bloomeries,— wordlessly and, as some may believe, patiently, they bide everywhere, these undeclared secular terms in the Equations of Proprietary Happiness."

Mason and Dixon, happening to be lost at nightfall (as they will later tell it), in the last possible light come upon a cabin, hardly more than a shed, of weathered fragrant old wood, beneath a sagging roof, showing no lights, to Apparition, abandoned for years,— yet, its ancient doorsill once traversed, the Surveyors find more room inside than could possibly be contained in the sorrowing ruin they believ'd they were entering.

To their alarm, Light shines ev'rywhere,— Chandelier Light, silver Sconce and Sperm-Taper Light,— striking them both to an all-but-sympathetick Squint. The Plafond,— as their slowly unclenching eyes ascend in wonder,— runs to a full spectrum of colors, depicting not the wing'd beings of Heaven, but rather the Denizens of Hell, and quite busy at their Pleasures, too....

"Yes yes very interesting indeed," Dixon hastily, "yet if it's all the same to thee, I think, having grasp'd the point, I, for one, am now arriv'd at the moment of D. Ahh. Oah,— and thee...?"

"There's no Moon," Mason reminds him. "Going out there now would be as dangerous as jumping into the open sea. We must shelter here, we've no choice." 'Tis only then that they hear the Music, though once acknowledg'd, it seems to've been playing all the time. Indeed it now emerges, that they have entered something long in Progress, existing without them, not for their Benefit, nor even their Attention. Some twenty or thirty musicians, by the sound of it,— new music, advanced music, as far from the Oboick Reveries of the Besozzis, as the Imperial Melismata of Quantz,— its modalities rather suggesting some part of the Globe distant from Britain, a dangerous jangling that nonetheless acts as an hypnotic Draught upon the Surveyors.

Cautiously, drawn, following a Gradient of loudness as best they can, they pass through doorways, cross anterooms filled with expensive surfaces and knick-knack intricacies they are moving among too briskly to examine, beginning to pick up the murmur of a Gathering, peaks of falsetto insincerity,— suddenly a grand Archway, above which, carv'd in glowing pink Marble, naked Men, Women, and Animals writhe together in a single knotted Curve of Lustfulness. The Surveyors have been gazing at it for somewhat longer than is considered sophisticated, when a Voice, from someplace they cannot see, announces them,— "Mr. Mason, and Mr. Dixon, Astronomers of London."

Mason snorts. "Congratulations."

Dixon pretends to look about for the Voice. "Really, I'm oahnly a county Surveyor...? He's the Astronomer...?"

"Overdoing the Rusticisms," Mason mutters. "And do try not to fling your head about so?"

Thus do they come stumbling into what, in London, is term'd an "Hurricanoe,"— a thick humidity of Intrigue and Masks realiz'd in locally obtain'd Fur and Plumage, clamorous with Chatter and what seems now more to resemble Dancing-Music,— dominated from one wall by a gigantic rococo Mirror, British Chippendale to the innocent eye, engrossing easily the hundredth part of an acre,— Dixon trying to stand his ground even as his partner has begun to walk away rapidly backward, for an Eye-blink there having pass'd over his Face a look of Alarm that has not possess'd it since the *Seahorse,* during the worst of that encounter.

"I cannot explain," as Dixon overtakes him, " 'tis a sort of Moral Panick."

"Manners first,— we must go in, as we can't offend our Hostess,— there's sure to be a Hostess...?" Dixon frantically resorting to what he knows of Climbers' Discourse. "If we offend her, she will at best behave inconveniently to her Husband,— at but slightly worse, she will advise him to have us expell'd from the Province. Are you there? Sheriffs will be instructed to make our lives even more difficult,— Children will play rude hoaxes upon us,— Water-Men will contrive to put us in the Water...."

"My Wig," Mason grasping and shifting it frantically about, "it doesn't feel quite...symmetrick,— no, and the Coat,— the moment we arose, I said it, remember? 'Shouldn't I wear the blue brocade?' But, in that case, I should have had to change the Breeches,— "

"Sir,— " a calm Voice at his elbow suggests, "take hold of yourself, lest another be obliged to."

"Aye? Another what?" Irascible Mason, known up and down the Churs of Stroud, on occasions like this, as a lightning Shin-Kicker, has actually begun shuffling to seek some purchase upon the gleaming floor, when he belatedly recognizes the notorious Calvert agent Captain Dasp, to smoak whose Dangerousness even those of an Idiocy far more advanc'd than Mason's require but an anxious few seconds.

"Gentlemen," advises this ominous Shadow, "— you have fallen, willy-nilly, among a race who not only devour Astronomers as a matter of habitual Diet, but may also make of them vile miniature 'Sandwiches,' and lay them upon a mahogany Sideboard whose Price they never knew, and *then forget* to eat them. Your only hope, in this room, is to impersonate so perfectly what they assume you to be, that instincts of Predation will be overcome by those of Boredom."

"I was just about to tell him thah'...?" nods Dixon.

Lady Lepton has appeared,— the Hostess there is sure to be one of. "Captain, how pleasant." With a gaze, met calmly by that of the agent, that invites at least Conjecture.

Dixon, ignoring the Captain's sensible advice, is giving her the once-over. "Eeh! Why, Lady, I've seen thee...?— years ago at Raby Castle, where tha came to visit. We were both about the same age...? still children, it was nearly winter,— Thee in a riding-habit, a sort of Brunswick style? scarlet and blue, and gold buttons,"— which is about where the Captain throws up his hands and walks off, shaking his head,— "a full skirt, a petticoat, and beautiful small boots of wine-colored Cordovan, with French Court heels...aye and a cocked hat with green Parrot feathers, all against a Winter Sky, and thine Hair, left loose, falling nearly to the saddle...."

Ordinarily their Hostess would have been expected to rejoin, "And you were the muddy boy at the side of the ditch with his hand upon his Willie," and everyone would have laughed gaily, except, of course, Dixon. Instead, she peers directly in his eyes, and whispers slowly, "Aye, you. At first I thought you were one of the Castle's Ghosts. Following me,— keeping just out of the Light. Even when I didn't see you, I felt you. They told me you were wild, poor, a Dissenter, an Outlaw, to pay you no attention. But I must have disobeyed, if, after all these years, I still remember you." Whereupon a golden Edge of Pleasure proceeds to bisect him upwardly all the way from his Ballocks to his Heart, which these days is a lengthy journey.

Tonight's Slave Orchestra includes the best musicians the Colonies, British and otherwise, have to offer,— for the melody-maddened Iron-Nabob has searched them out, a Harpsichord Virtuoso from New Orleans, a New-York Viol-Master, Pipers direct from the Forests of Africa,— and bought up their Contracts, as others might buy objects of art. The string instruments are from workshops in Cremona, the winds from France, and the music they are playing here for the guests at Castle Lepton, tho' at the moment little more than a suite of airs of the Street and Day, is nonetheless able somehow, perhaps in the unashamed prevalence of British modality,— that is, Phrygioid, if not Phrygian,— to lend weight to (where it does not in fact ennoble) even the most brainless conversation upon the great Floor,— which can usually be heard in His Lordship's vicinity, though nowhere at the moment near Dixon, who is finding all this, to his delight, dangerously interesting.

When they were still that young, he'd thought her bold as a Boy, and proud, with what he had already remarked, at a distance, as the proudness of Women. He'd stayed out, away from others, on a Lurk among the Towers and Gate-ways,— and in the shadows of Autumn, late-colored even in the mornings, had grown enjoyably obsessed. His Great-Uncle George, believing her a Witch, cast at young Jeremiah looks of sorrow and reproach. But the boy had watched her out on the Fell, riding so fast that her amazing hair blew straight back behind her, the same Wind pressing her Eyelids shut and her Lashes into a Fan, and forcing her Lips apart.... Long on a personal basis with the horses the Earl had given her to ride, Dixon sought their company now in the stables at night, stroking, feeding, talking it over gently with them. Indoors one day of early sleet, lurking in the damp and rodent smell of the mural passages, he looked out through the pierc'd paint Eyes of Nevilles and Vanes, costumed as shepherds, before a Castle glorified with an afternoon light that never was, to see her kissing one of the Chamber-Maids, who stood as under a spell, whilst ice sought entry, lashing at the tall Windows. At nightfall he heard her in the corridors far away singing something in Italian, "*Bellezza, che chiama...*," the sweet notes picking up from the stone Passages a barking Echo....

Somehow this fearlessly independent Girl had then gone on to marry the ill-famed, the drooling and sneering, multiply-bepoxed Lord Lepton, an insatiate Gamester who failed to pay his losses, forever a-twittering, even as he tumbled to ruin in one of the period's more extravagant Stock-Bubbles, summarily ejected from Clubs high and low, advised by friend and enemy that his only decent course would be to step off the Edge of the World.— Thinking they meant, "go to America," resolutely chirpy, he donn'd his sturdiest coat and breeches, took a false name and a public conveyance to the Docks, there indentured himself to a North Riding iron-master, and in good time sailed away (being kept with the other Slaves for the duration of the crossing, well below the ship's water-line) to far and fever-clouded Chesapeake, where he was brought up-country, to dig and blast in the earth, fetch and stoke in the service of the perpetual Fires, smell unriddably of Sulfur, drive the African slaves as basely as a creature of his Sort might be expected to do, be one day trusted with blasting-Powder,— an event that, given the state of his soul, counted as a major leap of Redemption,— and after three of these trans-Stygian Years, become Journeyman, and in two more, by then his own Master, make his next Fortune, returning to England but once more, not to the Mansions that had spurned him but to dark-skied Durham, to carry back to America the Woman who, mysteriously having allowed it to happen, stands here now, Chatelaine of Lepton Castle, almost as Dixon might remember her upon one of the old battered towers of Raby, pretending yet, surveying below the intricate Deployment not of fancied men and horses of long ago, but of present-tense Brussels Lace and Mignonette, of Brocades and flower'd Gauzes and unkempt rainbows of Satin across her own Ladyship's Parquetry, as the music complains inconsolably of loves at worst Hard-Labor, at best, impossible.

"…raving Lunatick of course," his Lordship fixing the Astronomers with a gleaming stare, "whatwhat?"

"Oh, aye," Dixon enthusiastically nodding whilst trying to kick Mason under cover of her Ladyship's Gown, whose elaborate Hem has somehow crept closer to his Person than he imagin'd etiquette to allow.

"Imbecile," Mason, he thinks amiably, suggests.

Lord Lepton reacts as though knifed. "Exactly the word he used,— or was it 'Idiot'? You, Dasp,— you were there, which was it?"

"If memory serves, My Lord, 'twas My Lord, that called him both of those." He pronounces each word separately, in a way that strikes the listener as unarguably foreign, tho' what strange Tongue may lie back of his English must remain a Mystery. He is gazing at Mason, and Dixon, too, so as to leave no doubt that this will be the last uncompensated Favor,— henceforth the Astronomers, unless the price be agreeable, are on their own.

"Tho', I say, look here," Lord Lepton has meantime been rattling, "everyone on about it, 'Great Chain of Being this, Great Chain of Being that,'— well frankly I'm first to say jolly good,— but,— now you see you have this rather lengthy *Chain,* don't you, and,— well damme, what's it for? Eh? What's it *do?* Is there something for example hanging?— *dangling* from its bottom end? Well! what happens if that something fails to hold on? Obviously it falls, but where, don't you know, and,— and how far?"

"Perhaps," Captain Dasp sibilantly entering the Game, "it is not a straight *vertical* line at all. Perhaps it is a Helixxx," gesturing in the air for Lord L.'s benefit, "and *wound about* something,— keeping it, let us say…chain'd in? Something not part of the Great Chain itself, but fully as enormous, something that must be kept in restraint. Which we pray may be only sleeping when, throughout the Chain's vast length, it is felt now and then…to stir."

"Yes!" cries his Lordship with a strange shiver, "flexing, writhing, perhaps beginning to snarl a bit, as one might suppose, deep within its Breast.…"

"Well, 'tis a horizontal Chain for me," Dixon beamingly raising his Punch-cup in Lord L.'s direction, drawing from his Partner a quick turn of the head,— *Why do you assist in this idiot's Folly?*— "such as Surveyors use. Which shall go before, I wonder, and which follow,— aye and which direction shall it point in?" A newcomer might have imagined he was talking about the Line, and that the answer was West. But the Nabob was feeling personally assaulted.

"You sound like one of these Leveler chaps," he mutters.

Dixon has about decided to reply, "Circumferentor, actually," when Lady Lepton interposes, sighing, "Ah, yet do recollect that Chain, more imprisoning than the Captain's, more relentlessly fiduciary than Mr. Dixon's." Her gaze fixing each, as she speaks his name,— then, meaningfully, Lord Lepton, but to no avail,— the object of her insinuation only continuing to nitter-natter…with a strange pointedness toward Dixon. "There's Coal out where you're going, you see. Already a brisk trade by way of the Indians, though they can't bring it in in volume, poor chaps. Pretty, magickal black Stone, for all they know of it. Yet we're not all Charcoal Hearths here, we've Coke as well. Produce our own,— Chambers and all here upon the Plantation.…"

Life for her in these forests has never prov'd altogether exhilarating, her Face, even with its Complexion still pale as a summer Moon just risen above the Staithes, having with the years form'd itself into an aspect of permanent disappointment. Thus, altho' like her husband she may laugh at anything, yet is the pitch of her voice as low, and its every inflection as bitterly preconsidered, as those of Milord are high and carelessly unrestrained. Sounding together, the two make a curious sort of Duetto.

'Twas alleged by wits of the day that she'd married him for his Membership in that infamous Medmenham Circle known as the Hellfire Club, resting thereby assured at least of a lively Bed-chamber. But as evidence that Milord's Tastes run to nothing much out of the ordinary, the Eye alert to the stirrings of a Gown, and adept at translating these into the true movements beneath the expensive surface and intervening Petticoats, may detect a Rhythm, a Damask Pulse, that speaks of Desires to cross into the forbidden.

It is difficult, in these days of closer-fitting Attire, to imagine the enormous volumes of unoccupied Space that once lay between a Skirt's outer Envelope, and the woman's body far within. "Why, there may be anything!" Capt. Dasp as if genuinely alarmed, "stash'd in there,— contraband Tea, the fruits of Espionage, the coded fates of Nations, a moderate-sized Lover, a Bomb."

"Yet the present-day bodice," remarks Lady Lepton, "can conceal secrets only with difficulty. A single key, perhaps, or the briefest of love-notes. Indeed, 'tis but an ephemeral Surface, rising out of the Spaces that billow ambiguously below the waist, till above melting...here, into bare *décolletage*, producing an effect, do you mark, of someone trying to ascend into her natural undrap'd State, out of a Chrysalis spun of the same invisible Silk as the Social Web, kept from emerging into her true wing'd Self,— perhaps then to fly away,— by the gravity of her gown."

"Oh, pishtush," comments her Husband, "Pshaw. Bodices are for ripping, and there is an end upon it."

The servants in the hall tonight are whitely-wigged black slaves in livery of a certain grade of satin and refinement of lace,— black Major-domos and black Soubrettes. One of the latter now passes by with a tray of drinks. "Milord's own punch receipt," advises the pretty Bondmaiden, gazing at Dixon intently. "Knock you on your white ass."

"Why, Ah would have brought me blahck one, but no one told me...?" She seems to know him. For a frightening moment, he seems to know her.

"Yes lovely isn't she, purchas'd her my last time thro' Quebec, of the Widows of Christ, a Convent quite well known in certain Circles, devoted altogether to the World,— helping its Novices *descend*, into ever more exact forms of carnal Mortality, through training as,— how to call them?— not ordinary Whores, though as Whores they must be quite gifted, but as eager practitioners of all Sins. Lust is but one of their Sacraments. So are Murder and Gluttony. Indeed, these two are combin'd most loathsomely in their Ritual of Holy Communion."

"Rest tha content with the way he's talking...?" Dixon whispers loudly into Mason's ear, and moistly as well.

"An Otick Catarrh was not in my day's Plan, Dixon?"

"Oh. Why, bonny. See if I confide anything to thee, anymore."

"Pray continue, Sir,— 'tis but his Idiocy again, recurs like an Ague, harmless, really.... And," Mason believes he must ask, "do they get...fat?"

"Fat? Ah," Captain Dasp assures him, "violent, greedy, treacherous. Needless to say, Men without number fall in love with them, pay them repeatedly enormous sums, becoming ruin'd in the process, whilst Las Viudas de Cristo continue to bloom and prosper."

In the instant, Mason later avow'd, he knew that the Captain was a French spy. The Peace of Paris has left a number of these adrift, the reduction of Canada having forced many of them South and West, to the Illinois and beyond. There be sightings of Pépé d'Escaubitte, and 2-A Lagoo, Iron-Mask Marthioly and the Boys from Presque Isle, too. Few but the foolhardy,— however admirably so,— have stay'd in Pennsylvania, and those ever within galloping distance of Maryland, with its Web of Catholic houses of Asylum,— not that anyone there looks forward to being ask'd.— "What, that bloody Frog again?"

"Chauncey, not in front of the *C-H-I-L-D!*"

"Oh Mamma, is that funny-talking man coming to visit again?"

"Yes but not a word or God will nail you where you stand, and probably with your Mouth open just like that."

"We promise! and shall he cook for us?" Upon such frail expectations, fugitive as the smell of a Roast through an open window, do the lives of these Renegadoes often depend.

Somewhere beyond the curve of a great staircase, Gongs, each tun'd to a different Pitch, are being bash'd. "At last," mumble several of the Guests as they make speed toward yet another Wing of Castle Lepton, converging at the entrance to a great dom'd room, the Roof being a single stupendously siz'd Hemisphere of Glass, taken from a Bubble, blown first to the size of a Barn by an ingenious air-pump of Jesuit invention, then carefully let cool, and saw'd in half. The sister Hemisphere is somewhere out in America, tho' where exactly, neither Lord nor Lady is eager to say. As no one at the moment has anything but Gaming of one sort or another in mind, the Topick is soon let go of.

Here is a Paradise of Chance,— an E-O Wheel big as a Roundabout, Lottery Balls in Cages ever a-spin, Billiards and Baccarat, Bezique and Games whose Knaves and Queens live,— over Flemish Carpets, among perfect imported Chippendale Gaming-Tables, beneath Chandeliers secretly, cunningly faceted so as to amplify the candle-light within, they might be Children playing in miniature at Men of Enterprise, whose Table is the wide World, lands and seas, and the Sums they wager too often, when the Gaming has halted at last, to be reckon'd in tears....

42

"Many Christians," comments the Rev[d], "believe Gaming to be a sin. Among Scholars, serious questions arise as to Predestination and the Will of God,— Who notes each detail of each life in a sort of divine Ledger, allotting Fortune bad and good, to each individually, even as He raiseth the storm at sea, lendeth the Weather-gage to the dark Dromonds of Piracy, provoketh the Mohawk against the Trader's Post. For He is Lord of All Danger. Yet others safe at home wager upon His Will, as express'd thro' the doings of these Enterprisers, exactly as upon a fall of Cards, or a Roll of Dice."

"Why, Wicks. You see us as no more than common 'Spielers'? Parasites upon the Fortunes of those willing to Risk all? Pray you, setting aside whose Hearth you are ever welcome at, tell me all."

"What alarms me most, Wade," proceeds Rev[d] Cherrycoke, "is the possibility of acquiring such vast sums so quickly. If a sailor may kill a Bully over a sixpence, then what disproportionate mischief, including Global War, may not attend the safekeeping of Fortunes of millions of pounds Sterling?"

"You're asking the wrong Merchant. I'm lucky if I clear'd a Thousand, this Year."

"Happen they all reach a point where they can't trust their Luck any more...? So they cheat."

"Bold as you please." Later, in their Rooms, too late the Gamer's Remorse, Mason working himself up, "He mark'd the cards. The Dice were of cunningly lacquer'd Iron, the playing-surface magnetickally fiddl'd,— Damme, he owes us twenty pounds,— more! what are we suppos'd to do, live upon Roots? 'twas the Royal Society's, belay that, the *King's own* money,— hey? right out of G. Rex's Purse it came, and don't it make a true Englishman boil!" 'Tis an Insult to Mason that cannot pass unanswer'd,— this runny-nos'd, titl'd Savage, tossing their Expeditionary Funds as airy Gratuities to the Slaves who stood all night with Coals kept ever a-glow, and with Bellows clear'd the immediate Air of smoke, that a player might see what Cards he held.

Insupportable. "We must take something worth twenty pounds, then...? Let the Rascal pursue huz...?" Dixon adjusts the Angle of his Hat. "Let's have a look. Here upon the wall, this Etching,— what's it suppos'd to be? Turkish Scene or something.... Wait,— Mason, it's people *fucking*...? Eeh! And look at thah'...?...Well,— we can't sell that in Philadelphia. What's this? Chamber-pot? Perhaps not. How about the Bed?"

"Might as well be taking that Tub over there," indicating a giant Bathing-tub with Feet, Bear Feet in fact, cast at the Lepton Foundry from local Iron.

"Why aye, that's it! The Tub!"

"Dixon, it's half a Ton if it's a Dram, we're not going to move it...? Even if we could, where would we move it to? And once there,— "

Dixon, a-mumble, is over examining the Tub. "Laws of Leverage...William Emerson taught things no one else in England knows. Secret techniques of mechanickal Art, rescued from the Library at Alexandria, circa 390 A.D., before rampaging Christians could quite destroy it all, jealously guarded thereafter, solemnly handed down the Centuries from Master to Pupil."

Mason's squint appears. "You shouldn't be showing these 'Secrets' to me, then, should you? No more than that Watch."

"Oh, thou would have to swear the somewhat ominous 'Oath of Silence,' of course, but we can do thah' later,— here, look thee." Dixon seems scarcely to touch the pond'rous Fixture,— yet suddenly, as if by Levitation, one end has rotated upward, and the great Tub now stands precariously balanced upon a sort of lip or Flange at its other end.

"That's amazing!" cries Mason.

"Simple matters of balance,— Centers of Gravity true and virtual,— Moments of Inertia,— "

"Have 'em all the time,— "

"— estimated Mass,— "

"— the Priest having enjoy'd a merry night before?" tho' yet a-squint. "What's this,— shan't I hear 'Magnetism,' as well? some deliberate omission?"

Dixon doesn't answer immediately, nor, as it will prove, at all, focus'd as he has become upon gently but fluently tweaking the giant iron Concavity across the room and toward the door,— through which it is not immediately clear how the Tub is going to, actually, fit. So sure is his touch that the floorboards barely creak. "Ah very nice, very nice indeed...? now I'll just have a look out at the stairs. And if *thoo* don't mind,— "

"Um,— ?" inquires Mason.

"This,— " indicating the looming Mass above them, "needs to be held at exactly the Angle it's at,— not just the Angle off the floor, do tha see, but also this exact Angle of Rotation about the long Axis? Try not to think of this as two separate Angles, but as One? Thou're following this?"

"I,— you want me to,— wait,— no, why not just lean it against the Wall, here?"

"Thah' Wall? eeh! eeh! it'll go *through* thah' Wall! No,— all I ask, is thah' thoo hold the Tub up, but for a minute, whilst I go reconnoitre."

"That's one minute,— you promise."

"Two minutes. At most. It's perfectly stable, so long as tha don't shift it about too much.... Good fellow, just slip in here, yes and thy hands go...there,— a unique resting-place for everything, Friend,— behold the Tub, perfectly quiescent, 's it not...? in maximum self-alignment, and quietly gathering Power. 'Twill see us free of this place,— eeh. Ideal. Now,— *don't move.* I'll be right back."

He vanishes, leaving Mason 'neath the Tub. Soon Mason detects the smell of Pipe-Tobacco,— Dixon's blend, indisputably. He's out there having a leisurely Smoke whilst Mason, squinting upward nervously, struggles to keep the Tub upon its Axes. After a while, as if to himself, lightly vocalizing, "It's gone two minutes and thirty-one seconds." The words gong loudly back and forth, painfully seeming to enter one ear, pass through his head, and depart out the other ear. In the after-hum he fancies he can hear Dixon's voice, and then another,— Lady Lepton's if he is not mistaken, tho' Words soon lapse, whilst Sounds continue. An overturn'd chair. Sighs. Fabric tearing. A merry Squeal. All at once, in chiming two-part Harmony and unnaturally accelerating *Tempo,* unmistakably, "O Ruddier than the Cherry." 'Tis the infamous Musickal Bodice, devis'd by an instrument-maker of London, wherein Quills sewn into its fastening, when this is pull'd apart, will set a-vibrating, one after another, a row of bell-metal Reeds, each tun'd to a specifick Note,— the more force applied, the louder the notes. "Ripping Tune!" Mason calls out. He has no idea how to disengage from Dixon's blasted Tub, tho' now would hardly seem the best time to do so, unless,— now that he's listening,— there no longer seems to be...hmm, quite as much sound from out there...

If, in fact, any. "Well,— fucking insane, wouldn't you agree!"

In the unpromising silence that slowly, gongingly, falls, Mason becomes aware of a measur'd Tapping upon the outside of the Tub, directly over the back of his Head. It progresses 'round the rim of the Tub until into sight comes the flush'd Phiz of an individual in an outdated Wig of foreign Manufacture, waving about a fantastickal Compass of Brass and Mahogany, rigg'd out with Micrometer Screws, dial-faces, enigmatickally wreath'd coils of Copper Wire. "Good day to you," he greets Mason. "Are you the one responsible for this quite astonishing Magnet?"

"What, this? 'tis a Tub, Sir." Hoping the Echo may give him an Edge.

" 'Tis damn' nearly Earth's third Pole," mutters the dishevel'd Philosopher. "Observe." He steps across the room, holds up a Building-Nail, and lets it go. It flies through the Air, in a curious, as it seems *directed,* Arc, hits the Tub with a solid *bong,* flattening its Point by an eighth of an inch, and fails to drop to the floor,— "Not unlike Hungarian Vampirism," snatching it loose and proceeding to dangle one by one a gigantick Loop of other Nails from it, "the Ability may be transfus'd from one Mass of Iron to another,— Excuse me. I am Professor Voam, Philosophical Operator, just at present scampering from the King's Authorities, for electrocuting at Philadelphia one of these American Macaronis who cannot heed even the simplest Caution, such as, 'Don't touch the Torpedo.' Ease of Compliance written all over it, not so? yet such is the Juvenility abounding upon these Shores, that the damn'd Fop must go feel for himself. Poh. Notwithstanding 'twas he who fell'd himself, a number of arm'd Citizens thought it better I depart.... Here,— shall you be much longer under there? Perhaps we could find some Coffee."

"I'm not sure how he got me under here," Mason a bit plaintive, "and even less sure about how to get out. Your mention of Coffee, withal, intensifies my Unhappiness."

"Someone *put* you beneath this Ferric Prodigy?"

"My Co-adjutor, Mr. Dixon."

"Of course! The Astronomers! Dixon and Mason!"

"Actually," Mason says, "That's— "

"Say, I hope you Boys ain't had a falling-out."

"He was demonstrating a Principle of Staticks, and became distracted. Apparently this Tub is resting upon some Axis invisible to all but Dixon."

The Professor has a Look-See, waving his Apparatus in mystickal tho' regular Curves at the Tub. "Fascinating. The Axis it's on is Magnetick. Good thing he didn't try to balance this mechanickally. Whoo! you'd be flatter'n a Griddle-Cake." He is carefully adjusting his Grip upon the Rim.

"Excuse me,— to what End? Gazing at it, as it fries? saying, Oh, you're so Circular...your Airr-Bubbles, they're so intrriguing,— "

"*Than, than,*— good, that's got it. Just help me lower it,— Q.E.D. and Amen. Say, pleasant Tub. This could be just the Article to keep Felípe in, now that I look at it."

"That's your...?"

"Torpedo. Lodging him in the Arabian-Gardens Pool for the moment, but 'twill soon be time to move on, and then...?"

Mason stretches and twists his Neck and Head about. "Grateful, Sir. Now perhaps may I direct you to Safety,— any number of Refugees having become attach'd to our Party,— all traveling under the joint guarantee of the Proprietors, and their Provincial Governments as well. To my knowledge, tho' there be Tailors, Oracles, Pastrymen, Musicians, Gaming-

Pitches, Opera-Girls, Exhibitors of Panoramic Models, bless us all, there is not yet an Electric Eel."

"You are kind,— yet the publick rooms of Philadelphia offering Insult a-plenty,— I am not sure the Practice would subside as we mov'd West."

"Yet, supposing Progress Westward were a Journey, returning unto Innocence,— approaching, as a Limit, the innocence of the Animals with whom those Folk must inter-act upon a daily basis,— why, Sir, your Torpedo may hold for them greater appeal than you may guess."

"Rural Electrification," the Professor sighs, "Seed-Bed of the unforeseen. Where is our choice? Come, and you shall meet Felípe."

After they are join'd by Dixon, emerging coprophagously a-grin from some false Panel in a Wall, *exeunt* the Premises, bringing along the Tub. One corridor's branching away from the Arabian Gardens, the Slave who spoke to Dixon earlier stands now abruptly in Mason's Path, obliging him to pause, quite close, Face to Face with her.

"Leaving me again, Charles?"

"It isn't you."

"I was abducted by Malays. Love-Jobbers. Walk thro' the Market with little Fly-Whisks, inspecting the Girls and Boys, striking this one, that one,— sooner or later, each is come for. When I felt the tiny Lashes, 'twas to be destin'd for Jesuit Masters, in payment of a Debt forever unexplain'd to me,— only then to be remanded, soon as we gain'd Quebec, to the Sisterhood of the Widows of Christ. Whence, after my Novitiate, kind Captain D. and I came to our Rapprochement."

"Your French has improv'd," whispers Mason. "I know who you are, and well before next Midnight, too. Ah, and as for 'kind,' why the man is at least a Flagellant, you Wanton."

She smiles not at all enigmatickally, turns and steps away, shaking those Globes,— too bad, Flagellants in the Region, she's here only on short-term Lease, in a Fortnight she'll be shaking them someplace else, and a glamorous International Life it's proving to be for her too, so far at least. Who says Slavery's so terrible, hey?

"Good-bye, Charles," beginning to blur, receding 'round the long curve of the Wall. Mason, Dixon and the Professor go poking in and out of one secret Panel after the next, but she is no-where to be found.... Instead, the Lads now encounter a Dutch Rifle with a Five-pointed Star

upon its Cheek-Piece, inverted, in Silver highly polish'd, shining thro'
the Grain upon the Wrist and Comb that billows there in stormy Intricacy, set casually above some subsidiary Hearth in a lightly-frequented
Room.— A Polaris of Evil...

"As it happen'd," relates Mr. LeSpark, "I was reclining right there, upon
a Couch, seeking a moment's Ease from the remorseless Frolick,— "

"Alone, of course," his Wife twinkling dangerously.

"As Night after dismal night, my green Daffodil, thro' the bleakness of
that pre-marital Vacuum, Claims of the Trade preëmpting all,— not least
the Society of your estimable Sex." In which pitiable state, he dozes off
and awakens into the Surveyor's Bickering as to the Rifle's Provenance,—
Mason insisting 'tis a Cape Rifle, Dixon an American one.

" 'Tis no Elephant Gun,— haven't we seen enough of these here by
now, Dear knoaws? Barrel's shorter, Stock's another Wood altogether."

"Your Faith being famous, of course, for its close Appreciation of
Weaponry."

"Ev'ry Farmer here has a Rifle by him, 'tis a primary Tool, much as an
Ax or a Plow...? tha can't have feail'd to noatice...?"

"Surrounded upon all sides, Night and Day, by the American Mob,
ev'ry blessed one of them packing Firrearrms,— why, why yes, I may've
made some note of that,— "

Wade LeSpark slowly arises, to peer at them over the back of the
Couch,— "Good evening, Gentlemen. I was just lying here, having a Gaze
at this m'self. Handsome Unit's it not? You can usually tell where one was
made, from its Patch-Box," reaching for the Rifle, turning the right side of
the Butt toward the Lanthorn, "— the Finials being each peculiar to its
Gunsmith, a kind of personal signature...look ye, here it is again, your
inverted Star, work'd into the Piercings, as a Cryptogram...withal, this
Brass is unusual,— pale, as you'd say,— high Zinc content, despite the
British embargo, and sand-cast rather than cut from sheet...."

"Lord Lepton hath an Eye,— Damme." He cannot release his Grasp
upon the thing. The octagonal Barrel is Fire-blu'd rather than Acid-
brown'd, the Lock left bright, despite its Length pois'd nicely when slung

from its Trigger-Guard, all brought narrow, focus'd, the Twist upon the Rifling inside a bit faster than one in forty-eight, suggesting in its tighter Vortex a smaller charge, a shorter range...a Forest Weapon, match'd to a single Prey, heavier than a Squirrel, not quite heavy as a Deer.... In the Purity as you'd say of its Intent, 'tis as Mr. Dixon surmises, American, yet not the Work of any Gunsmith known to Mr. LeSpark.

"Might ye be aware, Sir," inquires Mason, "of another such inverted Star,— in Lancaster Town, upon the sign of the Dutch Rifle?"

"Aye, and clearly meant, Sir, to depict a local Piece,— its own Finial, 's I recall, being in the form of a Daisy, which the Gunsmiths 'round Lancaster favor...tho' there remains a standing Quarrel, as to what Rifle may have serv'd as the Model,— that is, if any at all did,— too much, out here, failing to mark the Boundaries between Reality and Representation. The Tavern's Sign was commission'd of an unknown traveling Artisan, who left Town in the general troubles in 'fifty-five, as mysteriously as he'd come,— perhaps remov'd south, perhaps perish'd. One Story has it, that, lacking a Brush, he went out and shot a Squirrel, with whose Tail, he then painted the Portrait of the very Rifle us'd to obtain it,— that Star may've been put on later, out of simple Whim,— nor perhaps did he ever make a Distinction, between two points up, and two down."

"Again, Sirr,— perrhaps these Occurrences,— " Mason glowering, "as others, are *invisibly connected.*— Can you so lightly, Sirr, dismiss the very Insignia of the Devil,— Representations or no, allow'd to appear only by his Agents among us?"

"Many will believe all Firearms to be his Work, no matter how decorated," LeSpark replies, with enough Dignity in his voice to suggest to them an intimacy with the Trade, "whilst others with equal warmth declare these Pennsylvania Beauties to be about the Work of God,— therefore, a stand-off,— what matter?"

"But that small Devices," interjects Professor Voam, "may command out-siz'd Effects. This Pentacle, if valu'd for no more than the silent acts of Recognition it provokes, has more than earn'd back its Expense."

"As over-ponderous Tubs, Sir," replies Mr. LeSpark, "— may never recoup the Cost of conveying them anywhere. How far were you thinking of taking this one, for Instance?"

"Had we seen this Rifle first...?" Dixon, to appearance forthrightly, "we might be off with it instead,— that is of course unless our Host, the Sharper, be a partickular Friend of thine...?"

Mason, his Eyes protruding in alarm, tugs upon Dixon's Sleeve, hissing, "Don't you see, there's a Curse upon it, for Heaven's Sake, Dixon,— ?"

In an Exchange of Glances with Mr. Dixon, that Mr. LeSpark will remember even years later, however, each has soon reveal'd so far unconfess'd Depths of Admiration for the Rifle,— despite all the ill-fortune that might descend, from no more than touching it,— for its brutal remoteness nearly Classickal, as for the sacramental Fidelity with which it bodies the Grace peculiar to the Slayer,— no Object that fails so to carry Death just inside its Earthly Contours, can elicit Desire quite so steeply or immediately....

Mr. LeSpark has bargain'd with many a Quaker,— he knows the wordless Idiom Dixon speaks. The key point is that taking the Rifle will be far more dangerous, than taking the Tub, "— and as for the Tub," grins Mr. LeSpark, at length, "why, what Tub, don't ye know?"

"To accommodate Strangers so, 's it not risky?" Dixon puzzles. "Suppose we were desperate Outlaws...?"

"You don't know what I see back in this Country. Bribes, Impersonations, Land Fraud, Scalp-stealing, Ginseng Diversion. Each Day brings Spectacle ever more disheartening. You three are but Boys out upon a Frolick."

"Most kind, Sir, ever so kind...." Mason needlessly groveling.

"Then again," chuckles Wade LeSpark, "Lepton *is* an important Customer.... Maybe I should run right to him, with word of this Tub's Alienation. Maybe he'll send Dasp out with some Riders after you. Maybe this Rifle here'll belong to one of 'em."

"In that case we'd best be moving along."

"Proceed cheerily, Boys." And Mr. LeSpark, as he will come to tell the Tale, declines back into the Couch, seeking once again the comforts of celibate Slumber.

The last Door out opens to them. They make for the Arabian Gardens, Dixon coaxing the Tub slickly along over the Tile-work,— soothe the Harem Girls, collect the Torpedo,— who bears an impatient Expression, as if it's been waiting for them,— along with some pool water, and continue on to a convenient Ramp-way, where they transfer Tub and Torpedo to a Conestoga Waggon but lately unloaded, with fresh Horses hitch'd up,— "Yee-hah!" the Professor grabbing the Reins,— and Damme, they're off."

Clutching his Hat, swaying violently in his Seat, Mason shouts thro' the Wind of Passage, "Say, Dixon,— Did it seem like Austra to you?"

"If it was, she's chang'd...?"

"Striking Woman. Fancied me, as you must have seen. Not at all like the old Austra, who couldn't abide me.... Naahhrr,— can't be she, a Man can tell, for Woman's Distaste is incontrovertible, her clearest Emotion."

They reach the Wood-line without Incident, soon falling in with the Road to the Ferry, listening for Hoof-beats behind them. "A matter of time," mopes Mason.

"Why would they want huz? They've got the twenty pounds...?"

"Oh, not 'us,' Dixon. No, no. You.— I was under the Tub, remember?"

"A proper Show," cackles Professor Voam.

"Bearing up, Professor?"

"Ev'ry Time, this is how it turns out." He has been traveling Inn to Inn with this Giant Specimen of Guyana Torpedo, giving Lectures upon, and Demonstrations of, the Electrical Creature's mysterious and often life-altering abilities. " 'Tis styl'd the 'Torpedo,' tho' Scientifically speaking, the true Torpedo is a kind of Ray or Skate,"— men wearing Hats made of dead Raccoons wait him out, watching the Torpedo in its Tank,— " 'tis also known as the Electric Eel, yet Mr. Linnæus hath decided 'tis no Eel, neither, but a *Gymnotus*. Skate, Eel, or *Gymnotus*, 'tis ever 'the Torpedo' to me. 'Remember to feed the Torpedo today...wonder if that Torpedo's charg'd up yet'?— never is, o' course,— learn'd how to tell just by look-ing in its Eyes, how the Level is. *Sí, sí, Cariño*," as he reaches now into the great Tub and begins gently to sweep his hands close to the Creature's body, tail to head. The Torpedo remains calm, and presently grows appre-ciative, with a faint smile, much observ'd by Torpedo-Fanciers, about the V-shap'd Dimples at the Corners of its Mouth,— as if, in its grim and semi-possess'd life, it has found a moment to relax and let a Nonelec-trickal provide the Thrills for a change.

Sold to the Professor under the Name, "El Peligroso," or, "The Dan-gerous One," Felípe is quite large for a Surinam Eel, Five feet and two inches, and still growing. As he gets larger, the Dimensions of his Electrickal Organs change accordingly,— of particular interest being those of the Disks which are Stack'd lengthwise along most of his over-all length, each Disk being a kind of Electrickal Plate, whose summ'd Effect is to charge his Head in a Positive, as his Tail in a Negative, Sense. 'Tis necessary then, but to touch the Animal at both ends, to complete the circuit, and allow the Electrickal Fluid to discharge, its Fate thereafter largely contriv'd by the Operator, to provide onlookers with a variety of Spectacles Pyrotechnick.

"The Torpedo you see here,— fully charg'd, giddy, indeed as if drugg'd by the presence of the Electrickal, saturating ev'ry Corpuscle of its Being,— this is the classic El Peligroso," here the giant Eel smoothly assumes a new Attitude, as if posing for its Portrait, "the Torpedo the World sees, a strolling Actor, who nightly discharges into his Performance all the Day's dire Accumulation,— tho' the Mysteries of the Electrickal Flux within him continue to defy the keenest minds of the Philosophickal World, including a Task-Force of Italian Jesuits dedicated to Torpedic Study.

"You and I might consider it a repetitive life, routine beyond belief, yet El P. is nothing if not a Cyclickal Creature. _Sí_," to the apparently attentive _Gymnotus_, "_una Criatura Cíclica, así eres._... Departure and return have been design'd into his life. If he had to live the way we do, worrying about Coach schedules and miss'd appointments and Sheriff Thickley,"— cheers at the local Reference,— "believe me, he'd be one unhappy Torpedo. How do I know? I counted.— As a condition of Life, Felípe needs Rhythm.

"And so I believe do we. Did I see my Banjo somewhere?— ah, there 'tis." Striking up an Accompaniment curiously syncopated, he sings,

> Lads and Lasses, pass on down,
> 'Tis the world-renown'd Torpe-do,—
> Quite the Toast of London Town,
> Admir'd in far-off E-do,—
> Na-bobs, Kings and Potentates too, all
> Gawkin' at the shockin' sort of things he'll do, for
> A tuppenny, step up 'n' he will do, you, too,—
> The Torpedo, Voo-
> -Ly Voo!

Ev'ry Fop clear back to Philadelphia must be in Attendance this Evening, sporting bright glaucous Waistcoats, Suits of staggeringly tasteless Brocade, outlandishly dress'd Wigs, Shoes with heels higher than the stems of Wine-glasses, Stockings unmatch'd in Colors incompatible, such as purple and green, strange opaque Spectacles in both these shades and many others. They flourish Snuff-boxes and pocket-flasks about, and giggle without surcease. As to the Hats,— far better not even to open the subject. 'Tis as if to cross Schuylkill were to transgress as well some Rubicon of style, to fall from Quaker simplicity into the Perplexity, uncounted times broken and re-broken, of the World after Eden. "I can see it'll take a lot to shock a crowd like this!" cries the Professor.

All are pleas'd to hold the same Opinion, and cheer. At a gesture from his Exhibitor, Felípe stands straight up in his Tank and bows right and left. The Professor takes out an Antillean Cigar, bites the end off, produces two Wires, and with a supply of Gum attaches them precisely upon the Animal's body. Felípe allows it, though like any train'd beast he will make a half-hearted Lunge now and then toward the busy pair of hands, his Jaws stretching wide enough to allow Spectators to marvel and shiver at the Ranks of Dirk-sharp Teeth. The Professor moves the free ends of the wires slowly together,— suddenly between them leaps a giant Spark, blindingly white, into which the intrepid Operator thrusts one end of his Cigar, whilst sucking furiously upon the other, bringing it away at last well a-glow.

Mason stares, bedazzl'd. He is slow to respond to Dixon's hand upon his shoulder, shaking him. "Not a good idea to be staring directly into that Spark...?— Charles...?"

"Dixon," a passionately inflected Hiss, directed to something just behind his eyelids, "I saw,— "

"It's all right. It's all right."

"*I saw,—* "

"The Spark was too bright, Mason. All look'd away, but you."

In the hidden Journal that he gets to so seldom it should be styl'd a "Monthly," Mason writes, "I saw at the heart of the Electrick Fire, beyond color, beyond even Shape, an Aperture into another Dispensation of Space, yea and Time, than what Astronomers and Surveyors are us'd to working with. It bade me enter, or rather it welcom'd my Spirit,— yet my Body was very shy of coming any nearer,— indeed wish'd the

Vision gone. Throughout, the Creature in the Tank regarded me with a *personal stare*, as of a Stranger claiming to know me from some distant, no longer accessible Shore,— a mild and nostalgic look, masking, as I fear'd, Blood or Jungle, with the luminous Deep of his great Spark all the while beckoning....

"I can no more account for it than for the other Episodes. I do not choose these moments, nor would I know how. They come upon me with no premonition. Shall I speak with Dixon? Is it an hallucinatory symptom of a Melancholia further advanced than I knew? Should I seek the counsel, God help me, of the cherubick Pest, Cherrycoke? He will take down ev'ry Word he can remember. (Might it prove of use, in any future Claims for Compensation, to be recorded, at what's sure to be impressive Length, as having sought Spiritual Assistance?)

"How can I explain the continuing Fascination of the Torpedo? Were I it, I know I should have grown restless with the same set of Tricks night after night, and perhaps even disposed to Annoyance. But the Eel's facial expression is strangely benevolent and wise,— we spend a few minutes each morning sitting together whilst I take Coffee,— the Creature gazing in silence, relax'd, Fins a-ripple, enjoying these Quiescent hours of his Electrical Day for as long as he may...."

"For too soon the Charge," as the Professor declaims each night, "growing irresistibly, will be felt along the line of his Spine, to be follow'd closely by the emergence, from the great Shade outside the sens'd World, of the Other,— El Peligroso, whose advent the mild-manner'd Felípe you see here is quite helpless to prevent."

Meals consist so far mostly of locally caught fish, though Felípe is far from particular, having lately for example acquir'd a liking for Salt Beef. "Return to his native Hemisphere,— " the Professor mumbling, "strange variations in Salinity as in Diet, yet perhaps 'tis magnetickal, for as is lately discover'd, the Needle's Deflexion followeth, like Felípe, a Diurnal Cycle...." Yet behind the patter lurks the unspoken possibility that outside, perhaps even *just* outside, the widening sphere of Felípe's food interests, waits human Flesh.

Abandoning the Tub, the Professor builds a larger circular Tank, and mounts it upon wheels, so that daily it may be situated directly upon the Line. Felípe then slowly rotates until his head is pointing north.

Presently he has become the camp Compass, as often consulted as the Thermometer or the Clock.

" 'Cordin' to this Torpedo, north's over that way."

"Best keep an eye out tomorrow, next day, see if ol' Felípe changes his heading, we might be able to triangulate us in on to some big iron lode, quit this slavin', make our Fortunes quicker than loggin', quicker than Hemp-fields,— "

"Aye," comments Squire Haligast, who has join'd the Party, "for without Iron, Armies are but identically costum'd men holding Bows, and Navies but comely gatherings of wrought Vegetation."

"Cap'n, when we're rich, you can write all our business Letters."

"Put you in a sort of Booth, right out in front of the Mine, with a big sign overhead saying QUERIES."

"Shall I have a Pistol?" the Squire in a playful Tone.

"Why, a Cannon if you'd like. Just run you one up straight from the Comp'ny Forge."

"Boys, Boys," rumbles the imminent Overseer Barnes, "We aren't quizzing with the Squire again are we, we know the consequences of that well enough don't we by now?"

"They are Lads," says the Squire. "Having a dream together. No harm."

43

When at the end of February they arrive at Newark, the Surveyors find secure behind the Bar a pile of Correspondence forwarded to them by Mr. Chew, wherein lies news both cheery and crushing. There is the Possibility of further Engagement in America, measuring a Degree of Latitude for the Royal Society. There is also a letter from John Bird, with news of Maskelyne's elevation to H.M. Astronomer.

"You were expecting me to scream, weren't you?"

"No,— no, Mason, tha being a grown Man and all,— "

"Actually, I'm quite reliev'd. Didn't need that on my Mind, did I? Arh, arh! Let us be blithe about it, for goodness' sake! What a wonderful Omen under which to begin the West Line," Mason raising his Tankard with an abruptness advisable only in Rooms where one's Face is known. "At the very moment he was elevated, I lay flat upon a Back that for all I knew was broken, in a desert place in New Jersey."

"We're curs'd, you knew thah'...?" Dixon tries to bear down and attend closely. "And none could have foreseen,— "

"Oh, Maskelyne knew that Bradley was ill,"— Mason attempting to be chirpy is less easy to bear than Mason in blackest Melancholy,— "ev'ryone knew it, as ev'ryone knew that Bliss would come on only as Caretaker, for he as well was old, and ailing, yet there should be time enough left him, for each Aspirant to make his interest as he might...."

"Why aye, and yet you always knew he cultivated— "

" 'Cultivated,'— poh. Maskelyne caress'd, and slither'd, insinuating himself into an old man's esteem,— for having done nothing, really, one more lad from Cambridge, clever with Numbers, tho' none beyond that damn'd Tripos Riddling, who but happens to be Clive of fucking India's, fucking, Brother-in-law! Ahhr, Dixon! this seventh Wrangler, this bilious, windy Hypnotick in the Herbal of human character, this mean-spirited intriguer,— his usage of poor Mr. Harrison, and his Chronometer, how contemptible. Few are his ideas, Lunarian is his one Faith, to plod is his entire Project. He will never make any discovery on the order of Aberration, nor Nutation,— he is unworthy, damn him! to succeed James Bradley." His face is wet, more with Spittle than Tears.

"Eeh, Mason." Dixon by now has learn'd to stay at a respectful distance, and not to rely too heavily upon Touch as a way of communicating. "You believ'd... Really...?"

"Oh well, 'really,'— it's like a Woman, isn't it, you look at each other, you think Of course not, she thinks Of course not,— yet the Alternatives hang about, don't they, like Wraiths."

"Eehh, City Matters, would I knoah anything about thah'?"

"I was up there four years, I lost two women I lov'd, God help me. I lost Bradley, dear to me as well. Were Tears Sixpences, I'd have more invested in that miserable hilltop than Maskelyne could borrow, be the co-signer Clive himself. Well, let him never sleep. Let him pace those rooms, one after another, in the idled silence of the afternoons, till he hears the voices telling him he has no right there, and to go away. Let him stand at last in the Octagon Room, and shiver in the height of Summer. Let him fear to stay up for stars that culminate too late,— Aahhrrhh!"

"Mason,— aren't Maskelyne and Morton both Cambridge men? Wasn't it Morton who put his name forward? They must have wanted one of their own...?"

"The last three A.R.'s were all Oxford men."

"There's a difference?"

Mason stares, then says slowly, "Yes, Dixon, there is a difference.... *And* he went in as a bloody Sizar, I could have done *that*,— don't you think I was 'one of their own'? What, then, the Bastard Son? The faithful old Drudge in the Background? Haven't I any standing in this? Is that what this fucking exile in America's about then, Morton and his fucking Royal Society,— to get me out of the way so that Maskelyne can go prancing up to Greenwich freed of opposition,— "

"So, Ah'm dragg'd along in the wake of your ill fortune, eeh, another bonny mess...?"

"Might teach you to take care whom your name gets attach'd to. Ahrrhh! Ruin!" He pulls his Hat over his Eyes, and begins to pound his Head slowly upon the Table.

"According to this," Dixon soothingly, as if 'twere a Fan, waving a Page, enclos'd with the letter, clipp'd from the *Gentlemen's Magazine* of the December previous, "there were, it seems, ten, competing for the job,— Betts, Bevis, Short...so on. Any of those names light a Match?" Though reaching the outskirts of Forbearance, can he really continue? Yes, he ought to. Either Mason cannot admit there's a Class problem here, or, even this deeply compromised, he may yet somehow keep Faith that in the Service of the Heavens, dramatic Elevations of Earthly Position are to be expected of these Times, this Reign of Reason, by any reasonable man. Very well, "Mason, you are a Miller's Son. That can never satisfy them."

"What of it?" Mason snaps back, "Flamsteed was a Maltster's Son. Halley was a Soap-boiler's Son. Astronomers Royal are suppos'd to be social upstarts, for Mercy's sake. And I'd friends in the Company," inflecting this, however, with a Snort and a sidewise Tilt of the Head, assuming Dixon knows roughly how Sam Peach and Clive of India might sort out upon the Company's own Chain of Being.

"Did you and Maskelyne talk about any of this when you were together at St. Helena?"

"Are you insane?"

"Oh, off and on...? And thee?"

"Bradley's Name may have come up."

"And Maskelyne,— may I speculate?— said, 'Has he given Thought to a Successor?' "

"Why, that's amazing. You might have been there. What is it about you people, some mystickal Gift, I imagine."

"Ahnd,— he didn't say, 'Mason, though clearly I would welcome your support, I'm going to have this A.R. job with or without it,' anything like thah'?"

"Why are you trying to get me to re-live this? It was unpleasant enough the first time."

"So as to avoid it m'self, of course."

"I shall get thro' this, Dixon."

"Were I thee, I should make him feel guilty ev'ry chance I got. Perhaps he doubts his own Worthiness. Tha must never make it too obvious, of course, always the dignified Sufferer,— yet there is no predicting what Advantage tha may build, upon his Uncertainty."

"Why bless me, Sir,— you are a Jesuit, after all. Sinister Alfonso, move aside,— sheathe that Stiletto, wicked Giuseppe,— here is the true Italian Art."

"*I-o?* Why, I am simple as a pony, Sir...?— born in a Drift, a Corf for my cradle, and nought but the Back-shift for Schoolmasters there...?"

44

"Now, many is the philosophickal Mind,— including my own,— convinced that rapid motion through the air is possible along and above certain invisible straight Lines, crossing the earthly land-scape, particularly in Britain, where they are known as *Ley-lines*. Any number of devout enthusiasts, annual Stonehenge and Ave-bury Pilgrims, Quacks, Mongers, Bedlamites,— each has his tale of real flights over the countryside, above these Ley-lines. Withal, 'tis possible to transfer from one of them to another, and thus in theory travel to the furthest reaches of the Kingdom, without once touching the Earth. Something is there, that permits it. No one knows what it is, tho' thousands speculate.

"Here went we off upon the most prodigious such Line yet attempted,— in America, where undertakings of its scale are possible,— astronomically precise,— carefully set prisms of Oölite,— the Master-valve of rose Quartz, at the eastern Termi-nus. Any Argument from Design, here, must include a yearning for Flight, perhaps even higher and faster than is customary along Ley-lines we know. I try not to wonder. I must wonder. Whenever the Surveyors separate, they run into Thickets, Bogs, bad Dreams,— united, they pursue a ride through the air, they are link'd to the stars, to that inhuman Precision, and are deferr'd to because of it, tho' also fear'd and resented...."

— Wicks Cherrycoke, *Spiritual Day-Book*

March is snowy and frozen, clear nights are rare, and the Surveyors need ev'ry one they can get for Azimuth observations to find out the exact

Direction westward, to strike off in. Ev'rything upon the Ground, by April, as they're about to begin the West Line, must be sighted thro' a haze of green Resurrection.

"There'll be more out there than Stars to gaze at," says Mr. Harland, who's hired on as an Instrument-Bearer at five shillings a day. "Over Susquehanna,— once you've cross'd the York to Baltimore Road,— you'll see."

"I grew up west of that Road," adds Mrs. Harland, "and he ain't just hummin' 'Love in a Cottage,' either. 'Tis not for ev'rybody,— I know I lit East as soon's I was tall enough to cry in the right Uncle's ale-can, and it's also how I met the Wild Ranger here, who's never been west of Elk Creek. Maybe it's not even for you, Johnny."

"Tho' we do understand your Sentiments, Ma'am," Mason advises, "we are legally restrain'd from intervening in anyone's family business."

"Ah well, too bad, tried my best, fate is fate, Lord'll provide," she carols, bustling back into the House.

"Took it awfully well, I thought," says Mason.

"Maybe not," John Harland shaking his head as he follows her in. "Better go see."

"She never actually said she wanted him off the Crew," Dixon notes.

"It's what she meant. You have to understand them, Dixon, they've this silent language, that only men of experience speak at all fluently."

"Then why is it I've lost count of how many of my evenings tha've ruin'd, with thy talk of Cannibalism, or Suicide, or Bickering among the Whigs...? anything, but what 'they' wish to hear?"

"Unannounc'd blow."

Robert Boggs comes running by with fifty-weight of Harness hanging from each Shoulder. "Some Stranger over there by the Monument, acting peculiar." Off he runs again.

They go to see,— and there he is, up in the corner of Harland's field, curiously prostrated before the chunk of Rose Quartz where cross the Latitude of the south Edge of Philadelphia, and the Longitude of the Post Mark'd West,— the single Point to which all work upon the West Line (and its eastward Protraction to the Delaware Shore) will finally refer. All about, in the Noontide, go Waggoners and Instrument-Bearers in Commotion, preparing for the Translation south to Mr. Bryant's Field, and the

Post Mark'd West. Swifts come out in raiding-parties, but avoid the luminous Stone,— Dogs wait at what they've learn'd is a safe distance from it.

"Quite powerful," when they have coax'd him back at last to their own regime of Light, "— where'd you boys find this one? Whoo-ee!" He has been trying to find what in his Calling is known as the "Ghost," another Crystal inside the ostensible one, more or less clearly form'd. " 'Tis there the Pictures appear...tho' it varies from one Operator to the next,— some need a perfect deep Blank, and cannot scry in Ghost-Quartz. Others, before too much Clarity, become blind to the other World...my own Crystal,"— he searches his Pockets and produces a Hand-siz'd Specimen with a faint Violet tinge,— "the Symmetries are not always easy to see...here, these twin Heptagons...centering your Vision upon their Common side, gaze straight in,— "

"Aahhrrhh!" Mason recoiling and nearly casting away the crystal.

"Huge, dark Eyes?" the Scryer wishes to know.

"Aye.— Who is it?" Mason knows.

"The Face I see is a bit more friendly,— but then 'twould have to be, wouldn't it, or I'd be in some other line of Work."

His name is Jonas Everybeet, and in the time he travels with the Party, he will locate, here and there across the Land, Islands in Earth's Magnetic Field,— Anomalies with no explanation for being where they are,— other than conscious intervention by whoever or whatever was here before the Indians. "Anyone's Guess what they're for. And then your own very long Row of Oölite Shafts. Perfectly lin'd up with the Spin of the Earth. Suggestive, anyhow."

"Of what?"

"Think of Mr. Franklin's Armonica. Rather than a Finger circling upon the stationary Rim of a Glass, the Finger keeps still, whilst the Rim rotates. As long as there is movement *between* the two, a note is produc'd. Similarly, this Oölite Array, at this Latitude, is being spun along at more than seven hundred miles per hour,— spun thro' the light of the Sun, and whatever Medium bears it to us. What arises from this? What Music?"

Ev'ryone has a Point of View they wish to persuade the Surveyors to. "Sometimes you're the Slate," Mason observes, "sometimes you're the Chalk."

"Eeehh!" Dixon frowns. "And here again is that bothersome Crimp, O'Rooty." The Body-jobber offering them his Services, can arrange, he declares, for "any Work-force, at any level of skill, anywhere you want, when you want them. For instance I imagine you'll be needing some axmen. Hey? Do I know this Business? First thing to decide is how much you want to spend,— local Lads at three and six *per Diem*, or, for what prices out to but a few farthings more,"— picks up a couple of Powder-Horns, places them either side of his head,— "Scandinavians! yes, the famous Swedish Loggers, each the equal of any ten Axmen these Colonies may produce. Finest double-bit Axes, part of the Package, life-time Warranty on the Heads, seventy-two-hour replacement Policy, cus-tomiz'd Handle for each Axman, for 'Bjorn may not swing like Stig, nor Stig like Sven,' as the famous Timothy Tox might say,— Swedish Steel here, secret Processes guarded for years, death to reveal them, take you down a perfect swathe of Forest, trimm'd and cleared, fast as you're likely to chain the distance.— Parts of a single great Machine,— human muscle and stamina become but adjunct to the deeper realities of Steel that never needs Sharpening, never rusts,— "

"Oh, come, Sir!" the Surveyors exclaim together.

"So then take but one, take Stig here, on a trial basis only, pay what you think he's worth, if you don't like him, send him back.— "

Next in line behind O'Rooty comes a "Developer," or Projector of Land-Schemes.

"Kill him," advises Dixon, before anyone can get in a word. Mason risks a quick lateral Squint, but can neither see nor smell any sign of Intoxication. "And do it sooner rather than later, as it only gets more dif-ficult with time."

Since early in their acquaintance, the two have learn'd to mutter together so as to remain unheard beyond a Pipe-stem's Length. The Pro-jector, devotedly binocular and far too brisk, moves in an industrious Hop from one foot to the other, back and forth. "This is someone you know?" Mason not yet all that alarm'd.

"In general only. But work'd for enough of them, didn't I. Not proud of m'self for it. Needed the money." So abridg'd is this reply that Mason sur-mises some long and probably tangled Iliad of Woe back among the

Friths and Fells, which did not work out in Favor of Dixon, who continues, "Well, then...? Whah's thy preference?"

"Ehm,— what?"

"As to which of us will do the Deed."

"Deed...?"

"You know,— " cocking a rigid Finger toward their Visitor, who at last
grows aware of being under Discussion.

"Um, Dixon,— come back to the Tent for a moment, would you...
yes...yes there's a good chap,— just a word,— excuse us, please, small
technical Question, quite trivial really,— come along, good, there we go."
Mason, having visited Bedlam as well as Tyburn, in a profound Mime of
calm and Patience, Dixon playing his part with equal vigor, using as his
models any number of Lunaticks to be found in Bishop, any market day.

The first day of the West Line, April 5th, falls upon a Friday,— the least
auspicious day of the week to begin any enterprise, such as sailing from
Spithead, for example.

To stand at the Post Mark'd West, and turn to face West, can be a trial
for those sentimentally inclin'd, as well as for ev'ryone nearby. It is possible to feel the combin'd force, in perfect Enfilade, of ev'ry future second unelaps'd, ev'ry Chain yet to be stretch'd, every unknown Event to
be undergone,— the unmodified Terror of keeping one's Latitude.

They have been held up by the Weather,— first Snow, which by the
fourth day, even undrifted, has reached a depth of two feet and nine
inches,— then clouded Skies, which prolong the impossibility of Zenith
observations. Thursday night the fourth, the Sky is finally clear enough
for them to determine their Latitude exactly. The next day, the weather
holding, they decide not to waste the Friday, but to seize it, bad luck
and all.

A few wrinkles to be smooth'd. Messrs. Darby and Cope have left till
the last Minute, the Question of who's to go before, and who behind, upon
the Chain. The phrases "Good enough" and "More or less" must be dis-
couraged from the outset. Rules of precedence for Dixon's Circumferentor have to be work'd out, principally that, in case of Conflict, it must
ever defer to the Sector,— Astronomy before Magnetism.

At last, Mr. Cope pulls up his Bob, and gathers and stows his Plumb-line, thus removing his end of the Chain from the Post Mark'd West,— proceeding then in that Direction, across the snowy Field, to Mr. Darby's former Station. Detachment. The beginning of the West.

So they set off, the Chain a-jingle, Waggons a-rumble, farm Geese a-blare, heading into Farmland with a quiet Roll to it, watch'd by deer and kine, under the usual injunctions against trampling Garden patches or molesting Orchards, the Instruments, with a Tent of their own, stranger than anything the Party expects to see between here and Little Christiana,— which isn't much anyway, owing to the Trees, for which eleven more Axmen hire on, the second week.

"You'd think these Instruments were alive," Matthew Marine grumbles, "riding in Waggons upon feather Mattresses, whilst we slodge along behind, don't we?"

"May be they are alive, Matty."

"Aye and from someplace very far away 's well, Matty."

"Accounts for why they look all Brass and Glass and all…?"

"Boys now don't be telling me such things,— do you swear?"

Nodding solemnly, "Far, far away, Matt."

"Distant and strange."

"New-Jersey?"

"They do need tender Handling, boys," young Nathanael McClean tries sternly to advise the five-shilling Hands.

"Like your Mother's Pussy," is the reply.

"My Mother?" counters the young Swamper equably, "Say,—

Just saw your Mother, going out, to shoot,
Somebody stepp'd on her Infantry Boots,— "

"Aye? Well,—

I saw your Mother, and I Quiz you not,—
Drinking penny-Gin from a Chamber-Pot."

"Ladies, please, there are Gentlemen present," announces Overseer of the Axmen Moses Barnes ("Is ev'ry body 'round here nam'd Moses?"), seven and six per week, approaching with a heaviness of Step often felt minutes before his actual appearance. "Hark, is it Poetry? dear me Cedric, where've I put my Quill?" Those anxious to be his friends greet this with prolong'd Mirth. Barnes is a large Enforcer of Rules, with beefy undeluded eyes and a Reluctance to be far from the Cook Tent. Having long intimidated Commissaries into serving him gigantic piles of food, he has achiev'd a Mass 'twould shame a Military Waggon. Implicit in most of his dealings with the Axmen is the threat that should they fail to comply closely enough with his Wishes, this enormous yet mobile Weight may in some way unspoken,— and, 'tis further implied, unspeakable,— be directed against them.

Takes them less than a week to run the Line thro' somebody's House. About a mile and a half west of the Twelve-Mile Arc, twenty-four Chains beyond Little Christiana Creek, on Wednesday, April 10th, the Field-Book reports, "At 3 Miles 49 Chains, went through Mr. Price's House."

"Just took a wild guess," Mrs. Price quite amiable, "where we'd build it,— not as if my Husband's a Surveyor or anything. Which side's to be Pennsylvania, by the way?" A mischievous glint in her eyes that Barnes, Farlow, Moses McClean and others will later all recall. Mr. Price is in Town, in search of Partners for a Land Venture. "Would you Gentlemen mind coming in the House and showing me just where your Line does Run?" Mason and Dixon, already feeling awkward about it, oblige, Dixon up on the Roof with a long Plumb-line, Mason a-squint at the Snout of the Instrument. Mrs. Price meantime fills her Table with plates of sour-cherry fritters, Neat's-Tongue Pies, a gigantick Indian Pudding, pitchers a-slosh with home-made Cider,— then producing some new-hackl'd Streaks of Hemp, and laying them down in a Right Line according to the Surveyors' advice,— fixing them here and there with Tacks, across the room, up the stairs, straight down the middle of the Bed, of course,…which is about when Mr. Rhys Price happens to return from his Business in town, to find merry Axmen lounging beneath his Sassafras tree, Strange Stock mingling with his own and watering out of his Branch, his house invaded by Surveyors, and his wife giving away the Larder and waving her Tankard about, crying, "Husband, what Province were we married in? Ha! see him gape, for he cannot remember. 'Twas in Pennsylvania, my Tortoise. But never in Maryland. Hey? So from now on, when I am upon this side of the House, I am in Maryland, legally not your wife, and no longer subject to your Authority,— isn't that right, Gents?"

"Ask the Rev," they reply together, perhaps having noticed that Mr. Price is carrying a long Pennsylvania Rifle, two horns full of Powder, and a good supply of Balls.

"Eh?" the Rev[d], by all signs unaware of the trouble the Gentlemen are putting him to, not to mention in, beams at the so far but perplex'd back-Inhabitant. "I know but how to perform the Ceremony,— perhaps you need to consult an attorney-at-Law?"

"Separating Neighbors is one thing," Rhys Price declares, "— but separating Husband and Wife,— no wonder you people get shot at all the time. No wonder those Chains are call'd the D——l's Guts." He must struggle to work himself up into a Rage,— owing to an insufficient exposure, so far, to Evil and Sorrow, remaining a Youth who trusts all he may meet, to be as kindly dispos'd as he.

"What'll happen is," Alex McClean advises, "is you'll get hammer'd paying double taxes, visits all the time from Sheriffs of both provinces looking for their quitrents, tax collectors from Philadelphia and Annapolis, and sooner or later you'll have to decide just to get it up on some Logs, and roll it, one way or the other. Depends how your Property runs, I'd guess."

"...as North is pretty much up-hill," Mr. Price is reckoning, " 'twould certainly not be as *easy,* to roll her up into Pennsylvania, as down into Maryland."

"Where I am no longer your Wife," she reminds him.

"Aye, and there's another reason," he nods soberly. "Well then, let's fetch the Boys and get to it,— 'tis Maryland, ho!"

45

Back Inhabitants all up and down the Line soon begin taking the Frenchman's Duck to their Bosoms, for being exactly what they wish to visit their lives at this Moment,— something possess'd of extra-natural Powers,— Invisibility, inexhaustible Strength, an upper Velocity Range that makes her the match, in Momentum, of much larger opponents,— Americans desiring generally, that ev'ry fight be fair. Soon Tales of Duck Exploits are ev'rywhere the Line may pass. The Duck routs a great army of Indians. The Duck levels a Mountain west of here. In a single afternoon the Duck, with her Beak, has plow'd ev'ry Field in the County, at the same time harrowing with her Tail. That Duck!

As to the Duck's actual Presence, Opinions among the Party continue to vary. Axmen, for whom tales of disaster, stupidity, and blind luck figure repeatedly as occasions for merriment, take to shouting at their Companions, "There she goes!" or, "Nearly fetch'd ye one!" whilst those more susceptible to the shifts of Breeze between the Worlds, notably at Twilight, claim to've seen the actual Duck, shimmering into Visibility, for a few moments, then out again.

"I might've tried to draw a bead onto it,...but it knew I was there. It came walking over and look'd me thump in the eye. I was down flat, we were at the same level, see. 'Where am I?' it wants to know. 'Pennsylvania or Maryland, take your pick,' says I. It had this kind of *Expression* onto its Face, and seem'd jumpy. I tried to calm it down. It gave that Hum, and grew vaporous, and disappear'd."

Mason and Dixon attempt to ignore as much of this as they may, both assuming 'tis only another episode of group Folly, to which this Project seems particularly given, and that 'twill pass all too soon, to be replaced by another, and so on, till perhaps, one day, by something truly dangerous.

"They'll believe what they like," groans Mason, "in this Age, with its Faith in a Mechanickal Ingenuity, whose ways will be forever dark to them. God help this Mobility. They have to take all Projectors upon Trust,— half of whom have nothing to sell, who know nonetheless of this irrational need to believe in automatons, believe that they can sing and dance and play Chess,— even at the end of the Turn, when the latch is press'd and the Midget reveal'd, and the indomitable Hands fall still. Even as Monsieur Vaucanson furls back the last Silk Vestment,— no matter. The Axmen have a need for artificial Life as perverse as any among the Parisian *Haute Monde,* and this French toy, conveniently invisible, seems to— "

"Look out!" Dixon cries. Mason's Hat leaves his head and ascends straight up to the Tree-tops, where it pauses, catching the rays of the Sun, just gone behind tomorrow's Ridge-top. Faint Quacking is heard above.

"Very well," Mason calls, " 'Toy' may've been insensitive. I apologize. 'Device'?"

Armand comes running out. " 'Tis being playful, nothing more. Ah, *Chér-i-e,*" he sings into the Sky. "I'll guarantee their Behavior,— only please return the Gentleman's Hat, *Merci...*" as the Hat comes down Leaf-wise, zigging one way, zagging another, whilst Mason runs back and forth anxiously beneath.

"You'll guarantee what?" Dixon wants to know.

"Whilst advanc'd in some areas, such as Flight and Invisibility," Armand explains, "yet in others does the Duck remain primitive, foremost in her readiness to take offense. You must have notic'd,— she has no shame, any pretext at all will do. As her Metaphysickal Powers increase, so do her worldly Resentments, real and imagin'd, the shape of her Destiny pull'd Earthward and rising Heavenward at the same time,— meanwhile gaining an order of Magnitude, in passing from the personal to the Continental. If not the Planetary." Perhaps fortunately, no one present has any idea what he is talking about.

"I should have puzzl'd more," Mason now admits, "that Dr. Vaucanson was listed among those sent copies of Monsieur Delisle's *Mappemonde* for the Transit of Venus, showing us the preferr'd locations for observing the Event,— arriv'd at the Royal Society in the care of Father Boscovich, years late, owing to the state of the Rivalry,— I assum'd as ev'ryone did, that the great *Automateur,* having an interest in the Celestial Escapement above, and the date of the Event being sure as Clockwork, had early announc'd his intention to observe the impending Alignment,— or even more simply, that he enjoy'd Esteem at the *Académie.* But between the Invention of the Duck, and the observation of the Transit, there lies yet a logickal Chasm, as a temporal one, thirty years or more in Width, with no Bridge of Syllogism for Reason to cross, condemn'd rather to roam upstream and down, in search of a way, her Journey delay'd indefinitely upon the nearer side,— "

"The side of the Duck," Armand reminds him.

"Very well,— could it be, that in the Years since the Duck vanish'd, and despite the constant presence of the Duplicate the World knows, Monsieur Vaucanson, in his perusals of the Sky, has come to seek there wonders more than merely Astronomickal? For, having no idea of where or how far his Creature's 'Morphosis may've taken it, where look for Word of its Condition with more hope of success than among the incorruptibly divided Rings of Heaven?"

"Hold, hold," Dixon with exaggerated gentleness, "Mason, he... believes his Duck to've become a Planet, 's what tha're saying?"

"Why are you all edging away from me like that?" Mason's voice pitch'd distraughtly. "For a few moments among the Centuries, we are allow'd to observe her own 'Morphosis, from Luminary to Solid Spheroid...I don't know about you, but if I had a Duck disappear from me that way, I should certainly be attending closely the Categories of rapid Change, such as the Transit afforded, for evidence of the Creature's Passage." Even without the face full of discomfort Mason displays, Dixon would have understood this as yet another gowkish expression of grieving for his Wife.

"Someone's wrecking the Squash, I think," Armand backing into the Cook-tent, colliding with young Hickman emerging with a stack of Pots and Pans headed for the Scullery, which all promptly go scattering in ev'ry direction, more than once passing but inches from people's Heads.

"Nothing personal," both, nearly in unison, assure Mason.

Such is the Duck's Influence in the Camp, that several Axmen approach the Rev^d upon the Topick of Angels in general. "For instance," carols young Nathe McClean, lately dazy for a Milkmaid of the Vicinity, "tho' we know the Duck has been transform'd by Love, what of the Angels,— that is, may they...um..."

"Aye, they do that, Lad, and they drink and smoke, and dance and gamble withal. Thought ev'ryone knew that. Some might even define an Angel as a Being who's powerful enough not to be destroy'd by Desire in all its true and terrible Dimensions. Why,— a drop of their Porter? 'twould kill the hardiest drinker among ye,— they smoke Substances whose most distant Scent would asphyxiate us,— their Dancing-floors extend for Leagues, their Wagering, upon even a single trivial matter, would beggar Clive of India. And who's to say that Human sin, down here, may not arise from this very inadequacy of ours, this failure of Scale, before the sovereign commands of Desire,— "

"Sin as practis'd is not deep enough for you, Sir?" inquires Dixon.

"Why is it that we honor the Great Thieves of Whitehall, for Acts that in Whitechapel would merit hanging? Why admire the one sort of Thief, and despise the other? I suggest, 'tis because of the Scale of the Crime.— What we of the Mobility love to watch, is any of the Great Motrices, Greed, Lust, Revenge, taken out of all measure, brought quite past the scale of the ev'ryday world, approaching what we always knew were the true Dimensions of Desire. Let Antony lose the world for Cleopatra, to be sure,— not Dick his Day's Wages, at the Tavern."

46

When they may, they drink. So does ev'ryone else. Presently as they come more and more under the jurisdiction of the Night Sky, they drink less after Dark, finding it impossible to look out into *That,* however narrow'd the Field, with Vision in any way a-wobble, and be expected to work the micrometer, take readings, note the Time, and perform an hundred other tasks, most of them unforgivingly in need of Accuracy. Cloudy nights, of course, being exceptions to this Rule, are welcom'd by all.

Each ten Minutes of Great Circle, about ev'ry twelve miles, their Intention is to pause, set up the Sector and determine their Latitude, then figure the offsets to the true Line over the distance they've just come,— the true Line that has run along with them, at their left hands, an invisible Companion, but Yards away, in the Brush, outside the Fire-light.

Twelve miles from the Post Mark'd West, the Party crosses the Road from Octarara to Christiana Bridge, with a Farm-House close by, upon the Pennsylvania side. Here they set up camp, and begin their Latitude Work. Axmen set off in search of Food. The fragrant noontide so quiet you may hear the shuffling of Playing-cards.... 'Tis a Saturday, in that lull when all the Sellers have pass'd early into Town, and most of the Buyers, and families who dwell within a few hours by Waggon have not yet begun to head back home. Now and then, horsemen dismount at the

Tavern a few Chains up the Road, as others come wobbling back from it, sometimes deciding to sleep overnight here in Camp.

After half a dozen such have dropp'd into midday Slumber, "Do we encourage this?" Mason asks himself aloud, in Dixon's hearing. "Suppose but one of them is a French Agent, pretending to be drunk, perhaps even bent upon our Dissolution,— "

"As Christians, have we any choice but to allow all who wish, to enter freely?" offers Dixon.

"Ahrrh, well, as you put it that way...."

The Crew, now up to thirty Hands, having, in their first ten minutes of Arc, cross'd three Creeks and a River, and gone thro' one House, are dispos'd to a merry week-end, tho' mornings, when the demands of Recompense fall heaviest, are not to be altogether restful, so near is Octarara Road. Waggons-ful of Iron Products,— Bar and Rod Stock, Nails, Hatchets and Knives,— drawn by teams of Oxen, pass slowly, a-clank and a-creak, each step a Drama, left to right, right to left, across the Visto, all the Day. When Night falls, the Drivers unhitch and out-span their Teams, and make fires, and stay up drinking well past the Culminations of the later Stars, for Mason and Dixon, attending the Clock, the Plumb-line, the eternal Heavens, can hear them in dispute, often upon some point of religion. "Unco' Quantity of Iron upon the Road," comments Dixon. " 'Tis running me old Needle amok."

"Aye, as if the Prussian Army's about someplace," Mason none too pleas'd with any of it.

First thing Monday morning, they all come staggering from Bedrolls and Latrines to stand in loose Ranks and be tallied in. Overseer Barnes reads the Plan of the Day, the Rev^d comes by to say a short Prayer, then Special Requests are submitted, a few in writing, but most aloud and expected to be dealt with upon the Spot. Some mornings the Petitioning grows agitated indeed, with only the clanging of the Breakfast Alarm able to interrupt it.

"He's telling them Parrot Jokes again."

"Who is?"

"You know,...him."

"Ehud? is this true, what he's saying?"

"Mr. Barnes, Cap'n, Sir, all I said was, 'Sailor walks into a Tavern with a Parrot on his Shoulder, young Lass says,— ' "

"There! he's doing it again!"

" ' "What'll it be?" and the Parrot says,— ' "

"Two hours' extra Duty, Ehud. Yes, Mr. Spinney."

" 'Tis the Porridge again, Cap'n. As previously sworn, I can't abide an Oat mill'd that way, and they all know it in the Commissary, yet each morning, looking up at me from the Bowl,— faugh,— one more deliberate Insult. The cooks all snickering.... How long before I must begin to vomi', I'd like to know?"

"Then you must grind your own, Lad,— as the Indians do, between Stones. There's boiling water in the Cook-tent, ask politely and they may let you have some of that."

"Thankee Cap'n as ever, yet there abides the question of the Salt?"

"I'll have a word with 'em, Spinney. Now, is it...too much? or too little, Salt, exactly?"

"On second thought never mind, Cap'n."

"You're sure, now, 'tis no trouble.... Wonderful. And now whom do I see, but aye, Mr. Sweet, back again are we, how repetitious. Let me divine what your Request may be."

"My mate,— he was a Philadelphia Lawyer once, but gave it all up for the freedom of the Forest,— he says that, as an Expedition over land is like a ship at sea, Mr. Mason may, like a ship's Captain, exercise certain prerogatives,— "

"Ah," Mr. Barnes raising a huge hand, "and a lovelier lass was never seen this side of the previous cow-shed I'm sure, yet, how long can this go on, boy? Were you a woman, I'd say you were but flighty, and there'd be an end. But in a Lad, you know, it makes me apprehensive. Suppose you do marry one of them,— what happens when you meet the next?"

"Um...wait let me ask my Mate...."

"Chat with ye tomorrow, Sir? Lovely, and remember me to your Betroth'd. And your Mate, of course. Next? Mr. McNutley,— it's been near a year, man,— not another one in the works? All the best, and ye're such a scraggy Ancient, too."

"My thinking, Cap'n,— tho' some say hop to it just after the Harvest, so they'll give birth and be up again in time for next Harvest,— but I say just before Planting's better, so they can help wi' that, yet not be so far along by Harvest, that they can't help considerable wi' that, too. Howbeit, my Gwen, she's due in a month or two, I think, and I ought to be with her, pretty soon,— "

"Grow Titts," Mr. Barnes advises, "and learn to talk for an Hour without taking a Breath, and maybe as she grows more daz'd with her Pregnancy, she'll mistake ye for another Woman, taking from it what comfort she may. Otherwise, 'tis the Company of Women she needs, not the Author of it all, thumping about."

On they come, still too ill-assorted, too newly hir'd, to know what they may profitably expect, and what will ever remain hopeless,— tho' some will develop a taste for the exquisite discomforts of Rejection. Here is a protest, not the first, about Mrs. Eggslap's troublesome habit of extorting a higher fee once her Services are in Progress. This time 'tis Stig, the Swedish Axman. He speaks no English, Mr. Barnes no Swedish,— yet all have heard the dismal story before. At least once in every Sentence, Stig cries, "Yingle-Yangle! Yingle-Yangle!" denoting...Something of importance to him.

"Here is young Mr. McClean, he's just the one you ought to see, Stig,— yah yah, yoost the vun?"

Nathanael, the youngest of the McCleans, is here working during his summer "Vacation" from College in Williamsburg. At first, the Crew accorded him the Drone of intimate Insult, which is ever the Tender-Foot's Lot,— up to a point, at least, for his Father and Brothers are here, well in control of all aspects of the Expedition, from turning Angles to peeling Potatoes. Soon,— how, none can say,— the Axmen have assign'd to Nathanael a Character, closer to Macheath than to the diligent Factotum he knows himself to be, tho' he's tried to explain what in this Party he is and isn't,— yet do they expect him to take Bribes, to wink at Gambling, to keep local Justices of the Peace and Sheriffs satisfied,— above all, they continue to regard him as the Bully who protects Mrs. Eggslap and all her fair Colleagues, who some days have number'd in the Dozens. Hence Mr. Barnes's patent relief at Nathe's appearance now.

"He only *looks* like a kid,— but he's dangerous,— too dangerous for me." This from Moses Barnes, generally adjudg'd too dangerous for ev'rybody else. "Hello, Mr. McClean, quite another scorcher today, isn't it? Hope ev'rything's to your satisfaction?"

"Oh, come on, then," Nathe says, "I'm on my way to see Mo anyhow." They proceed to the Mess Tent, where Moses McClean is sitting in front of and frowning at a Pile of Accompts.

"As he is employ'd here but upon trial," Moses supposes, "his expenses may legitimately be withheld from the Books,"— and thus are they able to pacify Stig with a Sum whose Immediacy out-dazzles its Modesty. Yet Nathe is not quite free of the Matter, for Mrs. Eggslap accosts him in the muddy shade behind the cook-tent. "I do wish you wouldn't keep saying 'Extortion,' " she pleads more than once. Nathe makes the mistake of asking her, then, what does she think it is? "I knew we'd reach an understanding," grasping his hand and placing it upon her Hip, as if they were about to Dance.

"That Stig," Nathe blurts, "— you know he don't even speak English, Mizziz E. You took unfair advantage."

"Nathanael, my hasty Puddin', he brings that Ax to bed. He talks to it, and wants me to do the same. 'Oh,— oh how d'ye do, there,' says I to it, as so would you, were it being wiggl'd at you by some piece o' logging machinery with an Erection. Then he starts in with the 'Yingle-Yangle!' Right? 'Yingle-Yangle!' " I know *that* accent well, 'tis from the Neighborhood of Bedlam. Is that blushing, Nathe, or but the Sun in that innocent Face? Have ye never heard of Bonus Pay for hazardous Duty? that's what I was adding on."

"Fifty percent?" he's heedless enough to remind her.

"For you, my turtle-dove, I'd cap it at, oh let's say half o' that,— twenty-five?"

"It's still ext— well, exorbitant."

"Hmm. Five of it to you, of course."

"Five percent!"

"Oh, all right, ten, I never could resist a sweet Face." She swiftly kisses him, pressing into his hand some sort of Bank-note, and is off in a Wake of Jasmine Absolute.

As if waiting upon an invisible Queue, up next pops the Pass-Bank Bully Guy Spit, with another offer of a share in the Pass Bank proceeds. He is now offering 15 percent, up from 12. He believes Nathe to be a hard bargainer, holding out for more, when in fact the Youth is but trying to avoid an entire new mountain-range of worry in the Terrain already giv'n him to toil up and down in. But it throws all Mr. Spit's calculations out,— indeed, he assures Nathe, 'twould "threaten the very Arrangement," were he to refuse some share.

For all the Warnings Nathe has receiv'd as to avoiding Temptation, he'd not seen the true Article at first hand till this Swamper's Post fell to him, by virtue of his Family's favor with Mason and Dixon. " 'Twill be his salvation," Archibald McClean assur'd the Astronomers. "He is wasting too damn'd much time reading Books. He lives in some world all of us 'd be lucky to inhabit, but do not."

"And so, neither must he?" Mr. Dixon pretending astonishment. "Why, Heavens,— Books aren't going to hurt him…? Once he's found out about them, 'tis too late in any case. One way or another, he'll read whah' he needs to…?"

Mr. McClean, stung, cocks his head. "How many Sons have you, Sir?"

"Eeh, Friend, Ah have but *been* one…?"

"Howbeit, then," Mr. McClean shrugs, and seeks Dixon's Gaze. "Mostly that we'll need the extra Hand?"

Thus, soon, to his Father's unconcern, Nathe is as wildly a-spin, in unsuspected Engagement with Establish'd Greed, as any Nabobescent young Writer out in Bengal. Book-reading is no match, tho' he tries, being loan'd the choicest of limp, creas'd, and spatter'd books of erotick Pictures and Text, staying up to finish an extra chapter in *The Ghastly Fop,* to see how it comes out,— having, at last, no time to read, nor even look at Etchings. By the time he remembers how to unbutton his Breeches, he has fallen asleep. He is now falling asleep, usually face-first, with no warning, into not only his own bowl of Soup, but great Kettles of it as well,— and not only Soup, but Porridge, too. He also falls out of trees, off stools, and into card-games, scattering the hands and coins and usually getting thump'd for it. For days on end, press'd by continual demands, he may eat nothing but a fugitive Crust, sauc'd with the lees of some ale-jack and the Pipe-ash therein,— yet suddenly, as in a Spring flood, will he find himself devouring without pause, through the work-day, anything that comes to hand, or even too close. Mr. Barnes says he has seen Nathe eating in his Sleep, though this may be but more of the Overseer's great Wit.

"Ahoy Murray,— " Nathe writes to his School-friend back in Tidewater Virginia, "was there a Sermon about Greed? did I sleep through it? Nothing has prepar'd me for its Power how unabating, its Fertility how wild, Occasion for it being presented with ev'ry tally-mark, bottle astray, honest Favor, Milkmaid's Douceur, Diversion of Tobacco, exchange of Specie,— ev'ry Numeral utter'd, be it upon paper, or spoken low and allow'd to pass with the next breath into the Forgotten....

"They will forever do me favors I do not need, strings of iridescent Trout, July Cherries by the Bushel, with the Stones already out, land-transaction Advice that would put me in a Mansion upon Rappahannock with hundreds of Slaves and no worries forever,— i.e., rewarded as Pan-derers are, in every Form but Cash, a scarce enough commodity at the Coast,— becoming, further West, at last only another fabl'd American Substance.

"What's happening to me, Murray! This sordid haggling out in the open air, Axmen sidling by with knowing Grins, Girls peering apprehen-sively 'round corners, popping up from bushes to blow me Kisses of encouragement, even Mr. Mason with his Eyebrows up into his Hat, and Mr. Dixon whistling Airs from *The Beggar's Opera*. I am not the sinister Pimp they take me for.— Oh for someone understanding, out here in this endless Forest! We could ride our wing'd Pigs side by side through the Æther, and chat about it all.

" 'Sweet face'! Of course. That's it, without a doubt. They talk to me in high, sing-song Voices. Either I look younger than I am, or people assume I am some kind of Idiot. Is this what books call 'Wheedling'? I have heard my first Wheedling,— like discovering a new species of Bird. 'Tis this curse of being a grown Youth, well clapp'd to Life's Har-ness, yet looking as I did at three. Men don't trust it, more Women than I ever imagin'd find it desirable. I am oblig'd to behave as unnaturally

Male toward the one Sex, as Cherubickally Neutral toward the other. How is it I nonetheless covet ev'ry fair creature who happens, day by day, to appear in the Path of this Line? As it speeds its way like a Coach upon the Coaching-Road of Desire, where we create continually before us the Road we must journey upon, the Axmen as diligent and unobtrusive as the Tailor of Gloucester's Mice...."

47

The Instrument Carriers wait till Monday to go back to Mr. Bryant's and pick up the Sector. "Not so bad so far, d'ye think?" Robert Farlow, who is driving the empty Waggon, remarks to Thomas Hickman, beside him.

"Not bad for Fields we've all work'd in forever." Hickman, who is receiving a shilling more than Farlow this week, bears a worried look. The other six-shilling man, Matt Marine, took himself off up the Bridge Road sometime in the Dark, and hasn't been seen since,— leaving it upon Hickman's shoulders to make sure no harm comes to the Sector. Behind them, back in the dust and wood-smoke, the ringing of ax-bits diminishes with distance. John Harland, and John Hannings, and Kit Myers recline in the Waggon-bed among the Cushions for the Sector, the ragged breeze of their Progress bringing them the pleasing Scents of the Spring-tide, as they roll along the New-Castle Road, two to three miles south of the Line, and roughly parallel to it. Overhead, Birds carry twigs to secret destinations. Beside the Road, Children come running to stare, caps askew, Forks and Churns left to lie. Farmers in Waggons coming the other way wave or sometimes, knowing who they are, glare.

Each time, they set out slightly to the North of West, upon a Bearing that will describe Ten Minutes of Great Circle before intersecting again the true West Line. The Gentlemen know from calculation that the Angle to be turn'd off must be 0°08'18" to the Northward of perfect West. For a while they take Sky Observations to confirm this, Dixon as if in deference to Mason as Astronomer,— but presently they are turning the

Angle directly from the Plate of the Instrument,— a Surveyor's habit, that Dixon may feel more comfortable with, which they drift wordlessly into, beginning to learn, each at his own rate, that the choice not to dispute oftentimes sets free minutes, indeed hours, otherwise wasted in issueless Quarreling. Neither appreciates this at the time.

When they reach the end of each twelve-mile-or-so segment, they stop, and set up the Sector, to find the distances, in Degrees, of several Stars, at their highest points in the Night, from the Zenith. Bradley's Star Catalogue gives the Declination, or Celestial Latitude, for each Star. This value, plus the Zenith Distance, equals the Earthly Latitude of the Observing Point.

Owing to the error in taking Bearings, that ever accompanies the running of a real Arc upon the not quite perfectly spherickal Earth, the Sector will never be set up exactly in the Latitude of the true Line. So Off-sets are figur'd at each Mile, ranging from zero at the eastern end, to whatever the difference in Latitude might prove to be, at the other. These offsets must then be added to the purely geometrical differences, at each Mile, between the ten minutes of Great Circle actually run, and its Chord,— the Line itself,— each time increasing from zero to about twenty-one feet at the halfway point, then decreasing again to zero.

As Fortune had put their first Ten Minutes of Arc close beside Octarara Road, so does their next Stage west allow them to set up the Sector but twenty-six Chains short of the east bank of Susquehanna, a mile and a half of Taverns strung near and nearer along the way up to the Peach Bottom Ferry. On Sunday the twelfth of May, they begin their Zenith Obs again, continuing them till the twenty-ninth. It will be a brisk and pleasant Fortnight beside the broad River, which dashes and rolls 'round two small Islands directly in the line of the Visto. On days of cloud, they endeavor to project the Line across the River, whose breadth they take the occasion to compute,— tho' the task falls mostly to Dixon, being, as Mason informs ev'ryone, more Surveyor's Work, really.

Dixon and Mr. McClean, along with Darby and Cope, go trudging down to the River to have a look. Common practice would be to measure out a Base Line upon the further Bank, set up there, turn off ninety degrees, put a mark on the near side, come back across, set up at the mark there, and find the angle between the two ends of the Base Line,—

then, with the aid of a book full of logarithms, including those of "Trig" functions, 'twould take but a minute and a half of adding and checking, to find the distance across the River.

"That's how we learn'd in Durham," Dixon recalls, "to measure across places we'd rather not go. Not so much Rivers, of course, as unexpected patches,— sudden entire ranges of Spoil-heaps, or a Grove out in an empty Fell,— certainly nowhere near this d——'d many Trees."

"I've found little Joy in these Situations," offers Mr. McClean, whilst Darby and Cope nod at one another, silent as understudies in the Wings, moving their Lips no more than necessary. Sweating and muttering, all go tramping up and down the Bank, kicking up clouds of Gnats, crushing wild Herbs in Blossom, seeking a line of sight that will allow them to use a Right Angle,— a Fool's Errand, as it proves. At length, "Eeh, we'll have to use what Angles we can, then, that bonny with ev'ryone?"

And more than soon enough for the Chain-men, tho' Mr. McClean is shaking his head. "I never get the Figures right."

"Then let huz pre-vail somehow upon Mr. Mason, to review our computing,— Angles being the same,— so I surmise,— down here as Out There." Mr. McClean takes over the eighteen-inch Hadley's, and Dixon repeats his Sights with the Circumferentor, obtaining at last an ungainly Oblique Triangle, from which they calculate Susquehanna to be about seven-eighths of a mile across.

To Mason meanwhile has fallen the Task of projecting the Line across the River and setting upon its Western bank a point they might take up again from. Upon their last Saturday at Susquehanna, he writes, "...about sun set I was returning from the other Side of the River, and at the distance of about 1.5 Mile the Lightning fell in perpendicular streaks, (about a foot in breadth to appearance) from the cloud to the ground. This was the first lightning I ever saw in streaks continued without the least break through the whole, all the way from the Cloud to the Horizon."

Less formally, he comes running screaming into Dixon's Tent, just as Dixon is lighting his Evening Pipe. "Did you see that?"

"Bright as Day...?" Dixon nods.

"Lord, into what Sub-urbs Satanick hast Thou introduc'd me this time?— Thy Procedures not to be question'd, of course."

The Wind has begun to shake the Tents. The Surveyors hear the stumbling of Rain-drops against the taut Duck. Their Candle-flames are being torn to shining waxen wild-flowers. "I am assuming that I may be confident of my Safety here," Dixon puffing, "the entire issue of Lightning in America having been resolv'd by your Friend Dr. Franklin, who draws it off at will, easy as drawing Ale from a Cask.... Ah have got that correct, haven't Ah...? 'Tis certainly the right place for Lightning, eeh! Nothing like this in Staindrop! Lud Oafery did claim to've been hit once over by Low Dinsdale, but there were no other witnesses,— "

"Dixon, our, um, Lives? are in Danger?"

"Hardly enough to interrupt a perfectly good— " Here he is silenc'd by an immense Thunder-Bolt from directly overhead, as their frail Prism is bleach'd in unholy Light. "— Saturday Night for, is it I ask you...?" his Head emerging at last from beneath a Blanket, "Mason? Say, Mason,— are thee...?"

Mason, now outside, pushes aside the Tent-flap with his head, but does not enter. "Dixon. I will now seek Shelter beneath that Waggon out there, d'ye see it? If you wish to join me, there's room."

"Bit too much Iron there for me, thanks all the same."

"Interesting. Up to you of course,— " Another great blinding Peal. When Dixon can see again, Mason has withdrawn. Each Lightning-stroke another step across the landscape, the miles-high Electrickal Insect, whose footfalls are Thunder-Claps, proceeds at some broken, incomprehensible Pace, passing on toward Philadelphia and the Sea, and the Sky is restor'd to its pitiless Clarity, in time to obtain a good Zenith Distance for Capella.

Their latest orders, gallop'd in by Express, are to return to the Tangent Point, and run the three and a half Miles of Meridian, or North Line, needed to close the Boundaries of the Lower Counties. A Line must now be drawn Northward, from the Tangent Point, till striking the West Line at right angles, thus defining the northeast corner of Maryland. To obtain this last five miles of Boundary, the Parties have agreed, as if repenting close to the end of a long life of Error, to draw the Line at last due North and South.

Esteem'd Murray,—

Whatever else happens upon this Expedition, I am getting to meet an uncommon lot of Milk-maids. Every morning and evening they line up among the Tents, in the canvas alley-ways, clanking pails and kettles and whispering among themselves. And laughing. Ah! Laughter at the Outset of the Day. Some are lovely beyond the pen of this wretched apprentice. Some,— but even a 'Prentice must refrain from comparison. Gladly would I welcome attention from any of them,— alas, what am I to do?

Whilst, for their own part, the Lasses, often quite brazen about it, go on thinning the Milk with well-water, putting in Snails to make it froth, keeping it warm who knows how,— "Coy Milk-Maids" being a Game courtly as any back in the Metropolis, and like Dancing, exercis'd with ease and enjoyment, upon both sides.

> 'Tis Cream-Pot Love in the Morning Dew,
> Again at the Close of Day,
> One creeps about, like a Spider who
> Might covet some Curds and Whey...
> For...'tis...
> [Refrain]
> Dairy!— oh gimme that
> Dairy! the lengths that I'd
> Go to for its sake are extr'ordin-ary,—

"The step, you see, like this? And,— "

> I see a
> Cow 'n' just drool,
> Act like a fool,
> Any time a Cheese, roll by,—
> Butter and Milk,
> Foods of that Ilk,
> Make me shake my head, goin'
> Me-oh my!
> Polly's in the Penthouse,
> Molly's in the Mood,
> Ev'rybody lookin' for that
> Lactick Food,

Oh Dairy,
Though Seasons may
Vary, I'll ever be very
Enchanted, by you!

In the midst of teaching a long Queue of fair Purveyors the Steps of a Reel current at Williamsburg, Young Nathe is abruptly smit.

Miracle! after miserable nights in roadside hovels styl'd "Inns,"— the companionless sunsets turn after Planet's turn,— the days of regarding Daughters and even Wives of settlers with what I once imagin'd a Soulful Gaze (not always distinguishable, by she that receiv'd it, from an Offensive Stare),— unexpectedly to find, in the Day's first Dew, with the Light increasing so swiftly, apt, any instant, to reveal in her that decisive Flaw the Crepuscule had hidden (tho' steadfast beneath the Light, she but grew more Fair),— Her, whom I call, "Galactica,"— for she is one of the Purveyors, to this Expedition, of Dairy Products.—

"Poh!" I can hear you,— "another Tale of Cream-Pot Love,— " well aye, of course, as who has not practis'd it, in this Edenick Dairy-land,— yet Galactica, tho' *in* that larcenous Sisterhood, not truly *of* it.— What I'm in, is a Sailor's predicament,— far too soon must we extend the Line past any journey she can make in safety, or indeed find the time for. There is no question of her joining our Caravan. Her Duty here is as compelling as would be my own, were she to come, to deflect from her Person the attentions of up to an hundred men, including the implacable Stig.... So must I beseech Her wait till Winter, when we leave off and return Eastward,— then until we head West again in the Spring, and so on,— Moments too few, and the Waiting too heavy a burden, I fear, upon fair Galactica. For tho' I know next to nothing about the Sex, yet it seems, in my experience, that their reputation for Patience is gravely over-blown, and the faithful sailor's Sweetheart of song and Romance as mythical as a Mermaid....

48

On the Twenty-ninth of May, they turn eastward again, measuring off-sets and marking them as they go. Now they begin the Day sighting into the Sun, and watching their own Shadows at Evening, Surveyor and Tri-pod and Instrument stretching back, somehow, toward the past, toward more youthful Selves. Going west, even no further than Susquehanna, living by the simple Diurnal Rhythms,— going ever with the Sun, was not the same as this going against it. " 'Aye, very different indeed," remarks Dixon.

Mason is trying to wake up. The nearest coffee is in the cook-tent. "Pray you," he whispers, "try not to be so damn'd,— did I say damn'd? I meant so *fucking* chirpy all the time, good chap, good chap," stumbling out of the Tent trying to get his Hair into some kind of Queue. The Cof-fee is brew'd with the aid of a Fahrenheit's Thermometer, unmark'd save at one place, exactly halfway between freezing and boiling, at 122°, where upon the Wood a small Arrow is inscrib'd, pointing at a Scratch across the glass Tube. 'Tis at this Temperature that the water receives the ground Coffee, the brew being stirr'd once or twice, the Pot remov'd from the fire, its Decoction then proceeding. Tho' clarifying may make sense in London, out here 'tis a luxury, nor are there always Egg-shells to hand. If tasted early, Dixon has found, the fine suspended matter in the coffee lends it an undeniable rustick piquance. Later in the Pot, the Liquid charring itself toward Vileness appeals more to those looking for bodily stimuli,— like Dixon, who is able to sip the most degradedly awful pot's-end poison and yet beam like an Idiot, "Mm-*m m!* Best Jamoke west o' the Alleghenies!"— a phrase Overseer Barnes utters often, tho' neither Surveyor quite understands it, especially as the Party are yet east of the Alleghenies. Howbeit, at this point in a Pot's life-cycle, Mason prefers to switch over to Tea, when it is Dixon's turn to begin shaking his head.

"Can't understand how anyone abides that stuff."

"How so?" Mason unable not to react.

"Well, it's disgusting, isn't it? Half-rotted Leaves, scalded with boiling Water and then left to lie, and soak, and bloat?"

"Disgusting? this is Tea, Friend, *Cha,*— what all tasteful London drinks,— that," pollicating the Coffee-Pot, "is what's disgusting."

"*Au contraire,*" Dixon replies, "Coffee is an art, where precision is all,— Water-Temperature, mean particle diameter, ratio of Coffee to Water or as we say, CTW, and dozens more Variables I'd mention, were they not so clearly out of thy technical Grasp,— "

"How is it," Mason pretending amiable curiosity, "that of each Pot of Coffee, only the first Cup is ever worth drinking,— and that, by the time I get to it, someone else has already drunk it?"

Dixon shrugs. "You must improve your Speed...? As to the other, why aye, only the first Cup's any good, owing to Coffee's Sacramental nature, the Sacrament being Penance, entirely absent from thy sunlit World of *Tay,*— whereby the remainder of the Pot, often dozens of cups deep, represents the Price for enjoying that first perfect Cup."

"Folly," gapes Mason. "Why, ev'ry cup of Tea is perfect...?"

"For what? curing hides?"

For the next three weeks, they are occupied again with the enigmatick Area 'round the Tangent Point, seeking to close the Eastern boundaries of Pennsylvania and Maryland,— the Commissioners, to appearance, being anxious upon this score. "They all live upon this side of Susquehanna," Mr. McClean conjectures. "They don't want you across it just yet. Across it things are not so civiliz'd, so Anglican, begging your pardon, Sir, nor so Quaker, begging yours, Sir, or should I say, thine. Over Susquehanna begins a different Province entirely, and beginning at the Mountains, another differing from that, and so on,— beyond Monongahela, beyond Ohio,— tho' the betting in the Taverns is overwhelmingly against your getting quite that far."

"Won't that depend upon how far the Proprietors wish the Line to run?" inquires Mr. Mason.

"If by 'the Proprietors' you mean those who truly own it," remarks John Harland.

"The Indians," suggests Mr. Dixon.

"The Army," says Mr. Harland.

"I meant, rather, the Penns," Mason a bit starch'd, "— as Maryland's Grant ends just past Laurel Hill, from there West 'tis Penn's Line alone, dividing Penn lands from Virginia,— who bear none of the Cost."

"Five Degrees from the Atlantick Coast," opines Mr. McClean, "will include Fort Pitt, and the first few miles of Ohio before it bends south.... Iron deposits, Coal as well, underground mountain-ranges of it, burning down there for centuries, known to the Indians, perhaps us'd as well in connection with their mysterious Lead Mines in the Mountains. Right up your Street, Mr. Dixon."

The Surveyors soon discover, that the Meridian drawn north from the Tangent Point, will run slightly *inside* the Twelve-Mile Arc, crossing it twice, at points about a mile and a half apart,— producing now, between them, *two* boundary lines, one "straight," and one, about a thousandth of a Mile longer, "curv'd" (which will one day be declar'd the Legal Boundary, thus whittling a tiny Sliver from Maryland). The three and a half Miles to the West Line remaining can be run as a piece of pure Meridian,— to be styl'd, "the North Line."

"All I know", Mason shrugs. " 's I'm suppos'd to line up Alioth and Polaris with the Flame of a Candle, a mile away, being held by you, who at the same time must ever be bisecting the Flame perfectly with the string of your Plummet."

"Unless it sets the String on fire, of course." So Dixon is sent out into Darkness variable as the Moon, thick with predators bestial and human, Indians upon missions forever secret from European eyes, all moving easily among this Community of Night, interrupted only by the odd unschedul'd Idiot. Even Animals are late to arrive at Water holes, and so run into others in the Herd, away from whom the late-comers would as gladly have kept,— and Herd-Politics takes another strange and unforeseen turn. Through it all, there is the unsure and withal helpless Assistant, moving his Lanthorn about in the Air, whilst a distant voice through a Speaking-trumpet bids him go right, then left.

"Frankly," Mason chuckles, by way of what he fancies Encouragement, "were I watching from the Darkness, I shouldn't want to get too close to anyone in a peculiar Hat, shouting in a loud metal Voice? The Savages may be as frighten'd of you as were the People in Cecil County last winter."

" 'Twastn't I thah' frighten'd 'em…? They took me for the Apprentice, no more…?"

"I *saw* you, deny it all you like, I *saw* you conversing with that Torpedo,— "

"Nooah,— they were but more of thy *Visions,* Mason! tha were having them hourly, by then,— which is when, in fahct…? ev'ryone grew frighten'd of thee…? Another few days of bad weather, and…," he spreads his hands, with a pitying Gaze.

At last, on June 6th, in a meadow belonging to Capt. John Singleton, nearly 50 Chains east of Mr. Rhys Price's House, where the Meridian and Parallel intersect, the Surveyors sink in a Post, mark'd W upon the West Side, and N upon the North, and the Boundary is clos'd.

Here at the northeast corner of Maryland, the Geometrickal Pilgrim may well wish to stand in the company of his thoughts, at this purest of intersections mark'd so far upon America. Yet, Geomancer, beware,— if thy Gaze but turn Eastward by an Eye-lash's Diameter, thou must view the notorious Wedge,— resulting from the failure of the Tangent Point to be exactly at this corner of Maryland, but rather some five miles south, creating a semi-cusp or Thorn of that Length, and doubtful ownership,— not so much claim'd by any one Province, as priz'd for its Ambiguity,— occupied by all whose Wish, hardly uncommon in this Era of fluid Identity, is not to reside anywhere. As a peaceful and meadowlike Vista sweeps Southward, the Line and the Arc approach one another, one may imagine almost sensibly,

Bearing in from either Limb of Sight,
A-thrum, like peevish Dumbledores in flight

as great Tox has it, in his *Pennsylvaniad.*

Yet there remains to the Wedge an Unseen World, beyond Resolution, of transactions never recorded,— upon Creeksides and beneath Hedges, in Barns, Lofts, and Spring-houses, in the long Summer Maize fields, where one may be lost within minutes of entering the vast unforgiving Thickets of Stalks,— indeed, all manner of secret paths and clearings and alcoves are defin'd,— push'd over or stamp'd into being, roofless as Ruins, for but a few fugitive weeks of lull before autumnal responsibilities come again looming. The sun burns, the gravid short Forests beckon. The Soil, when enough is reveal'd, becomes another sand Arena. Anybody may be in there, from clandestine lovers to smugglers of weapons, some hawking contraband,— buckles, lockets, tea, laces from France,— some marking off "Lots" for use in some future piece of Land-Jobbery. Insect pests are almost intimidated into leaving, but sooner or later come back.

Nearby, withal, is Iron Hill, a famous and semi-magical Magnetick Anomaly, known to Elf Communities near and far, into which riskers of other peoples' Capital have been itching for years to dig,— but being reluctant to reward more than one set of Provincial Officials at a time, are waiting until the legal status of the Wedge becomes clear. Is it part of Pennsylvania? Maryland? or of the new entity "Delaware"?— which on paper at least belongs to Pennsylvania, William Penn's having leas'd it from the Duke for a term of ten thousand years,— tho' it has enjoy'd, for fifty of these, its own Legislature and Executive Council.

'Tis no one's, for the moment. A small geographick Anomaly, a-bustle with Appetites high and low, their offerings and acceptances.

The North Line quickly completed, the Surveyors are order'd back to Susquehanna, this time to continue the West Line "as far as the Country is inhabited." Legally this suggests as far as the Proclamation Line, at the Crest of the Alleghenies. Even before the Party reaches the River,—

as if 'twere a Fate neither could avoid,— Darby and Cope are pretending to be Mason and Dixon, tho' not always respectively. It begins when someone having observ'd the Chain, assumes the obvious,— "Mr. Mason! a-and this must be Mr. Dixon!"

"Not exactly," says Cope.

"He means," Darby hastily puts in, "that he's Mason, and *I'm* Dixon, isn't that right, 'Mason'?"

"I'd prefer to be Dixon," hisses Cope.

"Next time, all right?" The Links of the Chain cak'd with dried Dirt, and squeaking almost painfully....

"You'll want to take care," they're eventually warn'd by a friendly Tapster, "there're a couple of Lads about, pretending to be you two."

"Get on," says Darby.

"Why should anyone wish to be us?" wonders Cope.

Maidens in varying ratios of Indignation to Curiosity show up in camp, demanding to see Mason or Dixon, or both. Upon meeting the real Surveyors, "Well, but you're not him,— " "— nor you the other."

"Of course not," reply Mason and Dixon. When they have a moment to talk about it together, "It must be someone in camp," Mason suggests, "My guess is, 'tis Darby and Cope."

"How, then?"

"Well, they're never about, are they, when all these folk show up to complain? And their Names, like ours, are usually spoken together.... Yet you know more of Chain-men than I,— what think ye?"

"The Chain-man's Sorrows," it seems to Dixon, "all proceed from being forbidden, but upon sufferance of the Party-Chief, so much as to touch any Instrument, excepting the Chain,— with centuries of that word's poetic Associations adding to its Weight. Farmers in Durham aren't the only ones who call it the D——l's Guts.... Chain-men bear it, they hate it, they tend it carefully, their feelings ever in a muddle...they cannot keep from sliding queer covetous glances at the other Instruments. They understand the Surveyor's Injunction, yet touch they must, and will,— some honestly wishing to learn more of the Arts, others merely to fiddle with the Equipment. That Messieurs Darby and Cope, being, here in America, Surveyors fully competent with all Instruments, should now toil as Chain-men...?— under British supervision withal...?— invidious Situations arise, d'tha see."

"Then shall we break with Tradition, perhaps allow them to use our Surveying Instruments?— Or yours, rather, as I possess none of my own."

"Eeh! What,— My Circumferentor...? Why, 'tis another of my very Senses...? 'Twould be like letting someone else do my Smelling for me...?"

"Hum, so...You and this...Instrument are...quite close, then? D'ye have a Name, that you call it by?"

"Mason, the thought of either Darby's or Cope's Eye-ball dripping fluids all over the Lenses of my Old Circ,— "

"Ha! 'Old Circ'! How charming you people are, how child-like in your Attachments."

"Perhaps if the Tools of thy Trade had ever belong'd to thee, instead of to the King, tha might at least once have felt this simple, sentimental Bond,— quite common among the People in fact, though scarcely, I guess, among all those great Publick Zenith-Sectors and Telescopes and so forth, up there but a footfall from the Highest in the Land...?"

Mason drops his head in false apology. "Yet another Flaw! how many more, before my Character's too riddl'd for it to matter? Dixon, I know I am not worthy, to *carry* your esteem'd Instrument. Blessing upon you both, and much joy of your Relationship."

"Thankee, Mason, I mean that sincerely. As to our Chain-men,— they being qualified Lensfolk, might we not allow them some time with the Sector...? neither of us actually owning it."

"Fine with me, I've but its Custodians to report to. You must answer to its Maker."

"John Bird would do the same, I'm certain...?"

"Deferring as ever in matters of character," Mason making mock-French flourishes in the Air with his Hat.

"Why here are the Gents themselves, a Miracle, fetch me the Jesuit Telegraph, for I must report it to the Pope,— how now Boys,— "

"Far too truculent," mutters Mason. "Mr. Cope, Mr. Darby, well met."

"We prefer 'Darby and Cope,' actually," says Darby.

"He being the Head and all," adds Cope.

"Of course that's only east to west,— "

"Depending who ends up with the Stobs, really,— "

Going on to describe, in foul-copy Stichomythia, their Practice of exchanging ten small wood stakes, to keep the Chain-Count accurate, tho' between Mr. Darby's habit of keeping Stobs ev'rywhere about him, including in his Belt, Leggings, and Hat, and Mr. Cope's Forgetfulness in counting, they have grown so fearful of Stob-Loss, as to have begun Exchanging Stobs after eleven Chains instead of ten, with Mr. Cope then passing back only nine of his, and keeping one. Yet now one and now the other will forget, and revert to the old ten-Chain Method....

"We may be miles off by now," Dixon's eyes having grown very round.

"Save that thro' some dark miracle of Mathesis," says Darby, "our Errors have ever exactly cancel'd out."

"Else Susquehanna measur'd to Potowmack, Might haply 'maze the Trav'ler loxodromick,— "

"With phantom Leagues, too many or too few,— As if a very Hole in Space 'twere, too."

A pause. Not a mischievous Dimple 'pon either Phiz. "All content otherwise?" Mason as he imagines smoothly.

"Go easy, Mason, don't upset them...?— "

" 'Twas him made me do it!" screams Mr. Cope, as if yielding before a sudden Stress.

"Booby!" ejaculates Mr. Darby. " 'Twas you began it!"

"Yet Head Ev'rything must you ever be, mustn't you, leaving poor, miserable Cope to shift as he may,— "

"Made thee do what?" inquires Dixon.

"Aha! You see?" cries Mason, "— now are they confessing."

Actually, the Chain-men are fallen rather to thumping one the other, as Mason and Dixon look on. "Then again," confides Mason behind his Hand, "a turn at the Sector mightn't be such a good idea, not just now...."

There is Commotion up the Visto. A delegation of newly hir'd Axmen come marching in. "Here are the very Subjects!" cries one of these.

"Now then ye heathen, hold, 'tis not how we Christians settle our differences."

"Yet they *seem* like white men,— "

"Cleverly indeed fiendishly disguis'd, tho' 'Darby' and 'Cope' are not quite British Names, are they?"

"Why, they are as British as anyone here...?" Dixon points out.

"Not according to your pay-List,— see here, it reads, 'Darby and Cope, Chinamen.' "

"Thah's...'Chain-men'...?"

"Ah."

"Not the same,— "

"*Oh* dear."

"Is Mr. Barnes but fun-mongering, and we the Gulls?"

"Pity, really. None of us has seen a Chinaman before."

"Soon," promises the oracular Squire Haligast, in a Voice so charg'd with passion that immediately all but the most desperate of the Axmen believe him.

By the twenty-second of June they are back below the Peach Bottom Ferry,— another Saturday Night,— ready to start West again. There rushes the River,— both Surveyors understanding by now 'tis *not only* a River, being as well the Boundary to another Country. Next day, they measure southward about forty-five feet to correct their error in Latitude, "...and there placed a mark, and in the direction of this, and the Mark on the East Side of the River,...we proceeded to run the Line."

Just before they cross Susquehanna, a Parcel arrives for them by way of a lather'd Youth riding Express upon a black Barb, neither showing any sign of tiring,— with a terrible "Yee-hah!" the Youth sweeps off his Tricorne, wheels, and has gallop'd back into the Brush. In the Package is Fr. Boscovich's Book, *De Solis et Lunæ* at last, *Defectibus,* publish'd dispatch'd Transatlantickally by Maskelyne, who in the Jobation accompanying, invites their Attention to a great Variety of *Data* within, including a Warning as to the Attraction of Mountains,— "In Italy 'twas establish'd, that the Umbrian Appenines caus'd a very considerable deviation of the Plumb-line Northward, as the party, moving in that direction, drew ever closer."

"First the Iron-Lodes disable my Needle," moans Dixon, "now the Mountains are about to throw off my Plummet?"

"Obliging us, as Maskelyne and me at St. Helena, to take symmetrickal readings on the opposite sides of the Crests, and hope that the two errors will cancel out. I pray the Western Slopes of Allegheny may prove less distressing than the Windward side of that wretched Island...."

49

To Appearance, Trans-Susquehanna is peaceful enough,— Farm-houses, a School-house, a Road to York. At the third ten-minute segment of Arc, they calculate their probable error, change direction by an R.P.H. to the Northward, and continue to their next stopping-place, which once again shall place them conveniently,— this time beside the great inland Road between York and Baltimore, more real than any imaginary Line any would run athwart it. The earth hereabouts is red, the tone of a new Brick Wall in the Shadow, due to a high ratio of iron,— and if till'd in exactly the right way, it becomes magnetized, too, so that at Harvest-time, 'tis necessary only to pass along the Rows any large Container of Iron, and the Vegetables will fly up out of the ground, and stick to it.

Ahead of them in the next ten minutes of Arc lie a dozen Streams falling into Gunpowder Creek, which runs roughly parallel to the Visto, and about a mile south of it. The last of these Branches being close enough to another ten minutes West, upon crossing it, they need only calculate their error as before, and aim slightly north, so as to fall in again with their proper Latitude, ten minutes west of that...in such easy Hops thro' the summer fields and the German cooking, do they progress, Susquehanna to the Allegheny Mountain. Some mornings they awake and can believe that they traverse an Eden, unbearably fair in the Dawn, squandering all its Beauty, day after day unseen, bearing them fruits, presenting them Game, bringing them a fugitive moment of Peace,—

how, for days at a time, can they not, dizzy with it, believe themselves pass'd permanently into Dream...?

Summer takes hold, manifold sweet odors of the Fields, and presently the Forest, become routine, and one night the Surveyors sit in their Tent, in the Dark, and watch Fire-flies, millions of them blinking ev'rywhere,— Dixon engineering plans for lighting the Camp-site with them, recalling how his brother George back home, ran Coal-Gas through reed piping along the Orchard wall. Jeremiah will lead the Fire-flies to stream continuously through the Tent in a narrow band, here and there to gather in glass Globes, concentrating their light to the Yellow of a new-risen Moon.

"And when we move to where there are none of these tiny Linkmen?"

"We take 'em with huz...? Lifetime Employment!"

"But how long do they live?"

"Ensign Cheer."

As the Visto has grown longer behind them, the Philadelphiaward Fringe of the nightly Encampment has lengthen'd to a suburbs dedicated to high (as some would say, low) living. Gaming, corn whiskey, Women able to put up with a heap of uncompensated overtime, Stages knock'd together each nightfall and lanthorn'd into view, to a Murmur as of a great Crowd in Motion, only to be struck again each dawn,— as those for whom it is cheaper to follow than to abandon the Party for business elsewhere, groaning with the Night just past, hoping for a chance to sleep sometime during the Journey, prepare to follow the Axmen through another day. The fast-and-loose artist, the Quartz-scryer, the Vásquez Brothers' Marimba Quartet, who often play back-up for the Torpedo, to whom it is the musick of his Youth, his home Waters. The marimbas, in great towering Structure assembl'd each evening just outside of camp, pulse along, Chords and Arpeggiations swaying upward to their sharp'd versions, then back down again, sets of Hammers, Hands, and Sleeves all moving together along the rank'd wood Notes, nocturnal, energetic, remembrancing, warning, impelling.... The Anthem of the Expedition, as it moves into the Unknown, is "Pepinazos,"— marching, and rolling, but wishing rather to dance.

Pepinazos, nunca
Abrazos, Si me

Quieras, Sí
De Veras,
¡Oigamé!—
Déjaté,
Los Pe-pi-naa-zos!

All summer they labor in the service of the Line, over Codorus, Conewago,— pausing to set up the Sector, dodging inch-and-a-half hailstones, calculating Off-sets, changing Direction,— 'cross Piney Run and Monocacy Road, and the Creeks beyond, till just past Middle Creek, figuring they are about in their Latitude, without bothering to set up the Sector, the Surveyors turn off the Angle calculated to put them another ten minutes on,— at the South Mountain, in among all the ghosts already thick in those parts.

"We are Fools," proposes Dixon one night. The wind has shifted at about sundown to the SSE, heightening even minor stresses among the Company. "We shouldn't be runnin' this Line…?"

Mason regards his Cup of Claret. "Bit late for that, isn't it?"

"Why aye. I'll carry it through, Friend, fear not. But something invisible's going on, tha must feel it, smell it…?"

Mason shrugs. "American Politics."

"Just so. We're being us'd again. It doesn't alarm thee…?"

An accident of the late Light has fill'd Mason's Orbits with color'd shadows. "Resign? They would bring up the Letter. Immediately. Then?"

Dixon nods glumly, and Mason keeps on, more than he has to. "Tho' we're in this together, yet is it easier for you, being the Quaker and not expected to prove combative, than for me, who must accordingly bear double the burden of Bravery. Splendid. Did they team us up together like this *deliberately?* Are you my Penalty, precise to the Groat, for enjoying a Command of my own? For not having seconded Maskelyne at the Transit? Now I have to be Eyre Coote?"

"Bit steep, isn't i'…?"

Mason begins fiddling with his Queue, bringing it first over one Shoulder, then the other. "If it were all true,— ev'ry unkind suspicion, ev'ry phantastickal rendering,— would we, knowing all, nonetheless go on? Do what's clearly our Duty?"

"We sign'd an Agreement."

"If it meant our Destruction?"

"The ancient matter of the *Seahorse* must ever prevent us from Resigning. We've no choice, but to go on with it, as far as we may."

"Then as we've no choice, I may speak freely and share with you some of my darker Sentiments. Suppose Maskelyne's a French Spy. Suppose a secret force of Jesuits, receives each Day a summary of Observations made at Greenwich, and transcalculates it according to a system known to the Kabbalists of the Second Century as *Gematria*, whereby Messages may be extracted from lines of Text sacred and otherwise, a Knowledge preserv'd by various Custodians over the centuries, and since the Last, possess'd by Jesuit and Freemason alike. The Dispute over Bradley's Obs, then, as over Flamsteed's before him, would keep ever as their unspoken intention that the Numbers nocturnally obtain'd be set side by side, and arrang'd into Lines, like those of a Text, manipulated till a Message be reveal'd."

"Bit sophisticated for me. Tho' I don't mind a likely Conspiracy, I prefer it be form'd in the interests of Trade,— the mystickal sort you fancy is fair beyond me, I'm but a simple son of the Pit."

" 'Trade.'— Aha. You heard me mention Jesuits,— so now you're making veil'd allusions to the East India Company, in response,— I do see, yes…Drivel, of course."

"Come, Sir, can you not sense here, there, just 'round the corner, the pattering feet and swift Hands of John Company, the Lanthorns of the East…? the scent of fresh Coriander, the whisper of a Sarong…?"

"Sari," corrects Mason.

"Not at all Sir,— 'twas I who was sarong."

"Something's afoot with those Two, all right," says Dixon one day.

"Which two?"

"Frenchy and Mrs. Redzinger, they're scarcely together of late, 'd tha notice?"

As they draw nearer the Redzinger Farm, the presence of Peter Redzinger becomes quite sensible to both. Indeed, he's been back since the Winter,— he and the Boys have been working the place, lumbering about insomniack, eating whenever they happen to remember, tracking soil ev'rywhere, hardly speaking. To Luise he seems chasten'd, even at times dejected, yet innocent of all suspicion as respects his Wife, having long travel'd past the Conjugal Emotions,— belonging to the simple fact of another hard Pennsylvania Winter, the lowness and solidity of Sky, no day without its distress, roads that end in Thickets at nightfall. "Christ went away," he discovers at last how to tell her, one morning, the eaves a-drip, the bleary Sun irregularly brighter and dimmer, "one day, for no reason that I could see, Christ came to me and said, 'Peter, I am going away. You thought it was hard before this? Here is where it gets impossible.'

" 'Are you coming back?' I almost couldn't speak.

" 'You must live ever in that Expectation.— Come, spare Me that Face,— of course it is a lot to ask.' He seem'd in a dangerously merry State. Was it relief at being shut of me, at last?

" 'How do I proceed without you?'

" 'What have I been teaching you all this time?'

"I was smit dumb, Luise. I didn't understand the Question. 'Be more like You?' I tried. He'd been teaching me? All this time? *Wehe!*

" 'Alas.' His Smile, at least, was not a pitying one, nor was it quite as disappointed as I'd fear'd. He turn'd, for the first time I saw the back of His Robe. He had a Motto in German embroider'd fine as could be in Gold Threads, upon the back. I couldn't read what it said. He receded. He was gone."

"Peter."

"I feel cold, helpless, without him...*ah.* I believ'd I could count upon him forever, he was there, he was real, then he turn'd and went away. I have displeas'd Him,— but how? I lov'd him!" All day, half the Night, on he talks, stunn'd and sing-song. He does not weep as much as Luise expects. Armand has a swift look in from time to time, smiles understandingly, heaves a Sigh, withdraws. Luise waits to grow impatient. She considers the Frenchman for the first time with unrestrain'd Desire, having glimps'd the possibility that they may never have a chance to address it,— she can also appreciate how tiresome this listening to Peter is. Yet from some unexplor'd Region to her Spirit's West, like upland folk with goods to sell, come Messengers with the late News, that her destiny 'spite all may lie with this craz'd Christless wreck of a

Husband,— or, as she will also find herself asking in tears, upon any number of future occasions, "What else was I suppos'd to do? What? That Frenchman, and his Duck? I actually tried for a while to tell Peter about our little Trio. But I couldn't even do that, for he never heard me, he was too full of old adventures, out past Monongahela, with Christ, going about in various Disguises, Christ and his Hop-field companion Peter, upon missions of education. Christ and Peter visit the Indians. Christ reminisces about His Teen Years. Christ teaches Peter how to make Golems."

"Excuse me, Luise! Your Husband, he...?"

"Makes Golems,— oh, not the big ones, Lotte! No, Kitchen-size,— some of them quite clever, the Tasks they do,— one that peels and cores Apples,— *ja*, even pits Cherries,— "

"Luise, for Shame!" The women beam together mischievously. One day, however, Luise will show her. Peter will not mind.

> Pennsylvania is a place of spiritual Wonders amazing as any Chasm or Cataract. Among the German farmers of Lancaster, for example, are scores, perhaps hundreds, of truly, literally *Good People,* escap'd from a Hell we in our small tended Quotidian may but try to imagine,— entire Villages put to Flame, and Tortures worse than Inquisitorial,— disembowelments, bloodlettings,— a world without Innocence,— yet, escap'd here, into Innocence reborn,— something deeper and more intricate,— they call it "a new Life in Christ,"— it is their way of explaining it. Not a moment of their waking day passes, without some form of Christian devotion. Work, which the rest of us, at one time or another, have cursed and wish'd at an end, is here consider'd Sacred,— and this is only one of many Wonders....
>
> Never has Traveler encounter'd such personal Variety, where utter cleanness and sobriety may be seen immediately adjoining the most stupefied exhibitions of Hemp-field Folly. There are Germanickal Mystics who live in Trees,— not up in the Branches, but actually *within the Trunks,* those particularly of ancient creekside Sycamores, which have, over time, become hollow'd out, like Caverns. In the midst of these lightless Woods are gun-smithies where the most advanc'd and refin'd forms of Art are daily exercis'd upon the machinery of Murder by Craftsmen whose Piety is unquestion'd....
>
> — Wicks Cherrycoke, *Spiritual Day-Book*

DePugh recalls a Sermon he once heard at a church-ful of German Mysticks. "It might have been a lecture in Mathematics. Hell, beneath our feet, bounded,— Heaven, above our pates, unbounded. Hell a collapsing Sphere, Heaven an expanding one. The enclosure of Punishment, the release of Salvation. Sin leading us as naturally to Hell and Compression, as doth Grace to Heaven, and Rarefaction. Thus— "

Murmurs of, " 'Thus'?"

"— may each point of Heaven be mapp'd, or projected, upon each point of Hell, and vice versa. And what intercepts the Projection, about mid-way (reckon'd logarithmickally) between? why, this very Earth, and our lives here upon it. We only think we occupy a solid, Brick-and-Timber City,— in Reality, we live upon a Map. Perhaps even our Lives are but representations of Truer Lives, pursued above and below, as to Philadelphia correspond both a vast Heavenly City, and a crowded niche of Hell, each element of one faithfully mirror'd in the others."

"There are a Mason and Dixon in Hell, you mean?" inquires Ethelmer, "attempting eternally to draw a perfect Arc of Considerably Lesser Circle?"

"Impossible," ventures the Rev^d. "For is Hell, by this Scheme, not a Point, without Dimension?"

"Indeed. Yet, suppose Hell to be *almost* a Point," argues the doughty DePugh, already Wrangler material, "— they would then be inscribing their Line eternal, upon the inner surface of the smallest possible Spheroid that can be imagin'd, and then some."

"More of these…," Ethelmer pretending to struggle for a Modifier that will not offend the Company, "*curious* Infinitesimals, Cousin.— The Masters at *my* Purgatory are bewitch'd by the confounded things. Epsilons, usually. Miserable little,"— Squiggling in the air, "sort of things. Eh?"

"See them often," sighs DePugh, "this semester more than ever."

"What puzzles me, DeP., is that if the volume of Hell may be taken as small as you like, yet the Souls therein must be ever smaller, mustn't they,— there being, by now, easily millions there?"

"Aye, assuming one of the terms of Damnation be to keep just enough of one's size and weight to feel oppressively crowded,— taking as a model the old Black Hole of Calcutta, if you like,— the Soul's Volume must be an Epsilon one degree smaller,— a Sub-epsilon."

" 'The Epsilonicks of Damnation.' Well, well. There's my next Sermon," remarks Uncle Wicks.

"I observe," Tenebræ transform'd by the pale taper-light to some beautiful Needlewoman in an old Painting, "of both of you, that your fascination with Hell is match'd only by your disregard of Heaven. Why should the Surveyors not be found there Above,"— gesturing with her Needle, a Curve-Ensemble of Embroidery Floss, of a nearly invisible gray, trailing after, in the currents rais'd by Talking, Pacing, Fanning, Approaching, Withdrawing, and whatever else there be to indoor Life,— "drifting about, chaining the endless airy Leagues, themselves approaching a condition of pure Geometry?"

"Tho' for symmetry's sake," interposes DePugh, "we ought to say, '*almost* endless.' "

"Why," whispers Brae, "whoever said anything had to be symmetrickal?" The Lads, puzzl'd, exchange a quick Look.

50

Not all Roads lead to Philadelphia. Chesapeake means as much, and often more, to the Back Inhabitants as Philadelphia,— so Roads here seldom run in the same sense as the West Line, but rather athwart it, coming up from Chesapeake, and going on, to the North and the West. Soon, lesser roads, linking farms and closer Markets, begin to feed into these Line-crossing roads,— before long, on one or more of the Corners so defin'd, a Tavern will appear. It is thus, in the Back-Country, evident to all, however unschool'd in Euclid, that each time the Visto crosses a Road, there's sure to be an Oasis but a few miles north or south.

"Here's how we'll do it," proposes Mason. "Whenever we come to a Road, one of us goes North, the other South. The one not finding a Tavern in a reasonable Time, returns to the Line, where he finds either the other waiting, or that the other has not yet return'd,— in which case, he then continues in the same direction, either meeting the other returning, or finding him, already a dozen pints down."

East of Susquehanna, under this System, there prove to be Crossings where Inns lie both North and South of the Line, and on such Occasions, entire days may pass with each Surveyor in his own Tavern, not exactly waiting for the other to show up,— possibly imagining the good time the other must be having and failing to share. Later, across Susquehanna, there come days when the only Inns are worse than no Inn, and presently days when there are no Inns at all, and at last the night they encamp knowing that for an unforeseeable stretch of Nights, they must belong to this great Swell of Forested Mountains, this place of ancient Revenge, and Beasts outside the Fire-light,— the sun this particular evening as if in celestial Seal, spreading into a Glory, transgressing all Metes and Bounds, filling the Trees, lighting the Animals, their flanks averted, wash'd in its oncoming Flow, bringing to human faces a precision approaching purification, goading each soul, as if again and again, ever toward the Shambles of Eternity. The Axmen stand beneath it, no less bruised, worn or hungry than from any other day, blinking, turning away, then returning to this Radiance that flares from behind edges of Shapes uncertain,— the Creation they believe they know,— re-created.

Later, not all will agree on what they have seen.

Thus, as the Communication is a long sequence of Fortified remounting stations, so is the Line a long sequence of Taverns and Ordinaries, and absences of the same. One day, the Meridian having been closely enough establish'd, and with an hour or two of free time available to them, one heads north, one south, and 'tis Dixon's luck to discover The Rabbi of Prague, headquarters of a Kabbalistick Faith, in Correspondence with the Elect Cohens of Paris, whose private Salute they now greet Dixon with, the Fingers spread two and two, and the Thumb held away from them likewise, said to represent the Hebrew letter *Shin* and to signify, "Live long and prosper." The area just beyond the next Ridge is believ'd to harbor a giant Golem, or Jewish Automaton, taller than the most ancient of the Trees. As explain'd to Dixon, 'twas created by an Indian tribe widely suppos'd to be one of the famous Lost Tribes of Israel, who had somehow given up control of the Creature, sending it headlong into the Forest, where it would learn of its own gift of Mobile Invisibility.

"And...do you folk wear Special Hats, anything like that?" inquires Dixon. It sounds enough like the Frenchman's Duck to make him cautious. "Most of thee, in Speech and Address, I'd've guess'd to be Irish...I thought thee were known for *Little* People. This is a Wonder of the Wilderness, for fair...?"

"If, I say 'if,' you do see it," advises the Landlord, "you'll then talk of Wonders indeed."

"Sure that Golem,— you have to catch him when he's asleep," asserts a short red-headed woodsman in Deerskins, who is holding a tankard in one hand and a Lancaster County rifle in the other.

"Of course," adds a florid Forge-keeper who occupies the entire side of one Table, "that might not be for years." He chuckles, and the Tankards rattle upon the Shelves.

"Aye, some of us have never seen him, only heard his steps on the nights when there is no Moon, or his voice, speaking from above the only words he knows,— 'Eyeh asher Eyeh,' "— in on which, in Tones hush'd, though ominous, the others now join.

"That is, 'I am that which I am,' " helpfully translates a somehow nautical-looking Indiv. with gigantick Fore-Arms, and one Eye ever a-Squint from the Smoke of his Pipe.

"Tho' Rashi in his Commentary has, 'I will be what I will be,' as the Tense is ambiguous between present and future."

"Isn't that what God said to Moses?" Dixon inquires.

"Exodus 3:14. 'Tis what the Indians'll say to you, if you go far enough west,— being the Lost Tribes of Israel out there, whose Creature this is."

"In the Infancy Gospel of Thomas, you see, Jesus as a Boy made small, as you'd say, toy Golems out of Clay,— Sparrows that flew, Rabbits that hopp'd. Golem fabrication is integral to the Life of Jesus, and thence to Christianity."

"Nor is it any Wonder here by South Mountain, anyway. Sometimes the Invisible will all at once appear,— sometimes what you see may not be there at all."

"I am told of certain Stars, in the Chinese system of Astrology, which are invisible so long as they keep moving, only being seen, when they pause. Might thy Golem share this Property?"

The Company rush to enlighten Dixon. " 'Tis shar'd with this whole accursèd Continent," the quarrelsome Carrot-top lets him know, waving his Rifle and narrowly missing several Tankards upon the Table.

"— Which, as if in answer to God's recession, remain'd invisible, denied to us, till it became necessary to our Souls that it come to rest, self-reveal'd, tho' we pretended to 'discover' it...."

"By the time of Columbus, God's project of Disengagement was obvious to all,— with the terrible understanding that we were to be left more and more to our own solutions."

"America, withal, for centuries had been *kept hidden,* as are certain Bodies of Knowledge. Only now and then were selected persons allow'd Glimpses of the New World,— "

"Never Reporters that anyone else was likely to believe,— men who ate the Flesh and fornicated with the Ghosts of their Dead, murderers and Pirates on the run, monks in parchment Coracles stitched together from copied Pages of the Book of Jonah, fishermen too many Nights out of Port, any Runagate craz'd enough to sail West."

"All matters of what becomes Visible, and when. Revelation exists as a Fact,— and continues, as Time proceeds. If new Continents may become visible, why not Planets, sir, as Planets are in your Line?"

"Ye'd have to ask Mason, who should be here Hourly."

"Howbeit,— the Secret was safe until the choice be made to reveal it. It has been denied to all who came to America, for Wealth, for Refuge, for Adventure. This 'New World' was ever a secret Body of Knowledge,— meant to be studied with the same dedication as the Hebrew Kabbala would demand. Forms of the Land, the flow of water, the occurrence of what us'd to be call'd Miracles, all are Text,— to be attended to, manipulated, read, remember'd."

"Hence as you may imagine, we take a lively interest in this Line of yours," booms the Forge-keeper, "inasmuch as it may be read, East to West, much as a Line of Text upon a Page of the sacred Torah,— a Tellurian Scripture, as some might say,— "

"— 'Twill terminate somewhere to the West, no one, not even you and your Partner, knows where. An utterance. A Message of uncertain length, apt to be interrupted at any Moment, or Chain. A smaller Pantograph copy down here, of Occurrences in the Higher World."

"Another case of, 'As above, so below.' "

"No longer, Alas, a phrase of Power,— this Age sees a corruption and disabling of the ancient Magick. Projectors, Brokers of Capital, Insurancers, Peddlers upon the global Scale, Enterprisers and Quacks,— these are the last poor fallen and feckless inheritors of a Knowledge they can never use, but in the service of Greed. The coming Rebellion is theirs,— Franklin, and that Lot,— and Heaven help the rest of us, if they prevail."

"Yet," puts in a queer, uncollected sort of Townsman, who's been drinking so far in silence, "what of the way Mr. Franklin and his people stopp'd the Paxtonians before the City, as the Pope halted Attila before Rome,—

> 'Like Leo First, upon the Mincian Bank,
> Before that Horde, Rank after endless Rank...'

— yes and now, as then, the preponderant Question is, What kind of Arrangements were made? With conquest in their grasp and sight, our own Barbarians in like wise turn'd, and sought once again their wild back-lands, renouncing their chance to sack the Quaker Rome."

"Enjoy its Women." General Comment.

"Careful, Lad, some of them's us."

"Just so. What argument could have prov'd compelling enough to dissuade them?—

> 'The Kite, the Key, the mortal Thundering
> As Heaven's Flame assaults the hempen String,'

— Eh?— for they esteem Franklin a Magician. A Figure of Power. *We* know what he is,— but to the Mobility, he is the Ancestor of Miracle,— or, of Wonders, which pass as well with them,— without which, indeed, they would soon grow inquisitive and troublesome. For, as long as it remains possible to keep us deluded that we are 'free men,' we back Inhabitants will feed the Metropolis, open new roads to it, fight in its behalf,— we may be Presbyterian today, and turn'd only by the force of God, but after very few seasons of such remorseless Gulling, we must be weak and tractable enough even for the Philadelphian men of affairs, who themselves cannot be reckon'd as any sort of Faithful, but rather among Doubt's advancing Phalanx,— of whom one must ask, If they no longer believe in Bishops, where next, might their Irreverence not take them?"

"Now then, Lad.— 'Tis Patrick Henry, Sir, they've all got the Itch,— "

"Why, these Presbyterians need no Oratory from the likes of me, not men who ev'ry day face Savages seeking to destroy them, who will set and hold a Line of Defense quite well before Schuylkill,— though 'twill be Deists and Illuminati, and Philosophers even stranger than that, pois'd upon the Mountaintops between, to observe and, who can say? direct the Engagement.—

> 'In pale and Lanthorn'd reverie the Fair
> Of Philadelphia lounge, discussing Hair,—
> Whilst in the steep Shade of some Western Alp,
> A Presbyterian's fighting for his Scalp.' "

"These Lines thou keep quoting...? I know I should recognize them...? Is it Alexander Pope?"

"Why, 'tis Mr. Tox." A certain impatience of the Eye-brows.

"A Poet whom,— that is,— "

"In the Constellation '*Poesia*,' Sir, to frame it in more comfortable terms for you, even the Wasp of Twickenham must be assign'd the Letter Beta, for 'tis Timothy Tox who is its Lumina. I was quoting from the *Pennsylvaniad*, of course."

"Of course."

"Oh, go on, then, Tim, tell him."

"*Thoo* are— "

"Not so loud. This is not my Home. I am upon the Scamper, I fear, tho' none will speak of it. Like Mr. Wilkes, I have endanger'd my Freedom by Printing what displeaseth this King. Not 'the' King, you appreciate...." He peers at Dixon as a Physician might, waiting for some sign. "Only a Broadside. No more than a couple of hundred Copies. Went...something like,

> 'As legionaries once in Skirts patroll'd
> The streets of old Londinium, damp and cold,
> So Troops in kilts invade us now, unbeckon'd,
> Styling themselves "the Highland Forty-second."
> Who is this King that fires upon his own,
> Who are these Ministers, with heads of Stone,
> Holy Experiment! O where be Thou,
> Where be thy hopes, thy fears, thy terrors now?' "

489

Outside, great Percussions upon the Earth are heard, coming ever closer. Trees, push'd over, crash to the ground. Bears, Bobcats, and Wolves come fleeing before whatever is just behind. Pewter dances across the boards of the Tables. Ale trembles in ev'ry Can. Observing Timothy Tox's Brightness of Eye and steadfastness of Lip, Dixon pretends Astonishment. "Have thoo summon'd it here, with thy Verses?"

"Somewhat as ye may summon a Star with a Telescope. I pray no more than that."

"No Friend of the King, I collect...?"

"An American Golem. They thought the Black Boys who fought them at Fort Loudon were dangerous,— those were benevolent Elves in Comparison. Here as in Prague, the Golem takes a dim view of Oppression, and is ever available to exert itself to the Contrary."

Out the Window, great Mud Feet are seen to stir, tall as the Eaves. The Countrymen raise Tankards in their direction. "A sovereign Deterrent to Black Watch Plaid," declares Mr. Tox.

> "This Forest suffers not the Bag-Pipe's Scream,
> To stay away, the Brits it wiser deem."

51

South Mountain is the last concentration of Apparitions,— as you might say, Shape-'Morphers, and Soul-Snatchers, besides plain "Ghosts." Beyond lies Wilderness, where quite another Presence reigns, undifferentiate,— Thatwhichever *precedeth* Ghostliness....

Dixon takes to wearing a coonskin cap. Mason is alarm'd,— "That something has happen'd to your hair," is what he says aloud, whilst thinking, that Dixon has become a Werewolf, or even worse,— some New World Creature without a name, at home among the illimitable possibilities of Evil in this Forest,...some Manifestation to daylight denied.... Meanwhile Dixon, sensing in his partner but a lower order of Snakes-and-Bears Jumpiness, in Fun begins appearing at the Tent-opening with the tail of the Hat pull'd round in front of his face, screaming in a Pitman's Cant intelligible but to himself. Mason's reactions are all he is hoping for, and more. The Quill goes into a panicky skate off the page,— Mason looks frantically about for a weapon. Dixon quickly reverses the bushy Tail.

"Surprize!"

"Not funny."

"Don't like me Shappo? Well Ah hadn't done Punch's Voice yet...?" At Mason's blank look, "Tha mean, tha've never done this with thy Wig? The children love it."

"Fascinating. Apparently I was never allow'd the Opportunity,— my older son,— William,— having learn'd quite soon to remove mine from my head, and convert it into a toy Cudgel, with which, charmingly of course, he would pretend to smash his baby brother's head in. The powder always made him sneeze, altho' this did not affect the sincerity of his Assault."

But the word *always* has slipp'd in, fatal to any attempt at Wit, or even lightness of tone, and may be Mason's way of asking for sympathy, fully as supplicatory as a tremor in the voice, a fugitive tear. He has blunder'd on into a Remark about Hats, cock'd and not.

"Sir?" Dixon giving Beef.

"Surely, Sir, I meant no disrespect to the Quakers, among whom I number,— "

" 'Tis the dismissive Use of Metonymy, Sir. We are particularly earnest upon the Topick of Hats, having invested in them more than insurance against the Rain.— Our history as a Sect having begun with a Hat that remain'd upon its Head,— and mercifully the Head upon its Body,— "

Later, Mason seeks revenge. Dixon having drifted into a hypnagogic passage in which, amid a profligacy of stars rushing by, he is traversing straight upward, *Zenithward*,— "Eeh! Eeh!" He is awake and screaming. Mason is ringing a small iron Bell rapidly in front of his Nose. "Indians? Americans? Where's my Rifle? Whah'?"

" 'Tis Capella," smirks Mason, "about to culminate, and tho' I do prefer the Clock myself, as it *is* your, ye might say, Work-Station, reluctantly must I yield it to you, I suppose, and go clap me Eye to the old Snout once again."

"I wasn't asleep...?"

" 'Fair Blapsia, I am thine'? Pray you Sir, a moment's Mercy."

"Who said thah'...? Ah didn't say thah'...?"

Mason's look is pois'd between Pity and Annoyance.

"I've been awake. I remember when Farlow and Boggs came by...? with their Voucher Situation...? a lively whim-wham for fair."

"Boggs and Farlow didn't,— Hum, that is to say,— "

"Ha! Happen 'twas *thee* asleep then...? I puzzl'd that they spoke so quietly."

"I was *awake,* all the time, they were never here, you must have dream'd it."

"Oh, tha look'd awake, but Ah mind thy gift of sleeping with thine Eyes open wide."

"I can't help that, my father did it too, it's given me Nightmares for Years. I couldn't bear to look at it,— how can you? Doesn't it trouble you?"

"Me? Why, no. Why should it? Some individual pretending to stare at me, whilst his Soul's off God knows where, having Adventures imperfectly recall'd,— why should any of that trouble me, particularly the Question of what, in thy Absence, is doing the Staring for thee? What caretaker, what Verger of the Temple of the Self...? Eeh!"

"Yes. And, and the Stare you speak of,— do my Eyes, in a sense, *roll upward* into blind white Ovoids, and are your Dreams not invaded by that sinister unseeing Gaze, ever-charg'd with some imminent Act you must upon no account remain there to witness,— "

"Aye!" screams Dixon, "— aye, they're blank as boil'd Eggs, and worse,— for Irisless and unpupil'd yet do they go on *squinting* at me, as if,— "

"Yes, yes?"

"Eeh, never mind."

"No, pray you, I'm interested, very interested indeed." Wind shoves against the Tent. Rainwater somewhere drips into a kettle. The flames of the Tallow Dips are ever uncertain. From the Forest now proceed Sounds, real ones, that neither Surveyor has heard before, and that each is too embarrass'd to mention to the other. Dixon, having the finer tolerance for mysterious intrusion, breaks first. "All right, I know you hear it too. It's rhythmic, and high-pitch'd, aye? I say it's Indian Drums, and they're talking about huz...?"

"And I say, 'tis a Dog," Mason somber. "A particular Dog, with a syncopated Bark.... Oh yes, a Dog well known and much fear'd in this Region,— withal a Dog...."

"Eeh, wait then, wheer's my Flask, if we're having a Toast to the Animal...?" Outside something is creeping by. "Hold!" Dixon seizing a Pistol and diving out the tent-flap, into the rain with a smoothness Mason has rarely observ'd. There is some jingling and shuffling. "It's the young McClean!" cries Dixon.

"Felicitude," mutters Mason. "What next? Invite him in for a Drink, I suppose."

In pokes Dixon's head, considerably wetter. "Nathe's of your Mind,— thinks it's a Dog. I still say it's a Drum, though perhaps of unconventional Design,— say, how much of that Stuff in the Bottles is to hand?" They now are join'd by other crew members who have heard, and are unhappy with, the pulsing, uncertainly Distant Noise. Wearily Mason pulls on Oil-cloths, tugs his Service-Grade Beaver over his Nob, and emerges to mill about as perplex'd as the rest, hoping no one will look to him for Leadership. Soon the place is so full of Crew that they decide to move on into the Mess tent, where already Mr. Barnes and his Band have been conversing separately.

"Gents, we are all agreed," the Overseer greets them, " 'tis the," whispering for the first time since they've known him, "Black Dog."

"Probably out seeking to relieve himself upon one or more of his personal Trees," adds Matt Marine, "which will no longer be there, having been chopp'd down for our Visto. The B.D. will likely be very put out at this, for he does like his personal Trees, ye see."

"Shall he retaliate?" wonders Mason. "What Measures should we be taking?"

"Eeh, Mason...?"

"May I suggest that this is all but a form of Joint Mirage," offers the Rev[d], "something very like it having been reported in the *Philosophical Transactions* not long ago, as you may recall?"

Dixon's "Why, aye" and Mason's "I do not" are spoken simultaneously. The Surveyors glare at each other. "Someone wrote in to the R.S. about *this* Black Dog?" inquires Mason.

"Careful," warns Mr. Barnes, "you're not suppos'd to use any of Its names, really."

"Really? 'The Black Dog'? Can't say, 'The Black— ' "

"Sh-*shh!* 'Tis one of the Things That Are Never Said."

"Oh?" Dixon curious. "And the others are...?"

"An extended List, Sir."

"And of course tha'd rather not recite it aloud...? is it not yet enough, the Catholick axmen blessing their Bits each morning with holy water,— the Astrologites newly reluctant to work when the Moon is void of Course,— the Presbyterians ever brewing Potions, and scrying the entrails of Toads,— and now a List of Things That May Not Be Said?"

"Ahrr,— " Mason a-squint, "finely set these Days? Am I not given to understand that no Geordie can ever quite bring himself to pronounce the name of— "

"Don't say it,— "

"— of a certain farm animal? noted for its wallowing, and, and oinking,— "

"Be a Gent, Mason, I concede the point."

"And you promise not to say, 'The Black D— ' ehhp,— that is,— "

"Folk out here advise," says Dixon, "that all else failing, the Names most likely to matter, spoken aloud, are those of the Holy Trinity,— accompanied by a Cross, drawn in the air at the same time."

"Same time as what? as the Dog is leaping for my Throat?"

"Eeh,— disputes with Phantom Dogs are not in *my* Line, Mason. Dogs love me, I'm a Dog Person."

"Are you really."

"All my Life."

"So,— if I threw a Stick, and cried Fetch, you would actually run, and,— " Mason places a Finger crosswise between his teeth, and nods, inquiringly.

"No, no, not *that* kind of Dog Person.— Though happen I did see something like, once at Darlington Fair...?"

"Hark ye," calls Moses Barnes, "— Gentlemen. Has the Wind only shifted, or has this damn'd Howling come nearer?"

All attend the Night outside the canvas walls. "Ain't it more likely to be no Dog, but Indians pretending to be a Dog?" Mr. Farlow inquires calmly, thereby throwing the Company into a Panick. Countrymen set their fur hats mistakenly upon the Heads of others, or grab the wrong Rifle whilst it is yet in its Owner's Hands. Powder is spill'd, strewn, left by the Fire. Ev'ryone is shouting at once.

"Leadership," Mason mumbling to himself. Turning to Dixon, "One of us,— "

"Me. As usual." Pulling his Hat down over his Ears, he prepares to exit.

"Mr. Dixon is going out to have a look," Mason announces, quite chirpy. "If it is a Dog, he'll know what to do."

"What if it's Indians?"

"I'll bite them...?" Dixon lifts the Flap, clears his Sensorium, and steps outside. There is a long Silence. Mason has drifted into a curious daydream about Philadelphia, where he has just been elected Dog-Catcher, on the basis of his adventures upon South Mountain, when Dixon comes back.

"Wasn't the Creature yese spoke of. It was the Glowing Indian."

"What, the Glowing Indian of South Mountain? Hasn't been seen for years."

"Perhaps it was something else...?" Dixon accepts a Pewter Mug of Maize-Whiskey. "What would tha call a very large Native American, with a net output of light, comparable to that of a Forge?"

"Dunno...Glowing Indian?"

"Just so,— Hatchet and Musket-Barrel and Knife-Blades, all a-glow, Steam billowing up when he stepp'd in the Creek...?"

Mason has no command of his Tongue. He keeps trying to say, "Too far, Dixon, you never know where the Crease of Credulity's been set." He is disappointed at not having seen it, whatever it is,— believing it a Spiritual Demonstration, that Dixon almost certainly has fail'd to appreciate. Dixon, for his part, the further West they chain, finds himself with a need for some new Jostling daily to his Sensorium, and tonight's Glowing Indian, in this numbing torrent of American Stimuli, seems just the Ticket, tho' he wouldn't have minded some whim-wham with the Black Dog. "Wading down toward Antietam, last I saw. Seem'd a pleasant enough Lad. Not much to say. Too tall, of course...."

Over South Mountain, among the Springs that fall to Antietam Creek, on September 21st, they pause at 96 Miles, 3 Chains, near the House of Mr. Staphel Shockey, who tells them of a remarkable Cavern beneath the Earth, about six miles south of the Line. In the winter, English Church services are held in it. Mason's Hat begins to move, as from some Agitation beneath it. Accordingly, the next day, Sunday, they pay a visit, in company with Mr. Shockey and his Children, whilst Mrs. Shockey remains at home with a thousand Chores that Sunday does not release her from.

> The entrance is an arch about 6 yards in length and four feet in height, when immediately there opens a room 45 yards in length, 40 in breadth and 7 or 8 in height. (Not one pillar to support nature's arch)...On the Sidewalls are drawn by the Pencil of Time, with the tears of the Rocks: The imitation of Organ, Pillar, Columns and Monuments of a Temple; which, with the glimmering faint light; makes the whole an awful, solemn appearance: Striking its Visitants with a strong and melancholy reflection: that such is the abodes of the Dead: thy inevitable doom, O stranger; soon to be numbered as one of them.

"— So it reads in the Field-Book."

"They handed that *in?*" Ethelmer in surprise.

"Part of the official record," Uncle Ives's Eyebrows descending.

"However, where Mason saw a Gothick Interior, Dixon saw 'pon ev'ry Surface, ancient Inscriptions, Glyphs unreadable,— Ogham, possibly."

Mr. Shockey has little to add. "The Indians, it seems like they stay'd away from here,— bad Spirits or something. So if it's writing, it'd have to be older 'n them."

"Could've been Welsh Indians," offers one of his Sons. "Mov'd on West long before our Time, said to be cross'd beyond the Illinois. You'll be seeing Captain Shelby soon, he knows more."

Mason is looking about, precisely like someone planning to furnish a room. "Nor Summer's Heat," he will whisper later that Night, unable to quit the Fire "nor Winter's Freeze, need bother us, snug in the Earth...those Ceilings! high as Heaven...."

Dixon is not quite so entertain'd. The Cave oppresses him. He has mentally measur'd it, as Surveyors do, and is trying to imagine what form of Life might be calling something as spacious as this Home. And what might become of the Anglican Population out here, should the Dweller show up unexpectedly one Sunday, during the Service.

All the way back to the Visto, Mason is seiz'd by Monology. "Text,— " he cries, and more than once, "it is Text,— and we are its readers, and its Pages are the Days turning. Unscrolling, as a Pilgrim's Itinerary map in ancient Days. And this is the Chapter call'd 'The Subterranean Cathedral, or, The Lesson Grasp'd.' You must make sure I do not attempt to return. Didn't you feel anything? You people, with your second sight and Eldritch Powers,— why I've seen betterr at Painswick Fairr."

"Eeh, a Lad brings in a Well or two, and right away 'tis Wizard me this, Wizard me thah'…?"

"Can you stretch me a bit o' Chain today, do ye guess?"

"Thank thee for asking,— I'd been planning to crowd thee…?"

They neck-rein their Horses in opposite directions, till they're as far apart upon the Road as they can manage, and continue their return from the World beneath the World, to the Line beneath the Stars.

52

The crossing of Conococheague, with its dismal history, proves particularly unsettling. Providentially, no ten minutes of Arc terminate upon either Bank,— that burn'd and bloodied little huddle of Cabins, can provide no Object of Pilgrimage, any Prospect of lingering as much as a Fortnight, among these Ghosts, and the Desolation in which they wait, would have sent the Expedition on to some Station less haunted,— extra Chaining and Calculating and all.

Lancaster as a scene of horror had been bearable because of the secular Town upon ev'ry side, pursuing its Business, begging Attendance at ev'ry turn,— yet what in Lancaster was but an hour's Thrill, out here in this sternly exact Desert might become an uncontrollable descent into whatever the Visto was suppos'd to deny,— the covetousness of all that liv'd...that continued to press in at either side, wishing simply to breach the long rectified Absence wherever it might,— to insist upon itself.

Between two roads leading to different ferries across Potowmack, they calculate and change course, and at last, 117 miles, 12 chains, and 97 links west of the Post Mark'd West, they fetch up against the flank of the North Mountain, having enter'd the personal Zone of Influence of Capt. Evan Shelby. They pack the Instruments and leave them in his Care, for the Winter.

Not till they turn and head east again, do they find any time for rememb'ring anything. Going west has been all Futurity. Now, moving against the Sun, they may take up again the past.

Trudging one day into the wind, all hats impossible, hair in streams, struggling to keep the brass instrument on its tripod over one shoulder, Dixon at last saw the logic of Emerson's notorious back-to-front coat.

"Of course 'tis back-to front," Emerson had sigh'd, "Plutonians, give some Brain to it,— in all animals, isn't it the Ventral or Belly-side that needs most protection,— the Dorsal or Back-side being stronger and harder? And won't half the walking I'm to do in my Life, be into the Wind? Bonny. At such times, then, I'd rather be a few degrees above Freezing, thankee, and let me Back look after itself."

"Then why does ev'ryone else go about with Coats open in front?"

Emerson gazed upon the assembl'd young Scholars with a great pretense of mildness and forbearance. "My entire life as a Teacher, lesson after futile lesson, is time thus pitiably squander'd,— an old man's Folly. Not that I ever was a Teacher, really, I'm a Man of Science, between patrons at the moment, only doing this so I can pay my laboratory expenses, tho' Mrs. Emerson takes a slightly different View...' 'Tis the Grub-Street of Philosophy!' she laments. 'Durham Prison were better!' Howsobeit, the Question, mercifully, was not about Marriage.... The Modern Coat, as we know it," he explain'd, "is bas'd upon the attire of the Nobility and Gentry and other assorted Thieves, who could ever afford Servants to put their clothes on for them. At such intimate moments, 'twas believ'd more prudent to keep a Servant in front of one, than allow him behind. For today's Discussion, therefore, speculate for me if yese will, what might have happen'd to the Structure of England, had ev'rything fasten'd in back, obliging Servants,— let us here include America, the Indies, and black Slaves as well,— to spend more time behind their Masters than before, and so close as to be invisible?"

Long before the Soldiers came in sight, People in their Path could hear the drums, upon fitfully directed Winds, clattering off the walls of old quarries where Weld flower'd in glows of orange, yellow, and green, raking the hillside pastures all but empty, with the lambs just sold and the breeding ewes resting up for winter, their cull'd sisters off to auctions and fates less ritual, whilst the rams were soon to go up to spend winter in the hills. Vast flights of starlings, fleeing the racket, beat across the sky at high speed, like Squall-clouds,— Evening at Noon-tide. In the little one-street villages, women stood among the laundry they'd just put out, looking at the Light, reckoning drying time and marching time, and Cloud-speed, and how wet ev'rything might be when they'd have to bring it in again. Soon the mercilessly even drumbeat fill'd the Day, replacing the accustom'd rhythms of country People with the controlling Pulse of military Clock-time, announcing that all events would now occur at the army's Pleasure, upon the army's schedule.

"Then they began with the Bagpipes." For demonstrative purposes, Wolfe from time to time in the easy march up to Stroud would order his troopers to dismount, take up skirmish positions, and fire at whatever took their Fancy. Later, in Pennsylvania, deep within the Glades of Death, crossing the road upon which Braddock and his forces had met their unhappy end, Mason would wonder if the effects of the late Tragedy in America upon Army morale in general, and upon Wolfe in particular, might not also have play'd their part in this idle Musketry, which left splash'd behind them a path scarlet with hundreds of small innocent lives wild and domestic,— far beneath the notice of a dragoon, of course, but often of moment to local residents,— the Fowl running into the Fields, no sleep for fear of ev'rything that might happen....

"For all we know, Wolfe may have felt the same contempt for British Weavers as did Braddock for American Indians,— treacherous Natives, disrespectful, rebellious, waiting in Ambuscado, behind ev'ry stone wall."

"British firing upon British,— " Dixon charging his Pipe absently, "I thought thah' was all done with. Are your Weavers Jacobites, then?"

"They're people, Dixon, whom I saw daily, they work'd, they ate when they came off-shift, good for a Cob or a Batch-Loaf a day. Or a Mason's Bap,— that was my Dad's own specialty, baked upon the bottom of the Oven, white Flour in clouds, he'd sell 'em whole, or by the Slice.

"Some aspir'd to be master-weavers, most would have settl'd for a living wage, but their desires how betray'd, when in 'fifty-six the Justices of the Peace, upon easily imagin'd arrangements with the Clothiers, reduced by half the Wages set by law, and the troubles came to a head."

He pauses as if reaching a small decision. "Rebekah's people were weavers."

Dixon lighting his Pipe, "Hahdn't knoawn thah'."

"Wool-workers upon her father's side, silk upon her mother's,— she liked to say it accompted for the way she was."

Dixon puffs, nodding slowly, evenly, eyes cross'd as if scrying in the glow of his pipe-bowl.

And that wondrous night, in the High Street, they were all there, brothers and cousins and uncles,"— Mason's pause seems but for breath, tho' Dixon already is beaming an unmistakable inquiry,— "*I* was there, now that I think of it."

Dixon nods. "Been out upon the Pavement m'self…Tyne Keelmen, back in 'fifty. No business over there, understand, none at all, yet…"

Mason reaches for his Pipe. "Oh, aye."

"More than once, perhaps…?"

"I have look'd on Worlds far distant, their Beauty how pitiless."

"Yet thah' night,— "

"The Streets, Jere! thousands of angry men in Streets that ordinarily see no more than, oh, a dozen a day,— 'twas back'd up to Slad Brook! it spill'd out into both branches of the High Street,— " he puffs, in a sub-merriment Dixon recognizes, "— down the Lower Street, and up Parliament, and all that Hill-side between,— torches ev'rywhere, Looms dress'd in Mourning, songs of the 'Forty-five (their Throbbing within those prim corridors of Stone, how savage), effigies of hated Master Weavers, hang'd in their own Bar-chains so dishonorably set, and the Murmur,— ever, unceasingly, the great, crisp, serene Roar,— of a Mobility focus'd upon a just purpose."

"Aye…aye, of course in Newcastle 'twas more the Brick type of wall,— quite different sound,— more like Philadelphia…?"

"What did they do in Durham with the ones they caught?"

"The Keelmen? transported,— I know, not as entertaining as the gallows in Painswick,— yet, as we aren't quite such devotees of the Noose in Durham, a good many Tyneside Keel-men ended up in America,— hereabouts, in fact. If we'd stopp'd longer in Philadelphia, we'd've run into a few of 'em by now.…"

"And, would I've enjoy'd that?"

"Tha might not've been along...? I mean, of course, having at the last minute decided they weren't thy sort, all that coal-grime and ale-drinking and such,— nor as clean as thy Loom-worker, out there by the babbling Brook, neat as a Pin and All,— "

"Wait. You're saying that *ceteris paribus,* the Company of Keelmen is preferable to that of Weavers? That's clearly impossible, for 'tis widely allow'd, that Weavers are the soul of Jollification."

"You've nothing in Gloucester nay, nor in the Kingdom, to match the night Billy Snowball thought the Old Clasher's head was an Ale-Can! Eeh! Eeh! Eeh!"

Mason gazes until the laughter subsides. "Tho' evidently a source of Cheery Memories for you,— "

"Kept grabbin' him by his Noahse...? 'And whah's this?' Eeeh! Eeh!"

"— yet in Stroud, how ill-advis'd,— even in so tolerant and cosmopolitan a Room as The George Inn,— "

"Where, let us recall, back in 'fifty-six, tha witness'd a Congress of Clothiers leaping from the Upstairs windows,— "

"Thankee,— some indeed with their Punch-cups still upon their Fingers, and lit Pipes in their Mouths, and the Cards scatt'ring ev'rywhere,— "

At home he found his father in some Anxiety. "Weavers a-riot, troops coming in,— "

"I ought to stay, then."

"What'll you do, point your Telescope at them? You'll be worse than useless, they'll shoot you the moment you present them that vacant Face."

"Perhaps I can ask them at Greenwich for another— "

"Release yourself,— your mother and I will get through, between the thieving Mob and the thieving Soldiers, there're still places to hide an odd Loaf...but you,— better that you repair to Greenwich, Kent, young Sirr,— remain upon your Hill-top, farr from this poorr defeated place."

He sought his Mother's eyes,— receiving only a quick Sweep, as from a Broom, her face distress'd, as if whispering, You see how you distress him....

...

The open countryside seem'd made only to pull coal out of and run a few sheep on, and to harbor all the terrors imaginable to a boy. "I was only comfortable in the towns," Dixon one day would admit, "or in Raby, protected by the Castle,—yet never car'd for the territory between."

Mason looks on in some perplexity. "Rum affliction for a Surveyor, isn't it?"

"Say that it provided me an incentive, to enclose that which had hitherto been without Form, and hence haunted by anything and ev'rything, if you grasp my meaning,— anything and ev'rything, Sir."

"I was well acquainted with such terrors, whilst yet I crept and babbl'd, Sir. Despite the roads steep and toilsome, was I taken, like most children born in that part of Bisley Parish, truly bouncing Babes all, to Sapperton Church, to be Christen'd,— for Bisley lies across a great treeless Plain, known at our end as Oakridge Common, and at the other as Bisley Common, haunted by wild men and murderers, and its Wind never ceasing,— a source of limitless Fear."

"Cockfield Fell to the double-dot," Dixon recalls. "Ev'ryone put in great effort to avoid crossing it."

"When I got older and began watching the Stars, of course, 'twas another Story. The Sky was suddenly all there, in its full Display. I couldn't wait for Night, to be out under it."

"Eeh, stop, I'm a-shiver now."

"Nothing for Miles, unprotected 'neath those Leagues innumerable, in which, *at any moment,— *"

"Eeeehh!" Dixon, to appearance in a true Panick, runs about the Tent looking for someplace to hide, and finding nothing but a Feed-Sack handy, attempts to insert himself into it.

Emerson smoaked it all right away. "If it's but the empty places between the Towns," he advis'd Dixon, "your worries are at an end, for look what you can do. *You can get above it.*" He spoke these words with an emphasis Dixon cannot describe the full strangeness of. Something was up,— as so, shortly, would he and his classmates be,— but before they learn'd to fly, they had to learn about Maps, for Maps are the *Aidesmémoires* of flight. So Dixon came to discover as well the great Invariance whereby, aloft, one gains exactitude of Length and Breadth, only to lose much of the land's Relievo, or Dimension of Height,— whilst back at ground level, traveling about the Country, one regains bodily the realities of up and down, only to lose any but a rough sense of the other two Dimensions, now all about one.

"Earthbound," Emerson continued, "we are limited to our Horizon, which sometimes is to be measur'd but in inches.— We are bound withal to Time, and the amounts of it spent getting from one end of a journey to another. Yet aloft, in Map-space, origins, destinations, any Termini, hardly seem to matter,— one can apprehend all at once the entire plexity of possible journeys, set as one is above Distance, above Time itself."

"Altitude!" cried out a couple of alert youths,— as, in Emerson's class they were encourag'd to do.

"Altitude, being the Price we pay for this great Exemption, is consider'd as an in-house Expense, to be absorb'd in an inner term of a lengthy Expression describing Location, Course, and Speed. If you're interested, wait for my book upon Navigation, currently all but in Galley-proofs, for a detail'd Account."

Some were preoccupied with questions less modern. "Where is Hob Headless in this aerial View?" Dixon was not alone in wanting to know. "What of the Shotton Dobby, and the Old Hell-Cat of Raby with her black Coach and six? She can rise above the Land-scape too,— how does an innocent Cartographer deal with that?"

"Professional courtesy is the usual rule," Emerson replied. "You salute in the other her Gift of Flight, and move on. Briskly, if possible."

"And uhm, vice versa, too, you're quite sure of that, Sir...?"

"Tut, tut, alas and what shall we do, O the Lamentations of Jeremiah.— Have you then been squandering your precious Skepticism, over at Raby, upon this Gothickal Clap-trap?"

Why aye, and so he had, and even worse than that, he'd fallen into a Fascination with the "Old Hell-Cat" herself,— Elizabeth, Lady Barnard, who'd died back in '42 after a life of embitter'd family warfare over who was to inherit the Castle, whose Battlements she continued to walk with a pair of brass knitting-needles, whilst awaiting her Coach. The great thing, of these Needles, was, that they glow'd in the Dark, because they were Very Hot, hotter than a Coal-fire, more like the fires of Hell, which feed upon substances less easily nam'd. 'Twas as a further conundrum presented to them to solve (or not solve) that Emerson wonder'd aloud, What Yarn could she possibly be knitting with, that would not burn at the touch of Heat like that? Wool from a Hell-Sheep? Those who tried to imagine it were rewarded, though in ways they later found difficult to describe.

Many is the night young Dixon sees her up there, the angles between the two bright Lines ever varying as she paces to and fro.... One night at last, probably (he says he is no longer sure) disappointed in early Love, which is to say devastated, he decides, with nothing more to lose, that he'll go up and have a closer look. By now he knows the Castle like a Cat, no perch too precarious nor roof-slate too slippery, as he goes a-flowing one to the next among holds upon the facial features of Gargoyles known, perforce, with some intimacy, across Counter-scarps, to and through Machicolations in the Moon-light.... If the Spectre, without her Coach, be relatively slow-moving, how difficult shall it be to spy upon her?

That's if. As Dixon draws close, he can hear her muttering. "Never on Time. Always delay'd, always another excuse. The 'late' Lady Barnard, indeed. Yet what is the point of cursing the fool, Eternally curs'd as he was ever?" By now, there's a peculiar sound out in the night, bearing the same relation to Hoofbeats as pluck'd Strings to Drum-beats, and seeming to approach....

Dixon must suppress a Gasp. Assembling itself from the Darkness about them appears the most uncommonly beautiful Coach he's ever seen. Its curves are the curves of a desirable Woman, its Lacquering's all a-flash, Bright as a wanton Eye. Its coal-color'd Arabs, scarcely sighing, bring it in a glide to a spot near her Parapet, holding it then pois'd, hooves stirring in the empty Air, above the Grounds invisible in the Darkness below,— whilst the Coachman, with a face as white as his Livery is black, descends to the Parapet to open her Door.

"Late again, Trent."

"Sorry Milady,— traffick."

"Traffick!" she raises the Brass needles above her head, one in each trembling fist, as if to strike. "I've heard the lead horse went insane,—

I've heard the Wife she's not so clivvor this se'ennight,— I've heard, the Wind was in my teeth, and the Clock ran down, and the Dog made off with me Coachwhip, but this, Trent, this begins to approach the truly maddening. What possible Traffick can there be above Cockfield Fell? Are we not in fact the only flying Coach-and-six in the Palatinate?"

"They,— they come over from Hurworth, Milady,— swarms of them."

"Oh, it's Emerson and that lot. Ragged children. Swarms, quotha. You may as well have been delay'd by a flock of Ducks. Really, Trent, these excuses grow more and more enfeebl'd, and tiresome *pari passu....* What are you up to, honestly, when I leave you alone with this lovely Machine? Hmm? Trent? Come, come, you can tell Her Ladyship all." With an athletic readiness that surprises the young Lurker, she vaults up into the quilted black velvet interior, and Trent swings shut the Door and climbs smirking to his seat. Through the Window she leans then to stare back out, unmistakably and directly at Dixon, and calls, "Perhaps another time, Jeremiah." They are gone,— horses, perfect Shine, curves and all, leaving Dixon's nape and shoulders mantl'd in unearthly cold.

That is how he remembers first hearing of Emerson, though the Legend by then was well under way in Durham. Though he keeps chuckling it away, Dixon also suspects he sought out Emerson from his Desire to be one of those ragged Kids, and that "another Time" happen some Evening when he and Lady Barnard were both aloft. Down here she held too much advantage. Altitude might help his odds. He didn't know whether he was planning seduction, or combat,— these, at fourteen, being the only categories of Pleasure he recogniz'd. That it might have been something else altogether would never occur to him until years later, at Castle Lepton, in the wilderness of America, well entangl'd in gambling debts, Romantick Intriguing, and political jiggery-pokery, all punctuated by a Liver Episode he may have worried himself into, unless 'twas all that Drinking he was doing. "Ah Mason," he cried, tho' Mason, who in fact was not doing too much better, lay snoring in a Corner,— "she has it all,— Beauty, Money,...um...whatever else there is...."

．．．

Whilst yet in the steep Mountains, they take to Sledding in the Year's early snow-Falls, upon folded pieces of Tent-Canvas. One day, just as they start down a long slope neither can remember from earlier, coming the other way and climbing, an Autumnal Squall comes snapping up like a Blanket being shaken into a Spread of chill Cloud, and Snow begins abruptly, it seems, to fall. Both Surveyors feel their Velocity increasing ominously.

"Ehp, Dixon? Still over there? Can you see where we're going?"

"Snow's coming down too thick!" Dixon calls from someplace, because of the change of acousticks between them, unmeasurable.

Both shrill with the Predicament, blind, together, separate, they plunge down the imperfectly remember'd Steep. They pass the Commissary-Waggon, and one, then two more Supply-Waggons, each brak'd in its Snowy Descent by a late-fell'd Tree dragged behind, the Drivers looking 'round wildly, the Horses beginning to grow anxious, till Mason and Dixon are swept once again behind the stinging Curtain of Snow-Crystals. They hear voices ahead, then are suddenly zooming out of Invisibility, in among the Axmen, who, believing them pitiless crazy predators in this place lonely as any in Ulster or the Rhineland, scatter for their Lives back into the Trees. The Day is medium-lit, the Snow more Fall than Storm. The look of all things, thro' the white Descent, is amplified,— the Brass of Instruments back beneath Canvas, the droppings of the Horses, the glow of a clay pipe-ful of Tobacco…. Each is aware of how easily a Tree unfell'd, even a Stump left high enough to protrude from the Snow, rearing too quickly to swerve 'round, might mark their personal Termini.

"Dixon! Can you hear me?"

"I'm just here, tha' don't have to shout…?"

"Look ye, I am going entirely too fast, and as the *First Derivative* 'round here shows no sign of lessening, what I thought I'd do is self-brake,— that is, lean over gradually like this, until I fall o-o-o-ve-r-r-r!…," his voice abruptly fading behind, leaving Dixon alone to face whatever continues to rush upon him a Snowflake's breadth ahead of his Nose.

"Eeh, thah's a bonny Pickle tha've put me in, for fair...." His Reflections are interrupted by the seemingly miraculous Advent, directly in his Path, of a Pile of Cushions, usually located 'neath the Waggon-Canopy, where they intervene 'twixt the Instruments and the excursions of the secular Road-way, but here rather set in the Snow-fall to air out, lest the tell-tale Aura of Tobacco-Smoak testify to a slothful and indeed unacceptable proximity of Instrument-Bearers to Instruments. "Fate is Fate...?" he supposes aloud, opening his arms to embrace this by no means discomfort-free heap of Upholstery.

"Stogies, I believe...?" when all has subsided to a Halt.

"Sir," replies the Waggoner, Frederick Schess, "my personal Opinion of Tobacco,— "

"Freddie, consider the Crossing of Paths here,— why, it has likely sav'd my Life...? Miraculous, for fair...? How can I report thee? yet at the same time, how can I commend thee for it?"

"Cash is acceptable,— " calls Tom Hickman.

"Jug of Corn now and then'd be pleasant," adds Matty Marine.

They discharge the Hands and leave off for the Winter. At Christmastide, the Tavern down the Road from Harlands' opens its doors, and soon ev'ryone has come inside. Candles beam ev'rywhere. The Surveyors, knowing this year they'll soon again be heading off in different Directions into America, stand nodding at each other across a Punch-bowl as big as a Bathing-Tub. The Punch is a secret Receipt of the Landlord, including but not limited to peach brandy, locally distill'd Whiskey, and milk. A raft of long Icicles broken from the Eaves floats upon the pale contents of the great rustick Monteith. Everyone's been exchanging gifts. Somewhere in the coming and going one of the Children is learning to play a metal whistle. Best gowns rustle along the board walls. Adults hold Babies aloft, exclaiming, "The little Sausage!" and pretending to eat them. There are popp'd Corn, green Tomato Mince Pies, pickl'd Oysters, Chestnut Soup, and Kidney Pudding. Mason gives Dixon a Hat, with a metallick Aqua Feather, which Dixon is wearing. Dixon gives Mason a Claret Jug of silver, crafted in Philadelphia. There are Conestoga Cigars for Mr. Harland and a Length of contraband Osnabrigs for Mrs. H. The Children get Sweets from a Philadelphia English-shop, both adults being drawn into prolong'd Negotiations with their Juniors, as to who shall have which of. Mrs. Harland comes over to embrace both Surveyors at once. "Thanks for simmering down this Year. I know it ain't easy."

"What a year, Lass," sighs Dixon.

"Poh. Like eating a Bun," declares Mason.

53

The Ascent to Christ is a struggle thro' one heresy after another, River-wise up-country into a proliferation of Sects and Sects branching from Sects, unto Deism, faithless pretending to be holy, and beyond,— ever away from the Sea, from the Harbor, from all that was serene and certain, into an Interior unmapp'd, a Realm of Doubt. The Nights. The Storms and Beasts. The Falls, the Rapids,…the America of the Soul.

Doubt is of the essence of Christ. Of the twelve Apostles, most true to him was ever Thomas,— indeed, in the *Acta Thomae* they are said to be Twins. The final pure Christ is pure uncertainty. He is become the central subjunctive fact of a Faith, that risks ev'rything upon one bodily Resurrection…. Wouldn't something less doubtable have done? a prophetic dream, a communication with a dead person? Some few tatters of evidence to wrap our poor naked spirits against the coldness of a World where Mortality and its Agents may bully their way, wherever they wish to go….

— The Reverend Wicks Cherrycoke, *Undeliver'd Sermons*

She had found in her Kitchen, the Kitchen Garden, the beehives and the Well, a join'd and finish'd Life, the exact Life, perhaps, that Our Lord intended she live…a Life that was like a Flirtation with the Day in all its humorless Dignity…she was at her window, in afternoon peaceable autumn, ev'ryone else in town at the Vendue, Seth too, and the Boys, when They came for her,— as it seem'd, only for her. The unimagin'd dark Men. The Nakedness of the dark and wild men.

Water in a Kettle somewhere was crackling into its first Roll. She risk'd looking at their Faces. The only other place to look was down at the secret Flesh, glistening, partly hidden, partly glimps'd behind the creas'd and odorous Deer-skin clouts.... yet for them to come for her, this far East of Susquehanna, this far inside the perimeter of peaceable life, was for the Day to collapse into the past, into darker times,— 'twas to be return'd to, and oblig'd to live through again, something she thought she, thought all her Community, had transcended. Her Lapse had been to ignore the surprizing Frailness of secular Life. By imagining it to be Christian, she had meant to color it with the Immortality of her Soul, of her Soul in Christ, allowing herself to forget that turns of Fortune in the given World might depend upon Events too far out of her Power,...what twig-fall, Prey's escape, unintended insult, might have grown, have multiplied, until there was nowhere else for them to've come, no one else to've come for, even still as she was, and spiritless, before that violent effect of causes unknown....

The further they took her through the Forest, away from her home and name, the safer she began to feel. Sure they would have kill'd her back there, on the spot, if that's why they came? They were moving in a body, yet more slowly than they might have travel'd without her. Not at all angry, or cruel. Like a Dream just before the animals wake up, the German farms pass'd flowing by, the Towns, Equinox, New Cana, Burger's Forge, until, one morning, loud as the Sea, stirr'd to Apple-Cider turbulence from the Rains,— Susquehanna. How had they avoided the Eyes of all the Townsfolk and Farmers between, the gentry out riding, the servants in the fields, how had her Party found Darkness and Safety amid the busy white Densities? And now they'd come to it, how did they mean to cross the River?

There were boats waiting,— at the time she didn't find that as curious as their origins, for they were not Indian Canoes but French-built Battoes, fram'd in Timbers, she was later to learn, that grow only in the far Illinois,— And they cross'd then, as simply as the thought of a distant Child or Husband might cross the Zenith of a long Day. She knew the instant they had pass'd the exact Center-line of the River. As she stepp'd to the Western Shore, she felt she had made herself naked at last, for all of them, but secretly for herself....

Over the Blue Mountain, over Juniata, up into Six Nations Country, into the roll of great Earth-Waves ever northward, the billowing of the Forests, in short-Cycle Repetition overset upon the longer Swell of the Mountains,— a Population unnumber'd of Chestnuts, Maples, Locusts, Sweet Gums, Sycamores, Birches, in full green Abandon,— the song-birds went about their lives, the deer fell to silent Arrows, the sound of Sunday hymns came from a distant clearing, then pass'd, the days went unscrolling, the only thing she was call'd on to do was go where they went. They did not bind, or abuse, or, unless they must, speak to her. They were her Express,— she was their Message.

Northing, almost as she watches, trees, one after another, sometimes entire long Hill-sides of them, go flaring into slow, chill Combustion,— Sunsets the colors of that Hearth she may never again see, too often find her out, unprotected. Early Snowflakes are appearing. Enormous Flights of Ducks and Geese and Pigeons darken the Sky. The terrible mass'd beat of their Wings is the Roar of some great Engine above.... 'Tis withal a Snowy Owl Year,— the Lemmings having suicided in the North, the Owls are oblig'd to come further South in search of Food,— and suddenly white Visitors from afar are ev'rywhere, arriving in a state of Mistrustful Fatigue, going about with that perpetual frown that distinguishes 'em from the more amiably be-Phiz'd white Gyrfalcons. At the peaks of Barns, the Tops of girdl'd gray Trees, Gleaners of Voles soaring above the harvested Acres, with none of your ghostly *hoo*, hoo neither, but low embitter'd Croaking, utter'd in Syllables often at the Verge of Human Speech.

The Winds are turning meantimes ever colder, the leaves beginning to curl in and darken and fall. One day, having brought her to the Shore of some vast body of water that vanishes at the Horizon, they tell her she must get into a Bark Canoe,— and for the first time she is afraid, imagining them all rowing out together into this Yellow Splendor, these painted Indigo and Salmon Cloud-Formations, toward some miraculous Land at the other side of what, even with a mild chop, would soon have batter'd the frail craft to pieces. Instead, keeping the Shore ever in view, they continue North, till they enter a great River, fill'd with a Traffick of Canoes and Battoes and Barges, with settlements upon the Banks, smoke ascending ev'rywhere, white faces upon the Shore, and a Town, and another.... For many weeks now, she has neglected to Pray. She has eaten animals she didn't know existed, small, poor things too trusting to avoid the Snares set for them. Her Captors have told her when and where she may perform ev'ry single action of her life. It is Schooling, tho' she will not discover this till later.

When they arrive at last in Quebec, the Winter is well upon them. Tho' not as grand as its counterpart in Rome, yet in Quebec, the Jesuit College is Palace enough. Travelers have describ'd it as ascending three stories, with a Garret above, enclosing a broad central courtyard,— tho' were she ask'd to confirm even this, she could swear to nothing. (Perhaps there are more Levels. Perhaps there is a courtyard-within-a-courtyard, or beneath it. Perhaps a Crypto-Porticus, or several, leading to other buildings in parts of the City quite remov'd.) Her arrival here passes too quickly for her to take much of it in, so deep in the Night, in the snow, with the black nidor of the Torches for her first Incense, their Light sending shadows lunging from corners and crevices and window-reveals, the distant choiring like tuned shouts, the open looks of the men....

At dawn, separate, she is taken into the Refectory, where at each of the hundred places upon the bare tables is set an identical glaz'd earthen bowl of Raspberries, perfectly ripe, tho' outside be all the Dead of Winter, and upon each Table a Jug of cream fresh from the Shed. An old Indian serving-man, who moves as if wounded long ago, showing not a trace of curiosity, brings in a kettle of porridge,— she is not to have Raspberries (she thanks the Lord, for who knows what unholy Power might account for this unseasonable presence, in its unnatural Redness?).

The Courtyard produces a constant echoing Whisper that can be heard ev'rywhere in the great Residence, ev'ry skin seems immediate to ev'ry other,— into the morning, Scribes carry ink-pots and quills and quill-sharpeners, in and out of Cells of many sizes, whose austerities are ever compromis'd by concessions to the Rococo,— boys in pointed hoods go mutely up and down with buckets of water and kindling,— cooks already have begun to quarrel over details of the noon meal,— in his rooftop Bureau, an Astronomer finishes his Night's reductions, writes down his last entries, and seeks his Mat,— Vigil-keepers meanwhile arise, and limp down to the ingenious College Coffee Machine, whose self-igniting Roaster has, hours earlier, come on by means of a French Clockwork Device which, the beans having been roasted for the desir'd time, then controls their Transfer to a certain Engine, where they are mill'd to a coarse Powder, discharg'd into an infusing chamber, combin'd with water heated exactly,— *Ecce Coffea!*

She is taken, barefoot, still in Indian Dress, into a room fill'd with books. Père de la Tube, a Jesuit in a violet cassock, speaks to her with a thick French accent, and will not look at her face. Nearby, in smoothly kept Silence, sits a colleague whose relentless Smile and brightness of eye only the Mad may know. "Our Guest," the Frenchman tells her, "is a world-known philosopher of Spain, having ever taken interest, in heretick Women who turn to Holy Mother the Church. His observations upon your own case will of course be most welcome."

So silently that she jumps, another man now, slighter and younger, in black silk Jacket and Trousers, has appear'd in the room. When she makes out his face, she cannot reclaim her stare. As a small current of deference flows between the two Jesuits, the Spanish Visitor takes from the messenger a tightly folded sheet of paper, seal'd with Wax and Chops in two of the colors of Blood. The messenger withdraws. She watches for as long as she can.

"You have never before seen a Chinese, child?"

She has assisted at more than one Birth, has endur'd a hard-drinking and quarrelsome troop of Men-Folk,— who is this unfamily'd man in a Frock to call her child? She replies, "No, Sir," in her smallest voice.

"You must call me 'Father.' There'll be more than one Chinese here. You must learn to keep your eyes down."

The College in Quebec is head-quarters for all operations in North America. Kite-wires and Balloon-cables rise into clouds, recede into ærial distances, as, somewhere invisible, the Jesuit Telegraphy goes ahead, unabated. Seal'd Carriages rumble in and out of the *Portes-Cochères*, Horsemen come and go at all hours. Whenever the Northern Aurora may appear in the Sky, rooftops in an instant are a-swarm with figures in black,— certain of the Crew seeming to glide like Swifts ever in motion, others remaining still as statuary, the Celestial Flickering striking High-lights 'pon the pale damp faces. Rumors suggest that the Priests are using the Boreal Phenomenon to send Messages over the top of the World, to receiving-stations in the opposite Hemisphere.

"Twenty-six letters, nine digits, blank space for zero," a Sergeant's voice instructing a platoon of Novices, "— that suggest anything to any of you Hammer-heads?"

"An Array seven-by-five of, of— "

"Think, Nit-Wits, think."

"Lights!"

"Behold, ye Milling of Sheep.— " He swings a Lever. Above, against a gray Deck of snow-clouds, a gigantic Lattice-work of bright and very yellow Lights appears, five across by seven down. Briskly stepping along ranks and files of smaller Handles of Ebony, he spells out the Sequence *I-D-I-O-T-S* in the Sky above their gaping faces.

"Visible for hundreds of miles. Ev'ryone beneath, who can spell, now knows ev'rything there is to know about you.— But it's not all Spectacle, all Romance of Elecktricity, no, there's insanely boring Drudgery a-plenty too, *mes enfants,* for you're all to be sailors upon dry land," explaining that, as the whole Apparatus must stand absolutely still in the Sky, before Weathers unpredictable, it requires an extensive Rigging, even more mysteriously complex than that of a Naval Ship...lines must ever be shifted, individual Winches adjust constantly the tension in stays and backstays and preventers, as the changing conditions aloft are signal'd by an electrickal telegraph to those below. A Coördinator in a single-breasted *Soutane,* or Cassock, of black Bruges Velvet and lin'd with Wolverine Fur, stands upon a small podium, before the set of Ebony Handles and Indicators trimm'd in Brass, whilst Chinese attend to the Rigging, and specially train'd Indian Converts tend a Peat-fire so as to raise precisely the Temperature of a great green Prism of Brazilian Tourmaline, a-snarl as Medusa with plaited Copper Cabling running from it in all directions, bearing the Pyro-Elecktrical Fluid by which ev'rything here is animated. More intense than the peat-smoke, the smell of Ozone prevails here, the Musk of an unfamiliar Beast, unsettling even to those who breathe it ev'ry day.

In that harsh sexual smell, in the ice-edg'd morning, she is led past them, northern winds beneath her deerskin Shift, itching to risk raising her eyes, just once, to see who'll be watching. ("Do you think she understands?" The Visitor asks in rapid French. The other shrugs. "She will understand what she needs to. If she seeks more..." The two exchange a look whose pitiless Weight she feels clearly enough.) Men strain at cables that pitch steeply into the sky, the enormous Rooftops anxiously a-scurry, as before some Invisible Approach. Chinese seem to flit ev'rywhere. Voices, usually kept low, are now and then rais'd. He has her arm. The other priest is behind them. She could not break free,— could she?— reaching with her arms, run to the roof's edge and into the Air, up-borne by Friendly Presences, as by Brilliance of Will, away across the Roof-slates and Fortifications, wheeling, beyond the range of all Weapons, beyond the need for any Obedience,...the Sun coming through, the River shining below, the great Warriors' River, keeping her course ever south-westward. Nor might any left behind on the ground see her again,— would they?— passing above in the Sky, the sleeves of her garment now catching light like wings...her mind no more than that of a Kite, the Wind blowing through...

"Careful, her head."

She is upon her back, rain is falling lightly, a Chinese is squatting beside her, holding her forearm and talking to another Chinese, who is making notes in a small, ingeniously water-proof'd Book. 'Tis he,— the same man she saw in the Jesuit's Chamber.

He smiles. Or, 'tis something in his face she sees, and fancies a Smile.

"God protect us," P. de la Tube is saying, "from all these damnable fainting Novices, Day after Day, it never ends."

The Guest's ears seem to move. "And yet, how many of us, posted upon Missions more solitary, might find the Event intriguing, and your Situation here a Paradise of charming Catalepsies,— and wonder," his Manner bordering upon the strain'd, "whatever you had to com-plain of."

"Ah of course this isn't like the Field, is it, Father, where occasions of Sin are so seldom met with,— no, here are rather Opportunities without number,— none of which may, of course, be acted upon."

"Wouldn't that depend," baring his teeth in a smile, "upon whether she is to be a Bride of Christ, or stand in some other Connexion?"

"As...?" he hesitates, as if for permission.

"His Widow. A novice in Las Viudas de Cristo." Here the Spaniard kisses the Crucifix of his Rosary, and pretends to pray a moment for the success of the Sisterhood. "Have your Indians collected you enough of these *White Roses,* that you might spare one? Of course, if you have a particular interest in *this* one,— "

"No, who, I? not at all, in fact,— " fingering the Buttons down the front of his Costume like beads of a Rosary.

"— I would settle for another,— "

"But we wouldn't hear of it, Father,— Las Viudas must have her, no question. I shall do my best to speed the request up through Hierarchy."

"How very generous. I go to mention you in my next report."

The other inclines his head. She understands that she is being bar-gain'd for, having remain'd all the while upon her knees, disobediently gazing up at the men, waiting as long as possible to see which may be first to notice....

S. Blondelle is a Gypsy, a child of the Sun, whom men keep mistaking for the very Type of the British Doxy, blowsy and cheeky as any who's ever delighted us in Story, or upon the Stage. For a while indeed she worked as a Covent Garden Sprite, finding herself in the company of ev'ry sort of man imaginable and not so, from quivering Neophyte to deprav'd old Coot,— it did not take her long to accumulate a great Spoil-Heap of Mis-trust for the Breechèd Sex.

> Soldiers like Ramrods, and Sailors like Spars,
> Mechanicks and Nabobs, and Gents behind Bars,

Girls, there's no sort of Fellow I've ever pass'd by,—
Not even those Coolies, out there in Shang-hai....
'Tis...
[Chorus]
Men have the Sterling, and sixpences too,
So be where there's men, and 'tis meal-time for you,
Mind the Equipment as long as you can,
And don't sell yourself cheap, to some cheese-paring Man.

Ever since Adam stepp'd out of Eve's Sight,
And didn't get back till the following Night,
Men have been lying to Women they bed,
Care-free as felons, yet easy to shed, singing,—
[Chorus]

She is accompanied by a couple of Sisters, in close, yet, for those days, advanc'd, Harmonies. Beneath what seems but a tap-room Jig lies the same sequence of chords to be found in many a popular Protestant hymn. (Tho' I was not present in the usual sense, nevertheless, I am a clergyman,— be confident, 'twas an utterly original *moment musicale,* as they say in France.)

"Then," as Blondelle relates it, "just as I was about to give up Men, I discover'd Jesuits." It was like finding Christ at last,— a Bolt of Desire, to find herself, at last, beyond Desire. "Yet not like renouncing any-thing,— no, I lov'd the Streets, love 'em ever,— the Excitement, the Tale-a-Minute Scurrying, even the Bullies, and despite the Pox,— Girls stricken overnight,— Beauty,— gone.... Sure, Life's a gamble, just a day-and-night Pass Bank, isn't it? Why not look your best whilst the Dice yet tumble, 's how I see it, don't you?" She attends to her Hair. "Well. Would you like me to fetch a Mirror, 's what I mean."

"Oh..." For the first time since she was taken, her Voice stirs. She tries to smile but finds herself short of breath. "What must I look like...," whispering.

"Not quite ready for the Ridotto, are you," says Sister Grincheuse, with some Solemnity.

"These are from Berry-Vines?" the quiet and dewy Sister Crosier examining the scratches upon her body, closely.

She nods. "No marks from the Indians, if that's what you mean.... They were uncommonly gentle with me,— although..."

S. Grincheuse's eyes sparkle like Jasper. "Must we guess, then?"

"I star'd often at the many ways they had inscrib'd their own Skins, some of the Pictures being most beautiful, others arousing in me strange flashes of fear, mix'd with…it perplexes me to say…ow!"

"Speak up."

"…with feelings of Desire.…" She sets her Chin provocatively and gazes at them.

"Oh dear, just from a couple of Tattoos? Well, well, girls, whatever are we to do?"

" 'Twill be the Cilice for you, I'm afraid, my dear, and there's the first Lesson already,— *Never discuss Desire*. Get that one sorted out, you'll be a good Catholic in no time."

"But you bade me— "

"Shh. Here it is. Here is what disobedient Novices must wear." The Las Viudas Cilice is a device suggested by Jesuit practice, worn secretly, impossible, once secur'd, to remove, producing what some call Discomfort,— enough to keep thoughts from straying far from God. "If God were younger, more presentable," murmurs Crosier, "we'd be thinking about Him all the time, and we shouldn't need this,— " her Gaze inclining to the Hothouse Rose, deep red, nearly black, whose supple, long Stem is expertly twisted into a Breech-clout, to pass between the Labia as well as 'round the Waist, with the Blossom, preferably one just about to open, resting behind, in that charming Cusp of moistness and heat, where odors of the Body and the Rose may mingle with a few drops of Blood from the tiny green Thorns, and Flashes of Pain whose true painfulness must be left for the Penitent to assess.… Of course, this is all for the purpose of keeping her Attention unwaveringly upon Christ. "Considering what Christ had to go through," Jesuits are all too happy to point out, "it isn't really much to complain about."

S. Grincheuse stands behind her, gripping her by the arms. "It could have been worse," whispers little S. Crosier. "Not all Indians are so honorable." She kneels at the Captive's feet, holding the Device, her fingertips already prick'd and redden'd, and cannot keep from directing wide-eyed Glances upward.

"All right, Dear," nods S. Blondelle, "step right in, and mind those long Limbs."

She should be objecting, loudly if she must, but when has she ever done so before? and to offenses, it now seems to her, far more grave than this. Instead, her bare feet go creeping, one after the other, like docile birds, toward the waiting trap of the Cilice,— and then each, lifting, fluttering, passes into the Realm of Thorns.

Later they give her soothing Gums to rub into the tiny Wounds. The odor rises as the rubbing goes on, a single churchlike odor of incense, ungrounded by candle-wax or human occupancy, meant for Heaven, a Fume rising in Transmutation....

She is shorn of all hair, from head to Crux. "You must begin," they advise her, "absolutely naked. If you're good, if you learn what you are taught, you may someday be allow'd a Wig, a child's Wig of course, perhaps a Boy's, you look enough like one now,— "

"Farm work, Madame,— Aahh!"

"Don't be insolent."

Having already seen other Sisters going about in elaborate Wigs that she imagines must be quite in the current Parisian *Mode*, she is soon wondering how she might look in one of these powder'd Confections. One night she sneaks into the Room where, ranked upon Shelf after Shelf, all the Wigs are kept, each upon its elegant Wig-stand made of a strangely shaded Ivory. Mischievously she idles away one Cat-hour and then another, prowling, peering, crouching, hardly daring to touch the White bevortic'd Objects, each more desir'd than the last. When she does at length reach forward, take one to her Breast, slip it onto her own shaven Pate, and only then think of finding a Mirror, and then some Light to see by, she is flank'd in the Instant by strong Presences, whose faces she slowly recognizes in the Dark as those of Blondelle and Crosier.

"Took her time about it, I must say."

"Sooner or later, they all do it. Mistress Piety here's as Vain as any Portsmouth Whore."

"Yet prettier than most," whispers Crosier.

She blushes as they remove the Wig, in the near-Dark, and she supposes, with a private Frown, she'll never see it again. Her eyes follow it back to its Wig-Stand,— which, she notices for the first time, with a Chill, is directing at her a socketed Stare. She recognizes it belatedly

521

as a human Skull. Resolv'd never again to be call'd a fainting Novice, she looks about. Yes. Ev'ry gay elaboration in the room rests upon a staring Skull. She lets out her breath in a great Sigh. And refrains from fainting.

"The Model," the Wolf of Jesus addressing a roomful of students, "is Imprisonment. Walls are to be the Future. Unlike those of the Antichrist Chinese, these will follow right Lines. The World grows restless,— Faith is no longer willingly bestow'd upon Authority, either religious or secular. What Pity. If we may not have Love, we will accept Consent,— if we may not obtain Consent, we will build Walls. As a Wall, projected upon the Earth's Surface, becomes a right Line, so shall we find that we may shape, with arrangements of such Lines, all we may need, be it in a Crofter's hut or a great Mother-City,— Rules of Precedence, Routes of Approach, Lines of Sight, Flows of Power,— "

"Hold! Hold!" objects an Auditor, "is this not to embrace the very Ortholatry of the Roman Empire?— that deprav'd worship of right Lines, intersecting at right Angles, which at last reduc'd to the brute simplicity of the Cross upon Calvary— "

"Padre, Padre! which Rome is it, again, that Jesuits are sworn to?"

A grim smile. "What injury, that we are not in Spain." He is no longer surpriz'd at Impiety or Disrespect, having found them only too prevalent upon this side of the Ocean. Yet there remains little choice,— too much of Europe is unsafe now for any Jesuit. America is perplexing,— tho' all the world's expell'd and homeless be welcome here, no true soldier of Christ could ever find easy refuge among these People, for whom heresies flow like blood in the blood-stream, keeping them at the Work of their Day as Blood might keep others warm,— yet "Heresy" loses its Force in these Provinces, this far West, with Sects nearly as numerous as Settlers.— To pursue thro' the American Quotidian every act of impiety he might find, would be to fight upon more flanks than any could reckon,— where would time remain, for *la Obra?*

"Perhaps there is no Disjunction," he has nonetheless continu'd,— "and men, after all, want Rome, want Her, desire Her, as *both Empire and Church.* Perhaps they seek a way back,— to the single Realm, as it was before Protestants, and Protestant Dissent, and the mindless breeding of Sect upon Sect. A Portrayal, in the earthly Day-light, of the Soul's Nostalgia for that undifferentiated Condition before Light and Dark,— Earth and Sky, Man and Woman,— a return to that Holy Silence which the Word broke, and the Multiplexity of matter has ever since kept hidden, before all but a few resolute Explorers."

"Hold, hold! Is it a Chinese motif we begin to hear?"— an entire *Room*-full of Students transferr'd here from the University of Hell,— "If Chinese *Feng Shui* be forbidden, how may we study such Metaphysicks as this, without risk of reprimand?"

"The risk is not so much to your Backside as to your Soul. Can any tell me,— Why must we fight their abhorrent Magick?"

A ripple of giggling.

"*Pues Entonces*...I was a Student once, too. I remember passing around the same wither'd packets of Paper you have been reading in secret, now, unfolded and re-folded an hundred times,— 'Secrets of the Chinese Wizards'? Aha. Even to the Name. Some of you are learning how to paint the Symbols, perhaps even beginning to experiment with combining them in certain ways?— I know, Fellows, I know ev'rything that passes here.... Another of the thousand or so wonderful things about the Sacrament of Penance, is its Utility in group situations like yours. Someone always confesses. Or in plain Spanish, *Siempre Alguien derrama las Judías.*"

"What's he saying?"

"Something about scattering the Jewesses."

"Now 'tis Kabbalism, in a moment he'll be rattling in ancient Hebrew, and perhaps we ought to have a Plan."

"For subduing him, you mean?"

"Actually, I meant a Plan for getting out of the Room...."

"Why prevent the Chinese from practicing *Feng Shui?* Because it works," the Wolf of Jesus is explaining.

"How then,— if it works, should we not be studying it?"

"It carries the mark of the Adversary.— It is too easy. Not earn'd. Too little of the Load is borne by the Practitioner, too much by some Force

Invisible, and the unknown Price it must exact. What do you imagine those to be, that must ever remain so unreferr'd, and unreferrable, to Jesus Christ? And, as His Soldiers, how can we ever permit that?"

'Twas an earlier, simpler Time, Children, when many grew quite exercis'd indeed over questions of Doctrine. There is deep, throat-snarling Hatred, for example, as the Wolf of Jesus instructs them. "The Christless must understand that their lives are to be spent in Servitude,— if not to us, then to Christians even less Godly,— the Kings, the Enterprisers, the Adventurers Charter'd and Piratickal."

"What of those that we may Convert?"

The Priest makes a dismissive gesture, his knuckles flashing pale in the Candle-light. "Conversion is no guarantee of a Christly Life. Jews are 'converted.' Savages, English wives, Chinese, what matter?— once *con*-verted, all then *re*-vert. Each one, at the end of the day, is found somewhere, often out in the open, among ancient Stones, repeating without true Faith the same vile rituals,— and where is He, where are His Forgiveness, His Miracles?"

He is upon his knees, in apparent Consultation. The Students, after a while, begin to whisper together, and soon the place is chattier than a Coffee-House. The Spanish Visitor continues apart.

54

There came an evening during my novitiate when, after being fed but lightly, I was taken to a Chamber, and there laced into an expensive Corset, black as Midnight, imported, I was told, from Paris, from the very workshop of the *Corsetier* to the Queen. They painted my face into a wanton Sister of itself, showing me, in a Hand-Mirror,— 'twas a Woman I'd never seen before,— whom, upon the Instant, sinfully, I desir'd. I allow'd the *Maquilleuses* to hear my surpriz'd little Gasp as they brought out undergarments for me that might, Blondelle assur'd me, make a French whore think twice.

"The Chinaman likes these," they inform'd me, as firmly I was hook'd and knotted into this Uniform of most shamefully carnal intent, which fram'd, but did not veil, my intimate openings.

I went this way and that upon the balls of my feet, lace trimmings a-flutter, in tiny steps of Perplexity. "Chinaman? what Chinaman?"

"One of the principal Duties of a Widow of Christ is to charm the Chinese. Soon you'll begin your studies in their Language. Eventually you'll go there for a year or two."

"China?"

"Hold still.— *Oui*, ev'ryone here has serv'd upon that Station."

"You'll love it," cried Blondelle, "the food they eat there is delicious beyond belief,— Shrimps with Hot Chillies and Peanuts! Slic'd Chicken in Garlick and Black Bean Sauce! Cold Sesame Noodles! Sweet Biscuits with Messages folded inside upon Paper you can eat,— Ahh! making m'self hungry just thinking about it...."

The Wicked French Nuns all took a coördinated Dance-Step together, turn'd, and shook their fingers.

"Basest form o' Desire, Blondelle."

"Even to speak of it, suggests a failure of self-restraint I am all but oblig'd to report."

"Oh get on, 've ye never been starv'd for something that tastes like something, instead of this Gruel we're ever fed?"

"Nonetheless, Sister."

I took the moment to examine my new-adorn'd Limbs, running finger-tips where I could not see, trying to be my own looking-glass. It earn'd me a slap and some time upon my knees. Charming the Chinaman was serious business 'round here. "Time to bind those Feet, Child." It took a long time. I had never imagin'd my Feet as having quite so many distinct Parts, each able to feel in its own set of ways.... Chinese men, in my reveries upon the subject, grew more interesting as the binding proceeded. If *this* was what they lik'd...

Brae has discover'd the sinister Volume in 'Thelmer's Room, lying open to a Copper-plate Engraving of two pretty Nuns, sporting in ways she finds inexplicably intriguing...

"Oh, hullo, Brae,— aahcck...um, well what's that you're reading? Hmm," having a look, "something of Cousin DePugh's, I guess."

She gazes at him, for what seems to him a long time. "You left it for someone to find," she whispers at last.

"Perhaps I'd only imagin'd my room safe from the eyes, however big and innocent, of curious Cousins."

"You're full of Surprizes, 'Thelmer. Tho' I remain unclear, as to why a young University Gentleman should find Affection between Women at all a topic of interest."

"Why...sure there may be Renderings more pleasant to look upon...the Western Country at Sunset, probably,— Scenes of Religious Life, Hunting-Dogs, a Table-ful of Food...yet if one of you, beheld intimately, be all but unbearably fair, you see, imagine the sentimental Delight into which a Man might be thrown, at the sight of two of you."

"More than twice as much, I'd guess, wouldn't you?"

"Oh, something exponential, I've no doubt," her Cousin replies. "Besides that, 'tis the next in the Ghastly Fop series, I'm oblig'd in Honor to read them all in Line, ain't I?"

"Then you must first bring me up to Date, mustn't you."

'Thelmer blurts a Synopsis. "The Ghastly Fop. He's seen at Ridottoes and Hurricanes, close to Gaming-Tables, as to expensive Nymphs. But he speaks to no one. No one approaches him. 'Not I, thank you,— much too ghastly,' is the postventilatory Murmur among the Belles attending. He is reported to be the Wraith of a quite dreadfully ruin'd young man come to London from the Country, who can return neither there, nor to the World of Death, until sizable Debts in this one be settl'd,— and to reside, tho' not necessarily to live, in Hampstead."

The Ghastly F., true to his legend, is engaged in the long, frustrating, too often unproductive Exercise of tracking down ev'ryone with whom he yet has unresolv'd financial dealings. To some, he seems quite conventionally alive, whilst others swear he is a Ghost. That no one is certain, contributes to his peculiar Charm, tho' Admirers must ever sigh, for but. One Motrix commands his Attention and Fidelity,— the Account-Book. Some of those nam'd therein have cheated him of money he must collect, others are creditors whom he must repay, and so forth. On and on he goes, one to another, using these imbalances as a general excuse to pry into the finances of others, Fop-link'd or not. Some days he'll find a two-for-one. The Series runs to at least a Dozen Volumes by now, tho' no one is sure exactly how many,— forgeries have also found their way into the Market. Ghastly Fop sightings are increasingly reported, not only from Ranelagh or Covent Garden, but all over the Kingdom, Thornton-le-Beans, Slad, name your town, the Ghastly F. has either just been thro' or is schedul'd to arrive at any Moment. In his largely Paper Vengeance, he not only traverses England, but the World of Commerce as well, righting Injustices in Grub-Street, prematurely exploding Bubble-Schemes, making wild raids upon the Exchange, Gambling Stacks of what prove to be only Ghost-Guineas, losing all, straightening his Wig, and vanishing before the admittedly sleep-denied Eyes of the Company.

Somewhere, as some would say ineluctably, in this wealth-spangl'd Web, is a fateful Strand leading to the Society of Jesus. Of course, being a Financial Entity, Jesuits have the same difficulties with Stock-Jobbing, Land-holdings, Officials who may not stay brib'd for quite long enough,— that is, they seem submissive as any of us, before the commands of Time, tho' their Wonderful Telegraph gives them in that Article an Edge over the rest of Christendom, who have still advanc'd no further in the Arts of the Distant Message, than training Courier Pigeons,— or small Hawks to seize those of others out of the Sky, and bring the Prey back to their Handlers, before being allow'd their own Enjoyment.

"How far in the Book did you get?"

"Up to where she meets the Chinese Boy, and they plan their Escape."

"Awkward time to break off."

"I heard you out in the Hall."

They stand quite close in the small upper room, Relations stash'd orthogonally all about, invisible tho' now and then sens'd otherwise, behind wall-paper, plaster, laths, and scantlings,— Gazes attach'd,— unable, it dawns upon each, *not* to regard the other with just this steady Amusement.

"Say, the next Chapter's a Pippin," Ethelmer whispers. "May I read it to you? Promise I'll keep my voice down."

"Thoughtful as ever, 'Thel," Brae looking about now for some item of Furniture to sit upon other than the Bed, and finding none.

"We might sit upon the 'Magickal Carpet' in the Corner, as we did when children," he suggests.

"We might." Adverting to the Bed, rather, with a sure domestick Touch she sweeps Pillows and Bolsters into a longitudinal Berm more symbolick than practickal, and lies down upon one side of it. "Let us have another Candle first," says she, "that we not Ruin our Eyes in this Light."

"Nor fail to see in vivid Detail, what otherwise we'd merely have to imagine."

"Lament your own Imagination, Coz, but do not under-rate mine by quite so much."

"Say, nor's mine that feeble, Brae."

"Shh. Read away,— and if I fall asleep, pray do nothing rude."

"Fear not. All will be done with Refinement."

" 'Thel,— "

And so off they minuet, to become detour'd from the Rev^d's narrative Turnpike onto the pleasant Track of their own mutual Fascination, by way of the Captive's Tale.

One night I dream that I have come to a Bridge across a broad River, with small settlements at either approach, and in its center, at the highest point of its Arch, a Curious Structure, some nights invisible in the river mists, Lanthorns burning late,— a Toll-House. Not ev'ryone is allow'd through, nor is paying the Toll any guarantee of Passage. The gate-keepers are members of a Sect who believe that by choosing correctly which shall dwell one side of this River, and which the other, the future happiness of the land may be assur'd. Those rejected often return to one of the Inns cluster'd at either end of the Bridge, take a bed for the night, and try again in the morning. Some stay more than one night. When the Bills become too burdensome, the Pilgrims who wish strongly enough to cross, may seek employment right there,— at the Ale-Draper's, or the laundry, or among the Doxology,— and keep waiting, their original purpose in wanting to cross often forgotten, along with other information that once seem'd important, such as faces, and their Names,— whose owners come now to my rooms to visit, and to instruct me in my Responsibilities, back wherever it is I came from. They say they have known me all my life, and seek to bring me away, "home" to where I may at least be seen to by Blood. Perhaps there is a young man, professing with the skill of an amateur actor to be my husband. "Eliza! do tha not recognize me? The little Ones,— " and so forth. Someone I cannot abide. Stubbornly, I look for some explanation of this Order to live upon a side of the River I'd rather be across from than on.

"You're bold, I'll give ye that."

"I don't belong on this side."

"What do you know of these things? Go back to your Husband."

"He is not my Husband."

"Had you cross'd this Stream, you would have liv'd a life of signal unhappiness. Go, and survive for long enough to understand the gift we have made you."

One night the Wolf of Jesus understands,— in one of those thoughtlessly fatal Instants,— that Zhang has been fluent in Spanish all the while. Zhang watches him remember, one by one, the many Utterances he has felt free to make, in the Chinaman's hearing. The traditional next Step is simply to have Zhang dropp'd off the Roof during one of the night Drills,— the usual Tragedy. But then the Spaniard may see an opportunity to remove certain memories, and substitute others,— thus controlling the very Stuff of History.

To any mind at all Inquisitorial, an appealing turn of Fate,— yet the Spaniard is disappointed, soon bitterly so, at Zhang's willingness cheerfully to forget all he may have heard, to recite whatever catechism of the Past the Spaniard prefers. The Wolf of Jesus, perhaps never aware that Lies and Truth will converge, albeit far from this Place,— takes particular Pleasure in accusing Zhang of holding something back,— a Game which Mathematickally he cannot lose. "There was another such Remark. You remember it well. Damme if the *Baton* won't part it from ye, along with some Skin,"— such mention of Torture increasing day by day, as if his Alternatives had narrow'd to it. 'Tis then Zhang begins to plan his Departure.

Observing him, learning infallibly where he may be at any given Hour, she understands when he will leave, and in the instant decides to go with him,— dropping her Errands, as her Habit, stealing from the Indian Quarters a Boy's Breech-Clout, Robe, and Leggings, finding an unus'd Confessional Booth, sliding her unbound feet into soft Moccasins, dressing in deer-skin,— hoping to be taken for a Boy, she joins Zhang, who, with no choice but to take her, pretends no interest in her bared limbs and sleek muscles ever in motion, as the Fugitives cautiously seek exit from the City, in a Departure as bound to the Terrain as her dream'd one had been sky-borne.

In their Instruction of the Novices, the Jesuits spoke of early European Arrivals upon the Continent,— Winters, long and Mortal and soon enough productive of Visitants from beneath the Ice, have ever been among the Terms of Settlement here. This northern Desert was too cruel to winter in at all separately, the only way thro' till Spring was to gather as many people as possible into a Hall. "The Disadvantage to this Method," according to P. de la Tube, "being, that in crowded Quarters, one crazy Swede could lead to a deterioration in living conditions, up to and not excluding a House-ful of Corpses, come the Springtide."

What moral instruction does th' American Winter bring them, hiding upon the stark hill-side, the River remote as Heaven, below? Jesuits on horseback, in black riding-Habits with divided Skirts, patrol the Streets. From some avian drama above, long black Feathers blow one by one down toward where the Battoes once landed to take the City. The Wind keeps remorselessly Northern, and she wraps herself as she may into the Robe. She understands, at some turn in this, that she has not yet pray'd,— nor should she pray, not now. That is over. This is a journey onward, into a Country unknown,— an Act of Earth, irrevocable as taking Flight.

All the way down the River, keeping to the south shore, into Six Nations territory, not so much fleeing Jesuit pursuit, as racing their own Desire. One day, when they have gain'd the Mohawk, the Ice upon the River begins its catastrophic Rip and Boom, Blocks of it piling up into Pinnacles and Edifices, and Spring has caught up with them.

Guided by Captain Zhang's miraculous *Luo-Pan,* they proceed inland and south, to Fort Stanwix, and then on to Johnson Castle, above the Mohawk, arriving at the end of their Strength, moving down a Colonnade of Lombardy Poplars, slow as a Dream, observing about them Indian men smoking together in the clement Afternoon, or shaking Peach-Pits in a Bowl and betting upon the Results, whilst children run about with Sticks and Balls and women sit together with their Work, and there he is, himself the Irish Baronet, wearing Skins, and a Raccoon Hat, out among his People, the Serfs of Johnson Castle, moving easily among the groups, switching among the English, Mohawk, Seneca, and Onondaga Languages as needed.

The Chinaman presents him a curious sort of Metallick Plate, which Sir William scrutinizes, before relaxing into a less guarded Smile. The two exchange a complicated Hand-shake that seems to her to go on as long as an item of Town Gossip might, between Women. "And how is the old Pirate these days?"

"He bade me remind you,— "

"— of that which, as a cautious man, you may not mention immediately. Good. Who's this Lad with you? Bit weedy, 's he not? Could use a couple of Bear Chops, fry him some Mush, few Pints of Ale, be well on the way to recovery." Sir William approaches her. "Do you speak any English, boy?"

"Little," she whispers.

Something alerts him. He takes her chin gently by the side of his Index, and raises her Face, and narrows his Gaze. "The way of a Warrior is not to be chosen lightly," he advises her, "as a Girl might choose a Gown."

"She knew that," says the Chinaman. "That is, he.— He knew that."

"It's all right, Captain," in what she's surpriz'd to hear is her own Voice of old. "Sir, I am Eliza Fields, of Conestoga. This Gentleman has been kind enough to help me escape the French."

"Why bless me,— but he's not an Indian, either!" cries Sir William Johnson. "I am reputed the Soul of Subtlety in these parts, yet am I now the Bumpkin,— well, even a Churl may be taught, Sir. Tell me. What's the Story?"

They tell him.

"Then sure as Mahoney's Mother-in-Law there'll be a Jesuit Pursuit Party thro' here, and soon. Don't expect your Spaniard to wait for Summer. Blood that hot, they bring their own Seasons with 'em."

"I know him," says Zhang. "He is very patient."

"Howbeit,— a few more Mohawks about can't hurt. And you won't stay here forever. Will ye?"

"And you will of course present my Compliments to your Masonick Lodge," Capt. Zhang twinkling resentfully.

They arrange, thro' Sir William, for a safe-passage as far down the Delaware as they will need. In all the journey, the Chinaman has never attempted to force his Attentions upon her. Any Relief she may feel is undone by her anxiety over when and how the subject will arise,— that is, come up,— that is, one night in an abandon'd Beast-pen in New-Jersey, as they hold one another for warmth, feeling reckless, she reaches down, as she has been taught by the Order, and discovers his Wand of Masculinity in earnest Erection.

"Perhaps we'd do better to skip over this part," gallant 'Thelmer suggests.

"I've already read to the bottom of the next Page," coolly replies Brae, "so there's not much to do about it, save read on."

Thro' the Gloom, close enough for her to see, he smiles. Zhang does.

"Now then, Zhang," she whispers. "It's been there ev'ry day. Hasn't it."

"Yet,— observe." And as if at his Command, it wilts, no less dramatickally than it arose.

"What did I *do?*" she mutters.

"Mistress, to you and me, any, what we style, in Chinese, *Yin-Yang,* is forbidden," he tells her. "We were not born to play Theatrickal rôles assign'd us by others, for their Amusement."

"What are you talking about? The first man I approach in my life, and he says no. Aahhh!"

"Attend me,— I get into a lascivious state now and then.— I'm Chinese all the time. That doesn't make me a Lascivious Chinaman. Nor you, *mutatis mutandis,* a Debauch'd Heretick Maid."

"Yet,— suppose that's what we really are. Really ought to be."

"As you will, Mistress. Meanwhile, either we are trying to escape these Assassins, or we're not. Do you wish to return?"

For a moment she is all in a Daze. Her Eye-Lashes a-cycle, "What contempt you must have for me...."

"On the contrary," he whispers. "I adore you. Especially in that 'cute Deerskin Costume."

"Then...?— "

"It's a Sino-Jesuit Affair. Nothing you'd even wish to understand."

Well, then. Why didn't Blondelle mention anything like *this?* In his Particulars, Zhang corresponds to few, if any, of her Mentrix's detail'd Notions about the other Sex...Blondelle, whom she will never again climb into bed with as the cruel Rain assails the Windows.... That is, unless she be caught, and return'd. Somewhere in the Jesuit Maze, she's been told, waits a special windowless Cell lin'd entirely in Black Velvet, upon which wink various bright Metal Fittings...a mysterious Space she has more than curiously long'd to enter...'tis where they put the Runaways who come back. Who wish to come back.... Her thoughts thus in a whirl, she falls asleep in his Embrace, not waking till the Dawn of the cloud-drap'd Day, to feel him hard as ever, and press'd against her. She begins hoping they'll find some population soon.

The smell of wood-smoke is more and more with them, as often, thro' the newly green Trees, Cabins and out-buildings appear. They are challeng'd by Bulls, and chas'd by farm-dogs whose meanness is not improv'd by the doubtful Edibility of their intended Prey.

"That's what they call 'Chinese,' Buck."

"Not sure I'd want to eat that."

"Not sure you're going to catch that."

The other Dogs are pacing and posing like Wolves, putting on tight-lipp'd Smiles. "Well, they're fast, but,— "

"— not *that* fast...."

The fugitives learn to carry Staffs. Soon they look like Pilgrims, soon after that they begin to feel like Pilgrims. All the while, the *Luo-Pan* is trembling and growing hot to the Touch.

At last, as the Green Halations about the Hillsides reduce to material Certainty, they arrive at the West Line, and decide to follow the Visto east, and ere long they have come up with the Party. They are greeted by most of the Commissary, headed by Mo McClean,— the Hands more agog than they should be allowing themselves, by now, to be sent, by such Apparitions,— and assign'd Quarters separated by a good Chain and a Half's worth of Gazes, Stares, and Glares....

"Shall I see you more?" she mutters more than pleads.

"Shall you continue to question your choice?"

"Yes.— Pleas'd you're smiling, for a Change. You must think we're all amusing."

"What non-Chinese people find of Importance, may now and then be very amusing indeed.... Will you return to Canada?"

"It wasn't all bad there," she lets him know.

"Easy for you to say,— *Viudita.*"

"Sir."

"You are provoking me. My own experience was a bit different."

"Oh, you weren't having such a bad time of it, that I could see, missing few if any mess calls, indeed quite plump, and ever in good Humor, not as you are now. Why should you've ever wanted to leave, is past me."

"In China 'tis consider'd greatly unwise, to escape one Captivity in order to embrace another. To my Sins, so must I add Foolishness."

"Why, you're free as a bird. What Captivity,— " But he is gazing at her with those enigmatic Chinese Eyes she pretends she cannot read. She turns her head a bit, then looks back sidewise. "And will the Spaniard come after us?"

"Because he believes I stole you."

"Another Reason, then, for me to be upon my Way. Once, I would have sigh'd. Please, one Day, imagine me as having sigh'd."

"Shall you return to your Husband, then?"

"Either to the Jesuits, or to him?— That's my full list of Choices? Poh upon ye, Zhang, and poh upon your *Yin-Yang,* too." She twirls her Nose in the air, and departs.

She is bunking with Zsuzsa Szabó, the operator of the automatick Battle of Leuthen, a pleasant-looking young woman who, wearing the dress uniform of the Nádasdy Hussars, had one day, astride a splendid Arab Horse, overtaken the Party. "Hello, Boys,— it's Zsuzsa." She has a charmingly un-English way of saying this. Axmen arrest their swings, so violently that Axes stand still in the Air, their Recoils sending some of their axmen a-whirl the other way,— Indians crouch'd in the Brush gaze, and marvel at how she's painted her face, the Milk-maids whisper together at length. She has been on the move since the Battle of Leuthen, in 1757, in which, disguis'd as a Youth, riding in a detachment of light cavalry, she was not so much visited by understanding, as allow'd briefly to pay Attention to what had been there all the time,— seeing then her clear duty, to bring word of what was about to emerge into the World from the Prussian Plains. From a simple recital, with gestures, of the Events of the Battle, has develop'd a kind of Street-Show, with Accordion musick, Dog tricks and Gypsy Dancing, and an automatick miniature or Orrery of Engagement, displaying the movements of the troops as many times as the curious Student may wish.

Later, the Surveyors come by the Tent, each for a short Visit. Dixon, now that Eliza knows what to look for, seems to her fully as fascinated as the Chinaman, with her Deerskin Costume. As he leaves, backing out the tent-flap, all a-hum, he nearly collides with Mason, who mutters, "That likely, is it?" glaring Dixon upon his way before adverting to the young Woman,— whereupon he is seiz'd with what later he will describe to Dixon as an "Ague of Soul,"— fierce heat, deep shivering,— for a moment, she assumes 'tis the Indian turnout again, till she sees his so pale and sadden'd Face.

"Excuse me." He sits in an oblate Heap upon the tent-floor, removes his Hat, fans himself. "You resemble far too faithfully One whom I have not beheld,— not in Body,— for seven years. More than merely some general Likeness, Madam,— you are her *Point-for-Point Representation.*"

She runs a hand over her Crop. "I can't imagine her Hair was the same." This was how the Widows taught their Novices to Flirt. "Or,— " deciding Hair may be a safe Topick with this one, but little else, she doesn't go on.

"Allowing for all that, of course." His eyes shifting about in their Sockets like insects about Candle-flames.

"Sir...I am the elder daughter of Joseph Fields, of Conestoga Creek. Last Winter, I was taken by a band of Shawanese,— "

"Be easy, Child. I shan't insanely presume you to be she, I'm merely Torpedo-struck,— it's not only the separate Parts, but your Bearing of them as well...your bodily Gesturing, your Voice.... Attend me,— do you believe that the Dead return?"

"Sir, you are distraught, perhaps even about to behave irresponsibly?— Eeoo, Mr. Mason!— I think not!— Is there by chance a Chaplain attach'd to your Party?"

"Regrettably, yes. I try never to seek his Counsel."

"I meant, that I might wish to."

"Of course. Our Reverend Cherrycoke. Excellent man."

("You're making that one up," Uncle Lomax now wagging a Finger he eventually hits himself in the Nose with.

"And did she seek your counsel?" inquires Ives.

"Oh, I got into the matter, after a bit," recalls the Rev[d]. "Tho' Mason was the one who needed Spiritual Advice.")

"Is it Transmigration, Rev?" all but pleading, following me ev'rywhere, even out to the Latrine, "What are the Chances? Come, Sir. You can give it to me straight."

The Rev[d] cannot help having a fast look over at the Visto, and remarking in his own Tap-room cadence, "Around here? how else?" Squatting over the noisome Trench, as Mason paces to and fro, he speculates that the Resemblance so confounding Mason is less likely the Transmigration of a Soul, than the Resurrection of a Body,— in enough of its Particulars to convince him 'tis she. Yet the Soul he imagines as newly inhabiting their Guest, must in any case have forgotten its previous life as Rebekah Mason. "The Slate cleanly wash'd,— no way to prove who she's been. As in Plato's Tale of Er, she'll have drunk from Lethe, and begun anew."

"And if she comes,— or is sent,— as a sort of Corporeal Agent, to finish, in behalf of my Wife's Spirit, some Business that only the Body knows how to transact?" His Voice much too high and loud, about to careen upon him.

The Rev[d] runs thro' the possibilities, now and then, he fears, clucking. "Well I do hope not. That is, you are titular Party-Chief here, and may come and go as you please,— yet..."

"Yet I grow, I fear, not more bestial as you imply, but less,— even the activity you now so freely engage in, being denied me for longer than I now remember."

"Ye've taken Daffy's Elixir?"

"It means first asking Dixon, who holds the Key to the Dispensary. It thus means, as well, a certain Smirk, that I am not sure I can abide."

"He is, I collect, an Habitué of that Compound." The Rev^d, having wip'd his Arse with a handful of Clover, draws up his Breeches again.

"Just so. I have felt oblig'd to abstain from it, even as he superdoses himself,— for the sake of Equilibrium in the Party."

"Admirable, of course, as are all acts of self-denial. Usually. Are you certain you're telling me ev'rything?"

"Being clench'd in all other Ways," remarks Mason, "there likely is something I'm holding back."

That night, or perhaps the next, Mason wakes from a dream, one he has had before. Trying to get back to the mill in Wherr, he keeps being set down by carts and coaches farther and farther away...all at once he and Rebekah are traveling together, on foot, till they are pick'd up by a Stranger in a Coach and taken to a House whose residents she knows, where she is seduced, not entirely against her will, by this band of foreign, dimly political, dimly sinister men and women. She lies still, passive, allowing them all to handle her. Mason, in despair, watches a kind of lengthy Ritual. He does not intervene because she has told him, in painfully direct language, that he no longer has the right. Once she flicks her eyes toward him, as if to make sure he's looking...but only once, and briefly. Who are they? what is their mission? *their Name?*

Structur'd servitude, a fore-view of Purgatory, a Prison that works thro' bribes, threats, favors, with rules it may be fatal not to know...she, perhaps willingly, taken into it, under it,— he cannot follow. Can as little charm as sing his way in. He knows only straightforwardly squalid Pelhamite arrangements,— here all is illegible, in a light forever about to fail.

Worse, he shall have to return in dreams to this same place, again and again, the layout of the rooms ever the same, the same doors having but just closed, the invisible occupants having only just gone away,...the whispering across the Wall he can almost hear.... He wakes with his hands in fists, dried tears in cold lines 'cross his Temples. She is where the Frenchmen in their make-believe chateaux, perfum'd, intricately bewigg'd, stop all day at their toilettes, safe from the cold consensus that ignores dream in its Reckonings,—

France, French agents of Death,— at the worst of the fight between the *Seahorse* and *l'Grand,* in all that tearful fall from humanity, his Bowels seconds away from letting go, there had wrapp'd 'round him the certainty that whatever was come for him now, had also come for her then,— not in the way of a Bailiff or Assassin, at all selective, but rather as a Dredge, a Scavenger, foraging blind, unto which Mason sens'd himself about to be gather'd, as mindlessly as any seaman above-decks, forever to him nameless.

They were possessing her in ways more intimate than had ever been allow'd him...interfering at orders of minitude invisible to human Eye, infiltrated without need of light or Map, commanding the further branches of whatever flows in a Soul like blood,...she and her Captors whispering together incessantly, in a language they knew, and he did not, and what language could it be? not any French as he'd ever heard it,— too fast and guttural and without grace...they all spoke at incredible Speed, without pause for breath. For where breath has ceas'd, what need for the little pauses of mortal speech, that pass among us ever unnotic'd?

His father appear'd. "And give some thought to your spinsterr there, so abandon'd and gay. You're a genius at pickin' 'em, Boy. It has only now come to light, how she was the thrown-aside toy of a Leadenhall Street Nabob, who visits your dearr friends the Peaches now and then for East India business, and country Sport,— and their attentions to you are conditional upon your marrying her."

They were together in a room. She was about to depart. "I commend you upon your Forbearance, Madam. Most Christian."

"You mean considering all that your Father has said about me. Why, Sensibility,— 'tis nothing to me anymore. Pray release yourself."

He felt he had to go on. " 'Twas never you, 'Heart, 'twas me he wish'd to wound.— "

"On second thought," Rebekah swiftly return'd, "cherish your Antagonism. Let it freeze your souls, both of you. Either Choice lies far from me now."

Her representative in the waking world, pale and distant, squats by the Coffee, poking the Morning Fire. A little less solid each day, she is drifting toward her own Absence. She looks up warily as Mason makes a Loxodrome for the Pot.

"You've dreamt of her, again."

"Thankee. With your Hair growing in, you don't look like her that much anymore."

"I never did. Zsuzsa wants us to go off and be Adventuresses."

"Seth...quite out of the Picture, then, I take it?"

"If your Travels take you by Conestoga, put your Ears to the Wind, follow the sounds of merry Indulgence, and where they are loudest, there shall Seth be, and you will note how he mourns me."

"Ne'er met the Lad, of course,— "

"Good Morning, *kicsi káposta*," Zsuzsa striding in and embracing her co-adventuress-to-be from behind. They smile and stretch, glowing like cheap iron Stoves burning Heart-Wood in the Dark, just that distance from no light at all.

Rebekah, her eyelids never blinking, for where all is Dust, Dust shall be no more, confronts him upon surfaces not so much "random" as outlaw,— uncontroll'd by any apparent End or Purpose,— in the penumbra of God's concern, that's if you don't mind comparing his Regard with a solar Eclipse. Moving water,— Mason tries to go fishing whenever he can, for there is no telling what the next Riffle may present him,— the rock Abysses and mountainsides, leaves in the wind announcing a Storm,...Shadows of wrought ironwork upon a wall,...the kissing-crusts of new-baked loaves.... On the Indian warrior paths to and from triumphs, captivities, and death, in the lanes overgrown of abandoned villages at the turn of the day, in the rusted ending of the sky's light, in the full eye of the wind, she stands, waiting to speak to him. What more has she to say? He has long run out of replies. "Then I am not she, but a *Rep-*

resentation. This Thing,"— she will not style it, "Death." "I am detain'd here, in this Thing...that my Body all the while was capable of and leading me to, and carried with it surely as the other Thing, the Thing our Bodies could do, together...," she will not style it, "Love." Has she forgotten Words, over there where Tongues are still'd, and no need for either exists?

55

"Terrible *Feng-Shui* here. Worst I ever saw. You two crazy?"

"Because of...?" Dixon indicating behind them, in thickening dusk, the Visto sweeping away.

"It acts as a Conduit for what we call *Sha,* or, as they say in Spanish California, Bad Energy.— Imagine a Wind, a truly ill wind, bringing failure, poverty, disgrace, betrayal,— every kind of bad luck there is,— all blowing through, night and day, with many times the force of the worst storm you were ever in."

"No one intends to live directly upon the Visto," Mason speaking as to a Child. "The object being, that the people shall set their homes to one side or another. That it be a Boundary, nothing more."

"Boundary!" The Chinaman begins to pull upon his hair and paw the earth with brocade-slipper'd feet. "Ev'rywhere else on earth, Boundaries follow Nature,— coast-lines, ridge-tops, river-banks,— so honoring the Dragon or *Shan* within, from which Land-Scape ever takes its form. To mark a right Line upon the Earth is to inflict upon the Dragon's very Flesh, a sword-slash, a long, perfect scar, impossible for any who live out here the year 'round to see as other than hateful Assault. How can it pass unanswer'd?"

This is the third continent he has been doing *Feng-Shui* jobs on, and he thought he'd seen crazy people in Europe, but these are beyond folly. Whig country-homes, sinister chateaux, Adriatic villas, Hungarian hot springs, Danish harems in the Turkish style,— not one of their owners having hir'd him out of respect for the Dragon, nor for what he could do or find out or even tell them,— when 'twas not innocently to indulge a fascination with the exotic, 'twas to permit themselves yet one more hope in the realm of the Subjunctive, one more grasp at the last radiant whispers of the last bights of Robe-hem, billowing Æther-driven at the back of an ever-departing Deity. A people without faith,— very well, he could understand it, now and then even respect it,— yet here in America, is little *but* Faith,— church-spires on every town skyline, traveling ministers who draw congregations by the hundreds and thousands, across flooded pastures, beneath rain-combed skies and in under the outspread wings of their white tents, singing far off in the woods, full of fervent strange harmonies that grow louder as the traveler approaches....

Frowning at his *Luo-Pan,* the mystic Chinaman shakes his head and mutters, "Even the currents of Earth are with them."

" 'Them'?"

"I have an enemy in these parts, I believe,— a certain Jesuit who does not wish me well."

"French?" inquires Mason.

"Spanish, I believe. Father Zarpazo, the Wolf of Jesus, as he is known in his native Land, though I had the misfortune to meet him in my own. He has his Training directly from those who persecuted Molinos and his followers,— he is accordingly sworn to destroy all who seek God without passing through the toll-gate of Jesus. The Molinistas, as do certain Buddhists of my own land, believ'd that the most direct Way to the Deity was to sit, quietly. If this meant using Jesus as but a stage on a journey, or even passing him by, why so be it. Buddhists speak of finding it necessary, if the Buddha be blocking one's Way, to kill him. Jesuits do not like to hear this sort of thing, of course, it puts far too much into question. If access to God need not be by way of Jesus, what is to become of Jesuits? And the sheer amount of Silence requir'd,— do you think they could ever abide that?

"Zarpazo,— as relentless in his hatred of those he hunts down as they are indifferent, in their love of God, to the passions driving him. Jansenist Convulsionaries, Crypto-Illuminati, and Neo-Quietists alike have felt his cultivated Wrath, some taken before dawn by men in black, others accosted brazenly upon the steps of cathedrals,— clapp'd into iron and leather restraints, going along amiably enough, puzzl'd, sure it must be a mistake.

"European docility,— no one with Power has ever under-appreciated its comforts. So you may imagine the loss of morale, among visitors such as Padre Zarpazo, before the fact of China, as they see how far from Docility they have journeyed,— and what they have come into the midst of. Wild Chinamen! How could they ever have deem'd us ready for their Jesus? Somehow *Feng-Shui* became their principal Enemy. Without it in the World,— is this what they believ'd?— Jesus would have a better chance of finding converts in China. Accordingly, 'twould be a holy Service to destroy *Feng-Shui.*"

Zhang adverts to his *Luo-Pan,* and with fingers unhesitating proceeds to move various of its Rings forward and retrograde. Dixon, happening by, is drawn by the Instrument.

"Another Needle man,— so there's two of us. Ah hope Mason's not troubling thee upon the Topick,— he's unusually loyal to Heavenly Methods, is all."

"You would find even more congenial a Disciple of the Fuh-kien School, whose faith in the Needle is absolute,— whereas I am of the Kan-cheu School, which places the Dragon of the land above all else. Come, look. See here? These are the Moon-stations, the Stars fix'd and moving, signs of the Zodiack...we use all that,— but first comes the Dragon, and what the Needle responds to, is the Dragon's very Life."

"What Mason can't abide is that it never points to what he calls True North. As if the Needle's were False North."

"Zarpazo as well,— his Vows include one sworn to Zero Degrees, Zero Minutes, Zero Seconds, or perfect North. He is the Lord of the Zero. The Impurity of this Earth keeps him driven in a holy Rage.— Which is why he wants this Visto."

" 'Wants— ' "

"News of the Visto will bring him surely as a Gaze brings a Suitor. Purity of Azimuth is his Passion. He was in Italy when your Sponsor Le Maire was producing the Line from Rome to Rimini, he was in Peru with La Condamine and in Lapp-land with Bouguer,— 'tis his Destiny to inflict these Tellurick Injuries, as 'tis mine to resist them."

"I didn't know thah'. Thee come here, then, to oppose our Mission…? to seek our Failure…? Why, Sir? What possible ill Motives can we be serving, in marking out this tiny bit of a Lesser Circle?"

"Once, Monsieur Allègre had as little hesitation in slicing straight thro' the carcasses of Animals and viewing æsthetickally the patterns of Bone and Fat and Flesh thus expos'd. Now, no longer! Heaven has permitted him to see the distinction between Blade and Body,— the aggressive exactitude of one, the helpless indeterminacy of the other. In that difference lies the Potency of the Sin."

"Eeh,— but,— that's Jesuit talk, Captain.— The fell'd Trees aren't just lying there unus'd. There are plenty of Americans but a short trip away who come and fetch them for Firewood or Fences or building-Logs. How can tha think so ill of this Line? A fellow Surveyor. I cannot imagine it."

"Fret not,— my business is with the Jesuit. *We* happen to be the principal Personæ here, not you two! Nor has your Line any Primacy in this, being rather a Stage-Setting, dark and fearful as the Battlements of Elsinore, for the struggle Zarpazo and I must enact upon the very mortal Edge of this great Torrent of *sha*,— which at any moment either of us might slip, fall in, and be borne away, Westward, into the Vanishing-Point and gone."

"And Mason and I,— "

"Bystanders. Background. Stage-Managers of that perilous Flux,— little more."

"Eeh." Dixon thinks about it. "Well it's no worse than Copernicus, is it…? The Center of it all, moving someplace else like thah'…? Better not mention this to Mason."

P. Zarpazo being a master of disguise, Capt. Zhang, by now half insane anyway, becomes convinced that the Priest has actually penetrated the Camp, and only waits his moment to administer that poison'd Stiletto preferr'd by a Jesuit confronting Error. "It's got to be an axman," the Captain decides. "They come and go with entire freedom. Each possesses a Rifle and a choice of Blades. It could be Mr. Barnes. It could even be Stig. Yes! Yes that's it, 'tis Stig!"

"Friend Zhang," soothes Dixon, "Stig is in a number of difficulties at the moment, but none includes you. He could find neither the time, nor the repose of Spirit, to cause you harm in any way that a Jesuit would describe as at all useful. The same is true of the other Hands. Ev'ryone is too busy."

"He's here," insists the far too bright-eyed Geomancer. "If he's not an axman, then,— he must be one of the camp-followers,— Guy Spit the Pass-bank Bully, one of those Vásquez Brothers,— even one of Mrs. Eggslap's Girls. There is no limit to his ingenuity!"

"If he were one of the Ladies, Stig would have discover'd thah' by now."

"Stig could be a Confederate!"

"Captain, pray regard yourself."

The Oriental Operative thereupon grows bodily plumb and symmetrick,— his eyelids lower, his breathing decelerates, and presently he bows in Apology. "You're right, of course. I'm behaving like Chef Armand with his Duck. Which of us doesn't have an Unseen Persecutor? My case is probably no worse than your own."

"Mine...? Why," Dixon again fumescent, "I'm brisk as a Bee these Days. Not a care in the World. Who'd be after me?" Yet he avoids meeting Zhang's eyes.

" 'Tis widely assum'd that you are here on behalf of the Jesuit Le Maire, co-engineer with Boscovich, fifteen years ago, of yet another long, straight Europeans' Line, the Two Degrees of Latitude sliced across Italy from Rome to Rimini. Ever since then, *Sha* has flow'd unremittingly across that miserably Empoped and beduked and Dismember'd Peninsula, Tuscany and Milan taken by Austria, Modena and Genoa by the French, despotism ev'rywhere...."

"Come, come, beg to differ, even a simple child of the Pit country knows that since that last peace Treaty, why Italy's been enjoying a long and wonderful era of prosperity and improvement. If this be Despotism,...?"

"Go to Italy," scolds the Captain, "and look."

"Well,— what about Maria Theresa, then...?"

"The Jesuit Protectress,— a charming exception to the reign of Brutality uncheck'd, throughout the rest of Christendom,— whilst your Jesuits go on attempting to eradicate *Feng-Shui* from human awareness, and to promote the inscription upon the Earth of these enormously long straight Lines,— as in Lapp-land, in Peru, *Encyclopédistes* in expeditionary Costume, squirting Perfume about, and taking these exquisitely precise Sights whilst neglecting to turn their Instruments.... Tho' Degrees of Longitude and Latitude in Name, yet in Earthly reality are they Channels mark'd for the transport of some unseen Influence, one carefully assembl'd cairn, one Oölite Prism, one perfectly incis'd lead Plate, to the next,— when these are dispos'd in a Right Line aim'd at Ohio, it is natural to inquire, what other scientifick Workings may lie in the area.... Who'd benefit most? None, it would seem, but the consciously criminal in Publick Life as in Private, who know how to tap into the unremitting torrent of *Sha* roaring all night and all day, and convert it to their own uses. Howling like a great Boulevard of souls condemn'd to wander up and down the grim surfaces."

"Moreover," now interjects Mr. Everybeet the Quartz-scryer, "west of here, in the Hills 'round Cheat and Monongahela, are secret Lead Mines, which the Indians guard jealously." These Deposits occur not as Flats, as in Durham, nor as Veins, as in Derbyshire, but rather as spherickal Caverns, of wondrous Regularity, fill'd with a Galena, remarkably pure, nearly free of other Minerals. "Perfect Spheres of Lead ore, that is, are situated inside those Mountains, often dozens of Yards across, exerting Tellurick Effects unfathomable." Mr. Everybeet now produces a powerful Glass, beneath which he places samples of finely divided Rock. "The Limestone Matrix thro' which these Plumbaginous Orbs are distributed, proves to be of a peculiar sort, already familiar to you."

"Oölite," Mason and Dixon suppose.

"Plenty out here, ev'ryplace ye go, they sure didn't need to import it from England." The Surveyors have a look thro' the Glass, which reveals a fine structure of tiny Cells, each a Sphere with another nested concentrickally within, much like Fish Roe in appearance. "— Your own Linear Emplacement of Marker-Stones, whatever the reason, requires this sort of Fine structure, weakly tho' precisely Magnetick,— Lime, in certain of the Cells, having been replac'd with Iron,— whereas the fam'd Egyptian Pyramids, whose ever-mystickal Purposes, beyond the simply Funerary, are much speculated upon, requir'd Limestone with another sort of Fine Structure altogether,— containing numberless ancient Shells, each made up of hundreds of square Chambers, arrang'd in perfect Spirals."

He has been out to the secret Ore-diggings, at Night, amid a maze of Hills and Hollows, with Sentries at ev'ry turn of the Trail. Out-croppings of Limestone, whiter than they ought to be, shone in the Star-light. He was met by Native Vendors, with Coils, and Foils, and Bars of Lead, half-inch Balls and small unflattering Toy images including those of the King, and Mr. Franklin. The odor of Sulfur was ev'rywhere. The Valleys were lit with many small Fires, at each of which Ore was being burn'd to a Regulus of the Metal. Among the Indian smelters, Proximity to Fumes and Dust had produc'd a number of Ailments, from chronick Melancholy to haunting without Mercy, to early Death. They gap'd at the Scryer with blunted, sorrowing faces, some screaming words that no one offer'd to translate.

"Most unhappy," recalls Mr. Everybeet. "Not at all the Paradise one has been led to expect. Lead out here is a much-needed metal,— who controls Lead controls the supply of Ammunition, for all sides in ev'ry Dispute, not to mention a segment of the Tellurick-energy Market. Céléron's lead Plates may indeed have been but the visible Calibrating Devices for a much more extensive Engine below,— perhaps an Array of them, and a City to surround that...a Plutonian History unfolding far below our feet, all unknown to us above, but for occasional Volcanoes and Earth tremors. A complete, largely unsens'd World, held within our own, like a child in a Womb, waiting for some Summons to Light...."

"I consider'd myself not unacquainted with Mania," records the Rev^d, "but until the Spectacle I and, by now, ev'ryone else in camp are witnessing Capt. Zhang make of himself, I have known, I collect, as yet but few of its Flow'rings. 'I shall wear black robes,' he declares, '— if *El Lobo de Jesús* may, why so shall I.' And he does. Spanish phrases increasingly creep into his Conversation, and a small Beard is one day visible upon his chin."

"Spend enough time in these Mountains," as Capt. Shelby avers, "and sooner or later you see ev'rything. This has happen'd out here before, tho' they usually change into real Wolves...?"

"Well I can't understand it," frowns Mason, "— the Chinese are known far and wide as a learnèd and sagacious People, quite beyond behavior of this sort,— "

"Except," Dixon points out, "that this one *is* insane, of course."

Mason spreads his hands. "Which of us can say?"

"Falls a few Links short of a Chain, for fair...?"

"Yet,— if he were telling the truth? and there were a dangerous Spaniard on his way here? 'twould be trouble for the Party, without Doubt. Either way, we might have to ask the Captain to leave."

"Eeh,— now they're chucking Stilettos about, it's 'we' again...?"

"Look ye, Dixon, only you can get him to go. He already thinks you're a Jesuit Agent. All you have to do is advise him to stay, and he'll do the opposite."

"If he believes that his enemy may arrive at any moment, he'll prefer to wait, won't he...?— feeling safer, as who would not, among arm'd Protestants...?"

"*¡Ándale, mis Hijos!*" 'Tis the Chinaman himself. It had better be. Axmen nonetheless go scattering, spilling coffee, clutching what's left of evening Mess. Capt. Shelby puts on a Pair of Philadelphia Pebble-Lenses to verify what he seems to be seeing. Mason, making encouraging gestures, urges Dixon, "Go on,...go on," in loud whispers, as he takes himself behind the Cook's Waggon. Dixon stares. The Metamorphosis is alarming. Violet Piping outlines the Captain several times over against the perfect Black of the *Soutane*. He turns, revealing upon the back a gigantick and Floridly render'd Chinese Dragon, in many colors, including Heliotrope and Prussian Blue.

"By the time he finally arrives in this Camp," announces Capt. Zhang, "no one will be able to tell, which is the real Zarpazo. We Two will meet then in a struggle to the death, witness'd by all...the axmen will place bets...there will be beer and Dutch Pretzels, a bottomless Urn of Coffee, depending how long the contest takes, perhaps a free Luncheon as well."

"And if only one of you shows up...?"

"How could you ever be sure which one it was?— Oh, and meaning no offense,— for an Insolent Question like that, the 'real' Zarpazo would have you publicly aflame in the nearest Glade, before you even understood what you'd done. His Chinese impersonator might wait but a few minutes more."

"Mighty harsh talk, Captain," says Shelby. "But you know, I'm a Captain too, and now I wonder'd if I might just have a chat with you, Captain to Captain, as you'd say."

"You do me honor, Captain."

"What troubles us, Captain, about your Spanish friend, is his way of wanting to kill anyone who doesn't agree with him. Hardly do around here, you see. Likely, after a short while, to be no one left. Withal, if one of *us* gets lucky and prevails, then we have the problem of a dead Jesuit, thousands of miles from home, inside a Territory where he ought not to be. Others, some sooner or later with real power, will be making inquiries. In either case, you would have to flee."

"You are all safe, so long as I have,"— thumb and Index together, he twirls his wrist and is immediately holding up a dark Red sphere about the size of a Cherry,— "this. 'Tis a Pearl, yet not from beneath the Sea. Once it was a Cyst, growing within the Brain of a Cobra. None but experienc'd Harvesters are able to tell which Cobras bear them and which are not worth killing. The pearls are taken north into the Himalayan Mountains, where they find use in the Tibetan Medicine.... Therefore fear not the Advent of the Wolf, for here is the soul of the Cobra, yet living, yet potent."

"I'll buy one!" Dixon cries. Mason looks upward, patiently.

That night, at Zsuzsa's Exhibition, in Torchlight, before the gleaming eyes of lovesick Axmen, "Great Frederick has chang'd the face of War, created a new Power upon the Continent,...lo, the Prussian columns,— keeping ever their Intervals, and each precisely upon his mark, wheeling,...the Angles of the Hats, as of the Wigs, calculated as to the Field of Vision, for most efficient Fire."

When it is time for questions from the audience,— "Began at Ramillies, in fact," notes Professor Voam, to all nearby, "— 'twas well before the first Charles, that men envied and sought to copy, nay, outdo, the loos'd Locks of the other half of humanity. All the history of England since that discredited Dynasty has been about Hair,— and nothing else, the tied-back wigs of Marlborough's riflemen at Ramillies being so ideally Hanoverian, so perfected a compromise between the Stuart wantonness and the shorn Republican Pate, that today any hair worn forward of the shoulders, is but Jacobitism by means of Coiffure,— a wordless sedition, that places in question all our hard-won Arrangements."

"Do you mean," Zsuzsa cries, "a perfect balance between the Feminine and the Masculine? English Soldiers? My Brain,— ah, I must think...."

"My good young Woman." Captain Shelby flourishing his Brows. "Whilst Europe was enjoying such tidy doings as yours,— over here, in our own collateral wars, we rather suffer'd one by one, in terror, alone among the Leagues of Trees unending. The only German precision we know of's right here," patting the octagonal Barrel of his Lancaster Rifle, as if 'twere the Flank of a faithful Dog.

"Geometry and slaughter!" ejaculates Squire Haligast, "— The future of war, yet ancient as the mindless Exactitudes of Alexander's Phalanx."

"Perhaps," the Rev^d suggests, "we attribute to the Armies of old, a level of common Belief long inaccessible to our own skeptical Souls. Making the Prussian example all the more mystical,— whom or what can any modern army believe in enough to obey? If not God, nor one's King...?"

"They submit," Zsuzsa replies, "to the preëmptive needs of the Manœuvre,— a Soldier's Faith at last must rest in the Impurity of his own desires. What can Hansel possibly wish for, that Heinz in front of him, and Dieter behind, and a couple of Fritzes on either side, have not already desir'd,— multiplied by all the ranks and files, stretching away across the Plain? The same blonde from down the Street, the same Pot of beer, the same sack of Gold deliver'd by some Elf, for doing nothing. Who is unique? Who is not own'd by someone? What do any of their desires matter, if they can be of no use to the Manœuvre, where all is timed from a single Pulse, each understanding no more than he must,— "

" 'Tis he!" screams Capt. Zhang, leaping to the Platform and taking a position as if astride a Horse, extending his hands precisely before him. Zsuzsa, her eyes very wide, swiftly undoes some buttons of her Tunic, to reach for a Pistol of British make, and a Lady's Powder-Flask with a Stopper of strip'd blue Venetian Glass, purring, "Captain, Captain, not in here. Run along now, take it outside, you have all the Forest to play in."

"Reveal yourself, Wolf of Jesus. Zhang does not kill Fools, nor may he in honor kill you, whilst you linger within that contemptible disguise."

"What, this old *Rongy?*— Will someone explain this to me? Don Foppo de Pin-Heado, here, seems upset."

"Perhaps if Mademoiselle, as a gesture of good intent, would put aside her,— ehm,— " cajoles Mr. Barnes.

"We call it a Pistol, the same as men do," twirling the Weapon by its trigger-guard. "Now that you have spoken to the Lady in Breeches, perhaps you could have a word with the man in skirts."

"He's not a real Jesuit," Mason assures her.

"Or, perhaps all too real!" the Captain with a look of evil glee,— "for suppose I was never Zhang, but rather Zarpazo, all the Time! HA,— ha-ha!" His Laugh, tho' hideously fiendish enough, seems practis'd.

"Or," replies Mr. Barnes, "that you are neither, but yet another damn'd Fabulator, such as ever haunt encampments, white or Indian, ev'ry night, somewhere in this Continent."

"Too many possible Stories. You may not have time enough to find out which is the right one."

"Best thing's draw up a Book, for there's certain to be wagering upon the Question?" offers Guy Spit.

Ethelmer, downstairs, alone, at the Clavier, hair loos'd, apostrophizes a Thermometer,— throughout which the Listener may imagine a series of idiotic still-life Views, first of the Thermometer, registering some low temperature,— then of Ethelmer, singing to it, then back to the Thermometer again, and so forth.

> Say, Mister Fahrenheit,
> She doesn't treat me right, [advert to Thermometer]
> Wish you could warm up that Lady of mine,— [then back to
> 'Thelmer, &c.]
> Look at you, on the wall,
> Don't have a, care at all,—
> Even tho' our love has plung'd,
> To minus ninety-nine,— now, Doctor
> Celsius, and ev'ryone else, yes,

Say, you've plenty to spare,—
Don't let us freeze, can't you
Send some Degrees, from where-
-Ever you are, out there,—
Damme,
Mister Fahrenheit,—
Here comes another night,
I shall once again be shiv'ring through,
With no help from your Scale,
'Tis all Ice and Hail, and
I'll turn-into a Snow-man, too.

"Where's Brae, 'Thelmer?" DePugh, self-Mesmeriz'd, having lost his
way to the Larder.

"Dreaming. As to what, I can only say with certainty, that 'tis not of me."

"Romance, you did your best."

"Ah. But not my worst."

56

"Now here is something curious." The Rev^d produces and makes available to the Company his Facsimile of Pennsylvania's Fair Copy of the Field-Journals of Mason and Dixon, "copied without the touch of human hands, by an ingenious Jesuit device, and printed by Mr. Whimbrel, next to The Seneca Maiden, Philadelphia, 1776."

"Cycles, or if you like, Segments of eleven Days recur again and again. Here, in 1766, eleven days after setting out southward from Brandywine, is Mason paus'd at Williamsburg, the southernmost point of his journey,— next day he leaves for Annapolis, and eleven days later departs that City, to return to work upon the Line,— a very Pendulum. In April, just after crossing the North Mountain, they must wait in the Snow and Rain, from the sixth thro' the sixteenth before resuming. The culminating Pause, of course, is at the Line's End, between 9 October of '67, when the Chief of the Indians that were with them said he would proceed no farther west than the Warrior Path, and the 20th, when the Party, turning their backs for the last time upon the West, began to open the Visto eastward— unto their last Days in America,— " turning the Pages, "— from 27 August of '68, when accounts were settl'd and the work was officially over and done with, till 7 September, their last night in Philadelphia before leaving to catch the Halifax Packet at New-York. Again and again, this same rough interval continues to appear,— suggesting a hidden Root common to all. And Friends, I believe 'tis none but the famous Eleven Missing Days of the Calendar Reform of '52."

Cries of "Cousin? we beseech thee!" and "Poh, Sir!"

"Those of us born before that fateful September," observes the Rev^d, "comprise a generation in all British History uniquely insulted, each Life carrying a chronologick Wound, from the same Parliamentary Stroke. Perhaps we are compell'd, even unknowingly, to seek these Undecamerous Sequences, as areas of refuge that may allow us, if only for a moment, to pretend Life undamaged again. We think of 'our' Time, being held, in whatever Time's equivalent to 'a Place' is, like Eurydice, somehow to be redeem'd.— Perhaps, as our Indian brothers might re-enact some ancient Adventure, correct in all details, so British of a certain Age seek but to redeem Eleven Days of pure blank Duration, as unalienably their own....

"Pull not such faces, young Ethelmer,— one day, should you keep clear of Fate for that long, you may find yourself recalling some Injustice, shared with lads and lasses of your own Day, just as uncalmable, and even yet, unredeem'd."

Mason for a while had presum'd it but a matter of confusing dates, which are Names, with Days, which are real Things. Yet for anyone he met born before '52 and alive after it, the missing Eleven Days arose again and again in Conversation, sooner or later characteriz'd as "brute Absence," or "a Tear thro' the fabric of Life,"— and the more he wrestl'd with the Question, the more the advantage shifted toward a Belief, as he would tell Dixon one day, "In a slowly rotating Loop, or if you like, Vortex, of eleven days, tangent to the Linear Path of what we imagine as Ordinary Time, but excluded from it, and repeating itself,— without end."

"Hmm. The same eleven days, over and over, 's what tha're saying...?"

"You show, may I add, an unusual Grasp of the matter."

"Why then, as it is a periodick Ro-tation, so must it carry, mustn't it, a *Vis centrifuga*, that might, with some ingenuity, be detected...? Perhaps by finding, in the Realm of Time, where the Loop tries either to increase or decrease its Circumference, and hence the apparent length of each day in it. Or yet again not rotate at all, the length of the Day then continuing the same,— "

"Dixon. Everything rotates."

"A Vorticist! Lord help us, his Mercy how infrequent!" Emerson, believing Vorticists to be the very Legion of Mischief, had so instructed ev'ry defenseless young Mind he might reach.

"Very well,— if you must know,— lean closer and mark me,— I have been there, Sir."

" 'There,' Sir...?"

Mason is gesturing vigorously with his Thumb, at the Eye, much wider than its partner, that he uses for Observation.— "Tho' I've ever tried not to recollect any more than I must,— at least not till a zealously inquisitive Partner insists upon knowing,— yet the fact is that at Midnight of September second, in the unforgiven Year of 'Fifty-two, I myself did stumble, daz'd and unprepared, into that very Whirlpool in Time,— finding myself in September third, 1752, a date that for all the rest of England, did not exist,— *Tempus Incognitum.*"

"Eeh..."

"Don't say it,— I didn't believe it myself. Not until it happen'd, that is,— no Discomfort to it, only a little light-headedness. At the Stroke of the Hour, whilst I continued into the Third, there came an instant Translation of Souls, leaving a great human Vacuum, as ev'ryone else mov'd on to the Fourteenth of September."

"Not sure what that means, of course...."

"You'd have felt it as a lapse of consciousness, perhaps. Yet soon enough I discover'd how alone 'twas possible to be, in the silence that flow'd, no louder than Wind, from the Valleys and across those Hill-villages, where, instead of Populations, there now lay but the mute Effects of their Lives,— Ash-whiten'd Embers that yet gave heat, food left over from the last Meals of September Second, publick Clocks frozen for good at midnight between the Second and the day after,— tho' somewhere else, in the World which had jump'd ahead to the Fourteenth, they continued to tick onward, to be re-wound, to run fast or slow, carrying on with the ever-Problematick Lives of the Clocks...."

"Alone in the material World, Dixon, with eleven days to myself. What would you have done?"

"Had a Look in The Jolly Pitman, perhaps...?"

A look of forbearance. "Aye, as my first thoughts were of The George in Stroud,...yet 'twas the absence of Company, that most preoccupied me,— seeking which, in some Desperation, before the Sun rose, I set out. Reasoning that if I had been so envortic'd, why so might others— " breaking off abruptly, a word or two shy (Dixon by now feels certain) of some fatal confidence, that Rebekah would have stood at the heart of.

Young Charles was to reason eventually, that the pain of separation had lain all upon his side, for she was to bid him good morrow upon the fourteenth, as she had good night upon the second, without a seam or a lurch, appearing to have no idea he'd been away cycling through eleven days without her. Nor had whatever he liv'd through in that Loop, caus'd any perceptible change in the Youth she kiss'd hello "the very next day" in the High Street in Stroud, brazen as a Bell.

Meanwhile there he was, alone, with the better part of a Fortnight before he'd be hooking up again with his Betroth'd, as smoothly as if he'd never been gone,— and, Damme, he would be off. "Were there yet Horses about?" Dixon wishes to know.

"Animals whose Owners knew them, made the Transition along with them, to the fourteenth. 'Most all the dogs, for example. Fewer Cats, but plenty nonetheless. Any that remain'd by the third of September were wild Creatures, or stray'd into the Valley,— perhaps, being ownerless, disconnected as well from Calendars. I found one such Horse, a Horse no one would have known, as well as two Cows unmilk'd and at large. I rode past miles of Crops untended, Looms still'd and water-wheels turning to no avail, Apples nearly ripe, Waggons half-laded, the Weld not yet a-bloom, nor the Woad-mills a-stink, till at length from the last ridge-line, there lay crystalline Oxford, as finely etch'd as my Eyes, better in those days, could detect, nor holding a thread of Smoak in it anywhere...."

"You were making for Oxford...?"

"Aye, with some crack'd notion I'd find Bradley there.... Being a young Bradleyolator, as were all Lens-fellows of that Day, especially 'round Gloucestershire...tho' later, in my Melancholy, I might see more vividly his all-too-earthly connections with Macclesfield and Chester-field, and beyond them, looming in the mephitic Stench, Newcastle and Mr. Pelham. At that Moment, in my Innocence, I believ'd that Bradley, our latter-day Newton, insatiately curious, must have calculated his way into this Vortex,— with the annoying Question of why he should, kept beyond the Gates of conscious Entertainment."

"Did you find him there?"

"I found Something…not sure what. What surpriz'd me was the sensible Residue of Sin that haunted the place,— of a Gravity, withal, unconfronted, unaton'd for, lying further than simple Jacobite Persistence…. I'd of course collected, in some dim way, that Bradley had advis'd Macclesfield,— his great Benefactor, after all, perhaps even in partial return upon Milord's Investment,— as to ways of finding the movable Feasts and holy Days and so forth, under the New Style,— and that Macclesfield had taken credit for the philosophical labor, as Chesterfield for the Witticisms and *Bonhomie*, that it took eventually to bring the Calendar Act into Law. Yet, though Bradley seldom sought Acclaim, preferring to earn it, neither would he refuse credit due him, unless there were reason to keep Silence,— such as the unexpected depth of his complicity in an Enterprise so passionately fear'd and hated by most of the People."

Both reach for the coffee at the same time, Dixon elaborately deferring to Mason's over-riding need for any Antistupefacient to hand.

"I don't know that in the entire Cycle I caught a Wink of Slumber,— 'twere but a Devourer of precious Time, when all the Knowledge of Worlds civiliz'd and pagan, late and ancient, lay open to my Questions."

"Yet I guess I know this Tale,— 'tis the German fellow,— Faust isn't it?"

"But that he, at least, was able to live in the plenary World,— I, alas, was alone."

"Eeh…?"

"Well,…as it turn'd out, not alone, exactly…."

"I knew it,— some Milk-maid, out on a tryst, eeh! am I near it? stray'd too close to the Vortex? Whoosh! Pail inverted, Skirts a-flying,— So! how'd it go?"

"Pray you.— 'Twas something I never saw,— certainly not Mr. Bodley's Librarian, Mr. Wild,— and they were more than one. After Night-Fall, as I burn'd Taper 'pon Taper wantonly, only just succeeding in pushing back the gloom about me, would I hear Them rustling, ever beyond the circle of light, as if foraging among the same ancient Leaves as I."

"Mice, or Rats, maybe…?"

"Too deliberate. They seem'd to wish to communicate."

"And this was down among those Secret Shelves, where none but the Elect may penetrate?"

"You know about that?"

"Of course,— Emerson gave us a brief inventory. Aristotle on Comedy, always wanted to read thah',— all the good bits that Thomas left out of the Infancy Gospel...? Shakespeare's *Tragedy of Hypatia*...?"

"What sav'd me," impassively on, "was hunger,— an abrupt passage of indecipherable Latin returning my attention at last from lighted Page to empty Stomach. I recall'd that Pantries and Wine-cellars all over the Town lay open to my Hungers,— apprehensive, light-headed, I rush'd from the Library, too a-tremble to keep a taper lit, up ladders creaking in the absolute Dark, down corridors of high bookshelves,— Presences lay ev'rywhere in Ambuscado. I dared not lift my eyes to what all too palpably waited, pois'd, upon the ancient Ceilings, wing'd, fatal.... Then! a sudden great whir at my face,— scientifickally no doubt a Bat, tho' at the moment something far less readily nam'd,— provoking a cry of Fear, as at last I broke out into the open air of a Quadrangle, yellow in the Moonlight...."

"Wait! that's it! The Moon,— "

"Indeed, among any amateur Astronomer's first questions. How should the Moon behave, seen from inside this Vortex?"

"And, and?"

"Ever full,— ever fix'd upon the Meridian." An insincere Chuckle. "Yes, eleven days of Light remorseless, to be fac'd alone in a city of Gothickal Structures, that might or might not be inhabited, whilst from all directions came flights of the dark Creatures I hop'd were only...Bats."

"Tha don't mean,— "

"As the Timbres, nearly Human, of the ceaseless Howling I hop'd came only from...Dogs...."

"Not,— "

"Oh, and more.— 'Twas as if this Metropolis of British Reason had been abandon'd to the Occupancy of all that Reason would deny. Malevolent shapes flowing in the Streets. Lanthorns spontaneously going out. Men roaring, as if chang'd to Beasts in the Dark. A Carnival of Fear.

559

Shall I admit it? I thrill'd. I felt that if I ran fast enough, I could gain altitude, and fly. I would become one of them. I could hide beneath Eaves as well as any. I could creep in the Shadows. I could belong to the D——l, — anything, inside this Vortex, was possible. I could shriek inside Churches. I could smash ev'ry Window in a Street. Make a Druidick Bonfire of the Bodleian. At some point, however, without Human prey, the Evil Appetite must fail, and I became merely Melancholy again."

"Thee abandon'd thy Studies of the Ancient Secrets? For a mere Tickling of thy Sensorium, done with how swiftly...? Mason,— dear Mason."

"In fact," Mason unmirthfully, "I was prevented from ever returning. Exil'd from the Knowledge. As I cross'd into the Courtyard before Duke Humfrey's, I encounter'd a Barrier invisible, which I understood I might cross if I will'd, tho' at the Toll of such Spiritual Unease, that one Step past it was already too far. What that Influence was, I cannot say. Perhaps an Artifact of the Vortex. Perhaps an Infestation of certain Beings Invisible. I receiv'd, tho' did not altogether hear, from somewhere, a distinct Message that the Keys and Seals of Gnosis within were too dangerous for me. That I must hold out for the Promises of Holy Scripture, and forget about the Texts I imagin'd I'd seen."

"Tha didn't want to hear thah', I guess?"

Mason seizes, cradles, and hefts his Abdominal Spheroid. "Meditating upon bodily Resurrection, I arriv'd at the idea of *this* being resurrected, and without delay proceeded to a Bacchic interlude, in which you'd not be interested, being too prolong'd, and besides, too personal."

"Well...now...?"

"Gone was the Chance that might have chang'd my Life. It lay at the Eye of that Vortex,— to cross the Flow of Time surrounding it, was I oblig'd to aim a bit upstream, or toward the Past, in order to maintain a radial course to the Center...."

"And there, whilst with Taurean stubbornness tha kept at i'...?"

"Well now, odd as it may seem, soon as I'd penetrated the Barrier, I understood my Holiday was over,— I tried to pull back, but too late,— I was in the vortickal Emprise.... To my Relief, some, at least, of the dark Presences that had caus'd me such Apprehension, prov'd to be the Wraiths of those who had mov'd ahead instantly to the Fourteenth, haunting me not from the past but from the Future,— drawing closer, ever closer, until,— First I heard the voices of the Town, then at the edges of my Vision, Blurs appear'd, and Movement, which went suddenly a-whirl, streaking in to surround me, as in the mesh of prolong'd Faces, only hers stood firm.— And when I join'd her again, before I could think of what to say, she kiss'd me and declar'd,— 'Somebody got in late last night.'

"The only proof I had that 'twas not a Dream was the Bite I receiv'd whilst in my Noctambulation of the City.—

"This Life," runs the moral he is able by now to draw for Dixon, "is like the eleven days,— a finite Period at whose end, she and I, having separated for a while, will be together again. Meanwhile must I travel alone, in a world as unreal as those empty September dates were to me then...."

" 'Bite,' Mason?"

"Nothing, nothing. Likely a Dog."

"How likely?"

"What else? If the People of Stroud, pursuing ordinary Lives eleven days ahead of me, could 'morphose to such sinister Beings, why not their Dogs?"

"Show me."

"Well that was the rum thing, Dixon, for about ten minutes later,— "

"Eeh! I am the Sniffer sniff'd, as Parker said when he put his Head in the Bear's Den...?"

57

Early in 1766,— New Style,— reversing the Directions taken the year before, Mason sets off southward "to see the Country," whilst Dixon,— mention'd in the Field-Book only upon Mason's return, as having left Philadelphia, upon the eighteenth of March, to meet with the Commissioners at Chester Town,— in fact heads north for the lighted Streets of New-York.

At a Theater with no name, no fix'd address,— this night happ'ning to be upon Broad-Way,— printing no Handbills, known only by word of mouth, Dixon upon the advice of a Ferry-Companion attends a Stage performance of the musical drama *The Black Hole of Calcutta, or, The Peevish Wazir.* Before a backdrop of Fort William (executed with such an obsessively fine respect for detail, that during the Work's Longueurs, with the aid of a Glass, one may observe, pictur'd upon the Tableau, sub-ordinate Dramas as if in progress,— meetings of the Management, hands clutching throats or leveling Pistols, farewells by the landing, the steaming pale forever-unreachable Hooghly and the Ships waiting to go away, leaving behind the Unspeakable), a Corps of two dozen Ladies appear, strolling about in quasi-Indian Dress and singing, to the (as some would say) inappropriately lively Accompaniment of a small Orchestra,

> In the Black Hole of Calcut-ta,
> One scarcely knows quite what t'

Make of Things they groan and mut-ter,
Why, 'tis cheerier in the Gut-ter.—

Being dark and *ooh* so stuf-fy,
Little Su-gar for one's Cof-fee,
And the Na-tives, rah-ther huf-fy,—
And the Pil-lows far from fluf-fy,—

Ask of an-y, Bengal-i,
How's the Black Hole, to-night,—
Don't expect him, to be jol-ly,
For there's something, not-quite right! as

The Lamps begin to sput-ter,
All will not be Scones and But-ter,
When the door's at last been shut to
That Black Hole of Cal-cut-ta!
La,— la,— la-la, la-la, la-la...

The Story, as near as Dixon can make out, is about a British officer whose Rivalry with a comically villainous Frenchman for the Affection of a Nabob's Daughter, brings on the war in Bengal. There are some catchy Tunes, and an Elephant, promis'd in the first Act, which incredibly, at the very end of the Show, is deliver'd. The audience sits stunn'd in the vacuous Purity of not having been cheated. The Elephant, within its elaborate trappings of red, blue, and gold, watches ev'rything carefully,— someone's Elephant, perhaps, but no one's Fool. Girls emerge from the Howdah in impossible numbers, wearing Costumes as variously hued as the Rainbow, and as diaphanous. They place their stocking'd Toes precisely upon Elephant pressure points, long known to Chinese Healers, strung along his Ear Meridians,— the Elephant rolls his eyes appreciatively. 'Tis this part of the Show that the Girls, as well, enjoy the most, or so they tell Dixon afterward, when he wanders back-stage to see what might be up, in all Innocence following the Scents of Womanly Exertion, to the Dressing-Room.

"Here he is!"

"Took him long enough, for a Kiddy got up so flash."

"Oh ye'll bore him, Fiona! Come over here m' Darling, you can sleep later."

"Ooh! Cow."

"Anyone in here for a Turtle Feast? My foolish Lad has a Coach wait-ing?" Dixon is swept in a rush of Polonaises, Sacques, and Petticoats into the Vehicle, and with great cheering away they clatter, out the Greenwich Road to Brannan's and an unsequenc'd two days of Revelry, ever punctuated by someone rising to cry, "I haven't felt this excited,— " turning to the Others, who roar back, "— since Eyre Coote won the Battle of Wandiwash!"— being a famous Moment from the Comedy,— Party ending up back in the Town, at Montagne's Tavern, upon Broad-Way, near Murray Street, which proves to be Head-quarters of the local Sons of Liberty, as well as thick with Intrigue, regardless of the Hour.

He is soon aware of Captain Volcanoe, who in the Year since Mason saw him has been well in the Crucible of the Troubles attending the Stamp Act. Some of the old gang have fled,— others have decided to gamble ev'rything, unto their Lives, to see the British gone,— tho' beyond this, there is little agreement. "Even if this Act is repeal'd or in practice never enforc'd, any ministry of this King, even one that some-how includes Mr. Pitt, will be certain to tax us. 'Tis our Duty to resist, tho' it take up all our Days, and Nights as well. The Communications are now well establish'd, despite British Interceptions. We do well. More and more are resolv'd,— our Numbers ever growing. For the first time, we had a trans-Provincial Congress here in October,— yet, the Expense, reckon'd so far, must be borne most heavily by the warmer Sentiments, for we are become a colder lot. Tell your co-adjutor he was lucky we caught him last Winter, and not this, or Blackie might have had his way."

"From what he'll be pleas'd to hope a safe distance, then, Mr. Mason sends his Compliments to your Niece."

"She ran off with an Italian Waggon-smith," the Captain shaking his head, "and they went to live in Massapequa, upon Long-Island. His mother is teaching her to cook."

"Mason will be perplex'd."

"How do you think we feel? A sort of Club, at whose Gatherings she might meet a possible Husband,— that's all the use we ever were to her. Politics? Poh. She may never care about any of this. The road's not for ev'ryone, 's all's it is."

"Hallo, Cap'n. This un's a likely one,— hey?" A muscular, untended dark cloud of an Indiv. has appear'd upon Dixon's starboard Quarter.

"No, Blackie, he's another Astronomer,— you recollect the one last year? Well, this is his Partner."

"*Mais oui, mais oui,*" Dixon sweeping off his Hat and making his Notion of a Bow. "You hate Engleesh bastaird? Want to keel them, eh? Haw, haw! Me too!"

"Much rather kill you," sighs Blackie. "But, as I mayn't, you shall have to stand me a pint instead."

"Seems fair." Tho' by now broad daylight outside, in here 'tis forever Midnight,— Resolutions proper to the hour being made and kept all 'round them, Windows shutter'd, lamps few. Good thing I'm a jolly straight-ahead Lad, Dixon reminds himself,— or I'd start to imagine all kinds of things....

"To the 'Sixty-six!" Pewter clanking, ale spilling and commingling, much of it upon the Clothing of the Company.

"What d'ye think, then?" Blackie asks abruptly of Dixon.

"Eeh,— not Philadelphia, is it?"

"Nor Boston neither!" Blackie assures him, with a clap upon the shoulder. "Tho' it little matters."

"Aye,— ev'ry Province is agreed in this Business. All speak as One."

"What a terrible thing, that British Governments should mis-read us so, when we wish to believe in their Wisdom, their better grasp of History, as of Secular Likelihood,— yet they will keep finding ways to nourish our Doubts."

"Will their Stupidity prove beyond the reach even of Mr. Franklin, our American Prometheus?"

"Why bother to educate 'em? The stupider the better."

"Yet too stupid, and the only Choice left is Battle."

"There's the Ticket!" cries Blackie.

"At the Peak of the Riots, Blackie was running about a Thousand Sailors," remarks Capt. Volcanoe.

"And they're still in Town," Blackie with an eager Nod, "thanks to Cap'n Kennedy." Who, in Command of H.M.S. *Coventry,* is regulating Traffick in the Harbor, allowing ships to enter, but detaining as many as he may who attempt to leave with their Clearance Papers unstamp'd. "Here comes one of my Lads now, in fact."

Who does it prove to be but Foretopman Bodine, once of the *Seahorse*, who, as he now relates, having jump'd that ship in Madras, watching from shore as she sail'd away to the Capture of Manila, had then hir'd on to a China ship, which was set upon in mid-Ocean by Pirates, who took him to South America, whence he escap'd, making his way North, among Typhoons and Hurricanoes, Jungle and Swamp, Alligators and Boas, Indians and Spaniards, till fetching up in Perth Amboy in the company of a certain Roaring Dot, belle of the Harbor.

"Woman of my dreams," Fender-belly vilely chuckling.

"Nought but a Snotter waiting for a Sprit," his Lady controverts him. "Happen'd to be this 'un, 's all."

"Sav'd his arse from a musket ball before Fort George in November."

"Aye!" Blackie all a-grin, "What a Night! Thousands of us! A fierce Wind, coming in off the Harbor at our backs…Sparks from the Torches flying ev'rywhere!"

"Blackie kept imagining his Hat was a-fire," recalls the Captain. "All shouting up at them, 'Liberty!' Daring them to shoot Buggers. Tho' Major James could have ta'en easily a thousand Souls at the first Volley, he held his fire, and our War with Britain did not begin. But good Fender could have provok'd it, if anyone could." Whilst he was exposing his Hind-Parts to the Gaze of those in the Fort, prudent Dot, recognizing signs of Trouble ahead, remov'd a Sap from her Stocking, and bestow'd the Pygephanous Tar a Memento, from which he did not awaken until the next day, by which time he'd been convey'd to her Barge at the Amboys.

"Well met, Friend," says a quiet Voice at Dixon's Elbow. "I'll not tell if you won't." Peering thro' the Smoke, he recognizes Philip Dimdown, now as un-Macaronickal as possible, a serious young man upon a Mission whose end may not be predicted. They make their way to a Corner with a Clavier, from whose top Dixon must remove a Madeira bottle, two cold Chops, and a severely tatter'd Periwig in order even to lounge against it. "So, tha're not a Fop after all? I may pass Fop Remarks, make Fop-Joaks, without giving offense?"

" 'Twas the best way to get by them," Dimdown causing his Tankard to nod, amiably. "Rattling quite discomposes these Brits, some of whom may go for weeks without saying any more than they have to. Yet as no true Macaroni would, in non-Macaronick Company, behave too Macaronickally, in that was the impersonation you saw, defective. That is, I might have been more subdued about it."

"Fool'd me, for fair."

"I was probably indulging Fop Sentiments long kept under, unknown even to myself. Yet, even a Son of Liberty needs to have a little Diversion, given that scarcely a day passes when one doesn't have to step lively if one wishes to remain attach'd to one's Arse, and for me, say,— being a Fop's just the ticket. Right now I'm obsess'd with Wigs. I find I have to change them once a week at least in order to remain unidentified. What think ye of this one? Just snatch'd it up and threw it on,— in Town but for the night,— been trav'ling about in a French Bomb-Ketch, taken in the late War, *La Fougueuse,* two Mortars in the Cock-Pit, spot of Bother with the Trim in any kind of a Chop, dates back to 'forty-two, but she gets us where we want to go, she gets us 'round the Communications," seeming by this to denote, the total Ensemble of Routes by which Messages might in those days pass among Americans,— by which Selves entirely word-made were announc'd and shar'd, now and then merging in a plasma, like the Over-soul of the Hindoo, surging to and fro along the lanes, from hillside to bluff, by way of Lanthorn-Flashes, transnoctial hoofbeats, Sharpies and Snows, cryptograms curl'd among Macaronick Wigs, Songs, Sermons, Bells in the Towers, Hat-Brims, letters to the Papers, Broadsheets at the Corners, Criers at Town Limits facing out into the Unknown in the dead of Winter, in the middle of the Night, and shouting, never without the confidence that someone is listening, somewhere, and passing the Message along,— upon Water as upon Land, *La Fougueuse* in Company with Ferries coming and going 'round the Clock, linking coastal Connecticut, New-York, the Jerseys, all up and down Chesapeake, a single great branch'd Creature, impulses trav'ling Creeks and Coves at the speed of Thought,— Virginia, the Carolinas, well into and beyond the Mountains, into the water-Prairie of Ohio, and thence...

" 'Tis vast," Blackie assures Dixon. "Ain't never been nothing like it. Been living in Brooklyn all my life, seen some 'shit' some English Gents wouldn't even know if they stepp'd in it,…and by t'en, 'twould be too late. But what's going on wit' t'ese Lawyers," pollicating the Captain, "hey,— yese don't want to know. It's vast, all right? Know what I'm saying,— vast."

Dixon shrugging, shakes his head to indicate ignorance upon the Topick. "Christ's Return…?" he guesses.

"That's next, after us."

"Yese are paving the way?"

"Very likely put, Sir,— " cries an ecclesiastickal-looking Personage, "I should add, 'inspiringly' but for the prepond'rance of Deists among us, whom Christ makes uncomfortable. They will have their day. And later, a generation, or two, from now, when the People are at last grown disenchanted enough, 'twill be time for Christ to return to the Hearts of His own."

"Why Asaph, poh to ye and your 'they'! ye're a d——'d Voltaire Reader yourself, what kind of Thorns-and-Angels Stuff is this?"

"Mr. Dixon, being a Quaker, can hold little love for any King, Blackie, do calm down a bit,— tho' his love for Christ may be another matter, and 'twas that I was deferring to, that's if you don't mind?"

" 'Course not," Blackie replies with the smugness of one who believes he has scor'd a Point.

"Tho' rear'd a Friend," Dixon feels he must clarify, "I was expos'd at a receptive Age to a Rush of Deistick thoughts, aye very Deistick indeed…?— all in a great tumble, by way of Mr. Emerson of Hurworth,— so I've a Sentimental Foot in each, as tha'd say…?"

"As a Quaker, you'd surely rather see us independent of Britain?" inquires Mr. Dimdown.

" 'Tis not how British treat Americans," Dixon amiably rubescent, " 'tis how both of You treat the African Slaves, and the Indians Native here, that engages the Friends more closely,— an old and melancholy History…. My allegiance, as a Quaker born, would lie, above all Tribes, with Christ,— withal, as a Geordie, for reasons unarguably Tribal, I can have no sympathy for any British King,— not even one who's paid my Wages, bless 'im. Call me an ungrateful Cur, go ahead, I've been call'd worse.— Eeh, lo, thy Jack's empty...? Can't have thah', allow me, all who're dry, no problem, Mr. McClean shall enter each into his Ledger, and in the fullness of Time will all be repaid,— aye then, here they come! how canny, with those greeaht Foahm Tops on 'em, what do tha call thah'?"

"That is a 'Head,' " Blackie quizzickal. "They don't have that, back wherever you're from? What kind o' Ale-drinker are you then, Sir?"

"Shall we quarrel, after all?"

"Innocent question," Blackie looking about for support.

"Very well, as tha did ask,— I'm a faithful and traditional Ale-Drinker, Sir, who does thee a courtesy in even swallowing this pale, hopp'd-up, water'd-down imitation of Small Beer."

"Far preferable," replies Blackie, "— even if slanderously and vilely untrue,— to that black, sluggish, treacly substitute for Naval Tar, Sir, no offense meant, that they swill down over in *England?*" with a look that would have been meaningful, could it get much beyond a common Glower.

Dixon sighs. Ale Loyalty is important to him, as part of a pact with the Youth he wish'd to remain connected to. He lifts and drinks, as calmly as possible, the entire Pint of American Ale, without pausing for any Breath. Having then taken one at last, "O Error!" he cries, "How could I've so misjudg'd this?"

Blackie is as short of Time as anyone here. This thing that is now taking shape has an Inertia that may yet bear all before it...he can no longer indulge himself in what once, not long ago, would have prov'd a lively Contest,— nowadays, all energy, all attention, is claim'd by Futurity, unwritten as unscryable, the Door wide open.

Thus, "I once took Joy, 's a matter of fact, in many a British Pint," recalls Blackie, "and go ever in the Faith that so I shall again, some day. Meanwhile, as with our Tea, we brew American."

"Believe I'll have another of those...?" replies Dixon. "Would tha join me?"

58

Upon the Roads of Mason's journey South, the scene is alarming. In Maryland, in September, the Mob had pull'd down the house of Zachariah Hood, who, refusing to resign as the Province's Stamp Distributor, fled to New-York, and was granted refuge in Fort George, in time to witness Foretopman Bodine's Bi-Lunar Exhibition. Tho' 'twas now possible to clear Vessels out of Chesapeake Ports unstamp'd, pleading a lack of Stamps, Maryland was somehow among the last of the American Provinces to do so. As if, having paus'd self-amaz'd at their bold deed, the Mobility were now considering their next step. As Autumn rusted toward Winter, Youths went careering along the high roads firing long Rifles from Horse-back at any target that might suggest a connexion with stamp'd Paper, Puffs of Breath and Smoke decorating the way. Groups of farm Girls stood at crossroads and sang to them, "Americans All." Their Fathers, not always with better things to do, offer'd Jugs and Pipes, and their Mothers Tea. Traveling Sons of Liberty never had to pay a farthing for Drink,— and were ever the objects of Suggestions that, for even the liveliest of them, would have taken more time away from their Itineraries than Duty would allow. Massachusetts Bay accents were heard for the first time, out in the Allegheny, up in the Coves, or "Cöves," as Folk there were pronouncing it, purs'd as the Yankees were broad. New-Yorkers in Georgia, Pennsylvanians in the Carolinas, Virginians ev'rywhere, upon Horses perhaps better looking than suited to the Work,— all took time to appreciate the musick of Voices from far away, yet already, unmistakably, American.

> Out in the Field,
> Down by the Sea,
> The Hour has peal'd,
> Whoever ye be,
>
> Daughter of Erin,
> Scotia's Son,
> Let us be daring,—
> Let it be done.
>
> It is time for
> The Choosing,—
> Americans all,
> No more refusing
> The Cry, and the Call,—
> For the Grain to be sifted,
> For the Tyrants to fall,
> As the Low shall be lifted,—
> Americans all...
>
> Till the end of the Story,
> Till the end of the Fight,
> Till the last craven Tory
> Has taken to Flight,
>
> Let us go to the Wall,
> Let us march thro' the Pain,
> Americans all,
> Slaves ne'er again.

At Williamsburg, Mason, as well as being invited to the College of William and Mary, to inspect the Philosophickal Apparati, is introduc'd, at the State House, to a Party of Tuscarora Chiefs, upon a Mission to bring out the last of their people from the Carolinas, and conduct them safely back under the Protection of the Senecas, where they will join the rest of their Tribe, the sixth of the Six Nations.

The Escort have some apprehension about crossing Pennsylvania, with an hundred, perhaps two hundred, Tuscaroras, for they have heard

of the Paxton Massacres. But along the way they are to be join'd by Protectors from various Nations, principally Mohawks. Tho' their Territory
lies hundreds of Leagues to the North, the Six Nations are ever a-bustle
thro' the Forests of Pennsylvania, observing all Movement, regardless of
Size, vigilantly. "Any of Paxtonian Disposition," Mason tries to reassure
the Chiefs, "being usually bless'd with a Marksman's Eye, know who's
in the Woods, and why,— yet will not at ev'ry Opportunity choose to
engage."

He is staying at Mr. Wetherburn's. One morning a note appears tuck'd
into a Frame full of cross'd Ribbons, from Col° Washington, in Town and
seeking a quiet game or two of Billiards. Their Tranquillity is not long
preserv'd, as more and more arrive in Raleigh's Billiard-Room, 'round
the fam'd great Table.

"Even as Clearings appear in the Smoke of a Tavern, so in Colonial
matters may we be able to see into, and often enough thro', the motives
of Georgie Rex and that dangerous Band of Boobies.... Henceforth, it
seems, the Irish and the Ulster Scots are to be upon the same terms with
them as the Africans, Hindoos, and other Dark peoples they enslave,—
and so, to make it easier to shoot us, with all Americans,— tho' we be
driven more mystically, not by the Lash and Musket, but by Ledger and
Theodolite. All to assure them of an eternal Supply of cheap axmen,
farmers, a few rude artisans, and docile buyers of British goods."

"Not only presuming us their Subjects, which is bad enough,— but
that we're merely another kind of Nigger,— well that's what I can't forgive. Are you sure?"

"Civility, Sir! The word you have employ'd, here in this quiet Pool of
Reason, is a very Shark, which ever feels its Lunch-Hour nigh."

"Excuse me, do I hear that Word again? In this Smoak, 'twould seem,
so are we all."

"Eeh!" Washington grabbing Mason.

"Colonel, Sir," twitching away, " 'twould be far preferable,— "

"That voice, Mason! 'tis my Tithable, Gershom!"

"And furthermore, here's the latest news of the King." Several hoots
and whistles. "King goes in a Tavern, bar-tender says, what'll it be,
George, King says, I'm in disguise here, how'd you know who I was,—
bar-tender says, that Crown on your Head,— King says, Only a Madman

would walk around wearing a Crown,— bar-tender falls on his knees,— Your Majesty!"

Half the Company seem to believe this is a white Customer, impersonating an African. Others, having caught Gershom's act before, recognize him right away.

"Hey Gersh, do the one about the Crocodile that can talk."

"The Rabbit in the Moon!"

"Wait a bit, somebody say there's a real Negroe in here?"

"Hell, maybe even more 'n one."

For the rest of the evening, ev'ryone suspects ev'ryone else of being Gershom. Now and then someone, tho' the Bellows are never quite fast enough to reveal who, tells another King-Joak.

"King's Alchemist presents him with a Philtre that can transport him where'er he wishes.— "

Mason's turn to put the Clutch upon Washington. "Baby-Phiz Nathe McClean, or I'm a Sailor."

"King decides he'll journey to the Sun," the invisible Youth continues, "— Alchemist says, 'Your Majesty! The Sun?— it burns at thousands of Fahrenheit's Degrees,— far too hot there for anything to remain alive.' King says, 'So, where's the Difficulty?— I'll go at Night.' "

Young Nathe, back in Classes at William and Mary, daily more woven into Continental Realities, here, seen thro' what he and his School-mates style the Room-Brume, appears already less fit, more slothful than the narrow and restless Camp-Factotum of the summer previous. "I left that Party just in time," he confides. "I should have been crazy as Captain Zhang, had I remain'd a week more."

"Crazy enough," remarks his friend Murray.

"That bad, was it?" Mason a bit reserv'd.

"All respect, Sir, the Captain wasn't just Pipe-Smoking in the Article of that *Sha*. We all felt it, as, to Appearance, did you and Mr. Dixon. Surveying a Property Line, that may be one thing,— clearing and marking a Right Line of an Hundred Leagues, into the Lands of Others, cannot be a kindly Act."

"Should we have refus'd the Commission, then?" Mason in ever-sharpening Nasality, "— We didn't invent Parallels of Latitude. Your

Dispute is with Hipparchus, and Eratosthenes before him,— both, I believe, dead?"

"Perhaps no harm will come of it. So must we pray. Remember me to Mr. Dixon. Your Servant, Sir," as Nathe once more is subsum'd into Nicotick Vapors opaque as Futurity, leaving Mason feeling guilty as foolish, unable to rely as much as before upon Remembrances of the cheerful Boy who pass'd like a Shuttle, ever to and fro and amidst, as if weaving the very Party on into the West, Day upon Day.

59

The Surveyors return to the North Mountain at the end of March, to find the Shelby Seat engulf'd as ever in Turmoil. Six neighbors having but lately petition'd Governor Sharpe to remove him and his co-Adjutor Mr. Joseph Warford as Justices of the Peace, the Captain's secular Woes have multiplied sensibly toward a State of irremediable Chaos, owing to the great Scandal over the winter involving Tom Hynes, Catherine Wheat, and their Baby.

"You recall how last September,— not long before you Boys arriv'd,— Conrad Wheat, one of our Distillers hereabouts, 's Girl Catherine goes up before Cap'n Price holding in her Arms her newborn Baby, swearing under Oath that Tom Hynes is the Father. She doesn't appear at November Court in Frederick's Town, so the matter's put over till March."

Tom wonders what she's up to. Some other Swain behind the Smokehouse he don't know about? He's all perplex'd. His own father is happy to advise him. "This is my grandson. Know what that means?"

"Um, no Sir."

"A Grand-Son means a man can quit worrying at last. Means the chain goes on unbroken. The Miracle of Fatherhood. That's as long as the little sucker's Daddy ain't some contemptible Fool, who'd gladly run away, but for his own Father, who'd beat him so roundly he'd be running nowhere for a long while, o' course."

"Wha." Tom a-gape. "Marry the bitch?"

"We dwell among people of the Kirk, lad," advises the elder Hynes, "— recalling the Sampler your dear Mother made, that hangs o'er the Hearth,— "

" 'EXPECT INDIANS,' " nods Tom.

"Exactly in the same daily Spirit, must a man, aye and Woman too, at ev'ry Moment, expect Law-Suits out here, from any Direction, for any reason, or none. In a Presbyterian World, 'tis best to keep a tidy Life. Marry her."

"She...um, she'd never have me,— "

"Proving she's got good Sense,— all the more reason why you need to marry her. Now tonight I'm going to lock you in this Shed here,— "

"Dad!"

"To-night, Tom, you must be sober and alone with your Soul, not out rowdy-dowing. Take note I've been holding back the Hickory, so far. This is too important. Think about it."

So young Hynes obeys, tho' his Thoughts aren't quite as spiritual as his Father might have hop'd for. Rather, Tom thro' these dark Hours slowly pieces together what, even in the sunlight of the next day, to his redden'd eyes, continues to look like a clever Plan.

"Forget the Bitch," he announces, "we'll seize the Baby," dashing off before William can comment, to call upon Capt. Shelby and ask him, as Peace Commissioner, to write him a Warrant to repossess the Baby. The Captain, hearing the Story, is amus'd. His blood gets to racing at the possibility of yet another lawsuit. He goes thro' a great Rigmarole with good Paper, Pens and Inks of several Colors, and Wax Seals as well, and Tom, who can't read any of it, figures he's as good as got that Baby in his Hands.

That Monday Night, about nine or ten, they go to serve the instrument,— Tom, and the Constable, along with Moran, Dawson, a couple of others, Nathan Lynn, and John Gerloh, show up at Wheat's House, pretending at first they only want a Quart of Whiskey. Six of 'em, they're planning to share a Quart? The German, suspicious already, now spies Tom Hynes among the Company. "A Pint, I can only sell you."

"Well come on out here, Conrad, we want you to look at something." Conrad thinks about it,— there are women and children in the house, his nearest Pistol is too far away. He shrugs and steps into the night, leaving the Door open a little, with only the Thrusts of light from candles inside, moving to and fro, to see by. "We've come for the Baby, Conrad," says the Constable, Barney Johnson. "Will you give him up?"

"Why should I?"

"Court Order."

"May I see it."

"Too dark."

"Read it to me?"

Barney sighs. "Here, Moran, you've the Lanthorn,— "

What Shelby wrote proves to be a Search Warrant for Stolen Goods,— more of the Welshman's peculiar notion of Mirth. Catherine pops out the door to remind the Constable that her Child ain't Goods, stolen or however. Tom, jumping down off his horse, goes after her, and she slams the Door in his face. Ev'rybody's feeling edgy.

"Who sign'd this Order?" Conrad shouts.

"Don't tell him anything!" warns Tom in a Temper.

"Tom, 'tis all legal," says the Constable. "And Conrad, now,— the Warrant is Captain Shelby's, but,— "

"Shelby! Some Court Order, Barnett,— shame, so. Captain Shelby's Demand?— more of his Bullying,— it means nothing. My daughter has already given Security to Justice Price, and her Child is safe here."

"Catherine Wheat having fail'd to show up in Justice Price's Court last Month," Constable Johnson in a small hurried voice proclaims, "is deem'd in violation of the Law, and pending Disposition, for the good of the Child must I order my Deputies to lay hands upon it, forthwith."

"Lay hands upon this!" cries one of the Girls of the House, and shakes out a great Wing of Dish-Water, whose pinguid Embrace not all escape, whilst another sets the Hounds who live in the back, upon the Party. The House of a sudden is seen to be fill'd with more people than anyone might have imagin'd.

"Why then Conrad, I am personally sadden'd to think you would lie thus in wait for us,— " the Constable unable to finish his thought as he must struggle to remain atop his Mount. Out the Door, and a Window or two as well, come Barkley, Steed, and the Rush brothers,— Brooks and Flint remaining within, to see to the Ladies,— advancing upon the Constable's Men, who with back-Country Whoops come a-charging, Cudgels ready to strike, Tom in his not altogether subdued way screaming, "He's mine Bitch and I'll have him alive or dead!" One of Wheat's boys, roughly push'd, falls, is hurt. A sister swoops in to snatch the Baby, and bring him in his Swaddling, looking like a little stuff'd Cabbage-Leaf, back to the Kitchen, whilst the others in the House shut and bar the Door, tho' not for long, as the Rioters, close behind, begin breaking it in. The Boy has a compress of Arnica Tea upon his Thump by now, and will be all right. Conrad has a lot invested in the Door, which he's carpenter'd, carv'd, and hung all with his one set of hands,— he watches, not yet able to believe that these men he thought he knew could become a Band of Raiders who mean him harm, and his Grand-son as well, it seems, for now in this ear-batt'ring Kitchen Melee the Baby is suddenly become a Ball in a Game, being toss'd in short high arcs from one Party to another 'bout the House, as the Shelbyites go beating upon anyone in their Reach, injuring some so badly they won't make it in to Court. No more hazardous than the usual North Mountain Wedding. Young Tom is beating the Mother of his Child, informing her, in a Voice not entirely in his Control, of his intention to kill her,— passionate lad, tho' not in any way women are apt to find welcome, is it? Nathan Lynn grabs the Baby and runs out the Door, then one of Wheat's Women, chasing after, gets him back, runs on into the Field with Barney after her and John Gerloh close behind. They catch her and beat her till she gives the Child up, all out in the Dark where they can't see her as well as they could back in the Candle-light,— they've no sense of depth here, and don't know how hard to strike. All are Phantoms to one another. At last, she reclines in a frozen Furrow, weeping, trying to get one of them to look her in the face. Gerloh will not, and Barney is too occupied with the Baby,— who, upon assessing the Constable, has begun to cry.

Well, "cry" is perhaps not it exactly. All the way to Ralph Matson's House, that little Banshee lets out a Protest that echoes for miles off these Hills,— Irish Folk cross themselves, needlewomen drop Stitches not to mention Beaux. "For the Days then teeter'd 'round us all," comments Capt. Shelby, "— we'd soon enough ourselves be upon the March from Frederick Town down to Annapolis, riding as a Troop, two and three a-breast, with inexpensive Comparisons made to the Paxton Boys, tho' 'twas the Stamp Dispute that brought us out, and whether the Assembly would pass its Journal. Tom's domestick Drama gave us a practice run, as you'd say, for Acts of Publick necessity impending."

At last they convey the Goods successfully across to Matson's, upon the Pennsylvania side,— Capt. Shelby's there waiting, with Will Hynes,— the Baby crying to chill the Bones of Pontiac himself. "Give it here, Barney," says the Cap'n, "ye're doing that all wrong,— " and takes the Baby, who abruptly falls silent, gazing up at the Captain's Eyebrows. "Aye, you like that, do you? Can't say you look much like a Hynes. Just as well." He Orbs one by one the bleeding, dishevel'd Escort. "Do I take it the Mother was unwilling to give the Infant up?"

"I made the Dutch Bitch's blood fly," Tom Hynes informs the Company.

"Say it three times quickly, Tom, and we'll believe you."

"That, incidentally, is the Exclamation verbatim," Uncle Ives here asserts, "— see *Proceedings of the Council of Maryland,* for the Year 'sixty-five. Your Uncle has been telling the story as depos'd much later by people wishing to have Shelby dismiss'd as a Peace Officer, perhaps to get even for some wrong committed during the Crisis attending the Stamp Act, or perhaps more ancient. But here he crossed the Line,— a Pennsylvanian raid upon a Maryland Farmer. 'Twas more, than whose Warrant should have effect where,— Shelby ignor'd the Power of the Line, and chose to defy it. So it became a matter for Annapolis."

" 'Tis all there," allows the Rev[d], "the whole squalid Tale, transcending the usual Neighborly Resentment, tied in to that strange rising of Spirit throughout the Countryside,— from a certain cock of the Hat, to the Refusal of all further Belief in Boundaries or British Government,— a will'd Departure from History."

Captain Shelby's personal Peeve is the lack of respect for his Signature upon writs and orders, which he seems to run into at ev'ry Turn, either Side of the Line. The Law, in its Majesty, can look after itself,— 'tis the Disrespect for him personally, that Shelby cannot abide. "Damn the Dutchman, he'd better stay over there in Maryland or he'll be well thrash'd. Refusing my Writ! Good thing I wasn't along with you, Barney, I'd've burn'd his house down." No one reminds him that he wrote the Baby-Repossession Order in jest. He refuses in turn, to accept Security from Flint and Brooks on behalf of the Wheat girl,— "If my Writ means nothing over there, why should your Security mean any more over here?"— taking instead the Hyneses' Note for £100 as Bond to keep the Baby off the Parish.

The Captain's troubles are not over, for now Conrad Wheat brings Suit over the Riot at his House, obliging all Parties to show up at Justice Warford's House for a Hearing preliminary to Court. Tom Hynes the merry Bachelor, tho' bobbing Corklike as ever, beginning to feel remorse, no longer alludes to his recent blood-letting Activities. No one wants to hear about it anyway. When the moment to appear before the Justice arrives at last, he's all but desperate to see Kate.

Shelby comes in a-bellowing after a Warrant for Catherine Wheat's Fine. "Mrs. Warford advises against it," replies Joseph Warford, "her Gifts in this area being widely known,— and Evan don't try to squeeze this one dry, for there's not that much in it."

"Damme! Joe! My old Colleague-at-Law,— his worthy Wife at whose table I've ever been happy to dine. Betray'd! Who'd've thought it of either one, here, hey Will? Hey, Tom?— Tom?" Tom Hynes is not immediately visible.

Amazingly to all, Mrs. Warford and a resolute Candle-flame reveal the North-Mountain Casanova retir'd to a Stuft Chair in a dim corner, with Catherine Wheat upon his Lap, whilst he strokes her intently. "You wounded me," she is advising him, "I was bleeding,— I've the Marks yet,— here,— can you see my back?"

" 'Twas but a Willow Switch, and you were curl'd up so tight...I'd never harm you, Katie."

"Why, you lying snake, of course you would,— and you did."

"How was I suppos'd to feel?— ev'ryone staring,— without even telling me first, you just went to Captain Price.... I believ'd it our own secret child, the secret of our love, thah' no one need know— "

"Are you crazy?— hide a Baby! You know what Babies are, *net?* You've been in the House with ours, for even a Minute? *What* Secret?"

"Well,...maybe I know that now.... Maybe I was young then,— maybe even, even foolish."

"*Then* was three months ago, you could've just married me *then,*— sav'd us all this." She doesn't care by now who thinks what, not even Tom, whom she is looking *schlag* in the eye.

Firmly propell'd from behind by his Wife,— her Version of a suggestive Nudge,— Mr. Warford abruptly enters the *Tête-à-Tête*, rumbling, "Hynes as you have spoil'd this Girl, and taken her Credit from her, you ought to marry her."

Both young people regard the Avuncular Apparition, and the bobbing Arc of Faces behind, with strangely calm'd Expressions. She rests her head upon Hynes's shoulder, exhales, and continues to gaze at the Company, her face, if not smug, then at least innocently relaxing after a long struggle. "So, Tom," a confidence in her voice he's never heard, but were he quicker, might have felt concern'd about, "what d'ye think, my Boil'd Potato?"

"Oh," his Face drap'd in a slow Daze, "I haven't much against it. Sure, I'll consider of it."

Intending to offer twenty-five, but mov'd by the Spirit in the Room, Conrad Wheat declares, "Ye shall have thirty pounds from me. And a five-pound wedding, so."

"Hurrah," cries Mrs. Warford. "Now,— when were you thinking of, young man, exactly?"

"When." Tom Hynes, not sure what today's date is, notes, with some alarm, that all this whole Rioting, Baby-snatching, litigious Time, it has been Christmastide. Has Christmas come and gone and he's miss'd it in all the Commotion? "Before year's end, Miss's," he supposes.

"Just a minute," cries Capt. Shelby, who's been busy scribbling. The Merriment subsides. "There's yet this matter of the Girl's Fine. Joe, if ye'll not write me a Warrant, p'raps ye'll at least, kindly, sign one of my own, here?"

Mr. Warford peers over at his Wife, who for the second time tonight desuperpollicates, with a mischievous tho' unwavering smile for the Captain. "Sorry."

"I don't know how much more, as a man, I can really take of this," mutters the Welshman. "Damn'd Dutchman with his five-pound Ridottoes and his Indian-Corn Poison,— oh, much too grand to comply with my lawful Writ, and now, old Joe, you refuse me once, and then again,— this night am I thrice denied,— then Damme, I'll sign it myself,— there! Now someone, seize the young Lady forthwith!"

"My pleasure!" cries the dim Tom Hynes, clasping his sweetheart, who squeals.

Will Hynes frowns at Shelby. "What new Thievery's this?"

"I'll take your Note happily, Tom," the Captain prompts.

"Dad?"

"I think he wants you to be here for the Wedding," explains Will Hynes.

"Before the Year is out," intones Mrs. W.

Thus, upon the night of December 31st, all are gather'd at Mr. Warford's House, in clean Clothes and hopeful Spirits. Snow drifts in the corners of Window-panes distant from the Fire. Mrs. Warford has made a great dark, spirit-soak'd Fruit-Cake, and iced it for good Measure, in bridal White. Conrad Wheat has brought a Waggon-load of his lately run Conoloways White, whose drinking requires close attention, lest it prove but one more way of falling asleep. Stamp Act rumors fly among small gatherings of young Men, in and out of doors. An assortment of Calathumpians are there, with a full Battery of cowbells tun'd to the Pentatonick Scale, Drums with 'Possum-skin Heads, Whistles and Gongs and a Military Bugle found in the woods after Braddock's Defeat.

"Not as cold as last winter this time, d'ye remember?"

"Cold enough for me."

"Never hope to see another like that one."

"This morning my Dogs wanted to stay in."

"Your Dogs have to lean against the Wall to bark, Gus."

Captain Shelby recites the Service as if it were Poetry. "Will you Thomas Hynes, take Catherine Wheat to your lawful wedded Wife?"

"Aye, Sir, I will."

"And Catherine Wheat, Thomas Hynes to your lawful wedded Husband,— "

"I will."

"— Then, barring some further act of Disrespect toward yet another Signature of mine, acting within my Authority as Officer of the Peace, I am delighted to be able at last to pronounce,— Jump, Dog! Leap, Bitch! And I'll be damn'd if all the men on Earth, can un-marry you!"

"Tell 'em, Captain!"

"Oh, Tom you've broken my heart!"

"And several others as well!"

The Fiddler raises his Bow and attacks "The Black Joke." Feet rediscover Steps that are their own, and not those of the Day and its Demands.

When Tom wakes next morning, only slowly recognizing the bed Mrs. Warford is charging him five shillings for, the first thing he notices is the wallpaper, pattern'd all over with identical small blue Flowers, upon a Ground of glowing Vermilion. He lies there for a long time in the crescent light, doing nothing but regarding this floral Repetition. He finds that if he comes close enough to the Wall, and lets his eyes drift slightly out of Focus, each Blossom will divide in two, and these slide away to each Side, until re-combining with a Neighbor,— and that the new-made images appear now to have Depth, making an Array of solid Objects suspended in a quivering bright Æther.

It may have been a difficult night,— only one or two things stand out. He does recall Capt. Shelby performing the Marriage. He looks over beside him, now, and sure enough, there's Katie asleep, with an Egg-shap'd drop of Sunlight about to touch her Shoulder. So that was real.... He also recalls getting up in the middle of the night to piss, and being confronted with a Figure he at first imagines as the D——l, because it bears a Pitchfork,— but which he presently recognizes as Capt. Shelby.

"Been waiting, Mr. Hynes. Thought ye'd never come. Look at them, they're all asleep." In every dark nook lay revelers, under and upon the Furniture and Stairs. "All except me, I'm the only one who stay'd up, for I knew ye'd try to escape. Now,— get your Arse back into that Chamber, and if you dare to leave your lawful Wife, tonight or ever, this," waving the Fork, "gets jobb'd in your Guts, are we in Agreement?"

"Captain, all's I got up for was to piss,— and I was thinking more of outside the Judge's House than in?"

"Why didn't you say so? Come on, then. We'll see. We'll go piss in the snow."

Threading their way among snoring celebrants, trying not to blunder onto drooling Faces or disarrang'd Skirts, they go outside, and together piss in the Snow. Shelby writes his name, sweepingly, as if at the bottom of some Blank and all-powerful Warrant of the Winter, whilst Tom draws a simple Heart, unpierc'd, unletter'd, whose outline he fills in carefully, completely, and then some. The Captain looks over. "You certainly did have to piss. Hallelujah. Attend me. Give up the pleasures of Town,— those brick Defiles are not for you…your Fate lies rather to the West. When those Surveyors return in the Spring, they'll be needing Hands. You can be head of Shelby's Men, a sort of Party within the Party, what say you?"

"Did me a service," Tom Hynes will declare, when anyone asks. "I'm forever oblig'd to the Captain,— Catherine Wheat is the best thing that ever happen'd to me,— without her I'd be lost. He sure knew what was best."

They are reluctant to quit the freezing Night. Tom asks, quietly, "May she come along?"

"She'll be in Foal again. Hey?"

"Forgot about that."

Shelby regards him silently and at length. "I had ye calculated for a Renegado. Why ye're going to be another damn'd Grandfather Cresap, Tom,— you'll see."

60

In the strong twilight over the Mountains of Wales, draining of light League upon League of darkly forested Peaks…to the eye familiar, the occasional interruption of a Cabin or Plantation…chimney Smoke, a gray patch of girdl'd Trees amid the green pervading…a Shade ascending one hollow at a time, the wind acquires at the Dark a potency it did not possess in the light. An ax-bit's blow quench'd in living wood. A dog after a Squirrel. A percussive "Sandwich" of hammer, anvil, and the Work between. Night over all this watershed how vast, that covers each soul in it like a breathing Mouth, humid, warm, carrying the odors of living and dying, that takes back ev'rything committed upon the Land that Day, without appeal, dissolving all in Shadow.

They have caught up with this era in the settlement of this West. Though not in all ways insane, yet Capt. Shelby, avid for any occasion to quarrel, exhibits signs of mania upon the topic of Land-Disputes, being often preoccupied from well before sun-up till far into the early Darknesses with litigations great and petty, engrossments Ditto, with Boundary issues a particular Passion,— a fallen Tree, a wand'ring Chicken, the meanders of a Stream, any pretext, any least scent of Inconvenience, will do. He admires this West Line for its great Size, tho' he's puzzl'd as to why there can't be a few angles someplace, to accommodate a close friend, for example,— or even more than one.

"Kings," Mason with a what-can-we-poor-Sheep-do look, which Shelby declines to join him in. "This is how they reason, in Map-siz'd sweeps of the Arm. 'Divide it thus, I command you!' They can't be bother'd with the fine details."

"Having ink'd a Map or two, I know that impatience, tho' my Sympathy reaches no further. Out here the King has few to count upon, and his troops will be fools, to come much past Cumberland,— you be certain to tell 'em I said so."

"Tell whom?"

"Whoever may be asking."

"Do tha believe we're Spies, Captain...?" Dixon, with genial Tap-Room Menace, moving as if into Range.

"Sirs. I've been out here since before the late War, and have offer'd my Hospitality to many a Spy, of ev'ry persuasion, for, as Spies must travel, so, it follows, some Travelers must be Spies,— yet I bar my Door to no one. 'Tis a Pursuit of men, away in the distant World, no more sinful than the making of Rifles, or the charging of Quit-Rent, yet do I prefer an honest Quarrel out in the open, myself, 'tis more manly somehow, don't ye think?"

Dixon ambles closer, beaming. "Yet 'tis a gormless Spy indeed, who'd lurk where there are no more Secrets to steal."

"How so?"

"What is there that has not been visited, intentionally and not, an hundred times? Gathering Ginseng would be more profitable."

Shelby is of course also a Surveyor, who ranges these Mountains all about, bearing and wielding his Instrument like a Weapon. "Oh, I saw 'pon the Instant how this was," darkly to Dixon, "I saw how the ancient Sorcerers must have enjoy'd what they did. At our Pleasure, we may look thro' this brazen Tube, thro' Glass mathematickally shap'd, and whatever desirable Scene sweeps by as we turn it,— why 'tis ours for writing down the Angle! Good Heavens, what Power!"

There is a love of complexity, here in America, Shelby declares,— pure Space waits the Surveyor,— no previous Lines, no fences, no streets to constrain polygony however extravagant,— especially in Maryland, where, encourag'd by the Re-survey Laws, warranted properties may possess hundreds of sides,— their angles pushing outward and inward,— all Sides zigging and zagging, going ahead and doubling back, making Loops inside Loops,— in America, 'twas ever, Poh! to Simple Quadrilaterals.

"Eeh," Dixon nodding vaguely. He's never regarded his Occupation in quite this way before. His journeyman years coincided with the rage then sweeping Durham for Enclosure,— aye and alas, he had attended at that Altar. He had slic'd into Polygons the Common-Lands of his Forebears. He had drawn Lines of Ink that became Fences of Stone. He had broken up herds of Fell sheep, to be driven ragged and dingy off thro' the Rain, to Gates, and exile. He had turn'd the same covetous Angles as the Welshman,— tho' perhaps never as many, for Shelby seem'd seiz'd with Goniolatry, or the Worship of Angles, defining tracts of virgin Land by as many of these exhilarating Instrumental Sweeps, as possible.

"Thing's to survey your Domain. Even if you don't own it. Here at the Allegheny Crest, ye may stand and look either way, down mile after mile of the Visto ye've cut, and from your Eminence pretend that you own it. Ev'ry Girl, ev'ry Gambler, Tonick Salesman, and Banjo Player that comes down that Line, could easily be paying Tribute to somebody. Not a lot,— no worse than Quitrent,— a Nuisance-Levy really, even if it's a song or a Card-trick or ten minutes in the Hay-Loft."

Shelby accompanies them over North Mountain, whereupon it begins to rain and snow, and continues so for the next ten days. The Cards come out, and the Chap-books and Dice and Bottles. Mason goes to sleep, requesting that he be waken'd only in case of Spring. Dixon tries to learn from Capt. Zhang something of the *Luo-Pan,* in exchange for Instruction as to the Sector. "The Attention we are paying these Zenith-Stars," he suggests, "has brought me to imagine an *Anti-celestial, or backwards Astrology,* in which the Stars must be...projected inward, somehow...? mapp'd from the Celestial Sphere onto the Surface of our Globe...? At Greenwich, for example, the Zenith-Star is Gamma Draconis, putting Britain into the Terrestrial Sign of Draco, the Dragon."

"Just so!" The Geomancer twinkles.

"— Yet in Durham We mean something different when we say 'Dragon.' Ours are not at all the Chinese Variety. Some, like the Lambton Worm, lacking Wings and a fire-breathing Capacity, may indeed be of a distinct Species."

"You've seen such a Creature?"

"Heard the story, when growing up. As Lambton Castle lies almost upon the North Sea, we at Cockfield knew it as a Wear Valley tale, that like an ageless Salmon had work'd its way over the years upstream to us…. At the Market Square in Bishop, as at Darlington Fair, the Tale was often perform'd by troupes of traveling Actors, six of whom would be needed for the part of the Worm. The Drop was painted to suggest the Sea-Fret whispering along the walls, mysterious shapes in the Park beyond, as Romantick as you please. Today the country 'round Lambton is thick with collieries, and pretty much given over to staithes and shoots and waggon-rails,— but the river then was purer and wilder, not yet altogether converted to the service of the Christian God,— tho', as it happen'd, fishing in it on Sunday, in these parts, had long been forbidden." They take out Pipes, which Capt. Zhang fills with a Blend of cur'd Vegetation that he will describe only as "Chinese Tobacco,"— courteously igniting both, with Embers from the Fire.

"The heedless John Lambton, his Lordship's heir, a young man as malapert in company as he was masterly in a stream,— his own reach of the Wear in particular,— has long refus'd to honor this rule. One Sunday, instead of the salmon-trout he believes his due, he pulls in a small snakelike thing, with a double row of horrid little Vents either side of it, from its head down the body, gasping open and shut,— nine pair of them. At first he takes it for a Lamprey,— but Lampreys have only seven pair. This thing is different. He feels a strange cold at his temples,— a *conscious vibration* in the fishing-line. It seems to him almost that the creature is gazing into his eyes, with a look of intelligent Evil…."

Just then his friend Reginald comes galloping up, with a couple of pack-horses. "All right then John, come along, there'll be no Moors left by the time *we* get to Jerusalem."

"What?"

"The Crusade…? Oh, bother, you said you'd come. I say what's that on your line? Ghastly thing. Throw it back in, let's go bash old Abdul, whatwhat?"

"Yes but Reggie I'm not sure the River's quite the place for it, best interests of the fish and so on. Here, look ye, here's this hole, with some stones 'round the edge, I'll just chuck it in here, shall I."

"But,— isn't it someone's Well?"

"Some tenant or something, who cares?" and with one of those knightly flourishes, the young fool, damn'd in the instant, actually tosses the Worm into the Well.

"Oh, John," cries Reggie, "that's so amusing!" And thus cheerily, the lads are off to the East, where a number of desperate Adventures wait them.

Meanwhile the Worm is far from idle, having almost immediately begun, in that Womb of wet stone, to grow,— local people hear it thrashing about, and the bravest, as they peer down into the echoing dark, may almost see it. Soon, the water has acquir'd an unpleasant taste, metallic, sour, heavy with a reptilian Musk. Buckets let down do not come back up, creaking noises are heard at night as the well's Casing is brought under some enormous Force,— till one morning, as the Sun rises, so up over the Rim of the Well, appears a great blazing pair of Eyes, the closely set, purposeful eyes of a Predator. Slowly, with no appearance of effort, it begins to ascend from the Well, accompanied by a terrible, poisonous odor,— flowing up over the edge…indeed, it keeps coming for longer than it should. Everything living in the area, including the vegetation, stop what they're doing, and attend. The Worm seems quite hungry.

Taking its time, the Worm proceeds to one of the Batts or Islands in the River, where it sets up its base of operations. Its needs are simple,— Food, drink, and the pleasure to be had from killing. It eats sheep and swine, it drains milk from cattle nine at a time,— the number nine recurs in the Tale, tho' the reason is dark,— and careless dogs, cats, and humans are but light snacks to it. Around it, a circle of Devastation appears, pale and soil'd, which no one enters, and which the World must keep shifting for, a little at a time, as it goes on widening,— the Worm each day venturing a little further from its base, till at length the circle of terror advances to include a direct view of the Battlements of Lambton Castle itself, the final sanctuary, surely inviolable,— although the people in the Castle dare not try to organize an exodus, for the Worm when it must can travel at great speed, faster than horses can gallop,— they have watch'd in terror many Chases to the death across the Tide-Plain below, as, once alerted, the Worm has easily cut its Victims off in the open, far from any refuge or escape.

So there begins an Obsession by the Worm,— The Chapel is never empty now, the Steward has begun taking inventory, rationing lists are in early but serious negotiation. Days once idle are now fill'd with defensive chores. Engineers try to get the Trebuchet on the roof into working order, tweaking the shape of the Sling-Release Hook.... The Worm is by now grown so large that it may comfortably coil 'round the entire Castle. One day, there will come to it some Sign,— the call of a Raven, the exact shape of a Moon, the racing shadow of a cloud,— which will lead, by an unreadable train of Serpent thought, to a convulsive breaching of these walls and a merciless search within, a Face suddenly looming in the roofless Sky, a Feast. No one can say when. The Evil One has Lambton Castle literally in Its Embrace. The local folk keep a vigil, blending in against the brush on the somber hillsides, calculating how fast they'll have to move when the creature turns its attention to them. Days pass,— presently, weeks. The Worm continues to enlarge its Zone of emptiness, but with a change of Center,— returning now after each excursion to coil about the Castle, where it lies all night digesting loudly its day's predation. It is into this increasingly desperate Siege, that John Lambton now returns from his Crusade.

At first look, impaling foreigners seems to have agreed with him,— he is tann'd and fit and easy in the Saddle. But beneath the hearty Mask lies a Dread of what he will encounter. Approaching the Castle, he can smell the Worm long before he sees it. He would have much preferr'd a Dragon, Dragons having from time to time, in County Durham, chosen to infest the roads and lay desolate the countryside,— it falling, usually, to such known antidraconical families as the Latimers, Wyvils, or Mowbrays, to respond. But those creatures were winged and claw'd, fire-breathing, noble in conformation, the reptilian detailing ever harmless, almost an afterthought. Nothing like what John Lambton, rounding the last bend before home, beholds, recognizes, and understands as his own creation, something he must now before God deal with.

Time has not been kind to the Worm he threw in the well. It had been unpleasant enough to look at when only elver size,— now, despite what he has seen in the East, he must labor not to turn away. The eighteen vents have grown astonishingly, and hang, pulsating, each surrounded by a deep black annulus of something glist'ring and corroded. The Face has lost the youthful malevolence that Lambton remembers,— has rather become, deep in its abandonment, now purely a Weapon in the service of blood-lust, a serpent's gift for paralyzing its prey with a certain Gaze that the potential Luncheon, once returning it, is helpless to defy. Even Lambton, though at a safe enough distance, finds it strangely attractive.

He has not exactly been to the Holy Land,— where he ended up, in fact, was Transylvania,— this being one of the very last Crusades, taken up more in a privateering spirit by one Cardinal Cæsarini and a party of adventurers from many lands, who by breaking the Truce of Szeged and then losing at the battle of Varna, helped prepare the way for the Turks who were to capture Constantinople a few years later. During a long Iliad of hard soldiering and small, mortal, never-decisive engagements amid dramatic hilltops, haunted castles, mysterious flocks of Bats that always seem'd to be lingering about, Lambton one night, seeking diversion, had visited the encampment of a band of Gypsies, who included in their number a Sibyl widely respected for having successfully foretold every wedding, birth, adultery, and flow of wealth in this Locality for longer than anyone could remember. Solemnly, she inform'd him of the exact situation prevailing at Lambton Castle. "Then must I hasten home, to destroy this Monster. Shall I prevail?"

"*Bocsánat,*— I do not do Deaths. I am far too cheerful. You want to see a Roumanian for that sort of thing."

" 'Twould be little more than a sporting contest...?" young Lambton talking fast, "no more violent than jousting, really...?"

"Milord, please,— my time is as precious as yours. What I can do is bring in a priest here, divide the Fee, arrange an Oath for you."

"Anything," he assur'd her, "but quickly."

The Oath was fairly simple, he read it over a few times, couldn't find much wrong with it, so willingly knelt beside his sword and vow'd, that if God should allow him victory over the Worm, he would sacrifice unto Him the first living thing he then happen'd to see. "There are penalty clauses," the priest helpfully pointing them out, upon the long piece of parchment he'd just sign'd.

"If I prevail, then so drench'd in blood shall I be, that Bloodshed will weigh less upon my conscience, than it does even here, in Transylvania," avow'd the open-faced yet somber young Heir. "Therefore, I shall not default."

Once back in Durham, however,— having come to think of God under the aspect more of Fortune than of anything more Churchly,— he understands that his Duty also includes providing what he can, himself, on Earth, to shorten his odds.

Choosing from among the small crowd of youths always to be found, when the Worm is away, about the approaches to the Castle seeking Engagement as Runners, Lambton arranges for his father, immediately the Worm's destruction shall be signal'd by a blast upon a hunting horn, to send out one of the Castle Hounds. Neither Lambton thinks of this as cheating. It will be a legitimate sacrifice. Every one of those dogs is like family.

Young Lambton next rides up to Washington,— the Colonel's ancestral home, in fact,— to consult with the Armorsmith who fitted him out for his Crusade. Galloping toward the glow of the forge,— visible for miles, now and then reflected in the Wear,— he considers his basic tactical problem, which is the Worm's reported ability, even hack'd into separate pieces by conventional sword-work, to reassemble itself and fight on.

"I've been looking into this very difficulty," the Armorer greets him. "Glad you came by,— here, come and see." Inside the shop, lit by the lurid glow of the coals, with a sweating apprentice staring at them unfathomably, gleams a suit of Armor, to young Lambton's exact measurements, provided all over with hundreds of firmly attach'd sword-quality Blades, whose honed edges flicker with sanguinary light.

"Perfect. It won't be able to use its coils,— it'll have to come head-on, and happen I'll get lucky with m' Pike...?"

They discuss tactics far into the night. He returns with the Armor, pack'd in Straw. For the first Time, he understands that ev'rywhere about, for leagues, sleep Souls in real Bodies, mortal as any in Hungary, impossible longer to ignore, and that at Dawn, by way of their dreams, will all wake knowing what is to happen that day.

Young Lambton chooses to wait out upon the Worm's own Batt, the river flowing swiftly by on either side. Birds are subdued, treed. For the benefit of observers, of whom there are many, he kneels a moment, appearing to repeat his sacred Oath, before rising to put on, very carefully, piece by razor-keen piece, his bloodletting suit,— till all at last is ready. Then he hears it,— the unimagin'd tons of wet and purposeful Flesh, moving a-clatter through the reeds, ever closer, till out of the riparian mist emerges, towering, the savage Head, the deathlike Face, of the great Worm. It hisses, in a long exhalation. When the smell reaches him, young Lambton smiles grimly. "Plenty of time to vomit when we're done, thanks."

The fight is slow, bloody, repetitive. A Dream,— fever-shot, unwaking. It lasts most of the day. Small boys approach as close as they dare. Adolescent Rogues comment upon the weaponry, the suit, the hacking technique. Townsfolk watch from the Hill-sides the red, thrashing immensity filling the river, and the tiny, glitt'ring Knight. To his Obstinacy there seems no limit. Those who remember him as a flighty and lazy Child marvel at the change. "Before he went off to Jerusalem...?— he'd've run away, the bugger." Young Lambton fights on. At last, after too many cuts, deep and deeper, the Worm's capacity for self-repair is overcome, it lets out a series of last liquid hateful screams, echoing up the Valley all the way to Chester-Le-Street, and perishes, to be borne away, most of its blood ahead of it, already halfway to Dogger Bank, chunks of Flesh forever separate, out into the North Sea, where even the most voracious of the fish will only pick at it.

With the last of his strength, Lambton climbs to the now deliver'd Castle, stands before it, and blows upon his Oliphant. The dogs inside hear it and all start barking at once. They grow so agitated that none of the Lambton servants dares approach them. Meanwhile, blissfully having forgotten about the terms of the Oath, vertiginous in a Storm of emotions, the Elder Lambton can think only of seeing his son again. He is an agèd man, but he runs as he can over the drawbridge, arms held out. "John! Oh, my Boy!" He is of course the first living thing young Lambton sees.

"Eeh!" Young John just stands there, almost too tired to realize what has happen'd. Now, by the terms of his Contract, 'tis his father he must kill. It would be easy,— so foolish in his transport is the old man that a single embrace, folding him tightly but without mercy into the bladed Vambraces and Breast-Plate of the Worm-stain'd armor, would do the job. He could say he had been too exhausted to think. Then again, the Oath *was* taken in Hungary.... As God exempts England from many of Europe's less agreeable obligations to History, so, surely, must Oaths taken in foreign lands, at which foreign Priests and Gypsies attend, be without force here? He allows himself this sophistry,— it delays acting upon what he already knows,— that he cannot kill his father, that he must break the Oath, as he once consciously broke the Truce of Szeged...thus already corrupted, why shouldn't he? He lets go his sword, the image of the Cross he has sworn upon, lets it fall, turns, walks away, looking for someone who can help him out of the edg'd, and now perhaps even venomous, iron weapon he is wearing. Henceforth, when attending to internal business, he will put it on again and again, for the rest of his Life.

"The penalty stipulated in the Contract, to remain in force for nine generations,— one for each pair of holes in the Creature,— was that no Lord of Lambton die in his bed. Under this Gypsy curse, one by one, they drown'd, they were kill'd in battle,— Wakefield, Marston Moor,— sure 'twas, none died in bed. The last, the ninth Lord, was Henry Lambton, and one of my letters from Durham, brought me, whilst at the Cape, news that he'd died, three weeks after the Transit of Venus, riding 'cross the new Lambton Bridge in his carriage."

"Halfway between Shores," murmurs Mason, "his mortal Transit how brief. Never to reach Lambton, his own bit of Earth,— "

"Actually, he was heading the other way," says Dixon, "out over the Wear, into the world,— another Adventure."

"Cruelly serv'd," it seems to the Rev^d. "Nine innocent Generations. Whatever aid against the Worm young Lambton invok'd, its Source requir'd Blood Sacrifices. Because he spar'd his own Father's Life, it curs'd him and his Line most grievously for hundreds of years? What Agency could be so remorselessly cruel? Is it possible that at the battle in the Wear, the *wrong forces* won?"

"Why, Christ won, that Day...?" Dixon,— whose present state of religiosity is a puzzle to everyone,— appears to find it curious that anyone could think otherwise.

"Hum. Christians won, anyway," pronounces Capt. Shelby.

"Howbeit," Revd Cherrycoke suggests, "the Worm may have embodied...an older way of proceeding,— very like the ancient Alchemists' Tales, meant to convey by Symbols certain secret teachings."

" 'Tis that Worm in that Well, that's the Signature here.— " Set in an open doorway, twilight breeze off the Mountain flowing in around him, flaming autumn sky behind him, Evan Shelby is suddenly taller, more sly and cruel than he seem'd at first meeting, with a way of rolling his eyes to convey Celtic madness. "The Ancient figure of the Serpent through the Ring, or Sacred Copu-lation,— a much older magic, and certainly one the Christians wanted to eradicate."

"Thoughts that in my Line of work are too often denounc'd as 'Stukeleyesque,' or at the least 'Stonehengickal,' " adds the Rev^d.

"Not to mention 'Masonick,' " Dixon broadly pollicating his partner,— but Mason is hundreds of Chains remov'd into Morosity, accepting without full attention a glaz'd jug of the local white corn Whiskey from the Captain, who continues,—

"Nevertheless, Sir, the Serpent-mound which is at Avebury in England, looks very like one I have seen to the West of here, across Ohio. They might have been built by quite similar races of People."

"Red savages, in Britain?" Revd Cherrycoke a bit puzzl'd.

"Sir, when you go out there and talk to them about it," Capt. Shelby insists, "the Indians tell you that the Serpent, as the other earthworks unnumber'd of that Country, was *already ancient,* by the time their own people arriv'd. Indians speak of a race of Giants, who built them.... I had to hide all night once, within the Coils of some Serpent...they fancy the fiercer Animals.... All night, the Shawanese kept their distance, and I even managed to sleep,— briefly but in great comfort, somehow certain they would never venture close enough to find me. I woke strangely ener-giz'd, the Foe had vanish'd, the Dawn was well under way."

In the distance a Wench shouts, "There, Tom,— you've ripp'd me Bodice again!" Capt. Shelby rolls a paternal eye outdoors, in her direc-tion. Nothing that passes here must escape him.

The Surveyors, enjoying previous acquaintance, eastward of here, with wilderness Squires upon the model of Capt. Shelby, have already discuss'd his Character. "Large Eyebrows," Mason had opined, "betray a leaning to pugnacious eccentricity,— there is a passage in Pliny to that effect. Or, there ought to be."

"We're about as far from Philadelphia, here, as Durham from Lon-don," Dixon offer'd, "— much further, if you figure in the Trees and things, Precipices, Gorges,— and it seems quite like home, West being for Americans what North is for Geordies, an increasing Likelihood of local Power lying in the Hands of Eccentrics, more independence, more *Scotismus,* as tha'd say."

And, "Brows/ Of dauntless courage and considerate pride/ Waiting revenge...," the Rev[d] had quoted them Milton, upon Satan.

"And really the odd thing," the Captain's Eye now rolling back, fiendishly, to play full upon Dixon, "is that from the level of the ground, why, it seems but a high wall of dirt.— The only way even to make out the Serpent shape of it, is *from an hundred feet straight up.*"

Dixon reddens, believing, for no reason, that Shelby somehow knows of his childhood flights over the Fells. "There must be a hilltop...? a tall Tree, close by...?"

"Not close enough to 'spy down upon it from, regrettably, Sir." Anyone who wonders what Imps look like in their Middle Years would be perhaps more than satisfied with Shelby's Phiz at the moment,— Malice undiminish'd, with a Daily Schedule that leaves him too little time to express it.

"Then— " Mason catches himself about to ask how Capt. Shelby can know what the Plan View looks like, unless he has himself gain'd an impossible Altitude, noting also the thicketed eyebrows of the Welshman waiting, rearrang'd, for just this question.

"You must appreciate this is no idle Drudgery,— not some band of Savages, groping about earthbound for the correct Shape. Rather, 'tis a sure Artist's line, the Curves sweeping in preordain'd accommodation to the River,— if I grow too Rhapsodic, pray set the Dogs upon me. You would need to see one of these Works to understand."

61

So,— quite early the next morning there they both are, about to go visit one of the local Mounds with the possibly unstable Capt. Shelby as their Guide,— the frost along the Tent-Rigging bleach'd in the last of the Moon,— their breaths upon the Air remaining white for longer than 'twould seem they ought. Mason and Dixon step out of the Perimeter, into the Wild, now as entirely subject to the Captain's notions of Grace as any Romans, lur'd by promises of forbidden Knowledge, in the Care of an inscrutable Druid. "Come along," cries the Captain jovially. "We need to be there just at Sunrise."

"Folly," Mason mutters.

"Aye," Dixon replies, "you'd've pre-ferr'd the Moonlight, I guess, and an Owl or two." Down by the creek they fall in with the Path Shelby means to follow,— the North-Mountain rears above them, soon to catch the first light at its crest. Trees fill with whistling. Squadrons of cloud go rushing in the sky. The breeze has a cold edge. Dead leaves are everywhere. Soon all odor of woodsmoke has faded behind them. That of Ripeness, come and gone, enfolds them. And then something else.

"There's a new barrel-mill in the neighborhood,— smell it?" They are coming near the bank of a creek. Shelby, Eyebrows wrinkling together, takes hold of his Shot-Bag and begins to toss it lightly in his Hand. He seems eager to begin firing at any target that may present itself.

"Grist-millers," he declares, "discover there is more money in grinding out cheap barrels for rifles for the Savages. Philadelphia money. Here, up this way."

Mist is gather'd in the hollows, thick and cohering, blinding whilst carrying to each the Breaths and Mutterings of the others. Ev'rywhere between these white Episodes, the clarity of the Dawn slowly, piercingly, emerges. "This Ridge, another Valley," the Captain exhorts them, "and we are there." Over the crest and down to ford and then follow the creek through a gap in the hills to another Stream, where, in the angle of Confluence, its tip just catching the first rays of the Sun, stands Capt. Shelby's "Mound."

"Eeh!" cries Dixon. "Why, 'tis a great Cone!"

"Reg'lar as Silbury Hill," Capt. Shelby's head at an admiring angle.

Mason, slow to enthusiasm, sniffs the air. "No fermented Maize fumes about, but then, 'tis *Still*, so to speak, early in the Day."

"My Sacred Word," the Welshman rolling his eyes Heavenward, producing, however, an effect more of Madness than of Piety. "Come, Boys. Come." They are boys. They approach the giant Solid, alone upon its Promontory, as light slowly envelopes it, dyeing it a cold, crystalline Rose. Mason's first question, though he refrains from asking it aloud, is, Might it be under invisible Guard,— and how zealous are they? Shelby, watching his face, knows gleefully enough his Apprehensions.

"How do the Indians here about fancy Spectators like huz?" Dixon asks.

"They laugh. They but appear a solemn People,— worshiping Laughter, rather, as a serious, indeed holy, Force in Nature, never to be invok'd idly. This Mound is something they understand perfectly,— that white people do not, and show no signs of ever doing so, is a source of deep Amusement for them."

"Is there a way inside?"

"There shouldn't be, but there is." The Welshman's eyes tighten. "It was broken into years ago, perhaps by some larcenous Fool who had it confus'd with a Pyramid. His disappointment was the only good to come of it, for he found nothing,— no ancient corpses, nor even Copper bracelets or Tobacco-Pipes, for Indians never built it."

"Eeh!" cries Dixon, who's been peering into the opening. "D'yese see this, how these Layers are set in?— Mason! That Device Mr. Franklin show'd us,— his Leyden Jar! Remember thee all that Fancy Layering inside it...?"

"Yes," impatiently, "but those were Gold-leaf, Silver foil, Glass,— Philosophickal Materials," a quick glance toward Shelby, "whilst these,— " having a Squint, "— seem but different kinds of Refuse,— dirt...ashes...crush'd seashells...not likely to be an ancient Leyden Battery, Dixon, if that's what you're thinking."

"A Marvel no one taught you this, Mr. Mason, for there is lengthy Knowledge of such things,— according to which, alternating Layers of different Substances are ever a Sign of the intention to Accumulate Force,— not necessarily Electrical, neither,— perhaps, Captain, these Substances Mr. Mason so disrespects may yet be suited to Forces more Tellurick in nature, more attun'd, that is, to Death and the slower Phenomena."

Mason is shaking his head, having no idea how to control Ranting like this, genial though it be. He's long known that Leadership is not his best Quality. Captain Shelby is staring at them both, with apprehension more than curiosity, for he has seen the Deep Woods and its mysteries quite derange more than one visitor from the Sea-coast and beyond. Deciding to place his faith in Reason, "Ye'll note, how the Sun-light has been creeping down the Cone. A Progressive warming of the Structure. The Diameters of each infinitesimal Ring, at each moment, being the crucial values. Did either of you bring a Compass?"

"Here's one...eeh!" Dixon, regarding his Needle, feels himself begin to drift somewhere else, off at an angle to the serial curve of his Life.... Mason peers over his shoulder,— "Hum!" right into Dixon's Ear.

"Aagghh!" leaping away. "Mason, don't *do* that.— " He struggles to refocus,— in fact, to remember where he is. The Needle is swinging wildly and without pause, rocking about like a Weather-Vane in a storm, Dixon pretending to gaze at it knowingly.

Mason a-squint, "— Well, thank you for allowing us to witness your Experience, aye very helpful indeed...."

Shelby would have preferr'd the slow chatter of three Men, in the early morning, with nought more to discuss than the Day ahead. "This Structure happens to be quite in the projected path of your Line," he informs them, "— When at length your Visto is arriv'd here, the Mound will become active, as an important staging-house, for...whatever it may be," with an attempt at a Chuckle, tho' it comes out too loud, and imperfectly controll'd. "To quote Mr. Tox, in his famous *Pennsylvaniad,—*

> 'A "Force Intensifier," as 'tis styl'd,
> A geomantic Engine in the Wild,
> Whose Task is sending on what comes along,
> As brisk as e'er, and sev'ral Times as strong.'

— Welsh in origin, it goes without saying."

"How so? Welsh Indians?"

"Oh! Absolutely. Only a few days west and south of here.... 'Twas in *The Turkish Spy* but a few years since...?" The Cymry, Capt. Shelby explains, having first come to Britain from far to the East,— some say Babylon, some Nineveh,— their Fate ever to be Westering,— America but one of their dwelling-places, the Ocean nearly irrelevant. "Hugh Crawfford believes they are the Tuscaroras. Come along."

He leads them uphill again, to what seems the Ruin of a Wall, encircling part of the hill-top,— where he stoops and brushes away some Dirt. Here, inscrib'd in a roughly dress'd Stone, they see a Line of brief Strokes, some pointing up, some down, some both ways. "These are all over the British Isles,— 'tis a Writing call'd Ogham, invented by Hu Gadarn the Mighty, who led the first Cymrick Settlers into Britain. As ye'll note, 'tis useful for those who must move on quickly, yet do wish to scribble down something to commemorate their presence."

"What does it say?"

"Well...as nearly as I can make out,— 'Astronomers Beware. Surveyors too. This means you.' Of course I haven't read any of this for Centuries...yet 'tis indisputably Old Welsh."

"As you describe this Line," opines the Professor, back at Camp, "— the Marker Stones set at regular intervals,— a cascaded Array of Units each capable of producing a Force,— I do suspect we have the same structure as a Leyden Battery,— and, need I add, of a Torpedo."

"With the head aim'd close by New Castle?"

"Or the other way, were the Cascade reversible,— the emitted Blast, being as easily directed Westward as East? Either direction, 'twould be a Pip of a Weapon, even with your Marker Stones placed no further than Sideling Hill."

"Why fire at Sideling Hill?" Dixon all innocence.

"Not at the Hill," chuckles Capt. Shelby, "— at what's coming *over* the Hill."

"Pontiack? The French?"

"Too late for them. One day, one of you'll risk a Peep over the Ridge-line, and then you'll see."

"More mountains," says Mason.

"Exactly,— Mountains such as these, which may be liv'd among the year 'round. Therein ever rocks the cradle of Rebellion. Sooner or later, something up here will grow hungry or hopeless enough to want to descend to the plain, to stoop like Hawks upon rich Chesapeake, aye the Metropolis itself.... If the Black Boys so easily had their way with the British Regulars at Shippensburg, who knows what Wonders are yet possible out here, over the North-Mountain...."

Yet removing Trees to create a pair of perfectly straight Edges, is to invite *Sha,* as Captain Zhang, ever eager upon the Topick of the Line and its Visible expression upon the Landscape, with its star-dictated indifference to the true inner shape, or Dragon, of the Land, will be happy to indicate to them.

"They came from the Sky, they prepar'd to emplace these Webs of right lines upon the Earth, then without explanation they went away again. Their work is being continued by the Jesuits, inscribers of Meridians, whether in blind obedience to some ancient Coercion, long expir'd, or in witting Complicity with it, who can say?" Captain Zhang can of course imagine Jesuits guilty of anything, including conspiring with Extra-terrestrial Visitors, to mark the living Planet with certain Signs, for motives of their own, motives they do not discuss, especially not with their Jesuit hirelings.

"Hearken, Gentlemen,— Someone wants your Visto. Not your Line, nor the Boundary it defines. Those are but a Pretext for the actual clear'd straight Track. In the Domain of very slow Undulations we're discussing here, Wood is as much an Element as Air or Water,— living Trees in particular producing a Force that might interfere in too costly a way with whatever is to be sent up and down this Line.

"Earth, withal, is a Body, like our own, with its network of Points, dispos'd along its Meridians,— much as our medicine in China has identified, upon the Human body, a like set of Lines invisible, upon which, beadwise, are strung Points, where the Flow of *Chee* may be beneficially strengthen'd by insertions of Gold Needles. So, this arrangement of Oölite Shafts, at least partly inserted into the Earth,— you see, it is suggestive."

"Do we want to hear this?" Capt. Shelby inquires, plaintively.

"Hold, 'twill be legal evidence of his insanity, allow him to— ah, yes then Captain you were saying and how fascinating that you believe the Planet Earth to be a...living Creature? Hum?"

"Exactly as the creatures Microscopic upon your skin believe you to be a Planet. They may be arguing even now about whether or not you are a form of Life. Each time you step into a Tub, there comes upon them another universal Flood, with its Animalcular Noah, and another Reinhabiting, another Chain of Generations, to them how timeless, till the next Wash."

"Some reason that Bottle isn't moving more briskly?" Dixon wishes to know. "Thankye,— now Mason, don't ta'e the Hoomp, but the Captain's right,— "

" 'Right'?"

"Consider. We've an outer and an inner surface, haven't we, which mathematickally, 'tis easy, using Fluxions, to warp and smooth, by small, continuous changes, into a Toroid, with openings at either end, leading to— "

"Hold," cries Mason, "— An Inner Surface? Are you by chance seeking analogy between the Human Body and the planet Earth? The Earth has no inner Surface, Dixon."

"Have you been to its End, to see?"

"Tho' I come from pret-ty far North," Stig puts in, "yet there's a lot more North, North of even that,— out of which, now and then, a Sail will appear upon the Horizon, a Snow-craft approach, all the day long, and at Evening at last put in at our little Village,— Ev'ryone crowds into the Inn, by the light of bear-fat Candles, to drink Cloud-berry Flip, and listen to the Visitor's tales of a great dark Cavity up there, mirror'd overhead, as by a Water-sky,— Funnel-shap'd, leading inside the Earth...to another World."

"Grant me Patience O Lord," Mason with a bleak Expression, holding his head. "When 'tis not the Eleven Days missing from the New Style, or the Cock Lane Ghost, yet abides the Hollow Earth, as a proven Lure and Sanctuary to all, that too lightly bestow their Faith."

"Why," snorts Dixon, "half of all the Philosophers in Durham are Hollow-Earthers."

"That accounts for Emerson," hisses Mason. "Who was the other, again?"

"Lud Oafery," glowers Dixon, "marvelous chap, and he ever spoke highly of thee,— "

"Dixon,— pray you. Think. If Newton's figure is correct,— if the density of the Earth, on average, is between five and six times that of water, then the shell of this Hollow Earth of yours, be it hundreds of miles thick, would have to possess some quite impossibly high density to make up for the empty interior,— at least, say, twelve times that of water, maybe more. Where is the evidence of this? Solid Rock is but two and a half times as dense as water. What more could be down there?"

"Precisely what the Royal Society would wish to know."

"You've not, ehm that is, *mention'd* this to,— " pausing to consider how not to give offense.

"Some believ'd me, some didn't. Some took me for a Jes-uit Agent, angling for a Northern Expedition of some kind. Mr. Birch, bless him, immediately went off to make converts. Others asked questions tha'd have to term more or less rude...? My mining background, and so forth...? A Geordie descends into the Earth just once, and right away everyone starts to get ideas." Dixon on now like a tree-ful of ravens, with his Hollow Earth, an enthusiasm, Mason judges, too developed to be argued away without investing more time and patience than he possesses. Withal, he is too open himself to the seductions of Melancholy and its own comfortless phantoms, to call anything even as remotely hopeful as this into question,— no more Doubts for Mason just at the moment, thank you,— considering how ever less serviceable to him, as his days spin onward, they are proving to be.

"China may once have been another Planet," Capt. Zhang is now speculating, "embedded into the Earth thro' some very slow collision,— long ago, all populated, with its Language and Customs, arriving from the East Northeast, aiming for the Pacific,— over-shoots, plows into Asia, pushes up the Himalaya Range,— comes to rest intact, which is how, until the first Christian Travelers, it remains,— "

Taking this courteously if not perhaps seriously, Dixon replies, "Yet, from all we know, from Newton onward, how could the mechanism of its approach have been other than swift and Cataclysmick?"

"Why, if, within the last few miles of mutual approach, a Repulsive Force were to come into play, between the Earth and the Chinese Planet, acting counter to, and thus slowing, the Collision,— by analogy, of course, to Father Boscovich's Theory of Repulsion, at very close distance, among the primordial Atoms of Nature."

Dixon shakes his head, as if to clear some Passage within. "This is Jesuit physics. Why are you telling us this? Why must you ever be 'subtle'? Is this what Jesuits believe to be the origin of China?"

"Zarpazo does." The Chinaman beams and nods, as if Dixon has just understood a Joke.

The night before they set out westward again, Captain Shelby, from behind a can of his own Ale, brewed in the Shed adjoining, his face compos'd, inquires of them, Where is the Third Surveyor?

Mason, mistrustful, looks about as if this Newcomer might be at hand. Dixon, understanding Shelby to be posing a Riddle, is pull'd between loyalty to Mason and despair at his slowness in these matters. "Pray, Captain," he feels oblig'd to play in, "what Third Surveyor is that, for we are but two."

"Why," chuckles Shelby, "you are Wise Men from the East,— and ev'ryone knows they come in Threes!"

"Eeh, eeh! That's a canny one, for fair!"

Mason is less amus'd. The Captain's discourse verges upon Impiety.— Furthermore, it seems a bad Omen. "Well. It's like the Thirteenth Guest, isn't it."

Yet, reported sightings of the Supernumerary Figure now begin to drift in. He is seen often in the Company of an Animal that most describe as a Dog, though a few are not so sure, for its Eyes glow as if all the Creature's Interior be a miniature of Hell. The best time for a Sighting seems to be at around Sunset,— just as the Axmen are leaving off work and heading for the Mess Tent, the Wind changing, here in Pennsylvania, as between this World and the Next,— when one may catch him flitting across the Visto behind the Party, back at the edge of Visibility,— black Cloak, white Wig, black Hat, white Stock, black Breeches and so forth, on foot, carrying a three-leggèd Staff, with an Instrument of some kind affix'd. A rumor goes 'round that he is a Surveyor of Surveyors, independently hir'd by the Line Commissioners to keep an eye upon the first two. But where are the rest of his Party? Other interpretations are less Earthly. A Figure that might arouse no comment in Philadelphia, in these parts 'tis esteem'd a Wonder,— particularly as it shows no sign of having made the passage from there to here,— not, anyway, upon the Ground, nor through the Forest.

Presently, in camp, the phrase, "Resembles the old Gentleman," spoken low, is being heard, in reference to the Third Surveyor,— it having been long understood out here, as Capt. Shelby explains, that if one wishes to convey a certain Item of Spiritual Property in consideration of a Sum to be paid in advance, why, such a Contract may be arrang'd. "The old Gentleman is always interested, always buying,"— even this long at the Trade, as Shelby relates it, still resentful about his exile from the Infinite, descended here among the harsh Gradients of Space, subject to the cruel flow of Time,— denied the Future and the Past and thus his Omniscience,— whilst, as to drafting Contracts, left slightly worse at it than the average Philadelphia Lawyer.

"So when Brother Pritchard,— lives just over the Ridge, there,— without the Gentleman's noticing, decides to sneak in a *force majeure* clause that turns out to contain the phrase 'Acts of God,' why there's a legal crisis, the Gentleman wishing to nullify the Contract and get his money back,— Pritchard seeking to keep the money, and his Soul as well. Very, very expensive lawyers, all from Philadelphia, are engag'd by both parties. The Journals and Broadsiders get hold of the story, and quite excessive indeed grows the Commentary that follows, in Prose, Verse, and Caricature. The Gentleman, having virtually invented Publick Sensationalism,— which is reckon'd, indeed, upon his own torrid shores, as Entertainment,— has no illusions about anyone's motives, or the chances for great harm to his Case, yet naïvely, as others would say, disingenuously,— he clings to a belief in 'Justice.'"

"Well I don't know what you may have *heard* about what we *call* Justice up here," his Solicitor advises him, "but don't set your Hopes too high.— Just enjoy your Time in Town, visit the Shops, take in a Show...."

Hell, of late, has been growing so congested, that the Gentleman is happy enough to come up to Pennsylvania,— even Philadelphia in the Morning Rush seems to him a Prairie desolate,— and who even knows how many years this lawsuit may take? To him, as to the Deity, 'tis the blink of an Eye. "Damn'd Souls, you think I even *like* damn'd Souls? I go down to that Rout call'd 'Processing,' see them crowding in, more and more ev'ry day, I grasp the Situation, but don't *enjoy* it? Who could enjoy it?"

"Upon consideration, I think you're better advis'd not to sue in any of *our* courts. You could get fried like a Fritter, and Counsel along with you. Don't you have any, um, machinery for resolving this, out there in the Cosmos, wherever you come from?"

"A legal system? Us? Ha, ha, ha. What for? We're a Rubbish-tip, Sir! for all your worst Cases!— not that we get to pick or choose,— tho' we do have to deal with the Consequences for Eternity, of course,— yet, there I go, complaining again...oh and by the way, I'm anything but 'out in the Cosmos,' no no, being but Earth's D——l, local lad, working, in fact, *for* His Omnipotence these days, ha-hah yes, once an equal and respected Adversary, now but another contract employee. Ah, woe...and forget about Luncheon,— does he even write? once a century, maybe! If any of these damn'd Souls could see the misery I get, maybe they wouldn't groan so much."

"Howbeit, Milord,— my best advice is, Drop the case."

"Suppose we just go for the money. He can keep his Soul, but posting this kind of Debit isn't going to amuse my Commissioners."

"Style it an 'Investment.' Say the huge sum was to ensure his Corruption. You were developing a damn'd Soul."

"Already us'd that one too much, they shut me down a few sessions back, alas. But you seem like a Mortal of some ingenuity. Perhaps from time to time we could chat."

"Those would, of course, be billable Hours."

62

In the Conoloways, on the Twenty-second of April,— the first point of
Aries,— it snows all night, four inches of it upon the Ground when the
Axmen wake, and merrily begin to form it into Missiles or stuff it down
the backs of one another's Breeches. Springtide. Mason puts his head
out the Tent-Flap and is caught in an intimate Avalanche down the side
of the Tent. Dixon has his hat knock'd off by a Snowball, and goes chasing Tom Hynes 'round the Cook-Waggon.

"I dreamt of a City to the West of here," Dixon tries to recall, scrying
in his Coffee-Mug, the wind blowing Wood-smoke in his eyes, "at some
great Confluence of Rivers, or upon a Harbor in some inland Sea,— a
large City,— busy, prospering, sacred."

"A Sylvan Philadelphia...."

"Well...well yes, now tha put it thah' way,— "

"I hope you are prepar'd for the possibility, that waking Philadelphia
is as sacred as anything over here will ever get, Dixon,— observe you
not, as we move West, more and more of those Forces, which Cities upon
Coasts have learn'd to push away, and leave to Back Inhabitants,— the
Lightning, the Winter, an Indifference to Pain, not to mention Fire,
Blood, and so forth, all measur'd upon a Scale far from Philadelphian,—
whereunto we, and our Royal Commission, and our battery of costly
Instruments, are but Fleas in the Flea Circus. We trespass, each day ever
more deeply, into a world of less restraint in ev'rything,— no law, no convergence upon any idea of how life is to be,— an Interior that grows

meanwhile ever more forested, more savage and perilous, until,— perhaps at the very Longitude of your 'City,'— we must reach at last an Anti-City,— some concentration of Fate,— some final condition of Abandonment,— wherein all are unredeemably alone and at Hazard as deep as their souls may bear,— lost Creatures that make the very Seneca seem Christian and merciful."

"Eeh, chirpy today...? yet do I wish thee joy of thy dreams, Mason. I knaah the ones just before tha wake are most pleasant to thee,— having myself by then been long awake, from reluctance to re-visit the Horrors of my own, and so able to observe thee."

"How, then? Do I talk in my sleep, is that what you're saying?"

"Oh, aye. But tha needn't worry, no one would make it out, 'tis all another Language."

"I'm talking, another Language, in my Sleep,— *Dixon?*"

"Don't see what the whim-wham's about,— "

"Possession!— That is, somebody else's soul, possessing my body, whilst I sleep,— that's what it's *about!*"

"Why aye, whilst tha're away dreaming, that's what some would say, and others would add, What of it? Don't squint, ask the Reverend. Tha've a Dream-body, what use to thee's the solid one, for the time tha sleep? Here's some wand'ring Soul who may have been *centuries* without sleep, who may've indeed forgotten what sleep feels like, who, had Winding-Sheets pockets to carry it, might've offer'd pounds of Gold, for even a quarter-hour's rest...and here thy body is, as an Inn in the Wilderness, heated, drain'd, provision'd, and but for a beating Heart and a dormant Brain, vacant. Surely 'tis only the mildest of inconveniences— "

"Then tell me, Mirth,— where might this alien Ghost be, whilst I'm not dreaming? In what sort of humor?"

"Busy looking for another Habitation, I'd imagine...? Apprehensive...?"

"Well,— this won't do, will it."

"Not if tha feel this way. Here,— why not have Captain Zhang 'round someday to stand just outside, listen closely, and see what he can make of it...?"

"Too intimate."

"Half the Camp hears it. Some take it for Indians. Axmen say, if so, 'tis a Nation they have not yet encounter'd."

Later in the day, as they emerge from a Woodline, Mason gesturing eastward to where the encampment has swung into view, a Flight of sail,— "Something waits, directly in the Path of our Parallel,— too sure of itself to feel oblig'd to come forward and meet us,— and Lo,— what is to become of this rolling Gypsy village we've brought with us?" late sun, early Shadow in the tent-riggings. Pots a-clattering, kitchen smoke sucked out of Vents by the wind passing over. "None of this may be about either you or me. Our story may lie rather behind and ahead, and only with the Transits of Venus, never here in the Present, upon the Line, whose true Drama belongs to others,— Darby, Cope, Tom Hynes, Mr. Barnes, some new hire we don't even see,— and when 'tis all done I shall only return to Sapperton, no wiser, and someday wake up and not know if any of this 'happen'd,' or if I merely dream'd it, even this very moment, Dixon, which I know is real...."

"*Oh* dear....?"

For a while, at any rate, it appears to be the Drama of Stig, the Merry Axman, with ev'ryone else scurrying 'round out of sight, switching Wigs and Coats, appearing in the Proscenium only when needed,— "and whom has Stig ever needed?" as Mrs. Eggslap is apt to sigh, even in his hearing. But Stig, working diligently upon his Ax-bit, requires as near to perfect clarity of mind as he may achieve. It is this apparently single-minded concentration that at length draws the Attention of Light-Fingers McFee, in the midst of whose rummaging thro' Stig's Sea-Chest, Stig makes his Entrance, Ax in Hand.

"What is *this?*" he inquires.

"Ha! What is this?" brandishing an un-roll'd Sheet of Parchment cover'd with elaborate Seals and antiquated writing in some other Language, possibly Swedish.

Stig holds out his hand. "Give it."

McFee gazes at the Ax-Bit's shining Edge, considering. "Indians!" he yells.

"What does it mean, 'Indians'?" Stig asks, of an empty Tent, for McFee has zipp'd away. Stig roars and chases after him, as they go kicking over Laundry-Kettles, tripping over Tent-Guys and causing Tents to collapse, stopping at the Commissary to throw Potatoes and Onions at each other furiously for a full minute,— till in rides Capt. Shelby's co-officer out here, Mr. Joseph ("Continuation Joe") Warford, who detains them both, and after all have proceeded to the Cook-tent, has a look at the mysterious Parchment.

"Hum. Swedish is it, Stig?"

"Latin," Stig replies.

"Now then Stig, out with it," demands Capt. Shelby, "— or them yingle-yanglin' days is past and gone."

"Very well.— I am here on behalf of certain Principals in Sweden, who believe that the Penns, being secretly creatures of Rome, took illegally the original Svånssen land 'pon which Philadelphia would later come to sit,— and thus that the whole Metropolis has never ceas'd to belong, rightfully, to Sweden."

"What,— Swedish Jacobites!" exclaims Dixon, "sort of thing…why, Stig…?"

"Amid the glitter of your great World, the Flame of our cause may be easily overlook'd,…yet it burns hotly enough that certain Hands long accustom'd to Thievery durst not venture too close. Swedes have been here from the beginning, living among the Indians in peace, with no need to obtain their land falsely,— indeed, for Penn, Swedes were but another tribe of Indian, residing within his American Grant, whose Priority there he found no less irksome,— which is why, at bottom, there ever was a Boundary Dispute, and these Astronomers are come here at all."

"Stig," cries Mrs. Eggslap, "I had no idea! why, you can talk! I'll go bail for him gladly, Your Grace."

"Surely," protests the Camp-Lawyer Mr. Barnes, "if this be a Swedish claim, 'tis advanced in a less than timely way, Sir.— Eighty years and more, Kings have come and gone. How do you expect to fare in this?"

"I am but an Agent, Sir. For a greater View of Motive and Interest, beyond our own simple desire for Justice, you might ask among your Jesuitick acquaintance."

"If that's a remark about me,— " Dixon in full truculency.

"Gentlemen! Ladies!" cries the Justice of the Peace. "Must I read the Riot Act? I do so, I am told, most affectingly, having been compared indeed with Mr. Whitefield,— though I take in far less in donations, of course." (This seems to many a blatant request for a Bribe, tho' others maintain 'tis but innocent Joking.) "Now then Stig, give us your account, man."

"Do any of you know," Stig inquires, "what I have come down to you out of? The Frost eternal, the Whiteness abounding, beneath that all-night Sun? In the Royal Library in Copenhagen lies an ancient Vellum Manuscript, a gift from Bishop Brynjolf to Frederick the Third, containing Tales of the first Northmen in America, of those long Winters and the dread Miracles that must come to pass before Spring,— the Blood, the Ghosts and Fetches, the Prophecies and second Sight.... And the melancholy suggestion, that the 'new' Continent Europeans found, had been long attended, from its own ancient Days, by murder, slavery, and the poor fragments of a Magic irreparably broken.

"To enter the Capes of Delaware, was thus, for me, to pass the Pillars of Hercules,— not outward, into the simple Mysteries of an open Sea, but inward,— branching, narrowing, compressing toward an Enigma as opaque and perilous as any in my Travels. All day we ascended, and at dusk, finally approach'd *Philadelphia Irredempta*, ceaselessly a-clamor in the torch-light, headlong, as if in continuous Arrival from the Future,— the mesopotamian Idyll of the Svånssens, as vanish'd as Eden.

"As I stood among the hectic Mobility at Dock-Side, uncertain as to my next Step, a foreign Hand tapp'd at my mantle. A voice bade me good day, using my Christian name. I shiver'd, though I seldom do, ordinarily. 'Twas not a Voice I knew,— yet, terribly, *I knew it well.* Unprepared for any reception here, nonetheless I went with him through the necessary exchanges of Counter-seals and words that may never be written down and the like,— I stammer'd some kind of thanks for having been met. I can remember no longer what he look'd like. A closed Carriage approach'd,— "

"Hold," cries Capt. Shelby, "— what is this,— Elect Cohens, Bavarian Rosicrucians? Come, Stig, admit it,— you're not Swedish at all...are you?"

"Sir,— 'tis for you to work out,— let us say, that my people are of the North, Northern and very White, so white in fact that you British to us appear as do Africans, to you." He pauses, as one telling a Joak pauses for laughter, but all are silent, puzzling how white that might be. Stig presses on. "The first thing we learn to do, however, before we even learn to fish, is to *impersonate Swedes*,— for our Nation much prefer to remain unmolested, in return for sending south a few Emissaries now and then, like sacrificial youths and maidens, into the Sin-laden World, posing as Finns, Swedes, the odd Hungarian,— a Corps of Intermediaries for Hire, of whom I am honor'd to be one."

"Working as an agent for Swedish Jacobites unnam'd," Mr. Warford writing vigorously.

"My Contract runs for a year. By next year, Sweden, 'Dusky Olaf,' as we like to personify the place, may no longer wish to pursue his Claim. Then I shall have to be an A-gent for someone else." His Eye-lashes Stirrings of Light, his Brow pale and trackless as an Arctic Shore. "No Question I shall find Work with some American Province. After Mr. Franklin's success in London, Colonial Agents will be much in demand, as hard put to meet the Standards he has set."

"What I don't quite grasp," says Mr. Warford, "is how felling Trees all day is going to help the Swedes take Philadelphia back."

"Healthy Exercise," replies Stig. "Learning the Pioneer Arts,— in particular, the production of Vistoes. Ya, Vistoes to us may prove quite important,— as the Shape of a Lance once held within it the Shape of the Tilting-Lists wherein 'twould be us'd, so do these Lancaster County Rifles, with an amazing Fidelity, create their own Vistoes of moving Lead, straight as a Ray of Light for a Mile or more,— quite terrible for the unfortunate Squirrel over on the next Ridge-line, who imagines he has found safety."

"You anticipate an arm'd attack against Philadelphia?"

"Is that so fanciful? The Paxton Boys nearly succeeded last year, didn't they? and those were Scots, Welsh, Irish,— southern Races. Imagine next time, a Band, similarly arous'd, of healthy Swedes."

"Should you be sharing their Intentions this way, Sir?"

Stig shrugs genially. "Nothing is certain. Were the Time ever to come, the Continent should know."

"Aye, and you'll fare as well as Braddock did," declares Mr. Boggs, "for there's no room for your European Anticks over here in the Woods."

"Braddock's Vistoe was not wide enough," declares Stig. "Correctly prepar'd for and executed, techniques from the Prussian Plains, where

Science and Slaughter were ever fruitfully conjoin'd, remain unsurpass'd...."

"Tell 'em, Soldier!" adds Zsuzsa Szabó. "If it's not fit for Cavalry, it's not fit for war. The Future's out West, not creeping 'round these Woods."

"Bugs in your Hair," notes Eliza Fields.

"Too much green in the Day-light, as Grease in the Candle-light," adds Patience Eggslap. "Yet if it hadn't been for Trees, I'd probably never have found Stig."

"Was I lost?" Stig inquires. "When?"

Terrain begins to get "banky," as Dixon styles it. There are not as many Settlements, Forges, Saw-mills, or planted Fields. The last Market-Roads are cross'd,— the three between Antietam and Conococheague, the Fort Bedford Road, and finally, Braddock's Road,— Lingering prolong'd, gazing North and South, for whatever Traffick there might be,— each Road abruptly, too soon, behind them. They have enter'd that strewn and charr'd Theater of the late War, where Indians are still being shot by white men, and whites scalp'd by Indians, who yet pass upon their forbidden Trails, and watch invisibly from the Forests,— and there's no one who can tell the Surveyors whether or not 'tis a District any more in reach of the Treaty of Paris than were Pontiac and his Armies the summer before the Surveyors arriv'd in America.

Hickman, Gibson, and Killogh, veterans of Braddock's Defeat, depress the Spirits of the Company with Tales of that Tragedy, of how the Bears came out of the Trees to feed upon the Corpses of English soldiers, "A Defile of Ghosts growing, with the Years, more desperate and savage, to Settlers and Indians alike. You'd not wish this Line to pass too close to them, I shouldn't think."

"Do yese Damage," nods Alex McClean.

Their last ten-minute Arc-Segment, this time out, lands them about two miles short of the Summit of Savage Mountain, beyond which all waters flow West, and legally the Limit of their Commission. They set a Post at 165 Miles, 54 Chains, 88 Links from the Post Mark'd West and, turning, begin to widen the Visto, moving East again, Ax-blows the day long. From the Ridges they can now see their Visto, dividing the green

Vapors of Foliage that wrap the Land, undulating Stump-top yellow, lofty American Clouds a-sailing above, and, "This day from the Summit of Sidelong Hill I saw the Line still formed the arch of a lesser circle very beautiful, and agreeable to the Laws of a Sphere," as Mason records.

"Yet," he confides to Capt. Zhang, "this unremitting Forest,— it disturbs me. Far, far too many trees."

"Consider," replies the Geomancer, "— Adam and Eve ate fruit from a Tree, and were enlighten'd. The Buddha sat beneath a Tree, and he was enlighten'd. Newton, also sitting beneath a Tree, was hit by a falling Apple,— and *he* was enlighten'd. A quick overview would suggest that Trees produce Enlightenment. Trees are not the Problem. The Forest is not an Agent of Darkness. But it may be your Visto is."

"Are we in any danger at this moment?" Mason might be joking, but for an anxious under-tone.

"*Sha* takes time to accumulate and accelerate," explains Captain Zhang. "At this stage, only those of heightened sensitivity, like myself, can even feel it.— But I am uncomfortable. May we move off the Line a bit?

"To rule forever," continues the Chinaman, later, "it is necessary only to create, among the people one would rule, what we call...Bad History. Nothing will produce Bad History more directly nor brutally, than drawing a Line, in particular a Right Line, the very Shape of Contempt, through the midst of a People,— to create thus a Distinction betwixt 'em,— 'tis the first stroke.— All else will follow as if predestin'd, unto War and Devastation."

"Wait," objects Mr. Dixon. "It's as plain as pudding that Pennsylvania and Maryland are so different, that thy fatal Distinction was inflicted upon these Shores, long before we arriv'd,— "

"Poh, Sir," goads Mason, "the Provinces are alike as Stacy and Tracy."

"Except for the Negro Slavery upon one side," Dixon points out, less mildly than he might, "and not the other."

"If you think you see no Slaves in Pennsylvania," replies Capt. Zhang, his face as smooth as Suet, "why, look again. They are not all African, nor do some of them even yet know,— may never know,— that they are Slaves. Slavery is very old upon these shores,— there is no

Innocence upon the Practice anywhere, neither among the Indians nor the Spanish nor in the behavior of the rest of Christendom, if it come to that."

On June 14th, they stand atop the Allegheny Divide. From now on, any Settlers they find are here in violation of Penn's and Bouquet's Edicts. Here the Party will cross, not alone into Ohio, but into Outlawry as well. At last, running Water becomes the underlying unit of measurement,— Planets hold their Courses, Constellations stately creep on, Napier's Bones click in the Surveyors' Tents, and quietly, calmly, ev'rything keeps coming back to Water, how it inhabits the Land, how it gets on with the Dragon beneath. Mapp'd at last, "Maryland" is reveal'd as but a set of Lines meant to Frame Potowmack to the West, and Chesapeake to the East,— dry Land is included, but the Map is of Water. "Beyond the Dividing Mountain (Savage), the Waters all run to the Westward," Mason enters in the Field-Book. "The first of Note (which our Line would cross if continued) is the Little Yochio Geni, running into the Monaungahela, which falls into the Ohio or Allegany River at Pitsbourg (about 80 Miles West, and 30 or 40 North from hence).... The Ohio is navigable for small craft by the accounts I have had from many that have passed down it; and falls in to the River Mississippi (about 36.5 degrees of North Latitude; Longitude 92 degrees from London); which empties itself into the Bay of Florida." This is how far one Day at the Savage Mountain Summit takes his Desire, or his Quill.

"Who sent you boys out here like this?" There are about six of them. Some afterward will say seven. They are wearing Hats made from the fur of Raccoons, Opossums, Weasels, and Beavers,— and holding long Rifles with octagonal barrels, and packing a Pistol or two each. Even the Horses are glaring, all but carnivorously, at the Party.

A Dilemma. Say the name of either Proprietor, and they are agents of the Enemy. Say "Royal Society," and 'twill sound like working for the King, who's even less popular out here than the Penns. "Running a Line

East and West," Dixon finally says, "for some Gentlemen who'll pay for something that looks good on a Map."

"Lot o' Boys for just a simple straight Line, ain't it?"

"We could use more'n this," suggests Tom Hynes, perhaps not as aware as those Axmen who've taken refuge behind the Trees, how easily the Visitors may be provok'd. "Lot of Trees need fallin'. Ask the Steward, Mr. McClean. It's three and six the Day, and we'll keep ye fed."

"For how long?"

"Far west as they let us go. Could get day-to-day after a little,— "

"Hai-ll,— sounds good to me."

" 'Tis your Wife that's Good, Lloyd,— this is 'at damn Proclamation Line, 's what it is."

"No it ain't, that runs the other way, all along the Allegheny Ridge-Line. This is something else. Why're you chopping down all these Trees?"

"You're sure welcome to haul away what you need."

"This all right with Colonel Bouquet?"

Out here, the Col° would be a ruthless sort of chap to run up against. The Hero of Bushy Run has his own plans for America, and a good many friends among the high Whiggery as well,— as who must not, in these times. His Scheme is to tessellate across the Plains a system of identical units, each containing five Squares in the shape of a Greek Cross, with each central square controlling the four radiating from it,— tho' as to their Size, no one is agreed, some saying a mile on a side, others ten, or an Hundred,— Ohio, and the western Prairie beyond, presenting such Enigma, that no one knows what scale to work at.

"A Prison," suggests Capt. Zhang. "Settlers moving West into instant Control."

"Dozens of such Schemes each year," shrugs Capt. Shelby, "and they all fail."

"Bringing closer the day," replies the Chinaman, as if receiving Instruction from Elsewhere, "when one of them succeeds."

63

On August 4th, Mason reports a "great Storm of Thunder and Lightning: the Lightning in continued Streams or Streaks, from the Cloud to the ground all 'round us; about 5 minutes before the hurricane of wind and Rain; the Cloud from the Western part of the Mountain put on the most dreadful appearance I ever saw: It seemed to threaten an immediate dissolution to all beneath it."

"Thy sort of Weather," Dixon, chewing upon more than smoking a Conestoga Cigar, supposes.

"Look at that Cloud. Awful. Don't you pray, in situations like this?"

"Of course. But I didn't imagine Deists did, so much…?"

"This is no Pervading Influence, this is as personal as it gets, all it'd take'd be one Bolt of Lightning— " A huge, apocalyptick Peal strikes directly outside, arriving together with a Volume of light unknown even at mid-Day.

Again are the Party returning Eastward, into Memory, and Confabulation. The physickal World, from Gusts to Eclipses, must insist upon itself a bit more, so claim'd are the Surveyors in their contra-solar Return by Might-it-bes, and If-it-weres,— not to mention What-was-thats.

Next day, whilst yet west of Gunpowder, crossing Biter-Bit Creek, they pass near a House which is just reaching the Cusp of a Monthly, indeed Lunar, Whim-Wham they have on previous Occasions manag'd to avoid. It seems that each time the full Moon ascends to bathe in her flavid Stain the Steeps and Crevices of that country, Zepho Beck creeps from his

Bed, waking his Wife, Rhodie, who then waits for as many heart-beats as she may bear before stealing out after Zepho as he proceeds to the Creek-side and, selecting a young Birch of a certain Diameter, crouches before it, bares his Teeth, Finger-combing his hair back from his face with Creek-Water, approaching the Tree closely enough to sniff the Bark, and smell the Fluids of life coursing beneath, before falling upon it, and in a short tho' hideous turn of Gnawing,— his Eyes throwing crazed yellow flashes all about,— bringing it down....With his Wife watching secretly and in some Agitation, Zepho sheds his clothing to reveal a dense fur covering his Body,— enters the Water, dragging with him the slain Tree, and moves up-stream,— flapping his feet, now grown webb'd to propel and steer him,— sleekly 'round several bends, till coming upon a great Dam being built by legitimate Beavers, who of course all go swimming for their Lives as soon as they see Zepho, for they know him, as this has been happening ev'ry full Moon. Perhaps indifferent to their social Rejection, he sets to work separating his Tree into Poles, Sticks, and Withes, and placing them wherever in the Structures of Dam or Lodge he feels they need to go. The next morning he is found down-hill from his House, beside the fishing-Pond, lying among remnants of gnaw'd Shrubs, with fragments of half-eaten water-lilies protruding from his Mouth.

"Kastoranthropy," Professor Voam shaking his head, "And haven't I seen it do things to a man. Tragick."

"Yes and you might ask the Indians that you meet, how all the other Beavers like it," says Rhodie.

" 'Other,' Madam?"

"Well you've but to look at him, when he's...the way he is, the Hair, the Teeth? the *Tail*, for goodness' Sake, *they* seem to regard him as another breed of creek life,— welcoming his help with the Construction,— yet in the month's Lull before his next Fit, oblig'd to waste their Time putting much of it right again. I love him but Zepho's no Carpenter. Look at this place, Lord in his Mercy. And it gets worse. He believes that Indians are out setting traps for him, aiming to capture him and trade his Pelt for Weapons. Sometimes he does say 'Scalp,' but mostly 'tis 'Pelt.' "

"An advanc'd case," nods the Professor. They are in the Barn, where Zepho has been brought, much to the perplexity of the Animals there, who must conflate the Being who feeds them with this wild creature. "The Indians I have consulted, know ev'rything that's going on, and if it's any comfort, at least Zepho's not alone, there's been an Ulster Scot with a Taste for Swamp Maples, paddling about all summer, up Juniata,— a Son of Dublin, down by Cheat,— in fact, enough Kastormorphism among White folks out here, since we first started settling, to populate a good Lake of our own."

These Indians are certainly no strangers to the idea of a Giant Beaver. He figures importantly in Tales of how they and the World began,— he claims a fourth of the Delaware Nation under the Beaver Totem,— he is a protector, sustainer, worker of Miracles. Zepho during the Full Moon, however, is not exactly what they have in mind, failing somehow to be sinister or powerful enough,— nor, to be direct, do they ever find him quite Beaver enough, as the Phenomenon lasts but a Night and a Day, whilst beneath ev'ry other Phase of the Moon, he appears to be the Zepho of old.

"How can you go on wanting me as your husband?" he cries.

"Beaver for a Day don't seem like much, Zepho,— you've seen ev'rything I can turn into."

"Mighty kind of you, Rhodie,— in fact, too kind. What is it you're cooking up now?"

"Nothing, Zepho. Just how women flit from one daydream to another,— and all at once I had this idea for a Contest,— "

"Rhodie?"

"Make us a Fortune! Suppose you and that Swedish Axman Stig were to— "

"Wait, wait,— Dear, it wouldn't work,— a dozen things must be perfect,— the Bark has to taste right,— the age of the Tree,— its Vital Emanations,— "

"Nor's it quite fair," Professor Voam adds, "for Stig's indifferent to what he chops down, knowing he can fell anything with that Swedish Bit and custom Handle, a Hickory or an Alder, an Oak or a Peach, it matters little to Stig, the Equations are the same but for the Arboreal Coefficients,— Details of importance to a Beaver are absorb'd in a single brutal downswing,— after which, all is over."

"You're saying it's a mismatch? Listen, tree-for-tree I can match anything that Swede can do."

"There's the Zepho I married!"

And so, at the full Moon of August 5th, the two Lumbermen meet upon the Visto. Mason and Dixon bring out and carefully adjust the Royal Society Clock, winch up the Weight, and set the Pendulum a-tick. The Contestants are to proceed side by side, each being responsible for half of the Visto's Breadth. At the end of two perfectly measur'd Hours, the slain trees will be counted. If the numbers happen to be equal, then Zepho and Stig will each fell one more Tree, and the fastest will be Winner.

"All set?" booms Mr. Barnes, "— Gentlemen, let's clear us some Visto!"

A chorus of Mrs. Eggslap's young Ladies have turn'd out to lend support to Stig,— "Swing that Ax! Chop that Tree! On, Stig, on! To Victo-ry!" Stig strikes for them an athletick Pose, then another,— he has more than enough time, hasn't he, to get to work, and these girls are all so,—

"Stig!"

What is this? He narrows his Gaze, looking about. Zepho is already well out of sight, over the next Rise in fact, having left behind a five-yard Swathe of Trees horizontal, and neatly separated into Trunks, Branches, and Withes. Stig grips his Ax, assaulting his side of the Visto with so much Fury that the first Tree is coming down before he is really prepar'd to avoid it. One Limb in consequence catches him fairly across the Arse, sending him a-sprawl. He takes some time to arise, and when he does, he's limping. It proves but a Sprain, that he is able in the next two hours to work out, yet not enough to come up appreciably upon Zepho.

"I thought I was perfect," as Stig will recall later, "— what happen'd?"

"Sometimes," Mrs. Eggslap will begin, " 'tis hard, to be a Woman...."

By now 'tis well past Sun-set, and the Full August Moon has risen. Expecting its Rays further to enhance Zepho's performance, Guy Spit the pass-bank Bully is sending Agents 'round to make side-Wagers as to the total number of Trees fell'd. Imagine his consternation when Zepho, seeing the risen Orb, screams and runs for the nearest Shade.

"Impossible," mutters Professor Voam. "Unless..."

"The Light," Zepho screams, "— the Moon, Rhodie, it's almost,— aahh!"

Mason looks at Dixon. Dixon looks at Mason. "The Eclipse!" both cry at the same time. They have only now remember'd the Eclipse of the Moon, due to start later tonight. Zepho is 'morphosing back to Human, and not enjoying it much. Stig requests that the contest be declar'd void, and Guy Spit collapses in tears, his only intelligible Word, "Ruin."

" 'Tis well," murmurs Rhodie, trying to ignore the vast hands-ful of Fur Zepho is shedding all over her Apron. "There is a promising Lawsuit in this, if we can prove those Astronomers knew about it in advance."

"We assum'd the one would have no effect upon the other," protests Mason, "and we certainly didn't use the knowledge to win any money, did we?"

Dixon raises his eyes piously.

"How could they not be connected? Zepho, my own, speak to me!"

"Not even a Philadelphia Lawyer could win with an Argument like that."

"In ancient Days," notes Capt. Zhang, "they'd have been beheaded! Indeed, it nearly happen'd to a Pair of Astronomers legendary in China, nam'd Hsi and Ho." The next evening, Zepho yet in mental distress over his unpremeditated re-humanizing, and the Topick of Mason and Dixon's lapse having again arisen, the Captain tells,—

64

Once, so long ago that no one is sure of Dates anymore,— tho' some say it was during the reign of one of the Hia Emperors,— upon the first day of Autumn in the *Hsiu* or Moon-station of Fang, an eclipse of the Sun occurr'd, which the Court Astronomers, Hsi and Ho, fail'd to predict,— not just predict accurately, but predict *at all*. Instead of diligently observing the Heavens, and doing the calculations, they had been spending most of their time roistering into town at late hours, abusing wine, drunkenly pursuing notorious Courtesans, not all of whom were Women, falling into public Latrines, and losing great portions of their Royal Stipends to all sorts of thieves, from Adventuresses to Gaming-table Bullies,— until, one strangely-lit Noontide, clogg'd and neuralgick, weaving their way back to their quarters in the Palace, they notice something about the shadows of the trees.— The sunlight that is able to pass clear of the leaves and strike the Road-way, instead of the usual more or less round Dots amid a general shade, presents instead, a mindlessly repeated Spill of identical Crescents, each growing imperceptibly narrower and sharper, as the stupefied Philosophers watch,— slowly realizing that they are seeing the Moon, moving onto the Disk of the Sun, carpeting the Ground by the bleary shimmering tens of thousands, as far in ev'ry direction as they can see.

"We may be in trouble," says Ho.

"Thanks for doing the brain-work on that." They hurry on in the livid, decadent Noon, stepping among the slow-stirring bright lacework, their faces averted from the Event above. Dogs howl all over the City. Chickens stop what they are doing and fall asleep. Babies cry, Pigs briefly acquire the power of speech, saying, "Hush, hush." The Light continues to seep away, until all individual Shadows are dissolv'd in a general Gloom, tense and baleful.

Inside the Observatory, a great Tower of imported Rajputana Marble, a winding stairway leads upward to the Observing Platforms. Hsi and Ho ascend, bickering. "We did the Reductions correctly, didn't we? You look'd it over, right?"

"Well I didn't check ev'ry *Digit*, I assum'd that if you were doing your job, I wouldn't have to."

At the highest platform, they stand, two miniature rob'd wastrels, trying not to look into the black rays of Totality, whilst, far below, with an eruption of Cymbals and Fifes, a great Voice declares Hsi and Ho, henceforward unto Eternity, enemies of the Emperor,— and condemns them to death.

"For what?" Ho, terrified, squeals at his Partner. "What'd we do?"

"We made the Emperor look bad. As a Child of Heaven, he's suppos'd to know all about these Wonders in advance."

" 'Tis only an Eclipse,— only Shadows,— what harm to the Kingdom could result?"

Hsi cackles. "As above, so below. Eclipses indicate for all to see that something is wrong in the very Heart of the State,...tho' with this Emperor, if *anything* goes amiss, his shoes failing to fit, his Luncheon disagreeing with him, whatever it is, he'll blame it 'pon the Eclipse,— that is, upon us."

Ho groans. "Our heads, for a little indigestion?"

"Why they call them 'Heads of State,' I suppose...."

"Hsi! we are in Danger! What do we do?"

"Escape," reckons Hsi. Looking Earthward, they now see below them a body of men in dark, gleaming Armor, gathering into columns in the damag'd light.

"How," inquires Ho, his voice higher than usual, "— fly?"

"An excellent idea," Hsi now producing a gigantick sky-blue Kite, of some strong yet light silk Stuff, strengthen'd with curious Bamboo Ribwork, furnish'd with apparatus for steering. "Quickly!" They can hear the clamor of Soldiers' feet, echoing in the Stair-well.

"But will it hold our combin'd weights?" cries Ho, as his colleague, having attach'd these Wings, now roughly embraces him.

"Depends what you ate for Breakfast,"— as together they step from the Ærial platform into pure Altitude.—

"Well, I had the rest of the Duck, about six Dumplings with Pork Sauce, then— Aaaagh!" as they go plummeting toward the Terrain below, clutching each other in terror as, above them now, upon the Platform they lately occupied, appear the first of their Pursuers, gazing after them in that afflicted light, with faces too small to read any more. They wait for Arrows. Above stares the black Disk of the Sun....

In the reduced Visibility, the Astronomers have lost all sense of how fast they're falling,— indeed have no idea of how far they have already travel'd from the Palace and their Pursuers. It is really only after considerable time has pass'd, without having smash'd into the ground at high speed, that Hsi, the quicker of the pair, grasps that they have been gliding after all. By then the Lunar Visitor has begun to pass from the Sun's Face, and the landscape to grow increasingly readable again.

"Look!" Hsi pointing behind Ho, "some Army, and on the move! Look at that Plume of Dust!"

"Where?" Ho turns to look. "And,— coming our way, too! what do you suppose it is?"

"Wait," it occurs to Hsi. "Ho, 'tis *us*. Elementary Opticks! If we can see them…"

"Yes, yes?" Ho waits. Hsi waits for Ho. At length, "Oh of course, you mean,— then they can see us, too?"

"For this, I am risking my life? Why don't I just drop you off here? It would also make my escape that much easier."

"Suit yourself of course."

"And my arms are getting tir'd."

"Well, so are mine. Some embrace!"

"All right then, off you go," Hsi opening his arms abruptly. Ho clutches wildly back at Hsi but is already in midair, with nothing more to expect in the way of embraces, but the Wind of his Descent.

So intently have the Astronomers been bickering, however, that Ho has fail'd to notice how closely by now their Craft has laps'd to Earth. In fact, he falls no more than ten feet, and that into a small, willow-fring'd Lake belonging to the lands of Lord Huang, a very rich trader with seven eligible daughters. As Ho flounders about in the Lake, his partner lands on top of him, and then the pair of Wings upon them both....

They haul themselves to shore and stagger about, soaking wet, beginning, as their relief at being alive fades, to argue again. "You just let me drop?" Ho recalls. "Much higher, and you would have murder'd me?— This is strange! I'm here talking to not just *a* murderer, but *my* murderer!"

"*I* knew we were almost down," Hsi says. "Do you really think I'd drop you any more than ten feet?"

"Well,— I don't know. Would you have dropp'd me,— twenty feet? People can get kill'd falling twenty feet."

"Not into the water."

"Oh! Suppose it had been but a giant reflecting-pool, and only Inches deep?"

"I could see 'twas far deeper, by the color of the Water, not to mention Waves upon the Surface."

"So after this close assessment of our landing area, why did you not choose to share any of it?"

"You seem'd more interested in screaming,— I was reluctant to interrupt."

"But you let me *believe* you were killing me.— When I hit that lake, I thought, so, this is it, here it is, the world of the Dead.— Hmm, wet.... Cold, too. They don't let you breathe. So forth. Eventually realizing I was under Water, of course,— "

"Thank you, Ho,— but for the kind of help you need...your College must keep a list they can refer you to, and as I've said many times, there is no stigma, there are excellent remedial programs for cases like— excuse me, what are you doing?"

"Pissing." Somewhere out in the pale green Maze of the willows there's a chorus of merry comment, from the daughters of Huang, who customarily go about ev'rywhere in Company. Soon Ho has wander'd out of Hsi's sight, calling, "Girls! Girls! Here it is, over here!"

About then their Father shows up with a platoon of arm'd retainers, demanding to know how Hsi has penetrated so far inside his Boundaries. Unable to come up with another story on the Spot, Hsi tells the truth. The Lord thinks he is confabulating, but the Eclipse part of it has his interest. "Stargazer, eh? Can you predict when the *next* Eclipse will happen?"

"Of course. The Moon, you want Moon-Eclipses, I can do those too."

"I made more *yuan* on one deal today than you would ever have seen in your Life working for the Emperor,— all as the Result of your wond'rous Eclipse. A warehouse full of silk, let go for nothing, because its owner thought this was the End. If I'd known beforehand, I could have done more than one Deal like that. No wonder the Emperor wants your heads."

Reflexively Hsi grabs his Head, as if to assure himself of its continued Attachment. "Uh…"

"Needless to say, this would pay quite well. Same deal for your Partner, of course. Where is he, by the way?"

This is answer'd by a slow *crescendo* of Conversation, advancing upon them through the ornamental forest of Birches all around. "Keep those swords ready, Boys," advises Lord Huang, beginning to betray some Annoyance. Out of the trees bursts a dishevel'd and uncontrollably giggling Ho, his arm around the eldest of the girls, who is kissing him passionately whilst her sisters, aroar and roseate and smudg'd, frolick about them.

"Papa! This is Ho, and we wish to be married, this instant."

"Yes Papa, oh please," chorus the rest, as Li gives Ho a push, sending him staggering in her Father's direction. Ho's robes are torn, upon all expos'd skin are fingernail scratches, there is green scum from the Lake clinging to his hair. He leers in a friendly way at Lord Huang but isn't sure what to say.

"Have we a Deal?" mutters the Lord to Hsi, who shrugs. "I see no problem, then.— Welcome to the Huangs, my boy. Ho, is it? You, like your excellent co-adjutor here, have pass'd into a new Realm. Your Emperor was answerable to Heaven,— here must we answer to the Market, day upon day unending, for 'tis the inscrutable Power we serve, an invisible-Handed god without Mercy."

In the weeks and years to follow, Hsi and Ho, ever one step ahead of the Emperor's hir'd Blademen, travel far, gain respect, and make fortune upon fortune, not the least of their Successes being Erotick, at one time and another, in varying Combinations, too, some of them quite entertaining, *with all seven Daughters.* Hsi and Ho are frequently mistaken for one another,— in their early Careers an Inconvenience, in their later Years a source, ever fresh, of Occasion for Glee. Periodickally, one or the other, repenting of his life, makes Atonement to Heaven by forswearing Drink, or Gluttony, or Mah-Jongg,— as seldom, if ever, are both Astronomers repentant at the same time, at least one may pay his Duties close Attention. As a result, no longer do Hsi and Ho fail to plan for Eclipses, solar or lunar. Lord Huang, however, continues to extend himself upon a faith in the Astronomers ever in need of re-convincing, wagering ever more stupendous Sums upon the ecliptick Innocence of ev'ryone else, not only Silk-Merchants but presently Bankers, other Lords, and their Generals, until the terrible Day when Hsi or Ho, or both, whilst casting Calculations for an upcoming Total Solar Eclipse, with fingers Greas'd from the giant platter-ful of *Dim Sum,* which, having given their personal gold Chop-Sticks away as tokens of desire to the operatick Personage Miss Chen, they are absent-mindedly eating from by Hand, happen to mis-count enough critical Beads of the Abacus to throw their Prediction off by hours. Meanwhile, dress'd as a Chinese Sub-Deity in red, yellow, and blue and a number of Gem-Tones, having already commanded the Sun to darken, with no result, Lord Huang finds himself far from home, waiting before a fateful River-bank and a humorless Army. The contempt in the front ranks grows more and more open, as the loss of Huang's credibility spreads backward thro' the Host. The Sky continues as blank as a hir'd Astronomer's face, the Sun as relentlessly beaming as an Idiot. In one version of the Tale, Huang is sav'd just in time, and in his rage banishes Hsi and Ho, who end their lives in the western Desert, beggar'd and holy, living on what few drops of water and grains of Rice the Day may bring them,— in the other version, Huang is assassinated by his own fretful Troops, whereupon the Sun at last begins to darken, the Army is smitten with Terror and Contrition, and the Astronomers, who appear to have been waiting but this Moment all their lives, are easily able to take over Huang's Lands, Fortune, Army, and Harem of Daughters, who ageless as the Pleiades (which Chinese girls know as the "Seven Sisters of Industry") attend the Star-Gazers faithfully till their Days be run.

65

All the month of November, Mason and Dixon run the East Line, 11 miles, 20 Chains, 88 Links from the Post Mark'd West in Mr. Bryant's Field, now mark'd East as well,— eastward to the shore of Delaware, from which the five degrees of Longitude in the original Grant were to extend. It is a task they might have sub-contracted out to any of dozens of local Surveyors.

"Industrious Pair," speculates Capt. Zhang. "Unless you be, rather, jealous, to possess the Line in its entirety."

"As who would not?" Dixon replies. "Five degrees. Twenty minutes out of a day's Turn. Time enough for all sorts of activities,— eat the wrong Fish, fall in love, sign an order that will alter History, take a Nap...? A globe-ful of people, and not one is ignorant of the worth of twenty minutes, each minute a Pearl, let slip, one after the next, into Oblivion's Gulfs."

"Or twenty-one minutes, if you add another Quarter of a Degree," twinkles the Chinaman, "Crossing Ohio, as you might say. It was five and a Quarter Degrees that the Jesuits remov'd from the Chinese Circle, in reducing it to three hundred sixty. Bit like the Eleven Days taken from your Calendar, isn't it? Same Questions present themselves,— Where'd that Slice of Azimuth go? How will it be redeem'd? Perhaps your five Degrees of Visto were meant to be a sort of...Repository?"

The Surveyors exchange Grimaces. What now? Can he be serious? Have they another fictitious Spaniard in the Offing?

"Wouldn't each Degree simply've been widen'd by just a hair, to make up for the loss?" Dixon gently, in a voice Mason has heard him use with pack-horses that the Killogh brothers, their Pack-Men, vouch are "daft." "So that in some way, so should I imagine, congenial to the Oriental Beliefs...?, thy missing Degrees are distributed indistinguishably thro'out the Entirety of the Circle...?"

"And what may that slender Blade of Planetary Surface they took away, not be concealing?" Zhang dementedly on, oblivious, "— twenty-one minutes of Clock-Time, and eleven Million Square Miles,— anything may be hiding in there, more than your Herodotus, aye nor immortal Munchausen, might ever have dreamt. The Fountain of Youth, the Seven Cities of Gold, the Other Eden, the Canyons of black Obsidian, the eight Immortals, the Victory over Death, the Defeat of the Wrathful Deities? Histories ever Secret. Lands whose Surveys will never be tied into any made here, in this Priest-tainted three-sixty,— blue Seas, as Oceanick Depths, call'd into Being by Mathesis alone...without Shores, nor any but their own Weather blowing in from no-where upon the official Globe....

"*Nor* ought we to be forgetting the Heavens,— as above, so below!— Stars beyond numbering, Planets unsuspected, Planets harboring Life! Morally Intelligent Life! an extra sign of the Zodiack, tho' of course running a bit narrower,— yet might it stretch out North to South, perhaps even all the width of the Semi-Circle,— a Dragon? a Pennsylvania Rifle? a Surveyors' Line?"

"Am I content with this? Was that your Question, Dixon?"

"Ah didn't say anything...?"

"Of course you did. You were muttering over there, I heard it."

"Happen I may have audibly wonder'd, how one with so much Investment in the matter of the Eleven Days, could be much offended when the Hysteresis be express'd in Degrees...?"

"And taken at the correct Scale," declares Captain Zhang, "what is there to choose? both are Experiences of that failure of perfect Return, that haunts all for whom Time elapses. In the runs of Lives, in Company as alone, what fails to return, is ever a source of Sorrow."

"And a lively Issue among the Metaphysickal I am sure," Mason attempts to beam, "the even yet more compelling Question, just now, however, being, Are you planning on growing particularly violent any time soon?"

"You cannot shame me. I have lost Shame, as one loses a Bore at an Assembly, creeping behind, whispering, 'You should have left her in Quebec. Your Fate was never to bide this long, amid this Continental Folly.— Folly that you, yourself, are now fallen into.' "

"Sounds like half the Axmen," notes Mason.

"The half who aren't past themselves over that Zsusza...?" adds Dixon.

"This quite exceeds, Sirs, the unsophisticated Grunting of Back-Woodsmen,— She was the captive Ward of my Life's great enemy. Tho' any sight of her, even at a distance, begin in Delight, soon enough shall *his* evil features emerge from, and replace, those belov'd ones...yet do I desire...not him, never him...yet...given such Terms, to desire *her*, clearly, I must transcend all Shame,— or be dissolv'd beneath it."

"And you're doing an excellent job!" exclaims Mason, "Isn't he, Lads?"

They return to Harlands' in early December, and get busy with the Royal Society's Degree of Latitude. No telling if they'll ever take the West Line west of Allegheny. All is in the hands of Sir William Johnson.

"Pleasant Gentleman," recalls Capt. Zhang. "Tho' what in distant parts be judg'd Madness, the wanderer may not say, or even know." Like others of the Party, he is apt now and then to drop in without prior Notice, at the Harlands', who are ever happy to have the Company. Advent sees the forming of something near a Club, for the purpose of Discourse upon the Topick of Christ's Birth, repairing after dinner to the Horse-Barn, Capt. Zhang and the Revd Cherrycoke being observ'd among those in faithful Attendance. The Astronomers prove less consistent, tho' willing to pronounce upon points of Chronology, or Astronomy,— or both, such as the Star that brought the Magi.

" 'Twas either a Conjunction of Planets," Dixon opines, "or a Comet."

"In seven B.C., according to Kepler, Jupiter and Saturn were conjunct three times,— and the next year, Mars join'd them," Mason declares. "No one who was out at night could have fail'd to notice that. It must have been the most spectacular Event in the Sky."

"Again, in perhaps twelve B.C.," Capt. Zhang points out, "appear'd the late Comet of 'fifty-nine, whose return to our Era Dr. Halley predicted,— the Tail, taper'd ever toward the Sun, thus able to direct your Magi,— or perhaps mine,— after each Sunset, to the West."

"Gentlemen, surely," the Rev^d, as mildly as he may, advances, "Christ was not born any time Before Christ?"

"If," says the Geomancer, "like all Christian nations, you accept the reckoning of Dionysius Exiguus,— then, Herod died in four B.C.,— yet the Gospels have him alive when Christ was born,— the taxation decree that brought Mary and Joseph to Bethlehem may've been as early as eight B.C. There are a number of these...strange inconsistencies."

"Unless the death of Herod be wrongly dated,— for Dennis the Meager, as *we* know him,— was an agent of God."

"God should've found another Agent," remarks Dixon, in the same side-of-the-mouth delivery as Mason.

"Mr. Mason!" the Rev^d turning to shake his Index.

"I didn't say that," Mason protests, "— Did I?"

66

"Just talk, Stig...." Spring Winds howl outside the Tent. Mrs. Eggslap is in an Emerald-green Sacque with Watteau pleats, all disarrang'd at the moment, as is her Hair. A stout Candle of Swedish Wax burns in a Candlestick of Military design.

"To Thorfinn Karlsefni's settlement at Hop," relates Stig, who in lieu of smoking a Stogie, has begun to inspect his Ax-blade for flaws perceptible to him alone,— "at the mouth of one of the Rivers of Vineland, the Skrællings come, to trade pelts for milk. What they really want are weapons, but Karlsefni has forbidden anyone to sell them. Upon the second visit, Karlsefni's wife Gudrid is inside the House, tending Snorri the baby, when despite the new Palisado and the Sentries, a strange, small Woman comes in, announc'd only by her Shadow, fair-hair'd, pale, with the most enormous eyes Gudrid has ever seen, and asks, 'What is your Name?'

" 'My name is Gudrid,' replies Gudrid. 'What is your name?'

" 'My name is Gudrid,' she whispers, staring out of those Eyes. And all at once there is a violent crash, and the woman vanishes,— at the same Instant, outside, one of the Northmen, struggling with one of the Skrællings, who has tried to seize his weapon, kills him. With terrible cries, the other Skrællings run away,— the Northmen decide not to wait their return, but to go out to them, upon the Cape. The Sea roars against the Land, the Sea-Wind bears away the cries of the Wounded, Blood leaps, Men fall, most of those slain are Skrællings, their Bodies splay'd and vaporous in the Cold. None but Gudrid ever saw the woman whose visit announc'd this first Act of American murder, and the collapse of Vineland the Good,— in another year Karlsefni's outpost would be gone, as if what they had done out upon the Headland, under the torn Banners of the Clouds, were too terrible, and any question of who had prevail'd come to matter ever less, as Days went on, whilst the residue of Dishonor before the Gods and Heroes would never be scour'd away. Thereafter they were men and women in Despair, many of whom, bound for Home, miscalculated the Route and landed in Ireland, where they were cap-tur'd and enslav'd."

"Oh, Stig."

"These are Tales of the Westward Escapes, of Helgi and Finnbogi, and Thorstein the Swarthy, and Biarni Heriulfsson. Rogues and Projectors and Fugitives, they went without pretext, no Christ, no Grail, no expec-tation beyond each Day's Turnings, to be haunted by Ghosts more mate-rial, less merciful, than any they'd left at their backs.

"They found here, again, as in Greenland and Iceland, Firths and Fjords,— something Immense had harrow'd and then flooded all these Coasts.— "

"So that's why the Swedes chose to sail between the Capes of Delaware,— they thought it was another Fjord! You fellows do like a nice Fjord, it seems. Instead, they found Pennsylvania!"

"Some Surprize?"

"Some Surprize.— Stig?"

"Yah, Pa-tience?"

"Do we really need the Ax right here, like this?"

This Season, hanging just over the Horizon, spreading lightless Mantle and pale fingers across the sky, the great Ghost of the woods has been whis-pering to them,— tho' Reason suggests the Wind,— "No...no more...no further." Such are the Words the Surveyors have been able to bring to their waking Bank-side, from this great fluvial Whisper.

"Reminds me of a Lass from Escombe...," remarks Dixon. Jointly and severally, they have continu'd to find regions of Panick fear all along the Line,— Dixon, in the great Cave whose Gothicity sends his partner into such Raptures, but wondering, in some Fretfulness, what might be living in it *large enough,* to need so much space,— whereas 'tis Mason who stands sweating and paralyz'd before the great Death-shade of the Forest between Savage Mountain and Little Yochio Geni, "...a wild waste," he will write, "composed of laurel swamps, dark vales of Pine through which I believe the Sun's rays never penetrated," which evokes from Dixon, at his lengthiest, "Great uncommon lot of Trees about...?" Together, they are apt to be come upon at any stretch of the Chain, no telling when, by the next unwelcome Visitor that waits them. Nor,— tho' Night-fall is traditional,— will any Hour be exempt. This is none of the lesser Agents, the White Women or Black Dogs, but the Presence itself, unbounded, whose Visitations increase in number as the Party, for the last time, moves West.

One Day, having fail'd to fall asleep, and, as they often did, continue to sleep, through the nightly death of the Sun,— up instead, faces vermilion'd, amid the clank and bustle of preparations for the evening Mess,— Mason and Dixon hear the Voice, stirring the tops of Trees in a black swift Smear down the Mountainside and into the Shade, more to plead than to pronounce,— "You are gone too far, from the Post Mark'd West."

It is there. Neither Surveyor may take any comfort in Suspicions of joint Insanity. "Thankee," Mason mutters back to it, "as if we didn't already know."

"Myself...? Ah'd love to see the canny old Post again," adds Dixon, helpfully. They know by now where they are, not only in Miles, Chains, and Feet, but respecting as well the Dragon of the Land, according to which anyplace beyond the Summit of the Alleghenies, wherever the water flows West, into the Continental Unknown, lies too far from the Countryside where, quietly, unthreaten'd, among the tall gray stalks of the girdl'd trees, beneath Roofs tarr'd against the Rain, the Wives knead and flour, and the Dough's Rising is a Miniature of the great taken Breath of the Day,...and where voices in the Wind are assum'd into the singing of the Congregations, the Waggon's rumbling upon the roads of pack'd and beaten earth, the lowing, the barking, the solitary rifle-shot, close to supper-time, from over in the next Valley. Here the Surveyors,— as many of the Party,— have come away, as if backward in Time, beyond the Range of the furthest spent Ball, of the last friendly Pennsylvania

Rifle. The Implication of the ghostly Speech is clear to them both.— They will soon be proceeding, if indeed they are not already, with all Guarantees of Safety suspended,— as if Whatever spar'd them years ago, at Sea, were now presenting its Bill. Here, the next Interdiction, when it comes, will be not with the clamorous stench of Sea-Battle, but quieter than wind, final as Stone.

Abdominal Fear and Thoracick Indignation at the same moment visit both Surveyors. To have come this far…and yet, by the Scale it has assum'd, the Denial is so clearly meant to be heeded….

Be they heedful or not, 1767 will be their last year upon the Line. Conditions hitherto shapeless are swiftly reduc'd to Certainty. Having waited upon Sir William Johnson to negotiate with deputies from the Six Nations, assembl'd at German Flat, upon Mohawk, as to the continuation of the Line beyond the Allegheny Crest, the Surveyors loiter week upon week in Philadelphia, Drinking at Clubs, dancing with City Belles at Shore-parties, along the sand Beaches, playing two-handed Whist, their judgment in ev'rything from Fish to Pipe-Fellows grown perilously unreliable, as the Air oppressively damp,— howbeit, they get a late start this Year, not reaching the Allegheny Front until July, a full year since they left off their Progress West. Sir William Johnson is to be paid £500 for his Trouble.

Their last Spring out, passing by way of Octarara, they find the Redzingers and their neighbors all at a barn-raising nearby. A geometrick Maze of Beams, a-bang with men in black Hats. Luise waves to Peter up straddling a lower Girt, smiling over at one of the Yoder Boy's Hardware-Joaks. Mason and Dixon drop ceremonial Plumb-lines here and there, and Capt. Zhang pronounces the location acceptably within the Parameters of his *Luo-Pan*. He has re-join'd the Party after a mysterious Absence over the Winter, during which the Cobra-Brain Pearl he'd shown them has deflected at last the will of the Jesuit. Thro' its influence, there had appear'd in P. Zarpazo's path an irresistible offer to travel to Florida and be one of the founders of a sort of Jesuit Pleasure-Garden, of Dimensions unlimited by neighboring Parcels, tho' the Topick of Alligators has so far adroitly remain'd unaddress'd….

There are Parsnip Fritters, breaded fried Sausages, Rhubarb Dumplings, Souse and Horse-radish, Ham-and-Apple Schnitz und

Knepp, Hickory-Nut Cake and Shoofly Pies. Armand, bravely spruc'd up, even drops by,— tho' his heart, he will assure anyone who asks, is desolated,— with a strangely festive Pudding he has whisk'd together, loaded with Currants, candied Violets, dried apricots, peaches, and cherries chopp'd fine with almonds and rejuvenated in Raspberry Brandy. He is surrounded immediately by various small Children.

Luise leads her Husband over, by the hand with the sacred Finger, and the men meet formally at last. Armand finds himself looking upward at this very large German, who continues to grip the equally oversiz'd Hammer with which he has been whacking at Beams and Plates all day,— meanwhile regarding Armand as a Boy might a Bug. Or perhaps—

"How is the Duck?" Peter blurts. "She told me about it. Luise."

Armand almost blurts back, "The Duck is excellent," but wagering it is a religious question, replies, "I see the Duck seldom of late. Perhaps, by now, she has taken in her charge so many other Souls as troubl'd as my own, that there remains less time for me,— perhaps, as she has continu'd upon her own way, I have even pass'd altogether from her Care."

"But, Time, surely, by now, no longer matters to her?" Peter now curious, "— no longer passes the same way, I mean."

The Frenchman shrugs. "Yet we few, fortunate Objects of her Visits, remain ever tight in Time's Embrace," sighing, as if for the Duck alone....

"She, then,...enters and leaves the Stream of Time as she likes?" Luise, tossing her eyes vigorously skyward, slides away to attend to an Oven-Load of loaves and biscuits. The lads, whose flow of saliva has begun to escape the best efforts of their lower lips to contain it, proceed to eat their way from one end of a long trestle table to the other, thro' Hams and Fowl, Custards and Tarts, fried Noodles and Opossum Alamodes, all the while deep in discourse upon the deepest Topicks there are.

The instruments arrive on the seventh of July at Cumberland, throng'd and a-blare with skin-wearers and cloth-wearers ever mingling, Indian and White, French and Spanish. Ladies pack Pistols and Dirks, whilst coarser Sisters prove to be saintlier than expected. Poison'd by strong

Drink, Pioneers go bouncing Cheese-and-Skittle-wise from one Pedestrian to another, Racoon-Tails askew, daring Hooves and Wheel-Rims, and the impatience of a Street-ful of Business-Folk who must mind their Watch-Time, often to the Minute, all day long. Riflemen sit out on the Porches of Taverns and jingle their Vent-Picks in time to the musick of African Slaves, who play upon Banjos and Drums here, far into the Night. The Place smells of Heart-wood, and Animals, and Smoke. Great Waggons with white Canopies, styl'd "Conestogas," form up at the western edge of town, an uncommon Stir, passionate shouting, Herds filling the Street, as one by one each Machine is brought 'round, and its Team of Horses hitch'd on,— proceeding then to the end of a waiting line, where all stand, be it snow or summer, patient as cows at milking time.

"Thing about out here," cackles Thomas Cresap, when they go to pay him a visit, "is it's perfect. It's 'at damn U-topia's what it is, and nobody'll own to it. No King, no Governor, nought but the Sheriff, whose Delight is to leave you alone, for as long as you do not actively seek his attention, which he calls 'fuckin' with him.' As long as you don't 'fuck' with him, he don't 'fuck' with you! Somethin', hah? About as intrusive as Authority ought to git, in m' own humble Opinion, o' course. And there's to be sure the usual rotten apple among Sheriffs, that, 'scuse me Gents, Got-damn'd Lancaster Sheriff...Old Smith?...We had pitch'd musket battles with him and his Army of Pennite Refuse. 'Course back there you probably only heard their side of it."

"Mr. Sam Smith entertain'd us with an account, at Pechway, two, perhaps three years ago."

"We sure entertain'd him, that night."

"Said it was fifty-five to fourteen...?"

"Close enough."

"Call'd you the Beast of Baltimore."

"That I was and the Maryland Monster as well, and I'm even more dangerous today than I was then, for there's little I fear in this World, and nothing I won't undertake, long as these damn'd Knees don't betray me, that is. Ask any of these Louts how I do with a Pistol. Eh?" He produces a Highwayman's model, with a short, rounded-off grip and a twelve-inch octagonal Barrel. "All flash, you say, meant but to strike Fear,— "

"I didn't say that," says Mason. "Nor I...?" adds Dixon.

"Here, you,— Michael's one,— Get out there about to the first Fence and throw this,— here, this Jug up in the air for the old Bible Patriarch, 'at's a good boy."

"But it's full of— "

"Whatever your name is,— now we don't want to bore our guests, do we, with the details of the Tax Laws and how they differ as between the two Provinces, so just git your wrong-side-the-creek arse *out* to that Fence— " The boy is running, already halfway there. Cresap gazes after him. "See that Attitude? Don't know where he gets it. Just as happy to have a Sheriff about, if you want the truth. I thought I was an untamable kid, but that young Zack, there,— "

"Ready, Grampa!"

Patch, Ball, Grease, Rod, Powder fine and coarse, all in a strange blur, the fastest loading job anyone there, including the Rev^d, who's seen a number of them, can recollect. "Heads up!" hollers Cresap. The Jug sails slowly end-over-end in an Arc skyward, as Cresap, arm straight, aims, tracks and fires, whereupon, being struck, the Jug explodes in a great Ball of Flame whose Wave of Heat fans their astonish'd Faces.

"Sam'l Smith tell you about that one? That Army o' his started off with eighty-five men, but thirty ran away after the first couple of these Jugs exploded, so it was more of an even fight. I took a few precious Breaths to curse myself for ever settling so close to the limits of Maryland, yet, as I foolishly trusted, south of the Forty-Degree Parallel,— and wagering that the real Susquehanna would prove a more potent Boundary than any invisible Line drawn by Astronomers or Surveyors,— oh, that's right you're one of each in't you, so sorry,— and that surely no Sheriff of Lancaster would mount the naval Expedition he did. Gawwwd, Boats? There was sailboats and there was rafts, there was Battoes oar'd by match'd twenty-six-man African slave crews, there was even *Sailing Ships* out there upon broad Susquehanna that night in the dark of the Moon, thirty years ago now, but I'm no closer to forgetting it. For most of the settlers about, in the places they'd come from, troops of Horsemen upon the Roads late at night were far from rare,— but being invaded out of that midnight River, by a small Brigade,— betray'd by me own Bound'ry Line, as ye'd say, taken by total Surprize,— I suppose once in ev'ry lifetime it's necessary. They descended upon my Land with all the pitilessness of an Army in full Sunlight, and proceeded to build a camp and dig in to obsess us. And 'twas my young Daniel who was Hero of the Battle."

The younger Cresap, now forty, who's been eating enthusiastically though in Silence, pauses and shrugs. "Active sort of Lad," his father says. "Ran about making one mistake after another. They catch him, set him out of their way,— when they're not looking he finds their Powder, wraps what he can in his Handkerchief, throws it in the Fire."

Daniel grimaces, shaking his head. "Dove for cover, waited,— Nothing. The Handkerchief got a little charr'd. Then they were *really* angry,— what a sight they made, trying to retrieve that powder out of the Fire. Ev'rybody waiting for some great Blast. I didn't know if I should be laughing, or pleading for my Life. 'Twas their Call, as it is ever."

"Our house burn'd down, one of us murder'd with his hands in the air,— " Father and Son are exchanging Looks, "the rest dispers'd into the Woods,— they took me back across Susquehanna to stand trial in that dismal,— let me put it this way. If America was a Person,— and it sat down,— Lancaster Town would be plunged, into a Darkness unbreathable.

"On the way over the River, I was able to put one of my bold Captors in the water, where they all set upon him with Oars and Rifle-stocks, thinking 'twas me, some of them in their eagerness losing their balance and falling in as well. I couldn't get the Ropes off, and was trying to stay *out* of the River, in this water-borne Panick of Oxen. To be fair, 'twas vile Sam Smith sav'd my life, for most of them would as soon have tipp'd me in and let me sink. 'Twas only when we got to Columbia, across the River, that they plac'd me in chains, though I did knock the Blacksmith cold with 'em,— the Shame,— a Brother-immigrant, who more than any should have known better than to manacle another such, at the bidding of some jump'd-up Pea-wit working for the Penns. Sirs, that is my side of it. How does it match up with that of Smith, who must've known that sooner or later you'd see me?"

"He seem'd not quite as hale as you," Dixon recalls.

"Can I forgive him his Life? I've done with all my crying about that. And howbeit, I was releas'd at last,— Justice not so much prevailing, as Injustice, having early exhausted itself, retiring,— and leaving it to

640

Providence as to Sam'l Smith's capacity for further Harm outside of Lancaster County, my Family and I removed Westward, settling in Antietam, at that time upon the Frontier,— where, by trading honestly enough in skins and furs, we soon found ourselves at the Verge of a Fortune. Alas, our shipload of Pelts, upon which we had borrow'd heavily, approaching the Channel, was surpriz'd by one of Monseer's Privateers and like that, ta'en. Our creditors all show'd up in a single stern-faced crowd, so many that some were oblig'd to walk and stand in animal shit. I wav'd this very High-Toby Special about, appeal'd to their Shame, but we were all too perilously extended,— the seat by Potowmack, which at last I had begun to feel was mine, was thereupon seiz'd as pitilessly as our Fortune at Sea, and we must again reassemble, and take up our Lives and move West, eventually settling here, where Potowmack forks, and ways converge, from all over the Compass, and the Fort lies less than a day away. Perhaps I am not meant to govern a great Manor, like the scalp-stealing Fiend Shelby. Perhaps I am ready for this sort of Village life. Third-time-Lucky sort of thing."

"Nor must we ever be moving again." It is Megan, another of Michael's batch. Hair all a-fire, spirited, no respect at all for Traditional Authority. She knows how to read, and she is reading him Tox's *Pennsylvaniad.*

" 'Twas after Braddock fell, that times out here got very difficult indeed. Nemacolin and I put that road in, years earlier. Chopp'd damn near ev'ry tree. We were th' original Mason and Dixon. We cut our Visto too narrow for poor Braddock, but who was expecting an Army? We went by Compass. I felt that cold magick in the Needle, Sirs. Something very powerful, from far beyond this Forest, 'Whose Bark had never felt the Bit's Assault,' as Tox puts it so well. As for Nemacolin, I believe that he liv'd in a World where Magick is in daily operation, and the magnetick Compass surely is small Turnips."

"What will the Mohawks that are to join us think of our Instruments, then?" Dixon wonders.

"They'll be curious. Good idea to satisfy them on all questions. Wagering that they may not ask the fatal one,— 'Why are you doing this?' If that happens, your only hope is not to react. 'Tis the first step into the Quagmire. If you be fortunate enough to emerge, 'twill not be with your previous Optimism intact."

"Why *am* I doing this?" Mason inquires aloud of no one in particular, "— Damme, that is an intriguing Question. I mean, I suppose I could say it's for the Money, or to Advance our Knowledge of,— "

"Eeh,— regard thaself, thou're *reacting*," says Dixon. "Just what Friend Cresap here said not to do,— thou're doing it...?"

"Whine not, as the Stoick ever says? You might yourself advert to it profitably,— "

"What Crime am I charg'd with now, ever for Thoo, how convenient?"

"Wait, wait, you're saying I don't take blame when I should, that I'm ever pushing it off onto you?"

"Wasn't I that said it," Dixon's Eyebrows headed skyward, nostrils a-flare with some last twinkling of Geniality.

"I take the blame when it's my fault," cries Mason, "but it's never my Fault,— and *that's* not my Fault, either! Or to put it another way,— "

"Aye, tell the Pit-Pony too, why don't tha?"

"Children, children," admonishes the Patriarch, "let us be civil, here. Am I not a Justice of the Peace, after all? Now,— which is the Husband?"

This is greeted by rude Mirth, including, presently, Dixon's, though not even a chuckle from Mason, who can only, at best, stop glowering. This is taken as high Hilarity, and the "Corn" continues to pass 'round, which Mason is oblig'd to drink,— the unglaz'd Rim unwipably wet from the loose-lipp'd Embraces of Mouths that may recently have been anywhere, not excluding,— from the look of the Company,— live elements of the Animal Kingdom.

Dixon, being a Grain person, is having a generally cheerier Drinking Life than Mason, as, the further West they go, the more distill'd Grains, and the fewer Wines, are to be found,— until at last even to mention Wine aloud is to be taken for a French Spy. At Cumberland, as yet, Mason hasn't dar'd ask,— tho' if it's to be found anywhere, 'twill be at the Market, ev'ry day, Sundays as well, lying spread up to the gray stone Revetments, beneath the black guns, the shadows of the Bastions, the lookouts curiously a-stare, Indians from the far interior with not only furs to trade, but medicinal herbs too, and small gold artifacts,— drinking-cups, bangles, charms, from fabl'd Lands to South and West. Upland Virginians come with shoes by the waggonload, Philadelphia Mantua-makers with stitch-by-stitch Copies of the Modes of London and Paris, Book-sellers from the brick ravines of Frederick, with the latest confessions from Covent-Garden, Piemen and Milkmaids and Women of the Night, life stories spread upon blankets, chuck-farthing games in the Ditch, ev'rywhere sounds of metal, a-clang in the Forges, squeaking rhythmi-cally in the mud street,— bells in the church, iron nails pour'd in jin-gling heaps, Specie in and out of Purses. The skies are Biblically lit, bright yellow and slate-blue and purple, and the munitions waggons, whose horses in a former life were humans who traffick'd in Land, pass, going and coming, laden and empty, darkly gleaming in long streaks down their Sides, from what storm-light the condition of the Sky will allow...Dogs run free, feel hungry and accordingly impatient, often get together in packs, and hunt.

"Has no one heard of the Black Dog in these parts, then...?" wonders Dixon.

"The South Mountain Dog? He'd best step cautious 'round my Snake."

"Here's half a Crown says your Snake won't last a minute with my Ralph."

"Done, ye Bugger." No one of course is asking the Dogs, who would prefer sleep or a good meal. But these packs are running according to different plans. Life here is not quite so indulgent or safe as back East, in the Brick Towns. There, you forage for food already dead. Here, they encourage you to answer to the Wolf's Commandments to kill what you eat and eat what you kill. And somehow to try to resist the Jackal within, ever crying for carrion. Not all do. At the Fort you may always find com-missary garbage, tidbits from officers who want Favors,— more tempta-tion than a dog ought to resist. Ev'ry Dog upon the Post, at one time and another, has succumb'd. This helps enhance the Harmony within the Pack, for they are sharing a Sin.

Snake, who has a reputation as a Ratter, is less fond of eating his Prey, than of killing them. Chasing Rats is a good Pastime, combining Speed and the art of getting a step ahead, as well as perfecting solitary fighting skills, for he cannot depend on the Pack being there every time he might need it so, and he figures that if he can slay a rat, he can slay a Squirrel with no trouble, up a tree, down a hole, the idea being never to let it get there,— to interdict.

When Mason approaches him in a friendly way, he decides to trust him, rather than take the trouble to bare his Teeth for nothing. All about, the humans and their children come and go, eating upon the run, flirting, having disputes about money. The scents of food, small fires, and other Dogs are ev'rywhere.

"Hul-lo, Snake...?" the man down on his Haunches, keeping a fair distance, no wish to intrude. Snake raises his head inquiringly. "I'm assuming that Norfolk Terriers, like other breeds, maintain a Web of Communication among 'em, and I was but curious after the whereabouts these Days of the Learnèd English Dog, or as I believe he is also known, Fang."

Snake ponders,— his policy with strangers, indeed with his very Owner all these years, being never to reveal his own Power of Speech, for he's known others, including the credulous Fang in fact, who've trusted Humans with the Secret only to find themselves that very Evening in some Assembly Room full of Smoke and Noise, and no promise of Dinner till after they've perform'd. Not for Snake, thank you all the same. Something must be getting thro' by way of his Eyebrows, however, for the Man is now smiling, lopsidedly, trying to seem cognizant. "You are said to be fond of Rats. Our Expedition Chef, M. Allègre, is preparing, as we speak, his world-famous *Queues du Rat aux Haricots,* if that be any inducement."

More like an Emetick, Snake thinks, but does not utter. "Fond of Rats,"— who is this Idiot, anyway?

"All I'd require would be a Nod, after I say,— has he gone North? South? You haven't nodded.— East? Then, only West remaining, I'll take that as a Nod, shall I..."

"Mason," Dixon looming, vaporous of Ale, the bright Glacis behind him, "Are tha quite comfortable with the Logick of thah'?"

The man grumbles to his feet. "Snake, Snake, Snake. If there remain'd a farthing candle between us and Monongahela yet unsnuff'd, be certain, Ensign Enthusiasm here would find and snuff it. Yes once again Dixon you have sav'd me from my own poor small Hopes how relentless, thanks ever so much."

"Happen thy Impetuosity be no Candle, rather an ill-consider'd Fire...?"

From watching Humans out here over the Course of several Winters, Snake recognizes between these two a mark'd degree of Acidity. They walk away now, gesturing and shouting at each other. Snake puts his head back upon his Paws and sighs thro' his Nose. Old Fang. Who after all could claim to know Fang's true Story? Some saying he did it to himself,— others blaming the Humans who profited from his Strange Abilities. 'Tis not Snake's way to inform on another Dog, and withal, who knows what that Human was up to, wanting to see him after so much time?

The Surveyors face each other before a hazy Ground of blue Distance and Ascension,— the blue Silences that await them. "I know something is out there, that may not happen till we arrive.... I am a Northern Brit, a semi-Scot, a Gnomes' Intimate,— we never err in these things."

"Gone too far, as usual. When will he learn. Never."

"I know what tha wish to happen, what tha hope to find. 'Twould be the only thing that could've brought thee to America."

"And you say you think you can feel...?"

"Don't know what it is. Herd of Buffalo as easily as Light from Elsewhere,— something of about that Impact."

"You promise,— you're not just trying to be encouraging, in that cheery way you put on and off like a Wig...?"

"I wouldn't joak about thah'...? Not with thee...? With young Hickman perhaps, or Tom Hynes,— "

"Who are,— what? twelve? ten? They think they'll live forever, of course you can all joak about it."

The Gents locate an Ale-Barrel in the Shade. A Virginia Boy, seven or eight or thereabouts, comes running up to quiz with them. "I can show you something no one has ever seen, nor will anyone ever see again."

Mason squints in Thought. "There's no such thing."

"Ha-ha!" The lad produces an unopen'd Goober Pea-Shell, exhibiting it to both Astronomers before cracking it open to reveal two red Pea-Nuts within,— "Something no-one has seen,"— popping them in his mouth and eating them,— "and no one will see again." The Gents, astonish'd, for a moment look like a match'd pair of Goobers themselves.

67

Within the Fortnight, they are join'd by a Delegation of Indians, sent by Sir William Johnson, most of them Mohawk fighters, who will remain with the Party till the end of October, when, reaching a certain Warrior Path, they will inform the Astronomers that their own Commissions from the Six Nations allow them to go no further,— with its implied Corollary, that this Path is as far West as the Party, the Visto, and the Line, may proceed.

This will not come as an unforeseen blow, for Hugh Crawfford, accompanying the Indians, informs the Surveyors of it first thing. "Sort of like Death,— you know it's out there ahead, tho' not when, so you'll ever be hoping for one more Day, at least.

"We'll be crossing Indian trails with some regularity,— these don't trouble the Mohawks in particular. But ahead of us now, there's a Track, running athwart the Visto, north and south, known as the Great Warrior Path. This is not merely an important road for them,— but indeed one of the major High-ways of all inland America. So must it also stand as a boundary line,— for when we come to it, we shall not be allow'd to cross it, and go on."

"It'll take us a quarter of an hour. We'll clean up ev'ry trace of our Passage,— what are they worried about, the running surface? their deerskin shoes? we'll re-surface it for them, we'll give 'em Moccasin Vouchers,— "

"Mr. Mason, they treat this Trail as they would a River,— they settle both sides of it, so as to have it secure,— they need the unimpeded

Flow. Cutting it with your Visto would be like putting an earthen Dam across a River."

"And how far from Ohio?" with a slight break upon the word.

"Some thirty, forty miles," Crawfford as kindly as he can, having himself a history of disappointments out here, again and again, "yet the Path is over Monongahela," silently adding, "*Socko Stoombray,*" as he's heard the Western Spanish say,— one gets used to it. His is a face, however, difficult for Mason, or for many, to read much Sentiment in, so written upon is it, by so many years of hard Sunrises, Elements outside and in, left to rage as they might. "It's a fine road, I've had to use it now and then, if the wind and moon are right, you can fly along.... Sometimes they chas'd me, sometimes it was me after them,— we've chased these d——'d mountains through and through, canoeing for our lives down these mean little rivers,— made some respectable Fortunes, lost 'em in the space of a rifle-shot, as many of us taken or destroy'd over the years as got back safe. Ups and downs steeper'n the Alleghenies, Gents,— I've been captur'd, I've escap'd. We've been friends and enemies. They owe me years out of my life, parts of me not working so good,— you'd have to ask them what they think I owe back.— But I know 'em,— not in any deep or magickal way,— rather as you may know those that you've shar'd matters of life and death with,— and although on paper it may look like only a few short steps from the Warpath to the River Ohio, I beg you both, be most careful,— for Distance is not the same here, nor is Time."

"At least they told us beforehand...?" Dixon supposes.

Watching an Indian slip back into the forest is like seeing a bird take wing,— each moves vertiginously into an Element Mason, all dead weight, cannot enter. The first time he saw it, it made him dizzy. The spot in the Brush where the Indian had vanish'd vibrated, as an eddying of no color at all. Contrariwise, watching an Indian emerge, is to see a meaningless Darkness eddy at length into a Face, and a Face, moreover, that Mason *remembers.*

He grows apprehensive and soon kickish. "I respect them, and their unhappy history. But they put me in a State of Anxiety unnatural," he complains to the Rev[d], "out of all Measure. Unto the Apparition of Phantoms."

"How's that?"

"I see and even touch things that cannot possibly be there. Yet there they are."

"Can you give me examples?"

"There may lie a Problem, for I am closely sworn not to."

"Makes advising you difficult, of course."

"Yes, and some of them are Pips, too. Shame, really."

"Whilst you so amiably quiz with me," says the Rev[d], "Mr. Dixon seems quite content in their company."

"Who, Young Jollification? drinks with priests, roisters with Pygmies,— aye, I've seen that. What cares has he, as long as the Tobacco and Spirits hold out? And withal, throughout, from first Sip to empty Bottle, he is troubl'd by no least Inkling of Sin, nor question of Fear,— he is far too innocent for any of that. No,— 'tis I who am anxious before the advent of these Visitors how Strange, who belong so *without separation,* to this Country cryptick and perilous,...passing, tho' never close, as shadowy and serene as Deities of Forest or River.... So!" cries Mason, turning desperately to the Visitors, "— You're Indians!"

"Mason, that may not be quite— "

As Hugh Crawfford is translating,— they hope that's what he's doing,— the Mohawk Chiefs Hendricks, Daniel, and Peter, the Onondaga Chiefs Tanadoras, Sachehaandicks, and Tondeghho,— the Warriors Nicholas, Thomas, Abraham, Hanenhereyowagh, John, Sawattiss, Jemmy, and John Sturgeon,— the Women Soceena and Hanna,— all are examining Mason and Dixon, and the Instruments,— having earlier observ'd the Sector arriving in its pillow'd Waggon, mindfully borne by the five-shilling Hands, impressive in its assembl'd Size. Learning that 'tis us'd only late at Night, some, presently, are there each time to watch, as the Astronomers lie beneath the Snout, the Brass elongating into the Heavens, the great curv'd Blade, the Sweeps of Stars converging at the Eye, so easily harm'd even at play, hostage, like this, beneath the Instrument pois'd upon it....

The first time they see the Sector brought into the Meridian, the Indians explain, that for as long as anyone can remember, the Iroquois Nations as well, have observ'd Meridian Lines as Boundaries to separate them one from another.

"Not Rivers, nor Crest-Lines?" Capt. Zhang is amaz'd. "What did the Jesuits think of that?"

"We learn'd it of them."

"One Story," Hendricks adds. "Others believe 'twas not the Jesuits, but powerful Strangers, much earlier."

"Who?"

"The same," declares Zhang, "whose Interests we have continu'd to run across Evidence of,...who for the Term of their Absence are represented by Jesuits, Encyclopedists, and the Royal Society, who see to these particular Routings of *Sha* upon the Surface of the Planet by way of segments of Great or Lesser Circles."

"Shall we resign our Commissions? Is that what you're saying?"

"Then somebody else does the same thing," the Geomancer shrugs.

"Then tha'll go to work on them, for thy Commission is to stop it, not so? All thah' about Zarpazo was Snuff. He thah' would hang, after all, his Dog first gives out that he is mad."

"Excuse me," Mason says, "I think that's 'He who would *hang his Dog*, first gives out that he is mad.' "

"Why would anyone hang his Dog? No, 'tis he who wishes to hang, sends his Dog to run 'round acting peculiar, perhaps wearing Signs about its neck, or strangely costum'd, so that whenever its owner *does* hang, people can say, 'Yese see, 'twas Madness, for the Dog gave out he was mad.' "

"Yes that would all no doubt be true if that were how it goes, but 'tis not how it goes at all. It goes..."

And so on (records the Rev[d]). This actually very interesting Discussion extended till well past Midnight, that Night. If I did lose full Consciousness now and then, 'twas less from their issueless Bickering, than from the Demands of the Day, as part of the Tribute we must pay, merely to inhabit it.

That night I dream'd,— I pray 'twas Dream,— that I flew, some fifty to an hundred feet above the Surface, down the Visto, straight West. First dream I had that ever smell'd of anything,— cut wood, sap, woodsmoke, cook-tent cooking, horses and stock,— I could see below the glow of the coal we cut from outcrops so shining black they must be the outer walls of Hell, almost like writing upon the long unscrolling of the land, useful about the waggoners' Forge, a curiosity beneath Mr. McClean's Oven, and to Mr. Dixon, who knows his way 'round a bit of Coal, a quotidian delight. His brother George learn'd years ago how to make Coal yield a Vapor that burns with a blue flame,— and with a bit of ingenuity with kettles and reeds, and clay to seal the Joints, why it may even be done in the midst of this wilderness, as Mr. Dixon promptly demonstrated. And that is how I verify 'tis no Dream, but a form of Transport,— that unearthly blue glow in the otherwise lightless Desert night. The Indians come to look, but they never comment. They have seen it before, and they have never seen it before.

The Line makes itself felt,— thro' some Energy unknown, ever are we haunted by that Edge so precise, so near. In the Dark, one never knows. Of course I am seeking the Warrior Path, imagining myself an heroick Scout. We all feel it Looming, even when we're awake, out there ahead some-place, the way you come to feel a River or Creek ahead, before anything else,— sound, sky, vegetation,— may have announced it. Perhaps 'tis the very deep sub-audible Hum of its Traffic that we feel with an equally undiscover'd part of the Sensorium,— does it lie but over the next Ridge? the one after that? We have Mileage Estimates from Rangers and Run-ners, yet for as long as its Distance from the Post Mark'd West remains unmeasur'd, nor is yet recorded as Fact, may it remain, a-shimmer, among the few final Pages of its Life as Fiction.

Were the Visto to've cross'd the Warrior Path and simply proceeded West, then upon that Cross cut and beaten into the Wilderness, would have sprung into being not only the metaphysickal Encounter of Ancient Savagery with Modern Science, but withal a civic Entity, four Corners, each with its own distinguishable Aims. Sure as Polaris, the first struc-ture to go up would be a Tavern,— the second, another Tavern. Setting up Businesses upon the approaches, for miles along each great Conduit, there would presently arrive waggon-smiths, stock auctioneers, gun-makers, feed and seed merchants, women who dance in uncommon Attire, Lanthorns that burn all night, pavements of strange metaling brought from afar, along with all the other heavy cargo that now streams in both directions, the Fleets of Conestoga Waggons, ceaseless as the fabl'd Herds of Buffalo, further west,— sunlit canopies a-billow like choir-sung promises of Flight, their unspar'd Wheels rumbling into the soft dairy night-falls of shadows without edges, tho' black as city soot.

Festive Lanthorns, by contrast, shine thro' the Glass of the swifter passenger conveyances that go streaking by above the Fields, one after another, all hours of the day and night.... Aloft, these carry their wheels with them, barely scuff'd by Roadway, to be attached whenever needed. Singing and Gaiety may be heard passing thro' the Airy Gulfs above. Newcomers to the Ley-borne Life are advis'd not to look up, lest, seiz'd by its proper Vertigo, they fall into the Sky.— For' t has happen'd more than once,— drovers and Army officers swear to it,— as if Gravity along the Visto, is become locally less important than Rapture.

One night, yet east of Laurel Hill, Mason asks, "Where is your Spirit Village?" The Indians all gesture, straight out the Line, West. "God dwells there? At the Horizon?" They nod.

"And where is yours?" asks Hendricks. Mason rather uncertainly indicates Up.

Dixon cocks a merry eye. "What's this,— only at the Zenith...? Not something a little more...all-encompassing?" waving an arm to illustrate.

Surveyors and Indians have been out looking at the Stars, discussing the possibility of Life upon other Worlds, whether and how much our Awareness of such Life might figure in our Awareness of God, God, then, *vis-à-vis* Gods, and other Topicks, of such interest to my Profession that I felt oblig'd to listen in.

"What puzzles us about Star-gazing," says Daniel, "is that you are ever attending them, and never they you."

"Have They attended you?" Mason unprepar'd to believe it.

"Many times. Never all at once, usually but one at a time,— yet, they do come to us."

"Sounds like Fishing," supposes Dixon.

The Indians like that. "Sky-fishing," says Hanenhereyowagh.

"Shouldn't someone explain about the Bait?" young Jemmy whispers, loud enough to receive a number of Looks from his Party, ranging from amus'd to annoy'd.

"Eeh," Dixon encourages him. "Tell me and I'll give thee the secrets of my Amazing Bread Lure, famous the length of the Wear and beyond, for bringing them in."

"You spoke of it first," Hendricks reminds the Lad.

" 'Tis the Safety of your Soul," says Jemmy. He has lately been out upon his Trial of Passage from child to adult, having found his Protector,— a Bear, who walk'd toward him on her back feet, with her Arm extended in the precise Six-Nations Gesture for Peace. Now, however perilous the Trails may grow, She can be summon'd in an Instant. "Yet I had to risk all,— to bring her in, I had to fasten all that I was, upon a Line I could not break,— and wait, sleepless, starving not only with my Body but with— "

("Parsonickal interpolation!" shouts Uncle Lomax.

" '— my Spirit.' — What, Lomax, may not a Mohawk youth possess a needful Spirit?

" 'Thank thee, Jemmy,' at any rate, Dixon now replied. 'My Bread Lure's a bit safer than thah', and here's how it's done,— ' Whereupon they withdrew out of my hearing, so that regretfully I quite miss'd the Information."

"Oh, Coz, what Stuff."

"I have witness'd this Bait in action, Madam. I saw Dixon bring in fish not even native to the Region, let alone the Creek. Fish never seen before in those parts, Salmon-Trout out of farm-ponds you'd think couldn't hide a Frog, Chesapeake Rock-Fish well over the Allegheny Ridge,— the rarely encounter'd Inland Tuna...?— all with that miraculous Compound of his. I have personally taken with it Sea-Bass of weight unknown, but that it requir'd two of us to carry one back to the Cook-Tent,— withal, Trout innumerable, even as, close by, other Anglers drows'd at their Rods, hoping at best to intercept some unwary Perch. Believe me, if I knew the Secrets, I should be producing this Receipt from a Mill, by the Hogshead, and wallowing in Revenue.")

"See that group of stars over there?" Daniel points to the Big Dipper.

"We call it the Great Bear," Mason instructs them.

"So do we." Betraying no surprise. "And that bent Line of Stars by it?"

"The Bear's Tail."

The Indians are merry for some Moments. "Bears in your country have long Tails."

"That is a very long-tail'd Bear."

"Are you sure it's not something else?"

"Those Stars you call a 'Tail', are the Hunters who come after the Bear. Where are your Hunters?"

Mason indicates Boötes, and the Hunting Dogs. "So styl'd officially, tho' in practice we call 'em the Hounds."

Mason remembers from his youth a Market-Night, all of them in the bed of the Waggon, lumbering home late from Stroud. The Sun went down, and the Stars came out, and Charlie went on about the Stars. "The school-Master calls it Ursa Major, The Bigger of two Bears, and that's the Little one, there."

"My Father call'd it 'the Baker's Peel,' " his father told him.

"Mine always said 'Charles's Wain,' " recall'd his mother. "Charles was the Name of a great king, over in France."

"Hurrah!" cried Hester, "— here we all are, riding in Charles's Wain!" and it was one of the few times he could remember his Father laughing too.

Mason look'd up at his Parents' Faces, turn'd aside, under a great seeded Sky without a moon, under the unthinkable leagues of their Isolation. He would remember them all together like that, as if they liv'd at the edge of some great lighted Sky-Structure, with numberless Lanthorns hung and Shadows falling ev'rywhere, and pathways in, upon which once having ventur'd, he might account his life penetrated, and the rest of it claim'd.

He thought he knew ev'ry step he had taken, between then and today, yet can still not see, tho' the dotting of ev'ry last *i* in it be known, how he has come to the present Moment, alone in a wilderness surrounded by men who may desire him dead, his Kindred the whole Ocean away, with Dixon his only sure Ally. "Are we in danger?" he sees little point in not asking.

"Oh, sure and ask the Mohawk," cries Daniel, "— if the Topick be Danger, he knows all,— and let's not omit Violence, Terror, Weaponry, am I leaving anything out?"

"Sorry...I'm sorry," Mason mumbles.

Daniel sniffs and shakes his head. "Scalp but one White man, ev'ryone starts assuming things. Yes, of course you are in Danger. Your Heart beats? You live here?" gesturing all 'round. "Danger in ev'ry moment."

"May I ask about Vegetables, at least? Esculents notable for their Size,— that won't offend anyone?"

"I am not one of your Vegetable-wise Mohawks. You need to talk with Nicholas." All the way back to the Tents, Mason catches Daniel casting him glances, no longer of Curiosity, but of Judgment render'd.

In Camp, they find Nicholas conducting a Discussion upon the very Topick. He is amiable in responding to Mason's Inquiries, even when these carry an anxious under-surge. "Far, far to the North and West," Hugh Crawfford translates, "lies a Valley, not big, not small…a place of Magick. Smoke comes out of the Mountains…the Earth rumbles… Springs of Fire run ev'rywhere."

"Volcanickal Activity," Mason helpfully.

"In this Valley, plants,— Vegetables,— grow big,— very big. Big Corn. Each Kernel's more than a Man can lift. Big Turnip. Six-man crew to dig out but one. Big Squash. Big enough for many families to eat their way into, and then live inside all the Winter. *Very* big, BIG,— Hemp-Plant." The Mohawk is upon his feet, pretending to look in Astonishment at something nearly straight overhead.

Dixon, as if suddenly waking, inquires, "Well how big's that, Nicholas…?

"Late in the Season, to climb to the top of a Female Plant is a Journey of many Days, Red Coat."

They beam mischievously at one another, a Look that Mason in his Excitement does not pick up, babbling, "Because of the Volcanick Soil, obviously. A Marvel! Crawfford, ask him about Carrots."

"Big," the Indian replies directly, smiling and nodding. Mason notices that ev'ryone is nodding.

"Hemp-Plant," Dixon reminds Nicholas.

Many people, he explains, even from far away, make the Journey and Ascent. In earlier times, they climb'd to a Limb wide enough not to roll off of, and camp'd there overnight. But 'twas a fix'd season, and a growing Demand,— soon the great Limbs grew crowded. Some Travelers were not careful with their campfires, starting larger fires soon put out, tho' not before producing lots of Smoak. *Big* smoak. Depending upon the Winds, often climbers were delay'd for days.

The first long-houses began to appear upon the sturdier Branches, each season's Pilgrims sleeping in them overnight, then traveling on upward, others remaining to wait for them, smoking meanwhile Resin broken from some Bud nearby, and wrapp'd in a piece of Leaf, the whole being twisted into a great Cigar. Soon sheds were added to the Limb-side Inns, serving as Depots for the Jobbers who buy direct from the Bud. Bands of Renegadoes arrive to attack and rob the Enterprizers, who accordingly must band together in arm'd Convoy. Yet desperate men will assault even these vertical Caravans. 'Tis a lively time out there upon the Stalks.

"This Valley,— how far away is it?" Dixon with a dark breathlessness, as if, upon the right answer, he will immediately rush off into the night.

Gesturing toward gentle Alioth, "Too far. You would not go, Red Coat."

"Perhaps I might."

Nicholas is laughing now. " 'Perhaps' no need to." Patiently, he tells the story of the Giant Hemp-Plant again, making his Voice loud on words such as *Jobber,* and *Resin.*

Mason gets a Glimmer. "He's trying to sell us something."

Frantic now, the Mohawk is making wild smoking gestures, puffing imaginary Smoak right in their Faces. "Smoak?" says Dixon. "Thee mean, *Smoak?* O sublime Succedaneum!"

"He thinks he's back at the Cape," Mason's eyes cast skyward. "Where he grew so abstracted that I had to keep reminding him of the date of the Transit, aye, even upon the Day itself. How he attended the Clock and Telescope as closely as he did, remains a Mystery."

"*Dagga* hath many Mysteries," Dixon replies.

One being, that talking about things, while not exactly causing them to happen, does cause something,— which is almost the same, tho' not quite. Unless it is possible to smoke a Potatoe. That is, the first of the Giant Vegetables does not seem all that large,— remarkable at some Fair in the Country perhaps, but hardly the Faith-challenging Specimens that lie yet a Ridge-line or two away, further West, where they are soon to be found ever larger, abandoning the Incremental, bringing into question the very Creation....

"Ah don't see it," Dixon apologetick. "There'll always be a few very large Specimens of anything tha like...."

"This is Acre upon Acre, and cannot be God's Work."

West of Cheat, they discover Indian Corn growing higher than a Weather-cock upon a Barn. What they take for a natural Hill, proves but the Pedestal for a gigantick Squash-Vine thicker than an ancient Tree-trunk, whose Flowers they can jump into in the mornings and bathe in, sometimes never touching the Bottom. Single Tomatoes tower high as Churches and shiny enough to see yourself in, warp'd spherickal, red as Blood, with the whole great sweep of Forest and River and Visto curving away behind. And the Smell, apotheckarial, œstral, musk-heavy,— one must bring along a Bladder fill'd with fresh Air, and now and then inhale from it, if one does not wish to swoon clean away, in these Gardens Titanick.

"Did ye hear someone going Fee Fie Fo Fum?" Mason frowns.

"And yet…might these not be the products of Human Art…?"

"Folly. No philosopher, however ingenious, not Mr. Franklin himself,— look at it, for Heaven's sake! You can't see the top! Like some damn'd Palm Oasis here!"

"My guess is it's the top of a Carrot," replies Dixon, "tho' of some Size, of course,— yet let us further imagine, that where there is a vegetable patch, there must be someone,— some thing,— tending it. I suggest we— "

"Too late."

"You're welcome, Sirs, tho' you're not suppos'd to be here." 'Tis a group of Farmers despite whose middling Age and Height, Proximity to any of the Plants in their Care, gives the look of serious Elves. "Rifle's back at the Barn, so I can't kill ye. Yet you're Brits by the look of ye, so we cannot trust yese neither."

"Why keep it a Secret? Why not rather notify the *Pennsylvania Gazette?*"

"We but look after these, for Others who are absent, pending their Return, in the meantime being allow'd the free use of all we may grow." They are invited to follow.

The Seeds are stor'd in Sheds especially built for them, each able to shelter one, at most two, for the Winter. In the Spring, planting but a few of them is a communal Task, easily comparable to a Barn-Raising. Last Year's Potatoe, lying in the giant Root-cellar dug beneath the nearer Pasture, is assaulted by Adze and Hatchet, and taken by handcarts to the Kitchen to be boil'd, bak'd, or fried in as many ways as there are Wives on hand with personal Receipts. "Nothing!" cries the Head Gardener. "Wait'll yese see the Beet!"

The Beet is of a Circumference requiring more than one Entry-way. All who pass much time going in and out, whether for reasons of Residence, or Investigation, or indeed Nutrition, eventually acquire a deep red-indigo Stain that nothing can wash away.

"Like Geordie Pitmen, tho' more colorful," it seems to Dixon. "And which is less reasonable, all 'round,— ever to place thy Life's Wagers upon a large tho' finite Vegetable upon the Earth, or a like-siz'd Vein of Coal beneath it? The Beet, at least, yese can see...?"

"Yet, does it live," declares their Guide.

"You don't mean,— " Mason markedly less eager to have a look inside now.

"We are as Garden Pests, to It. It suffers us. We being unworthy of Its full Attention."

"It...understands what we say?" Mason's eyes fallen into an Alternating Squint, with one right-left-right Cycle taking about a Second.

"There are schools of Thought, as to that. Another Lively Question is, Does it remember the Days, when we were *bigger* than Beets, yes, by about the same Proportion, 'd you notice, that Beets are now bigger than us? Now that the Tables are turn'd, do, do they harbor Grudges? Do they have a concept of Revenge, perhaps for insults we never intended?"

68

By this time, they're making a mile or two per day. On the seventh of August, they cross Braddock's Road at 189 miles and 69 Chains. Thirty-two Chains further on, they cross the Road a second Time. The next Day, a Mile and 35 Chains beyond that, they cross it a Third Time.

"I'm not content with this, Dixon, not at all."

Three agents for Philadelphia land-speculating Interests are said to be out here this summer, scouting real estate,— Harris, Wallace, and Friggs. The Metropolitan cabal back there, 'tis said, goes upon the hope of the next Purchase of the Indians, of as much trans-Alleghenian Land as possible. The settlers having been serv'd Eviction Notices last year by Capt. Mackay and the Highland Forty-second, and withal Surveying itself about to be proclaim'd a Crime,— fifty Pounds' fine and three months in Jail,— these Gentlemen suppose they may take over the Rights out here for virtually nothing.

"Three months for Surveying!" Mason marvels. "And if someone's been doing it all his Life? A-and think of the Money! Is that fifty Pounds per Act of surveying? Per Diem, perhaps?"

"Thankee, Friend Mason."

Before crossing the Big Yochio Geni, in the evening after Mess, the Surveyors gather all who've follow'd the Party undaunted this far.

"Now like Prospero must I conjure you all away, for from here to the Warpath, we'll have no time for gentle recreations, but must stand Watch and Watch for as far west as we may."

"Whah',— no musicians? The Indians love our Musick."

"The Indians will need their Ears for other Tasks."

"We must go back to that Fort, then."

"We'll wait for them at Cumberland."

"A long way, sister. So far we've enjoy'd an Escort of Mohawk fighters, best in the Land. Who'll be protecting us on the way back?"

"Might get lucky and hook up with a band of Axmen headed home?"

"They'll be long gone. Absorb'd like Hail-Stones into the Earth."

"Well I'm not languishing by the Banks of Potowmack, I'm for someplace with Lamps outdoors, and purses full of idle Specie. Anybody for Williamsburg?"

They arrange to keep the Sector at the House of Mr. Spears, where Braddock's Road meets the Bank of the Yochio, and go in search of the Ferryman, Mr. Ice. "They expect a Ferryman to be silent," announces he, his eyes a-glimmer. Taking his Coat and draping it over his head so as to hood his face, "Well. Welcome aboard. Smoking Lamp's lit on this Craft." On shore his brother-in-law is letting out the line, allowing them to be taken by the Stream, as his Nephew upon the further side waits to begin hauling them in. Exactly at the middle of the River, for a moment, no one can see either Father or Son. To appearance, the passengers stand upon a raft in a boundless body of water.

"Now here is what they did to me, and mine,"— and the last Ice proceeds to tell ev'ry detail of the Massacre that took his family, in the dread days of Braddock's defeat. Time, whilst he speaks, is abolish'd. The mist from the River halts in its Ascent, the Frogs pause between Croaks, and the peepers in mid-peep. The great black cobbles of the River-bed stir and knock no longer. The Dead are being summon'd. The Ferryman's Grief is immune to Time,— as if in Exchange for a sacrifice of earthly Freedom, to the Flow of this particular Stream.

"You think this is some kind of Penance? Hey, I enjoy this. Such looks on Passengers' Faces, when they hear how the Flesh and Bones of those I lov'd were insulted! They are us'd to tales of Frederick's rank'd Automata, executing perfect manœuvres upon the unending German Plain,— down here in the American Woods, that same War proceeded silently, in persistent Shade, one swift animal Death at a time...no Treaty can end it, and when all are dead, Ghosts will go on contending. 'Twas the perfect War. No mercy, no restraint, pure joy in killing. It cannot be let go so easily."

The Youghiogheny, cov'd and willow'd and Sycamor'd, has no Fish in it that Mason has been able to learn of. "Yah, you'll hear that," says Ice,— "Yet ev'ryone up and down this River knows of the great School of Ghost-fish that inhabit it, pale green, seldom seen, two sets of Fins each side and a Tail like a Dragon's. They travel unmolested where they will, secure in the belief that no Angler in his right mind would dare attempt to catch any of them. And that, Sir, could be where you come in."

Dixon is trying to nudge Mason alert, but owing to the Darkness, not always connecting. Mason is already simpering like a Milk-maid. "Who, Sir? I am but a Country coarse-fisher, after the odd Chub or Roach, whatever the Mills haven't kill'd or chas'd off, actually, is usually what I settle for, and goodness, why this Fish of yours sounds far too much for my light-rod skills, being so very, as ye might say, *big*,— "

"Mason," Dixon, not often a Mutterer, mutters.

"Up to five, some say six foot long," Ice avows, "big as a man or Woman, pale as a floating Corpse,...yet these do live...tho' few have dar'd, some of us out here have taken Ghosters,— I could show you more than one, stuft and mounted,— no question of eating them, of course...indeed, no question trying to hang one over the Hearth, given the Wives who object to looking at them for long.— Or at all.

"The Yochio as it comes down off the Mountains of Virginia descends very rapidly, very dangerously. You might not want, or even be able, to wade in it. Some think it's the Fall, the very Speed of the Flow, that creates those Ghosters. No one knows. Their entire lives are engulf'd unceasingly in change. They never come to rest. They never know an Instant of Tranquillity. One wonders, what must their idea of Death be," Ice's feign'd Smile nearly unendurable, "how are they going to deal with eternal Rest? unless this World be already their Purgatory, and they no longer classifiable as living Fish."

"And what of those who seek them?"

"Ghosters are accorded a respect comparable to that shewn the Dead.... If we get out upon this River tonight," says Mr. Ice, "perhaps we'll see a few. They like it just after the rain. In the sun-light, they show up against the black rocks of the River-Bed. In the Dark, they glow some,— for one another, they do. Us,— they pay no mind. In a way, that could prove an advantage...to an Angler bold enough."

"Pray you," Mason's hands upon his Bosom.

Mr. Ice abruptly turning to Dixon, "Forgive me, Sir, if I stare. Yours is the first Red Coat to be seen in these parts since Braddock's great Tragedy,— the only ones out here with Opportunity to wear one, being the Indians who from the Corpses of English soldiers, took them. Even to these Savages, even intoxicated, 'tis too much shame, ever to put a Red Coat on."

"Yet I find it a means, when in the Forest, of not being innocently mistaken for an Elk...?"

"Nor should any mistake me for a tearful fool," advises Immanuel Ice, "merely upon observing how I must battle against a daily Sadness. The Graves of my Family are in back of the Cabin, up that Meadow, near the line of Cedars...I visit ev'ry Day,— yet, Grief too Solitary breeds madness. At my Work I meet a good many of the Publick, who travel in these parts, who will sometimes, like you, let me bend their Ears with my particular Woes. It keeps away the Madness. Hey? You think it's over out here, Redcoat? It's not over. The Fall of Quebec was not the end, nor Bouquet's Success at Bushy Run, nor the relief of Fort Pitt,— for there is ever a drop in the cup left, another Shot to be fir'd, another life to be taken off cruelly, in unmediated Hate, ev'ry day in this Forest Life, somewhere. The last Dead in this have not yet been born. Young Horst will now pass among ye with a Raccoon Hat, the Contribution is sixpence. Thanks to Audiences like you, this place is proving to be an Elves' Treasury."

"But,— this is horrible," protests Mason, "— Mr. Ice, how can you use your private Tragedy for the mere accumulation of sixpences?"

"How sinful is that?" Mr. Ice wishes to know. "Were any of you out here then? Not since Westphalia, such Evil. Without Restitution, what's the Point? Here's my opportunity to redeem some of that terrible time, to convert enemy Rifle-Balls to Gold. How can any Person of Sense object to that? Meanwhile, there all of you are, accosting Strangers in Taverns, spilling forth your Sorrows, Gratis. One day, if it be his Will, God will seize and shake you like wayward daughters, and you will thenceforward give nothing away for free."

Between Laurel Hill and Cheat, the Account-book shows at least III Hands on the pay-list, not including the Surveyors, various McCleans, and those forever omitted from the official Books. Once over Laurel Hill, they are in the Country of the Old Forts,— all across these hilltops are the Ruins, ancient when the Indians first arrived. Broken Walls, fallen nearly to Plan Views of themselves, act as Flues that the Wind must find its way past, in a long Moan with a Rise at the end of it, as if posing a Question. The Fort at Redstone lies upon the site of one. The Creek below is crowded with Rocks with lines of Glyphs inscrib'd on them. Nobody can read them, but all believe they are Grave Markers.

"The old stories say the Forts were built and later abandon'd by a Nation of Giants, who possess'd a magick more powerful even than that of the English or the French."

"Fortifications?" says Dixon. "Against what?"

The Indians laugh. "Each other, maybe."

"Now and then you'll find these Gigantick Bones," says Hugh Crawford.

"Human?" inquires Mason.

"Sure seem to be. Been there a long time."

Ev'ryone out here knows of the Old Forts. When it becomes very Dark, and Thunder-Gusts come sailing in over the Ridge-line, fanciful Uncles tell Nieces and Nephews that the Giant People are back, loud as ever, seeking to reclaim their Country. Redeem it. Some bite at this, some do not. Within the broken Perimeters lie Monoliths that once stood on end,— recumbent, the Indians believe, "— they are dead or sleeping,— upright, they live,— likenesses neither of Gods, nor of men,— but of Guardians...."

"Guardians,— of...?"

"Helpers. They live. They have Powers."

"In England, you see," Mason feels impell'd to instruct the Indians, "They mark the positions of Sun, Moon, some say Planets, thro' the Year.... They are tall, like Men, for the same reason our Sector is Tall,— in order to mark more closely these movements in the Sky."

"Small Differences mean much to you. There is Power in these?"

"The finer the Scale we work at, the more Power may we dispose. The Lancaster County Rifle is precise at long range, because of microscopick refinements in the Finish, the Rifling, the ease with which it may be held and aim'd. They who control the Microscopick, control the World."

"Listen to me, Defecates-with-Pigeons. Long before any of you came here, we dream'd of you. All the people, even Nations far to the South and the West, dreamt you before ever we saw you,— we believ'd that you came from some other World, or the Sky. You had Powers and we respected them. Yet you never dream'd of us, and when at last you saw us, wish'd only to destroy us. Then the killing started,— some of you, some of us,— but not nearly as many as we'd been expecting. You could not be the Giants of long ago, who would simply have wip'd us away, and for less. Instead, you sold us your Powers,— your Rifles,— as if encouraging us to shoot at you,— and so we did, tho' not hitting as many of you, as *you* were expecting. Now you begin to believe that we have come from elsewhere, possessing Powers you do not…. Those of us who knew how, have fled into Refuge in your Dreams, at last. Tho' we now pursue real lives no different at their Hearts from yours, we are also your Dreams."

As they have come West, the Visto has grown sensibly wider, and the Hands have tended more and more to be in it as little as they may, in the Day-time, as to sleep up and down its Center-Line at Night.

The Axmen begin to depart unannounc'd,— as the Army might say, desert. Cheat is the Rubicon, Monongahela is the Styx. At last there are the Indians, and fifteen Axmen newly hired, and Tom Hynes ("Somebody has to cook…"). And after the first terrible Poker invisible up the Arse, after allowing themselves a moment to see if they wish to begin screaming and flinging themselves about, Mason and Dixon notice the Indians, politely enough, yet unarguably, watching them, to see how they will react.

Hendricks seems fascinated. "What do they believe waits them, on the other side of the River, that sends them away so fast?"

"They said Shawanese, Delawares, Mingoes,— someone said, a tribe whose Name they've never heard."

"A Tribe with no name?" He translates quickly for his Companions, as if trying to finish before being careen'd by the gathering Sea of Mirth.

"We know that Tribe,— we are afraid of them, too, the Tribe with no Name." The Indians sit and smoke, continuing to laugh for what, to Europeans, might seem a length of time far out of proportion to the Jest. The Day passes, the night deepens, the Absence of the Axmen is felt at Ear-drums and Elbow-joints, as in the sleeplessness attending Watch and Watch, as the Days of their Westering, even the most obtuse of the Company can see, are rapidly decremented, as in a game of Darts, to Zero, waiting moment upon moment the last fatal Double.

69

One day, yet east of Cheat, a light Snow descending but scarce begun to stick, several of the Party observe a Girl chasing a Chicken across the Visto, when an odd thing happens,— smack at the very Center, directly upon the Line, the Chicken stops, turns about till its head points West and Tail East, and thenceforward remains perfectly still, seemingly fallen into a Trance. The Girl, after Guarantees from both Surveyors of the Chicken's Safety, moves on to other chores, whilst the day wheels over and down into Dusk, and ev'ryone in the Crew comes by to have a look at the immobile Fowl, for as long as their Obligations may allow.

" 'Tis well known," various ancient Pennsylvanians and Marylanders assure the Surveyors, "that placing a Chicken 'pon a Straight Line'll send it nodding faster than ever a head put under a wing." The Girl, returning to fetch her Hen, agrees briskly. "Chicken on a Line? Thought ev'rybody knew that."

Dixon's idea of Thrift is offended. "Well that's an attractive nuisance, isn't it? what's to keep them *all* from wandering in at any moment...? ev'ry Clucker clear to Ohio and back to Cheapeake,— lining up, going into a Daze, presently throngin' the Visto? We could have a Chickens' Black Hole of Calcutta, here,— except that, being in America, they'd all have to be remov'd gently, one by one, wasting Days, lest any fowl-keeper whose stock has suffer'd even a Feather's molestation call down, among these Lawyer-craz'd People, a Vengeful Pursuit after Reimburse-ment, upon a Biblical scale, that may beggar our Mission."

Mason groans. "Shall wise Doctors one day write History's assessment of the Good resulting from this Line, *vis-à-vis* the not-so-good? I wonder which List will be longer."

"Hark! Hark! You wonder? That's all?" One of the Enigmata of the Invisible World, is how a Voice unlocaliz'd may yet act powerfully as a moral Center. 'Tis the Duck speaking, naturally,— or, rather, artificially. "What about 'care'? Don't you care?"

"This Visto…is a result of what we have chosen, in our Lives, to work at," Dixon bewilder'd that the Topick is even coming up, "— unlike some mechanickal water-fowl, *we* have to, what on our planet is styl'd, 'work,'…?"

"Running Lines is what surveyors *do*," explains Mason.

"Thankee, Mason," says Dixon. "And one of the few things Star-gazing's good for, is finding out where you are, exactly, upon the Surface of the Earth. Put huz two together with enough Axmen, you have a sort of Visto-Engine. Two Clients wish'd to have a Visto for one of their Bound-aries. Here we are. What other reason should we be together for?"

"Thankee, Dixon," says Mason.

Later that night, and, as he hopes, out of the Duck's Hearing, Mason says, "I've been thinking about that Chicken today."

"Aye, Ah knoah how lonely it gets out here, tho' aren't they said to be moody…?"

"Only a moment, dear Colleague, pray you.— Suppose Right Lines cause Narcolepsy in *all* Fowl, including,— "

"— the Duck," Dixon exclaims. "Why aye! As in the Chinaman's Refrain, there's all thah' Bad Energy, flowing there night and Day,— bad for us, anyhow. But for the Duck? Who knows? Mightn't it, rather, be nourishing her? helping to increase her Powers,— even…uncom-monly so?"

"Exactly. 'Twould explain her relentless Presence near it, …humm… yes, the trick,— should we wish to play it,— would be to see to her per-fect location upon the Line,— symmetrickally bisected."

"Facing East, or West?"

"What matter? she can turn upon a farthing however fast she goes."

"Pond-Larvæ," offers Armand, feeling like a Traitor, "— she still fan-cies them.…"

"A Decoy. We need a painted Wood representation of a Duck."

"Tom Hynes is the very man, Sir, hand him a Pine Log and he'll carve ye a Quacker ye can't tell from real even close enough to scare it away."

"It must look like an Automatick Duck, not a natural one."

Tom does a better job on the Decoy, than he knows. Soon the Duck is spending hours, still'd, companionably close to the expressionless Object. One day, in an Access, she throws herself upon it, going to beak-bite its Neck, and of course the Truth comes out. "Wood." For a moment it seems she will sigh, ascend, accelerate once more, back into her Realm of Velocity and Spleen. Instead, "Well, it's a beginning," she says. "It floats like a Duck,— it fools other Ducks, who are quite sophisticated in these matters, into believing it a Duck. It's a Basis. Complexity of Character might develop, in time...." Quiet, good-looking, ever there to drop in on after a long Tour of Flying,— and where there's one withal, why, there's more of the same...Famine to Feast! Who needs bright Conversation?

"...and that's why, around those foothills, some nights when the Wind is blowing backwards and the Moon's just gone behind the Clouds, you can hear the Hum of her going by, due West, due East, and that forlorn come-back call, and then folks'll say, ' 'Tis the Frenchman's Duck, out cruising the Line.' "

"Why doesn't somebody set her free," the children of settlers up and down the Line want to know. "Go in, get her, bring her out?"

"Not so easy. Anybody finds a chance to try it, she disappears. She's like a Ghost who haunts a house, unable to depart."

"A Ghost usually has unfinish'd Business. What, think you, detains the Duck?"

"A simple, immoderate Desire for the Orthogonal," in the Opinion of Professor Voam, "which cannot allow her even the thought of life away from that much Straightness, the Leagues of perfect straightness, perfect alignment with Earth's Spin,— flying back and forth, East and West, forever, the buffeting of the Magnetick currents, the ebb and flow of Nations over the Land-Surface, the Pulse and Breath of the solid Planet, the Dance with the Moon, the entire great Massive Progress 'round and 'round the Sun...."

For a while after becoming a Resident of the Visto, the Duck accosts Travelers for Miles up and down the Line, ever seeking Armand. For a chance at Revenge, it is worth slowing into Visibility,— besides giving her an opportunity to chat. "Here,"— producing from some interior Recess a sheaf of Notices in print, clipp'd from various newspapers and Street-bills,— "here,— *voilà,* with the Flauteur, and the Tambourine-Player? in the Center, 'tis *moi, moi....* Listen to what Voltaire wrote about me, to the Count and Countess d'Argental,— '...*sans la voix de la Le More et le Canard de Vaucanson, vous n'auriez rien que fit ressouvenir de la gloire de la France,*' all right? Le More, who's that? some Soprano. Fine, I'm a big-hearted sort of *Fille,* the Glory of France certainly knows how to share a Stage. You think it was easy ev'ry night with those two Musicians? Listening again and again to that Ordure? You'd think now and then a little Besozzi, at least,— *any* Besozzi would've done. Relief? forget it, not in the Rooms *we* work'd. Took all my Stage Discipline not to start quacking along with those grand high C's. One admires the man, genius Engineer, but his taste, musickally speaking, runs from None to Doubtful.

"The true humiliation came at the end of each Exhibition, when Vaucanson actually open'd me up, and show'd to anyone who wish'd to stare, any *Bas-mondain,* the intricate Web within of Wheels, levers, and wires, unto the last tiny piece of Linkage, nay, the very falling Plummet that gave me Life,— nowadays, itself 'morphos'd, so as to fall without end.... They pointed, titter'd, sketch'd exquisitely in the air,— Indignity absolute. He would never allow anyone the least suspicion that I might after all be real. Inside me lay Truth Mechanickal,— outside was but clever impersonation. I was that much his Creature, that he own'd the right to deny my Soul.

"His undoing was in modifying my Design, hoping to produce Venus from a Machine, as you might say. My submission was not yet complete enough. In the years before the late War, as Publick tastes veer'd in quite another Direction and we were left becalm'd, each in the Company of few but the other, his demands grew less and less those of a Man of Science. He wish'd, rather, to hear Sounds of affection and contentment, in his presence. He got nothing more abandon'd than Wing Caresses, perhaps a Beak-Bite...a limited Repertoire, but all the same, one felt...compromis'd. He wish'd to control utterly, not an Automaton, but a creature capable of Love, not only for Drakes and Ducklings, but for himself. The approach of his middle years, the winds blowing as from an untravel'd North..."

'Tis on their way back East for the last time, that the Duck learns to hold perfectly still in the Air, at any altitude, and remain there whilst the earth Spins beneath her. She understands that she may now shift north or south, to any Latitude she likes, without being restricted any more to the Line and its Visto. But she is curious about where else the Parallel goes. She ascends, one evening after Mess, and as the Party, with their Tents, all go rolling away into the Shadow, they in their Turn watch her, pois'd above the last lit Meridian, recede over the Horizon and vanish. Next morning here she comes roaring in at well over seven hundred miles per hour, coasting to a smooth stop and settling upon the Cook-tent's Peak with not a Feather out of place. "Interesting Planet," is her comment. "I have been o'er the Foot of the Italian Boot, close by Bukhara and Samarkand,— "I can't wait to do the Equator. Ye have tapp'd into but five degrees of three hundred sixty, twenty minutes of a Day it would cause you Astonishment and Distress to learn of your minor tho' morally problematick part in."

"A Global Scheme! Ah knew it!" Dixon beginning to scream, "what'd Ah tell thee?"

"Get a grip on yerrself, man," mutters Mason, "what happen'd to 'We're men of Science'?"

"And Men of Science," cries Dixon, "may be but the simple Tools of others, with no more idea of what they are about, than a Hammer knows of a House."

("Ah," sighs Euphrenia, "all too true. The Life of an Automaton cannot, however conceiv'd, strike anyone as enviable."

"Excuse us, Aunt," ventures DePugh, "but did we understand you to say,— "

"Don't get her started!" Brae hisses.

"Have you, Aunt," Ethelmer fiendishly pretending Interest, "really shar'd the Life of— "

"Shar'd! Why, in my own Student Days, in far-off Paris, France, I was oblig'd to keep Starvation off my Sill, by pretending to *be* an Automaton Oboe player. My Manager, Signore Drivelli (actually, under the Statutes of the Two Sicilies, we were man and wife), not only charg'd Admission, but also took bets on the side as to how long I could play between breaths."

"Zabby," pleads Mr. LeSpark, "speak with her about this sometime, could you please, it being your Family?"

"What was your best Time?" asks Ethelmer.

"Never went longer than twenty minutes or so, but I could've easily tootl'd on all night, the secret being to sneak Charges of Air in thro' your Nose, using the cheeks as a Plenum, for Storage, as 'tis in the Bag-Pipes,— The Musick written for Oboe is notoriously lacking in places to breathe. The Notes just keep coming, sixteen or thirty-two of 'em ev'ry time you tap your foot, not to mention the embellishments you're expected to put in yourself, for no extra Fee of course,— the principal Reason so many of us go insane being, not from forcing air into a small mouthpiece, but in all the sneakery and diversion of Attention requir'd to keep blowing,— in India they understand how important the breath is,— being indeed the Soul in different form,— and how dangerous it is to meddle unnaturally with the rhythms proper to it....")

As Dixon becomes possess'd by the Horizon, Hugh Crawfford is seen to walk to and fro shaking his head, presently muttering softly. Mason corners him behind a Waggon. "Out with it, Sir,— things are too precarious here for you to be concealing your opinions from me."

"Not concealing. Withholding, maybe,— " Mason, losing his composure, lunges for and attempts to strangle the Guide. They slip and stagger in the newly fallen Leaves. "Very well,— Mason! off, off, attend me, this is a Mountain Dulcimer, that I put together by Hand once, when there wasn't much else to do,— " and in a wild Note-scape, almost minor, almost Celtick, commences an uncommonly amazing Hammering and Plucking. When Mason appears soothed enough, "Now, I've seen Mr. Dixon's Ailment before,— yes,— with trappers, with traders,

> With rangers and strangers, the
> Frenchies out there call it
> '*Rap-ture de West*,' Brother,
> Sooner or later,
> It's go-ing, to take ye,

Away to the sunset,
Along with the rest,

So 'tis hey, ye Dirt-Farmers,
I'm gone, for the Prairies,
And over, the Mountains, and
Down to the Sea, if I
Get back some Day, tho' the
World shine as Morning, yet
Ever will sunsets be
Beck'ning to me....

But out under the Moon, Chestnut Ridge and Cheat behind them, and
Monongahela to cross, into an Overture of meadow to the Horizon, low-
lands become to them a dream whilst under a Spell, the way it gives back
the Light, the way it withholds its Shadows,— who might not come to
believe in an Eternal West? In a Momentum that bears all away? "Men
are remov'd by it, and women, from where they were,— as if surrender'd
to a great current of Westering. You will hear of gold cities, marble cities,
men that fly, women that fight, fantastickal creatures never dream'd in
Europe,— something always to take and draw you that way," Mr. Crawfford puffing meanwhile upon an Indian Pipe, whose Bowl, finely carv'd
of soft stone, by a Quebec Frenchman he had dealings with years ago,
depicts a female head of Classical beauty, her Locks spilling beyond
obsessiveness, all blacken'd with fire and grease, smok'd out of for all
those years, having held a thousand Stems, from Reeds stirr'd by the
Mists of Niagara, to Cane at the mouth of the Mississippi, "— you recall
to me myself, in my first days out here, up all night, going West by way
of the Stars. It's said some have a gift for it, like dowsing, and can run
true bearings indefinitely under the most obscur'd of Skies. Many of
Colonel Byrd's Companions running the Line 'twixt Virginia and Car-
olina possess'd the gift,— when the Party split, with half going 'round
the Great Dismal and half right across, becoming detain'd in that
Cypress Purgatory for weeks, 'twas the Westering Certainty that got 'em
thro' safe.... I've even managed to keep my Latitude for the odd few seconds, so I take an amateur's Interest, and thus far, by my estimate, you
are hardly the width of a pipestem out. As to what draws Mr. Dixon,— I

don't mean to present it lightly. We say the Westering's 'got' him. And I also tell you this so you'll know that when"— here Mason draws a sharp breath,— "something requires an unpremeditated cessation to the Line, well,— Mr. Dixon…may not be inclin'd to stop."

"He wouldn't take a chance with his— " but the Guide has put a hand upon Mason's arm, motioning with his head as Dixon comes into view,— he has been wandering among the tents and Waggons, looking troubled, very tall and out of scale in the uncertain dinner-time light. By the time he's out of earshot again, it has occurr'd to Mason, "You said what? an unpremeditated,— "

"Cessation."

"Is there something else I should know?"

There is, nor does it take long in coming. Mortality at last touches the Expedition. William Baker and John Carpenter are kill'd by the Fall of a single Tree, on September 17th, a Thursday. 'Tis possible they'd sign'd up together, and work'd together,— their names are enter'd together in Mr. McClean's records. The next week, Carpenter's is enter'd by mistake, to be follow'd by a trailing Line over to a row of Zeros, for Days work'd in the Week. Mo must have forgot,— so may the Book-keeper's Page be haunted,— a Ghost-Entry, John Carpenter's Soul lingering,— William Baker's, to Appearance, having mov'd on.

"This is a Disaster," Mason curl'd as a dying Leaf, dispos'd to give it all up. "You agree, don't you, Jeremiah, you know it doesn't happen, it never happens, that two are kill'd in the fall of a single Tree?"

"Their People have them,— they'll be safe?" too vex'd in Reassuring himself, to see Mason's Point.

"You were the one looking for a Sign, weren't you, well there's your miserable Sign, why aren't you reading it."

" 'Twas a tall old Chestnut, they set their Wedges wrong, and then it fell where they hadn't guess'd it would. What else, pray?"

"Damn'd right, pray," snaps Mason, "— somebody'd better, around here."

They sit in the Tent, Coffee growing cold, Mason waiting for the Sector to arrive, Dixon waiting for Mason to burst forth with "Well what's the fucking Use, really?" to which Dixon will have to come up with an answer, and not take too much time, either, doing it.

Geminity hath found a fleshless Face,—
No second Chance, 'tis Death that's won the Race
Between the Line in all its Purity,
And what lay, mass'd, within the mortal Tree…
— Timothy Tox, *The Line*

No question, beyond Cheat they move in a time and space apt, one instant to the next, to stretch or shrink,— as a Chain's length may, upon the clement Page, pass little notic'd, whilst in an Ambuscade, may reckon as, perhaps, all,— or nothing.

When the Sector arrives, they set up upon a Bluff overlooking Monongahela, and watch the Culmination of Stars in Lyra and Cygnus, correcting for seconds plus and minus of Aberration, Deviation, Precession, and Refraction, whilst in Cabins nearby the Wives of the new-hir'd Axmen gather, and those Axmen who may, come thro', and out the back, to take White Maize Whiskey out of a Tin Cup.

Soon as the Party have stept West of Monongahela, Indians of Nations other than Iroquois begin showing up to have a look at them. The Delaware Chief Catfish, his Lady, and his Nephew arrive in the first days of October, all dress'd as Europeans might be, and confer apart with the Mohawks, exchanging Strings of Wampom with them. Stranger and Native alike confess ignorance of Catfish's Mission in these parts, far from his Village, and as if Disguis'd, in Coat, Waistcoat, Breeches, and Cock'd Hat. "Looking for Business," is how Hugh Crawfford translates it, adding, "It is usually best in these cases, not to inquire too closely." A few miles further on west, eight Senecas, going south to fight the Cherokees, come and stay over in Camp, obtaining Powder of Mo McClean, along with some Paint. "Materials of War,— I'm not sure we can write these off," Mason cautiously suggests to him. The Commissary glares, as if presented with an opening for some Violence. "Well they're southern Indians," he explains instead. "They are Snakes down there,— poisonous, no human feeling. Whereas, these Seneca, well, they're *our* Indians,— we live in, as off, the same Forests,— if we can help 'm along, it ever pays to have a friend or two out here, Gents." And at the final Station by Dunkard Creek,— as Mason records in his "Memoranda," for 1767,— the venerable Prisqueetom, Prince of the Delawares and brother to their King, pays them a call, and is presently describing for them the

673

great unbroken Meadow of the West, whilst Indian Visitors pass by in all directions, staring or amus'd, sometimes in Drink as well, regardless of the hour,— all Figures relating to their daily ration of Spirits having been negotiable since the Party cross'd Monongahela.

"It's like Covent Garden on Saturday Night," Mason grumbles, "— what are we become,— a Show they all must see, or lose credibility among...whatever Indians have for Fops? I ought to just go over and inform that old Coot,— "

"Mason, he's eighty-six...? And why should Traffick not be Brisk? These People freely travel an Arrangement of High-Roads, connected upon a Scale Continental, that nothing we know of in North Britain can equal...? Making huz little different from the Strollers who work the Inns along the Coaching Roads of more civiliz'd Lands.... Can't speak for thee, but I rather welcome all this mix'd Society. Not as...formal, this way, as it might become,— " swinging his head westward. "Heaven help us if we run out of Whiskey. As it is, Mo's got distillers clear back the other side o' Monongahela working back-shifts by the light of the moon, and Waggons that do and don't make it thro', all so that our Guests here'll be taken care of...?"

"Peace, Merriment,— take joy of thy rude Hurricanoe, give no thought to what may lie beyond thy moment's mean Horizon. *Fatum in Denario vertit,* but don't let that stop you, allow me rather to assume as well thy *own* Burden of Worry, being a self-sacrificing gent, in a curious sort of way,— "

"Eeh, Mason, mind thy Wig now, for these are all good Lads, they drink but in moderation, no more riotously than in Wapping, I am sure...?"

"Arrhh...now am I entirely sedate, thankee."

"Safest thing's to act insane, of course," Mr. Crawfford advises.

"How's that?"

"We style it, 'Doing a Chapman.' " A trader by that name, captur'd near Fort Detroit, at the time of Pontiack's rising, famously having escap'd execution by feigning to be mad. "These folk respect Madness. To them 'tis a holy state."

"As I told thee, Mason,— nothing for thee to worry about...?"

"I'd notic'd them stepping lightly 'round you."

Hitherto, as if by Conscious Agreement, Withdrawal into Folly by the one Surveyor would have unfailingly provok'd an Embrace of Sobriety by the other. So, up till now, has the Line been preserv'd, day to day, from frenzied Impulse, as from reason'd Reluctance,— allowing it to proceed on its Way unmolested. Here, as it draws to its last Halt, if anywhere, might both Gentlemen take joy of a brief Holiday from Reason. Yet, "Too busy," Mason insists, and "Far too cheerful for thah'," supposes Dixon.

"As the Stars tell you where it is you must cut your Path, so do the Land and its Rivers tell us where our Tracks must go."

"Yet the Stars, in their Power," Mason's Melancholia so advanc'd that he is not fully aware of sitting wrapp'd in a Blanket arguing Religion with a Mohawk Warrior with whom he is scarcely upon intimate Terms, "that only the Mightiest God may command, deserve at least the one small, respectful Courtesy, of allowing their Line to cross, without a Mark, your Nations' own Great Path...."

"Come," says Daniel.

"Eeh," Dixon looking up from his Pipe.

"Come where?" says Mason.

"Out on the Path. We'll take a Turn down toward Virginia and back again."

"Am I in Condition for this?" inquires Mason, of no one in particular. "And what of all these Catawbas I keep hearing about?"

"Will we be allow'd to smoak?" Dixon wants to know.

The Indian is gazing at them doubtfully. "You must see, what it is you believe you may cross so easily. Follow me, tho' I am not entirely pleas'd with my Back to either of you."

They proceed along Dunkard Creek, abandoning their short-term Destinies to the possibly homicidal Indian. The Forest life ever presenting Mystery to them,— too much going on, night and day, behind ev'ry Trunk, beneath ev'ry Bush,— how many new Pontiacks may even now be raising forces, planning assaults, perhaps in the Market for a couple of English Surveyors to style a *casus belli* and publickly torture before putting to death,— yaagghh!— yet isn't this man entirely vouch'd for by Sir William Johnson? Or, actually, *said to be* vouch'd for. Hum. Perhaps the first item of the neo-Pontiackal uprising, would be to put Johnson to Death? Perhaps this has already occurred? So busy are the Astronomers with these Apprehensions that they nearly miss their Guide's Hand-Signal to slow down and approach with Caution what lies ahead.

The Moon has not yet risen. The Indian steps off the Path, motioning to them, to do the same. "This is troubling. They've been this far up already. See what you nearly stepp'd on." He crouches and fleetly retrieves a long, slender tho' not easily broken, Sliver of something from the Trail. "Swamp Cane. It doesn't grow up here,— they gather and splinter it, catch and kill Serpents, dip the Points into the venom,— set them in the Trail, aim'd toward us." Having gather'd as many of the deadly Points as he can find, he bends close to a small patch of untravel'd Ground. "Forgive me, for what I must now beg you to bear at my hands." Carefully he pushes each Point into the Earth, till only bits of the blunt ends remain.

"These Catawbas," Mason falling increasingly short of perfect nonchalance. "How close are they, I wonder?"

"Whoever set these, they weren't more than two, and they were moving fast. The main body could be anywhere south of here."

" 'Twould be useful to know how far south...?" Dixon supposes.

"He means, let us go on, into sure Ambuscado and Death," Mason hastily, "he's a bit, what do you people call it?" Tapping his Nob and twirling his finger beside it. "Pray do not suppose all Englishmen to be quite so free of care."

"By the time we get anywhere to tell anyone, they'll be someplace else. We'd better go back. For now, say nothing more, and try to move quietly."

Mr. Barnes is troubl'd at the Depth of the Silence that reigns. "No longer frets th' intemperate Jay," he mutters, "— withal, the Siskin chirpeth not."

"Cap'n, what the fuck *is* going on?"

At either end of the Warrior Path, the heat, the agitation, the increasing Tension grow. Never in memory, they are assur'd by their Mohawk Escort, have Iroquois and Catawba each wish'd so passionately the other's Destruction. Any new day may bring the unavoidable Descent.

With Indians all 'round them, the Warpath a-tremble with murd'rous Hopes, its emptiness feeling more and more unnatural as the hours tick on, into the End of Day, as the latent Blades of Warriors press more closely upon the Membrane that divides their Subjunctive World from our number'd and dreamless Indicative, Apprehension rising, Axmen deserting, the ghosts of '55 growing, hourly, more sensible and sovereign,— as unaveng'd Fires foul the Dusk, unanswer'd mortal Cries travel the Forests at the speed of Wind. Ah Christ,— besides West, where else are they heading, those few with the Clarity to remain?

They both dream of going on, unhinder'd, as the Halt dream of running, the Earth-bound of flying. Rays of light appear from behind Clouds, the faces of the Bison upon close Approach grow more human, unbearably so, as if just about to speak, Rivers run swifter, and wider, till at last the Party halts before one that mayn't be cross'd, even by the sturdiest Battoe,— that for miles runs deeper than the height of a Conestoga Waggon. Upon that final Bank, an Indian will appear silently, and lead the party past a forested Bend to a great Bridge, fashion'd of Iron, quite out of reach of British or for that matter French Arts, soaring over to the far Shore, its highest part, whenever there are rain-clouds, indeed lost to sight,— constructed long ago by whatever advanced Nation live upon the River's opposite side.

"May we cross?" asks Dixon.

"May we not cross?" asks Mason.

"Alas," replies the Son of the Forest, "not yet,— for to earn Passage, there is more you must do."

"Why show it to huz at all?" wonders Dixon.

"If I did not, your Great Road thro' the Trees would miss it. You move like wood-borers inside a Post in a great House, in the dark, eating and shitting, moving ever into the Wood and away from your shit, with no idea at all what else lies Without."

"In the Forest," comments Mr. Crawfford, "ev'ryone comes 'round in a Circle sooner or later. One day, your foot comes down in your own shit. There, as the Indians say, is the first Step upon the Trail to Wisdom."

They wake.

70

At the moment of the Interdiction, when their Eyes at length meet, what they believe they once found aboard the *Seahorse* fails, this time, to appear. It is not a faltering on either man's part, or the mistaken impression of one, or any moral lapse,— 'tis a difference of opinion. Mason, stubborn, wishes to go on, believing that with Hugh Crawfford's help, he may negotiate for another ten minutes of Arc.

"But Mason, they don't know what thah' is…?"

"We'll show them. Let them look thro' the Instruments or something. Or they can watch us writing."

"They don't want any of thah'? They want to know how to stop this great invisible Thing that comes crawling Straight on over their Lands, devouring all in its Path."

"Well! of course it's a living creature, 'tis all of us, temporarily collected into an Entity, whose Labors none could do alone."

"A tree-slaughtering Animal, with no purpose but to continue creating forever a perfect Corridor over the Land. Its teeth of Steel,— its Jaws, Axmen,— its Life's Blood, Disbursement. And what of its intentions, beyond killing ev'rything due west of it? do you know? I don't either."

"Then,— just tidying these thoughts up a bit,— you're saying this Line has a Will to proceed Westward,— "

"What else are these people suppos'd to believe? Haven't we been saying, with an hundred Blades all the day long,— This is how far into your land we may strike, this is what we claim to westward. As you see what we may do to Trees, and how little we care,— imagine how little we care for Indians, and what we are prepar'd to do to you. That Influence you have felt, along our Line, that Current strong as a River's,— we command it.... We might make thro' your Nations an Avenue of Ruin, terrible as the Path of a Whirl-Wind."

"But those are Threats we do not make."

"But might as well make. As the Indians wish, we must go no further."

"No. We must go on."

For eleven Days, from the ninth thro' the nineteenth of October, they linger beside Dunkard Creek, the Indians keeping their distance, looking to their Weapons, as to their Routes of withdrawal, whilst the White Folk dispute. Some of the Hands are back east of here, cutting the Visto to Breadth, as Autumn closes in and ev'ryone is eager to be away, for there are other Tasks that claim each in the Party, including the Surveyors,— who at some point exchange Positions, with Dixon now for pushing on, razzle-dazzling their way among the Indians at least as far as Ohio. "Cheer's the Ticket. Let them have more than their daily Ration of Spirits. They'll be Sports."

"Wait,— you think you'll be getting through on *charm?* Indians all the way up into the Six Nations and down to the Cherokee know about that Coat,— many have their Eye upon it, and you are but the minor inconvenience from which 'twill have to be remov'd."

The Indians grow coy and sinister. The Women stare openly, steadily amus'd. Mason and Dixon are allow'd to cross the War-path, and three more Turnings of Dunkard Creek, before they can climb to a Ridge-top high enough to set up the Sector. At last the Dodmen have reach'd their Western Terminus, at 233 Miles, 13 Chains, and 68 Links from the Post Mark'd West. "Damme, we're only a few miles shy."

" 'A few'! Forty miles?"

" 'Tis easy country. We're over the last ridge. We're in the Ohio Country."

Mason has seen it from the top of Laurel Hill, "...the most delightful pleasing View of the Western Plains the Eye can behold,"— the Paradise once denied him by the Mills, now denied him by, he supposes,

British American Policy ever devious. They decide to travel light and fast,— not to take the Sector, nor any other Instrument. "Mustn't tie thah' River in, just yet...?"

"Aye, let them all be free while they may."

Mason is Gothickally depressive, as Dixon is Westeringly manic. Dixon's Head, like a Needle forever ninety degrees out, tho' it wobble some, remains true to perfect West, whilst Mason might as well be riding backwards, so often does he look behind, certain they are about to meet an abbreviation of Braddock's Fate. Mason withal, via the happenstances of God's Whimsy, is riding Creeping Nick, the same crazy animal that threw him on to the Jersey Ice. Departing at Sun-down, keeping their Latitude as best they may by Polaris, growing more fearful with ev'ry Mile, they travel thro' the Night, trans-Terminal America whirling by, smelling of wildflowers and Silt, and immediate Lobes of Honeysuckle-scent apt to ambush the unwary Nose, amid moonlight, owls, smears of nocturnal Color somewhere off-center in the Field of Vision,— they make it to the great River just at Dawn,— the Rush of the Water loud as the Sea,— stunn'd by the beauty of it they forget, they linger, they over-stay all practickal Time, and are surpriz'd by a Party of Indians in elaborate Paint-Work.

"Far from your Tents, Red Coat." It is Catfish and his Nephew, and some Friends, who reluctantly lower their Rifles.

"Having a Look at the River, Sir," Dixon replies.

"There are Catawba Parties about. Mingoes, Seneca. Good thing we saw you first. How'd you sneak out past Hendricks? He never sleeps."

Mason sees it first,— then, tipp'd by his frozen silence, Dixon. Catfish is packing a Lancaster Rifle, slung in a Scabbard upon his Saddle, with an inverted Pentacle upon the Stock, unmistakable in the Moon-light. Mason looks over, on the possibility that Dixon has a Plan, and sees Dixon already looking back at him, upon the same deluded Hope.

"Actually," says Dixon, "we only just arriv'd, so it isn't as if we've 'seen' the River, if that poses any sort of problem,— "

"— and it certainly isn't as if we're planning to settle here,— "

Catfish with one huge hand slides the Rifle out and holds it up before him, noticing the Sterloop as if for the first time. He smiles without mirth at the Surveyors. "You think this is my Rifle? No! I took this Rifle! From a White man I have wish'd to meet for a long time. He was a very bad man. Even White People hated him. Beautiful Piece, isn't it?"

"The Sign on it has evil Powers," Mason warns. "You should take a Knife or something, and pry it out."

"What happen'd to its owner?" Dixon with a look of unsuccessfully feign'd innocence.

The Delaware is delighted to share that information with them, pulling from a Bag he carries a long Lock of fair European Hair so freshly taken, 'tis yet darkly a-drip, at one end, with Blood. "This very day, Milords. Had you been earlier, you might have met."

Either Mason or Dixon might reply, "We've met,"— yet neither does. "It didn't feel complete to me," Mason admits later, "I expected he yet liv'd, screaming about the Woods, driven to revenge at any price, a Monomaniack with a Hole in the top of his Head,— "

"— looking for that Rifle back," adds Dixon.

Coming back, setting in the last Marks, crossing Jennings Run, little Allegheny, Wills Creek, Wills Creek Mountain, the Road up to Bedford, Evitts Creek, Evitts Mountain, at all the highest Points in the Visto, they put up Cairns, as the ancient British Ley-builders and Dodsmen before them, as later the Romans, for purposes more Legionary than commercial. The Hands keep leaving, without notice. With those who stay, the Astronomers, transiting from Weightless Obs to earthly back-wrenching Toil the Obs demand by way of Expression, set Posts ev'ry Mile, these being large segments of Tree, roughly squar'd, twelve by twelve inches, and five or sometimes six or seven foot long. First the Crew dig a deep Post-Hole, put in the Post, fill back the Hole, tamping down the Earth scientifickally, one shovel-ful at a time, then bring more Stone and Earth to make a Cone about the Post, leaving perhaps six inches of it visible. That is the Surveyors' estimate of the Mark's Longevity,— tho' of course Angles of Repose vary,— and withal, Mason and Dixon will bicker, by now, over anything.

On November 5th, two things happen at once,— the Visto is completed, and the Indians depart,— as if, as long as a Tree remain'd, so might they. At last the Axmen have clear'd the Visto back to the Post marking their last Station of the Year previous,— east of which all lies clear, all the way back to Delaware. "There being one continued Visto," Mason writes in the Journal, "opened in the true Parallel from the intersection of the North Line from the Tangent Point with the Parallel to the Ridge we left off at on the 9th of October last.

"Mr. Hugh Crawford with the Indians and all Hands (except 13 kept to Erect Marks in the Line etc.) Left us in order to proceed Home."

The departing Axmen roam about peering at, poking, and buying Blankets, Kettles, Milch Cows, Grindstones, anything Mo McClean thinks he may sell to lighten the load, before the Mountains, no offer too insulting. The Vendue is a protracted Spectacle of sorrowful farewells, Debts settl'd or evaded, Whiskey Jugs a-swing, upon ev'ry Index, and a Squirrel Stuffata from the Commissary Tent without equal this side of the Allegheny Ridge. At length, the last of the Farmers, new-bought pots and pans a-clank, goes riding off into a dusk render'd in copper-plate, gray and black, the Hatching too crowded to allow for any reversal, or return...leaving gather'd by the Waggons, smoking Pipes, gray with fatigue and winter sky-light, Mr. Barnes, Cope, Rob Farlow, the McCleans, Tom Hynes, Boggs Junior, John and Ezekiel Killogh,— and the others of that faithful Core who stay'd across Monongahela, to the Warrior Path, and the westernmost Ridge, and back again.

None of the Hands is feeling that well. Dixon has been giving out opiated Philtres to all who would but gesture toward their Noses,— as Mo McClean is writing at furious speed, Chits upon Philadelphia Money-Boxes as if he'll never see the place again, so what's it matter? Suddenly Expenditures are above £100, then £200, per week. Fiscal insanity has visited the Commissary Tent. Sensing opportunity, Farmers with goods to sell appear from Horizons all swear have been empty for Hours.

The snow drives in relentlessly. From the ninth to the nineteenth of November,— another eleven-day Spin,— there is little in the Field-Book,— suggesting either a passage so difficult that there was no time for nightly entries, or events so blameworthy on all sides that they were omitted from the Account.

In fact, such was the level of Engagement requir'd to answer to the Elements, as to mark the Line, that there was no time for bad behavior. This is the Gradient of Days in which the Party must work their way up to the Allegheny Crest, hastening as they may, the early Winter having caught them west of the Mountains. Here lie the most difficult Miles of the long Traverse, this ascent out of Ohio and out of the West. Unsettl'd by the abrupt Absence of Mohawks, with whom they have come to feel almost secure, as so seldom in this Continent of Hazard, the Skies, night upon night, too clouded over for Observations, both Surveyors, cast into Perplexity, Drink and play Whist for Sums neither will ever see all in one place at the same time,— the Crew meanwhile deserting Day upon Day, their replacements taking ever more exorbitant Wages,— yet, whilst they bide in this Realm of the Penny-foolish and Pound-idiotick, till the Moment they must pass over the Crest of the Savage Mountain, does there remain to them, contrary to Reason, against the Day, a measurable chance, to turn, to go back out of no more than Stubbornness, and somehow make all come right...for, once over the Summit, they will belong again to the East, to Chesapeake,— to Lords for whom Interests less subjunctive must ever enjoy Priority.

They have lost their Race with the first Snows,— now they pray they may get all the Cairns dug and pil'd before the Ground freezes too hard. The Snow is already a foot deep. Traces break, a Waggon skids back down the Slope on its side, the Canvas bellying, the Animals fearfully trying to fight clear,— Tent-Poles and Spades a-clatter, a Lanthorn against the low-lit Day, falling and smashing upon the Ice, tiny trails of Flame borne instantly away. Here are the last Cadre, out in the uninterrupted Visto,— from a certain Height, oddly verminous upon the pale Riband unfolding,— fairly out in the Hundred-League Current of *Sha*, where ev'ry Step is purchas'd with a further surrender of Ignorance as to what they have finish'd,— what they have left at their Backs, undone,— what, measuring the Degree of Latitude next Spring, they shall be newly complicit in,— tho' if it takes them much longer to get over the Ridge, even if they escape freezing solid, they may yet have journey'd further into Terrestrial Knowledge, than will allow them to re-emerge without bargaining away too much for merely another Return following another Excursion, in a Cycle belonging to some Engine whose higher Assembly and indeed Purpose, they are never, except from infrequent Glimpses, quite able to make out.

...

Turn'd in Retreat Eastward again, watch'd from Cover at ev'ry step, with Apprehensions, instead of lessening, rather mounting, Ridge by Ridge, the Party feel the Warrior Path engrossing more of their sentimental Horizon, even as it recedes into the West. Immediately upon the deaths of Baker and Carpenter begin a string of mishaps between Men and Trees, some nearly lethal, none unconnected.... Felling-Mates try to keep as close as they may, often conversing more in a day than they have in all the time since they team'd up. Spending precious Minutes in daily Rituals of Protection, all pay Tolls at the Gate of Sunrise, good but for the one Day that must be got thro'.—

Mason and Dixon look in again at The Rabbi of Prague, inquiring in partickular after Timothy Tox. "He is mad," Countrymen are soon explaining to them. "What he now styles, '*His* Golem,' does not exist." Mr. Tox looks on with a tolerant Smile.

"Because he heard it speak the same words as God out of the Burning Bush, Tim nowadays imagines himself Moses,— with a Commission from God, to bring another People out of Captivity."

"Out of the City," declares Timothy Tox, "where Affliction ever reigns, must the Golem deliver them, over Schuylkill, out of that American Egypt."

"You don't want to be going into Philadelphia, Lad," they warn him, "— carrying Folk off and so forth. Nor, particularly, confiding in too many of those Cits about the Goah-lem, now, for to many of them, the Old Knowledge is an Evil they'll be as content to execute ye for, as lock ye away."

"I am quite undeluded," the Forest Dithyrambist replies, "as to the Philadelphians,— before all, the Lawyers,— come, come, does no one recall,

> ' 'Tis only by the Grace that some call Luck
> That anyone can quite escape the Muck.—
> As e'er, 'mongst Wax, and Wigs, and Printer's Ink
> Seepeth the creeping sly Suborner's Stink.— ' "

"There he goes!"
"So do ye summon it, Tim, we're *on* to that by now?"

"It will protect me, as it will protect them it sets free."

" 'Twas ne'er your Creature to command, Tim."

"Just so. It is our Guardian."

Mason and Dixon, each revisiting The Rabbi of Prague for his distinct Reasons, attend this Discussion closely. Dixon has already propos'd offering Mr. Tox the Protection of the Party as far as Newark, near the Tangent Point.

"So long as he doesn't bring the Golem," stipulates Mason. "He brings the Golem,— well,— what do they eat, for example? What are their sanitary Requirements? How shall Mo McClean, who's already striking himself daily upon the Pate with his own Ledgers, find the additional Resources?"

"Yet, mightn't we turn the Creature to some useful work,— say upon the Visto? Pulling up the Trees by their Roots,— clearing out all those un-sightly Stumps?"

"The Axmen would never hear of it. Next two-story House we came to, we'd both be taken upstairs and defenestrated. Nay,— I know what you seek,— the Neighborhood of Prodigy,— the Mobility Awe-struck,— Entry to Saloons you have previously been unwelcome in,— " Whilst Mason himself, of course, is angling quite a different Stream. Here is a Creature made of Water and Earth,— Clay, that is, and Minerals,— as if an Indian Mound of the West, struck by Lightning, had risen, stood, and, newly awaken'd, with the *Vis Fulgoris* surging among all its precisely fashion'd Laminæ, begun, purposefully, to walk. An American Wonder, one's own witness of which might even be brought back across the cold Sea, to the true, terminable World again. Mason can think of no way to ask the obvious Question, as he did of the Learnèd Dog, and has been reluctant to of the Frenchman's Duck. Now withal, Time for this grows short,— just outside, in the Forest, articulate as Drumming, can be heard the rhythmick approach of the Kabbalistick Colossus Mr. Tox has summon'd. Mason and Dixon place their Heads upon the Table, and regard each other solemnly, in joint awareness of how much Effort will be needed, this time, to believe Mr. Tox's Testimony, as to whatever is about to appear....

As 'twill prove, the closer they escort Mr. Tox to the Metropolis, the less Evidence for his Creature's existence will they be given, till at length they must believe that the Poet has either pass'd, like some Indian Youth at the Onset of Manhood, under the Protection of a potent tho' invisible Spirit,— or gone mad. They leave him upon the New Castle Road, standing among the late purple Loosestrife by the Ditch, glancing upward from time to time, waving his Arm,— then growing still, appearing to listen. Just before he has dwindl'd around the last bend in their own Road, Mason and Dixon see a Conestoga Waggon, with an exceptionally bright Canopy, and drawn by match'd white Horses, stop beside him. Timothy Tox without hesitation goes around to the Tail-Gate, and climbs up under the luminous Canvas, vanishing within, as if confident that the Golem, whose Strides are at least as long as a Team and Waggon, will contrive to stay close to him, wherever he is taken, and whatever may befall him there.

71

Back again, Tavern-crawling near the Wharves upon Delaware, Ale-stuporous, the Surveyors enter The Crook'd Finger Inn,— "We both know what it is, Dixon," Mason is instructing his Partner, "— your hour is come, your Innings, for Retributive Poultrification,— at last, you must prepare, mustn't you, for all that Expression of Jesuit Interest so long-deferr'd,— this next Commission being, after all, the one they were engineering all along, isn't it, yes, another Degree of Latitude to put with the others they've appropriated, this is what it all's been leading to, correct? Wondrous! Now shall you,— at least,— finally learn, perhaps even via the Jesuit Telegraph, *why you are here,*— a Blessing extended to how few. Anything I can do to help, of course.— "

"Eeh, but whah's the use, the fuckin' use?" Dixon resting his head briefly tho' audibly upon the Table. "It's over...? Nought left to us but Paper-work...?" Their task has shifted, from Direct Traverse upon the Line to Pen-and-Paper Representation of it, in the sober Day-Light of Philadelphia, strain'd thro' twelve-by-twelve Sash-work, as in the spectreless Light of the Candles in their Rooms, suffering but the fretful Shadows of Dixon at the Drafting Table, and Mason, seconding now, reading from Entries in the Field-Book, as Dixon once minded the Clock for him. Finally, one day, Dixon announces, "Well,— won't thee at least have a look...?"

Mason eagerly rushes to inspect the Map of the Boundaries, almost instantly boggling, for there bold as a Pirate's Flag is an eight-pointed Star, surmounted by a Fleur-de-Lis.

"What's this thing here? pointing North? Wasn't the *l'Grand* flying one of these? Doth it not signify, England's most inveterately hated Rival? France?"

"All respect, Mason,— among Brother and Sister Needle-folk in ev'ry Land, 'tis known universally, as the 'Flower-de-Luce.' A Magnetickal Term."

" 'Flower of Light'? *Light,* hey? Sounds Encyclopedistick to me, perhaps even Masonick," says Mason.

A Surveyor's North-Point, Dixon explains, by long Tradition, is his own, which he may draw, and embellish, in any way he pleases, so it point where North be. It becomes his Hall-Mark, personal as a Silver-Smith's, representative of his Honesty and Good Name. Further, as with many Glyphs, 'tis important ever to keep Faith with it,— for an often enormous Investment of Faith, and Will, lies condens'd within, giving it a Potency in the World that the Agents of Reason care little for.

" 'Tis an ancient Shape, said to go back to the earliest Italian Wind-Roses," says Dixon, "— originally, at the North, they put the Letter *T,* for *Tramontane,* the Wind that blew down from the Alps...? Over the years, as ever befalls such frail Bric-a-Brack as Letters of the Alphabet, it was beaten into a kind of Spear-head,— tho' the kinder-hearted will aver it a Lily, and clash thy Face, do tha deny it."

"Yet some, finding it upon a new Map, might also take it as a reassertion of French claims to Ohio," Mason pretends to remind him.

"Aye, tha've found me out, I confess,— 'tis a secret Message to all who conspire in the Dark! Eeh! The old Jesuit Canard again!"

At which Armand runs in looking anxious. "The Duck is doing something...*autoerotique,* now?" They re-phrase,— unconsol'd, Armand wanders away. Becoming reaccustom'd to this City's Angular Momentum is costing him daily Struggle. He appears to miss the West Line, and the Duck it has captur'd and denied him.

"Perhaps, for this Map alone," it occurs to Mason, "as East and West are of the Essence, North need hardly be indicated at all, need it? Or, suppose you were to sketch in something...less politickal?"

"This has been my North Point," Dixon declares, "since the first Map I ever drew. I cannot very readily forswear it, now, Sir, for some temporary Tradesman's Sign. It does not generally benefit the Surveyor to debase the Value of his North Point, by lending it to ends Politickal. 'Twould be to betray my Allegiance to Earth's Magnetism, Earth Herself if tha like, which my Flower-de-Luce stands faithfully as the Emblem of...?"

Making no more sense of this than he ever may, Mason shrugs. "It may sit less comfortably with the Proprietors, than with me."

"Oh, they're as happy to twit a King, when they may, as the next Lad,— "

"Hahr! So that *is* it!"

"Thy uncritical Worship of Kings, with my inflexible Hatred of 'em,— taken together, we equal one latter-day English Subject."

"Much more likely Twins, ever in Dispute,— as the Indians once told us the Beginning of the World."

"Huz? I'm far too jolly a soul ever to fight with thee for long...?"

"Because you know how your Shins would suffer...." Mason is able to inspect the long Map, fragrant, elegantly cartouch'd with Indians and Instruments, at last. Ev'ry place they ran it, ev'ry House pass'd by, Road cross'd, the Ridge-lines and Creeks, Forests and Glades, Water ev'rywhere, and the Dragon nearly visible. "So,— so. This is the Line as all shall see it after its Copper-Plate 'Morphosis,— and all History remember? This is what ye expect me to sign off on?"

"Not the worst I've handed in. And had they wish'd to pay for Coloring? Why, tha'd scarcely knaah the Place...?"

"This is beauteous Work. Emerson was right, Jeremiah. You were flying, all the time."

Dixon, his face darken'd by the Years of Weather, may be allowing himself to blush in safety. "Could have us'd a spot of Orpiment, all the same. Some Lapis...?"

"It is possible," here comments the Revd Cherrycoke, "that for some couples, however close, Love is simply not in the cards. So must they pursue other projects, instead,— sometimes together, sometimes apart. I believe now, that their Third Interdiction came when, at the end of the eight-Year Traverse, Mason and Dixon could not cross the perilous Boundaries between themselves."

Whatever happen'd at the Warrior-Path, the Partners are to remain amicably together, among the cheerless Bogs of Delaware, thro' nearly another Year, busy with the Royal Society's Degree of Latitude, chaining a Meridian over the same ground as the Tangent Line, shivering in the Damp of Morning after Morning, both fending off the Ague with the miraculous willow-bark powder discover'd by the Rev^d Mr. Edmund Stone, of Chipping Norton,— return'd to the vegetational Horizons, the Sumach whose Touch brings misery, the deadly water-snakes coil'd together like the *Rugæ* of a single great Brain, the gray and even illumination from the Sky.

Their Agreement to un-couple may easily have come, not after all during the crisis of the Year before, at the Warrior-Path, but rather here, somewhere upon this Peninsula, wrapp'd in the lambent Passing of any forgotten day of mild Winds, the Day as ever, little to distinguish it from others before and after but the values enter'd for Miles, Chains, and Links,— and why not here, especially with leisure and opportunity at last to talk of Plans for the second Transit, the possibility of return to America...?

The Story among Dixon's Descendants will be that Uncle Jeremiah wish'd to emigrate and settle here, and that his Partner did not,— tho' in the Field-Book, as late as June 9, Mason is to be found rhapsodizing in writing about Mr. Twiford's seat upon Nanticoke, as he does thro'out the Book as to other Homes, other Rivers, or Towns upon them. To Dixon,— "Aye how pleasing in all ways. Yet address any of it too intently, and like Dreams just at the Crepuscule, 'twill all vanish, unrecoverably."

"Shakespearean, correct?"

"Nay, Transcendence,— 'twas but Masonick."

Dixon gazes at the River, the gentle points and Coves in the mist, the willows and Loblolly Pines, desiring, whilst humiliated at how impossible it is to desire any Terrain in its interminable unfolding, ev'ry last Pebble, dip, and rain-path. For Mason, the Year of Delaware is all passing like a Dream. He can believe in this Degree they are measuring but in the way he believes in Ghosts,— for all its massless Suggestion, Number is yet more sensible to him, than this America that haunts his Progress. "Stay? Here? Christ, no, Dixon.— 'Twas an Odyssey,— now must I return to the Destiny ever waiting for me,— faithfully,— her Loom now mine to sit and toil at, to the end of days, whilst she's out, no doubt, with any number of Suitors, roaring and merry."

("Well," suggests Uncle Lomax, "It's Pope and Lady Montague all over again, isn't it? A touchy race, the Brits, unfathomable, apt to take offense at anything, disputes can go on for years."

"Yet 'twas never *that* cold," declares the Rev^d.) Each seem'd to be content in postponing a return to England, and thereby to what others there expected. Measuring the Degree, they may have intended to hide somehow, inside the Work-day,— surrendering, as openly as they ever could, into a desire to transcend their differently discomforted lives, through what, at the end of the Day, would be but Ranks and Files of Numerals, ever in the Darkness of Pages unopen'd and unturn'd, Ink already begun to fade, from Type since melted and re-cast numberless times,— all but Oblivion,— The Delaware country their Refuge,— no steep grades,— "as level for 82 Miles," they wrote to the Royal Society, "as if it had been formed by Art," a phrase later to be found in Maskelyne's introduction to their publish'd Observations (1769),— no hostile Indians, fresh food, Cities in easy reach, Obs themselves straight-forward and not even all that many,— to the World's Eye, two veteran Wise-Men, coasting along between Transits of Venus, soon to be off again for more glamorous foreign duty where the Seeing's perfect and the Food never less than exquisite, and Adventures ever ahead and unforeseen, Boscovich and Maire all over again,— a Godly pursuit, and profitable withal, if only in the Value of Commissions to come.".

Yet at the same time, silently parallel to the Pleasantries of teamwork, runs their effort to convince themselves that whatever they have left upon the last ridge-top, just above the last stone cairn, as if left burning, as if left exhibited in chains before the contempt of all who pass, will find an end to its torment, and fragment by fragment across the seasons be taken back into the Tales preserv'd in Memory, among Wind-gusts, subterranean Fires, Over-Creatures of the Wild, Floods and Freezes... until one day 'twill all be gone, re-assum'd, only its silence left there to be clamor'd into by something else, something younger, without memory of, or respect for, what was once, across the third Turning of Dunkard Creek, brought to a halt....

But it does not die. It comes out at nightfall and visits, singly obsess'd with a task left undone. Newcomers choose other Ridge-lines to settle in the Shadows of, Indian Priests proclaim it forbidden Ground, even unto the Lead-Mines beneath,— Smugglers of Tobacco, Dye-stuffs, and edg'd Implements flee their Storage-Cabins in the middle of the night, leaving behind Inventories whose odd scavengers prove as little able to with-stand the disconsolate spirit prevailing here, as if 'twere the Point upon which was being daily projected, some great linear summing of Human Incompletion,— fail'd Arrivals, Departures too soon, mis-stated Inten-tions, truncations of Desire. Even the uncommonly stolid Stig feels it, in his Perplexity resorting more and more often to the Handle of his Ax for Re-assurance,— Captain Zhang each night in his Tent, shivering, con-tinues to express concern as to the *Sha* Situation. "Returning from here will be not much better. In *Sha* there is no up- nor down-Stream,— rather a Flow at all points sensible, equally harmful, east or west. Our Sorrows shall persist and obsess for as long as we continue upon this ill-omen'd Line."

Too often, back here, they find themselves chaining through wet-lands, the water usually a foot and a half to two feet deep,— Daylight somewhere above them, indifferent, the Gloom in here forcing them to shorter sights, more set-ups, closer Quarters. As they stand in the muck of the Cypress Swamp, black and thinly crusted, each Step breaking through to release a Smell of Generations of Deaths, something in it, some principle of untaught Mechanicks, tugging at their ankles, voice-less, importunate,— a moment arrives, when one of them smacks his Pate for something other than a Mosquitoe.

"Ev'rywhere they've sent us,— the Cape, St. Helena, America,— what's the Element common to all?"

"Long Voyages by Sea," replies Mason, blinking in Exhaustion by now chronick. "Was there anything else?"

"Slaves. Ev'ry day at the Cape, we lived with Slavery in our faces,— more of it at St. Helena,— and now here we are again, in another Colony, this time having drawn them a Line between their Slave-Keepers, and their Wage-Payers, as if doom'd to re-encounter thro' the World this pub-lic Secret, this shameful Core.... Pretending it to be ever somewhere else, with the Turks, the Russians, the Companies, down there, down where it smells like warm Brine and Gunpowder fumes, they're murder-ing and dispossessing thousands untallied, the innocent of the World, passing daily into the Hands of Slave-owners and Torturers, but oh, never in Holland, nor in England, that Garden of Fools...? Christ, Mason."

"Christ, what? What did I do?"

"Huz. Didn't we take the King's money, as here we're taking it again? whilst Slaves waited upon us, and we neither one objected, as little as we have here, in certain houses south of the Line,— Where does it end? No matter where in it we go, shall we find all the World Tyrants and Slaves? America was the one place we should *not* have found them."

"Yet we're not Slaves, after all,— we're Hirelings."

"I don't trust this King, Mason. I don't think anybody else does, either. Tha saw Lord Ferrers take the Drop at Tyburn. *They execute their own.* What may they be willing to do to huz?"

72

First they have to mark a Meridian Line, then clear a Visto, then measure straight up the middle of it, using "Levels," great wooden Rectangles twenty feet long by four feet high, and an inch thick, mostly of Pine Boards, with iron and Brass securing the reinforcing Bands,— which would have serv'd handsomely in many of these Fens as Duck-Boards or Rafts, but must instead be carried carefully upright, being compar'd most dutifully ev'ry day with how close to eight times a five-foot Brass Standard might be fit in the length of the two Levels set end to end,— and into the Daily corrections needed, the Temperature reckon'd and enter'd as well. Each Plumb-line is protected from the Wind by a three-foot Tube. When tilted until the Plumb-line bisects a certain Point drawn at the bottom, the Level is level. 'Tis then necessary only to set it with its Mate, together in a forty-foot Line easily kept true by sighting down its Length toward the farthest point of the Visto they can see, on the assumption the Visto has been truly made.

"Back in Durham we style this a Squire's Line,— using the Equipment of the Gentleman who hires thee, easy Terrain, careful work, turning the Telescope over and over, bit of fancy artwork upon the Plane-Table Drafts. Careful and slow."

"Slow, 'tis certain." Mason has long dropp'd all pretense at Patience. There are days when the Routine has him livid with boredom. "As Lady Montague said of Bath, the only thing one can do upon this Engagement, that one did not do the Day before— "

"Bad Luck, don't say it!" shouts Dixon thro' his Speaking-Trumpet, tho' they are close enough not to require any, causing Mason to wince.

"Never mind when,— *shall* it end? Set a Mark before, set a Mark behind, swing the Instrument, do it again the other Way, 's fucking Body and Blood, Dixon, I am beside myself."

Dixon, approaching a few steps, gazes intently a foot and a half to Mason's right. "Eeh,— why, so yese are. How does thah' feel, I wonder...?" Switching his eyes to Mason, then back to the Spot beside Mason, "Well, why don't one of thee go ahead, and the other behind me, makes it much easier to line up the Marks...?"

"Ahrrh! Like a giant Eye! ever a-stare!" He is referring to the Target, a Board about a Foot Square, with Concentrick Circles drawn on both sides, rigg'd to be slid in two grooves, at the distant gesturing of the man at the Telescope, till it should line up precisely upon the central Wire, previously brought into the Meridian,— whereupon the other Surveyor hammers in his Stake immediately below, drops his Plummet-String along the center-line of the Target, and marks with a Notch exactly where, atop the Stake, the Bob-Point touches. Then the Transit Instrument leap-frogs the Target and goes ahead of it, its operator sets up, and takes a Back-sight at the Eye upon the Board's Reverse. Then they do it all again.

"I find little serious Astronomy in any of this," Mason complains.

It may be the level'd and selfless Pulse of it that enables them, at the end of June, the Measurement done, at last to travel South together, across the West Line, into Peril however differently constru'd, leading to Baltimore and the moment when Dixon will accost the Slave-Driver in the Street, and originate the family story whose material Focus, for years among the bric-a-brac in Hull, will be the Driver's Lash, that Uncle Jeremiah took away from the Scoundrel....

"No proof," declares Ives. "No entries for Days, allow'd,— but yet no proof."

"Alas," beams the Rev[d], "must we place our unqualified Faith in the Implement, as the Tale accompting for its Presence,— these Family stories have been perfected in the hellish Forge of Domestick Recension, generation 'pon generation, till what survives is the pure truth, anneal'd to Mercilessness, about each Figure, no matter how stretch'd, nor how influenced over the years by all Sentiments from unreflective love to inflexible Dislike."

"Don't leave out Irresponsible Embellishment."

"Rather, part of the common Duty of Remembering,— surely our Sentiments,— how we dream'd of, and were mistaken in, each other,— count for at least as much as our poor cold Chronologies."

The Driver's Whip is an evil thing, an expression of ill feeling worse than any between Master and Slave,— the contempt of the monger of perishable goods for his Merchandise,— in its tatter'd braiding, darken'd to its Lash-Tips with the sweat and blood of Drove after Drove of human targets, the metal Wires work'd in to each Lash, its purpose purely to express hate with, and Hate's Corollary,— to beg for the same denial of Mercy, should, one day, the rôles be revers'd. Gambling that they may not be. Or, that they may.

Dixon has spoken with him already, the night before, in the Publick Room of his Inn. The Slave-Driver is announcing a Vendue at the Dock, twenty Africans, Men and Women, each a flower of the Tribe they had been taken from. Yet he is calling them by names more appropriate to Animals one has come to dislike. Several times Dixon feels the need, strong as thirst, to get up, walk over to the fellow and strike him.

"And so I hope ev'ryone will come down and have a look, dusky children of the Forest, useful in any number o' ways, cook and eat 'em, fuck 'em or throw 'em to the Dogs, as we say in the Trade, imagine Gents, your very own Darky, to order about as you please. You, Sir, in the interesting Hat," beckoning to Dixon, who raises his Brows amiably, at the same time freezing with the certainty that once again he is about to see a face he knows. Someone from the recent past, whose name he cannot remember. "A fine young Mulatto gal'd be just your pint of Ale I'd wager, well tonight you're in luck, damme 'f you're not."

"Not in the Market," replies Dixon, as he imagines, kindly.

"Ho!" drawing back in feign'd Surprize, "what's this, not in the market, how then may I even begin to educate you, Sir, or should I say, *Friend,* upon this Topick? The news, Friend, being that all are in the

Market,— however regrettably,— for ev'ryone wants a slave, at least one, to call his own...."

"Sooner or later," Dixon far too brightly, "— a Slave must kill his Master. It is one of the Laws of Springs." The Herdsman of Humans, who has been staring at Dixon, now looks about for a line of Withdrawal. "Give me Engines, for *they* have no feelings of injustice,— sometimes they don't exist, either, so I have to invent what I need...," at which point the Enterpriser has edg'd his way as far as the door.

"Remember, tomorrow, midday at the Pier!" and he is off like a shot.

Attention shifts to Dixon, whose insane demeanor has vanish'd with the Dealer's Departure.

"Will you be there, Sir?" inquires a neighboring Drinker, more sociably teasing, than wishing to sting. "Being one of our Sights down here, of interest to a Visitor,— you might find it diverting. Not quite as much as a Horse Auction, o' course."

Dixon vibrated his Eye-balls for a while. "That's it? Slaves and Horses?"

"Why, and Tobacco! Ye've never been to a Tobacco Auction? Say, ye'll never listen to an Italian Tenor the same way again."

In '55, at the grim news of Braddock's Fate, Pennsylvanians had come flying Eastward before the Indians, over Susquehanna, in a panic,— here in the Chesapeake Slave country, rather stretch'd long nights of Apprehension, the counting of Kitchen Knives, Fears conceal'd, Fears detected, Fears betray'd, of poisons in the food, stranglings at midnight, Women violated, Horses and Cash, House and Home, gone,— as their Spoliators into the boundless Continent,— and everywhere the soft Weight of the nocturnal Breath, above that water-riddl'd Country.

In his heart, Mason has grown accustom'd to the impossibility, between Dixon and himself, of Affection beyond a certain Enclosure. They have spent years together inside one drawn Perimeter and another. They also know how it is out in the Forest, over the Coastal ranges, out of metropolitan Control. Only now, far too late, does Mason develop a passion for his co-adjutor, comparable to that occurring between Public-School Students in England.—

"Oh, please Wicks spare us, far too romantick really," mutter several voices at once.

Say then, that Mason at last came to admire Dixon for his Bravery,— a different sort than they'd shown each other years before, on the *Seahorse*, where they'd had no choice. Nor quite the same as they'd both exhibited by the Warrior Path. Here in Maryland, they had a choice at last, and Dixon chose to act, and Mason not to,— unless he had to,— what each of us wishes he might have the unthinking Grace to do, yet fails to do. To act for all those of us who have so fail'd. For the Sheep. Yet Mason offer'd his Admiration, so long and unreasonably withheld, only to provide Dixon fodder for more Rustick Joakery.

"All...? Pray thee, Mason, shall I have a special U-niform for thah'? Something with a Cloak to it,— Mantua-length would be better, wouldn't it, than all the way down, for I would need access to my Pistol,— "

There unavoidable in the Street is the Slave Driver. And he's driving about half his Drove, who thro' some inconvenient behavior, remain unsold. He is screaming, having abandon'd all control, and Striking ev'rywhere with the Whip, mostly encountering the Air, even with the movements of the Africans limited by the Chains, having fail'd to inflict much Injury. "You *fuck'd* up my Sale, you *fuck'd* up my day, you *fuck'd* up my business,— *Now* I owe money, *plus* another night's Lodging, *plus* another night's Victualling,— "

"I'll just seek Assistance, then, shall I?" Mason making as if to flee.

"Mason, thou're the only one nearby who knows how to watch my Back,— would tha mind, frightfully?" And before Mason can stir, Dixon is down the Steps, and into the Street.

"That's enough." He stands between the Whip and the Slaves, with his Hat back and his hand out. Later he won't remember how. "I'll have that."

"You'll have it to your Head, Friend, if you don't step out of my Way. These are mine,— I'll do as I damn'd please with my Property." Townsfolk pause to observe.

Dixon, moving directly, seizes the Whip,— the owner comes after it,— Dixon places his Fist in the way of the oncoming Face,— the Driver cries out and stumbles away. Dixon follows, raising the Whip. "Turn around. I'll guess *you've* never felt this."

"You broke my Tooth!"

"In a short while thah's not going to matter much, because in addition, I'm going to kill *you*...? Now be a man, face me, and make it easier, or must I rather work upon *you* from the Back, like a Beast, which will take longer, and certainly mean more discomfort for *you*."

"No! Please! My little ones! O Tiffany! Jason!"

"Any more?"

"— Scott!"

Dixon reaches down and tears, from the man's Belt, a ring of keys. "Who knows where these go?"

"We know them by heart, Sir," replies one tall woman in a brightly strip'd Head-Cloth. With the Driver protesting the usefulness of his Life, the Africans unchain themselves.

"Now then!" cries Dixon merrily.

A not at all friendly crowd by now having form'd,— "And as we're in the middle of Town, here," the Africans advise him, "Sheriff's men'll be here any moment,— don't worry about us,— some will stay, some'll get away,— but you'd better go, right now."

Despite this sound Counsel, Dixon still greatly desires to kill the Driver, cringing there among the Waggon-Ruts. What's a man of Conscience to do? It is frustrating. His Voice breaks. "If I see *you* again, *you* are a dead man." He shakes the Whip at him. "And dead *you'll* be, ere *you* see again this Instrument of Shame. For it will lie in a Quaker Home, and never more be us'd."

"Don't bet the Meeting-House on that," snarls the Driver, scuttling away.

"Go back to Philadelphia," someone shouts at Dixon.

"Good Withdrawal-Line or two here, yet," reports Mason.

Thrusting the Whip into his red Coat, Dixon steps away, Mason following. At the first brick Prow of a house to block them from View, they take to their Heels, returning by a roundabout and not altogether witting route to the Stable where their Horses wait. "Eeh, Rebel, old gal, Ah'm pleas'd to see your Face...?" Dixon has brought a small apple from a fruitmonger's barrow, but the Horse dives anyway beneath the giant flaps over his Coat Pockets and goes in to inspect, lest something should have been overlook'd. At that moment of Equine curiosity, with Mason occupied in saddling up, Dixon understands what Christopher Maire must have meant long ago by "instrument of God,"— and his Obligation henceforward, to keep Silence upon the Topick.

They are very conscious of leaving Town,— with Luck, for the last time,— observing ev'rything as thro' some marvellous "Specs," that make all come sharp, and near. Sailors sit upon curb-stones outside the front doors of the Taverns that have intoxicated them, vomiting the Surveyors on, with a strange elation. Traffick in the Street brings and takes its own Light, Lanthorns upon carriages projecting, in swooping Shadows upon the crooked Meridians and Parallels of the brick walls, ev'ry leafless Tree, ev'ry desire-driven Pedestrian and Street-wary Dog. In low-ceiling'd Rooms at right angles to the street, Waggon-drivers stand in glum rows, drinking as if out of Duty, protected from the snow that promises at any moment to begin, tho' from little else, least of all the Road, and its Chances. Women pull their shawls in against the Night. Young people singly and pair'd, bound for twilight Assignations, sweep up and down the steps of Row-Houses, and along the curb-sides, from which the Steps rise, in all the traceless Promise of first Lanthorn-Light. Now that the Surveyors must leave, they wish to stay. In an onset of Turning-Evil, Mason imagines the Streets full of Row-Houses multiplying like loaves and fishes, whirling past like Spokes of a Giant Wheel, whose Convergence or Hub, beyond some disputable Prelude to Radiance, he cannot make out.

They are soon enough upon the York Road, the deeply magnetiz'd Fields to either side, in the Dark, tugging at Bits, Buckles, Pen-Nibs, Compass-Needles, and the steel strands of the Driver's Whip. They feel cover'd with small beings crawling and plucking ev'rywhere, neither kindly Remembrancers, nor wicked Spirits. "Do you feel that?" calls Mason in the Dark. "You're the Needle-Master,— what is it?"

"Mysteries of the Magnetick...?"

After a bit, "Aye? Instances of those being...?"

"Ah don't know, Mason, 'tis why I say 'Mysteries'...?"

Lanthorn-Lights ahead. Soon they can hear a night-Congregation singing. Reaching a small wood Moon-color'd Chapel, as if by earlier arrangement, the Surveyors pause to listen.

Oh God in thy Mercy forever uncertain,
Upon Whom continue Thy Sheep to Rely...
Pray keep us till Dawn,
Be the Night e'er so long—
All Thy helpless Creation,
Who sleep 'neath the Sky...

For the chances of Night are too many to reckon,
And the Bridge to the Day-light, is ever too frail...
When the Hour of Departure shall strike to the second,
Who will tend to the Journey? who will find us the Trail?

As once were we Lambs, in a Spring-tide abiding,
As once were we Children, eternal and free,
So shepherd us through,
Where the Dangers be few,—
From Darkness preserve us, returning to Thee.—
For the chances of Night &c....

Having acknowledg'd at the Warpath the Justice of the Indians'
Desires, after the two deaths, Mason and Dixon understand as well that
the Line is exactly what Capt. Zhang and a number of others have been
styling it all along— a conduit for Evil. So the year in Delaware with
the Degree of Latitude is an Atonement, an immersion in "real" Science, a Baptism of the Cypress swamp, and even a Rebirth,— not some
hir'd Cadastral Survey by its nature corrupt, of use at Trail's End only
to those who would profit from the sale and division and resale of
Lands. "Guineas, Mason, Pistoles, and Spanish Dollars, splendorously
Vomited from Pluto's own Gut! Without End! All generated from thah'
one Line...? Yet has any of it so much as splash'd or dribbl'd in our
Direction?

"The one thing we do know how to do, is Vistoes. Let's give 'em some-
thing they'll journey from other Provinces, down Rivers and Pikes in
Streams ever-wid'ning, to gaze upon,— " as the Visto soon is lin'd with
Inns and Shops, Stables, Games of Skill, Theatrickals, Pleasure-
Gardens...a Promenade,— nay, Mall,— eighty Miles long. At twilight
you could mount to a Platform, and watch the lamps coming on, watch

the Visto tapering, in perfect Projection, to its ever-unreachable Point. Pure Latitude and Longitude.

"I am a student of 'Blind Jack' Metcalf, if it please you," declares one of the Axmen, overhearing them.

"West Riding Lad! Blind Surveyor! he was famous in Staindrop even when I was a Lad."

"Applying the methods I learn'd whilst a member of his Crew, we could build a Modern Road here, straight up this Visto, eighty Miles long, well drain'd its entire length, self-compacting, impervious to all weather, immovable 'neath Laden Wheels be they broad or narrow,— true there's nothing much *at* the Middle Point, not today as we speak, but with the much improv'd Carriage from the other end, itself convenient to Philadelphia, New Castle, the entire heart of Chesapeake, why a Metropolis could blossom here among the Fens of Nanticoke that might rival any to the North."

"*Sha!*" warns the Chinaman. "Think about it!"

"Very well,— yet Right Lines, by minimizing Distance, are highly valu'd by some,— Commanding Officers, Merchants, Express-Riders? Must these all be Creatures of *Sha?*"

"Without Question. Officers kill men in large numbers. Merchants concentrate wealth by beggaring uncounted others. Express-riders distort and injure the very stuff of Time."

"Then why not consider Light itself as equally noxious," inquires Dixon, "for doth it not move ever straight ahead?"

"Ah!" a gleam as likely Madness as Merriment appearing in his Eye. "And if it moves in some other way?"

"Ev'ry Survey would have to be re-run," cries Dixon. "Eeh,— marvellous,— work for all the poor Dodmen till Doomsday!"

"Excuse me, Sir," Mason addresses the Geomancer. "Is this an article of common Faith among the Chinese, which I must remedy my ignorance of,— or but a Crotchet of your own I assume I may safely disregard? no wonder the Jesuits find you Folk inconvenient."

"What's that you're writing? Looks like Verse...?"

"My Epitaph. Like to hear it?

'He wish'd but for a middling Life,
Forever in betwixt
The claims of Lust and Duty,
So intricately mix'd,—
To reach some happy Medium,
Fleet as a golden Beam,
Uncharted as St. Brendan's Isle,
Fugitive as a Dream.

Alas, 'twas not so much the Years
As Day by thieving Day,—
With Debts incurr'd, and Interest Due,
That Dreams were sold to pay,—
Until at last, but one remain'd,
Too modest to have Worth,
That yet he holds within his heart,
As he is held, in Earth.' "

That other Tract, across the Border,— perhaps nearly ev'rything, perhaps nearly nothing,— is denied him. "Is that why I sought so obsessedly Death's Insignia, its gestures and formulæ, its quotidian gossip,— all those awful days out at Tyburn,— hours spent nearly immobile, watching stone-carvers labor upon tomb embellishments, Chip by Chip,— was it all but some way to show my worthiness to obtain a Permit to visit her, to cross that grimly patroll'd Line, that very essence of Division? She only wishes me back in the stink of mills, mutton-grease, Hell-Clamor, Lanthorns all night, the People in subjection, the foul'd wells of Painswick, Bisley, Stroud, styling it 'Home,'— Oh, is there no deliverance!"

She accosts him one night walking the Visto. "Seems sad, doesn't it," she chuckles. "Trust me, Mopery, there are regions of Sadness you have not seen. Nonetheless, you must come back to our Vale, 'round to your beginning,— well away from the sea and the sailors, away from the Nets of imaginary Lines. You must leave Mr. Dixon to his Fate, and attend your own."

"You don't care for him, do you?"

"If we are a Triangle, then must I figure as the Unknown side.... Dare you calculate me? Dead-reckon your course into the Wilderness that is now my home, as my Exile? Show, by Projection, Shapes beyond the meager Prism of my Grave? Do you have any idea of my Sentiments? I think not. Mr. Dixon would much prefer you forget me, he is of beaming and cheery temperament, a Boy who would ever be off to play. You were his playmate, now that is over, and you must go back inside the House of your Duty. When you come out again, he will no longer be there, and the Dark will be falling."

On their last visit to New-York, at the very end, waiting for the Halifax Packet, they dash all about the town, looking for any Face familiar from years before. Yet they are berated for their slowness at Corners. Carriages careen thro' Puddles the size of Ponds, spattering them with Mire unspeakable, so that they soon resemble Irregulars detach'd from a campaign in some moist Country. The Sons of Liberty have grown even less hospitable, and there is no sign of Philip Dimdown, nor Blackie, nor Captain Volcanoe. "Out of Town," they are told, when they are told anything.

"Let's drink up and get out of here, there's no point."

"We can find them. That's what we do, isn't it? We're Finders, after all."

"The Continent is casting off, one by one, the Lines that fasten'd us to her."

Yet at last, seated among their Impedimenta, Quayage unreckon'd stretching north and south into Wood Lattice-Work, a deep great Thicket of Spars, poised upon the Sky, Hemp and City Smoak, two of a shed-ful of somberly cloak'd travelers waiting the tide, they are aware once more of a feeling part intra-cranial, part Skin-quiver, part fear,— familiar from Inns at Bridges, waiting-places at Ferries, all Lenses of Revenance or Haunting, where have ever converg'd to them Images of those they drank with, saw at the edges of Rooms from the corners of Eyes, shouted to up or down a Visto. This seems to be true now, of ev'ry Face in this Place. Mason turns, his observing Eye protruding in alarm. "Are we at the right Pier?"

"I was just about to ask,— "

"— I didn't actually see any Signs, did you?"

They are approach'd by a Gentleman not quite familiar to them. A Slouch Hat obscures much of his Face. "Well met," he pronounces, yet nothing further.

"Are ye bound for Falmouth?" Mason inquires.

"For Pendennis Point, mean ye, and Carrick Roads?" His tone poises upon a Cusp 'twixt Mockery and Teasing, which recognition might modulate to one or the other,— yet neither can quite identify him. "*That* Falmouth?"

"There is another, Sir?" Dixon, maniatropick Detectors a-jangle, gets to his feet, as Mason Eye-Balls the Exits.

"There is a Falmouth invisible, as the center of a circle is invisible, yet with Compasses and Straight-Edge may be found," the Stranger replies. At that instant, the company is rous'd by a great Clamor of Bells and Stevedores, as the Packet, Rigging a-throb, prepares to sail. There will be perhaps two minutes to get aboard. "We must continue this Conversation, at Sea,"— and he has vanish'd in the Commotion. Each Day, on the Way over, Mason and Dixon will look for him, at Mess, at Cards, upon ev'ry Deck, yet without Issue.

Mason's last entry, for September 11th, 1768, reads, "At 11h 30m A.M. went on board the Halifax Packet Boat for Falmouth. Thus ends my restless progress in America." Follow'd by a Point and long Dash, that thickens and thins again, Chinese-Style.

Dixon has been reading over his Shoulder. "What was mine, then...? Restful?"

73

As all History must converge to Opera in the Italian Style, however, their Tale as Commemorated might have to proceed a bit more hopefully. Suppose that Mason and Dixon and their Line cross Ohio after all, and continue West by the customary ten-minute increments,— each installment of the Story finding the Party advanc'd into yet another set of lives, another Difficulty to be resolv'd before it can move on again. Behind, in pursuit, his arrangements undone, pride wounded, comes Sir William Johnson, play'd as a Lunatick Irishman, riding with a cadre of close Indian Friends,— somehow, as if enacting a discarded draft of Zeno's Paradox, never quite successful in attacking even the rearmost of the Party's stragglers, who remain ever just out of range. Yet at any time, we are led to believe, the Pursuers *may* catch up, and compel the Surveyors to return behind the Warrior Path.

Longer Sights, easier Grades, wider Night Skies, as the landscape turns inside-out, with Groves upon the Prairie now the reverse of what Glades in the Forest were not so many chains ago. Far less ax-work being requir'd, soon the Axmen are down to Stig alone, who when ask'd to, becomes a one-man assault force on behalf of the Astronomers. The Musick, from some source invisible, is resolutely merry, no matter what it may be accompanying.

One late Autumn, instead of returning to the Coast, the Astronomers will just decide to winter in, however far west it is they've got to…and after that, the ties back in to Philadelphia and Chesapeake will come to mean that much less, as the Pair, detach'd at last, begin consciously to move west. The under-lying Condition of their Lives is quickly establish'd as the Need to keep, as others a permanent address, a perfect Latitude,— no fix'd place, rather a fix'd Motion,— Westering. Whenever they do stop moving, like certain Stars in Chinese Astrology, they lose their Invisibility, and revert to the indignity of being observ'd and available again for earthly purposes.

Were they to be taken together, themselves light and dark Sides of a single Planet, with America the Sun, an Observation Point on high may be chosen, from which they may be seen to pass across a Face serene and benevolent at that Distance, tho' from the Distance of the Planet, often, Winter as Summer, harsh and inimical.

Into the Illinois, where they find renegade French living out a fantasy of the Bourbon Court, teaching the Indians Dress-making, Millinery, Wine-Growing, *Haute Cuisine,* orchestral Musick, Wig-Dressing, and such other Arts of answering Desire as may sustain this Folly. They believe Mason and Dixon to be Revolutionary Agents.

Descending great bluffs, they cross the Mississippi, the prehistoric Mounds above having guided them exactly here, by an Influence neither can characterize more than vaguely, but whose accuracy is confirm'd by their Star observations, as nicely as the Micrometer and Nonius will permit. They stay at villages of teepees where Mason as usual behaves offensively enough to require their immediate departure, at a quite inconvenient time, too, for Dixon and his Maiden of the day, who've both been looking forward to a few private moments. Instead, the Astronomers spend the rest of their Day running from the angry Villagers, and only by Fool's Luck do they escape. They subsist upon Roots and Fungi. They watch Lightning strike the Prairie again and again, for days, and fires rage like tentacles of a conscious Being, hungry and a-roar. They cower all night before the invisible Thunder of Bison herds, smelling the Animal Dust, keeping ready to make the desperate run for higher ground. They acquire a Sidekick, a French-Shawanese half-breed Renegado nam'd Vongolli, whose only loyalty is to Mason and Dixon, tho' like the Quaker in the Joak, they are not so sure of him. When they happen across an Adventurer from Mexico, and the ancient City he has discover'd beneath the Earth, where thousands of Mummies occupy the Streets in attitudes of living Business, embalm'd with Gold divided so finely it flows like Gum, it is Vongolli, with his knowledge of Herbal Formulæ, who provides Mason and Dixon with the Velocity to avoid an otherwise certain Dissolution.

Far enough west, and they have outrun the slowly branching Seep of Atlantic settlement, and begun to encounter towns from elsewhere, coming their way, with entirely different Histories,— Cathedrals, Spanish Musick in the Streets, Chinese Acrobats and Russian Mysticks. Soon, the Line's own *Vis Inertiæ* having been brought up to speed, they discover additionally that 'tis *it,* now transporting *them.* Right in the way of the Visto some evening at Supper-time will appear the Lights of some complete Village, down the middle of whose main street the Line will clearly run. Laws continuing upon one side,— Slaves, Tobacco, Tax Liabilities,— may cease to exist upon the other, obliging Sheriffs and posses to decide how serious they are about wanting to cross Main Street. "Thanks, Gentlemen! Slaves yesterday, free Men and Women today! You survey'd the Chains right off 'em, with your own!"

One week they encounter a strange tribal sect, bas'd upon the worship of some celestial Appearance none but the Congregation can see. Hungry to know more about the Beloved, ignoring the possibility of a negative result, recklessly do they prevail upon the 'Gazers to search scientifickally, with their Instruments, for this God, and having found its position, to determine its Motion, if any. It turns out to be the new Planet, which, a decade and a half later, will be known first as the Georgian, and then as Herschel, after its official Discoverer, and more lately as Uranus. The Lads, stunn'd, excited, realize they've found the first new Planet in all the untold centuries since gazing at the Stars began. Here at last is the Career-maker each has dreamt of, at differing moments and degrees of Faith. "All we need do is turn," cries Mason,— "turn, Eastward again, and continue to walk as we ever have done, to claim the Prize. For the first time, we may forget any Obligations to the current Sky,— for praise God (His ways how strange), we need never work again, 'tis t'ta to the Mug's Game and the Fool's Errand, 'tis a Royal Entrance at Life's Ridotto, 'tis a Copley Medal!"

"Eeh!" Dixon amiably waves his Hat. "Which half do thou fancy, obverse or reverse?"

"What?" Mason frowning in thought, "Hum. Well I rather imagin'd we'd...share the same side,— a Half-Circle each, sort of thing...."

Yet by now they can also both see the Western Mountains, ascending from the Horizon like a very close, hitherto unsuspected, second Moon,— the Circumferentor daily tracking the slow rise in vertical angle to the tops of these other-worldly Peaks. They are apt to meet men in skins, and Indians whose Tongue none of the Party can understand, and long strings of Pack-Horses loaded with Peltry, their Flanks wet, their eyes glancing 'round Blinders, inquiring... Survey Sights go on now for incredible Hundreds of Miles, so clear is the Air. Chainmen go chaining away into it, and sometimes never come back. They would be re-discover'd in episodes to come, were the episodes ever to be enacted, did Mason and Dixon choose *not* to turn, back to certain Fortune and global Acclaim, but rather to continue West, away from the law, into the savage Vacancy ever before them....

"The Copley Medal!" Dixon trying to get into the spirit of things.

"Attend me,— *nothing would lie beyond our grasp.* We would be the King's Own Astronomers, living in a Palace, servants to obey our desires! Weighty stipends, unlimited Credit! Wenches! Actresses! Observing Suits of gold lamé! Any time, day or night, you wanted,— what do you people eat? Haggis! You want a Haggis after Midnight, all you need do is pull upon a bell-cord, and hi-ho!"

"Tha've certainly sold me," nods Dixon, gesturing with his broad hand at the Sun-set, which happens tonight to be wildly spectacular. "Yet all those,— "

Mason nods back, impatiently. "They will have to live their lives without any Line amongst 'em, unseparated, daily doing Business together, World's Business and Heart's alike, repriev'd from the Tyranny of residing either North or South of it. Nothing worse than that, whatwhat?"

"How, then. Should we never again come West?"

"Should we ever be permitted to? Either by the King, or by the Americans? Think not, Lensfellow. If we do turn, and go back now, 'twill have to be a Continental D.I.O., forever."

"How Emerson will despise me...."

"As you've already taken money from the Royal Society,— isn't that, in his View, unredeemably corrupted?"

"Thankee, I'd nearly forgotten...?"

"Lethe passes to each and all,— yet vivid in Attention must the Degree of our Day's Sinfulness be ever kept."

"What ever did Sinners do, before there were those to tell them they were sinning?"

"However blissful their Ignorance, why they suffer'd."

"Bollocks. They enjoy'd themselves," Dixon mutters. "I was there. Another expell'd from Paradise, another Lad upon the North Road, seeking his daily Crumbs...."

Countryfolk they meet again are surpris'd to see them, sometimes shock'd, as at some return of the Dead. Mothers drive their small ones like Goslings away to safety. Bar-room habitués reprove them at length,— "You weren't ever suppos'd to be back this way,— "

"Ev'ryone said you'd done with all that to-and-fro by 'sixty-eight, left it to the other side of th' Ohio, and 'twould be Westward from there and then on, for you two, or nothing."

"We took yese in among us,— allow'd ye to separate us, name us anew,— only upon the Understanding, that ye were to pass through each of our Lives here, but once."

"We believ'd you exactly *that* sort of Visitor, not...the other sort. We've enough of those here, the Lord knows, already,— Indian, White, African, aswarm well before the Twilight,— we hardly need more."

"How dare you come back now, among these Consequences you have loos'd like Vermin?"— and so on. Babies take one look at them and burst into tears inconsolable. Boys but recently initiated to the ways of the Rifle take playful shots at them. A recently wed couple assault them, screaming, "Yes you came the proper pair of bloody little Cupids, didn't you, then just went polka-dancing away, leaving us to sort out *his* mother, the recruiting Sergeant, the Sheriff, the other Girl,— "

"— whilst ev'ry low-life you gentlemen caus'd to be suck'd into town in your Wake is ogling the Queen of Sheba, here, who never could keep her eyes to herself, and say what you will, Wife, my dear Mother has ever shewn the born grace and sense of the true lady."

"D'you hear that then, you miserable cow? once again as I've ever been telling all you Scum, none of you's good enough for my Boy Adolphus, 'specially not you, fifteen stone of unredeem'd Slut, my gracious just look at you,— "

"Bitch!" the wife two-handedly swinging at her mother-in-law's Head a great Skillet, which none of the men present are hasty in rushing to deflect,— the older woman dodges the blow, and from somewhere produces a Dirk. In a moment, someone will have to load and prime a Pistol. All this having resulted from the award-winning "Love Laughs at a Line" episode, which seem'd but light-hearted Frolick that first time through.

In the next Village east, the Creature they thought they had so rationally and with up-to-date methods prov'd to be but a Natural phenomenon has re-emerged, and holds in its sinister emprise the lives of that half of the Populace living upon one side of the Line...yet for some reason, it is reluctant to cross and continue its depredations upon the other. The Line is believ'd to present some Barrier, invisible but powerful enough to hold back the Being, to preserve those across it from the Fate of their former Neighbors. Brave townsfolk slip out after dark, dig up and move the Boundary-Stones, as far as they dare, some one way, some another. The Line thro' here soon loses all pretense to Orthogony, becoming a Record in Oölite of Fear,— whose, and how much,— and of how a Village broke in two.

In some Towns they are oblig'd to turn back Westward, often waiting until Dark to creep cautiously eastward again, for the Population will hear of them in no other way but Westering. When it seems there's a Chance that someone may listen, Mason and Dixon both try to explain about the new Planet,— but very few care. It breaks slowly upon the Astronomers, that with no time available for gazing at anything, this people's Indifference to the Night, and the Stars, must work no less decisively than their devotion to the Day, and the Earth for whose sake something far short of the Sky must ever claim them, a stove, a child, a hen-house predator, a deer upwind, the price of Corn, a thrown shoe, an early Freeze.

At last the Post Mark'd West appears. A Joint Delegation from the American and Royal Societies, alerted by Jesuit Telegraph, is there to greet them. A new and iridescent generation of Philadelphia Beauties in full Susurrus and Chirp line both sides of the Visto. A Consort of Crumhornes is on hand, playing Airs and Marches. 'Tis the Ineluctable Moment of Convergence. Will somebody repent, ere they arrive?

When they reach the Post Mark'd West, one swerves a bit North and the other South of it, and on they go, together, up the East Line, to the shore of Delaware, into a Boat and across, dropping by, that day, to visit the McCleans at Swedesboro.

"Heard some Tales, Gents,— what'll yese do now?"

"Devise a way," Dixon replies, "to inscribe a Visto upon the Atlantick Sea."

"Archie, Lad, Look ye here," Mason producing a Sheaf of Papers, flapping thro' them,— "A thoughtful enough Arrangement of Anchors and Buoys, Lenses and Lanthorns, forming a perfect Line across the Ocean, all the way from the Delaware Bay to the Spanish Extremadura,"— with the Solution to the Question of the Longitude thrown in as a sort of Bonus,— as, exactly at ev'ry Degree, might the Sea-Line, as upon a Fiduciary Scale for Navigators, be prominently mark'd, by a taller Beacon, or a differently color'd Lamp. In time, most Ships preferring to sail within sight of these Beacons, the Line shall have widen'd to a Sea-Road of a thousand Leagues, as up and down its Longitude blossom Wharves, Chandleries, Inns, Tobacco-shops, Greengrocers' Stalls, Printers of News, Dens of Vice, Chapels for Repentance, Shops full of Souvenirs and Sweets,— all a Sailor could wish,— indeed, many such will decide to settle here, "Along the Beacons," for good, as a way of coming to rest whilst remaining out at Sea. A good, clean, salt-scour'd old age. Too soon, word will reach the Land-Speculation Industry, and its Bureaus seek Purchase, like some horrible Seaweed, the length of the Beacon Line. Some are estopp'd legally, some are fended directly into the Sea, yet Time being ever upon their Side, they persist, and one Day, in sinister yet pleasing Coral-dy'd cubickal Efflorescence, appears "St. Brendan's Isle," a combination Pleasure-Grounds and Pensioners' Home, with ev'rything an Itinerant come to Rest might ask, Taverns, Music-Halls, Gaming-Rooms, and a Population ever changing of Practitioners of Comfort, to Soul as to Body, uncritickal youngsters from far-off lands where death might almost abide, so ubiquitous is it there, so easily do they tolerate it here.

'Tis here Mason and Dixon will retire, being after all Plank-Holders of the very Scheme, having written a number of foresighted Stipulations into their Contract with the Line's Proprietor, the transnoctially charter'd "Atlantick Company." Betwixt themselves, neither feels British enough anymore, nor quite American, for either Side of the Ocean. They are content to reside like Ferrymen or Bridge-keepers, ever in a Ubiquity of Flow, before a ceaseless Spectacle of Transition.

Three

Last Transit

74

Perhaps all was as simple as that,— that Dixon wish'd to remain, and Mason did not,— could not. So Dixon return'd as well, and on 15 December 1768, at a meeting of the Royal Society Council, according to the Minute-Book, there they are, together in the Room. Both have chosen to wear gray and black. "Messrs Mason and Dixon attending with proposals relative to the aforesaid intended observations, were called in; And Mr Dixon acquainted the Council, that he was willing to go to the North Cape or Cherry Island; Mr Mason rather declined going; but added, that if he was wanted, he should be ready to go."

Was their Appearance all pro forma, did Dixon know, did they have it all work'd out beforehand, or was it sprung upon him, and thus less forgivable than the accustom'd Masonickal behavior? The meaner of spirit might translate it into, "Of course I'll go, but not with Dixon,"— a clear Insult, Dixon was often advis'd,— Would he not care to respond? "Ah've grown so us'd to it," Dixon assur'd his Comforters, "that often Ah neglect to take offense...?"

Privately, his Sentiments are of a more hopeful turn. He knows enough of Mason to recognize by now most of the shapes his Pursuit of the Gentlemanly takes on, as well as the true extent of his progress beyond the socially stumbling Philosopher-Fool he began as. That is, 'tis possible that Mason, honestly believing Dixon ready for, as deserving of, his own command, is willing to risk looking ungracious, if it will advance that end. And so this "rather-decline-yet-if-I-am-wanted" Formula is but more of his inept Kindness.

They leave together. Out into another Christmastide, each for his own reason seeking the brightest Lights. Some horrible Boswell pursues them, asking questions. "Known of course as the Reluctant Lensmen of the Cape Expedition to observe the first Transit of Venus in 'sixty-one, and despite the generally excellent quality of your Work, neither of you has been voted to membership in the Royal Society. Mr. Mason, we've heard you're the one here who's unhappy with that, whilst Mr. Dixon takes the more philosophickal View."

"Only the long view, Lad."

How could the elder Charles have forgiven Mason for leaving his children with his Sister, dumping them really, going off to the Indies with another man, another Star-Gazer, coming home only to turn about and sail off to America, *with the same man?* Dixon sees the pattern, the expectation, the coming Transit of Venus. Mason sees it, too. "If we went off a third time together,...he hates me enough already.... I study the Stars against my Father's Wish,— but do I remain among 'em, only at the Price of my Sons? That is what I face,— some Choice!" So he declines the North Cape, and another posting together, symmetrically as ever, to that end of the world lying opposite their first end of the World. "Someone must break this damn'd Symmetry," Mason mutters.

For years, as he found his way further into the wall'd city of Melancholy, he dream'd,— tho' presently no longer sure if he had been asleep, or awake,— of the North Cape he would never see,— an unexpectedly populous land, where the native people were enslav'd by a small but grimly effective European team, quarter'd and mostly restricted to an area within easy reach of their boats, upon which indeed many of them preferr'd to sleep. The only industry there, was mining the Guano of the sea-birds and shipping it to lower latitudes, to be process'd into Nitre, for Gunpowder, which was in great demand, as it seem'd that far Below, a general European war had broken out, for dynastic, racial, and religious reasons Mason, and Dixon, who was also in the Dreams, realiz'd they were ignorant of, having been out of touch with any kind of periodical news for eight or nine years now. They arriv'd at the North Cape to find the mines working day and night shifts, and the mood turning unpleasant as white overseers demanded more and more from workers who were not making enough for it to matter what the warring nations Below did to each other, nor on what Schedule.

The Guano deposits and hence the mining were upon rocks off the Coast, often quite far out to Sea, where the Light was crepuscular and clear. The Guano was carried out to the Ships in Scows of soak'd, black, failing Timbers. Loading these vessels directly from the Rocks was perilous work. Weather often swept in, carrying away ships and Souls. The Natives, who were dark-skinn'd and spoke none but their own tongue, deserted when they could and many times contriv'd their own Deaths when all else had fail'd to deliver them....

At Maskelyne's Behest, Mason agrees to observe the Transit from South Ulster, where he obtains the ingress of Venus upon the Disk of the Sun, but not her departure. "The mists rise up out of the Bog. There she is, full, spherickal...the last time I shall see her as a Material Being...when next appearing, she will have resum'd her Deity." Maskelyne will edit this out, which is why Mason leaves it in his Field Report.

Shall Ireland be his last journey out, his last defiance of Sapperton,— which is to say, Rebekah? There's no place for him in London. The city has never found his Heart, and 'tis his Heart that keeps a residue of dislike for the place ever guarded. Likewise must he allow himself to let go of Dixon, soon now.... He sees nothing but Penance ahead, and Renunciations proceeding like sheep straggling back, gathering to shelter. He sits alone in brand-new Rooms of which he may be the very first Occupant, in the smell of Plaster and Paint and Glue, the Paper upon the Walls an assault of Color,— Indigo, Cochineal Red, Spanish Orange, the rarely-observ'd Magenta and Green...the Day outside unable to emerge from Mourning. Rebekah, whom he expects to visit, does not appear. He waits, trying to see his way ahead, suddenly sixteen again. He tries to think of how, short of suicide, he may put himself in her way. He is furious about ev'rything, he screams at length about transient setbacks however slight.

"Misses his Family," the Servants tell it. "No sleep."

The House is large, inexpensively Palladian, with beds in ev'ry room, not only the Parlor and the Drawing Room, but the Kitchen and the

Music Conservatory as well. Shadows are ev'rywhere unpredictable. Mason tries each room in turn. Other Guests are out upon the same Pilgrimage,— they meet in the Halls and mutter Civilities. In the Musick-Room, he wakes during the Night and mistakes the Clavier for a Coffin, with somebody in it, withal...who may or may not be another Sleeper. Out in the Bogs, Fairy Lights appear. He hears a Note from the Cas'd Instrument, then another. He much prefers the Kitchen, or the Observatory out back. There he is hypnagogickally instructed all night long in the arts of silent food Preparation, the "Sandwich" having found here a particular Admiration, for the virtual soundlessness of its Assembly.

In a letter dated November 9th, close to Mason's departure from Donegal, Maskelyne as A.R. is wallowing in the pleasure of good Instruments to work with at last. The defective Bob-Suspension is now but a distasteful Pang of Memory, causing him at his Morning Shave to grunt, and avoid his Eyes in the Mirror. The Sector Telescope he finds "charming." "I have also used a 10-foot telescope with a micrometer. Your moral reflections on the subject I approve of, as becoming an astronomer, who ought to make this use of these sublime speculations."

"What was he talking about?"

"In Maskelyne's Letter, which we have, he says he's responding to a letter of Mason's dated October fifteenth, which no one can locate, including me,— indeed, I've not found any of Mason's Letters, tho' there are said to be many about."

"Make something up, then,— Munchausen would."

"Not when there exists, somewhere, a body of letters Mason really did write. I must honor that, mustn't I, Brother Ives?"

Ives snorts and chooses not to contend.

"Why not gamble they'll never be found?" wonders Ethelmer.

"Just because I can't find them doesn't mean they're not out there. The Question may be rather,— Must we wait till they are found, to speculate as to the form 'moral reflections' upon a ten-foot telescope, with a Micrometer, might take?" The Presence of this Device, as well as the Instrument's Length, suggests an accuracy to perhaps two further degrees of Magnitude, than the Instrument it replac'd at Greenwich. "Sublime speculations"? Accuracy and Sublimity? Is the A.R. being ironickal? Whatever Mason had to say, almost certainly included G-d.

Was he off the deep end again? "Make this use..." suggests Mason had advanc'd some Program. Suppose he'd written to Maskelyne,—

"...'Tis the Reciprocal of 'as above, so below,',...being only at the finer Scales, that we may find the truth about the Greater Heavens,...the exact value of a Solar Parallax of less than ten seconds can give us the size of the Solar system. The Parallax of Sirius, perhaps less than two seconds, can give us the size of Creation. May we not, in the Domain of Zero to One Second of Arc, find ways to measure even That Which we cannot,— may not,— see?"

"Many of us in the *parsonical* line of work," admits Wicks Cherrycoke, "find congenial the Mathematics, particularly the science of the fluxions. Few may hope to have named for them, like the Reverend Dr. Taylor, an Infinite Series, yet such steps, large and small, in the advancement of this most useful calculus, have provided us a Rack-ful of Tools for Analysis undreamed-of even a few years ago, tho' some must depend upon Epsilonics and Infinitesimalisms, and other sorts of *Defective Zero*. Is it the Infinite that tempts us, or the Imp? Or is it merely our Vocational Habit, ancient as Kabbala, of seeking God there, among the Notation of these resonating Chains...."

"Reminds me of America. Strange, some mornings I get up and I think I'm in America." Half Mountain, half Bog, ev'ry other Soul in it nam'd O'Reilly, Oakboys with night Mischief in mind all about, this is frontier Country again, standing betwixt Ulster and the Dublin Pale, whilst of neither,— poor,— at the mercy of Land-owners...such as Lord Pennycomequick, the global-Communications Nabob, who now approaches Mason upon the Lawn, carrying in Coat-Pockets the size of Saddle-Bags four bottles of the Cheap Claret ev'rywhere to be found here, thanks to enterprising Irishmen in Bordeaux. "In my family since the Second Charles," he calls in greeting.

"Isn't a hundred years consider'd old for Wine?" Mason having risen kickish this morning.

"Oh, but I meant the Coat?" Pennycomequick having decided, with Legions before him, that Mason, because he speaks in the hurried and forc'd Rhythms of at least a Tickler of Children, is a professional Wag of some sort. "Aye, 'tis call'd a Morning Coat, the yellow symbolizing the Sun, I imagine,— several theories about these Aqua bits, here," examining them the way we examine our Waist-coats for spill'd Food, "being of course our famous historically subversive Color Green,— should have been a hanging Offense as long ago as Robin Hood, if you ask me,— yet disguis'd cleverly, you see, by the addition of Blue. Perhaps a touch of Buff as well. Ha! ha ha do not look so concern'd, Sir, being all Whigs here staunch and true, yes well do come along, ye've not seen the Folly yet have ye."

What cannot escape Mason's notice, as they come round the Butt End of the Topiary Elephant, is a sudden Visto of Obelisks, arrang'd in a Double Row too long to count, forming an Avenue leading to the Folly. In this Sunlight they have withdrawn to the innocence of Stone, into being only Here enough, to maintain the Effect of solemn Approach...yet it isn't hard for Mason to imagine them in less certain Light, at a more problematick time of day, taking on more Human shape,— almost Human Shape...somewhat larger than human size...almost able to speak,—

"There 'tis. What do you think?" The Lord has halted, Pockets a-sway, to help Mason admire it, this being a task inadvisable for but one person.

"You can't say it isn't something," is Mason's comment.

"Of course if you've read Mr. Halfpenny's *Rural Architecture in the Chinese Taste,* you'll recognize those bits there at the Roof-corners... our Great Buddha, half-scale regrettably.... Here,— therapeutick Pool, Peat Baths, good morning, Rufus, I trust your good woman has recover'd...Excellent! (She ran that Department, Chaos since she left),— Ah! the Electrick Machines, yes a good many of them, all the way down to the end there, can you make it out? On the rare chance you have an appetite when you emerge, lo, a Summer-Kitchen, complete with gesticulating Chef,— Yes yes, *Soup du Jour,* Armand! clever fellow, claims to know you, 's a matter of fact,— "

"Meestair Messon! Meestair Messon!" 'Tis the very Frenchman,— is it not? yet why then is his figure illuminated so much *less* than ev'rything else about, this time of Day?— why is he moving so smoothly, as a Boat upon still Water, looming ever closer, aiming, it now becomes apparent,

a Kiss at Mason's Cheek, his Color at close range aberrating toward Green, as he sweeps in a cold wind, upon and past the shiv'ring Mason, with an echo, like an odor, trailing after. Mason turns,— the Lawn is empty. At some moment he has fail'd to mark, Lord Pennycomequick has left him. He stands by an Oven, with Moss between its Stones, that he wishes upon no Account to look into.

The Rain has rais'd in ev'ryone an insomniack Apprehension, in which all talk of Bog-bursts is avoided,— yet 'tis but a Question of where the black Flood shall break thro'. The longer it rains, the higher too the level of Nerves and Vapors. No-one here, or for miles, will need to be awak-en'd for it. At last, one Midnight,—

"Bog-burst! Out upon McEntaggart's piece,— good evenin' to ye Sir, and regretfully must I now be tellin' ye,— ye've been, as they say in yeer Royal Navy, impress'd, Sir."

"Oh, I am impress'd," Mason agrees, "really,— the efficiency with which you are able to turn all these Wretches to, is nothing short of impressive, indeed."

"Excuse me, Sir,— 'tis me English no doubt,— I meant, that you too must come out and work in the company of these very 'Wretches.' "

"Of course,— Man of Science, ever happy to advise. Restoring the Berm, is that how we'll be at it?"

"Someday when all's calm, I'd love to chat over wi' ye the finer points of Bog-Burst Management,— yet now, would I suggest Boots and Gloves, Sir, and smartly too, if ye'd not be mindin'?"

Little McTiernan at the Door is giving out short-handl'd Peat-Cutters styl'd, by the Irish, "Slanes."

"Not sure I know how to cut a Sod," mumbles Mason.

"Quickly's best,— before he can pick up a Weapon...?"

"Let him be, Dermy,— not his fault he's English."

"Bogs," Mason to himself, as they go along, bearing Candles in hol-low'd out Turnips, not certain if he is speaking aloud, "are my Destiny. I imagin'd Delaware, not merely the end, but years past the end, of this sort of Journeyman's Humiliation...even fancied that I had earn'd pas-sage, at last, into a purer region, where Mathesis should rule, with nothing beyond an occasional Ink-Smudge to recall to me that unhappy American Station of the Cross. Arrh! Stars and Mud, ever conjugate, a Paradox to consider,— one...for the Astronomer-Royal, perhaps?" His current scheme being, to assail Maskelyne's Sanity, by now and then posing him Questions that will not bear too much cogitating upon— most lately, *Über Bernouillis Brachistochronsprobleme*, 17 oz, by Baron von Boppdörfer ("Mind like a Spanish Blade. Read it at the Risk of your Self-Esteem.") having almost done the Trick.

Slodging the wet Tracks, dress'd all in the local Frieze, Mason, by Neep-Lantern light, looks like a wet, truculent Sheep. The rain comes down. They cross the River, passing 'round Keadew and Kinnypottle, where more come creeping from sleepless Dwellings to join them. Mason might be traveling with a Herd of Ghosts, felt but invisible, bearing him into Country Unknown. The Sky tonight has nothing to show him. Now and then, very much closer to the Earth, he begins to see Lights, moving, flickering, soon gone. "Who are they?" Mason inquires of his faceless Companions.

"Hush," come a half dozen voices at once. "They are going their Way, as we go ours," whispers someone behind his right Ear. "They are not often out in the Rain, nor particularly helpful in a Slide."

Soon they have reach'd one Shore of the liquefied Peat-Flow, thro' some Mirage blacker than the neighboring Night. "McEntaggart's been after that Tath for a Year, and now 'tis his, for nothing."

"He kept still, and the Premises mov'd!"

"Look out, here comes more of it!"

"What, a Re-Peat!"

In Irish perversity all a-quip, they set to work finding and cutting out Peat Sods not yet saturated by the Rain. Other countrymen appear now and then bearing Rocks, piling them laboriously against the Burst, thro' the drizzling of the Night. Cottagers, daz'd, come wobbling down the Hill. Dawn finds the tops of the Hillsides obscur'd, each Shift-mate a wan Spectre in the Vaporous Bog.

"Mr. Mason!"

"Your servant, sir."

" 'Tis the Well of Saint Brendan, if you please,— "

"Thought he was a Galway Lad."

No, he pass'd thro' Cavan once, on his way to the Sea, looking for Crew, and from the spot where he slept, came forth the very water they drank in Eden, so lovely is it to taste,— now, in the general Relocation, has it vanish'd. "Tho' we've Dowsers a-plenty, yet are all in Perplexity, not to mention humility, in begging the Application of your London Arts, in discov'ring and restoring it."

"I've the very thing," Mason replies. Among his Equipment at the Pennycomequick Manor is the *Krees* from his Dream in Cape Town, which he has kept ever by him. "Have you water from this Spring?" He pours and rubs it over the Blade, returning to the Bog-burst, where immediately he senses a Traction, a warmth, a queer high whine along the Blade, tho' 'tis none of these..."Here, I believe."

He helps them to dig. At no great Depth a Spring is encounter'd, whose Perimeter is quickly shor'd against re-collapse. One by one Countryfolk taste the Water. Some say it is the very Spring of the Saint, others say it isn't. In fact, there is so wide a difference of opinion, that presently what will be the first of many Blows are exchang'd.

In an ordinary Dream, Rebekah appears. "No need to feel pleas'd with yourself. What you found was not their sacred Well, but only *a Representation* of it." He wakes up into a midnight sadness, trying to say, I have tasted it, yet he has not tasted it. Now he is afraid ever to, lest his Spring be discover'd as soil'd as the Holy Wells of Gloucestershire, and therefore the *Krees,* and therefore his Dreams.

He prays to see her Face in the new Comet,— each night, this time, in terror of *not* seeing it. He tries to will it there, yet is amaz'd that for some Minutes now, he cannot even remember her Face. Yet at last arrives a clear night of seeing, so clear in fact that sometime after Midnight, supine in the Star-light, rigid with fear, Mason experiences a curious optical re-adjustment. The Stars no longer spread as upon a Dom'd Surface,— he now beholds them in the *Third Dimension* as well,— the Eye creating its own Zed-Axis, along which the star-chok'd depths near and far rush both inward and away, and soon, quite soon, billowing out of control. He collects that the Heavenly Dome has been put there as *Protection,* in an agreement among Observers to report only what it is safe to see. Fifteen years in the Business, and here is his Initiation.

Now, nothing in the Sky looks the same. "As to the Comet,— I cannot account for how,— but there came this night, to this boggy Miasmatick place, an exceptional Clarity of the Air,…a sort of optickal Tension among the Stars, that seem'd ever just about to break radiantly thro'…. And there. In Leo, bright-man'd, lo, it came. It came ahead. And 'twould be but Prelude to the Finger of Corsica,— which now appear'd, pointing down from Heaven. And the place where it pointed was the place I knew I must journey to, for beneath the Sky-borne Index lay, as once beneath a Star, an Infant that must, again, re-make the World,— and this time 'twas a Sign from Earth, not only from Heaven, showing the way."

"Quite so…. Yet I'm not terribly sure this ought to be in your report," says Maskelyne, "— objections from the Clergy,— readily imagin'd, what-what?— leaving aside the question of, actually, well what does it mean?"

"No Idea. I was in a kind of Daze. Have ye never fall'n into one of those Cometary Dazes, with the way the Object grows brighter and brighter each Night? These Apparitions in the Sky, we never observe but in Motion,— gone in seconds, and if they return, we do not see them. Once safely part of the Night Sky, they may hang there at their Pleasure, performing whatever in their Work corresponds to shifting jibs and stay-sails, keeping perfectly upon Station, mimicking any faint, unnam'd Star you please. Do they watch us? Are they visits from the past, from an Age of Faith, when Miracles still literally happen'd? Are they agents of the absented Guardian,— and are these Its last waves, last Beckonings, over the tops of the Night Trees? An Astronomer in such a State of Inquiry's apt to write nearly anything. How about yourself?"

"Of course there are things one wishes to leave in, often yearns to. Then again, there are things one leaves in,— "

"Wondrous! Let's strike the Passage, by all means. Now, what about the part 'round July, where I compare the Aurora Borealis to jell'd Blood,— do ye want that out, too?"

"I was just coming to that. They've been frightfully picky of late about that Word. No one knows why."

"What? 'Blood'? Well. Too bloody bad, isn't it?" The Octagonal room echoes with indignation imperfectly mock'd. "Bloody *Hell*, now ye come to it,— "

Maskelyne looks about nervously. "Pray ye, Mason. There's ever someone listening."

"What of it? You arre the A. Rrr.,— arrre ye not? Tell 'em bugger off."

He receives a long Look from Maskelyne he can't recall ever having seen before. " 'Tis not the same Office, as it was in Bradley's day...and your own. There will nevermore be disputes like this current one over *his* Obs,— 'tis said it may run on for years."

His Obs. Mason, who perform'd many of these Observations himself, and is consequently in the middle of the Quarrel, snorts, but does not charge.

"Instead of the old Arrangements, we've now a sort of...Contract... rather lengthy one, indeed...in return for this,— " gesturing 'round, yet keeping his elbow bent, as if unable to extend his Arm all the way, "— they own my work, they own the products of my thinking, perhaps they own my Thoughts unutter'd as well. I am their mechanickal Cuckoo, perch'd up here in this airy Cage to remind them of the first Day of Spring, for they are grown strange, this Cohort, to the very Wheel of Seasons. I am allow'd that much usefulness,— the rest being but Drudging Captivity."

"Hum. Difficult Life. Excuse me, what's this thing where the Astronomer's Couch us'd to be?"

" 'Tis styl'd, by the knowing, a '*Péché Mortel.*' One of Mr. Chippendale's. Elegant, don't you think? Clive bought it for me," defiantly, the small eyes tightening for some assault, the lips remaining steady.

"Who? Clive of *India?*" is all Mason says.

"I meant, 'for the Observatory,' of course," replies Maskelyne.

"What would you do with Mortal Sin? when you wouldn't know it if it came over and bought you a Pint."

"I have learn'd to simulate it, however, by committing a greater than usual number of the Venial ones."

Mason, trying not to stare too openly, has just realized that Maskelyne, direct from the Astronomer's Couch, is wearing his favorite Observing Suit, a garment of his own design that his brother-in-law the famed Clive of India sent him from Bengal, where the Nabob had had it cut and sewn with painstaking fidelity to a thirty-page List of Instructions from Maskelyne. It is a three-piece affair, everything quilted, long jacket, waistcoat, and trousers, which have Feet at the ends of them, all in striped silk, a double stripe of some acidick Rose upon Celadon for the Trousers and Waistcoat, and for the Jacket, whose hem touches the floor when, as now, he is seated, a single stripe of teal-blue upon the same color, which is also that of the Revers.... It is usually not wise to discuss matters of costume with people who dress like this,— politics or religion being far safer topicks. The Suit, Mason knows, is but one of a collection of sportive outfits from the Royal-Astronomical Armoire, run up to Maskelyne's increasingly eccentric specifications by the subcontinental genius Mr. Deep, and his talented crew, and shipped to him express by East Indiaman, "the third-fastest thing on the Planet," as Mun lik'd to say, "behind Light and Sound."

Nevil seems to miss the life, sleeping or drinking in the daytime, starting to come alive around Dusk, quickening with the Evening Shift. He and Mason pace about, the window-lensed afternoon sun heightening the creases beneath their chins, amid motes of wig-powder drifting in the glare of the beams. He exhibits a morally batter'd Air, and is not shy about discussing its origins. Once more the Harrison Watch, like an Hungarian Vampire, despite the best efforts of good Lunarians upon the Board of Longitude to impale it, has risen upon brazen wings, in soft rhythmic percussion, to obsess his Position, his dwindling circle of Time remaining upon Earth, his very Reason.

"It reach'd its Peak in 'sixty-seven. The B. of L. in its Wisdom kept insisting on one trial after another, finally they hung it around *my* neck,— new in the job, what was I suppos'd to do, say no?— to oversee trials of the Watch at *Greenwich,* for G-d's sake, for nearly a d——'d Year." Maskelyne had been observ'd glaring at the lock'd case, to which he held the key, apostrophizing the miserable watch within that could render moot all his years' Trooping in the service of Lunars, with more of the substance of his Life than he could healthily afford, stak'd upon what might prove the wrong Side. "Were Honor nought but Honor's Honor kept," some thought they heard, "All Sins might wash away in Tears unwept...."

"Couldn't believe it," reported the room-steward Mr. Gonzago, "like watching Hamlet or something, isn't it? Went on like that for weeks,— he wanted to break in, he didn't want to break in, he spent hours with scraps of paper, elaborating ways to damage the Watch that would never be detected,— he liv'd in this Tension, visible to all, between his conscience and his career."

("Bringing it to Greenwich upon an unsprung Cart over the London Lanes might have done the job alone," Mason suggests to Maskelyne, none too gently.)

Retir'd Navigators and Ship's Carpenters crept up the Hill to witness this, feeling like Macaronis who've paid their threepence at Bedlam. "Yesterday, so vouches my Mate, Old Masky, he scream'd and rav'd for quite an Hour."

"Let's hope he's not too tired to give us some kind of Show."

"I'd settle for a London Minute…?"

"Look at my side of it," Maskelyne would blurt at them (too passionately, as he saw right away). "That is," untying his Queue and commencing to scratch his Head furiously and at length, "they've put me in an impossible Position, haven't they, I mean it isn't a Secret of State that I've an interest in Lunars, nor that this blasted Harrison Watch is the sole Obstacle, between your servant, and the Prize he has earn'd fairly, at the cost of his Vision, his sleep, his engagement with Society. Ordinarily I'm the last one that ought to be giv'n *any* Authority over it, let alone the Key permitting Access. Yet if you ask why, you will hear,— 'We are ensuring his Honesty this way,— he dasn't fiddle with it now.' And, 'If the watch comes thro' despite Maskelyne's Curatorship, why then has it seen the Fire, and conquer'd it.' How am I suppos'd to feel? The Burden upon me is more than anyone should justly be made to bear."

"Like being the Swab who holds the Anchor-Pool."

"Aye! The Purser of Time!"

"He looks a bit furtive to me, what say ye, Boats?"

"Like settin' a Spaniel to guard the Prize Cock."

"Gentlemen," Maskelyne, according to some, scream'd. "Why this unfriendly Attendance? Is it the per Diem, is that it? You wish,— what? sixpence more? A Shilling?"

Sham'd, disappointed in him, the Veterans of Cartagena and Minorca began to move sighing and mutt'ring away.

"I am of Mathematickal Mind,— 'twould be an afternoon's work,— recreation, rather,— to devise a way to destroy the Watch's Chances forever,— and yet there is bound to be some Enquiry,— wherein each of my moments, since I was laden with this impossible Duty, must be accounted for,— yet already too many have pass'd in solitude, unwitness'd by others, such as your good Selves,— a Blank Sheet that invites Fiction and her vulgar Friends, Slander and Vilification, to sport upon it.— "

"Dodgy."

"Then why not be hung for a Sheep as a Lamb?" Maskelyne continued. "— I often find myself asking, not of G-d, exactly, but of whatever might be able to answer the Question. If the World already believe me party to a Fiddle, when I'm not, you understand, then why not go in there with a Hammer, heh, heh, so to speak, and really do a Job?"

"Classickal," grumbles Euphrenia.

"Easy to find fault with the Reverend Dr. Maskelyne," her brother agrees, "though with our Eleventh Commandment, I must not speak ill of another Clergyman. His behavior toward Mason was ever consistent with that of a brotherly Rival for the love of, and the succession from, their 'Father,' Bradley. Did he, in posting Mason out of England, employ a Code,— to Cavan in order to put him once again among Ulstermen as he'd been upon the Pennsylvania frontier...to Schiehallion out of some mean desire to remind him of the error Cavendish pointed out, due to the Allegheny Mountains,— or, Cavendish being after all more Enemy than friend, were these rather simple Kindnesses in standing by an old colleague and ally? The long-winded Letters to Mason in the Field, tho' surely meant to assert his personal Authority, may reveal nothing beyond the desire, out of resentments unvoic'd, to bore their Recipients into compliance,— at Cambridge he had been now and then upon the receiving end of a 'Jobation,' or lengthy Reproof, and perhaps this was his way of reasserting in his Life a balance (having been born beneath the Scales) that would otherwise have been set a-lop by an excess of Patience. It also appears that he did what he could to support Mason's claim to Prize money from the Board of Longitude for his Refinements to Mayer's Lunar Tables, whilst seeking none for himself. And he back'd the younger Harrison's admission to the Royal Society, despite the ease with which his opposition might have been understood and excus'd. Nor was his Approach to the Longitude ever the most congenial to've taken,— the method of Lunars being by no means universally lov'd, its tediousness indeed often resented, and not only by Midshipmen trying to learn it,— many wish'd for a faster way, willing to cede to Machinery a form of Human Effort they could've done without."

Maskelyne fancied that, when he became Astronomer Royal, there might be an Investiture, a Passage, a Mystery…an Outfit. He began designing, with the utmost restraint and taste of course, ceremonial Robes for himself, bas'd upon the Doctors' Robes at Cambridge, Rose upon Scarlet, a black Velvet Hat, Liripipes, Tippets, Sleeves to the ground,— decorated all over with Zodiackal Glyphs, in a subdued Gold Passementerie. But to whom could he show it? The Royal Society might not approve. The King might be offended. When, at all, might he have occasion to wear it? Perhaps an occasion could be proclaim'd. Star Day. Ev'ryone up all night. No flame allow'd. Food misidentified in the Star-light, Lovers a-tip, and something glamorous, like the Pleiades, upon the Rise.

And the King would place in his hands something preserv'd from the days of the Astrologers,— a Prism, an Astrolabe, a Gift of Power,— he would be sworn to secrecy. Of course he would use it wisely.…

Mason has almost presum'd to think of them as old Troopers by now, with the Transits of Venus behind them, Harrison's Watch, battles budgetary and vocal lost and won,— weary veterans of campaigns in which has loomed as well the amiable bean-pole Dixon, secretly afraid of what they were all caught up in doing, as if at the Behest of the Stars, which somehow had begun to take on for him attributes of conscious beings ("Seen it before," quoth Maskelyne, "— Rapture without a doubt,— for some reason Dissenters are particularly susceptible…"), attacked by Vertigo if he continu'd too long at the eye-piece, lost in terror before the Third Dimension, indeed running, when there was a choice, to Earth rather than to Fire, desperate to pretend all was well, face kept as clear as the bottom of a stream in August, nothing visible at the fringes of readability,— who knew him, truly? What might wait, at the margins of the pool, mottled, still, river-silt slowly gathering upon its dorsal side?

At the end of the day, all Mason knows of Maskelyne, is how to needle him. "Maskelyne,— I cannot go,"— yet as if uncertain as to how much Maskelyne intends to make him plead. "That is," he cannot help adding, "if it pleases Your Grace."

The Astronomer Royal is not prepared. "Again you renounce me," he does not exactly intend to blurt, his scowl appearing slowly, like a blush. "Bloody infuriating, Mason."

"I know. Why not have another bowl of *café au lait?* And,— look ye here, a lovely iced bun."

"Here,— suppose you go to Scotland only as a sort of Scout,— look at likely possibilities, report back to us."

" 'Us'?"

"Pay Mr. Dixon a visit upon your way, for Heaven's sake."

"I've your Permission for that, have I."

"Mason,— "

"Half a Guinea a Day."

"Gentlemen usually accept a single Honorarium."

"Plus daily expenses."

"This might be quite in your Line, Mason."

"Try not to say 'Line,' Maskelyne. Ehp,— that is,— "

" 'Mask,' then," flirtatiously, "plain old 'Mask.' "

75

"At the request of Maskelyne, I am coming North a Mountain of suitable Gravity to seek, whose presum'd Influence might deflect a Plumb-line clearly enough to be measur'd without Ambiguity.— Tho' given the A.R.'s difficult History with Plumb-lines, I feel Apprehension for the Project.

"Having determin'd after deep study in Mr. C. Dicey's County Atlas that it is impossible to travel from here to Scotland without passing your doorstep, I should be oblig'd for any recommendation of a good Inn for the night, whence I shall beg leave to make ~~You~~ Thee a brief visit.

"I pray that thou suffer no further from the Gout. I am well enough,— in Body. Our Afflictions are many, proceeding from an unilluminated Region deep and distant, which we are us'd to call by Names more reverent. 'Twill be four years, Brother Lens. I hope it is not too long,— nor yet too soon."

To which,— "The Queen's Head is Bishop's best,— yet, my own house being around but a couple of corners, I would have to insist that thou improve the emptiness of one of its chambers. Besides, at The Queen's Head, despite the excellence of its Larder and Kitchen, strict insistence is kept upon appearing on time at the Table, which might prove inconvenient to thee.

"We'll find the Carp shy of human company, the Dace fat and slow, but none so much as

Thy svt,

J."

Mason finds Dixon still gloomy about the death of his Mother back in January. Tho' they had finally found the time to be together, sometimes 'twas too much, and they fell to bickering. "Tha should have gone when tha had the chance...? Jere, tha never were one for Pit work, nor it for thee, and Father, tha know, never was expecting it of thee."

"Bonny time to be tellin' me thah'...?"

"You were the Baby, the Baby can do no wrong, don't you know thah'?"

"So Dad came to an agreement," Jeremiah press'd, "with Mr. Bird."

"Dear knaahs, Jeremiah."

"How could he repay Mr. Bird," Dixon asks of Mason, years later. "Thah's what I can't see."

Of course it matters to him. Mason has his own mysteries in this regard,— what could the Miller of Wherr have done for the Director-to-be of the Honorable E.I.C.? Bread? "Coal?" he speculates.

"A few pence off upon the Chaldron,— 'twould add up. Yet in that Quantity,— "

"Suggests a need for high heat, sustain'd over time. Glass? Iron?"

Mason is content for the moment simply to sit, inside The Jolly Pitman and a Carousing of Geordies, feeling settled, quietly plumb, seeing against the neutral gray of the smoke all the sun-flashes from the Day, the clear slacks, the sand bottoms, the nettles and rose bay willow-herb, the sudden streak of light as the most gigantic Carp he'd ever run across in his life, keeled, what in legend will be recalled as but inches from his foot. It was the notoriously long-lived Canny Bob, said to've been chased by the Romans who once encamped up above Binchester. "But as you froze there, seemingly the object of Torpidinous assault," Dixon tells him, after Bob has made his escape, "I hesitated to approach you, for fear of electrocuting myself. At least I was able for once to observe him at some leisure,— he strangely seem'd to *like* you, Mason. I've never had that good a chance at him, no one I know has been as close as you. The Romans 'round here used to say, '*Carpe carpum,*' that is, 'Seize the Carp'."

"All right. I waited too long. But think how embarrassed all your friends would have felt, had a Stranger taken him,— and my first time on the river, too. Just as well, really." There is a fragility about Dixon now, a softer way of reflecting light, such that Mason must accordingly grow gentle with him. No child has yet summon'd from him such care.

"Tha must attend closely to the Dace up here as well, for they look exactly like Chub, yet are they night and Day when it comes to the fight they'll put up...?"

"Excuse me, one looks at the Fins. 'Tis fairly obvious which is which."

"Not here, I fear. Nor will River Wear Chub have much to do with the Bread-baits you no doubt learn'd to use down in Gloucester."

"What then? Some rare Beetle, I imagine."

"Some rare Beef would better do the Trick...? They are blood-crazed, and feral."

Despite their best Efforts, talk will ever drift to their separate Transits. "Maskelyne kept me over there," says Mason. "Nothing but Weather, Day after Day. Couldn't get enough Obs for him. Would have taken the projected age of the Universe. Brought me back upon a meat-ship...."

In the Hold were hundreds of Lamb carcasses,— once a sure occasion for Resentment prolong'd, now accepted as part of a Day inflicted by Fate, ever darkening,— exil'd to which, he must, in ways unnam'd,— perhaps, this late, unable to include "simply,"— persist. In the heavy weather of late November, the carcasses thump'd against the Bulkheads, keeping exhausted and increasingly irritated Mason from sleep. Deep in the mid-watch, his Mental Bung at last violently ejected by the Gases of Rage, he ran screaming to undog the hatch into the forward cargo space, and was immediately caught, a careless Innocent at some Ball of the Dead, among a sliding, thick meat Battery, the pale corpses only a bit larger than he, cold as the cold of the Sea that lay, he helpfully reminded himself, just the other side of these Timbers curving into candle-less blackness,— oof! as the ship roll'd, some dead Weight, odorous of sheep-fat, went speeding by headed for the Port side, nearly knocking Mason upon his Arse, and obliging him immediately to spin away upon one Foot, whilst the Ship pitch'd heavily, down and up,— fine Business. His intention, a true Phlegmatick's, having been but to locate the offending Carcass,— being unable to allow in his *Data* more than one,— and secure it, somehow, imagining the Meat-Hold well supplied with any Lines and Hardware he might need.

Fool. Here were the Representatives of ev'ry sheep he had ever spoken ill of,— and now he was at their Mercy. But they are dead, he told himself. Aye, but *not only* dead. Here was a category beyond Dead, in its pointless Humiliation, its superfluous Defeat,— stripp'd, the naked faces bruis'd and cut by the repeated battering of the others in this, their final Flock, they slither'd lethally 'round him. He had a clear moment in which he saw them moving of their own Will,— nothing to do with the movements of the Ship,— elaborately, the way dancers at Assemblies danc'd.

"Well I certainly wouldn't want to be a Disruption, here!" Mason roar'd at them, waiting, blind as a Corn in a Mill, to be crush'd. The situation held little hope for him,— wherever he stepp'd, he slipp'd, there being no purchase upon the Deck, owing to the untallied Tons of Fat that had long made frictionless ev'ry surface,— Mason instantly recognizing the same proximity to pure Equations of Motion as he had felt observing Stars and Planets in empty Space, with only the beautiful Silence missing now....

"However'd tha get out of thah' one?" Dixon wonders.

"Ahrrhh! the Smell alone might have done for me. Quite snapp'd me back, yes it did, like a Spring, back to that damn'd Cape. I recall being very annoy'd, that my last Earthly Memories should be of that dismal place. Purgatory has to be better, I told myself, maybe even Hell.— Fortunately, just then, a Party of Sailors, who for some reason were neither on Watch nor asleep, seeming indeed almost furtive in Demeanor, rescu'd me. I noted too a puzzling air of Jollification, some of it directed at me. 'How is it in there?' one of them ask'd, with what, upon Shore, would certainly've been taken as an insinuating Leer. Not 'How *was* it,'— which is odd enough, no, what this Sailor distinctly said— "

"Why aye, Mason, tha see it, don't tha ...? they *were* Sailors...? 'Tis probably a standard practice, upon those Meat-Voyages...? Something a foremast Swab, in his Day's unrelenting bleakness, might have to look forward to, when the Midnight Hour creeps 'round...?"

"What.— Do you mean,— Oh, Dixon, really."

Dixon shrugs. "If a Lad were wide awake, kept his wits about him, why the pitch of Danger...? eeh, eeh! at thah' speed, thah' lack of Friction...? and one's Mates in there as well,— might be just the Thing,— "

"And then at the Dock," Mason continues brusquely, "— at Preston,— for the Captain declared that he 'would not risk Liverpool,'— this enormous crowd were waiting,— some of them quite fashionable-looking indeed, significant Wigs and so forth, running about, screaming, setting fire to Factors' Sheds, and now and then, to one another. 'Twas the Food Riots,— the same having pitch'd, as I'd thought, to full fury when I sail'd for Ireland, now a year later, far from having abated, reach'd even to Proud Preston. And what of the rest of England? My Father? Had they burn'd down the Mill yet?

"No one was there to meet me. The Sunlight abovedecks was smear'd, the Shadows deeper than Day-time's. The Mob, many of them small and frail from Hunger, yet possess'd by a Titanic Resentment that provided them the Strength, storm'd the Ship, and began removing Lamb carcasses (the Abasement of these not yet complete), and throwing them into the Water,— casting away food they might rather have taken with them, and had to eat. The loud insanity, the pure murderous Thumping. Thou wouldn't've wish'd to go out there at that moment, either. The Captain allow'd me to shelter in his Quarters, till it should be safe to emerge,— proving meantime an engaging conversationalist, particularly upon the Topick of Mutton, as to which he seem'd most well inform'd, and even strangely...affectionate,— "

"Of course,— being, as tha'd say, the Sultan of the Arrangement."

"Well, it never occurr'd to me. Too late to do anything about it...."

"Pity...? Tha might've had a bit of Fun in there, at least...?"

"Aahhrr.... With its Corollary, that whatever I do imagine as Fun, invariably produces Misery...."

"Not only for thee," adds Dixon, pretending to scrutinize the Fire, "but for ev'ry Unfortunate within thy Ambit, as well."

"Gave thee a rough time, didn't I, Friend." Reaching to rest his hand for a moment upon Dixon's Shoulder, before removing it again.

"Oh," Dixon nodding away at an Angle from any direct view of his Partner's Face, "as rough times go,...the French were worse...? Then five Years of Mosquitoes, of course...." The old Astronomers sit for a while in what might be an Embrace, but that they forbear to touch.

"Quite a Lark, you must have had.... I returned from the North Cape in some Con-fusion,— wishing but to put distance between my back and

Hammerfost, a-Southing I went, in a true Panick, all the way to London. Hoping the while, that I had only slamm'd my Nob once too often upon the roof-beams of that Dwarf's Hovel the Navy styl'd an Observatory…. Would have welcomed the chance to see thee, to talk, but Maskelyne was being a Nuisance as ever, and thou were yet in Ulster….

"Bayley went to the North Cape. I was put off about seventy miles down the coast, at Hammerfost, on Hammerfost Island. The Ground was frozen so hard it took a week to dig a hole for a Post to fix the Clock to. Then it snow'd for a week, sometimes with violent Winds, and Hail. The days just before the Transit were hazy, and now and then very hazy indeed. On the morning of the Transit, the first sight I had of the Planet, she was already half immerg'd. Ten minutes later, for one instant, thro' a thin cloud, it seem'd she was upon the Sun. Yet no thread of Light. Six hours on, the same thing. Caught her going off the Disk, internal Contact was already past,— one swift View, and then the Clouds came in again. Got the Eclipse later, next day took the Dip to the Horizon. Here was the World's Other End,— one stood upon a great Bluff and look'd out upon the Arctic Ocean, the Horizon strangely nearer than it ought to've been. 'Twas amid this terminal Geometry, that I was visited." Mason appearing to hear no resonance, "— Taken, then,— yet further North."

"Ah.— " Can Dixon see the Apprehension in his Face? "How far was that?"

"Hours…? Days…? He appear'd with no warning. Very large eyes, what you would call quite large indeed. I had no idea who, or how many, might have been dwelling in this desolate place. 'You must come with me,' quoth he.

" 'I have a ship leaving in a few hours, man,' I mumbl'd, and kept on with my paper-work.

" 'H.M.S. *Emerald,* Captain Douglas. There will be no wind until we return. Come.' I looked up. He was undeniably there,— I had not been upon the island long enough for Rapture of the North to have set in. For a moment I thought 'twas Stig, a Shadow of Stig, you recollect our mystickal Axman, with his Nostalgia for the North, so in command of him…. Yet my Visitor's eyes were too strange even for Stig,— his aspect, his speech, were nothing I recogniz'd. We descended to the Shore, and went out upon a great Floe of Ice, and so one Floe to another, until all had frozen into a continuous Plain. In his movement he seem'd as much a Visitor as I in this Country. From his Pack he unfolded a small Sledge of Caribou Hide, stretch'd upon an ingeniously hinged framework of Whalebone, and from a curious black Case produced a Device of elaborately coil'd Wires, set upon Gimbals, which he affix'd to the Prow of the vehicle. 'Hurry!' I had barely climb'd aboard when the whole concern spun about, till pointing, as a Needle-man I surmis'd, to the North Magnetick Pole, and began to move, faster and ever faster, with a rising Whine, over the Ice-Prairie. 'Sir,' I would have shouted, had the swiftness of our Travel allowed me breath, 'Sir, not so far!' when I'd really meant to say, 'not so fast.' We sped thus northward in perpetual sunlight. Night would not come to that Latitude. The Sun up there, from mid-May to late July, does not set. The phantoms, the horrors, when they came, would not be those of Night.

"Nor, as things turn'd out, would it be a Journey to the North Pole. The Pole itself, to be nice, hung beyond us in empty space,— for as I was soon to observe, at the top of the World, somewhere between eighty and ninety degrees North, the Earth's Surface, all 'round the Parallel, began to curve sharply inward, leaving a great circum-polar Emptiness," as Mason shifts uncomfortably and looks about for something to smoke or eat, "directly toward which our path was taking us, at first gently, then with some insistence, down-hill, ever downward, and thus, gradually, around the great Curve of its Rim.— And 'twas so that we enter'd, by its great northern Portal, upon the inner Surface of the Earth." A patiently challenging smile.

Mason sits rhythmickally inserting into his Face an assortment of Meg Bland's Cookies, Tarts, and Muffins,...pretending to be silent by choice, lest any phrase emerge too farinaceously inflected.

Dixon continues cheerfully.—

"The Ice giving way to Tundra, we proceeded, ever downhill, into a not-quite-total darkness, the pressure of the Air slowly increasing, each sound soon taking on a whispering after-tone, as from a sort of immense composite Echo,— until we were well inside, hundreds of miles below the Outer Surface, having clung to what we now walked upon quite handily all the way, excepting that we arriv'd upside-down as bats in a belfry...."

The Interior had remain'd less studied philosophickally, than endur'd anxiously, by those who might choose to travel Diametrickally across it,—

means of Flight having been develop'd early in the History of the Inner Surface. "Their God, like that of the Iroquois, lives at their Horizon,— here 'tis their North or South Horizon, each a more and less dim Ellipse of Sky-light. The Curve of the Rim is illuminated, depending on the position of the Sun, in greater or lesser Relievo,— chains of mountains, thin strokes of towers, the eternally spilling lives of thousands dwelling in the long Estuarial Towns wrapping from Outside to Inside as the water rushes away in uncommonly long waterfalls, downward for hours, unbrak'd, till at last debouching into an interior Lake of great size, upside-down but perfectly secured to its Lake-bed by Gravity as well as Centrifugal Force, and in which upside-down swimmers glide at perfect ease, hanging over an Abyss thousands of miles deep. From wherever one is, to raise one's Eyes is to see the land and Water rise ahead of one and behind as well, higher and higher till lost in the Thickening of the Atmosphere.... In the larger sense, then, to journey anywhere, in this *Terra Concava*, is ever to ascend. With its Corollary,— Outside, here upon the Convexity,— to go anywhere is ever to *descend*."

With great Cordiality and respect upon all sides, Dixon was taken to the local Academy of Sciences, and introduc'd to the Fellows.

"Nothing to do with your actual Appearance," Dixon said, "but all of thee have such a familiar look,— up above, we hear many Tales of Gnomes, Elves, smaller folk, who live underground and possess what are, to huz, magickal Powers? Who've min'd their ways to the borders of our world, following streams, spying upon us from the Fells when the light of the Day's tricky enough.... Is this where they come from, then?"

"They are we." One of the inner-surface Philosophers removing his Hat and sweeping into a Bow, the others, in Echelon, following identickally, Hat-Brims all ending up in a single, perfectly imbricated Line.

"Your servant, Sirs."

"You receive Messages from us, by way of your Magnetic Compasses. What you call the 'Secular Change of Declination' is whatever dimm'd and muffl'd remnant may reach you above, of all the lives of us Below,— being less liv'd than waged, at a level of Passion that would seem, to you, quite intense. We have learn'd to use the Tellurick Forces, including that of Magnetism,— which you oddly seem to consider the only one."

"There are others?" Mason perking up.

"That's what he said. All most effective and what we'd style 'miraculous,' down there,— tho' perhaps not as much so, up here.

"Thy trip to Scotland will be closely watch'd, Mason, *from below....* 'Once the solar parallax is known,' they told me, 'once the necessary Degrees are measur'd, and the size and weight and shape of the Earth are calculated inescapably at last, all this will vanish. We will have to seek another Space.' No one explain'd what that meant, however...? 'Perhaps some of us will try living upon thy own Surface. I am not sure that everyone can adjust from a concave space to a convex one. Here have we been sheltered, nearly everywhere we look is no Sky, but only more Earth.— How many of us, I wonder, could live the other way, the way you People do, so exposed to the Outer Darkness? Those terrible Lights, great and small? And wherever you may stand, given the Convexity, each of you is slightly *pointed away* from everybody else, all the time, out into that Void that most of you seldom notice. Here in the Earth Concave, everyone is pointed *at* everyone else,— ev'rybody's axes converge,— forc'd at least thus to acknowledge one another,— an entirely different set of rules for how to behave.'

"We happen'd to be looking through a Telescope of peculiar design, for hundreds of yards around whose Eye-piece, Specula of silver, precisely beaten and polish'd to a Perfection I was assur'd had cost the sanity of more than one Artisan, were spread like sails for catching ev'ry least flutter of Luminosity, conveying to a central set of Lenses the images they gather'd in. With this Instrument one could view any part of the Hollow Earth, even places directly across the Inner Void, thousands of miles distant. Tho' Light through the Polar Openings north and south varied as the Earth traveled in its orbit, 'twas never more than low and diffuse, hence the enlarged eyes of these inner-surface dwellers, their pale skins, their diet of roots and fungi and what greener Esculents they might go to harvest out in the more arable country 'round the Openings, though the journeys back inside were fraught with peril and inconvenience from arm'd Bands of Vegetable Pirates. Leaves in here were nearly black in color, fruit rare. The Wines," Dixon shaking his head, "are as austere as anyone can imagine."

"You've not become a Grape person, Dixon?"

"The damn'd Gout. Wine's not as bad."

Mason bleakly exhales. "No Hell, then?"

"Not inside the Earth, anyway."

"Nor any…Single Administrator of Evil."

"They did introduce me to some Functionary,— no telling,— We chatted, others came in. They ask'd if I'd take off as much of my Clothing as I'd feel comfortable with,— I stepp'd out of my Shoes, left my Hat on…? They walk'd 'round me in Circles, now and then poking at me…? Nothing too intrusive."

"Nothing you remember, anyway," Mason can't help putting in.

"They peer'd into my Eyes and Ears, they look'd in my Mouth, they put me upon a Balance and weigh'd me. They conferr'd. 'Are you quite sure, now,' the Personage ask'd me at last, 'that you wish to bet ev'rything upon the Body?— *this* Body?— moreover, to rely helplessly upon the Daily Harvest your Sensorium brings in,— keeping in mind that both will decline, the one in Health as the other in Variety, growing less and less trustworthy till at last they are no more?' Eeh. Well, what would thoo've said?"

"So, did you— "

"We left it in abeyance. Arriv'd back at the Observatory, it seem'd but minutes, this time, in Transit, I sought my Bible, which I let fall open, and read, in Job, 26:5 through 7, 'Dead things are formed from under the waters, and the inhabitants thereof.

" 'Hell is naked before him, and destruction hath no covering.

" 'He stretcheth out the north over the empty place, and hangeth the earth upon nothing.' "

Upon the doorstep, horses waiting him in the Street, Mason grasps Dixon's Hand. "If they don't kill and eat me up there, shall we do this again?"

"We must count upon becoming old Geezers together," Dixon proposes. They are looking directly at one another for the first time since either can remember.

"Let us meet next Summer…. You must come stay in Sapperton."

"I may not travel far." Immediately reaching out his hand to Mason's arm, lest Mason, in his way, take too much offense. "I wish it were not so."

Mason, as he long has learn'd to for Dixon, refrains from flinching. "No loss, perhaps,— thanks to the damn'd Clothiers, no one can guarantee what, if anything, swims in the Frome anymore," avoiding any prolong'd talk of Frailty, which he can see is costing Dixon more than his reserve of cheer may afford. "The Mills, curse them all.... Dixon, I shall be happy to see you wherever you wish." He turns to the Straps securing the Transit Instruments, ignoring what is just behind his Eyes and Nose. "Mind thyself, Friend."

76

"Now, Dr. Johnson, along with Boswell acting as his Squire, happen'd, in August of 'seventy-three, to be crossing into Scotland as well, upon their famous Trip to the Hebrides."

"More likely," snorts Ives, "they didn't pass within a hundred miles of Mason."

Yet (speculates the Rev^d), did they hesitate, upon the Border, at some rude Inn, just before taking the fatal Step across into the Celtick Unknown?... Sitting at a table, drinking Ale, observing the Mist thro' the Window-Panes, Mason forty-five, the Cham sixty-four. "You seem a serious young man, with Thames-side intonations in your Voice, if I'm not mistaken."

"Sir, I saw you at The Mitre Tavern, once."

"Royal Society, are you."

"As your own Intonation already implies, Sir, not bloody likely, is it? tho' I have contracted with them, and more than once."

"You're the Star-Gazer, what's his name."

"Mason," Boswell informs him.

"Damme 'f that's not it exactly," says Mason. "Thankee, Gents, altho' this time I am come upon an Errand of Gravity." He explains to them his search for a Scottish Mountain, suiting as many as possible of Maskelyne's Stipulations.

"Hum..." Boswell's gaze bright'ning, "he's Clive of India's Brother-in-law. Do you suppose the Nabob wants to buy a Mountain?"

"Good Lord,— Maskelyne, working in Confidence, as a Land-Agent? I never thought of that."

"Then you are not as corrupted as you believe you are, at least according to the creases of your Phiz, Sir," somewhat brusquely announces Dr. Johnson. "Such relative Innocence may be a sacred Asset, yet a secular Liability. May you ever distinguish the one from the other. Oh, and Mason?"

"Your Servant."

"Be careful."

"Of what, Sir?"

"Of the Attention you'll be getting up there, if your Principal's illustrious Relation becomes widely known," warns Mr. Boswell, himself a Scot.

"Upon the Map I carry," declares Dr. J., "nothing appears, beyond here, but Mountains,— in Practice to examine them all is a task without end,— and ev'ry Scot you meet will be trying to sell you at least one, that he,— and ignore not 'she,'— happens to know of. These people are strong, shrewd. Be not deceiv'd by any level of the Exotick they may present you, Kilts, Bag-Pipes sort of thing. Haggis. You must keep unfailing Vigilance."

Mr. Boswell bows elaborately, whilst keeping his Eye-balls upon the Roll.

Out there in the Fog brimming and sweeping now over Ridge-tops and into the Glens, somewhere it waits, the world across the next Line, in darkness and isolation, barren, unforgiving, a Nation that within Mason's lifetime has risen to seize the Crown, been harrow'd into submission, then been shipp'd in great Lots to America. "I imagine there's yet a bit of...resentment about?"

The Doctor snorts. "The word you grope for is *Hatred,* Sir,— inveterate, inflexible Hatred. The 'Forty-five lives on here, a Ghost from a Gothick Novel, ubiquitous, frightfully shatter'd, exhibiting gallons of a certain crimson Fluid,— typickal of the People, don't you see."

"Aye, he means me," sighs Mr. Boswell. He picks up the Bone remnant of a Chop and gestures with it. "Soon he will commence with the Cannibalism-Joaks, pray you, miss it not, 'tis more hilarious than may at first seem likely. All his lifelong Enmity, emerging at last in this way. No one knows why, but he intends to go to the Hebrides, to the furthest Isle, to view the Dark Ages upon Display."

"The uncomplicated People, laboring with their primitive Tools," gushes Mason, "— the simplicity of Faith, lo, its Time reborn."

" 'Tis fascinating, this belief among you Men of Science," remarks Dr. J., "that Time is ever more *simply* transcended, the further one is willing to journey away from London, to observe it."

"Why, Mason here's done the very thing," cries Boswell. "In America. Ask him."

Mason glowers, shaking his head. "I've ascended, descended, even condescended, and the List's not ended,— but haven't yet *trans*-cended a blessèd thing, thankee."

"The Savages of America," intones the Doctor, "— what Powers do they possess, and how do they use them?" As if here, at the Edge of the World, they might confide what no one would ever say aloud in London,— with Boswell a-bustle to get it all scribbl'd down into his Quarto.

The abruptness of the Doctor's Question reminds Mason of himself, addressing the Learnèd English Dog, a dozen years ago…his mouth creeps upward at the corners, almost achieving an Horizontal. "Would that my co-adjutor Mr. Dixon were here," says Mason (missing Dixon as he speaks), "for the Magickal in all its Occurrences, to others of us how absent, was ever his Subject…. Potions, Rain-Making, the undoing of Enemies remote,— that Mandeville of Mohawks would be sure to enlighten you. I can myself testify to little beyond the giant Mounds that the Savages say they guard as Curators, for some more distant Race of Builders. I have fail'd to observe more in them, than their most impressive Size, tho' Mr. Dixon swears to Coded Inscriptions, Purposive Lamination, and Employment, unto the *Present Day*, by Agents Unknown of Powers Invisible.

"Yet appropriately enough, what compels me out under the Elements once again now, is yet another damn'd Species of Giant Mound,— and after hoping I'd seen my last in America. Woe, it seems I've acquir'd a Speciality,— and the Elevated, the Chosen, go on assigning me to these exercises in large-scale Geometry. This Mountain I'm about to seek must be regular as a Prism, as if purposely constructed in days of old by Forces more powerful than ours…powerful enough to suggest that God (whatever that may be) has not altogether quit our own desperate Day."

"You're not pleas'd with His Frequency of Appearance," frowns Johnson. "Sir, be wary,— for the next step in such Petulance, is to define Him as some all-pervading Fairy-Dust, and style it Deism."

"D'ye think I wasn't looking, all that long arse-breaking American time? Mounds, Caverns, things that went across the Sky?— had you seen one of those, 'twould've made y' think twice…. Even giant Vegetables,— if it had to be,— seeking Salvation in the Oversiz'd, how pitiable,— what of it, I've little Pride, some great Squash upon the Trailside? I'll take it, won't I."

"I'd've been happy with the Cock Lane Ghost," Johnson mutters.

"Happy," Mason nods. His eyes far too bright. "You were ill-treated, Sir, in that matter."

"Be careful to note, Boswell, how even a Lunatick may yet be civil. Thank you, Sir. Or is it Your Holiness?"

"I?" All but pleading for someone's Judgment of madness, as if desiring to be admitted to that select company, select as the Royal Society, which did not want him, either.

"I had my Boswell, once," Mason tells Boswell, "Dixon and I. We had a joint Boswell. Preacher nam'd Cherrycoke. Scribbling ev'rything down, just like you, Sir. Have you," twirling his Hand in Ellipses,— "you know, ever…had one yourself? If I'm not prying."

"Had one what?"

"Hum…a Boswell, Sir,— I mean, of your own. Well you couldn't very well call him that, being one yourself,— say, a sort of Shadow ever in the Room who has haunted you, preserving your ev'ry spoken remark,— "

"Which else would have been lost forever to the great Wind of Oblivion,— think," armsweep south, "as all civiliz'd Britain gathers at this hour, how much shapely Expression, from the titl'd Gambler, the Barmaid's Suitor, the offended Fopling, the gratified Toss-Pot, is simply fading away upon the Air, out under the Door, into the Evening and the Silence beyond. All those voices. Why not pluck a few words from the multitudes rushing toward the Void of forgetfulness?"

The Mountain he finds for Maskelyne will be too regular to be natural,— like Silbury Hill, it will have the look of ancient Earth-Work about it. And 'twill be Maskelyne who goes to Schiehallion, after Mason refuses the Assignment again, and becomes famous for it, not to mention belovèd of the Scots people there, the subject of a Ballad, and presently a Figure of Legend, in a strange Wizard's turnout bas'd upon an actual Observing Suit he will wear whilst in Perthshire. A plaid one, in fact, of Maskelyne's own Design,— "A Tartan never observ'd in the World," he explains, "that no one Clan up there be offended."

"Or ev'ry one," Mun is quick to point out.

Mason will go back to waking day after day in Sapperton, piecing together odd cash jobs for the Royal Society, reductions for Maskelyne's Almanack,— small children everywhere, a neat Observatory out in the Garden, a reputation in the Golden Valley as a Sorcerer, a Sorcerer's Apprentice, who once climb'd that strange eminence at Greenwich, up into another level of Power, sail'd to all parts of the Globe, but came back down among them again,— they will be easy with him, call him Charlie, at last. Another small-town eccentric absorb'd back into the Weavery, keeping a work-space fitted out someplace in the back of some long Cotswold house, down a chain of rooms back from the lane and out into the crooked Looming of those hillside fields.

77

So when they meet again, 'tis in Bishop, and any third Observer might note in an instant the deterioration the Year intervening has brought to each,— Dixon's pronounc'd limp and bile-stain'd Eyeballs, Mason's slow retreat, his steps taken backward, only just stubborn enough to keep facing the light, into Melancholy.

Increasingly ill at ease with change of any kind, be it growing a year older or watching America,— once home to him as the Desert to a Nomad upon it,— in its great Convulsion, Mason has begun to dream of a night-time City,— of creeping among monuments of stone perhaps twice his height, of seeking refuge from some absolute pitiless Upheaval in relations among Men.

'Twas Stonehenge, absent 'Bekah and Moon-Light. The Monuments made no sense at all. They were not Statues,— they bore no inscriptions. They were the Night's Standing-Stones, put there by some Agency remote not in Time but from caring at all what happen'd to the poor fugitives who now scurried among them, seeking their brute impenetrability for cover. Whoever their Makers had been, they were invisible now, with their own Chronicles, their own Intentions,— whatever these were,— and they glided on, without any need for living Witnesses.

Were this but a single Dream, wip'd out as usual by the rattling Quotidian, Mason might even have forgotten it by now. But it keeps coming back,— more accurately, he return'd to it, the same City, the same unlit Anarchy, again and again, each time to be plung'd into the middle of whatever has been going on in his absence. At first he visits fortnightly, but within the year he is journeying there ev'ry night. Even more alarmingly, *he is not always asleep*...out of doors against his will, a City in Chaos, the lights too few, the differences between friend and enemy not always clear, and Mistakes a penny a Bushel. Reflection upon any Topick is an unforgivable Lapse, out here where at any moment Death may come whistling in from the Dark.

"Well Hullo, Death, what's that you're whistling?"

"Oo, little Ditters von Dittersdorf, nothing you'd recognize, hasn't happen'd yet, not even sure you'll live till it's perform'd anywhere,— have to check the 'Folio as to that, get back to you?"

"No hurry,— truly, no hurry."

"You 'cute Rascal," Death reaching out to pinch his Cheek.... Sometimes Mason wakes before traversing into the next Episode,— sometimes the bony Thumb and Finger continue their Approach, asymptotickally ever closer, be he waking, or dreaming something else.

"Their visits," wrote the Rev[d], on unnam'd Authority, "consisted of silence when fishing, fever'd nocturnal Conversation when not. Though even beside the Wear, or in it, are they ever conversing. In their silences, the true Measure of their History."

Mason arrives one day to find Dixon sitting there with giant Heaps of Cherries and Charcoal. "Have some," offering Mason his choice.

"Excuse me. The Gout is eas'd by things that begin with 'Ch'?"

"Why aye. They don't know that down in Gloucestershire?"

"Chicken?"

"In the form of Soup, particularly."

"Chops? Cheese? Chocolate?"

" 'Tis consider'd an entertaining Affliction, by those who have not suffer'd it."

"Oh, Dixon, I didn't mean,— " Ev'ry turn now, a chance for someone taking the hump. "Here, your Cushion,— may I,— "

"First thing!— is, you mustn't touch...the Foot, thank thee. Bit abrupt, sorry, yet do I know this, by now, like a County Map,— where the valleys of least Pain lie, and where the Peaks to avoid. Ev'ry movement has to be plann'd like a damn'd Expedition.... Meg Bland is the only mortal, nothing personal, who may even breathe too close to it."

"Lucky me," says she, in the door straight as a Swift, a tall ginger-hair'd Beauty disinclin'd to pass her time unproductively. Margaret Bland gave up on marrying Dixon long ago, indeed these Days is reluctant, when the Topick arises, even to respond. "We'll have the Wedding just before we go to America," he said,— and, "We'll go to America as man and wife." For a while she was a good sport, and allow'd herself to be entertain'd with his Accounts of what Adventure and Wealth were there to seize, in that fabl'd place. But there soon grew upon her, as she had observ'd it in her mother, a practical disillusionment before the certainty of Death, that men for their part kept trying to put off as long as possible. She saw Jere doing just that, with his world of Maps, his tenderness and care as he bent over them, as herself, resign'd to tending him,— no different than man and wife, really.

"I love her," he tells Mason. "I say thah'.... Yet to myself I think, She's my last, my...how would tha say...?"

"She's a good Woman," Mason says, "thou must see that."

"Bringing me Cherries ev'ry day. For this," pollicating the Toe. Shaking his head, laughing in perplexity, he looks over at Mason, finds Mason looking at him,— "The Girls are mine."

Mason, who rarely these Days smiles, smiles. "Well.— Well, well, in fact." They sit nodding at each other for a while.

"Tha must've seen it in their Faces, in Mary...and Elizabeth, for fair...?"

"So *that's* what it is,— well, they are beautiful Young Women despite it all."

"Thy Boys,— they must be nearly grown?"

Mason nodding, "Oh, and I got married again. Forgot to mention that. Aye. Then we had Charles Junior, then two weeks after he was born, my *Dad* got married again. We both married women nam'd Mary. Tha would like them both, I know. Mine in particular."

"She's young...?"

"Amazing. How do these People— "

"Strange Geordie Powers, Friend,— and I know thou need as many Children as possible, as a Bridge over a Chasm, to keep thee from falling into the Sky."

"Charlie the Baby's the very Image of my Dad, that's what's so peculiar. The Boys look like Rebekah, but the Baby,— the resemblance makes me jumpy. I expect him to start shouting at me...sometimes he does. Can't understand any of it of course, but then I can't make out my Dad either."

"Eeh. Then all's fairly as usual...?"

"I come to the Mill ev'ry morning, and he gives me one Loaf. 'Take thee this day, thy daily bread,'— ev'ry time,— 'tis Wit. 'Tis great fun for him. How inveterate a Hatred shall I be able to enjoy, for someone who looks like my baby son?"

"Tha seem disappointed."

"Next worst thing to unrequited Love, isn't it? Insufficient hate."

"And yet it's done thee a world of Good...? the months, often years, of Time tha didn't know tha had...?"

"Ahrr. Years off my age."

"And we've another coming in right about Harvest time.— How do you know that about me? Maybe I hate children."

"Then feel free to ignore my wish of much Joy, Mason. Shouldn't tha be in Sapperton, with thy Mary?"

"Her mother is there, and they are just as content to have me away."

They are dozing together by Dixon's Hearth. Both their Pipes are out. The Fret has gather'd in the waste places, cross'd them, and come to the Edge of the Town. Anything may lie just the other side, having a Peep. There is jollity at The Queen's Head, tho' here in Bondgate, for the moment, the Bricks are silent.

Each is dreaming about the other. Mason dreams them in London, at some enormous gathering,— it is nam'd the Royal Society, but is really something else. Some grand Testimonial, already some Days in progress, upon a Stage, before a Pit in which the Crowds are ever circulating. Bradley is there, living and hale,— Mason keeps trying to find him, so that Dixon and he may meet, but each new Face is a new distraction, and presently he cannot find Dixon, either....

Dixon is dreaming of a Publick performance as well, except it's he and Mason who are up on the Stage, and whoever may be watching are kept invisible by the Lights that separate Stage and Pit. They are both wear-

ing cheap but serviceable suits, and back'd by a chamber orchestra, they
are singing, and doing a few simple time-steps,—

> It...was...fun,
> While it lasted,
> And it lasted,
> Quite a while,—
> [Dixon] For the bleary-eyed lad from the coal pits,
> [Mason] And the 'Gazer with big-city Style,—
> [Both] We came, we peep'd, we shouted with surprize,
> Tho' half the time we couldn't tell the falsehoods from the lies,
> [M] I say! is that a— [D] No, it ain't! [M] I do apologize,—
> [Both] This Astronomer's Life, say,
> Pure as a Fife, hey,
> Quick as a Knife, in
> The Da-a-ark!
>
> [M] Oh, we went,—
> Out to Cape Town, [D] Phila-
> Del-phia too,
> [Both] Tho' we didn't quite get to Ohi-o,
> There were Marvels a-plenty to view...
> Those Trees! Those Hills! Those Vegetables so high!
> The Cataracts and Caverns,
> And the Spectres in the Sky,
> [M] I say, was that— [D] I hope not! [M] Who
> The Deuce said that? [D] Not I!
> It's a wonderful place, ho,
> Nothing but Space, go
> Off on a chase in the Dark...."

Dixon wakes briefly. "It had damn'd well better be Bodily Resurrection's all I can say...?"

One final Expedition, Dixon believ'd, a bit more Gold in the Sack, and
he'd be free to return to America, look up Washington and Franklin,
Capt. Shelby, and the other Lads, find the perfect Seat in the West.

He knows where the Coal is, the Iron and Lead, and if there's Gold he'll
witch that out of the Earth, too. The Trick lies less in hollowing out the

Wand, or putting in the tiny Samples of ev'rything you're not looking for, than in holding it then, so as to adjust for the extra Weight.... Let George have all Cockfield Fell,— in America is Abundance, impossible to reach the end of in one lifetime,— hence, from the Mortal point of view, infinite.

By the time he might have emigrated at last, Mary Hunter Dixon had grown ill, and in January '73, she pass'd to a better place. Busy with rebellion, America drew back toward the edges of Dixon's Frame, where the shadows gather'd. In the meantime, the demand for Coal in Britain promising to ascend forever, there seem'd to Dixon no reason to abandon too quickly a sure source of Work, in order to cross the Ocean and settle in a wilderness of uncertainty.

American reports that reach'd him mention'd Shelbys fighting in the West, and all the McCleans joining the Virginia Militia,— by then Dixon had survey'd the Park and Demesnes of the Lord Bishop's Castle at Bishop Auckland, and the Year after that all of Lanchester Common,— wilderness enough for him, tho' no longer is he sent quite as much into Panick'd Incompetence at the Alidade, by Moor-land unenclos'd,— as if he has found late protection, or at least toleration, from the Fell-Beasts of his younger days. At the Plane-Table, he erases his sketching mistakes with bits of Bread he then keeps in a Pocket, not wishing to cast them where Birds might eat the Lead and come to harm. Now and then, only half in play, he will take a folding Rule and measure the ever-decreasing distance between the tip of his Nose and the Paper, for among Surveyors, 'tis said, that by the degree of Proximity therebetwixt, may you tell how long a draughtsman has been on the Job,— and that when his Nose at last touches the Paper, 'tis time to retire.

He continu'd to postpone the American Return, whose mere Projection had separated him from Mason, and to recognize more clearly, as the Days went along, that his Life had caught up with him, and that his Death might not be far behind, and that America now would never be more real than his Remembrance, which he must take possession of, in whatever broken incompleteness, or lose forever.... "I was sure my Fate lay in America,— nor would I've ever predicted, that like thee I would swallow the Anchor and be claim'd again by the Life I had left, which I had not after all escap'd,— nor can I accurately say 'twas all Meg's doing, and the Girls', for I was never like thee, never one for Duty and so forth, being much more of a flirtatious Bastard, tha see, yet I couldn't leave them again. Thah' was it, really."

"To leave home, to dare the global waters strange and deep, consort with the highest Men of Science, and at the end return to exactly the same place, us'd,— broken...."

"No-body's dream of a Life, for Fair."

"You always wanted to be a Soldier, Dixon, but didn't you see, that all our way west and back, aye and the Transits too, were Campaigning, geo-metrick as a Prussian Cavalry advance,— tho' in the service of a Flag whose Colors we never saw,— and that your behavior in hostile territory was never less than..."

"Aye?"

"...Likely to be mention'd in Dispatches."

"I'll take it! Gratefully."

"The only hope, I suppose, is if we *haven't* come home exactly,— I mean, if it's not the same, not really,— if we might count upon that fail-ure to re-arrive perfectly, to be seen in all the rest of Creation...."

"Eeh,— I *hope* thah's not the only hope?"

They have been nymphing by Moon-light in the Wear, hoping for Sea-Trout, tho' finding none,— now, upon the bankside, Mason and Dixon sit, smoking long white Clay Pipes, whose stems arch like Fishing-Poles, and bickering about the Species eluding them,— Dixon seeming to Mason far too eager to lecture, as if having assum'd that Mason has never seen a Sea-Trout,— which, tho' true in a narrow sense, doesn't rule out his having felt them, once or twice, at the Bait....

"Whilst not as shrewd as the Carp," Dixon declares, "yet are they over-endow'd with Pride, and will have thee know, there are things a Sea-Trout simply will not do, such as waste his time upon an insect that dares the Flow too briskly, there being too much Humiliation for him, should he attempt capture, and fail...?"

"Humiliation before whom, Dixon? Frogs? Grebes? You have...dis-cuss'd this with the Sea-Trout here personally, 've you, perhaps even... more than once?"

"I ken them, Sir...? I see into their Minds...? 'Tis how I know, that tha must leave aside thy own Pride, and learn to feign with thy Bait weakness, uncertainty, fatigue,— " They hear swift footsteps close by,—

and in a moment behold, approaching them, sniffing industriously, a Norfolk Terrier, of memorable Appearance.

"Well, God's Periwig," whispers Mason. " 'Tis he!"

"Can't be,— what's it been? fifteen? sixteen years? and this one's scarcely a year old…?"

"Yet, see how he holds his head…old Fang's way to the Arc-Second …yes it's all right, lad, come on…?"

The Dog, as if not wishing to intrude, waits, Tail a-thump.

"Why, he's the very Representation…? Might he've been with those Strollers lately at The Queen's Head, that vanish'd in the middle of the Night…? happen they left him behind…?"

"We'll not insist that ye speak for your Supper," offers Mason.

"Not at all. Come back with us, and we'll see about thah', shall we?"

The Dog accompanies them to Dixon's House, dines unselectively tho' not gluttonously, and, having made amiable acquaintance with the Dogs already resident there, stops overnight.

"Quite at home, to appearance," Mason remarks next morning.

"Nay…? clearly, 'tis thee he fancies…?"

"He's a Town Dog, he'd much rather stop with you, than journey all the way to Sapperton."

"Eeh, why cannot tha see he can't wait to be back upon the Road, touring again?"

"A modest wager, perhaps."

"We never settl'd for thah' great race in Chester Town ten years ago 'twixt Selim and Yorick…?"

"Really. Which Horse won? Who'd I bet upon?"

The Dog listens to them for as long as he may, before standing, stretching, and trotting away to explore Bishop, nor reappearing till that night, 'round Suppertime.

"There you are again," Meg Bland stooping to greet him. "I've been making him those fried American corn-meal Ar-ticles of yours, Jere, to have with his Fish…? What'll his name be?"

"Fang," says Mason.

"Learnèd," says Dixon.

The Dog ignores both, however, as if his true Name is one they must guess. Each day the weather allows, he accompanies Mason and Dixon to the River, and watches whilst they fish. He does not venture to speak, indeed barking only once, when Lud Oafery,— an otherwise unremarkable person of middling age,— comes down out of the Willows and into the water, pretending to be a Pike in fierce Descent upon the Dace-Shoals, attempting to send all the Fish he may, into a Panick'd Stampedo.

"Sacrilege, where I come from," mutters Mason.

"Eeh, 'tis but Lud's bit of Diversion, whenever he's above ground...? throw him a Chub, and he'll be off...?"

As Mason's departure nears, Dixon can see he's growing more and more anxious upon the Topick of canine Speech. "How then? coerce him? shame him?"

"Think not...?"

"Yet one would expect, wouldn't one," the Dog, as ever, bright-eyed and companionably attending, "that out of professional Obligation, at least,— "

"Eeh, Mason...? really."

"All right, all right,— ever so sorry,— "

Close to dawn, dreaming of America, whose Name is something else, and Maps of which do not exist, Mason feels a cold Nose at his ear.

"When ye wake," whispers a youthful, South English voice, "I'll have long been out upon the Darlington Road. I am a British Dog, and belong to no one, if not to the two of you. The next time you are together, so shall I be, with you."

They wake early,— the Dog has gone. Dixon reports the same Nose, the same Message.

"Did we both dream the same thing?"

"I was awake...?"

"As certainly was I,— "

"Then must we see him again, next year...?"

78

Now 'tis very late, Dawn is the next event to consider, candles have been allow'd to burn all the way out, no one has uncork'd a Bottle in some while, Tenebræ slumbers beneath the Canopy of the Chinese Sofa, whilst her Cousins, sprawl'd in Chairs, are intermittently awake and listening. All seems to them interrupted by Enigmata, blown thro' as by Winds it is generally better not to be out in.

"What I cannot quite see to the end of," confesses Euphrenia, "is Mason's Return to America,— abruptly,— as if, unable to desert his Family again, what choice has he, this time, but to present them with the sudden voyage by sea, and carry them all to Philadelphia. Yet, what could have brought him here again?"

"Or else,— What frighten'd him away from Gloucestershire?"

"Plague? There was ever Plague. The weight of Rebekah's Ghost? How, if she were content to have him in Sapperton? Unless— "

"*She* came at last to wish him gone? Even at the Price of knowing they would never be buried together,— as he must also have known,— yet at the end she could not abide him as he had come to be, and so she turn'd terrible, as she had ever been a shadow's Edge away from doing anyway. The fear,— the Resolve? Poor Mason. He gather'd them all with the force of his Belief,— "

"Poh. 'Twas madness."

"You have look'd upon madness, have you, young 'Thelmer?"

"Any Saturday night down at the Hospital, Sir, a Spanish Dollar to the Warder purchases you more entertainment than your Ribs may bear, my Guarantee upon it."

"What! Bedlam in America! Mind yourself, lad."

When the Hook of Night is well set, and when all the Children are at last irretrievably detain'd within their Dreams, slowly into the Room begin to walk the Black servants, the Indian poor, the Irish runaways, the Chinese Sailors, the overflow'd from the mad Hospital, all unchosen Philadelphia,— as if something outside, beyond the cold Wind, had driven them to this extreme of seeking refuge. They bring their Scars, their Pox-pitted Cheeks, their Burdens and Losses, their feverish Eyes, their proud fellowship in a Mobility that is to be, whose shape none inside this House may know. Lomax wakes, sweating, from a poison'd Dream. Euphrenia has ascended the back Stairs, as the former Zab Cherrycoke those in front, to Slumber. Ethelmer and DePugh, Brae and the Twins, have all vanish'd back into the Innocence of Unconsciousness now. Ives is off at his Midnight Junto,— only Mr. LeSpark and the Rev^d remain. The Room continues to fill up, the Dawn not to arrive.

> And if it all were nought but Madmen's Sleep?
> The Years we all believ'd were real and deep
> As Lives, as Sorrows, bearing us each one
> Blindly along our Line's relentless Run....

"Who was that," Lomax LeSpark in a stuporously low-level Panick. "I know that Voice...."

"He's in here!" his brother Wade marvels. Blurry as a bat in this candle-stump flicker, "— Damme. How's he do it? He's suppos'd to be either in Chains, or out upon the Roads. Not in this House."

"Have a Cup, Tim," the Rev^d offering his Brother-in-Law's best Sercial. "Ever fancied the opening Lines to Book One, m'self...."

"You mean," the Poet nodding in thanks,

At Penn's Ascension of the Delaware,
Savages from the banks covertly stare,
As at the Advent of some puissant Prince,
Before whom, Chaos reign'd, and Order since...."

Proceeding, then, to recite the *Pennsylvaniad, sotto Voce* as he wanders the Room, among the others, the untold others....

"Will you be leaving before Christmas, Wicks?"

"What do I say? Your Servant, Sir."

"I meant, that I should welcome your Company, as your Mediation, in visiting with Mr. Mason's widow and Children, if they are yet in Town, tho' I am d——'d if I can see how to do it much before Epiphany, there being an Alarm Clock even next my Chamber-Pot, these Days."

"Thanks to the American Society, they are here, and car'd for. I have heard that Mrs. Mason will return to England with the younger Children, whilst William and Doctor Isaac will remain."

"Then I should like to meet them, in particular. Perhaps I may find a way to help."

"Brother, you have Moments."

"Aye,— we call 'em Philadelphia Minutes."

On entering Mason's Rooms at The George Tavern, Franklin is greeted by an Odor he knows and would rather not have found. He resists the impulse to take out his Watch, ever Comforter and Scripture to him. He hears Children, gather'd somewhere in their own Rectangle invisible. Mary stands before a window looking upon an Alley-way. "What a desperate Night it's been. I don't know if he really wants to see you, or if it's more of his Illness. He sleeps now, but he's dreaming and talking, so I expect he'll be with us soon."

"I receiv'd his Letter.... Having this year been much vex'd...this godawful disintegration of Power...'twas only now,— but forgive me, Mrs. Mason,— I whine."

She sinks with a sidewise contraction of her body onto a Couch design'd more to encourage the Illusions of Youth, than to console the Certainties of Age. Outside rackets the Traffic of Second Street.

"Please excuse me if I do not immediately sit,— at eighty, it requires some advance work,— so, my Sympathies must precede me."

She manages for him a Smile, whose muscular Cost he can feel in his own Face. He leans upon his Cane. "We met in times easily as dark as these,— we transacted honorably some items of Philosophick Business,— I put him up for Fellow in our American Society, tho' his desires were ever fix'd upon the Royal. He wanted them so to want him as a Member. We were but colonials, amusing enough in our way,— and of course he was touch'd,— yet, Philadelphia is not London."

"Upon Rebekah's Tomb-Stone he has put 'F.A.S.' after his own Name. So it means much to him. I expect you are surpriz'd, at,"— gesturing behind her as a wife might at her house, half apologizing, half welcoming,— "yet 'twas over-night." One moment they were at their own Table, in from cotes and stone walls and mud lanes,— the Loaf steaming, the Dishes going 'round,— the next, they were all in some kind of great loud Waggon, bound for Southampton. Money they'd had sav'd...

"But why?"

"I ask'd him why, ev'ry day, till I saw it was making him worse. 'We must go to America,'— that was nearly all he'd say. He has a way of saying 'America,' in his Father's Voice. Rrr. 'We all must go togetherrr.' Is it for leaving William and Doctor Isaac behind, all those years ago? I would gladly have remain'd in England with the Children, but at *my* age, Sir, it is a terrible choice. To find, and sweep from the last Corners of Sapperton and Stroud,— from Bisley!— some pitiful little heap of Mercy, or to remain with him and his Madness, which grows ever less hopeful, in our utter dependence upon the Board of Longitude. Praise Heaven, a fine Choice."

"Surely the Royal Society,— "

"Alas. Tho' he has friends there,— the Reverend Maskelyne has been truly gentle with Charles, has remain'd by him ever,— Charles believes inflexibly that the Society could not forgive him the Letters he wrote them from Plymouth, so long ago now,— that too many resented him for speaking up then, for daring, from his lower Station, to suggest another Plan."

To speak of the final seven years, between Dixon's death and Mason's, is to speculate, to uncertain avail. Obituaries mention a long descent, "suffering, for several years, melancholy aberrations of mind." His illness at the end was never stipulated. Yet 'tis possible, after all, down here, to die of Melancholy.

He had return'd to his earthly Father, yet never reconcil'd,— in his Will, Charles forgave Mason the price of the Loaf he'd taken ev'ry Day for his Table, and that was all. Mason had married again, and become the father of five more boys and a girl, yet he never put Rebekah to Earth…tho' she herself, to appearance, might at last sigh, relax, and move on,— one would think,— with Old Mopery come to rest where he'd started out from. It is the way journeymen became masters, and the ingenuous wise,— it is a musickal piece returning to its Tonick Home. Nothing more would be expected of him now, than some quiet Coda.

His efforts at refining the Longitude tables of Mayer avoided any risk of looking into the real Sky,— as if, against his father's wishes having once studied the Stars, now, too late, he were renouncing them,— tho' he got out under the Heavens ev'ry now and then, sometimes alone, usually with children along, for whom he adjusted Oculars and Screws, and peer'd only rarely, gingerly, Star-ward.

As Rebekah withdrew into Silence eventually complete, Mason's Melancholy deepen'd. If she was no longer to be found in Sapperton,— if he insisted that her Silence be Rejection, and not Contentment,— that may have help'd push him away, back to America,— whatever it was, his despair by then was greater than Mary had ever seen, or could account for. "I thought I knew him a little,— Children all over the place, Charlie bent over his logarithms all night, a new Stomach Onset arriving with each Post,— "

Doctor Isaac had had his Father back for ten years, yet still he relied upon Willy to help him along, as his older Brother had ever done, coming to accept it as naturally as the Day. "He will never speak of her," Willy said once. "Nor will Aunt Hester, much."

"They ought to, you know? It isn't fair. It's as if they're asham'd of her for something. Grandfather, when he is displeas'd with me, says that I— "

"I heard him. He should never have said that."

"And he said I was nam'd after the Doctor who lost her. That Dad hated me that much, he wanted it always on me, like a notch upon a Pig's Ear."

"Grandfather is a sour and beggarly old fool. You are nam'd for New-ton, whom Dad admires greatly."

Neither has ever denied the other his direct gaze. "Who told you 'twas Newton?" Doc keeps on, finely quivering, resolute.

"Aunt Hettie."

"On your Oath, Will."

"Ask her."

"I did. Mindful as ever, she went on, as, 'The name may've come up. Who knows? Your Father talks unendingly, but I can't recall much of anything he's said,— So now, I really shall have to take your sworn Word, Willy. And hope you do understand, how serious this is.'"

"How,— should I ever lie to you? 'Tis I,— remember me? the taller one?"

Without considering, Doc reaches up, for the Hand that is not there,— finding his brother's shoulder instead, which will have to do.

When news reach'd Mason that Dixon had died, he went about for the rest of the Day as if himself stricken. "I'd meant to see him this Sum-mer," he repeated over and over. At last, "I must go up there."

"I'll come with you," offer'd Doctor Isaac.

"The Boy works for his Bread," the elder Mason growl'd, "— he's not a Man of Science,— leave him be."

"Hire a Weaver for a Se'nnight,— there are plenty of them to choose from. I'll pay ye back any sum it loses ye."

"With what? Stardust?"

Presently, curses ringing in their Ears, Mason and his son were out upon the North Road together, bundl'd against the Cold, stopping in at ev'ry Tavern upon the Way. Mason, for some reason, found himself unable to stop looking at Doc, recalling that the Lad had never been out of these Hills, nor even down to Oxford. Out on the Road like this, he seem'd sud-denly no longer a Child. They stopt overnight in Birmingham, and again in York, they ate and drank with Waggoners and Fugitives and commer-cial travelers.

As they lie side by side in bed, Mason finds he cannot refrain from telling his Son bedtime stories about Dixon.

"He was ever seeking to feel something he'd hitherto not felt. In Philadelphia he was fascinated by Dr. Franklin's Leyden Jar, as with the Doctor's curious History, cheerfully admitted to, of self-electrocution thereby, on more Occasions than he can now remember...."

"Here's the Lumina of the Lab," leading the Surveyors among Globes of Glass, Insulators of Porcelain, a Miniature Forge, a Magnetizing Station, Gear-trains of Lignum Vitæ, and Engine out of which protrudes a great Crank, Bench-tops strewn with Lenses, Lamps, Alembicks, Retorts, Condensers, Coils,— at length to a squatly inelegant wide-mouth'd Vessel, in a dark corner of the Work-room. "Three-inch Sparks from this Contrivance are routine. And when ye hook a Line of 'em up,s in Cascade? Well. Many's the time I've found myself out upon the Pavement, no memory of Removal from where I'd been, and a Hole in the Brick Wall between, about my Size and Shape. Here now, just take hold of this Terminal,— "

Mason, aghast of course, and not about to touch any Terminal, withdraws, upon the Pretext of Business with Dr. Franklin's Assistant, a gnomelike Stranger nam'd Ingvarr, whose unsettling Grin and reluctance to speak provoke from Mason increasingly desperate Monologue,— whilst for his part, Dixon is eagerly hastening to handle all the Apparatus he can find, that might have Electrick Fluid running thro' it.

"*EEHH* aye, thah' was a good one! And here, whah's this, with the three great Springs coomin' out?"

"Ah. Yes, two go into the Ears, thus,— and the other, with this Y-Adapter, into your...Nostrils, there we are! Now, then!"

"Master! Master!" Ingvarr scuttling near.

"Not now, Ingvarr...unless of course you'd like to assist in a little...Spark-length Calibration?"

"Aiyee! No, Master!"

"There now Ingvarr, 'tis but a couple of Toes,— callus'd quite well I see, more than enough to withstand the 'lecktrick Tension...try not to squirm, there's a good fellow,— "

"It tickles!"

"Fine with me, as Howard says to Howard, only please try not to kick that Switch to the main Battery, lest Mr. Dixon,— oh, dear.— Ingvarr. What did I just say?"

So forcefully that his Queue-Tie breaks with a loud Snap, Dixon's Hair springs erect, each Strand a right Line pointing outward along a perfect Radius from the Center of his Head. What might be call'd a Smile, is yet asymmetrick, and a-drool. His Eyeballs, upon inspection, are seen to rotate in opposite Senses, and at differing Speeds. Releasing Ingvarr, who makes himself scarce, Franklin opens the Switch at last, and Dixon staggers to a Settee. "Sir," the Doctor in some concern, "I trust you've not been inconvenienc'd unduly?"

"Suppose I us'd Tin-Foil," Dixon, upon his back, replies, "— instead of Silver,— how many of these Jars should I need, to...reproduce that Effect?"

Next morning, at Breakfast, Doc is curious to know, "Did you ever cast his Horoscope?"

"Quite early on, tho' I never told him. His natal Moon, in Aquarius...? and in Leo, the sign of his Birth, he's bless'd with a Stellium, of Mercury, Venus, and Mars,— Mars being also conjunct his Sun,— tho' both are regrettably squar'd Jupiter *and* Saturn. His Bread, that is, ever by the sweat of his brow...so did it prove to be,— yet *Vis Martis* enough, and more, for the Journey.... He may've done my Horo on the sly, for all I know. Rum thing not to know of someone, isn't it? But he knew how to cast a Chart, and had the current Year's Ephemeris by Memory.... Damme, he knew his Astronomy,— tho' I teas'd him with it now and then...."

"Meant to bring you to see him one day. He'd heard enough about you...."

"You spoke of me?"

"You, Willy, the Babies. We talk'd about our Children. He had two Girls, young Women I should say,— "

"Arrh...and you were hoping...?"

"Who? What? D'you take me for a Village Busybody such as your Aunt Hettie?"

"Two Sons," explains Doc, "Two Daughters. And a Father wishing, as Fathers do, to be a Grand-Father."

"Sure of that?"

"Mason-Dixon Grand-Babies." He risks casting at his Father a direct look of provocation, that Mason finds he may no more flinch from, than answer to. For the next Hours, then, neither speaks more than he must,— at ease, for the first time together, with the Silence of the Day. 'Twas what Dixon ever wish'd from him,— to proceed quietly.

"I thought if ever I did this," Doc tells his father later, out upon the Road, " 'twould be alone. And headed the other way,— to London."

"You're like me. At your Age, I couldn't wait to be out of the Vale."

"Why'd you ever come back?"

"You were here, and Will...and your Mother...."

Doc flashes him a thoughtful look. "You never speak of her." Here they are, fallen upon the Drum-head of the Day.

" 'Tis twenty years. Perhaps I've pass'd beyond the need to."

"But then,— "

Mason sees the struggle the Lad is having between going on, and keeping silence. "Of course. We must speak of her. Whatever you wish to know of her. I shall try."

"It doesn't have to be right away."

Snow is nearly upon them, and night soon to descend. Shelter has not so far presented itself. At the last of the Day-light, providentially, at the Edge of York, they smell wood-smoke with a sensible Fat Component, and follow their Noses to The Merry Ghosts, which is in fact a Haunted Inn, as the apple trees planted too close to it testify, growing directly away from the Structure, as far as their roots will permit, often at quite unstable Angles.

"Not promising," mutters Mason.

"What choice?"

As they step into the busy Saloon, all, to the wiping of Mouths, falls dead silent. Faces gather'd in a Circle about a Dark-Lanthorn and a Heap of stolen Purses, look up in varying degrees of annoyance. A gigantick and misanthropick Tapster comes out of the Shadows. "Private Party tonight, Gents."

"Where's the next Inn?" Mason is about to inquire, when Doc speaks up,— "Here then, Coves, 'tis Mason and Mason, High Tobers of Greenwich, rambling Bearward, and Zoot Cheroot sez me early-and-late, or 'tis be-wary of the Frigidary, for the Gloak that quiddles.— Oh and Pints for all, that's if we may…?"

" 'We'?" inquires Mason. The Tapster withdraws, the Bitter flows, those staring resume Business. Mason and Doc find a Corner where they may pretend themselves confederates upon the Toby, plotting Deeds dark enough to allow them to be left in Peace.

" 'Tis a Ring," explains Doc. "They're dividing up the Day's Spoils. Later we'll see the night Brigade come on."

"How do you know all this?"

"Read about it in *Ghastly Fop*. 'Tis a Weekly, now, did you know?"

"I didn't."

"The Coach brings it to Stroud."

'Round the Footpads' table perplexity rules. "What did he say?" asks the Brum Kiddy. "Is that London Canting?"

"Clozay le Gob," he is advis'd. "You're too young, yet."

"But what's it mean?" the Kiddy persists.

"Here's what you do, Kid,— just go over there and ask 'em what they said."

Mason and Mason get an identifiable Joint for Supper, and the best room upstairs to sleep in. "They'll murder us in our sleep, suggests Mason.

"We're not going to sleep." By and large Doc is correct. The Traffick in front, as back in the Courtyard, of The Merry Ghosts is prodigious and unceasing. Confidences at best dangerous to hear are scream'd heedlessly back and forth all night.

"I thought it was suppos'd to be haunted," Mason objects. "How can anyone tell, in this Tohu-Vabohu?"

"Unless…" Doc looks out the Window. Among all the roarings, whistles, wheel-rumbling, and low Song, there is not a Visible Soul below. The snow is falling now. Mason sits by the window waiting for traces of these outspoken Spirits to show up against the white Descent. At some point, invisible across the room, Doctor Isaac will ask, quietly, evenly, "When did you meet? How young were you?"

At Bishop they learn'd that Dixon had been buried in back of the Quaker Meeting-House in Staindrop. Doctor Isaac stay'd with his Father, step for step. At the grave, which by Quaker custom was unmark'd, Mason beseech'd what dismally little he knew of God, to help Dixon through. The grass was long and beaded with earlier rain. A Cat emerg'd from it and star'd for a long time, appearing to know them.

"Dad?" Doc had taken his arm. For an instant, unexpectedly, Mason saw the little Boy who, having worried about Storms at Sea, as Beasts in the Forest, came running each time to make sure his father had return'd safely,— whose gift of ministering to others Mason was never able to see, let alone accept, in his blind grieving, his queasiness of Soul before a life and a death, his refusal to touch the Baby, tho' 'twas not possible to blame him.... The Boy he had gone to the other side of the Globe to avoid was looking at him now with nothing in his face but concern for his Father.

"Oh, Son." He shook his Head. He didn't continue.

"It's your Mate," Doctor Isaac assur'd him, "It's what happens when your Mate dies."

Solitude grew upon him, despite his nominal return to the social Web-work. Neighbors near and far, including owners of textile mills he would once never have spat upon, believing him vers'd in ev'ry Philosophick Art, kept bringing him repair jobs. The work-shed grew clutter'd with shafts and weft-forks, pirn winders and pistons, silk-reels and boiler gauges. Scents of Lavender, wild Roses, and Kitchen-Smoke pass'd in and out with Bees and Wasps, thro' the unmortar'd walls, pierc'd ev'rywhere with bright openings to the sunlit Garden outside, and the abiding Day. Mason might be found sitting at a Pine Table, bow'd over a curious Mirror. The beings who visited had names, and Titles, and signs of Recognition. Often they would approach through Number, Logarithms, the manipulation of Numbers and Letters, emerging as it were from among the symbols....

His principal income in those years came from pen-and-paper Work, laborious, pre-mechanickal, his only Instrument a set of Logarithmick Tables,— reducing and perfecting Mayer's solar and lunar *Data*. These form'd the basis of the Nautical Almanac, which Maskelyne edited, and in whose Introduction the A.R. was generous in acknowledging Mason's work. Mason came to believe that thro' Taurean persistence he had refin'd the values to well within an error that entitl'd him to the £5,000

Prize offer'd by the Board of Longitude. But "Enemies" succeeded in reducing it to an offer of £750, which he refus'd, upon Principle, tho' Mary at the news withdrew in Dismay.

Did he now include among his Enemies Maskelyne?

The A.R. had shar'd with Mason his delight over the new Planet,— he had taken it for a Comet,— wishing Mr. Herschel joy of his great Accomplishment. Suddenly the family of Planets had a new member, tho' previously observ'd by Bradley, Halley, Flamsteed, Le Monnier, the Chinese, the Arabs, everyone it seem'd, yet attended to by none of them. 'Twas impossible to find an Astronomer in the Kingdom who was not wandering about in that epoch beaming like a Booby over the unforeseen enlargement of his realm of study. Yet to Mason was it Purgatory,— some antepenultimate blow. What fore-inklings of the dark Forces of Over-Throw that assaulted his own Mind came visiting?— small stinging Presences darting in from the periphery of his senses to whisper, to bite, to inject Venoms...Beings from the new Planet. Infesting.... Mason has seen in the Glass, unexpectedly, something beyond simple reflection,— outside of the world,— a procession of luminous Phantoms, carrying bowls, bones, incense, drums, their Attention directed to nothing he may imagine, belonging to unknown purposes, flowing by thick as Eels, pauselessly, for how long before or after his interception, he could never know. There may be found, within the malodorous Grotto of the Selves, a conscious Denial of all that Reason holds true. Something that knows, unarguably as it knows Flesh is sooner or later Meat, that there are Beings who are not wise, or spiritually advanced, or indeed capable of Human kindness, but ever and implacably cruel, hiding, haunting, waiting,— known only to the blood-scented deserts of the Night,— and any who see them out of Disguise are instantly pursued,— and none escape, however long and fruitful be the years till the Shadow creeps 'cross the Sill-plate, its Advent how mute. Spheres of Darkness, Darkness impure,— Plexities of Honor and Sin we may never clearly sight, for when we venture near they fall silent, Murdering must be silent, by Potions and Spells, by summonings from beyond the Horizons, of Spirits who dwell a little over the Line between the Day and its annihilation, between the number'd and the unimagin'd,— between common safety and Ruin ever solitary....

The Royal Society by then had divided into "Men of Science," such as Maskelyne and Mr. Hutton, and "Macaronis," such as Henry Cavendish and Mr. Joseph Banks, a Dispute culminating for Maskelyne, with his own set of Enemies, at the Instant he found his name absent from the List of Royal Society Council Members for 1783–84, and had an Excursion into Vertigo unsought. At this Cusp of vulnerability, Mason, with the Exquisiteness of a Picador, launch'd his Dart.

At The Mitre, of all Places, amid pipe-fumes and the muffl'd ring of pewter upon oak, they ended up waving half-eaten Chops in lieu of pointed Fingers. From an innocent discussion of the Great Meteor of the Summer previous, they abruptly surrender'd to Earthly Spite.

"If they are Souls falling to Earth," becoming incarnate, then 'tis of Moment, which Point of the Zodiack they appear to radiate from."

"Like most of them that night, this had its Radiant in Perseus. If that's any help to you."

Mason mimicking the preacherly rise and fall, "Perseus, home to most baleful Algol, the Ghoul-Star,— when upon its Meridian, directly above New-York, the American Sodom,— the Star that others nam'd Lilith,— or Satan's, or Medusa's, Head...would the Soul I seek, emerge and fall from a region so attainted? Never. You know that very well. You little Viper. What have you ever lost?"

Even Mun, who loved a brisk Punch-up as well as the next truculent Sot, now chose rather to pull his Brother away, first to another Table, and presently out the Door and on to another Tavern altogether. "You'll not dismiss me again," cried Mason. "I fail'd to see Hatred for what it was,— believing you but a long-winded Fool, ever attempting to buy my regard with Gifts in your power,— "

"I may have priz'd your good opinion," Maskelyne in that meek Tone Mason knew promis'd a Stab unannounc'd.

Striking instead, "Why should it matter to you? Certainly not out of Respect for the better Astronomer,— "

" 'Twas plain Recompense, no more than that. Schiehallion, which you rejected,— Day-Labor for the B. of L., without which your Family should have starv'd,— all in my humble Gratitude, for being allow'd, once, to approach Bradley,— "

"Better we'd starv'd,— for you came closer than you ought,— the worse for him."

"An Usurper? Is that what you make of me? Must I now be slain? Can you never get beyond it?"

"No need to slay a Man who isn't *There.*"

Maskelyne understood that Mason meant, *not There upon the Royal Society Council.* His parsonical Scowl dropp'd from forehead to Eyes, as we clench our Faces sometimes, against Sentiment. No records survive, however, of when Nevil Maskelyne did, or did not, weep. What he did do now, was turn away from Mason, and for the first time, and the last time, not turn back to face him. The last Mason saw of him was the back of his Wig. The next year, after several dramatick Votes and Skirmishes, tho' not all that many Stick-enhanc'd Injuries, ev'ryone in the Royal Soc. ended most frightful Chums, and Maskelyne was back on the Council, remaining so thereafter, Year upon Year, till his Passing.

Mason struggles to wake. He arises, glides to the Door, and emerges from an ordinary Modern House, in one of the plainest cities on Earth, to find ascending before him one single dark extended Petroglyph,— a Town-enclos'd Hill-side, upon which lie the all-but-undamag'd remains of an ancient City, late Roman or early Italian temples and public buildings, in taupes and browns, Lombardy Poplars of a Green very dark.... There is writing on some of the Structures, but Mason cannot read it. Does not yet know it is writing. Perhaps when Night has fallen, he will be able to look up, to question the Sky.

"I think he's waking." She is up and a-bustle, the children secreting themselves in corners, older ones shepherding younger ones to nearby rooms. Mary beckons Franklin in.

Mason is gone gray, metallic whiskers sprout from his Face, even his eyelashes are grizzl'd. Franklin is surpriz'd to find that Mason has lost his Squint, that as the years have pass'd, his Face has been able some-how to enter the Ease of a Symmetry it must ever have sought, once he abandon'd the Night Sky, and took refuge indoors from the Day.

"I trust you will soon be out of this Bed, Sir."

"Whilst I'm of use," Mason says, "they shan't seek my dissolution, not in the thick of this Dispute over the Bradley Obs so-call'd, these being, many of them, my own. No one wants to repeat what went on between Newton and Flamsteed. Excepting perhaps one of Kabbalistick Turn, who believes those Arrays of Numerals to be the magical Text that will deliver him to Immortality. Or suspects that Bradley *found something,* something as important as the Aberration, but more ominous,— something as important as the Aberration, but more ominous,— something France may not have, or not right away, and Jesuits must not learn of, ever,— something so useful and deadly, that rather than publish his suspicions, or even reduce the *data* any further, Bradley simply left them as an exercise for anyone strongly enough interested. And what could that be? What Phantom Shape, implicit in the Figures?"

"Ah, you old Quizzer," Franklin tries to beam, Mason continuing to regard him, not pleading, but as if it didn't matter much what Franklin thinks.

" 'Tis a Construction," Mason weakly, "a great single Engine, the size of a Continent. I have all the proofs you may require. Not all the Connexions are made yet, that's why some of it is still invisible. Day by day the Pioneers and Surveyors go on, more points are being tied in, and soon becoming visible, as above, new Stars are recorded and named and plac'd in Almanacks...."

"You've found it, have ye? This certainly isn't that Curious Design with the trifling Cost that you sent me along with your Letter."

"Sir, you have encounter'd Deists before, and know that our Bible is Nature, wherein the Pentateuch, is the Sky. I have found there, written ev'ry Night, in Astral Gematria, Messages of Great Urgency to our Time, and to your Continent, Sir."

"Now to be your own as well, may an old Continental hope, Sir."

Mary looks in. "Well, young Mary," Mason's eyes elsewhere, unclaimable, "it turn'd out to be simple after all. Didn't it."

"You're safe, Charlie," she whispers. "You're safe." She prays.

Mary would return to England with the younger Children,— William and Dr. Isaac, Rebekah's Sons, would stay, and be Americans. Would stay, and ensign their Father into his Death. Mr. Shippen, Revd Peters, Mr. Ewing, all Commissioners of the Line twenty years earlier, now will prove, each in his Way, their Salvation upon this Shore.

"Since I was ten," said Doc, "I wanted you to take me and Willy to America. I kept hoping, ev'ry Birthday, this would be the year. I knew next time you'd take us."

"We can get jobs," said William, "save enough to go out where you were,— "

"Marry and go out where you were," said Doc.

"The Stars are so close you won't need a Telescope."

"The Fish jump into your Arms. The Indians know Magick."

"We'll go there. We'll live there."

"We'll fish there. And you too."